FRENCH FAIRY TALES

FRENCH FAIRY TALES

FRENCH FAIRY TALES

Retold by Jan Vladislav

Illustrated by
Ota Janeček

HAMLYN
London · New York · Sydney · Toronto

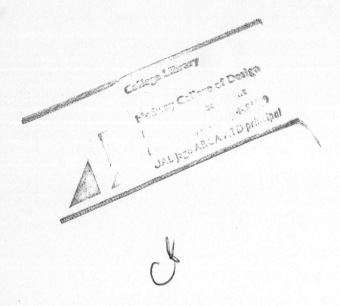

Translated by Vera Gissing and Joy Kohoutová

Designed and produced by Artia
Published 1971 by The Hamlyn Publishing Group Limited
London · New York · Sydney · Toronto
Hamlyn House · Feltham · Middlesex · England
This edition © 1971 by Artia
Illustrations © 1970 by Ota Janeček
Graphic design by Bronislav Malý
ISBN 0 600 33419 8
Printed in Czechoslovakia by Svoboda
1/01/13/51

CONTENTS

A Fairy Tale about Fairy Tales   7
The Half-a-Cockerel and the Evil King   8
Mr Wolf, Mrs Fox and the Clever Little Goat   14
The Fairy Toad   17
Mr Wolf and his Pipe   21
The Fisherman and the Queen of the Fishes   23
The Miller's Three Sons   28
The Snowchild   34
Strong Fourteen   36
The Shepherd and the Flying Princesses   42
The Black Ship   48
How the Blacksmith became the Son-in-law and
   Heir of the French King   55
Joseph and Beautiful Sunflower   60
The Dragon King and the Sleeping Princess   76
The Godson of the French King
   and the Princess of Tronkolen   88
The Prince with the Black Scarf   107
Captain Tulip and the Princess from Bordeaux   126
The Blacksmith and Golden-legged Robert   142
The Two Gifts   157
Beautiful Mona and the King of the Morgans   160
The Miserly Farmer and the Artful Farmhand   170
The Adventures of Jack Bragger   174
The Animal even the Devil could not Recognise   187
How Johnny Pancake did not marry a Princess   190
Balderdash and Fiddle-Faddle   202
The Six Lazy Brothers and Princess Goldenlocks   205
How Old Tom tried to Barter   214
How the Little Boy and the Little Girl went for a Walk
   in the Mud or The Longest Story in the World   217

A FAIRY TALE ABOUT FAIRY TALES

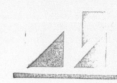

One day I went to see my grandmother:
'Please, Grandmother, tell me a story!'
'I'll tell you a story, but first you must bring me a mug of milk.'
So off I went to see the cow:
'Please, Cow, give me a mug of milk!'
'I'll give you a mug of milk, but first you must bring me a basket of hay.'
So off I went to the meadow:
'Please, Meadow, give me a basket of hay!'
'I'll give you a basket of hay, but first you must bring me a sharp scythe.'
So off I went to speak to the blacksmith:
'Please, Blacksmith, give me a sharp scythe!'
'I'll give you a scythe, but first you must bring me a side of bacon.'
So off I went to see the pig:
'Please, Pig, give me a side of bacon!'
'I'll give you a side of bacon, but first you must bring me a sack of acorns.'
So off I went to speak to the oak:
'Please, Oak, give me a sack of acorns!'
'I'll give you a sack of acorns, but first you must bring me a blustery wind.'
So off I went to visit the sea:
'Please, Sea, give me a blustery wind!'
The sea gave me a blustery wind for the oak, the oak gave me a sack of acorns for the pig, the pig gave me a side of bacon for the black-smith, the blacksmith gave me a sharp scythe for the meadow, the meadow gave me a basket of hay for the cow, the cow gave me a mug of milk for Grandmother, and Grandmother began to tell me stories, one after another, and then some more, until I had two whole aprons full.

And here are the stories she told me.

7

THE HALF-A-COCKEREL
AND THE EVIL KING

Once upon a time there were two old women who shared a tiny little cockerel between them. One day, one of the old women said to the other:

'What are we going to eat today? We have no milk, we have no flour, all we have is our little cockerel. Let's make a pot of soup out of him.'

'No,' said the other old woman. 'Let him hop and peck around the courtyard.'

'Soup,' said the first old woman.

'No!' said the second.

'Well, then, I'll make soup out of my half,' said the first old woman.

'Go ahead,' said the second, 'but I'm going to let the other half hop and peck around the courtyard.'

So the first old woman made soup out of her own half of the cockerel, but left the other half to hop and peck around the courtyard. The half-a-cockerel hopped around on a single foot, pecked the gravel with half a beak, and waved a single wing. As it hopped and pecked on the ash heap, it suddenly uncovered a purse full of gold coins.

The half-a-cockerel hopped for joy on its single foot.

'Cock-a-doodle-doo, look what I've found.

A purse full of coins, all shiny and round.

I found it on the ash heap, cock-a-doodle-doo,

I'll give it to my mistress, that's what I'll do.'

So the half-a-cockerel hurried to the old woman to give her the purse of gold coins. But as it hopped on its single foot, the king himself rode by in a golden carriage. When he saw the half-a-cockerel with the big purse in its little half-beak, he jumped up and ordered the coachman to stop the horses. He turned to his servants and said:

'What does that rooster have in its beak?'

'A purse full of gold coins, Your Majesty.'

'Bring it to me!'

So the servants caught the half-a-cockerel, took the purse, gave it to the king, and drove away as fast as the horses could gallop.

The little half-a-cockerel was very unhappy.

'Cock-a-doodle-doo, a purse of gold I found.

A purse full of coins, all shiny and round.

The king came and took it, cock-a-doodle-doo,

But, I'll get it back, that's what I'll do!'

So the half-a-cockerel set out for the king's palace to get its purse of gold coins back. On the way, it met a fox.

'Where are you going, half-a-cockerel?' asked the fox.

'I'm going to get back the purse of gold that the king stole from me.'

'I'll go along with you if you like,' said the fox.

'Come on then,' it said.

So they set out for the king's palace. After a while, the fox was exhausted.

'Half-a-cockerel, I can't take another step,' said the fox.

'Then crawl under my wing!'

The fox climbed under the half-a-cockerel's wing, and the brave little bird went on and on, until it met a wolf.

'Where are you going, my fellow?' enquired the wolf.

'I'm going to get back the purse of gold that the king stole from me!' said the half-a-cockerel firmly.

'I'll go along with you if you like,' said the wolf.

'Come on then,' said the half-a-cockerel.

So they set out for the king's palace. After a while, the wolf was exhausted.

'Half-a-cockerel, I can't take another step,' said the wolf.

'Then crawl under my wing!'

The wolf climbed under the half-a-cockerel's wing, and the brave little fellow went on and on, until it met a swarm of bees.

'Where are you going, half-a-cockerel?' asked the bees.

'I'm going to get back the purse of gold that the king stole from me!'

'We'll go along with you if you like,' said the bees.

'Come on then,' said the half-a-cockerel.

So they set out for the king's palace. After a while, the bees were exhausted.

'Half-a-cockerel, we can't fly another inch,' said the bees.

'Then crawl under my wing!'

The bees climbed under the half-a-cockerel's wing, and the brave little bird went on and on, until it came to a river.

'Where are you going, half-a-cockerel?' asked the river.

'I'm going to get back the purse of gold that the king stole from me!'

'I'll come along with you if you like,' said the river.

'Come along then,' said the half-a-cockerel.

So they set out for the king's palace. After a while the river was exhausted.

'Half-a-cockerel I can't flow another foot,' said the river.

'Then crawl under my wing!'

The river climbed under the half-a-cockerel's wing, and the brave little fellow went on and on, until at last it came to the king's palace.

'Good morning, King, cock-a-doodle-doo,
Give me back my coins please do!'

'Tomorrow,' cried the king. 'But first you must spend the night in my royal chicken-coop!'

The king's servants threw the poor half-a-cockerel in the chicken-coop. The king thought his royal chickens would peck the strange little bird to death during the night. And they would have done — they started to peck and peck, and they would have pecked the poor little half-a-cockerel to death, but it cried:

'Fox, come out, come out I say!

Cock-a-doodle-doo, and save the day!'

The fox jumped out from under the half-a-cockerel's wing, gobbled up half the royal chickens, bit off the heads of the other half and went on its way.

When the king came to the royal chicken-coop in the morning he almost fainted. All his royal chickens were dead.

The half-a-cockerel cried:

'Good morning, King, cock-a-doodle-doo,

Give me back my coins, please do!'

'You'll get them tomorrow. But first you must spend the night in the royal sheepfold,' said the crafty king.

The king's servants threw the poor half-a-cockerel in the royal sheepfold. The king thought the royal rams would trample the little half-a-cockerel to death overnight. And they would have done. No sooner had the royal shepherd brought them back to the fold, and the sun began to set, than the royal rams began to stamp and tramp until they almost trampled the little bird to death.

But the half-a-cockerel cried:

'Wolf, come out, come out I say!

Cock-a-doodle-doo, and save the day!'

The wolf jumped out from under the half-a-cockerel's wing, ate up half the royal rams, smothered the other half, and then ran away.

When the king came to the royal sheepfold in the morning he almost fainted. All his rams were gone.

The half-a-cockerel cried:

'Good morning, King, cock-a-doodle doo,

Give me back my coins, please do!'

'Tomorrow,' cried the king. 'Servants, take the half-a-cockerel to my throne room!'

The king thought he would get rid of this persistent bird during the night. Hardly had it grown dark when the half-a-cockerel sitting on the king's throne grew very drowsy. The king came and sat down on the bird, almost stifling it to death. When the half-a-cockerel felt this, it cried:

'Bees, bees, come out I say!

Cock-a-doodle-doo, and save the day!'

The bees flew out from under the half-a-cockerel's wing and began to sting the king so hard that he crawled under the bed, crying and moaning, and left the half-a-cockerel alone. Only then did the bees go their own way.

When the king woke up the next morning he was as fat and swollen as a barrel.

The half-a-cockerel called:

'Good morning, King, cock-a-doodle-doo,

Give me back my coins, please do!'

'You'll get them back tomorrow. Wife, put the half-a-cockerel into the oven for the night!'

The king thought he would light the oven in the morning and roast the bird. As soon as dawn broke the servants lit a fire under the oven and almost roasted the half-a-cockerel to death. When the half-a-cockerel realised what was happening it cried:

'River, river, come out I say!

Cock-a-doodle-doo, and save the day!'

The river rushed out from under the little cockerel's wing and began to flood the oven, then the kitchen and finally the whole palace. First the king had to climb up on his throne, then on a cupboard and finally on the roof.

And the half-a-cockerel ran after him crying:

'Good morning, King, cock-a-doodle-doo,

Give me back my coins, please do!

If you don't give them back to me,

You'll surely drown, you will, you'll see!'

The king realised at last that he would not be able to fob off the half-a-cockerel. He pulled the purse of coins from his pocket and threw it at the cockerel:

'Here you are!'

Only then did the river fall back and go its own way. The little cockerel snatched up the purse full of coins and rushed off to give it to the old woman for allowing him to run around her yard. And if it hasn't died yet, then it is still running around the yard, pecking away at the gravel heap, and singing:

'Cock-a-doodle-doo, cock-a-doodle-doo,
I found some coins, shiny and true.
My coins and purse the king did steal,
But I paid him back and brought him to heel!'

MR WOLF, MRS FOX AND THE CLEVER
LITTLE GOAT

Uncle Matthew had three goats, a black one, a striped one and a white one. When it was warm the goats had a good time, for Uncle Matthew left them to graze in the lush meadows by his farm, where the goats ate and ate until their stomachs were ready to burst. But when autumn came and the wind began to whistle over the fields, there was no more grass and Uncle Matthew had nothing left to give the goats to eat. All he could do was to sell his goats on market-day, but he kept the youngest, a little white one. He tied him to a post in the garden behind the house, and every day he brought him a few crusts of bread so that he didn't die of hunger.

But the little white goat did not like being in the garden behind the house. He kept bleating and nibbling at the rope, because he wanted to go into the forest over the hill, where the grass was sweeter.

'Be reasonable, Little White Goat,' Uncle Matthew pleaded with him. 'It is winter, there are wolves and foxes over there, and they will eat you up. And the grass has turned yellow a long time ago.'

The little white goat did not believe Uncle Matthew.

'He's only saying that to make me afraid,' he thought, and secretly nibbled at the rope until one evening he was free. The little white goat slipped under the fence, and ran straight into the forest.

While it was still daylight the little goat had a wonderful time. He ran wherever he wanted, ate a little grass when he felt like it, even though it was yellow, and nibbled a few leaves even though they had withered, and thoroughly enjoyed his freedom. But as soon as it began to grow dark, the little white goat thought longingly of Uncle Matthew's cottage. He ran down the hill then suddenly came to a dead stop. From the path ahead, two green eyes gleamed in the twilight.

'A fox,' thought the little white goat in panic, and he was not mistaken. On the path, barring his way, stood Mrs Fox.

The little white goat turned round instantly hoping to run away. But hardly had he taken three steps when again he came to a halt. On the path two yellow eyes were gleaming in the twilight.

'A wolf,' thought the little white goat in panic, and he was not mistaken. On that side of the path stood Mr Wolf.

The little goat knew that his end had come, poor little fellow.

Mrs Fox licked her lips:

'Well, fancy that! Uncle Matthew's little goat! That will make a tasty dish, Mr Wolf!'

Mr Wolf ran his tongue over his teeth:

'A tasty dish indeed, Mrs Fox! Shall we eat him at once?'

But Mrs Fox was fussy:

'Not at once! Let's take him to your cottage and cook him properly!'

Mr Wolf agreed:

'That's a good idea, Mrs Fox. I've never tried a cooked goat.'

He grabbed the rope with his teeth and led the poor little goat to his cottage, with Mrs Fox following behind.

Once inside the cottage, Mrs Fox got busy. She lit a fire in the stove, but there was not enough wood.

'Mr Wolf, I haven't enough wood!'

'I'll go to the forest for some!' offered the little goat in a timid voice.

'What do you think of that!' laughed Mr Wolf gruffly. 'Thinking of running away, are you? I shall go for the wood myself!'

He came back in a little while with a bundle of sticks.

Mrs Fox added some more wood to the blaze, and put the kettle on the fire, but she did not have enough water.

'Mr Wolf, I haven't enough water.'

'I'll go to the well for it!' offered the little white goat in a timid voice.

'What do you think of that!' laughed Mr Wolf gruffly. 'Thinking of running away, are you? I shall go for the water myself!'

He took a long time about it, but at last he was back with a pail of water.

Mrs Fox poured the water into the kettle, and began to add spices to it, but she did not have enough.

'Mr Wolf, I haven't enough spices!'

'I'll go to the shopkeeper for them!' offered the little white goat in a timid voice.

'What do you think of that!' laughed Mr Wolf gruffly. 'Thinking of running away, are you? I shall go for the spices myself!' And he ran to the shopkeeper.

But it was a long way to the shopkeeper's, and Mr Wolf was a very long time.

'Where can that wolf be,' grumbled Mrs Fox. 'There'll be no water left by the time he comes back. Little White Goat, look into the kettle and see if I still have enough!'

But the little white goat answered wisely:

'Just look yourself, Mrs Fox! I'm afraid of falling in!'

Mrs Fox smiled:

'Why should you fall in, you silly goat! All you have to do is to get up on this little table, lift the lid and look inside!'

And Mrs Fox got up on the little table, lifted the lid and leaned over the kettle.

The little white goat hesitated no longer. He jumped up and pushed the fox from behind with all his strength, and old Mrs Fox fell into the kettle. The little goat put back the lid.

Footsteps were now heard outside, on the path leading to the cottage. Mr Wolf was returning from the shopkeeper's with the spices. The little white goat quickly leapt to the door and closed the latch. The wolf banged on the door:

'Mrs Fox, open the door. I've brought the spices.'

But the little white goat replied cleverly:

'Mrs Fox is not here. She locked me in and took the key with her while she went for some cream. She said you will have to climb in down the chimney!'

'The chimney?' grumbled Mr Wolf. 'Then take the kettle with the water away so that I won't get burnt.'

'Of course I will!' said the little white goat, but he left the kettle under the fireplace and took the lid off the pot. Then there was a noise in the chimney as Mr Wolf came flying down and fell straight into the boiling water. The little white goat had only to pop the lid back on the kettle!

No one knows what happened to Mr Wolf and Mrs Fox under that lid. But the little white goat returned to Uncle Matthew that very night and since then has never wanted to leave his garden.

THE FAIRY TOAD

Once upon a time there was a poor widow, and all she had in the world was an old cottage and a young son. The cottage was near a forest and the boy, who was called Willie, would go into the forest to collect sticks and sell them. His mother did odd jobs in the village and so they just managed to earn their living. But it was quite impossible for Willie to go to school. They needed the money he earned and, anyway, they could never afford the books he would need for school.

So little Willie, instead of going to school, went to the forest, and instead of carrying books under his arm he carried bundles of firewood on his head. One day, he was returning home from the forest when suddenly he heard something crying plaintively. He had never heard a voice like it.

Willie was not afraid. He threw down his bundle of sticks and ran in the direction of the sound. He had only taken a few steps when he saw the reason for the cries. There, on the path, a fox was crushing a beautiful green toad with its paw.

Willie felt very sorry for the toad. He seized a stick and chased the fox, till it ran away. The toad stayed where it was on the path. Willie bent down, lifted it up carefully and, seeing that it was still breathing, put it inside his shirt. With the bundle of sticks on his head he set off for home.

His mother was already out looking for him.

'Look what I have brought,' Willie called to her, showing her the toad.

'But that's just an ordinary toad,' said Willie's mother. 'There are lots of them everywhere.'

'There is only one toad as beautiful as this!' said Willie and told his mother how he had found it.

'Certainly, I have never seen such a lovely toad!' his mother admitted when she looked more closely. 'Since you have saved it, you can keep it. But you must take good care of it!'

His mother did not have to tell Willie to look after his new pet. He found an old bowl for it to live in, and making it comfortable with gravel, a bed of moss and a little water, put it on the window sill. Every morning and evening he fed it and the toad quickly settled into its new home. So much so, in fact, that the toad did not want to leave the cottage even after it had recovered from its terrible wounds. Willie often used to carry it out of the house into the garden, but the toad always hopped back in again, so Willie and his mother decided to keep it with them in their cottage at the edge of the forest.

And they did not regret it. From the time the toad came to the cottage, fortune began to shine on Willie and his mother. Once the wind blew down the old willow tree in the garden behind the cottage and the poor widow found a jug full of silver coins in its roots. Another time a distant relative remembered her and left his entire fortune to her in his will. And so things continued.

'Willie's toad has brought us good luck' the widow told her neighbours and the whole village really believed it.

In the meantime Willie was growing up, and since there was enough to eat and drink in the cottage he was able to go to school. He was a good pupil and soon no one could rival him at his lessons.

But even after he had finished his schooling and travelled through half the world, he did not grow too proud to remember the little cottage by the forest. On his return from his travels, he went straight home, to his mother and to the green toad.

When he reached the cottage and jumped off his horse in front of the door, his mother hardly recognised this strong and handsome young man. Willie kissed his mother and then hurried to the bowl on the window-sill. He pulled out the toad, placed it on the palm of his hand and said happily:

'Thank you for everything, Toad, on behalf of my mother and myself. We shall celebrate this evening and you will sit with us at the table!'

The little toad, looking as though it understood, began to jump for joy on Willie's hand.

That evening Willie's mother prepared a special meal. When the table was set, Willie pushed a chair to the head of the table, put a pillow on it and sat the toad on the pillow. Then he and his mother took a seat on either side of the table, wished each other a hearty appetite and poured out the soup from the tureen. The little toad was served first.

But as soon as the bowl was filled to the top there was a quiet sigh and Willie and his mother stared in amazement. Instead of the green toad, there sitting between them was a beautiful girl in a beautiful green dress and with still more beautiful green eyes.

'Do not be frightened, good people,' said the girl. 'It is I, your toad. Willie saved my life, and because of that I remained with you in order to help you. But now you no longer need my help and I must return home to the forest, to my fairy friends.'

'Do you no longer wish to stay with us, Toad?' asked Willie sadly.

'I like being with you,' replied the fairy toad, 'but you are grown up now. Soon you will marry and then I would only be in your way.'

'I shall marry,' said Willie firmly, 'but only if you will have me for a husband! Tell me, Toad, will you marry me?'

'If you really mean that, Willie, then I will marry you,' replied the fairy toad.

'I do mean it truly,' said Willie. 'I am only afraid that I am too poor for you. Everything we had was used to pay for my education.'

'That's no problem,' smiled the fairy toad. 'Just look!' She took a handful of lentils from the plate, held them up high and then let each seed fall, one by one. Instead of lentils, gold coins dropped on the table with a ringing sound.

And so all their worries were over. Within a week the wedding was held, and Willie took as his bride the girl with the most beautiful green eyes in the world. All their children and their children's children, for seven generations, inherited those beautiful eyes.

THE WOLF AND HIS PIPE

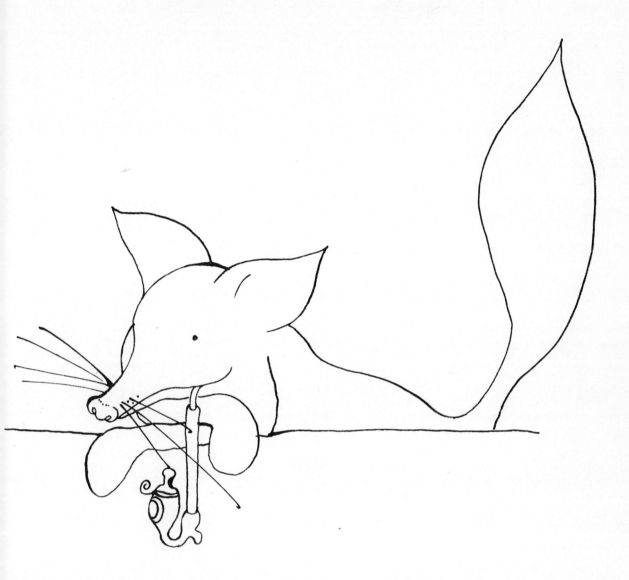

One day, Mr Fox was sitting in his doorway smoking a handsome pipe.
Mr Wolf his neighbour, who happened to be passing by, saw the
pipe and stopped to ask:

'What are you doing, Mr Fox?'

'I'm smoking, Mr Wolf!'

'Is it enjoyable, Mr Fox?'

'Of course it is Mr Wolf, otherwise people wouldn't smoke.'

'You're right, Mr Fox, I must try it too. If only I had something to
smoke!'

'That's no problem, Mr Wolf, you can get a pipe very easily. Over there, near the forest, a farmer is ploughing and he has left his jacket lying under a bush. I'll bet anything you like that you'll find a pipe and tobacco there.'

'Then let's go and see, Mr Fox!'

'All right!' said Mr Fox, and he ran with Mr Wolf to the bush. In the grass lay the jacket and under it a gun.

'This is a beautiful pipe, Mr Wolf,' cried Mr Fox. 'It's bigger than mine but you'll get a better smoke. Just try it.'

He pushed the barrel of the gun into the wolf's mouth.

'Now I'll fill it and light it for you Mr Wolf. You must keep still and take a breath.'

Mr Wolf stood still and took a breath as he was told, and Mr Fox pulled the trigger. There was a loud bang and Mr Wolf dropped to the ground. His three best teeth were gone.

'I won't let you get away with this, Mr Fox,' he howled as he ran into the forest. 'Even though you've taken my three best teeth, I still have enough left in my mouth to tear you to pieces!'

'So that's all the kindness I get for my troubles, Mr Wolf! I wanted to teach you to smoke and in return you want to pull me to pieces. Is it my fault if smoking does you such harm?'

THE FISHERMAN AND THE QUEEN
OF THE FISHES

Once upon a time there was a fisherman who had nothing in the world except an old boat, a miserable cottage, a wife and lots of children. Every day the fisherman set out to sea and whatever he caught he always divided into two parts. The larger part he sold at the market and the smaller he brought home so that there would be something to eat. But try as he might, there was never enough money or fish, especially when the children and their appetites began to grow.

One day, as usual, the fisherman went out to sea but had no luck. Although he had been fishing from the break of dawn, and the sun was now high over the sea, he had not caught a single fish. The poor fisherman did not know what to do, so he took his last piece of bread, crumbled it up into the water to attract the fish and lowered his net. When he hauled the net in, it was empty save for a beautiful little golden fish thrashing about at the very bottom. The old fisherman had never seen such a fish in his life. He reached for it and was holding it in his hand when suddenly the fish spoke:

'Let me go, Fisherman! I was caught by your piece of bread but if you let me go I shall reward you richly. I'll give you so many fish for each day's fishing that you and your whole family will be well off for the rest of your lives. And if something bad should happen to you at sea, just remember me and I shall help you, because I am Queen of the Fishes.'

The old fisherman felt sorry for the fish. He threw it back into the sea and the Queen of the Fishes disappeared immediately. But she kept her promise. Hardly did the fisherman lower his net than it was so full that it almost tore under the weight. That day he brought home more fish than he had ever done before. And from that time forward, luck was with him for every catch. Within a year or two the poor fisherman had become a wealthy and important man.

But he did not become too proud, for apart from buying a larger boat and a better net, he carried on the same as before, fishing just as hard as ever.

One day while fishing he was caught in a storm. The fierce wind raised huge waves and the boat was tossed about like an eggshell. The old fisherman had lived through many things at sea, but he had never been caught in such a fierce storm before. He knew that his end was near because the boat was rapidly filling up with water. In his desperation the old fisherman remembered the golden fish.

'Only the Queen of the Fishes can help me now,' he sighed. And at that moment he saw in the black waves the glitter of the golden fish.

'Fear nothing, Fisherman,' she said, 'I shall help you.'

She flapped her tail, splashing the water everywhere, so that the poor fisherman swallowed quite a mouthful! But as soon as he swallowed the water he discovered that he was sinking into the waves and swimming quietly and contentedly after the golden fish, to the depths of the sea, just as though he was walking along the street on his way home. In a little while he found himself in a beautiful city. It stood on the bed of the sea, with streets paved with gold and houses made of precious stones, and all kinds of fish were swimming everywhere. The fisherman could not take his eyes off all these riches and every once in a while he would bend over and pick up a piece of gold or a precious stone lying on the ground. In a short while his pockets were full. The golden fish said:

'This is the capital city of my kingdom. If you wish, you can stay here until the end of your life.'

But the fisherman shook his head:

'I would like to stay, Queen of the Fishes! But you know that I have a wife and children. What would they do without me?'

'You are right,' said the golden fish. She blew on a gold whistle and suddenly there was a large dolphin standing before him.

'Dolphin,' the golden fish ordered, 'carry this fisherman on your back and take him to a rock so that someone out fishing will find him!'

Then she said goodbye to the kind fisherman and as a parting gift gave him a bag full of gold coins:

'This will last a lifetime, Fisherman! For every coin you use, there will be another one to replace it.'

The old fisherman thanked the golden fish, said farewell to the city at the bottom of the sea, climbed on the dolphin's back and in a short while was sitting on a rock in the sea not far from his own village. Soon a fishing boat came sailing by. The fisherman waved to it. The boat stopped but when the crew saw the fisherman they almost fainted. They

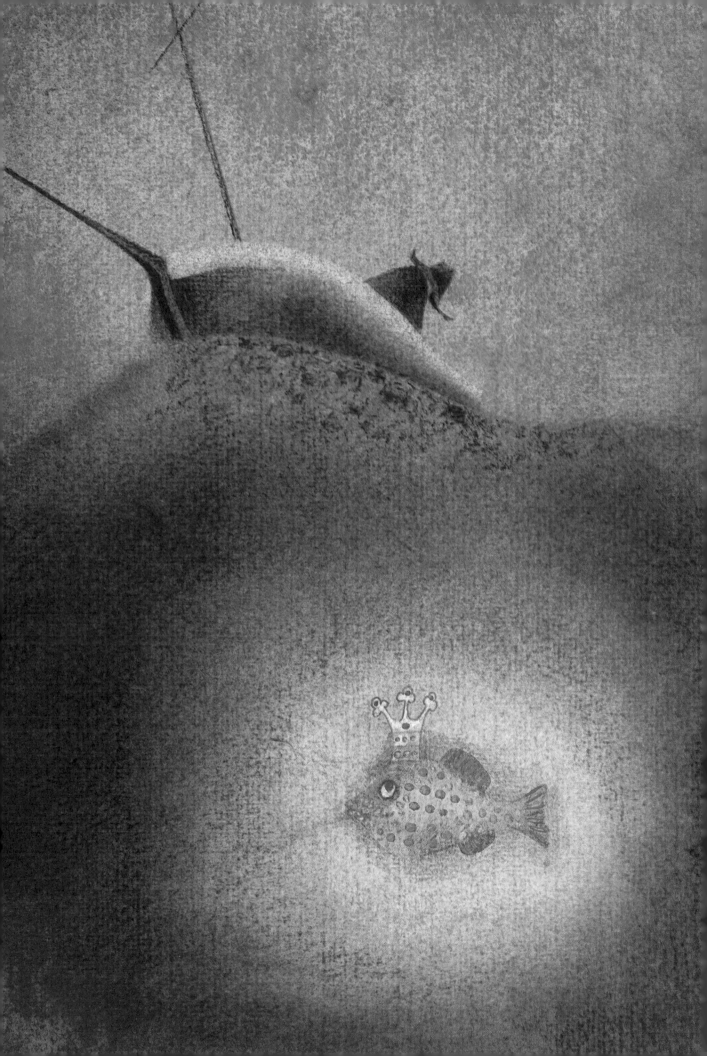

thought he was a ghost because the old fisherman had disappeared into the sea more than a year before.

'But I've only been away one day,' thought the fisherman at first, but then he remembered that one day at the bottom of the sea is the same as a year on dry land.

At first the fishermen could not believe what their old friend told them. But when he showed them his pockets full of precious stones and when he showered the whole village with the gold coins from his bottom-less bag, they believed him. Ever since then, the fisherman no longer goes fishing. He has received enough riches to last him a lifetime and he does not want to be ungrateful to the fish who had welcomed him so kindly in their city at the bottom of the sea.

THE MILLER'S THREE SONS

Once upon a time there was a miller who was so poor that when he died he left his three sons, John, James and Jack nothing but an old tomcat, a rooster and a scythe.

What about the mill in which he ground the flour and the donkey who carried the grain, you may ask? Well, the mill belonged to the lord of the castle and the poor hardworking donkey died three days before the miller himself.

When the sons returned home from the cemetery after the funeral, they asked each other sadly what was to become of them now.

'All that we can do,' said the eldest son, John, 'is to divide what our father left among us and go out into the world. We shall get along somehow there, whereas we shall certainly die of hunger here.'

'You are right,' said James and Jack. 'Since you are the eldest, you shall divide our inheritance!'

'Right,' said John. 'Jack, you take the scythe. James you'll get the rooster and I shall keep the tomcat.'

The brothers agreed to this. Jack threw the scythe over his shoulder, James took the rooster under his arm and John called to the tomcat to follow him. So the miller's three sons set out into the world.

A short way from the village they came to a crossroads.

'There are three of us and here are three paths. Let us each take a different path,' said John. 'We shall meet again at this place in a year and a day to see what luck we have had.'

The brothers nodded in approval, said goodbye to each other and set off.

The eldest, John, trudged with his tomcat many a weary mile, until he came to a king's castle. What a strange sight met his eyes there! Two thousand of the king's servants with all sorts of sticks and clubs in their hands were chasing mice and rats. There were so many mice and rats in this kingdom, eating whatever they found that the poor people were left without a morsel of food. The king's servants had already been chasing the mice and rats for half a year, yet all they had killed were three tiny mice, nothing more.

When John saw them all running and jumping about and bumping into one another, while the mice merrily scampered between their legs, he had to laugh. One of the servants stopped and said:

'You can afford to laugh, Stranger, but if you were in our place you wouldn't laugh long.'

'Why?' asked John.

'Why? Don't you see how we are trying to catch these terrible mice and kill them?'

'You are making a very hard job of catching a mouse,' said John. 'My tomcat can do that easily.'

He put the tomcat on the ground. The tomcat crouched then suddenly leapt, and landed on the first mouse running by and gobbled it down in a split second.

All the servants cried out in surprise:

'Good heavens, what miraculous animal is that?'

'It is a tomcat,' said John. 'He will catch all the mice in your kingdom all by himself.'

'A tomcat?' said the servants in amazement. 'We have never seen such an animal before. Won't it eat people?'

'Have no fear,' said John, 'it only eats mice and rats.'

'Then we must show this wonderful animal to our king,' said the servants. 'He will want to buy it at once. But do not be foolish and ask a low price for our king is rich,' they all advised him.

They immediately took John and his tomcat into the castle and led him before the king himself in the throne room.

When the king heard what his servants had to say, he frowned sternly and said:

'Stranger, I have been informed that the animal you have under your arm can catch mice and that it does not eat people. Is this true?'

'True as truth can be, Your Majesty,' said John. 'If you wish I will show you at once.'

A lot of mice were running around the throne, between the chairs and in and out of the cupboards. John put the tomcat on the floor and the poor animal, hungry after such a long journey, crouched and then pounced and pounced, until in a little while he had packed away a good half-dozen mice.

The king was amazed.

'How much do you want for this wonderful animal?'

But John was a clever lad and he said:

'My tomcat is not for sale. It is the only animal of its kind in the world and I cannot live without it.'

'But I will give you half my kingdom,' said the king, 'if you will let me have it.'

'I could not do that,' said John, 'unless you gave me your daughter, the princess, for my wife.'

The king did not take long to make up his mind and gave John the beautiful princess in exchange for the miraculous tomcat. The wedding took place that very day and so John received the king's daughter and half the kingdom.

But what happened in the meantime to the middle brother, James? He, too, had walked and walked with the rooster tucked under his arm until after a long journey he came to the castle of another king. It was growing dark and out of the castle gate came a huge hay-wagon drawn by black horses.

'Where are they going with that hay-wagon?' James asked one of the servants.

'Where are they going?' he replied. 'For daytime, of course! Don't you have daytime in your country or is it always night there?'

James asked no more, but thanked the servant and waited to see what would happen. The next morning he awoke early, just as the clock on the castle tower struck five. He peered out of the window but it was pitch dark, even though it was the middle of summer. Then the clock struck six, seven, eight, but outside it was still night. At about nine o'clock the sound of creaking wheels could be heard from a distance, and shortly after that the hay-wagon appeared, the very one he had seen leaving the castle gate the evening before. The hay-wagon was bringing daytime.

'Ah, so that's it,' said James. 'They probably don't have any roosters in these parts if they have to go and fetch daytime. We shall see this evening.'

At night he secretly let his rooster into the yard. At about three o'clock in the morning the rooster awoke, shook its wings and merrily crowed:

'Cock-a-doodle-doo! Cock-a-doodle-doo! Cock-a- doodle doo!'

In a little while it began to grow light and in half an hour it was daylight. Everyone in the king's castle was amazed. At first they thought that the hay-wagon had unexpectedly returned early, but then they realised something else had happened. The servants were questioned and one of them finally revealed what had happened. The young stranger who had been given a place to sleep in the castle had put some kind of a bird in the yard during the night and the bird kept on crying out until daylight arrived.

The king had James brought before him, looked at him sternly and said:

'Are you the one who brought daylight, young man?'

'Yes, I did, or rather my bird did,' replied James, pointing to the rooster he had under his arm.

'What is the name of your bird?' asked the king.

'It is called a rooster, Your Majesty. All it has to do is to crow in the morning and daylight comes,' answered James.

'Where can one get such a wonderful bird?' asked the king.

'This is the only such bird in the world,' said James, who was no fool.

'Sell it to me,' urged the king, 'and I will give you whatever you want for it, even as much as half my kingdom.'

'My rooster is not for sale, at least not for gold or silver, since I cannot live without it,' said James. 'But if you want it so badly I will make a suggestion. Give me your daughter, the princess, in exchange for it.'

It did not take the king long to make up his mind and he exchanged the beautiful princess for this miraculous bird. So James won the king's daughter and half his kingdom.

And what happened to the youngest, Jack? He thought he had received the worst share of the legacy and at first he wanted to throw his scythe in the bushes at the side of the road. Luckily he did not do this but kept on walking until he came to a king's castle. Around the castle were large fields of corn, and thousands of harvesters were reaping the grain in such a way that they kept bumping into one another. They were working hard, but most of their efforts were wasted, as much of the grain fell from the stalks on to the ground.

Jack looked at them in amazement and could not believe his eyes. Finally he went over to the field, showed the harvesters his scythe and with one swing reaped a good armful of corn.

'What is that wonderful thing?' cried the harvesters. 'We must tell our king about this.'

They went to tell the king about the wonderful tool which the stranger had.

The king wanted to see this miracle and went with the harvesters to the field to find Jack. When he arrived, he asked the miller's son to show him his magic tool.

'It is a scythe, Your Majesty,' said Jack and began to cut the corn. In a short while the whole field of corn was cut.

The king could not take his eyes off this wonderful work and said:

'Stranger, sell me your scythe!'

But Jack was not stupid. He said:

'I cannot, Your Majesty, my scythe is not for sale. But I might leave it with you if you give me your daughter, the princess, for my wife!'

'I will, I will with pleasure,' replied the king, and so even the miller's third son received a king's daughter for a bride and half a kingdom.

When a year and a day had passed, the three brothers kept their promise to each other and came to the crossroads near the village where they had once parted. What a joyful occasion it was when all three came riding in their golden coaches with royal crowns on their heads! And who did they have to thank for all this? Their poor father and his legacy, the tomcat, the rooster and the scythe!

THE SNOWCHILD

Once upon a time there was an old man and his wife who had no children although they dearly wanted them. While they were still young they did not mind so much, because they kept hoping that they would eventually have children. But when they grew old, they realised that they would be alone until the day they died and this made them unhappy. Who would comfort them and who would look after them when they were too old to look after themselves?

One winter's day the old man called on a neighbour to smoke a pipe and have a chat with him. In the meantime, the sky clouded over and soon it began to snow. The flakes fell so thickly that it looked as though everything was hidden under a quilt of eiderdown. There had not been such a heavy fall of snow in the village for a long time. The children rushed into the street and began to play in the snow.

Just at this time, the old man was returning home from his neighbour's. When he saw the children happily rolling a big ball of snow in order to make a snowman from it, an idea occured to him. He rushed home and called to the old woman.

'Wife, wife, come outside quickly! If we cannot have a real child, we'll make a child out of snow. For a few days at least, we'll have something to be thankful for.'

The old woman took a fancy to her husband's idea.

'You're right, husband! Let's make a snowchild.'

No sooner had she said this, than they set to work. They rushed out into the street, made a ball from the soft snow and began to model a snowchild from it. In a short while the whole village had turned out to watch them. The children were delighted, but the older people laughed and said to each other that the poor old man and his wife had lost their wits.

But in a little while they stopped laughing. The old man and the old woman had made a snowchild so pretty and so lifelike that it looked as if it was about to move and speak. When the old man and his wife each put a piece of coal in its face for the eyes, all of a sudden the snowchild really did move and really did begin to speak. It flung its white arms around the necks of the old man and woman in turn and cried:

'Daddy, Mummy! At last I have real parents of my very own!'

The great wish of the old man and the old woman was fulfilled! They had a son with hands and legs as white as snow and eyes as black as coal. People came from everywhere to look at him and could not believe their own eyes.

Really and truly they had never seen such a delightful child.

As long as it was cold outside the lovely snowchild was happy and gave his old parents nothing but pleasure. But when the days grew longer and the snow began to disappear, first from the fields and then from the hillsides and mountain peaks, the snowchild began to waste away and make his parents more and more worried. He went around like a body without a soul, avoiding the sun, seeking shade and darkness, and with tears flowing incessantly from his eyes.

'Tell us, what is the matter with you, snowchild,' said the old man and the old woman, but the lad did not answer and hung his head. Matters became worse and worse. He stopped going out during the day, and only went out in the evening. When the sun had set and the cold moon had climbed up into the sky, he slipped out like a shadow to stand for a moment in front of the house.

Now summer had arrived and the boys and girls in the village were preparing to celebrate midsummer's eve with a bonfire. They made a pile of branches in the meadow near the forest, and when it grew dark they set fire to the bonfire and began to dance around it. The snowchild who was with them suddenly seemed to come to life again and merrily danced with the other children.

When the bonfire had almost burnt out, the children began to jump over the flames. Laughing and shouting, they jumped, first one, then another, then yet another, and finally even the snowchild jumped. But alas, no sooner did he touch the flame than the fire flickered and hissed as it does when you throw a piece of ice on it, and the snowchild disappeared. Only a little water remained on the arms of the children who had held his hands.

So once again the old man and the old woman were alone without even their child made of snow.

STRONG FOURTEEN

O nce upon a time there was a woman whose husband died soon after the birth of their son. The woman looked after the child as best she could and cared for him for seven whole years. At the end of the seventh year the boy said to his mother:

'I am going to the mountain to see if I am strong enough. If the wind blows me down you must look after me for another seven years.'

When the boy climbed to the top of the mountain a strong wind almost blew him over. 'I'm not strong enough,' he told himself and returned home.

At home his mother cared for him for another seven years. At the end of his fourteenth year the boy said to his mother:

'I shall go to the mountain again to see if I am strong enough. If the wind blows me down you must look after me for another seven years!'

When he climbed the mountain there was a strong wind blowing, but Fourteen did not even quiver.

'Now I am strong enough,' he told himself and returned home.

'Mother, I am strong enough now and shall go out into the world to seek my fortune.'

He went straight to the King, and said:

'Your Majesty, do you need a stable boy?'

'I do,' replied the King, 'mine has just left. But what do you expect me to pay you?'

'Only as much grain as I can carry, so that my mother will have something to eat.'

'Agreed,' said the King. 'But first you must cut down that forest.'

He gave him an axe. But Fourteen said:

'What's this? It can't be an axe, it must be a fly swatter. I need something solid.'

'All right,' said the King. 'Go to the blacksmith and tell him to make you a special giant axe.'

As soon as the special axe was ready, Fourteen tied it to his little finger and went into the forest. Once he got there he lay down in the forest and went to sleep. In the morning a young girl brought him breakfast. Fourteen ate it and then lay down to rest. Then the girl brought him lunch. Fourteen ate it and spent the afternoon doing nothing.

The King was watching from a castle window and became so furious that he almost reached for his gun.

'You scoundrel, not doing anything. Only eating and drinking. I don't need such good-for-nothings here.'

'Take him one more meal,' he said to the girl, 'and ask him whether or not he intends to do something. If he doesn't I shall throw him out!'

The girl brought Fourteen a meal and said:

'The King wants to know whether you are going to do anything. If you won't, you will be thrown out.'

'I will, of course I will, but there's no hurry,' said Fourteen. 'First I have to make a handle for my axe.'

He ate his meal and then set to work.

With a few blows the best oak tree fell to the ground, and Fourteen made a handle from it.

'And now to work,' he said, rubbing his hands together, and began to fell the trees.

In a quarter of an hour almost the entire forest was cut down.

The King looked out of the window and saw nearly all his trees lying on the ground.

He called out quickly to the girl, 'Run and tell him to stop, that's enough wood. Let him just bring me some wood for the fire.'

Fourteen took the two largest oaks, and bent them, binding them round all the wood he had cut.

When the King saw Fourteen carrying a whole forest on his back towards the castle, he took fright and said to the girl:

'Tell him to pile it behind the castle.'

Fourteen threw down the firewood in the courtyard. The whole castle shook and the poor old Queen fell from her chair on her knees, almost tumbling into the fireplace.

The King realised that things were bad.

'What shall I do with this lad?' he asked the Queen. 'He will ruin us.'

'A fine mess you've made of everything,' said the Queen. 'But wait.

You know that in our village the miller is a devil and always robs us when grinding our grain. Why don't you order Fourteen to stop him doing that. The devil will certainly carry him away and then you'll have no more trouble.'

'You're right,' said the King and ordered Fourteen to come before him. 'Listen,' he said, 'our miller is a devil. Take him the wheat from all my estates, but do not let him rob you of any of it or things will fare badly for you.'

'Don't worry, Your Majesty, he'll not rob me of a single kernel!'

He seized the sacks of grain and trotted along to the miller's.

'Here, grind this grain,' he told the miller. 'But do not try to rob me of a single kernel or things will fare badly for you!'

The miller-devil was afraid of strong Fourteen, so he did not steal a single kernel from the King's sack.

'Your Majesty, here is the grain,' said Fourteen to the King and threw the sacks of flour on the ground. 'You can weigh it, and you will find that not a grain is missing.'

The King weighed the sacks and, indeed, not a grain was missing.

'What shall I do with him now?' he asked himself angrily. Then he remembered something and said:

'You've done very well, but the Queen has never seen a devil and would like to have a look at this miller. Go and fetch him.'

'Your Majesty, if the Queen wants to see the devil, she shall. Just give me a strong pair of Turkish tongs.'

'All right,' said the King. 'Go to the blacksmith and tell him to make you some Turkish tongs.'

As soon as the tongs were ready, Fourteen set out to find the devil.

'Bang, bang, bang,' he pounded on the gate.

'Who's there?' asked the devil.

'It is I, Fourteen.'

The devil opened the gate:

'What do you want?'

'I want you to come with me! The Queen wants to look at you!'

That made the devil angry.

'You beware of me,' he cried.

But Fourteen was not frightened. He seized the tongs, caught the devil between them and said:

38

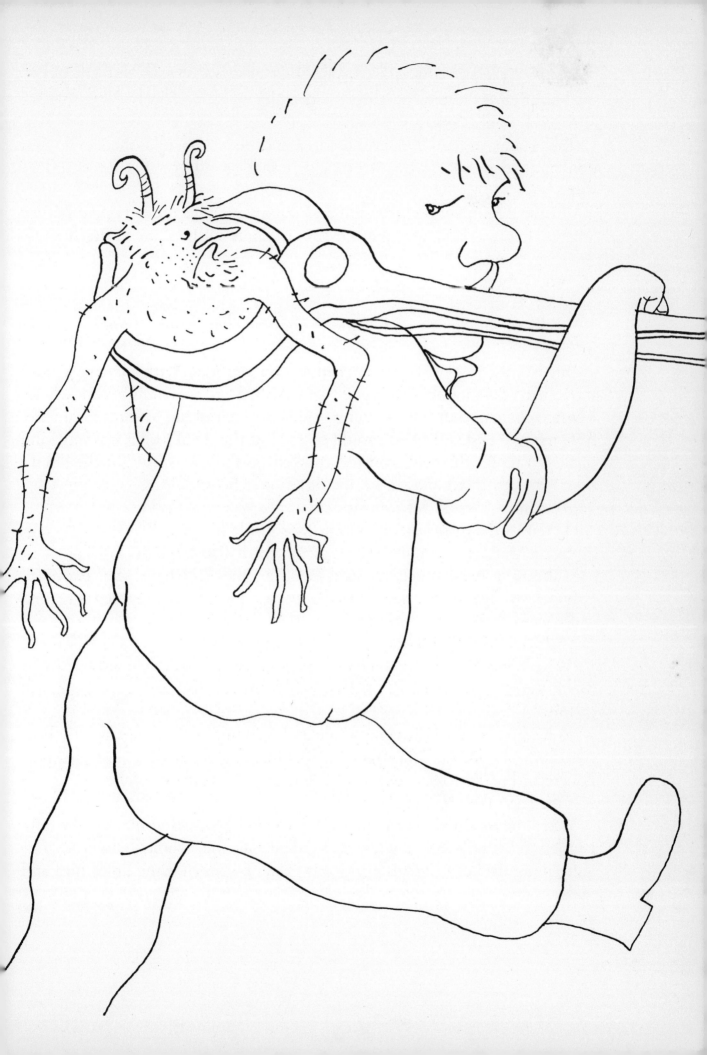

'You're coming with me whether you want to or not. Off we go!'

And he threw the devil over his shoulder.

After a while, Fourteen stopped.

'I'm going to put you down for a moment,' he told the devil, 'but don't you dare run away. If you do, I shall go after you and you'll be sorry.'

But the devil paid no attention and ran away. This made Fourteen very angry. He raced back and pounded on the gate with all his strength:

'Bang, bang!'

'Who's there?'

'It is I, Fourteen!'

'Lock all the gates and doors!' shouted the devil. 'Don't let him in!'

But it was no use. Fourteen banged on the gate with his tongs until it opened. He ran in, but the devil had vanished and was hiding somewhere. Fourteen began to turn everything upside down looking for him. Suddenly he came to a bed and what should he see but the devil's long nose sticking out from under the bed! Fourteen picked up the tongs, caught the devil's nose between them and threw the devil over his shoulder.

'And now I won't let you go!'

He ran to the castle. As soon as he was inside he cried:

'Your Majesty, come and look at the devil I've brought you!'

'Take him away quickly!' shrieked the Queen. 'I have seen enough!'

Fourteen threw the devil on the floor. The devil breathed fire and smoke and flew up the chimney.

The poor King did not know where to turn next.

'What shall I do with this lad?' he pondered. 'Where would I get as much grain as he can carry? That will ruin me forever. I must get rid of him.'

So he gave Fourteen a crazy mule and sent him to fight against a whole battalion of soldiers. The soldiers kept shooting from rifles and pistols at Fourteen, but Fourteen just carried on, grumbling to himself:

'Oh, these flies do sting!'

When he reached the soldiers, he seized the mad mule by the tail, twirled it round like a stick and killed off the whole battalion. The King hung his head, for his army was gone. Fourteen came up to him and said:

'Your Majesty, you deserve to be cut up into little pieces too, but you're the King and I'm your subject, so I'll not hurt you. Give me my grain and I'll go.'

The King could do nothing but give Fourteen as much as he could carry! A whole barn of grain, a whole cellar of drink and food, and a whole treasury of gold and silver.

When Fourteen brought all this home, his mother praised him:

'I have a good son!'

Later, Fourteen got married and a big feast was prepared. There was so much food that everybody could eat as much as they wanted, and the wine flowed like a stream from the glasses, so that everyone could drink as much as they wanted. I was there too, eating and drinking with the rest, but it's a pity it lasted such a little while because now our story has come to an end.

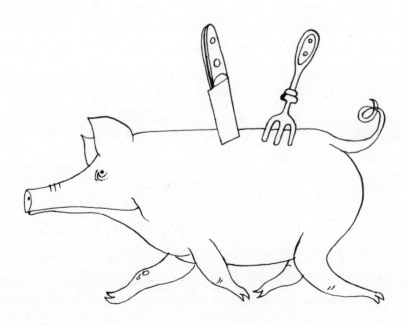

THE SHEPHERD
AND THE FLYING PRINCESSES

Once upon a time there was a boy called Pipi Menu. He was an orphan who had nobody in the world except a grandmother. Granny was already old, and she sat at home by the fire all day spinning while Pipi Menu took the sheep to pasture. That was their only source of income.

Pipi Menu often took his sheep to pasture in the meadows, but most of all he liked to take them up on the hill behind the village. On the other side of the hill, in the midst of a forest, lay a deep, clear lake and in the late afternoon, before the sun set, large white birds would fly to the lake. The little shepherd had never seen such beautiful birds.

'What can they be?' he asked himself over and over again, until one day he decided to find out. He left the sheep in the care of his faithful dog and all alone he crept closer to the lake. What a surprise he had! Before the sun had set, three white birds circled round the lake, flew down to the grass, and shook their wings. At that moment their skin and feathers fell from them and there on the shore of the lake stood three beautiful girls in white gowns.

The beautiful girls went into the water, and swam, dived and frolicked like ducks while the sun was still setting. Then they jumped out on the shore, put on their skins with the white feathers and immediately became three swans again. The swans rose, circled round the lake and flew away.

That day, Pipi Menu returned home, his head full of thoughts.

'What has happened to you, child,' his grandmother asked. She stopped whirling the spindle between her fingers and turned from the fire to her grandson.

'Tell me, what is troubling you, perhaps I can help.'

'I don't think you can help me, Granny,' said Pipi Menu. 'But perhaps you know who those three beautiful girls are that I saw today near the lake.'

He told his grandmother what he had seen. Granny shook her head:

'My dear Pipi, it would have been better if you hadn't seen them! Now listen to me! Those three swans are princesses, the daughters of a powerful magician. They live in a castle made of solid gold and precious stones and the castle hangs from four golden chains, very very high above the blue sea.'

Pipi Menu asked:

'Can an ordinary person like me get into that castle?'

'He can, my boy,' said grandmother, 'I remember when I was a girl, a shepherd like yourself from our village set out for the castle and even came back. He was the one who told us all about it.'

'What must a person do to get there?' asked Pipi Menu.

'First of all you must be a brave lad who isn't frightened easily,' said his grandmother. 'You must hide near the lake until the princesses come, and then hide the feathers of one of them. The princess will beg, cry, plead and cajole, so you must not give way but insist that she takes you to the castle. Only when the princess promises that can you return her feathers, and then the princess will really carry you in the air to their palace. When you get there you must make up your mind about what to do.'

Pipi Menu listened and was fascinated. The whole night long he dreamed about the swan princesses and about the castle suspended in mid-air on golden chains above the broad, blue sea.

The next morning Pipi Menu took his sheep out to pasture but, in fact, he had already made up his mind to try his luck with the beautiful princesses. Towards evening he sent the herd home with his faithful dog and went to the lake himself.

He arrived in time, as the swans had not yet come. The little shepherd hid in the bushes near the place where they shed their skins and waited. In a little while, the three beautiful white birds appeared over the lake. They circled over the water, sank down to the grass, shook their wings and there on the shore of the lake stood three girls dressed in white gowns. They seemed even more beautiful than before, but the youngest pleased him most. He watched carefully where they left their feathers and while the princesses were frolicking in the water and playing far from the shore, he ran over to the skins, seized one and hid it in the bushes.

In a short while the sun had set and the princesses came out of the water. But on the shore there lay only two swan skins, for the third one was gone. The two elder princesses quickly put on their swan feathers, shook their wings and rose above the lake.

But the third princess began to weep and run along the shore looking for her feathers.

Pipi Menu came out of his hiding-place. When the princess saw her feathers in his hand she ran up to him and began to beg him:

'Shepherd, Shepherd, please give me back my feathers. I will give you as much gold and silver as you want!'

But Pipi Menu was not to be persuaded:

'I will return your feathers only if you carry me to your castle!'

'I cannot!' cried the princess. 'Father would be angry with me and would tear you to pieces. Please give me back my feathers or I'll take them from you!'

But Pipi Menu was not frightened by her threat and insisted on having his own way.

'I will return your feathers only if you carry me to your castle!'

The princess realised that she could not dissuade the shepherd.

'All right,' she said, 'but if something happens to you don't blame me!'

So Pipi Menu returned the feathers to the youngest princess. She put them on, changed into a swan and took the shepherd on her broad back. In a moment or two they could see the sea, and above it, high up over the clouds, there was a magnificent castle suspended on four golden chains. It glittered so brightly with gold and precious stones that it almost hurt their eyes.

The white swan put the shepherd down in the castle garden.

'You must not go into the castle. If father finds you there it will be the end of you,' she told the lad. 'Help our gardener, and I shall come to see you from time to time.'

Then she flapped her wings and flew into the castle through an open window. It was very late now!

So Pipi Menu became a gardener. All day long he helped the old gardener and all through the night he dreamed about the beautiful swan princess. He thought hard and long about how he could speak to her in secret.

Things were no better with the lovely princess. She just could not get the shepherd out of her mind, dreaming about him for nights and days on end and thinking hard and long about how to speak to him in secret. It was not easy because ever since the evening she had returned home late she had never been allowed to leave the castle with her sisters.

At last, however, they did manage to speak to one another. The old queen, the princess's mother, used to send a basket on a rope down to the garden from the castle window. During the day the old gardener filled it with fresh fruit and vegetables and in the evening the queen would pull the overflowing basket up to the castle and through the window. When Pipi Menu saw this, he gladly offered to help the old gardener and so it happened that the gardener's helper was put in charge of the basket. In the first basket he sent, in addition to fruit and vegetables, he put a beautiful bouquet of flowers.

The old queen was surprised.

'Our gardener has never sent such a bouquet before,' she said, and put it in her room.

The queen was surprised about the bouquet of flowers, thinking it had been sent by her old gardener. But her youngest daughter immediately understood who had sent them, so she offered to send the basket down and pull it up every day. The old queen willingly consented and from that time on the princess and Pipi Menu saw each other for a little while every morning and every evening. In the morning the princess let the basket down from the window and Pipi Menu stood below in the garden and waited for it. In the evening the princess pulled up the basket and Pipi Menu stood in the garden and waited until the basket and the princess disappeared from sight.

One evening the princess came to the window but could not see the shepherd below in the garden, and the basket was so heavy that she could hardly pull it up. No sooner had she put it on the floor in her room, and pushed aside the leaves that covered the basket than out of it jumped Pipi Menu himself.

'Do not be frightened, Princess,' said Pipi Menu, 'I only wish to talk to you.'

'And I with you,' said the princess and hid the shepherd behind a curtain.

From that time on, Pipi Menu talked to his beloved every day. In the evening the princess would draw him up in the basket and in the morning she would let him down into the garden. So they met to talk and laugh and sing together and no one knew anything about it. Only the two other princesses suspected anything at all. Their younger sister, who used to

45

be so sad, suddenly became very gay, and every evening a strange voice was to be heard coming from her room.

'Tell us who comes to see you,' they urged their sister. 'If you don't tell us we will tell mother and father!'

The princess knew that they would do so. When her shepherd came to see her that evening she put two little bundles in his hand, and said:

'Dear Pipi Menu, we must go away or something terrible will happen to us. Here are two little bundles: one of them contains my gold and precious stones, the other contains my older sister's spindle, my eldest sister's distaff, and my mother's thimble. We shall need them. And now sit on my back and fear nothing.'

The princess put on her swan skin, shook her wings and, with the shepherd on her back, flew up into the air.

In a moment or two a dark cloud appeared on the horizon behind them. It spread all over the sky and almost reached them. The white swan looked round and cried:

'Pipi Menu, throw the spindle behind you or we shall be in trouble! That is my older sister!'

Pipi Menu put his hand in the bundle, grabbed the spindle and threw it behind him, and the dark cloud fell to the ground like heavy rain.

The white swan with the shepherd on her back flew on. A moment later a darker cloud appeared on the horizon. It spread all over the sky and almost reached them. The white swan looked round and cried:

'Pipi Menu, throw the distaff behind you or we shall be in trouble! That is my eldest sister!'

Pipi Menu put his hand in the bundle, grabbed the distaff and threw it behind him, and the dark cloud fell to the ground like hail.

And the white swan with the shepherd on her back flew on. A moment later the third and darkest cloud of all appeared on the horizon. It spread all over the sky and almost reached them. The white swan looked behind and cried:

'Pipi Menu, throw the thimble behind you or it will be our end. That is my mother!'

Pipi Menu reached into the bundle, grabbed the thimble and threw it behind him, and the black cloud fell to the ground like a storm, with thunder and lightning.

Then the white swan, with the shepherd on her back slowly sank to the ground. Pipi Menu saw the lake under him where the swans had gone to swim, the hill where he took the sheep to pasture, and the cottage where he lived with his grandmother.

Granny happened to be standing in the yard and looking at the sky. Out of the sky she heard a sound above her head, and before she knew what had happened, there standing beside her, was her grandson, Pipi Menu, holding a beautiful princess by the hand.

Ever since then the shepherd has lived happily and contentedly with his beautiful wife in his grandmother's cottage. Pipi Menu continued to tend the sheep, while his beautiful wife stayed at home and cooked, cleaned, and spun. Grandmother looked after the grandchildren and told them, evening after evening, about the castle hanging from four golden chains, high, high above the clouds and the wide blue sea.

THE BLACK SHIP

Once upon a time there was a merchant who had one son, called Johnny. Johnny was a good boy and when he began to grow up his father sent him to the town of Saint-Malo to be trained as a proper seaman, since they say that the best sailors in the world used to come from Saint-Malo. The boy did not disappoint his father, and in a few years young Johnny grew up to be the brave and able Captain John. The old merchant gave him his best ship and a good-sized bag of gold so that he could buy cargo and then sail the seas and sell his goods.

Captain John thanked his father, bought the goods, fitted out the ship and then chose thirty of the best seamen in Saint-Malo. No one had ever had such a crew before!

When everything was ready, Captain John bade farewell to his father and set sail for India. The journey was long and tiring, but the sailors were content. They ate with the captain at one table like his officers, they received the same food that he ate, and drank wine from the same cask. They could hardly have wanted more; and they would have jumped into fire for their captain, if he had asked them to.

The trip to India ended successfully. They sold the rich fabrics and pearls they had brought, and bought coffee and tea, and when they reached Saint-Malo after a year and unloaded their cargo, all the merchants came running, eager to buy, and Captain John made a mountain of money. His old father was pleased and John's seamen were too, because each of them got a good share of the earnings.

This was repeated year after year. Year after year, Captain John sailed to India or to America, year after year he returned richer and year after year his old father would say:

'If only you would marry, I could close my eyes in peace. You have already chosen a bride!'

It was true. Captain John had long since met a beautiful girl, lovely Jane, the sister of one of his officers, but he did not wish to marry yet.

'When I find the golden island, then I'll get married,' he always told his father. On one of his journeys to India he had heard about a secret

48

island made of gold. Many captains had set sail for it but not one of them had returned.

'But I shall return and then all of us, myself and my sailors, will have enough to live on until the end of our days,' Captain John decided. At last he began to prepare for the journey. This time he took no goods with him but filled the ship with bread, rusks, smoked meat, fruit and wine, enough supplies for a year's trip.

Captain took leave of his father, said goodbye to lovely Jane and gave the order to set sail.

'When I return we'll be married,' he called cheerfully to Jane as the ship began to move, and the crew cheered as though they were already returning home.

A very long journey lay before them. They had left the shores of India behind, the last island had disappeared from view, and they no longer saw birds on their sails, and still not a sign of the golden island. Nineteen whole months passed since they had left Saint-Malo to begin their journey, and still they could see no trace of the golden island.

'Who knows if such an island even exists,' the discontented sailors began to grumble, and they would have been happy to turn back. But Captain John refused to be beaten.

'Since we have sailed for nineteen months let us go on for still another month,' he said. 'You'll see that we will find the island.'

And believe it or not, in the end they did find it. One day a sailor in the lookout cried:

'Land, land!'

Something on the horizon glittered like a second sun about to rise, or a great fire burning. But it was neither the sun nor a fire, but the island they were seeking. It sparkled in the sun and really was made of gold. Within seconds the crew was on deck, cheering joyfully.

But their joy did not last for long. The island itself was empty and bare, without a living soul on it, but around the island sailed a flotilla of heavily armed ships. They were guarding the island, and as soon as Captain John came within firing range they welcomed him with a cannon salvo.

Captain John realised that he could do nothing against a whole flotilla with only one ship.

'The devil take them!' he swore on the captain's bridge and ordered the ship to be turned around. 'We tried so hard, and now we have to go home with empty hands! I would give my soul to the devil if he would help me land on that island!'

Hardly had he said this than a ship appeared behind him on the horizon. It was completely black, with six masts so tall they almost reached the sky. The bow and stern of the ship consisted of prison cells and the upper deck was lined with taverns. Carts moving along cables were carrying sailors from one place to another.

When Captain John saw this ship, his heart tightened with fear, although usually he was not afraid of anything, even the most terrible storm. But he could not turn back now for the black ship was soon at the side of his own craft, which looked like a nutshell compared with this ship. At the wheel of the black ship stood an old sailor, older than the world itself. He called to Captain John:

'Captain, throw me a rope, and I'll tow you over to the golden island!'

In a moment one of the sailors had thrown a rope over to the deck of the black ship, which towed Captain John's ship swiftly behind it. In three hours they were back at the golden island. Then the old captain of the black ship put a black whistle to his lips, and when he blew it it seemed that shots were being fired. The guard ships raced away in all directions and the way to the golden island was open.

'Now you can land, Captain, and fill your boat with gold,' said the old man. 'Are you satisfied?'

'I am,' answered Captain John. 'I don't know how to thank you for all this.'

'You need not thank me,' said the old man, as old as the world. 'Just don't forget what you promised me!'

Captain John hung his head.

'I won't forget,' he said. 'A promise is a promise, and I shall keep my word.'

'Good, good,' said the old man, 'but just to make sure would you please put it in writing.'

'I'll do that,' said Captain John, 'but only when you deliver us alive and healthy with our cargo at Saint-Malo.'

'Now look,' said the old man, 'before my ship can turn round seven years will have passed and you would long be home by then. Just fill up your ship with gold and I'll show you the way.'

So Captain John and his sailors landed on the island. It had no grass, no people, no animals, no houses, no trees, only gold. The sailors filled the ship with gold and then set sail for home. At the wheel stood the old man, as old as the world. Under his guidance the ship flew like an arrow. After only three months the towers of Saint-Malo came into view. The ship dropped anchor in the bay. From the harbour came a boat to welcome the crew. In it were Captain John's father, Jane the captain's betrothed, and the wives and sweethearts of all the sailors.

Captain John heartily welcomed them, and when he showed them the treasure they were all delighted. But Captain John hung his head sadly as though something was worrying him.

His betrothed, the lovely Jane, noticed this at once. As soon as she found the right moment, she asked:

'What is the matter, Captain John, that makes you walk so sadly?'

'Nothing,' replied Captain John.

But Jane did not believe him.

'Please tell me, Captain John. You know that joys shared are twofold joys, and sorrows shared are half the sorrow. Perhaps I can help you in your troubles.'

'How could you help me when the devil has me in his power,' sighed Captain John and told Jane everything that had happened about his foolish promise to the devil in return for taking him to the golden island. 'And tomorrow, when we anchor in the harbour and unload all the gold, I must pay my debt because a promise is a promise.'

'That is true,' said the lovely Jane. 'But don't worry, even the devil cannot compete with a woman's wiles. I shall help you. Just be sure that I am there when you sign the contract.'

The next day Captain John's ship reached the dock and the sailors began to unload the bags of gold. The old man, as old as the world, stepped into the captain's cabin holding a piece of paper in his hand.

'I fulfilled my promise, Captain John. Your ship and cargo have reached Saint-Malo safe and sound,' he said. 'It is time for you to keep your promise. Here is the contract for you to sign.'

Captain John took the contract, signed it and was just about to give it to the old man, as old as the world, when Jane, who was sitting on a chest in the corner, seized the contract before the old man could take it, and said:

'Captain John fulfilled his word. But there is one more debt to be paid.'

'Which one?' said the angry old man, as old as the world.

But Jane was not frightened:

'On what ship did you come to the town of Saint-Malo?' she asked the old man.

'On Captain John's ship,' replied the old man, as old as the world.

'Then you are in debt to him for the journey!' said Jane. 'What will you give him for it?'

'Whatever he wants!' said the old man, as old as the world, furiously.

'That's good,' said Jane. 'The captain wants nothing but this piece of paper.' And she tore the contract into pieces and burned them in the flame of a candle that stood on the table.

'You caught me, there, lovely Jane,' said the old man, as old as the world, gnashing his teeth. 'But you haven't won yet! If I ever find your captain on the open sea, not even your cleverness will help him!' and he disappeared in a cloud of smoke. Only a bitter smell was left behind in the cabin.

And that was how the lovely Jane saved brave Captain John. When they divided their treasure of gold into twenty-one equal parts, the sailors and their captain became the richest men in Saint-Malo. For the rest of their lives they did not have to go to sea again. And for the rest of his life the brave Captain John did not set sail although he often longed for the wide seas. Whenever he thought about them, his lovely Jane reminded him of the black ship and the threat of the old man, as old as the world.

HOW THE BLACKSMITH BECAME THE SON-IN-LAW AND HEIR OF THE FRENCH KING

Once upon a time there was a French king as rich as the ocean, as brave as a lion and as true as steel. Yet the French king was not happy, for his only daughter was as beautiful as a sunny day and as wise as a book, but she was so sad that she never, never smiled. This was why she was called Princess Sad-Face.

But that was not all. The French king had yet another problem. Although he had seven hundred beautiful horses as black as night in his stable, he loved his one white horse most of all. And this horse was so wild that not even the best blacksmith in the kingdom could shoe it. This was why it was called White Breakiron.

The French king worried and worried about his daughter and his horse until one day he could not stand it any longer and sent for the town-crier of his royal city. When the town-crier came, the king gave him a hundred gold coins and said:

'Town-crier, here are one hundred coins. Go into the wide world, from city to city, from village to village, from house to house and let it be known that whoever can make Princess Sad-Face smile just once and can shoe White Breakiron, will become the son-in-law and heir of the French king!'

The town-crier gave a roll on his drum and said:

'Your Majesty, your orders shall be obeyed.'

He left straightaway for the wide world, and wandered from city to city, from village to village and from house to house to announce the king's message.

From that moment, from all corners of the world, suitors who hoped to make the princess smile and to shoe the white horse arrived at the king's castle. Many came but they all left without success.

At this time in a village in the French kingdom, a brave young blacksmith lived with his mother. One evening at supper the young blacksmith said to his mother:

'Mother, tomorrow I shall go to the king's court to make Princess Sad-Face smile and to shoe White Breakiron so that I shall become the son-in-law and heir of the French king.'

'Go ahead, Son,' his mother replied, 'may the Good Lord go with you. Here are four silver coins and one gold one for your journey.'

Then the mother went to sleep, but her son stayed awake. He took his silver and gold coins and instead of putting them in his bag for the journey he set to work on them with his blacksmith's hammer. He made four silver horseshoes from the silver coins, and twenty-eight nails from the gold one, seven for each horseshoe. Only then did he go to bed.

At dawn the young blacksmith said goodbye to his mother and set out for the royal court wearing a beret on his head, holding a stick in his hand and carrying a bag over his shoulder containing a hammer, the silver horseshoes, the golden nails, a piece of bread and a flask full of wine.

When he had walked for the whole morning, the blacksmith became hungry. He sat down by the roadside, opened his bag and began to eat. But,

56

just at that moment, in the nearby field, a cricket, black as tar, was singing. As soon as it saw the blacksmith it hopped up to him and said:

'Chirr, chirr, chirr! Good day, Blacksmith.'

'Good day, Cricket,' replied the blacksmith. 'What can I do for you?'

'Chirr, chirr, chirr! Blacksmith, I want to know where you are going.'

'Cricket, I am going to the royal court to make Princess Sad-Face smile and to shoe White Breakiron in order to become the son-in-law and heir of the French king.'

'Chirr, chirr, chirr! Blacksmith, take me with you. I may be of service to you.'

'Why not, Cricket! Come and catch hold of my beard.'

The cricket jumped and caught hold of the blacksmith's beard and the blacksmith went on. When he had been walking almost the whole day he grew hungry. He sat down by the roadside and began to eat. In the nearby field a little mouse was nibbling away at some grain. As soon as it saw the blacksmith it ran up to him and said:

'Squeak, squeak, squeak! Good day, Blacksmith.'

'Good day, Little Mouse,' replied the blacksmith. 'What can I do for you?'

'Squeak, squeak, squeak! Blacksmith, I want to know where you are going.'

'Little Mouse, I am going to the royal court to make Princess Sad-Face smile and to shoe White Breakiron in order to become the son-in-law and heir of the French king.'

'Squeak, squeak, squeak! Blacksmith, take me with you. I may be of service to you.'

'Why not, Little Mouse! Come along, catch hold of my beret.'

The little mouse jumped and caught hold of the blacksmith's beret and the blacksmith went on.

When it was dark, he stopped at an inn to sleep for the night. Towards morning he suddenly woke up, for something had bitten his nose.

'Blacksmith, get up, get up. You've slept enough, you lazybones!'

In great surprise the blacksmith said:

'Who are you? How is it that I can hear you but cannot see you?'

'Blacksmith, I am Mrs Flea and I want to know where you are going.'

'Mrs Flea, I am going to the royal court to make Princess Sad-Face smile and to shoe White Breakiron in order to become the son-in-law and heir of the French king.'

'Blacksmith, take me with you. I may be of service to you.'

The blacksmith agreed and with the cricket in his beard, the mouse in his beret and the flea at the tip of his nose he went straight to the royal court.

Three hours after the sun had set he was sitting on a stone seat near the main gate of the king's castle.

The servants hurried past and asked him, mockingly:

'Blacksmith, where are you going?'

But the blacksmith was not upset.

'Good people, I have come to speak to the French king and Princess Sad-Face.'

'Blacksmith, the king is over there, just coming out from church.'

And indeed the king had just come out of the church with Princess Sad-Face.

The blacksmith boldly went up to the princess and said:

'Good day, Princess Sad-Face! I have come to make you smile in order to become your husband. Good day, French King! I have come to shoe White Breakiron in order to become your son-in-law and heir.'

When Princess Sad-Face saw this young man with a cricket on his chin, a mouse in his beret and Mrs Flea at the tip of his nose, she began to laugh gaily.

But the blacksmith only said:

'French King, the first half of my work is finished. Princess Sad-Face has smiled for the first time in her life.'

'Blacksmith, you are right!' said the French king. 'But now you must go to the stable and shoe White Breakiron.'

The young blacksmith was not frightened and replied:

'French King, your order will be obeyed!'

And all three set out for the stable. Once there, the blacksmith took the four silver horseshoes and twenty-eight golden nails out of his bag. The French King and Princess Sad-Face opened their eyes wide.

'Blacksmith, such horseshoes and nails cannot be found anywhere in the world!'

'Well, I'm no ordinary blacksmith, Princess Sad-Face. You'll see what I can do!'

But big White Breakiron was not ready to give in so easily. As soon as he saw the blacksmith he began to rear up, to kick and to snort so loudly that he was heard a good seven miles away. But the blacksmith was not to be put off either and he said:

'Cricket, Mouse, Flea, to work!'

The cricket jumped into White Breakiron's ear and began chirping, the mouse jumped into his other ear and began squeaking, and the flea took a bite of his nostril. Poor White Breakiron was so tormented that finally he gladly consented to be shod if only these creatures pestering him would go away.

The blacksmith shod him properly, put on a bridle, fastened a saddle and then, without fear, he mounted White Breakiron.

'Giddyap, giddyap!' he cried and the horse galloped into the court-yard.

Then the blacksmith said:

'French King, the second half of my work is done. White Breakiron is shod and now I wish to become your son-in-law and heir.'

'And so you shall,' said the French king. 'Princess Sad-Face will be yours today. Steward, go for the priest. And you, servants, prepare a wedding feast the like of which the world has never seen.'

The steward fetched the priest, the servants prepared the feast and there was a wedding the like of which the world had never seen. Everyone in the castle and the town was invited together with the blacksmith's mother from the village. Nor were the cricket, the mouse and the flea forgotten. The cricket chirped at the wedding until the fiddlers were worn out, the mouse ate at the wedding and almost had too much of the delicious cake, and Mrs Flea drank so much wine that she became tipsy. And that was how the young blacksmith became the son-in-law and heir of the French king.

Once upon a time there was a woodcutter. His wife had died, and all he had left in the world was one son, Joseph. Joseph was still a little boy and the kind woodcutter thought it would be a good idea to marry again so that the boy would have a new mother. But alas, the new wife hated Joseph and one evening, when Joseph was lying in bed, his stepmother said to the woodcutter:

'Husband, I cannot bear to even look at Joseph any more. He eats so much that one day he'll eat the two of us. Take him into the forest tomorrow, and leave him there, so that he can never, never come back to us.'

What could the poor woodcutter do? He feared the evil woman as much as the devil and so he only nodded sadly. But Joseph was still awake and had heard everything. Early, very early the next morning he slipped out of bed and ran to his grandmother:

'Grandmother, my stepmother has told father to take me into the forest so that I can never, never return! What shall I do?'

'Don't be afraid, Joseph, just fill your pocket with little stones and then drop them along the way. You'll find your way home easily by following them.'

So Joseph filled his pocket with pebbles near the stream and ran home. There his father was waiting for him in front of the door, with an axe on his shoulder:

'Come, Joseph, let's go to the forest.'

'I'm coming!'

They set off, and when they came to some thick bushes, the woodcutter said:

'Wait for me here, Joseph, and pick some strawberries. I'm going to have a look round and I'll come back soon!'

But it wasn't true, and the woodcutter did not return. Poor Joseph waited and waited, but when the sun began to set in the west, he started to run home. The little stones he had secretly dropped led him all the way back to the cottage. He crouched under the window and listened. His father and stepmother were sharing a bowl of steaming hot soup and the woodcutter sadly sighed:

'If only my Joseph were here, he would enjoy it so. He loved soup. Where is he now, I wonder?'

Joseph tapped on the window:

'Here I am, father!'

The kind woodcutter was happy to see Joseph home again and immediately poured him a brimming full plate of soup. But the stepmother frowned, and when Joseph had gone to bed she said:

'Husband, I cannot bear the sight of that Joseph. He eats so much. He ate up all our soup today and one day he'll eat the two of us. Take him into the forest tomorrow, and leave him there so that he can never, never come back to us.'

What could the poor woodcutter do? He feared the evil woman as much as the devil and so he only nodded sadly. But Joseph was still awake and had heard everything. Early, very early the next morning he slipped out of bed and ran to his grandmother:

'Grandmother, my stepmother has told father again to take me into the forest so that I can never, never return. What shall I do?'

'Don't be afraid, Joseph, just fill your pocket full of ashes from the fire and drop them behind you as you go. You'll find your way home easily by following them.'

So Joseph filled his pocket with ashes and ran home. There his father was waiting for him in front of the door, with an axe on his shoulder:

'Come Joseph, let's go to the forest.'

'I'm coming!'

They set off, and when they reached some thick bushes, the woodcutter said:

'Wait for me here, Joseph, and pick some raspberries. I'm going to look round and I will be back soon!'

But he did not return. Poor Joseph waited and waited, but when the sun sank low in the sky he started to run home. The ashes that he had secretly dropped led him all the way back to the cottage. He crouched behind the door and waited. His father and stepmother were just sitting down to steaming bowls of porridge and the woodcutter sadly sighed:

'If only my Joseph was here, he would enjoy it so! He loved porridge! Where is he now, I wonder?'

Joseph knocked on the door:

'Here I am, father!'

The woodcutter was delighted to see Joseph again and immediately placed a brimming full bowl of porridge in front of him. But the stepmother frowned, and when Joseph had gone to bed, she said to the woodcutter:

'Husband, I cannot bear the sight of Joseph. He eats so much. He ate up all our porridge today and one day he'll eat the two of us. Take him into the forest tomorrow, and leave him there, but this time make sure you really do or something evil will happen!'

What could the poor woodcutter do? He feared the evil woman even more than the devil and so he only nodded sadly. But Joseph was still awake and this time, too, he had heard everything. Early, very early the next morning he slipped out of bed and ran straight to his grandmother:

'Grandmother, for the third time my stepmother has told father to take me into the forest and to really leave me there forever. What will happen to me now?'

'Don't be afraid, Joseph, just fill your pocket with grain from the pantry and drop it behind you as you go. You'll find your way home easily by following it.'

64

So Joseph filled his pocket with grain from the pantry and ran home. There his father was waiting for him in front of the door, with an axe on his shoulder:

'Come, Joseph, let's go to the forest.'

'I'm coming!'

They set off, and when they reached the thickest bushes, the woodcutter said:

'Wait for me here, Joseph, and pick some blackberries. I'm going to look round and I will be back soon!'

But he did not return. Joseph waited and waited and when the sun was almost behind the trees, he decided to run home. But alas, this time there was not a trace of the path, because the birds had eaten all the grain.

What now? Poor Joseph realised that he was lost in the middle of the deep forest and that night would soon fall. He quickly climbed to the top of the highest pine tree and looked round in all directions. Everywhere he looked there was forest. He saw not a house, not a village, absolutely nothing. Only in the distance, far, far away a pale light blinked amidst the trees.

Joseph walked in the direction of the light. He walked and walked until he came to a large house set in the middle of a beautiful garden. Joseph bravely knocked on the door:

Knock, knock, knock!

'Who is knocking on our door?' came a voice from within.

'It is I, Joseph. I have lost my way in the forest and am looking for kind people to put me up for the night,' said Joseph.

The door opened slightly, and from behind it peered a girl, who was as beautiful as the sun. For this reason she was called Beautiful Sunflower.

'Go away quickly, Joseph, you will fare very badly here! Don't you know that my father is a giant?'

'But where shall I go, Beautiful Sunflower! It is night and I'm so tired I can hardly move!'

Beautiful Sunflower took pity on Joseph:

'Come inside then. I'll hide you somehow for the night, and then we'll see.'

Beautiful Sunflower led Joseph to her mother in the kitchen, gave him something to eat and drink and then hid him under the bed:

'Here is a mouse's tail. When Father returns and asks to see your little finger, show him this tail instead. But don't forget, or he'll eat you up.'

At midnight the giant returned and from the doorway he shouted:

'What's this, I smell human flesh! Wife, who is here?'

'No one, Husband dear,' his wife soothed him. 'A stranger did stop by, but only a little boy. He is lying under the bed, but he is no good to you, for he is still small, only skin and bones!'

'I'll take a look myself,' muttered the giant and leaned down to Joseph: 'Show me your little finger!'

Joseph poked out the mouse's tail. The giant felt it and grumbled:

'You're right, Wife, that's nothing yet. He must grow a bit more!'

So the giant left little Joseph in the room. He sat down at the table, ate a whole roast joint in one bite and then went to sleep. When Joseph woke up next morning the giant had long since gone. Joseph thanked Sunflower for the supper and sleep and said he would leave her now.

'Where can you go?' said Sunflower. 'Stay with us, for at least it will make me happier.'

'But what about your father, Sunflower? When he sees me he'll eat me,' said Joseph.

'Don't worry, we'll think of something, and I certainly won't let him eat you,' said Sunflower, and so Joseph remained. They talked together for days on end in the garden or at home, and at night Joseph always hid under Sunflower's bed.

But all good things must come to an end. One day the giant returned home more than an hour sooner than he was expected. And what did he see? His Sunflower walking in the garden with Joseph beside her.

'Just look how quickly that little wanderer has grown! Wife, get up very early tomorrow morning and bake him for me!'

Sunflower knew that matters were very serious. She ran to the giant and said:

'Father, why don't we keep Joseph! Do that for me, if you love me! If you eat him I will have no one to talk to, and I will be sad, so sad!'

There were tears in her eyes, and the giant weakened:

'All right, Sunflower, I shall do it for you. But if he wants to stay with us he must work. Tomorrow let him dig a well in the garden for me. By evening I shall expect to have a jug of cold water from it on the table. Otherwise, let him beware. Here is a shovel and a spade for him.'

In the morning Joseph took the shovel and spade and began to dig the well in the garden. But alas, no sooner did he push the spade into the ground than it broke in two, and hardly had he taken a shovelful of soil when the shovel broke, too. Sadly, Joseph sat down on a stone:

'If I carry on like this, I shall never get the well dug.'

At noon, Sunflower said to her mother:

'Mother, I shall take Joseph some soup.'

'No, no, Sunflower, Father has ordered me to take it to him myself.'

'Father need not know everything, Mother! Just give me the soup, I'll take it to him!'

Sunflower seized the pot of soup and ran into the garden. Joseph was sitting there with his head hanging low, on the verge of tears.

'What is the matter, Joseph, that you look so miserable?'

'What isn't the matter, Sunflower? I only touched the spade to the ground and it broke in two, I only took a shovelful of earth and the shovel broke too. I shall never get the well dug.'

'Don't be miserable, Joseph! I'll see what can be done, but don't hang your head. Eat up, while I take your place.'

She drew out a wand from her belt and waved it three times:

'Magic wand, listen to me: before the sun goes down, let there be a well in the garden. Before the sun goes down, let there be a jug of water from the well on the table.'

Before Joseph finished his soup, there was a deep well in the garden, and before the giant sat down to supper, there was a jug of cold water from the well on the table.

The giant poured out a full glass, drank and then said:

'Sunflower, Sunflower, this is certainly your work!'

'It is not, Father!'

'Well, well, we shall see. Tomorrow let your Joseph plant some wheat in the garden, and by evening I shall expect to eat fresh-baked bread from it! Otherwise, things will be bad for him. Here is a spade and a scythe for him. And now, Wife, show him where he is to sleep!'

The giant's wife led Joseph into a little room with a bed made of burning coal. At the last minute, Beautiful Sunflower came running:

'I'll make the bed, Mother!'

'No, no, Sunflower, Father has ordered me to make the bed.'

'Father need not know everything, Mother! Just go to bed and sleep.'

When her mother had gone away, Sunflower whispered to Joseph:

'You go and lie down in my bed, and I shall sleep here alone.'

In the morning, Joseph took the spade and scythe and began to sow the grain in the garden. But alas, no sooner did the spade touch the ground than it broke in two, and as soon as he lifted the scythe it broke as well. Joseph sat down on a stone sadly:

'If I carry on like this, I shall never get the grain harvested!'

At noon, Beautiful Sunflower came running with the soup:

'What is the matter, Joseph, that you look so unhappy again?'

'What isn't the matter, Sunflower! I only touched the spade to the ground and it broke in two, I only took the scythe in my hand and it broke as well. I shall never get the grain harvested.'

'Don't be miserable, Joseph! I'll see what can be done.'

She drew the wand out from her belt, and waved it three times:

'Magic wand, listen to what I say: before the sun goes down let the grain have ripened in the garden, and before the sun sets let there be freshly baked bread from it on the table.'

Before Joseph had finished his soup, the grain had ripened in the garden, and before the giant sat down to supper, fresh bread had been baked from it.

The giant cut himself a good slice, ate it and then said:

'Sunflower, Sunflower, this is certainly your doing!'

'How could you say such a thing, Father!'

'Well we shall see. Tomorrow let your Joseph plant some grapes in the garden. By evening I shall expect a bottle of wine from the grapes to be on the table. Otherwise, things will be bad for him! Here is a hoe and a pick for him. And now, Wife, show him where he will sleep.'

The giant's wife led Joseph into a little room with a bed made of ice. At the last minute, Beautiful Sunflower ran in:

'I'll make the bed for him, Mother!'

When her mother had gone, Sunflower sent Joseph to sleep in her bed and she lay down on his.

In the morning, Joseph took the hoe and pick and began to plant the grapes in the garden. But alas, no sooner did the hoe touch the ground than it broke in two, and hardly had he started to break ground with the pick than it broke as well. Joseph sat down on a stone sadly:

'If I carry on like this, I shall never get these grapes planted.'

At noon Beautiful Sunflower came running with the soup:

'What is the matter, Joseph, that you look so unhappy again?'

'What isn't the matter, Sunflower! I only touched the hoe to the ground and it broke in two, I hardly started to use the pick when it broke as well. I shall never get the grapes planted.'

'Don't be miserable, Joseph! I'll see what can be done, so don't be sad. Eat up while I take your place.'

She drew out the wand from her belt and waved it three times:

'Magic wand, listen to what I say: before the sun goes down let the grapes ripen in the garden, and before the sun sets let there be a bottle of wine from them on the table.'

Before Joseph had eaten his soup, the grapes had ripened in the garden, and before the giant sat down to supper a bottle of good wine from them was on the table.

The giant poured himself a good glass, gulped it down and said:

'Sunflower, Sunflower, this is certainly your work!'

'Not at all, Father!'

'Well then, we shall see,' said the giant and poured himself a second glass, then another and another, until he had drunk all the wine, and then he fell on his bed like a dead man.

When the giant's wife had also gone to sleep, Beautiful Sunflower came to Joseph:

'Joseph, we must go away, there is nothing else to be done. Tomorrow Father will certainly bake you. Get up and let us go!'

Then she put a stick in her bed and a broom in Joseph's bed, and waved her wand over them three times so that they would answer for them until morning. Then very quietly, she and Joseph stole out of the house.

At midnight the giant's wife cried out in her sleep. She was having a bad dream. The giant turned over in bed and said crossly:

'What's the matter, Wife?'

'I had a dream that Joseph wants to run away and take our Sunflower with him!'

The giant sat up in bed:

'Sunflower!' he called.

'What is it, Father?' replied the stick in Sunflower's bed.

'Joseph!'

'What can I do for you?' replied the broom from Joseph's bed.

The giant grumbled:

'Do you hear that, Wife? They are in bed and sleeping. You go to sleep too and leave me in peace!'

An hour later, the wife cried out in her sleep again. The giant turned over in his bed crossly:

'What is it now, Wife?'

'I dreamt that Joseph was running away and taking Sunflower with him!'

The giant sat up in his bed:

'Sunflower!' he called.

'What is it, Father?' replied the stick.

'Joseph!'

'What can I do for you?' replied the broom.

The giant grumbled:

'Do you hear, Wife? They are in bed and sleeping. You go to sleep too and leave me in peace!'

An hour later the giant's wife cried out in her sleep for the third time. The giant turned over in his bed crossly:

'What is it, Wife?'

'I dreamt that Joseph ran away and took our Sunflower with him!'

The giant sat up in his bed:

'Sunflower!' he called.

But the stick did not reply because it was already morning.

'Joseph!'

But the broom did not reply because daylight was outside the window.

The giant's wife cried:

'You see they have escaped! Get up quickly and go after them!'

The giant jumped into his seven-league boots and ran after the runaway pair.

Joseph and Sunflower were already far away. They were sitting on the shore of a lake, resting a little. Sunflower was making a wreath out of forget-me-nots when Joseph cried:

'Look, there is your father in the woods!'

'Don't worry, Joseph,' said Sunflower and drew out her wand. She waved it three times and Joseph was instantly transformed into a drake and Sunflower into a duck. They gaily jumped into the water and began to swim in the lake.

70

The giant ran right up to the shore of the lake and called:

'Drake, Duck, did you see Joseph and our Sunflower running this way?'

The drake and the duck only replied:

'Quack, quack, quack! Quack, quack, quack!'

The giant learned nothing else from them. Frustrated, he ran home.

'Well,' asked the giant's wife, 'have you brought them?'

'I haven't! I didn't meet a living soul on the way except for a drake and a duck on a lake, but all they did was to quack, quack, quack, quack!'

'You fool, that was Joseph and our Sunflower! Go back for them, quickly!'

The giant jumped into his seven-league boots and ran after them.

Joseph and Sunflower were already far away. They were sitting in a meadow, resting for a while. Sunflower was weaving a daisy chain, when Joseph cried:

'Look, there is your father!'

'Don't worry, Joseph,' said Sunflower and drew out her wand. She waved it three times and Joseph was instantly transformed into a finch and Sunflower into a goldfinch. They flew gaily from bush to bush.

The giant ran to the meadow and called:

'Finch, Goldfinch, did you see Joseph and our Sunflower running this way?'

But the finch and the goldfinch only chirped:

'Tweet, tweet, tweet! Tweet, tweet, tweet!'

The giant learned nothing else from them. Frustrated, he ran home.

'Well,' asked the giant's wife, 'have you brought them?'

'I haven't! I didn't meet a living soul on the way except for a finch and a goldfinch in a meadow, but all they did was to chirp tweet, tweet, tweet, tweet!'

'You fool, that was Joseph and our Sunflower! Go back for them, quickly!'

For the third time the giant jumped into his seven-league boots and ran after the runaways.

Joseph and Sunflower were very far away now. They were sitting by a stream, resting for a while. Sunflower was picking marigolds when Joseph cried:

'Look, there is your father in the meadow!'

'Don't worry, Joseph,' said Sunflower and drew out her wand.

She waved it three times and instantly she became a foot bridge across the stream and Joseph was the railing on the bridge.

73

But this time Sunflower had made a mistake. The giant remembered that at this spot there had never been a foot bridge.

'Sunflower, Sunflower, this is certainly your work. This time you won't get away, and nor will your Joseph!'

But Joseph and Sunflower did manage to escape him. Just as the giant was about to seize the railing and jump on the bridge, the railing turned into a bull and the bridge into a frog. Before the giant knew what had happened, the bull ran into the other meadow and the frog hid somewhere in the rushes. Only Sunflower's magic wand was floating on the water. The giant seized it and said:

'Well, Joseph! You are a bull now and will remain a bull for six years! And, Sunflower! You are a frog now and for seven years will remain a frog! We'll see after that whether you'll still want each other.'

And he returned to his forest.

For six years, day after day, Joseph, in the shape of a bull, went to the edge of the stream, and for six years, day after day, the frog would hop out of the rushes over to him, so that they could talk for a while. After six years, the bull changed into a strong, healthy young man who no longer paid any attention to the frog in the rushes. He went out into the world and never again returned to the stream.

A year passed, and so did the curse on Sunflower. Instead of a frog in the rushes, once again she was a beautiful young girl. But she was alone and abandoned, and had no idea where Joseph was. Beautiful Sunflower set out to find him. She went from village to village, from town to town until she once came to a city, and there in a house near the market a wedding was being prepared. Sunflower stopped in the yard to watch, and saw to her amazement that the groom was none other than her Joseph!

Sunflower went into the kitchen:

'Good day, Mistress, do you need some help?'

'I could do with some, girl, every hand is welcome when a wedding is being prepared!'

So Sunflower helped in the kitchen, she cooked, baked and carried the food to the table.

When the wedding party had reached its height, Sunflower made a pigeon and a pigeon-hen out of dough, placed it on a dish and brought it to the table, right in front of the groom.

The wedding guests were surprised because they had never seen anything like it before. But in a while they were even more surprised because suddenly the pigeon began to coo like a live pigeon:

'Coo, coo, pigeon-hen, give me a kiss!'

But the pigeon-hen replied:

'Coo, coo, pigeon, I will not! You would then forget me as Joseph forgot his Sunflower!'

When the groom heard this, he suddenly remembered everything and immediately recognised in this clever cook his own beloved Sunflower. He ran to her, threw his arms round her neck and kissed her in front of everybody:

'This is my Sunflower, this is my true bride!'

That was the end of that wedding. Sunflower led Joseph away and after their own wedding they lived happily until the end of their days. And they did not leave one another for a moment, so that never, never again did they have to search for each other.

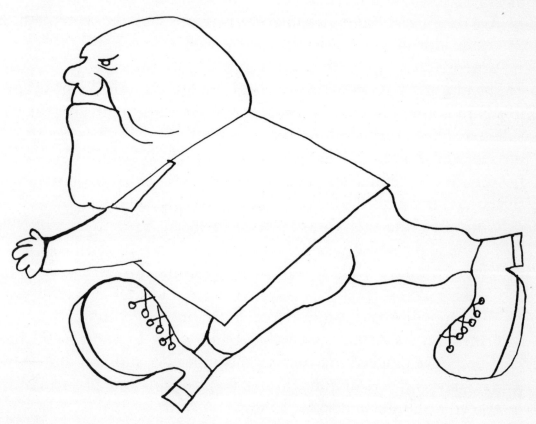

THE DRAGON KING
AND THE SLEEPING PRINCESS

Once upon a time there was a king who had three beautiful daughters. The most beautiful of all was the youngest: the first two were as beautiful as the day, but the third was as beautiful as the sun itself. As you can well imagine, the king was very proud of her and yet, strangely enough, though he loved all his daughters, the youngest and most beautiful occupied the last place in his heart, perhaps because she was the shyest. Whenever the king went anywhere, he always brought back expensive presents for the two elder sisters, everything they wanted. But because the youngest never asked, the king never brought her anything. After a time this made the youngest princess unhappy. One day when the king was preparing for a journey, the youngest princess went up to him and said:

'Dear Father, I see that you are preparing for a journey and I would like to ask you to bring me back a present.'

'With pleasure, Daughter,' said the king. 'Just tell me what you would like?'

'Anything you think is suitable, Father,' said the youngest princess. 'If you like, it need be only a pretty flower.'

'You shall have it,' said the king and set off.

The journey was not a long one and in a few days the king was preparing to return home. As usual, he bought many beautiful gifts for the two elder princesses but forgot about the youngest. Only when he was already on his way home and happened to pass by a beautiful garden full of flowers did he remember the gift for her. He reined his horse, went into the garden and picked a beautiful flower for his daughter.

Suddenly there was a noise above his head, as though a big bird was flying by, and a voice said:

'King, you have plucked my most beautiful flower!'

The king was surprised:

'Who are you that I can hear you but cannot see you?'

'I am who I am, and you will see me when I choose,' said the voice. 'But you have plucked my most beautiful flower and you must pay me for it. You have three daughters. Either you give me one of them as my wife or else you will die and so will they.'

What could the king do? He promised to speak to his daughters and to bring one of them back with him. Only then was he allowed to go home.

At home his daughters were waiting impatiently for him and the first thing they did was to ask about the gifts. The king gave each of them what he had brought; to the two eldest he gave clothes and jewels and to the youngest the beautiful flower, and said sadly:

'Listen to what happened. Your gift almost cost me my life. When I plucked this flower in the garden of a castle, I heard a voice and that voice asked for one of you for a wife. Otherwise, it threatened all of us with death. Which of you wants to have the gentleman from the castle for a husband?'

'I don't Father,' said the eldest. 'Not for anything in the world!'

'I don't either, Father,' said the middle sister. 'Even if it means taking my life.'

'Then I will have him,' said the youngest. 'I don't want anything evil to happen to you because of me.'

The next day the king sat his youngest daughter in front of him on his horse and took her to the garden where he had plucked the beautiful flower. In the middle of the garden was a magnificent castle. The king rode up to the gate, lifted his daughter off the horse and bade her farewell:

'Goodbye, Daughter, I hope you will be happy.'

He then kicked his spurs into the horse's side and rode away.

With tears in her eyes, the poor princess went up to the castle door. Hardly had she touched the door when it opened by itself and as she entered it closed behind her. The castle was even more beautiful inside than outside. There were fires burning in all the rooms, in the hall the table was set for dinner, in the bedroom the bed was prepared, but not a living soul was to be seen.

The princess ate, drank and then went out into the garden to see the flowers. She walked in the garden and picked the flowers until evening. When it began to grow dark, a sound was heard in the air, as though a big bird was flying by. The princess was frightened and threw away the flowers, but a soft voice said:

'Pick the flowers, my sweet one, gather flowers since it gives you such pleasure!'

The princess was surprised:

'Who are you that I can hear you quite clearly but cannot see you?'

'I am your betrothed,' said the voice. 'If you are not afraid, tell me and I will show myself to you.'

'Why should I fear my betrothed?' replied the princess.

There was a flash of lightning and thunder and before the princess there appeared a winged dragon, as big and strong as a poplar tree:

'Here I am, my sweet! Do you still want to take me for a husband?'

'I do, Dragon,' said the princess. 'I keep my promises. I shall marry you whenever you wish. Only give me three days to sew my wedding dress at home.'

'So be it,' said the dragon. 'But you must not tell your family what I am! Come back in three days as you promised, otherwise I shall die of grief and your dear ones at home will die with me. Here, take my gold ring. If it whitens that is a sign that I am ill, if it blackens it means I am dying. And now I will take you home.'

The dragon seated the princess on his back, spread his wings and carried her a hundred times faster than a swallow. In the twinkling of an eye they were in front of the castle of the old king.

'Do not forget, my dear,' said the dragon. 'Say nothing and in three days come back to me or things will go badly. If you need anything, take a handful of leaves and burn them in a corner of the garden and I shall come!'

The dragon flew up into the sky and the princess went into her father's castle. You can imagine how surprised everyone was and all the questions they asked the princess! But the princess did not tell them very much. She talked about the dragon's beautiful castle and his wonderful garden, but did not say a word about her betrothed.

'You'll see him yourself, when the time comes,' she replied and sewed her wedding dress. 'But now you must leave me, I must be ready in three days.'

The sisters realised that something was wrong and to prevent their youngest sister from leaving in three days, at night they undid the stitches she had sewn during the day. Three days passed and the princess's wedding dress was still not ready.

'Don't worry,' her sisters consoled her, 'if you do not return, your betrothed will come for you.' The princess let herself be persuaded and remained.

But that was a foolish thing. On the fourth day, when she looked at the dragon's ring she saw that it was completely white. The dragon lay ill in his castle and the princess's parents were ill with the same illness. The princess wanted to run away to the castle of her betrothed, but again her sisters did not let her.

'Wait until tomorrow when father and mother are better,' they persuaded her and the princess agreed.

But that was a foolish thing. When she awoke on the fifth day and looked at the dragon's ring, it was completely black. The dragon lay in his castle, deathly ill, and the princess's parents also became deathly ill. The little princess knew that things were very bad so she ran into the garden, put some leaves in a corner and lit a fire. Just then, out of the smoke, came a dark figure and before the princess stood her dragon.

'You did not keep your word, my dear,' said a weak voice, 'and I am dying. If you do not marry me, I shall die by the time the sun sets and your father and your mother will die with me!'

'Forgive me, my dear,' the princess wept. 'My sisters persuaded me to stay and I obeyed them. But now I shall go with you wherever you wish, if only you will make my father and mother well again.'

'Go and fetch your wedding dress,' said the dragon, 'and everything will be all right!'

The princess ran home and, indeed, the king and the queen — as if by a miracle — had become better and the wedding dress, from out of nowhere, was ready too. The princess put it on, ran into the garden and seated herself on the dragon's back. The dragon flew away with her a hundred times faster than a swallow. In the twinkling of an eye they found themselves before a chapel where three candles were burning. The dragon led the princess to the altar. An old pilgrim was waiting there. When the bride and groom came up to him, an organ sounded and the pilgrim bound their hands with a scarf and the dragon and the princess were married. Then the bridegroom said softly:

'My dear, look to the left and tell me what you see!'

The princess looked and said:

'I see a dragon's skin and wings lying there.'

Then the bridegroom said again:

'My dear, now look to the right and tell me what you see!'

The princess looked and said:

'I see a young prince standing there at my side, as beautiful as day.'

Then the bridegroom said:

'It is I, your bridegroom and king. Because you took me for a husband you have freed me from an evil curse. But our trials are not yet over and the power of my enemy, the evil sorcerer, is still not broken. Listen carefully to what I say! Take the dragon's skin and wings and leave the chapel. My servants will be waiting for you in front of the chapel with a carriage to take you to my castle. When you get there, lock yourself in our room and burn the skin and the wings in the fire, until the very last scale is destroyed. If you do what I say things will go well and I shall come to you at the stroke of midnight and then nothing will ever part us again. But if you do not take care, if a single scale remains from the skin and wings, things will go badly for us both.'

'King, I shall obey your command!' said the princess, taking the dragon's skin and wings, and she left the chapel. Outside, a golden carriage with six white horses was waiting for her. The servants took the princess to her lord's castle. It was full of people now, and the walls resounded with cries of laughter. Everyone was delighted to think that the lord of the castle had happily married. The princess locked herself into the bridal chamber and threw the dragon's skin and wings into the fire. In a little while all that remained of them was a handful of ashes. Only one single scale did not burn but turned into a beautiful flower, the very kind of flower that the princess's father had brought her as a gift from his journey. The princess liked the flower so much that she forgot what the young king had told her. She took the flower, put it into a golden vase and then lay down to sleep.

A quarter of an hour before midnight the window opened and into the room flew the evil sorcerer on a great black raven. When he saw the beautiful flower in the vase, he was pleased and said:

'The dragon's skin has not all burnt, the bride did not obey, and so he is still in my power. Young King, you shall never, never see your wife again!'

Then he took the sleeping princess in his arms, placed her on the back of the black raven and flew out of the window into the dark night.

At the stroke of midnight the young king knocked on the door saying:

'It is I, my dear, it is I, the young king, your husband!'

But the door did not open and no sound came from the room.

The young king became frightened and knocked on the door for the second time:

'Open the door, please, Wife, open it, while there is still time!'

But the door did not open and not a sound came from the room. The young king waited no longer, but pressed his shoulder against the door, pushed it open and entered the room. Inside the scent of the beautiful flower in the golden vase filled the room. In a flash, the king understood what had happened:

'This was certainly the work of my enemy, the evil sorcerer! He has carried away my wife, but I shall find her even if I have to travel the wide world over!'

The very next day, the young king set out on his journey. A year and a day later he came to a pilgrim's cottage in a deep forest.

'What are you looking for in the forest, young King?' the old pilgrim asked in surprise when the king reached him.

'My beloved wife,' replied the king. 'She was carried away by my enemy, the evil sorcerer! But I shall find her even if I have to travel the whole wide world. Do you know where she is, wise Pilgrim?'

The pilgrim shook his head:

'I do not know, young King. But my older brother will surely know about her.'

The pilgrim put a whistle to his lips and blew it. At that moment an eagle as big as a bull flew out of the clouds. The pilgrim said:

'Eagle, you know what I wish, obey my command!'

The large eagle seized the young king in his claws and flew with him up into the clouds. Within seconds they had flown over a thick forest and came down to earth at the foot of high mountains. There was the cottage of the pilgrim's older brother.

'What are you looking for, young King?' asked the old man in surprise when the king stood before him.

'My beloved wife,' said the young king. 'She was carried away by the evil sorcerer. Do you know where she is, wise Pilgrim?'

The old man shook his head:

'I do not know, young King. But our eldest brother will surely know.'

The old man put a whistle to his lips and blew it. At that moment, an eagle as big as a bull flew out of the clouds.

'Eagle, you know what I wish, so obey my command!'

The large eagle seized the young king in his claws and flew with him up to the clouds. In a split second they had flown over the high mountains and came down to earth on the shores of a large sea. There was the cottage of the oldest pilgrim.

'What are you looking for, young King?' asked the pilgrim in surprise when the king stood before him.

'My beloved wife,' said the king. 'She was carried away by the evil sorcerer. Do you know where she is, wise Pilgrim?'

'I know, young King,' said the pilgrim. 'Your wife is on a high mountain in the centre of an island far out in the wide sea. She is sleeping there in the shade of a huge oak tree and will sleep there until you awaken her. But before you can do that you must get to that island and it will not be easy. Your enemy, the evil sorcerer is on guard day and night. He is the king of the fishes and rules the sea and the sky. Listen to what I tell you. When I still lived among people, I was a fisherman and had a good ship and a gold fishing rod. That ship and fishing rod are still standing by the shore. Get into the ship and it will take you safely to the island of the king of the fishes. When you get near to the island, the king of the fishes will whip up a storm at sea and a tempest in the sky. You must fear nothing, but put a piece of human flesh on the gold fishing rod, and as soon as you throw it into the sea, the king of the fishes will be caught. He will try to pull you into the water, but hold on fast and do not let go of the rod, even though he will come out of the water six times, each time in a different shape. The seventh time he will take on the form of a man and that will be your moment. Boldly draw out your sword and cut off his head. The rest you will be able to do very easily yourself.'

Then the pilgrim put a whistle to his lips and blew it. An eagle as big as a bull flew out of the clouds. The old pilgrim said:

'Eagle, you know what I wish, so obey my command!'

The large eagle seized the young king in his claws and flew with him up to the clouds. In a few seconds they were over the bay where the ship rocked at anchor. The eagle set the young king down in the ship and flew away.

'Thank you, great Eagle,' cried the young king and then began to look around for the fishing rod and bait. He found the gold fishing rod easily, it was lying at the bottom of the ship, but it was harder to find the bait of human flesh. Suddenly he spied a shepherd with a herd of sheep in the meadow a short distance away. The young king looked at him for a while but then said:

'No, I cannot kill that lad. I cannot take such guilt upon myself.'

And he left the shepherd with his sheep. Shortly afterwards, he saw a beggar in the distance. The young king looked at him carefully, but then said, as he had the first time:

'No, I cannot kill this old man! I cannot take such guilt upon myself.'

And so he set out to sea without the bait.

As long as the island of the fish king was far away, the young king sailed calmly and contentedly. But as soon as he began to approach the island, the waves began to rise as big as mountains and a tempest began to blow. The ship bobbed up and down in the water like an empty nutshell. It was time to throw the fishing rod in the water with the bait of human flesh. Without hesitation, the young king seized a knife, cut out a piece of flesh from his thigh and pinned it on to the gold hook. No sooner did he throw the fishing rod into the water, than the line grew so taut that the young king almost fell in. But he held the line with all his strength until, finally the king of the fishes rose from the water in the shape of a dragon.

The young king cried:

'Your efforts are in vain, King of the Fishes, I know it is you and I shall not let go!'

The king of the fishes was furious. He dived to the bottom and in a while appeared again in the form of a wreath made of seaweed. But the young king was not to be fooled and cried:

'Your efforts are in vain, King of the Fishes, I know it is you!'

The king of the fishes was furious. He dived to the bottom and in a while appeared again in the form of a beautiful water fairy. But the young king was not to be fooled and cried:

'Your efforts are in vain, King of the Fishes, I know it is you!'

The king of the fishes was furious. He dived to the bottom and in a while came up again in the form of an ugly beast. The young king was not to be fooled and cried:

'Your efforts are in vain, King of the Fishes, I know it is you!'

The king of the fishes was furious. He dived to the bottom and in

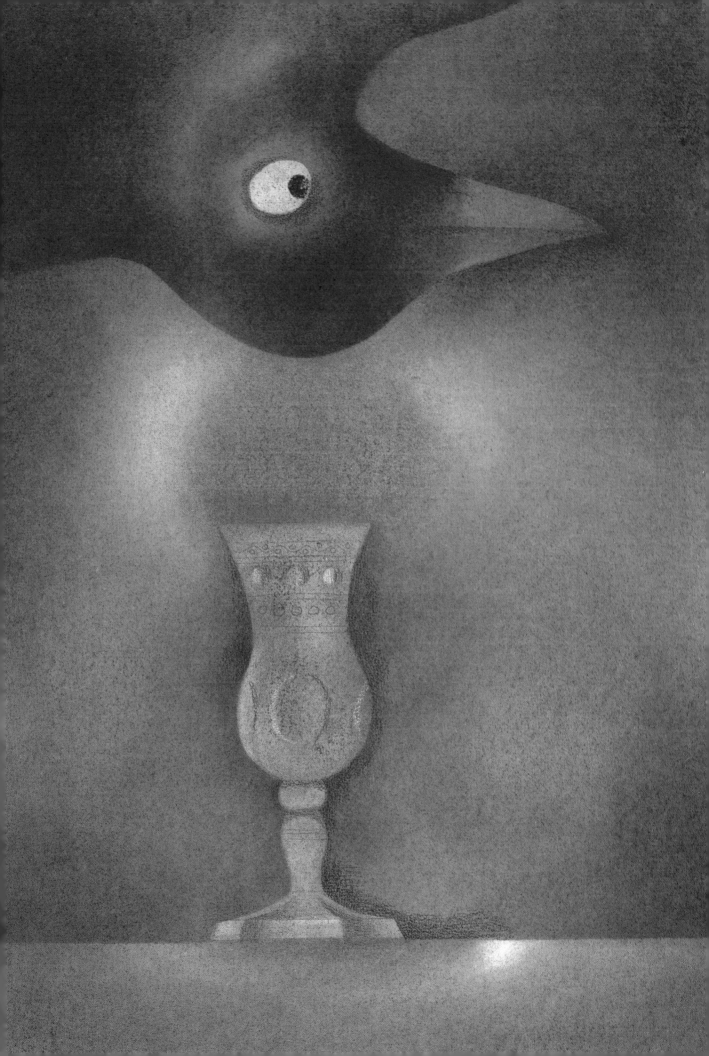

a while appeared in the form of a cloud of steam. The young king was not to be fooled and cried:

'Your efforts are in vain, King of the Fishes, I know it is you!'

The king of the fishes was furious. He dived to the bottom and then appeared in the form of the king's young wife. But not even this time was the king fooled and he cried:

'Your efforts are in vain, King of the Fishes, I know it is you!'

The king of the fishes screamed and dived down for the last time. When he appeared on the surface again, he was in the form of a man. This was the young king's moment. With his left hand, he seized the king of the fishes by his hair, with his right hand he pulled out his sword and with a single blow cut off his head. At that very moment the storm died down and the young king was able to reach the island. On the mountain, sleeping in the shade of a tall oak tree, lay his beloved wife. The young king leaned over and kissed her. At that moment the princess opened her eyes and sighed:

'I have slept a long time.'

'You would have slept forever if I had not awakened you!' said the young king pointing to the head of the evil sorcerer and king of the fishes. 'But now our trials are over. Come, let us go home. Everyone is waiting for us!'

When the ship with the young king and his beautiful wife reached the shore, after sailing seven days and seven nights, there was a golden carriage with six white horses waiting for them. In a few moments it carried the happy groom and bride to the king's castle where a wedding feast was ready. After the wedding feast the young king and his lovely wife lived happily in love and contentment for ever and ever.

THE GODSON OF THE FRENCH KING AND THE PRINCESS OF TRONKOLEN

Once upon a time there was a poor collier who already had twenty-five children when his twenty-sixth was born. He was a boy, a lively and good-looking baby, but the poor collier did not know whom to ask to be the child's godfather. When someone has twenty-six children there is always something to worry about!

'What can I do but go out into the world and seek a godfather,' said the collier. So taking a walking stick in his hand, he set out on his journey.

Luck was with him. As soon as he left the forest and came out on the royal highway, what should he see but a golden carriage carrying the French king himself along a white path in a green meadow! The collier knelt down in the dust and greeted the king respectfully. The French king replied kindly to this greeting as he threw the collier a gold coin with his portrait on it:

'Here is a souvenir for you, my good man.'

The poor collier said:

'Thank you, French King, a gold coin with your portrait will always come in handy for a poor man, but I need something else.'

The French king asked:

'And what do you need, good man?'

The poor collier summoned up courage and said:

'I already had twenty-five children, French King, and now my twenty-sixth has been born. He is a boy and a fine looking child, but I cannot find a godfather for him. All my neighbours have already acted as god-parents and so I have set out into the world to seek a godfather.'

The French king was surprised:

'Twenty-six children, my good man? No French king has ever had so many! But since you have them, I shall act as your son's godfather. Await me tomorrow!'

The next day the French king really came. He acted as godfather to the collier's son and since the king was called Louis, the child was named after him. In the evening after a gay celebration, when the French king was about to leave, he gave the poor collier a full purse of gold:

'This is for my godson! When he is seven, send him to school so that he will not disgrace my name!'

The collier thanked the king for his gift, but that was not all. In addition to the purse of gold, the king also gave him half of his royal ring:

'When he is eighteen, send him to my court in Paris with this ring. I shall recognise him by it and will then see that he is looked after.'

Having said this, the French king left.

He went to his palace in Paris and the collier's son remained at home in his own forest. The years passed like water under a bridge, and in a little while the boy was seven and began to attend school. He was a good pupil and certainly did not bring shame on the king's name. When he was eighteen, his father called him home, gave him half of the king's ring and said:

'Go and take this half of the ring to your godfather, the French king. He will see that you are looked after. When things go well with you, remember your old father and your twenty-five brothers.'

'I shall remember,' the lad promised. Then he kissed his father and his twenty-five brothers, one after the other, and set out for the town of Paris to see his godfather, the French king. His father had given him an old, stubborn horse so that he would not have to go the whole way on foot. The young man wrapped the half of the king's ring in his mother's scarf.

The lad mounted the old horse and at the edge of the forest waved to his father and his brothers for the last time and then came out on the royal road. After a while he passed a white-haired old man. He was walking but it was clear that he could hardly take another step. The young man leapt off the horse and said:

'Good day, old man! Would you like to ride some of the way?'

'Why not, Louis, why not, godson of the French king?' said the old man and climbed up on the horse.

The young man was surprised that the old man knew him but he said nothing and led the horse by the reins so that it would behave.

After an hour or two, the old man drew up the nag:

'Thank you, kind lad! Because you were kind enough to carry me I shall give you some good advice: do not make friends with strangers, and do not go near water, even if it is only a well, with people you don't know.'

The lad thanked the old man, said goodbye to him kindly and rode on towards his godfather, the French king, in the city of Paris. He had hardly reached a turn in the road when a horse and rider appeared behind him:

'Hello, Louis, hello, godson of the French king, wait for me!'

The godson of the French king was surprised:

'Who can it be that he knows me but I do not know him?'

He slowed down and in a few moments the rider caught up with him. He was a young man with a handsome face and a good horse, but with an ugly smile on his lips.

'I am glad that I caught up with you,' he said to the godson of the French king. 'Don't you remember me? We went to school together!'

The godson of the French king did not really remember this stranger but since he said that they had gone to school together he thought it was probably true. He greeted the young man, but then urged his horse forward:

'I must go on, I am heading for Paris!'

'I am too,' said the stranger. 'But why the hurry? Here, near the forest, there is a well. Let us have a drink and a talk for a little while.'

At first the godson of the French king did not want to go to the well. True, he was thirsty, and his horse needed a rest but, when he remembered the old man's advice, he shook his head:

'I'm in a hurry, friend.'

'I am too,' said the stranger and took Louis's horse by the reins. 'But a moment of rest will make us feel better.'

Reluctant though he was, the godson of the French king jumped down from his horse and followed the stranger. They soon reached a well. The stranger knelt down, drank deeply and said with a laugh:

'Drink, godson of the French king, and you will not be sorry.' Poor Louis paid no attention to that laugh. He leaned over the well and cupped the cold water in the palms of his hands, but before he could take a drink he was pushed head first, into the well. The stranger pulled the scarf with the king's ring from Louis's pocket and then pushed him down with all his might.

The stranger thought that the godson of the French king would drown in the well. He mounted his horse, dug his spurs into its side and galloped to the road and then along the road towards the French king in the city of Paris. But Louis did not drown. True, he swallowed much of the water before he remembered what had happened, but then he pulled himself together and climbed out of the well. He was wet through and through, then leapt on his horse and galloped after the stranger. But the stranger had a better horse than Louis and so the poor godson of the French king caught up to him only at the gate to the king's castle.

'Give me back my ring,' he cried to the thief. But the stranger only turned around mockingly and said:

'What ring? This ring belongs to the godson of the French king and I am that godson. If you say another word, I shall have the guard lock you up. But if you are sensible, I shall ask my godfather, the king, to find a job for you looking after the horses.'

What could poor Louis do? He bowed his head and was silent, angry with himself for not listening to the old man's advice.

'But everything is not over yet,' he told himself afterwards and entered the king's castle.

The stranger boldly went up to the French king and gave him half of his ring:

'Here is your ring, French king. I have come as you ordered.'

The French king recognised the ring but not his godson. He expected a modest collier's son and, instead, here was a proud gentleman in fine dress with an ugly smile on his lips. The young lad who had come with him pleased the King more.

'Who is that with you?' he asked the false godson.

'That is a lad from our village. He latched himself on to me and would not go away. He says he wants to serve the French king! It would be best if you gave him some work looking after the horses!'

'Good,' said the French king and sent poor Louis to the stable.

Louis worked hard in the royal stable, rubbing down the horses, giving them fodder and cleaning up the dung, while the false godson paraded through the king's rooms, ate well, drank well and went wherever the king went. And why not, since the king had no children of his own, the king's godson might well become heir to the throne overnight? Only one thing clouded the false godson's prospects and that was young Louis. He pondered a long time on how to get rid of him and finally one day, he said to the king:

'I wonder if you know, Godfather, what your new stable boy was boasting about today?'

'And what did he boast of, Godson?' asked the French king.

'That, if he wishes, he will go and ask the sun why it is so red when it rises in the morning,' lied the false godson of the French king. 'I should also like to know that,' said the French king. 'But since he is so bold, I shall send him there at once, tomorrow.'

'That is a good idea, Godfather,' said the false godson. 'But don't let him wriggle out of it by trying to make excuses!'

'Let no one try to use any excuses with me!' said the French king. 'Either he goes, or his head comes off. Bring him here to me!'

So poor Louis was brought before the French king.

'I hear that you have been boasting that you would ask the sun why it is so red in the morning,' the French king said to him sternly.

'I never said any such thing, French King.' Louis defended himself and pleaded, but it was no use.

'Either you set out at once, tomorrow, or I shall have your head cut off!' the French king commanded.

Louis had no choice. He saddled a good horse, put some food and a few coins in a bag for the journey and sadly set out for the east. After a while he met the white-haired old man on the road.

'Where are you going, Louis, where are you going, godson of the French king?'

'To the edge of the world, old man, to the Sun,' answered Louis sadly.

'You see, if you had taken my advice you would not have to go there,' said the old man. 'But you cannot undo what has happened and it's no use to cry over spilt milk. You had better mount that wooden horse and it will take you to the glass mountain where the sun has its castle. Once there you'll manage by yourself. Your own horse will not get you there even if you travel till the end of time.'

In the bushes near the road stood a wooden horse with wings on its shoulders. Louis leapt up on it and pressed its sides, and the horse rose into the sky. The godson of the French king hardly had time to thank the old man.

'Thank you, thank you, old man, I shall never forget you for this!'

In a moment or two the wooden horse had flown over the wide sea and come down on a beautiful island, at the foot of the glass mountain. On the mountain, the sun's castle glittered with gold. Louis reached the foot of the mountain in the twinkling of an eye, but the climb to the castle took a whole day. He reached it just before evening. The castle shone so brightly that it almost blinded the godson of the French king. The lad knocked on the gate made of pure gold.

'Knock, knock, knock! Open up, good people!'

He heard steps inside the castle and at the gate there appeared an old woman. It was the sun's mother.

'What do you want, Louis? What are you seeking here, godson of the French king?'

Louis bowed respectfully and greeted the old woman:

'Good day, old woman, I came to ask if the sun is at home.'

'He is not at home, Louis, but he will soon return,' said the old woman.

'Then I shall wait for him, if I may,' said the godson of the French king.

'Of course you may,' said the old woman. 'But when my son returns he will be so hungry that he will eat you up without mercy. I must hide you somewhere. Come in here!'

She led Louis into the golden castle and hid him in the kitchen under the large kneading trough. Immediately afterwards there was a terrible noise outside the door and into the kitchen stepped the golden sun.

'Mother, I'm hungry!' he thundered. 'I'm hungry and I smell human flesh. Bring it to me and I'll eat it up!'

'Whatever are you talking about?' said the old woman. 'Here is your supper. Eat it up, I tell you, or I shall give you a hiding!'

The sun was frightened. He hung his head down between his shoulders and as obediently as a child he sat down and ate. When he had eaten, the old woman nodded to Louis to show himself.

The godson of the French king did not have to be told twice. He jumped out from under the kneading trough, bowed respectfully and said:

'Good day, Sun, good evening, bright Sun! I came to ask you why you are such a beautiful red colour when you rise in the morning!'

'I'll tell you at once, Louis, godson of the French king!' said the sun. 'Next to my island is Tronkolen Island, where the Princess of Tronkolen has her castle. The Princess of Tronkolen is so beautiful that she almost outshines me and so, every morning, I have to appear before the world at my best. But now run along, I must go to sleep!'

'Thank you Sun, thank you bright Sun, and you too, old woman,' said the godson of the French king. He said goodbye and went down the glass mountain. At the foot of the mountain he got on his wooden horse and in the twinkling of an eye was carried across the sea. At the road, waiting for him, was the white-haired old man and his own horse.

'Well, how did you get on, Louis, godson of the French king?' asked the old man.

'I got on well, old man. The sun told me what I wanted to know. Thank you for your help.'

'Not at all, come again,' said the old man and disappeared round the bend in the road.

In the morning, Louis came before the French king and his false godson. The French king was surprised:

'Are you back already? Well, tell us why the sun is red when it rises in the morning?'

'Because on the neighbouring island of Tronkolen, where the Princess of Tronkolen has a castle, the Princess is so beautiful that she almost puts the sun in the shade. That is why the sun must appear before the world at his best every morning!'

The French king was satisfied and gave Louis a bag of gold for his information. But the false godson was certainly not pleased, and pondered for days on how to get rid of Louis for ever. One day he hit upon an idea and said to the king:

'I wonder if you know, Godfather, what your new stable boy was boasting about again today?'

'And what did he boast of, Godson?' asked the French king.

'That if he wishes he will fetch the Princess of Tronkolen and have her for his wife,' lied the false godson of the French king.

'I will have her for my own wife,' said the king. 'But since he is so bold, send him to get her at once, tomorrow. Bring him here to me, now!'

So poor Louis was brought before the French king.

'I hear you have been boasting that you would fetch the Princess of Tronkolen,' the French king said to him sternly.

'I have never said any such thing.' Louis defended himself and pleaded, but to no avail.

'Either you set out at once, tomorrow, or I shall have your head cut off!' the French king commanded.

Poor Louis had no choice. He saddled a good horse, put some food and a few gold coins in a bag for the journey and sadly set out for the east. A short distance from town he met the white-haired old man.

'Where are you going, Louis, godson of the French king?'

'To the island of Tronkolen, old man, to the Princess of Tronkolen. The French king wants her for his wife,' replied Louis sadly.

'You see, if you had taken my advice in the first place you would not have to go there,' said the old man. 'But what has happened is over and done with, and it doesn't help to cry for ·yesterday. Better return to the king and tell him you will need a ship with a load of wheat, bacon and beef, otherwise you will not be able to fetch the Princess of Tronkolen. When you receive the ship, I'll tell you what to do next.'

So Louis returned and told the French king what he needed.

'You shall have it,' said the French king and ordered a ship to be made ready for him. When it was moored to the pier, ready to sail, the godson of the French king stepped ashore and the first person he saw was the white-haired old man.

'Well, you have your ship, Louis, godson of the French king. Now take this white stick with you and listen to what I say.

'This stick will lead you. When you have it in your hand your ship will always have enough wind in its sails and will ride as swift as an arrow. First you will come to the island of ants. You will give them the wheat because you will need their help. Then you will come to the island of lions. You are taking them the bacon since their gratitude will soon be useful. And finally you will come to the island of hawks. The beef is for them, for without their assistance you would get nowhere. Then the way to Tronkolen Island will be open to you. But beware, Louis, be careful, godson of the French king, that the Princess of Tronkolen does not see you before you see her. If she sees you first, she will put you under a spell and that will be the end of you. And now be off, and good luck!'

The godson of the French king took his place in the ship and raised the white stick, and the boat leapt forward with full sails, as sharp as an arrow. Louis hardly had time to thank the old man:

'Thank you, old man. I shall never forget you!'

In a moment or two a large black mountain appeared on the horizon. It was the island of ants. When Louis had docked, he went to their king and said:

'King of the Ants, I have brought you a gift, a load of wheat.'

The King of the Ants was happy:

'Thank you, Louis, thank you, godson of the French king, your wheat has saved us from hunger. We had nothing left to eat.'

He ordered the wheat to be unloaded. The sailors let down a ramp and along it ran a stream of ants, one stream going this way, the other that way. Each carried one kernel of wheat but there were so many ants that in a little while all the wheat was ashore. Then the King of the Ants said to Louis:

'Because you have helped us in our need, we shall help you too. When you need us, think of me and I will come to your assistance with all my ants.'

The godson of the French king took leave of the ants and raised his white stick, and the ship leapt forward with full sails, as sharp as an arrow. In a moment or two a black mountain appeared on the distant horizon. It was even bigger than the one before, and was the island of the lions. When he landed, Louis appeared before the king and said:

'King of the Lions, I have brought you a gift, a load of bacon.'

The King of the Lions was happy:

'Thank you, Louis, thank you, godson of the French king, your assistance has come just in time. We had nothing left to eat.'

He ordered the bacon to be brought ashore.

The sailors let down a ramp and along that ramp ran a stream of lions, one stream going this way and the other, the other way. Each carried a good-sized slab of bacon and in a while all the bacon was ashore. Then the King of the Lions said:

'Because you have helped us in our need, we shall help you too. When you need us, think of me and I will come to your aid with all my lions.'

The godson of the French king took leave of the lions and raised his white stick, and the ship leapt forward with full sails, as sharp as an arrow. In a moment or two on the distant horizon there appeared a black mountain even bigger than the other two. It was the island of the hawks. When he landed, Louis appeared before the king and said:

'King of the Hawks, I have brought you a gift, a load of beef.'

The King of the Hawks was delighted:

'Thank you, Louis, thank you, godson of the French king, your assistance has come just in time. We had nothing left to eat.'

He ordered the meat to be brought ashore.

The sailors did not even have to let down a ramp. One flock of hawks came down on the ship while the second flock flew away, each hawk with a good-sized piece of beef in his beak. In a while all the beef had been brought ashore. Then the King of the Hawks said to Louis:

'Because you have helped us in our need, we shall help you too. When you need us, think of me and I will come flying to your aid with all my hawks.'

The godson of the French king took leave of the hawks and raised his white stick, and once again the ship leapt forward like an arrow. In a moment or two a beautiful island appeared out of the waves and in the centre of the island was a shining crystal castle, the castle of the Princess of Tronkolen. Louis had a boat lowered from the ship, and he rowed it to the shore. Then he set out for the castle. Surrounding the castle was a large garden. In the garden was a spreading orange tree and beneath it sparkled a well. Louis stole up to the orange tree, softly climbed to the top and waited. In a while, a beautiful young girl came walking along the path to the well. She sat down under the tree, took the crown off her head and began to comb her long, golden hair. Instead of using a mirror she looked into the surface of the well.

The godson of the French king could hardly take his eyes off the beautiful picture reflected in the water. But when he had looked hard and long enough, he plucked a ripe orange and threw it into the well. The blue water formed ripples and the princess's image disappeared. When the surface became calm again, the Princess of Tronkolen saw in it the face of a handsome young man. She smiled at his image in the water and said:

'Is it you, Louis? It must be you, godson of the French king! Come down from the tree and come with me to my castle.'

So Louis climbed down from the orange tree, bowed to the lovely Princess of Tronkolen and went with her to the castle.

In the castle, time passed as quickly as in a fairy tale for the godson of the French king. Day after day went by full of singing, laughter and talking with the princess and before Louis knew what had happened two weeks had passed. Then he remembered why he had come:

'My master the French king has sent me to you, beautiful Princess of Tronkolen, and I am to take you to his castle. Will you come with me?'

'I will, Louis, I will, and gladly, godson of the French king,' replied the Princess of Tronkolen, 'but first you must be worthy of me and perform three difficult tasks. If you perform them, then everything will be fine, but if you do not, things will go ill for both of us!'

The next day, the princess set Louis his first task. She led him to a huge loft in the castle and showed him a mountain of grain — wheat, oats, barley and rye.

'Do you see the grain, Louis? Do you see the mountain of grain, godson of the French king? Before the sun sets you must divide the grain into four piles, but in such a way that not a single grain is in the wrong pile. Otherwise we shall fare badly.'

Then she left. Poor Louis set to work, but by noon, he had only managed to share out three handfuls of grain.

100

'If I carry on like this, I will be here for a hundred years,' he sighed sadly, and then he remembered the King of the Ants. 'If he does not help me it will be the end of me!'

No sooner did Louis think of the ants than their king stood before him and said:

'What would you like, Louis? What do you need, godson of the French king?'

'Help me to share out this grain,' said the godson of the French king. 'Otherwise it will be the end of me!'

'Only this and nothing else?' said the King of the Ants. 'It will be ready before you can say Jack Robinson!'

And it really was! The king of the Ants called all his ants and they set to work with such a will that in a moment or two all the grain was divided into four piles and not a single grain was on the wrong pile. Louis could calmly stretch out in the corner of the loft and take a nap.

When the sun began to set, the Princess of Tronkolen entered the loft and saw that the first difficult task was done perfectly.

'Louis works tremendously hard, he must be a marvellous boy,' she said in wonder and kissed the young man on his forehead.

The next day the Princess set Louis his second difficult task. She placed a woodcutter's axe in his hand, led him behind the castle to an avenue of tall, aged oak trees and said:

'Do you see the trees, Louis, do you see the great, aged oak trees, godson of the French king? Before the sun sets you must cut down the oak trees. Otherwise, we shall fare badly.'

Then she left. Poor Louis set to work. By noon he had cut down only one oak tree.

'If I go on like this I will be here for a hundred years,' he sighed sadly and remembered the King of the Lions. 'If he does not help me it will be the end of me!'

No sooner did Louis think of the lions when their king stood before him and said:

'What would you like, Louis? What do you need, godson of the French king?'

'Help me to cut down these oak trees,' said the godson of the French king, 'otherwise it will be the end of me!'

'Only this and nothing else?' said the King of the Lions. 'It will be ready before you can say Jack Robinson.'

And it really was! The King of the Lions called all his lions and they set to work with such vigour that in a moment or two all the oak trees were lying on the ground. Louis could calmly stretch out on the grass and take a nap.

When the sun was sinking down to the horizon, the Princess of Tronkolen came to the avenue and saw that even the second difficult task had been accomplished. All the oak trees were lying on the ground.

'That Louis is quite a lad. He must be a very diligent worker,' she said in wonder and kissed the lad twice on his forehead.

The next day the princess set Louis the third and most difficult task. She gave him a shovel, led him to a high mountain behind the castle and said:

'Do you see this hill, Louis, do you see this high mountain, godson of the French king? It throws too large a shadow on my castle and garden. Before the sun sets you must level the mountain to the ground. Otherwise, we shall fare badly!'

Then she left. Poor Louis set to work, filled a wheelbarrow once and dumped the earth into the sea, filled the wheelbarrow a second and third time and it was already noon.

'If I go on like this I will be here for a hundred years,' he sighed sadly and remembered the King of the Hawks. 'If he does not help me it will be the end of me!'

No sooner did Louis think of the Hawks than their king flew down and said:

'What would you like, Louis? What do you need, godson of the French king?'

'Help me to level this mountain to the ground,' said the godson of the French king, 'otherwise it will be the end of me and of the Princess of Tronkolen too!'

'Only this and nothing else?' said the King of the Hawks. 'It will be ready before you can say Jack Robinson.'

And it really was. The King of the Hawks called all his hawks and they set to work with such energy that almost immediately the whole mountain was in the sea. Louis was able to stretch out on the level ground and take a nap.

When the sun had sunk down to the blue waters of the horizon, the Princess of Tronkolen came to see if the mountain was levelled to the ground and she saw that the third and most difficult task was accomplished.

'When I marry I shall only have Louis for a husband,' said the Princess and kissed the lad three times on his forehead.

Louis awakened and said:

'Are you content now, beautiful Princess? Are you content, Princess of Tronkolen?'

'I am, and I shall go with you wherever you lead me,' said the Princess.

'I shall take you to my master, the French king,' said Louis and set out with the Princess of Tronkolen to the coast. There his boat was waiting for him. Louis jumped into it and led the princess to a seat and in a while they had reached the ship. When they were on deck, the godson of the French king raised his white stick and the ship leapt forward with full sails, sharp as an arrow, heading for the shores of France.

The white stick and the good wind took them swiftly across the wide sea. At the French coast, the white-haired old man was waiting for them. He called from a distance:

'Welcome, Princess of Tronkolen, who will soon be married, welcome, godson of the French king, who will soon be the king's heir!'

'Thank you, old man, for without you I could never have done it,' replied Louis.

Then they went to the castle of the French king. As soon as the French king saw the Princess of Tronkolen he could hardly take his eyes off her and his face became rosy with happiness. But his false godson was green with jealousy. Not even now had he rid himself of Louis! He pondered for days on how to revenge himself and finally had an idea. When everyone was seated at the table, he leaned over to the French king and said:

'I wonder if you know what your stable boy has been boasting about? That he will have the Princess of Tronkolen for his own bride!'

'No he won't!' decided the French king. 'A king shall have her for a wife!'

Without hesitation he rose and in front of the whole court asked the Princess of Tronkolen for her hand in marriage.

But the Princess of Tronkolen laughed:

'What are you saying, dear sir? What are you saying, French King! Why, you are old enough to be my grandfather! I shall take a younger man for my husband!'

'If you want a younger one then you shall have him,' decided the French king. 'Take my godson and my heir.'

And he pointed to the false godson sitting by his side. But the princess laughed again:

'I shall have your godson with pleasure, but not this liar and traitor. Your real godson is sitting next to me,' and she pointed to Louis.

The false godson of the French king grew even more green. It was enough just to look at him to know that he was a liar and that the princess was right.

'But where did he get half of my ring?' thundered the French king.

'He stole it from me,' said Louis and related what had happened.

The French king heard this and decided on the spot:

'Guard, take him away and cut off his head in the courtyard. Prepare everything for a wedding feast in the castle. My real godson will be married to the Princess of Tronkolen.'

So, finally, everyone got what he deserved. The liar and traitor had his head cut off, Louis was given the Princess of Tronkolen for a wife, and the French king officiated at the wedding. But grateful Louis did not forget those who had helped him. On one side of the wedding table, next to the French king, sat the white-haired old man, on the other side the old collier, opposite him the three powerful kings — the King of the Ants, the King of the Lions, and the King of the Hawks — and Louis's twenty-five brothers. Never before had there been such a splendid wedding. Afterwards they all lived happily together for ever and ever.

THE PRINCE WITH THE BLACK SCARF

Once upon a time there lived a very wealthy king of France, who had the wisdom of an owl and the courage of a lion. When he was young he had been a brave soldier, and when he grew older he was a wise ruler. His people loved him dearly, just as much as did his kind and beautiful queen and their little prince.

The prince was a healthy, lovely boy and it was a joy to see him grow steadily into a strong, handsome youth. The years flew by and soon he had reached his seventeenth year.

Up till then he had given the king and queen only pleasure, but now, alas, he changed completely and caused them much worry. He chose bad friends who led him astray, he roamed through the streets for days and nights, he gambled with dice and took to drink — it really was a shame! When his behaviour showed no sign of improvement, the Elders of the kingdom gathered together and confronted their king:

'Good day, King of France!'

The king welcomed them:

'Good day, my friends. What brings you to me?'

The wise men bowed their heads and replied:

'We come with an unpleasant duty, our Lord! Your son — our Prince — has fallen into bad habits; he has some nasty companions, wanders about like a tramp, gambles with dice and drinks — what more need we tell you. One day he is to be our master, our king! Please reason with him, King of France, to mend his ways, so we will gain a wise ruler like yourself!'

The king hung his head in shame:

'Thank you friends, I am glad you have been so honest with me. I shall reproach my son.'

This he certainly did. Messengers were sent throughout the city, and when they all confirmed that the prince really had fallen into such bad ways, the king sent not only for his son, but also for the executioner.

'What is this I hear?' he stormed the moment the prince came before him. 'Your behaviour is not fitting for a son of mine or for a future king! How will you be able to reign over others when you have no control over yourself? You will receive one hundred lashes as a warning. Perhaps this will knock some sense into you. If it does not, you will go to prison, though you are a prince. Executioner, carry out your task!'

The executioner gave the prince one hundred lashes, and for a while afterwards the prince behaved better. Unfortunately this did not last, for only a couple of weeks later he was carrying on worse than ever before. The Elders of the kingdom met again and for the second time confronted their king:

'Good day, King of France, we are here once more!'

'Good day, my friends,' the king greeted them. 'What brings you to me?'

'Nothing very pleasant, Your Majesty. Your reproof was of no use. Your son — our prince — is misbehaving worse than ever. Try and make him mend his ways. After all, one day he will be our king.'

The king hung his head in shame:

'Thank you my friends, I am glad you have been so honest. I assure you I shall do what is necessary. Return to your homes in peace.'

He sent for his son immediately and called the executioner.

The moment he saw the prince, the king raged:

'What is this I hear? My reproofs and punishments have had no effect, for you are behaving worse than before, acting as if you were neither a prince or a future king. You will receive one hundred lashes and will spend a whole year in prison, fed only on bread and water. Perhaps this will knock some sense into you! And if this does not work, you shall go to the gallows — even though you are the prince and my son! Executioner, carry out your task!'

The executioner gave the prince one hundred lashes, then locked him in a dark cell of the prison, where he remained for a whole year, fed only on bread and water, so he had plenty of time to learn his lesson. However, only a month or two after his release he was misbehaving worse than ever before. As this went on and on, the Elders of the kingdom met once again and confronted their king for the third time:

'Good day, King of France! We are here again, for the third time!'

'Good day, my friends!' the king welcomed them. 'What brings you to me?'

The wise men replied fearlessly:

'An unpleasant duty, our Lord! We are sorry to say your reproof and punishment had no effect even this time. Your son — our prince — is carrying on worse than ever before. Try and make him mend his ways. He is, after all, supposed to be our king one day when you are no longer with us.'

At this the king blazed with anger:

'Thank you, friends, for telling me this, but I shall not try to reason with my son again! I gave my word he would go to the gallows if he did not mend his ways, and I shall not break it, even though he is a prince and my own son and heir.'

The wise men tried to calm the king's anger, but he would not change his mind. He sent for the executioner and ordered him to fetch the prince.

The prince happened to be away from home, roaming the streets and drinking in the inns with his bad friends. As it was, the queen and not the guards found him first. With her face wet with tears, she led him secretly into her room.

'My son, you are in danger! Your father, the King of France, is very angry with you, because you have behaved so wickedly. He gave his word he would send you to the gallows, but I believe there is goodness in your heart. Take this purse of gold coins, and this sword, mount your horse and ride into the world. Perhaps somewhere you will find your true path. Remember this, I do not want to see you until you have found it.'

She kissed him then and led him through a hidden gate into the garden, where a saddled horse was waiting. The prince jumped onto his back and galloped off into the dark night. Soon only the sound of hooves could be heard, then the noise faded, and only silence remained.

In the morning the queen went to her husband, the King of France:

'My lord, I feel very guilty. I have given our son — the prince — a purse of gold, a sword and a horse, and have secretly sent him away, so you could not send him to the gallows. Forgive me and do not be angry.'

'I am not angry,' the king sadly replied. 'You are his mother and you did what your heart begged of you. But I am a king and I must act accordingly; I must proclaim I never ever wish to see our son again. If I lay my eyes on that good-for-nothing son, I shall indeed let the executioner have him!'

Then he kissed the queen on both cheeks.

In the meantime the prince was galloping on his strong horse farther and farther away from the palace; and by that evening he had reached a forest. Dismounting from his horse, he tied the reins to a tree and sat down on the mossy ground. Suddenly he caught sight of a hawk as it swooped down from the air onto a mouse in the grass. He killed it with a single blow of his beak, but before he could fly away, a vixen hidden in the bushes jumped onto his back. She bit through the hawk's neck and was just about to drag her prey away, when a smartly dressed huntsman rode by. In his hands he held a taut bow and with a well-aimed arrow he slew the vixen instantly. However, when he bent down from his saddle to pick up the vixen, the string of the bow snapped, hitting the horse on his side. The startled horse galloped away, dragging behind him his rider, who was trapped by his foot in the stirrup.

The huntsman was dead before the prince had a chance to come to his aid.

Then the prince thought very deeply about all he had just seen, and he realised that evil creates only evil, and every bad deed must be punished in the end, even if the guilty one wears smart clothes, even if he is a mighty prince or a king.

'My father the King of France was quite right to scold and punish me,' he said to himself. 'But I shall prove to him that I am after all worthy to be his son.'

The prince rode into the nearest town. He sold his horse, and gave all his gold to the poor people, keeping only his sword with him. Then he put an old beggar's cloak over his beautiful clothes, masked his face with a black scarf, which had two holes for his eyes and one for his mouth, and in this fashion he set out into the world.

After walking for seven weeks he found himself in a deep forest. In the middle of it was a clearing, where stood a wooden hut, the home of a white-haired hermit.

'Welcome, Prince of France,' the hermit greeted the traveller in the black scarf.

The prince was most surprised:

'How do you know who I am?' he asked the old man.

'Not only do I know who you are,' was the hermit's reply, 'I also know why you are out in the world, and what is worrying you. I can offer you some very good advice: leave me your sword, your princely clothes and your black scarf, then travel further along this path. When after seven days you come to a farm, ask for some work. The rest will depend on you. When you need your sword, your clothes and your scarf, return here for them; I shall keep them for you. Now go — and luck be with you!'

The Prince of France took the old man's advice and leaving his sword, clothes and black scarf behind, he bade farewell, then continued on his journey. Seven days later he came to the farm, where he knocked upon the door:

'Good day, good folk! Could you use a man for work perhaps?' he asked.

'We certainly could,' the farmer answered. 'We need a man to drive a herd of pigs to pasture.'

'I should be very happy to look after your pigs for you,' the prince replied — and that is how the prince became a swineherd. Every morning he drove a hundred pigs out of the farmyard down the pastures of the forest, which stood above the sea, and every evening he drove them back to the farm again. Time passed, and the farmer was very satisfied with his swineherd. He had never known such a hard-working, honest and vigorous fellow. Everyone on the farm liked him, and the good swineherd was a true friend to one and all.

One evening as he was returning with his pigs from their pasture, he heard a piercing scream coming from the edge of the forest. In the meadow just beyond, a poor old woman had been looking after her goat, when suddenly a large wolf had pounced upon her helpless animal. As he was just about to drag his victim into the bracken the good swineherd moved swiftly to block his way. Raising his crook he struck the wolf with such strength and so fearlessly that it decided to drop the goat and take to his heels and flee.

'Thank you, swineherd, thank you, French Prince!' said the old woman. 'You have done me a great service and I should be happy to repay you. Look at this hollow tree. When you are in need of anything, do not hesitate to come to it; knock on the tree three times, and shout: Shepherdess of goats, help me! — and I shall come to your aid.'

Then the kind old lady and her goat melted away, just like a small cloud of steam in the sunshine.

That same evening, when the swineherd returned to the farm and sat down to his supper, he noticed that his master looked rather sad.

'What has happened, master, that your head is hung in sorrow?' asked the swineherd.

'How can I feel happy!' replied the farmer. 'Bad times have fallen upon the French kingdom. A giant at least six hundred feet tall has descended upon it. He has a gleaming diamond eye in the middle of his forehead. From morning till night he roams through the countryside, and wherever he goes, everything dries up and dies under his piercing gaze. If he is not stopped, he will turn our whole country into wasteland. Our poor old king is worried to death about it!'

'Has no one come forward to stand up to the giant?' wondered the swineherd.

'Many tried,' answered the farmer. 'A whole army of brave men set out against him, but they were helpless, because the fiery giant cannot be destroyed. They all lost their lives in vain.'

The good swineherd listened carefully without saying another word. The next day, as he was driving his pigs to their pasture as usual, he stopped when he reached the hollow tree by the edge of the wood, and he knocked on it three times, shouting:

'Shepherdess of goats, help me!'

Before he had time to shout for the third time, a beautiful lady dressed in white appeared as suddenly as if she had been swept there by the wind.

'Good day, swineherd, good day, French Prince. I know what is troubling you and I will gladly help you. Listen carefully to me: if you wish to slay the fiery giant, you have to strike him hard with your sword in his diamond eye. Go and fetch your sword, your clothes and your black scarf from the hermit, then follow the midday sun for seven days and seven nights, until you reach a dry, deserted plain. There you will find the desolate ruins of a castle. Hide inside and wait. When night falls, the fiery giant will come. He will stretch his body across the plain, lean his head against the castle, and go to sleep. Wait till he is sound asleep! Rise with the stroke of midnight, strike him with all your might in his diamond eye with your sword, and the fiery giant will die. And now, goodbye, for you will never see me again.'

The beautiful lady disappeared as if she were blown away by the wind, before the swineherd could say thank you, so he turned his herd round and drove it back to the farm at once.

'Master, the time has come for us to part, for I must be off on a long journey,' he said.

'In that case go and return safely; remember you are always welcome here,' said the farmer, and gave the swineherd a purse of silver. 'Here are your wages, and good luck to you.'

'Thank you, master, but please keep it for me. If I do not return by the end of six months, give the silver to the poor. And now goodbye!'

The swineherd set forth on his travels. After seven days and seven nights he reached the hermit's wooden hut. The old man was already waiting for him:

'Welcome, Prince of France! What brings you here?'

'I need my sword, my clothes and my black scarf,' said the prince.

'They are here, all ready for you,' answered the hermit, passing the prince's belongings to him.

The swineherd put on his princely clothes, secured his sword, masked his face with the black scarf and set out in the direction of the noon sun. He travelled for seven days and seven nights, till he reached the bare, burnt out plain and the bleak ruins of the castle. Night was falling, so the prince hardly had time to hide amongst the tumbledown walls before he heard a thunderous noise, as if a whole army was approaching. It was the fiery giant! He spread his massive body over the plain, propped his head against the castle and began to snore so loudly that the stones fell off the walls. It seemed as if he was truly sound asleep, but the prince took no chances and waited till midnight, for by the stroke of twelve the fiery giant really was asleep. The prince then leapt from his hiding-place, unsheathed his sword and struck the diamond eye with all his might. The fiery giant sighed a mighty sigh and was no more. Then his body changed into thick black smoke and only a shining diamond was left on the ground, so the prince picked it up and put it in his pocket:

'At least I can prove I killed him now,' he thought, and set out to the castle of the French king. As his face was masked by the black scarf with the three holes, no one recognised him, not even the queen who sat by the window gazing into the distance, wondering if her son would ever return home.

Then the prince came to his father and said:

'Good day, French King!'

'Good day, man in the black scarf,' his father greeted him. 'What brings you here to me?'

'I slew the fiery giant and am bringing you the diamond from his eye,' answered the prince at once.

'Thank you, man in the black scarf,' said the king. 'For the great service you have done me, and for the shining diamond, I will reward you with one hundred thousand gold coins.'

'I did not fight the giant for wealth but for honour,' the prince answered. 'If you do not need the one hundred thousand pieces of gold, give them to the poor!'

'I can see you are not only brave but also noble, man in the black scarf,' commented the king. 'Show me your face.'

'That I cannot do, King of France,' the prince replied. 'My father never again wishes to see my face, so you also cannot see it.'

'Your father should be proud of such a son,' the king said sadly.

'My own son turned out so very differently, he is a failure, a good-for-nothing — he will surely end up on the gallows!'

'I know your son, King of France,' the prince remarked. 'He changed for the better a long time ago.'

'I do not believe you, man in the black scarf,' said the king firmly. 'I do not believe you at all, and if I so much as lay my eyes upon him, I shall let the executioner have him, as I vowed!'

When the prince heard this, he took his leave of the king at once, waved to the queen who still sat by the window, and went quickly on his way. After seven weeks he reached the old hermit's hut again.

'Welcome, Prince of France,' the hermit greeted the traveller in the black scarf. 'How did you get on may I ask?'

The prince told the old man how he had killed the giant and called on the King of France, ending regretfully:

'But my father is still very angry with me.'

'That is because your test is not yet finished,' said the hermit. 'Leave me your sword, your princely robes and your black scarf, and return to your work.'

The Prince of France obeyed the old man, left his possessions behind, said goodbye and went on his way along the now familiar path. After seven days and seven nights he arrived at the farm and knocked on the door:

'Good day, farmer, I am back again!'

'Good day, swineherd,' his master replied. 'Welcome back! If you wish, you can carry on here as before.'

So the good prince stayed on, and once again worked as a swineherd as before. Every morning he drove his pigs to the woodland pastures above the sea, and every evening he took them back to the farm. Everybody was pleased with his work. Such a reliable, hardworking and capable young man they had never known!

Then one day as he was resting under a tree, a beautiful golden bird perched on a branch above his head. The golden bird sang sadly and spoke to him with a human voice:

'I am the Golden Bird, swineherd, I am the Golden Bird who will live till the end of the world, Prince of France. Every hundred years, however, I must take a drink of human blood, otherwise I shall perish, mark you. It is exactly one hundred years ago today since I had my last drink of blood. Please help me, give me a little of yours or I shall die!'

'I will help you, Golden Bird. I will give you all the blood you want,' said the prince. 'Fly to me and drink.'

The kind swineherd took out his knife and stabbed his arm. The Golden Bird flew down to the ground and drank greedily till its thirst was quenched. Then it turned to the prince:

'Thank you, swineherd; you have done me a great service and I shall gladly reward you. If ever you need anything, come to this wood, clap your hands three times and shout: "Golden Bird, help me!", and I shall come to your aid.'

The Golden Bird fluttered its wings happily and soared into the sky. That evening, when the swineherd returned to the farm and sat down to supper, he noticed his master sitting with his head hanging sadly again.

'What has happened this time sir, to make you so unhappy?' asked the swineherd.

'How can I be happy!' cried the farmer. 'Once again bad times have fallen upon the French kingdom. A fierce dragon more than one thousand feet long, with a golden crown upon his head, has settled in the kingdom — goodness knows where he came from! He roams over the country from morning till night, eating people and cattle and goodness knows what! If this continues, there won't be anyone left alive in the whole kingdom. Our poor old king is worried to death.'

'Has no one yet come forward who would be willing to fight the dragon?' asked the swineherd.

'Many were brave enough to face him,' the farmer answered. 'But the dragon ate every one of them, for an ordinary man is helpless against such a beast.'

The good swineherd listened, but said no more. The very next day, as soon as he had driven his pigs into the forest, he clapped his hands three times and shouted:

'Golden Bird, please help me!'

Before he had time to repeat it for the third time, the Golden Bird flew to a branch of a nearby tree.

'Good day to you swineherd, good day to you, Prince of France. I know what is troubling you and I will gladly help you. Listen carefully. Here is one of my feathers. If you place it in your mouth, you will turn into a bird but the moment you spit the feather out, you will change back

118

into a man again. Return to the hermit for your sword, your princely robes and your scarf, then travel for seven days and seven nights in the direction of the midnight moon till you reach some very high mountains. Hide in a cave and wait for the dragon. You can kill him only by piercing his heart with your sword. No human power can cut through his strong tough skin. But when he opens his enormous mouth, turn into a bird, fly bravely into his throat, and then you will be able to pierce his heart quite easily. Now goodbye, for we shall never meet again.'

Before the swineherd could thank the Golden Bird, it disappeared. So he turned to his herd and drove his pigs back to the farm at once.

'Master, the time has come for us to part again, for I must be off on a long journey once more.'

'I wish you a safe return and remember that you are always welcome here,' said the farmer, handing him two purses of silver. 'Here are you wages.'

'Thank you, master,' the princes answered, 'but please keep the money for me. If I do not return by the end of six months, give them to the poor. And now, goodbye!'

So the good swineherd began his journey. After seven days and seven nights he reached the hermit's hut. The old man was already waiting for him as before.

'Welcome, Prince of France! What brings you here?'

'I need my sword, my princely robes and my black scarf,' the prince replied.

'I have them here all ready for you,' said the hermit.

The prince dressed in his smart clothes, fastened his sword, masked his face with the black scarf, and set out in the direction of the midnight moon. Then he walked for seven days and seven nights till he reached the high mountains. There he found a cave and waited for the dragon. When night was falling, the dragon stormed to the mountains. Altogether he was a good thousand feet long. On his head he wore a golden crown and his mouth opened like an enormous gate. But the prince was quite unafraid. He put the feather from the Golden Bird in his mouth and turned into a bird at once. Disguised in this way, he flew through the wide mouth to the regions beyond. When he reached the dragon's heart, he spat the feather out and was a prince once again. Then lifting his sword without any hesitation, he plunged it with all his might into the dragon's heart. The dragon sighed a mighty sigh and was no more. He also dissolved into thick black smoke and all that was left was a golden crown upon the ground. The good prince picked it up and placed it in his sack at once.

'At least I can prove I have killed the dragon,' he thought and set forth to the castle of the French king. As his face was masked by the black scarf with the three holes, no one recognised him even this time. Only the queen, who again sat by the window looking out for her absent son, turned her glance three times in his direction, as if he reminded her of someone she knew.

The good prince came before his father:

'Good day to you, King of France!'

'Good day to you too, man in the black scarf,' the king greeted him. 'What brings you to me again?'

'I have slain the dragon and I have brought you his golden crown,' the prince answered.

'Thank you, man in the black scarf,' said the king. 'For this great service and for bringing me the golden crown, I shall give you two hundred thousand gold coins.'

'I did not fight for wealth, but for honour, my Lord,' the prince replied. 'If you do not need the two hundred thousand pieces of gold, give them to the poor!'

'I see you are not only courageous, but also noble, man in the black scarf,' commented the king. 'Show me your face!'

'That I must not do, King of France,' the prince answered. 'As I told you last time, my father never again wants to see my face, so you also cannot see it either.'

'Your father should be proud of such a son,' said the king sadly. 'I am afraid my own son did not turn out so well. He is a failure, a good-for-nothing, and is sure to end on the gallows as I said before.'

'I know your son, French King, and you are being unjust to him. He mended his ways a long time ago and wants to return to you. Shall I tell him that he may?' asked the prince.

'I do not believe you, man in the black scarf,' replied the king, shaking his head. 'I do not believe what you say and if I lay my eyes upon my son, I shall hand him over to the executioner, as I vowed.'

When the prince heard this and realised the king would not weaken in

his resolve, he bowed to the king, waved to the queen by the window and departed. After travelling for seven weeks he reached the hermit's hut again.

'Welcome, French Prince,' the hermit greeted him. 'How did you get on?'

The prince told the old man he had killed the dragon with the golden crown and visited the King of France.

'But my father has not yet forgiven me.'

'That is because your test is not yet finished,' said the hermit. 'Leave me your sword, your robes and your black scarf, and return once more to your work.'

The French prince obeyed the old man, took off his robes, his sword and his black scarf, bade the hermit goodbye, and set out along the familiar path from the wood. After seven days and seven nights he arrived at the farm and knocked on the door:

'Good day farmer, I am back again!'

'Good day swineherd,' his master answered. 'Welcome back again, and if you wish, you can stay on as before.'

And so the good prince once again worked happily as a swineherd. Each morning he drove the pigs to the woodland pasture above the sea and each evening he drove them back to the farm. Everyone was glad to have him back, for they never had such a hardworking, honest and brave worker!

Then one day when the swineherd was sitting on the shore of the sea, a huge vulture swooped from the air right to the water's edge, and grasped in its claws a big gold fish. The fish wriggled and tried hard to escape, but the vulture was the stronger. It lashed out with its wings at its prey and was just about to soar into the sky with the exhausted fish when the good swineherd, with one mighty blow of his crook, knocked the vulture into the waves, and the gold fish swam to the shore:

'Thank you, swineherd, thank you, French Prince. You have done me a great service and I shall repay you. When you need me, throw three handfuls of sand into the sea and shout: "King of Fish, help me!" and I shall come to your aid.'

Then the gold fish disappeared into the sea.

The very same evening when the swineherd returned to the farm and sat down to his supper, he noticed a worried frown on his master's face:

122

'What has happened sir, to make you look so worried?' the swineherd inquired.

'How can I stop worrying,' the farmer replied. 'Once again disaster has struck the French king, and even greater than ever before. Black Plague is spreading through the kingdom, and people are dying like flies. The old king is gravely ill too.'

'Has no doctor been found who could help?' the worried swineherd asked.

'Many have tried to help,' the farmer answered. 'But no one can find the cure for the Black Plague; even the doctors are dying one after the other.'

The swineherd realised the situation was really serious. He rose and said:

'We must part for the third time, and for ever. A very long journey lies before me.'

'In that case I wish you luck, and remember you are always welcome here,' said the farmer as he handed him three purses of silver coins. 'Here are your wages.'

'Thank you master!' the swineherd replied, 'but give the money to the poor, for I have no need of it. As I shall never return again, I wish you well and bid you goodbye!'

Then the good swineherd hurried to the shore of the sea, threw three handfuls of sand into the waves and shouted:

'King of Fish, help me!'

Before he had time to shout for the third time, the large gold fish swam to the surface.

'Good day swineherd, good day French Prince!' said the King of Fish. 'I know what is worrying you and I will gladly help you. There is only one cure against the Black Plague and that is the Golden Flower, which has the scent of balsam and the voice of a nightingale. As soon as you plant it in the grounds of the king's castle everyone will be cured. But the Golden Flower grows on a distant island in the middle of a stormy ocean. Whoever tries to reach it is swept away by angry seas and strong gales. But I will take you there in safety. Jump on my back and do not be afraid!'

The good swineherd obeyed, jumped onto the fish's back and the King of Fish shot away like an arrow. Although mountainous waves rose around them and the gale howled angrily, drowning even the sound of their voices, they reached the island of the Golden Flower very swiftly.

'This is the place,' said the King of Fish. 'Go along, French Prince, dig out the Golden Flower and return quickly, for we have very little time to spare.'

The prince leapt onto the shore and out of the earth dug the Golden Flower which had the scent of balsam and the voice of a nightingale. Then he returned quickly to the King of Fish. They rode away as fast as lightning, though mountainous waves rose around them and the gale howled angrily, drowning even the sound of their voices. In a moment or two they came to the shore near the old hermit's hut.

'We have arrived,' said the King of Fish. 'Now that I have helped you, I no longer owe you anything. As we shall never meet again, I bid you goodbye, French Prince!'

Before the good prince had a chance to thank him, the King of Fish disappeared in the deep waters.

The prince, with the Golden Flower in his hand, turned towards the hermit's hut. There the old man was waiting for him:

'Welcome, Prince of France! Here are your sword, your robes and your scarf. I know you are in a hurry, so I have already saddled your horse. If you were to go on foot, it would take you seven weeks, but on horseback you will be there in a flash.'

'Thank you, old hermit,' said the prince. 'As we shall never meet again, I wish you well and bid you goodbye. I shall never forget all your help.'

Then the Prince of France put on his princely robes, fastened his sword, masked his face with the black scarf, and with the Golden Flower in his hand he mounted his horse. Very soon he was standing in front of the king's castle. The prince quickly dismounted, dug a hole in the ground and planted the Golden Flower in it. Immediately the scent of balsam perfumed the air and the flower started to sing like a nightingale. All the town and all the kingdom came to life again. The sick rose from their beds and the healthy rushed to the king's palace. The good prince went into the palace, but he found an empty throne. The king was not to be seen. Only the old queen sat by the window gazing into the distance, just in case her son should return. When she saw the man in the black scarf come through the doors, she rose and ran to him, crying:

'Welcome, my son, welcome, Prince of France! It is you after all!'

'Yes, I am your son,' replied the prince as he embraced her fondly. Then they hurried to the king's room, where the old king lay on his bed, gravely ill. Candles burned by his head, as though he was dead already. The moment the prince entered the room, his father raised his head:

'Welcome, man in the black scarf! What brings you to me?'

'I have brought you the Golden Flower which perfumes the air with the scent of balsam and sings with the voice of a nightingale,' answered the prince. 'I have chased the Black Plague away!'

'Thank you, man in the black scarf,' said the old king. 'For this great service and for the Golden Flower I shall give you my throne and my crown. My son is a failure, a good-for-nothing, and will never become a king.'

'I know your son well, King of France, and you judge him unjustly,' the prince insisted. 'He has mended his ways a long time ago, and is no more a good-for-nothing than I am. He would dearly like to return to you, if you could forgive him.'

'I would like to believe you, man with the black scarf,' said the king. 'I would so like to believe you, and if my son really is no more a good-for-nothing than yourself, I shall gladly welcome him.'

'Then welcome him now,' cried the prince and tore the black scarf from his face.

The old king realised only then who the man with the black scarf really was, and he embraced and kissed the good prince with joy.

From that moment they all lived together happily and peacefully till the end of their days. When the old king died, the good prince took over the reign of the kingdom and ruled just as wisely and fairly as his father before him.

CAPTAIN TULIP AND THE PRINCESS
FROM BORDEAUX

O nce upon a time there was an orphan boy, called Tulip, perhaps because he grew straight and strong — in spite of being poor and needy — with cheeks like two red tulips and eyes like two bright stars.

Young Tulip's life was not easy, but he managed as best he could. When he reached his eighteenth birthday, he joined the army and went to war with the King's Dragoons. After three years of fighting he returned alive and well and was promoted to a captain.

One day Tulip's regiment came to the town of Bordeaux. Captain Tulip was strolling with two of his friends through the port, when a handsome carriage drawn by two pairs of black horses drove past them. Inside the carriage sat the most beautiful princess he had ever seen.

'What a lovely princess,' cried Captain Tulip. 'What would I give to have the honour of sitting next to her.'

The carriage stopped suddenly. The princess had heard the words of the captain and had asked her coachman to halt the horses.

'Which one of you spoke?' she asked the Dragoons.

Captain Tulip was dumbfounded; the sight of the lovely princess made him lose his tongue. His friends, however, did not stay silent:

'It was our friend, Captain Tulip!'

The lovely princess turned to Tulip and said sadly:

'Captain Tulip, if you were to sit by my side, you would fare very badly.'

The good Captain Tulip shook himself from his stupor:

'Lovely Princess, if you would only care to ask me, I will gladly sit in your carriage even if I would pay for it with my life!'

'No, Captain Tulip, I must not ask you,' said the princess. 'I bid you goodbye, but we shall meet again!'

The carriage drove off as if a sudden gust of wind had blown it away, and was never seen again in Bordeaux. Captain Tulip searched for it throughout the port every day, but in vain; he asked everyone about the princess, but in vain; no one knew her. Captain Tulip grew more sad every day. At last he went to see his general:

'Good day, General!'

'Good day, Captain Tulip! Speak, what do you want?'

'I have served for three years, General, and now I should like to go on a long journey. Please give me your permission!'

'You have my permission, Captain Tulip. I wish you good luck and every success!'

'Thank you sir! Either I shall return in seven years' time, or you will be hearing about me.'

The captain left the general, said goodbye to his friends, and in less than an hour he and his faithful servant were galloping astride their strong horses into the wide world. So began his search for the beautiful princess from Bordeaux.

Captain Tulip looked for her for six long years; he travelled the world for six long years; he asked everyone about her for six long years, and he found no trace of her for six long years. When the seventh year began, he and his faithful servant arrived one fine evening at a very large castle. An avenue of tall trees led up to it, a lovely garden full of flowers surrounded it, and the main doors were open wide:

'Hullo, good people, is anyone at home? Hullo, good folk, may we come in?'

But the castle stood silent. Not a single sound was heard, except an echo repeating as if in invitation:

'Come in!'

Captain Tulip did not wait to be asked again. He entered fearlessly and what do you think he saw? In the middle of the room was a table laid for two. In one corner a bright fire was burning merrily in the hearth and in the opposite corner stood two beds already made up. Captain Tulip asked daringly:

'Hullo, good people, where are you? Hullo, good folk, may we eat and drink?'

But the castle remained silent. Not a sound could be heard, except the echo repeated as if in invitation:

'Eat and drink!'

Captain Tulip did not need to be asked twice. He immediately sat at the table with his faithful servant and ate with relish. After supper he asked for the third time:

'Hullo, good people, is anyone at home? Hullo, good folk, may we sleep here?'

Once again the castle remained silent. Not a sound was heard, except the echo repeated as if in invitation:

'Sleep here!'

Captain Tulip did not wait to be asked again even this time. He jumped into one of the comfortable beds and his servant into the other. They both slept soundly till the break of dawn.

The next morning they breakfasted, then explored the castle. When they came into the garden filled with flowers, Captain Tulip heard a strange moaning near a tall black cypress tree, as if someone under the earth was sobbing and crying:

'Alas, alas! Alas, alas!'

128

'Can you hear those moans, my faithful servant? Whatever can it be?'

'I don't know, Captain Tulip, for all I hear is the murmur of the grass.'

Then the strange cry was heard again:

'Alas, alas! Alas, alas!'

'You must have heard it that time, my faithful servant!'

'I did not, Captain Tulip! I can only hear the whisper of leaves.'

Then the cry was heard for the third time:

'Alas, alas! Alas, alas!'

Captain Tulip said:

'Speak, tell me who you are and what you want of me!'

A voice from under the earth replied:

'It is I, your princess from Bordeaux. This is the seventh year that I have waited here for you to come and set me free. An evil magician buried me alive in this spot. Anyone who wishes to set me free must undergo terrible torture for three nights. Please try and bear them, Captain Tulip, but take care: if you utter a single word, if you once cry out, I shall be doomed for ever and so will you.'

'Do not worry, lovely princess. I, Captain Tulip, will not let you down.'

That evening the good captain dined with his servant, then slept fitfully till midnight. All was silent, but at the stroke of twelve the wicked magician burst into the room with his helpers.

'Here is this human worm! Take him and drag him up and down the staircases of the castle till the cock crows! We shall see if he does not cry out!'

The magician's assistants grabbed poor Captain Tulip by his feet and dragged him ceaselessly up and down the staircases till Captain Tulip felt as if all the bones in his body were broken. But he uttered no sound, and at last was freed by the first crow of the cock.

The faithful servant had no idea what had happened. He saw nothing, heard nothing, and slept soundly all night. In the morning he found his master on his bed bruised and battered.

'What has happened to you, Captain Tulip?'

'I hardly know, my faithful servant! Help me. See if you can find some ointment for my legs and arms.'

The servant looked around and, strangely enough, found a jar of sweet-smelling ointment on the table beside the bed. Then the faithful servant rubbed his master with it from head to toe, and, lo and behold, his master was fit and well again. He got up and hurried into the garden. The beautiful princess was still buried under the tall cypress tree, but now only up to her shoulders.

'Faithful servant, look over here! Can you see the lovely princess?'

'I cannot, Captain Tulip; I can see only the tall black cypress tree and a bush underneath it.'

Although the faithful servant saw nothing and heard nothing, Captain Tulip saw and heard very well indeed.

'Thank you, Captain Tulip! I know what you had to suffer because of me, but this night your torture shall be even worse to bear. Please endure it, Captain Tulip, but do take care: for if you utter a single word, if you cry out only once, I shall be doomed for ever, and so will you as well.'

'Do not be afraid, beautiful princess! I, Captain Tulip, will not let you down!'

That evening the good Captain Tulip dined with his servant, then they retired to bed. All was quiet till midnight, but with the stroke of twelve the magician burst into the room with his assistants:

'Here is this human worm! Take him, chop off his nose and ears, and comb him with the iron comb until the cock crows.'

The assistants of the wicked magician seized poor Captain Tulip, cut off his nose and both his ears and combed his body with the iron comb till the first crow of the cock set him free.

The faithful servant had no idea what had happened. He heard nothing, saw nothing and slept soundly till the break of day. Then he found his poor master in a dreadful state.

'What has happened to you, Captain Tulip?'

'I hardly know myself, my faithful servant! Help me quickly, soothe my pain with some ointment or something!'

The faithful servant looked around and strangely enough found a new jar of scented ointment next to the captain's bed. He rubbed it on his master's body from head to toe and then a second time, and, lo and behold, the nose and ears of Captain Tulip were firmly back where they belonged and his wounds were all healed! Then he rushed into the garden with his servant to the lovely princess who was still buried under the tall black cypress tree, but only up to her knees.

130

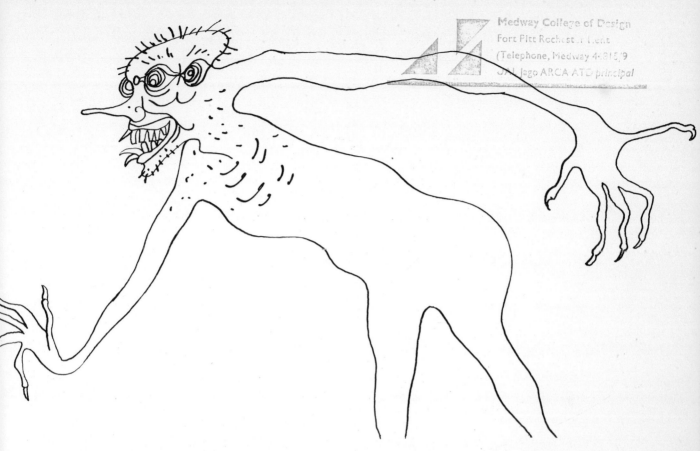

'Look over there, faithful servant! Can you see the lovely princess?'

'No Master! I see only a tall black cypress tree with a strange bush underneath.'

Though the faithful servant saw nothing and heard nothing, Captain Tulip saw and heard very well indeed!

'Thank you, Captain Tulip! I know what you have had to bear on my account, but tonight your suffering will be worse by far. Try and endure it, dear captain, but take care: if you utter a single word, if you cry out even once, I shall be doomed for ever, and so will you!'

'Do not worry, lovely princess, I shall not make a sound. I, Captain Tulip, will never let you down.'

That evening the good Captain Tulip dined again with his servant and then they peacefully went to bed. All was silent till midnight, but with the stroke of twelve the wicked magician rushed in with his assistants:

'Here is the human worm! Take him, chop off his hands and feet and roast him slowly over a low fire until cock crow!'

131

The wicked magician's assistants took hold of the poor captain, chopped off his hands and feet and roasted him over a low fire until the first crow of the cock set him free from his great pain at last.

The faithful servant had no idea what had happened. He saw nothing, heard nothing and slept soundly till morning. Then he found the poor, lifeless body of his master.

'What has happened to you, Captain Tulip?'

But the Captain remained motionless and did not answer. The faithful servant looked round, and saw yet another jar of sweet-scented ointment by the side of the bed. He rubbed his master's wounded body from head to toe, once, twice, and a third time, then, lo and behold, Captain Tulip's hands and feet grew back again and he was alive and well! He ran with his servant into the garden. Under the tall cypress tree stood the beautiful princess, surrounded by flowers.

'Look over there, faithful servant! Can you see the lovely princess?'

'I can see her now, master! Her dress is made of sunbeams, and she wears a crown of stars in her hair!'

The princess came over to them and said:

'Thank you, Captain Tulip! Your bravery has put an end to my suffering. Servant, go to the stables and saddle the three strongest horses!'

The faithful servant did as he was told and when the horses were saddled, the princess, Captain Tulip and the servant mounted and rode away from the castle into the sunset. When dusk fell, the princess came to a halt in front of another tall castle.

'Wait for me here, Captain Tulip. Take these three apples, as red as poppies. The master of this castle will ask you to dine with him, but he will put poison in your food. Do not be afraid, for if you eat one of these apples afterwards the poison will do you no harm. Take care though: after you eat your apple, do not drink, even if you have a searing thirst! I will come to fetch you at midnight and will take you to my parents.'

'Do not worry, lovely princess. I, Captain Tulip, will not let you down!'

The princess spurred her horse and was gone. The captain and his faithful servant knocked on the castle doors and entered. The master of the castle came to greet them and invited Captain Tulip to dine with him. The food was plentiful and good, but Captain Tulip plainly saw the master of the house add poison to it. The minute he was alone in his bedroom

with his servant, he ate one of the apples, as red as poppies. Suddenly he was very thirsty, so unendurably thirsty that he completely forgot about the princess's warning, and reached for a glass of water. But, alas, as soon as he took one sip, he fell into a drugged sleep.

At the stroke of twelve the princess appeared, but Captain Tulip was still sound asleep and the faithful servant tried to wake him in vain.

'Faithful servant, your master did not keep his word! Tell him he has one year in which to find me in the City of the Seven Towers.'

Then the princess put a scarf of blue silk over his face and was gone.

When the sun rose, Captain woke up and found the blue silk scarf on his face:

'Faithful servant, where did this scarf come from?'

'It was left by your princess, master. She came at the stroke of midnight, but you were sleeping like the dead. She left this message: you have one year to find her in the City of the Seven Towers.'

'How dearly I must pay for that single sip of water,' sighed the captain. 'But what can be done? Let us be off!'

For a whole long year, day in and day out, Captain Tulip and his faithful servant searched the world, but no one could tell them where they could find the City of the Seven Towers. On the very last day of the year they climbed to a castle on a high mountain. The Green Lord, the master of all flying creatures lived in it.

'Good day, Green Lord! Do you know where we can find the City of the Seven Towers?'

'I have no idea, Captain Tulip, but I shall ask all my subjects.'

The Green Lord whistled three times. Straight away the air hummed with the flutter of wings, as all the flying creatures in the world came to rest on the mountain.

'Flies, do you know where the City of the Seven Towers lies?'

'We know not, Green Lord!'

'Butterflies, do you know where the City of the Seven Towers lies?'

'We know not, Green Lord!'

'Birds, do you know where the City of the Seven Towers lies?'

'We know not, Green Lord!'

'What about you, great eagle, don't you even know where the City of the Seven Towers lies?'

'I know where to find it, Green Lord!'

'Then I command you to take these two travellers there without any further delay!' You must make the greatest possible haste!'

'Your wish is my command, Green Lord, but give me plenty of raw meat to sustain me on the journey.'

The Green Lord killed a ram, skinned it and then gave the meat to the eagle:

'Here is your food for the journey!'

The eagle placed the meat and the travellers on his wide back and soared into the sky. Countries and seas flashed by under them, as if the wind carried them away. Now and then the eagle shouted very loudly:

'Meat, meat!'

Very soon there were only the bare bones of the ram left, but by this time the City of the Seven Towers could be seen on the horizon. The eagle, however, kept shouting deafeningly:

'Meat, meat!'

As there was no meat left, Captain Tulip without hesitation unsheathed his sword and cut off a piece of his own thigh.

'Here you are, eagle!'

The eagle swallowed the meat and flew downwards to the main square of the City of the Seven Towers. Then he spat out the last mouthful of the flesh:

'Captain Tulip, you are indeed a brave man, and your flesh is very tasty, but have this piece back. Put it on your wound and you will be whole again!'

The eagle flew away. Captain Tulip put the piece of flesh on his wound, and, lo and behold, his thigh was healed! He looked up and before him stood the princess! She was leading three saddled horses.

'Welcome, Captain Tulip! Mount your horse quickly, for a long journey lies before us.'

The captain, his faithful servant, and the beautiful princess mounted their horses and galloped away into the sunset from the City of the Seven Towers. When dusk fell, the princess stopped in a meadow by a silver well.

'Wait for me here, Captain Tulip! If you and your servant are hungry, share the two remaining apples, as red as poppies. I will come back for you at midnight and will take you to my parents. But take care:

once you have eaten the apple, do not drink, even if your thirst is unbearable!'

'Do not worry, lovely princess. I, Captain Tulip, will not let you down!'

The princess prodded her horse and was gone. The captain and his servant stretched out in the grass, ate an apple each and rested. After a while Captain Tulip felt so parched, so unendurably thirsty, that he quite forgot the princess's warning, and drank water from the silver well. But, alas, as soon as he swallowed the first mouthful, he collapsed into the grass and slept like the dead.

At the stroke of twelve the princess appeared by the well, but the captain was sound asleep. The faithful servant tried hard, but in vain, to wake him.

'Faithful servant, once again your master did not keep his word. Tell him I give him just one day to find me where the West Wind blows. Instead of horses I shall leave you a mule with a load of gold. You will need it!'

Then she covered Captain Tulip's face with a scarf of red silk and with a scarf of white silk, slipped a gold ring on his finger and disappeared with the horses.

Captain Tulip woke at daybreak and was surprised to find the two scarves, one red, one white, on his face, and a gold ring on his finger.

'Faithful servant, where did this ring come from?'

'It was left by your lovely princess, Captain Tulip! She came at the stroke of midnight, but you were sleeping like the dead. I am to give you this message: you must find her in a single day — somewhere where the West Wind blows. She took our horses and left this mule with a load of gold.'

'How dearly I must pay for my sip of water,' sighed the Captain. 'But what can be done? Let us be on our way!'

They walked all through the day, leading the mule with the load of gold. An hour before sunset they came to a high mountain, so steep and smooth that not even an ant could climb to the top of it, certainly not a man, nor a mule. At the foot of the mountain stood an old woman, black as coal and withered with age.

'Good evening, Captain Tulip. Why do you look so gloomy? Tell me, for maybe I can help you.'

'It would be hard for you to help me, old woman as black as coal and withered with age! I am searching for the Castle of the Four Winds; I need to talk to the West Wind.'

'That is an easy task, Captain Tulip, for I am the mother of the Four Winds, and this castle on top of the mountain is their home. In a minute they will return home, but I am afraid they will be furious, for I have nothing to give them for their supper.'

'Your worries are over, old woman as black as coal and withered with age. Take a hundred pieces of gold and go and buy whatever food you need.'

The old woman took the hundred pieces of gold and with one puff blew the two travellers and their mule with the load of gold up the mountain-side right to the Castle of the Four Winds. Soon after that she joined them laden with bread, meat and wine.

'Come in, Captain Tulip. You can eat and drink with your servant, then hide in this small room, so my sons do not see you when they return.'

Captain Tulip drank and ate with his faithful servant, and then they hid in the small room behind the kitchen. Soon a thunderous sound could be heard, as if all the castle was about to crumble, and the four winds entered the kitchen:

'Mother, give us food, for we are hungry!'

The old woman as black as coal and withered with age brought bread, meat and wine to the table. Her sons were delighted for they had not dined so well for quite some time.

'What will you do tomorrow, my four sons?' the old woman enquired. 'Tell me, North Wind!'

'I will fly to the ancient city of Rome and ring all the bells in the towers.'

'What about you, South Wind?'

'I will fly to the city of Paris and blow tiles off the roof of the French king's castle.'

'What about you, East Wind?'

'I will fly to the town of Bordeaux and blow all the boats out of the harbour!'

'What about you, West Wind?'

'I will fly to Jerusalem to play with the trees in the hills.'

At last Captain Tulip and his faithful servant knew where the West Wind was going to fly!

When they had eaten, the Four Winds discarded their wide cloaks and took off their huge boots, then went to sleep. With the stroke of midnight they were up on their feet. Good Captain Tulip and his faithful servant came out of hiding and addressed the West Wind:

'Good morning, West Wind! Would you like another tasty meal today, like the one you ate last night?'

'Of course I would, Captain Tulip!'

'Then you can keep this mule with its load of gold which will buy all the food you want. It is yours, West Wind, if you promise to lead us to Jerusalem.'

'I will gladly lead you, Captain Tulip, but I fear you will not be able to keep up with me.'

'Let that be our worry, West Wind!'

'In that case, let us be off, Captain Tulip! I will just put on my cloak and my boots.'

While the West Wind wrapped the wide cloak round his shoulders, Captain Tulip and his faithful servant hid, one in each boot! The West Wind put his feet in them and flew on his way.

'Captain Tulip and you, faithful servant, can you keep up with me?'

'Of course we can, West Wind! Carry on!'

The West Wind raced through the clouds and every now and then he asked in his thunderous voice:

'Captain Tulip and you, faithful servant, can you keep up with me?'

'Of course we can, West Wind! Carry on!'

At day break the West Wind came down on the roof of the most beautiful castle in all Jerusalem. Inside the castle was Captain Tulip's lovely princess. He and his faithful servant climbed secretly out of the boots:

'Thank you, West Wind! We have yet another request. Whistle hard and break the window of my princess's room.'

The West Wind howled and the window shattered, ringing merrily.

'Here you are, Captain Tulip. Now I must be off. Goodbye!'

'Goodbye, West Wind! Remember me to your mother, the woman as black as coal and withered with age!'

The West Wind flew away. The captain looked through the broken window into the room, and saw his lovely princess fast asleep on her bed. He tiptoed in and covered her face with the three silk scarves which she had given him, and then he crept away.

When the princess awoke in the morning, she saw the three silk scarves which she had given to Captain Tulip.

'Thank goodness! Captain Tulip must be here! Now my troubles really are over!' she said to herself thankfully.

Meanwhile Captain Tulip and his faithful servant were strolling through the town, which was buzzing with excitement and gaily decorated. White drapes hung from houses and windows, the streets were strewn with flowers and all the bells in every spire were ringing merrily.

'Excuse me, good people, but what are these celebrations about?'

'Don't you know, Captain Tulip? Today at midday the wedding of an English king and a beautiful princess will take place. The Archbishop of Jerusalem is going to marry them. Come to the service in the cathedral, for you will not have a chance to see such a ceremony again.'

Captain Tulip and his faithful servant entered the cathedral where the English king was already waiting with his attendants. Captain Tulip found a seat near him. Then there were sighs of awe and sounds of pleasure, for his princess was walking up the aisle with her attendants! Dressed all in white, she wore a crown of lilies in her hair, with a long beautiful veil. When she saw Captain Tulip, she smiled happily.

The Archbishop of Jerusalem waited. When the bride and groom came to stand before him, he said in a powerful voice:

'The English king wishes to marry this lovely princess. Is there anyone present who has any objections?'

Captain Tulip stepped out:

'I object, your Grace.'

The English king put his hand on his sword:

'How dare you, Captain Tulip! If we were not inside the cathedral, I should strike you with my sword! Come outside and we shall see who is the stronger.'

'I would do so with pleasure, English king! But first let me ask you one question, then let the Archbishop of Jerusalem be our judge!'

'Ask away, Captain Tulip, I shall answer you! Archbishop of Jerusalem, listen and give us your verdict, and I will do what you decide!'

Captain Tulip then began:

'I served the princess from Bordeaux, and then she gave me three silk scarves — a blue one, a red one and a white one. Tell me, English king, could she take them away from me, if I wanted to keep them?'

140

'She certainly could not, for a gift is a gift, and a promise is a promise.'

'You have answered fairly, English king! But you have also passed a sentence upon yourself. As it happens I gave the scarves back to the princess, because I wanted to. But the princess also gave me her word that she would take me for a husband. This promise I shall not give back!'

The lovely princess turned to the Archbishop of Jerusalem:

'Captain Tulip speaks the truth, your Grace. I gave him the three silk scarves for his services, a blue one, a red one and a white one, and Captain Tulip did return them to me. I also gave him my word and a promise that I would marry him. He has not returned this promise and I am glad he did not! Now your Grace, please judge and give us your verdict.'

The Archbishop of Jerusalem gave his verdict:

'Captain Tulip is in the right, English king.'

'I can see he is in the right, your Grace,' said the English king. 'I also came to the same conclusion. And as a promise is a promise and right is right, marry them and I, myself, will be their witness.'

So the Archbishop of Jerusalem married the good Captain Tulip to his beautiful princess from Bordeaux. Afterwards there were great feasts and celebrations, to which all the people of Jerusalem were invited. While the rejoicing was at its height, Captain Tulip and his lovely bride drove off to the princess's own kingdom, where they lived happily and merrily till the end of their lives.

THE BLACKSMITH
AND GOLDEN-LEGGED ROBERT

Once upon a time there was a poor widow who lived in a cottage with her only son Robert. He was a handsome lad, strong as a horse and brave as a lion, though he was barely fourteen years old.

One evening during supper Robert said to his mother:

'Mother, I will never make my fortune here at home; we have always been poor and I can't see things changing. I will go as an apprentice to the blacksmith.'

The poor widow was horrified:

'What are you saying, my son! The blacksmith! Don't you know what they whisper about him? He is a sorcerer! Seven boys already have gone to train as apprentices and not one lived to tell the tale. Only the black wolf as big as a bull, who works the bellows, has managed to survive.'

'I will survive too,' Robert said. 'When I have finished my apprenticeship, I shall be the best blacksmith, silversmith and goldsmith in the whole wide world!'

The poor widow realised that Robert's mind was made up. With tears in her eyes she gave him permission to go and then blessed him.

The blacksmith had a forge by the four crossroads above a turbulent river. He was an enormous fellow with skin the colour of soot. His hair and his thick beard were as prickly as a hedgehog and his eyes gleamed with the same fierce glow as his furnace. People were afraid of him and no one dared to go inside his workshop. If they needed his help, they called him to come outside in the garden. Though everyone was so frightened of the blacksmith, he did not lack customers, because such a clever craftsman was not to be found anywhere else. He not only worked with metal, but also with silver and gold and with precious stones, and his furnace burned brightly from morning till night. Robert certainly could not have chosen a better teacher.

When Robert reached the forge he called out fearlessly:

'Hullo, Blacksmith!'

The blacksmith came out of the forge:

'What do you want, Robert?'

Robert answered, unafraid:

'I would like to be your apprentice, Blacksmith.'

The blacksmith laughed till his white teeth gleamed under the black moustache.

'Come in then, if you are not afraid.'

Robert was not, so he followed the blacksmith into the forge. In the middle of the floor stood an anvil and under the chimney the furnace was burning brightly. In one corner a black wolf the size of a bull circled round and round as he worked the bellows.

The blacksmith said:

'Show me first how strong you are!'

Robert took hold of the anvil and threw it as if it was a small stone.

The blacksmith said:

'Good, and now show me how clever you are!'

Robert carefully removed a thick spider's web from the corner of the workshop, unwound it completely and proceeded to rewind it into a ball, but so cleverly that he did not break the thread, not even once.

The blacksmith said:

'Good, and now show me how daring you are!'

Robert went over to the bellows, where the blacksmith's black wolf was circling round, and when the wolf jumped upon him, he caught his neck with one hand and grasped a hammer with the other. Then he held the wolf down on the anvil and hammered at him as if he were a horse's shoe.

The blacksmith said:

'Good, I can see that you are equally strong, clever and daring. Put the wolf back to work at the bellows, then go home and come back in three days. Then we shall start your lessons! I shall teach you all I know and will pay you well.'

'Thank you, Blacksmith. I will return in three days' time,' Robert promised. On his way home he thought:

'My mother is right, the blacksmith is a sorcerer. I must take care and find out what he is up to during the day and all through the night.'

At home he said to his mother:

'Mother, we are not going to be poor any more. The blacksmith has accepted me as his apprentice, and I begin work in three days. But first I want to take a look at the world. Please give me enough food and drink to last me three days.'

His mother was delighted and prepared food and drink for her son:

'God be with you, my son, and return safely!'

Robert bade her goodbye and slung the sack of food over his shoulder as if he was setting out on a long journey, but he did not go very far. He hid near the forge in a haystack, and no one could hear nor see him, though he could hear and see everything.

In the evening, as soon as the sun went down, the blacksmith locked the forge and everything was very still. But Robert stayed on patiently, and it was just as well he did! When the stars showed that it was eleven o'clock, the blacksmith crept out quietly, looking round him to make sure he was not seen. Then he hummed just like a cricket:

'Can you hear me, daughter? Can you hear me, Queen of all Snakes?'

Out of the darkness slithered the Queen of all Snakes, at least eighteen feet long and as wide as a sack of seeds. Her head was marked with the shape of a black lily.

'Here I am, Father, here I am, Blacksmith!'

The blacksmith and the Queen of all Snakes kissed and embraced.

'Tell me, Father, have you a new apprentice?'

'Yes, I have, Daughter: he is starting in three days. He is as strong as a horse and as brave as a lion.'

'I know, Father, I know, Blacksmith, for I have seen him. I like him very much and want him for my husband,' said the Queen of all Snakes.

'You shall have him, Daughter, you shall have him, Queen of all Snakes, when he finishes his apprenticeship and grows up. And now go, for my hour of midnight is approaching!'

The Queen of all Snakes slithered away into the darkness. The blacksmith ran towards the river, and Robert came out of his hiding-place and followed him, unseen. The blacksmith took off all his clothes and placed them in a hollow tree, then waited. When from a distance he heard the stroke of midnight, he slit his skin from head to toe with a ring, peeled it off, just like a snake! Under his human skin was the coat of an otter! He did the discarded skin with his normal clothes in the hollow tree, and with one leap dived into the river. Robert could see him swim, dive, bob up with fish in his mouth, and then dive again for another catch — and so it went on until daybreak. When the cock started to crow, the big otter hurried out of the river, slipped on its human skin and clothes and once again became the blacksmith. Before the sun climbed in the sky, the blacksmith was back in his forge. He had no idea that he had been followed and watched by his apprentice.

The next night Robert again hid in the haystack, and once again saw the blacksmith talk to his daughter, Queen of all Snakes, and saw him turn into an otter at the stroke of midnight and swim and fish in the river till dawn.

The third night was the same. When Robert returned from his watch, he thought:

'Now at least, I know who my master really is and what to guard against. The time has come for me to work, for three days have passed and the blacksmith must be expecting me.'

The blacksmith was waiting for him:

'Come in, Robert, let us begin!' he greeted the youth when he saw him walk up the path. 'If you work hard, you will learn all I know in less than a year.'

Robert learned faster than the blacksmith realised. By the end of the year he was more skilful than his master, but he was careful not to show it. He was afraid it would make the blacksmith cross — and he was right!

One evening the blacksmith said to his apprentice:

'Listen to me, Robert! In three months time the French king's elder daughter is to marry the King of the Sea Islands. The bride is to have a chest of jewels for her dowry, and her father has ordered us to make them. Tomorrow you must go with all your tools to the Palace. You will be given all the gold, silver and precious stones that you need. Work hard and use all the skill you have gained. I shall come to see what you have done a month before the wedding, and will help you to finish your task.'

'I will do as you ask,' said Robert, and early next morning he travelled with all the necessary tools to the Palace of the King of France.

They were already expecting him. They fed him well, then led him to his workshop. Robert was given all the gold, silver and precious stones he needed. When he saw all this wealth, he thought:

'Now you will see, Blacksmith, what a craftsman your apprentice is!'

He worked very hard. He hammered, chiselled, cast and sawed and set the precious stones. The jewellery which his hands created — beautiful rings, ear-rings, brooches, necklaces and bracelets — was of such beauty as the world had never seen. Everyone in the Palace from the lowliest page to the mightiest king, especially the bride whose dowry he was making, marvelled and praised the skill of the young apprentice. The bride's younger sister was the only person who did not offer a single word of praise. She was a young girl as lovely as the day and as wise as the world. She spent her days by Robert's side, watching him work, but always remained silent.

After almost two months, when Robert had nearly finished his task, the beautiful little princess spoke for the first time:

'You do make some lovely things, Robert; you do make the loveliest of jewels, handsome apprentice, but they are all for my elder sister. Tell me, would you make something as beautiful for someone else?'

'I certainly would,' Robert replied. 'If I were making something for my promised bride, I would create the most beautiful necklace under the sun!'

'Describe this necklace, Robert! Describe this gold necklace, handsome apprentice!' begged the little princess.

'If I were making a necklace for my bride,' Robert began. 'It would be made of gold as bright as the sun. When I took the molten gold out of the furnace, I would mix some of my own blood with it. Then if I were to place the necklace round my promised bride's neck, it would grow into her skin and flesh, and no one would ever be able to take it away from her. Once the necklace became a part of her, my promised bride would think of no one but me, and whilst I remained happy, it would remain shiny and bright.'

'What if something were to happen to you, Robert, what if some misfortune was to befall you, handsome apprentice?' the little princess wanted to know.

'If some misfortune overtook me, the necklace would darken to the colour of blood,' Robert replied. 'My bride-to-be would then have three days in which to prepare herself. She would go to her parents and say:

"I am going to die, dear parents, but when I die, bury me dressed as a bride in white robes, with a garland of lilies on my head and a veil, and a posy of flowers at my waist.' On the third day she would fall into a deep slumber and everyone would believe she was dead; they would bury her as she had requested. But my promised bride would not be really dead, only asleep and waiting. If I died, she would wait for ever. But if my misfortunes passed, I would awake her and claim her for my wife.'

The little princess exclaimed:

'Make your gold necklace, Robert. Make your gold necklace for me, handsome apprentice!'

It took seven hours to make the necklace of gold as bright as the sun. Then Robert threw it into the burning furnace, stabbed his arm with a knife, filled a basin with his blood and dipped the red-hot necklace into it. Afterwards he fastened the necklace round the throat of the little princess, and the necklace was immediately firmly embedded in her skin and flesh, so that no one could ever take it off.

'From now on I am your promised bride, dear Robert, from now on I shall think only of you, my handsome apprentice, come what may!' the little princess vowed, then kissed Robert and returned to her room. No one knew what had happened, not even the lowliest page, nor the mighty king.

The following day the blacksmith came to the Palace of the French king:

'Good day, Robert, what have you made during the last months, my apprentice? I have come to see if all is in order and to finish whatever is necessary. Show me your work!'

'Here it is,' Robert said and placed before the blacksmith everything he had created, the rings, ear-rings, bracelets and necklaces, the like of which the world had never seen before.

The blacksmith examined everything most carefully, then laughed loudly, till his teeth gleamed through his black moustache:

'I can see, Robert, there is nothing left to teach you. I can see, my apprentice, that you are more skilful than I, your teacher. Now you can work on your own. But I should be glad if you stayed on with me for another three months.'

'I will stay for as long as you wish, master,' replied Robert.

The blacksmith gathered all the jewellery Robert had made and went with him to see the French king:

'Good day, King of France! Our task in finished. My apprentice has done better than I myself could have done. Here is his work; the pay shall be his.'

Then the French king gave Robert a purse of gold:

'Here are a thousand gold pieces, apprentice.'

But Robert would not accept the payment:

'Thank you, King of France, but I want nothing for my work. If you do not need this gold, give it to the poor.'

Robert and the blacksmith bade the French king goodbye, and set out for the forge at the four crossroads.

A week later the blacksmith turned unexpectedly to Robert and said:

'Listen Robert, the fair has come to our town today. We must go and see it, so let us have a drink first, then go.'

He poured out two glasses of wine. Robert lifted his glass, saying:

'Your health, master!' and drank.

'Your health, apprentice,' the blacksmith smiled till his teeth gleamed under the black moustache, but he did not touch his wine, for he had drugged it with a strong sleeping draught.

The moment Robert took a drink his eyes grew heavy and he fell into a deep sleep. He had no idea how long he remained asleep, but when he came to, he was lying on the floor of the forge, his hands and legs tied with a chain and his mouth gagged. The furnace glowed brightly under the chimney and he caught a glimpse of a shiny new saw.

'So you tried to be more skilful than I, your master! Now you are in my power, Robert, and no one can help you. If you do not obey me, you will have to bear unbearable torture. Now tell me that you are willing to marry my daughter, the Queen of all Snakes!'

Robert was unable to speak as his mouth was gagged, but he shook his head vigorously.

'In that case . . .' muttered the blacksmith, and took the red-hot saw out of the furnace and sawed Robert's left leg right off. Then he threw in into the fire which soon turned it into ashes. He spoke again:

'So you wanted to be more clever than I, your master! Now you are in my power and no one can help you. Tell me, are you willing to marry my daughter, the Queen of all Snakes?'

Robert was still unable to speak, but he shook his head even more vigorously.

'In that case . . .' muttered the blacksmith, took the new saw and cut off Robert's right leg. He threw it into the furnace where it turned to ashes. Then he tried again:

'So you wanted to be better than I, your master! But now you are in my power and no one can help you. Are you going to marry my daughter, the Queen of all Snakes?'

Robert shook his head most vigorously. The blacksmith realised he would get nowhere.

'In that case . . .' he muttered, threw Robert on to a cart, covered him with straw and cracked his whip. His black horse raced like lightning over mountains and valleys, forests and rivers, meadows and fields, till they came to a desolate country near the sea, called the Kingdom of Snakes. In the middle of the wilderness, surrounded by sand, rubble and stones, stood a high tower made of rock and mortar. It had no roof, no doors, and no windows, but it did have a special well and a secret opening so narrow that only the Queen of all Snakes could slither through it before it closed behind her.

The Queen of all Snakes was expecting the blacksmith:

'Here is this scoundrel!' shouted the blacksmith to his daughter, who called the giant eagles from the Black Mountains:

'Listen to my command, giant eagles from the Black Mountains! Take this wretch and throw him into the Tower. He will remain a prisoner there until he agrees to marry my daughter, the Queen of all Snakes!

The hard floor will be his bed, the sky his cover. He will drink water from the well and eat bread which he must earn. But he will get as much gold, silver and precious stones as he needs. For he will make me such rings, ear-rings, bracelets, brooches and necklaces as have never been seen before. Bring me all he makes, and bring him bread for his toil. He must earn every crust, every mouthful a hundred times over.'

Such was Robert's punishment.

The giant eagles from the Black Mountains obeyed the command, and so Robert was thrown into the Tower, where he remained for seven long years. He slept on the bare floor and the sky was his cover; when he was thirsty, he drank from the well; when he was hungry, he ate the bitter bread. He had to earn each crust a hundred times over with his work for the blacksmith, but he did have as much gold, silver and precious stones as he wanted. Everything his clever hands made was taken by the giant eagles from the Black Mountains to the blacksmith.

Robert had not been such a clever pupil for nothing. He did not only work of his old master. He dug out a deep hollow under the anvil and hid the articles he worked on when the giant eagles from the Black Mountains were not there to watch him. He made such wonderous things for himself as the world had never known.

First of all he made an axe, strong and sharp. Then he made a wide belt, with three firm hooks. And he made a pair of legs of pure gold, so perfect that they were identical to those the blacksmith had sawn off and burned to cinders. Last of all he made a pair of large gold wings, as light as a feather. It took him seven years to complete all this.

For seven years Robert worked endlessly for the blacksmith and for himself and for seven long years he was visited each night after sunset by the Queen of all Snakes, who slithered in through the door which closed immediately behind her, and who said on each occasion:

'As soon as you agree to take me for a wife, Robert, your suffering will end.'

Robert always replied:

'Go away, Queen of all Snakes! I have already chosen my bride and I shall never change my mind!'

So it went on for seven years. But when Robert's secret work was completed, when the hollow under the anvil contained his axe, his belt, his legs and his wings, he answered differently. When the Queen of

all Snakes asked as usual if he would not have her for his wife, he replied:

'I will marry you, Queen of all Snakes! I had chosen another to be my bride, but I shall not even think of her ever again.'

The Queen of all Snakes was overjoyed:

'Robert, your sufferings are at an end. Tomorrow, when the sun sets, I shall come and lead you away.'

Robert pleaded:

'Queen of all Snakes, please come quickly, for I can hardly wait till then!'

The next day shortly before sunset, Robert thought:

'Now I shall have some fun!'

From his hiding-place he took the strong, sharp axe; round his waist he fastened the belt with the three hooks; he put on his beautiful legs made of gold, and stood guard by the spot where the Queen of all Snakes appeared every evening.

When the sun went down, the Queen of all Snakes slithered through the secret opening. Robert was waiting and as soon as he saw her head, he placed his foot firmly on her neck. The Queen hissed and bit Robert's leg, but to no avail, for his leg was made of gold. With one sharp blow of the axe Robert cut off her head and hung it on the first hook of his belt, and her body on the second. He fastened the gold wings, as light as a feather, to his shoulders, and flew into the night from the top of the Tower. The stars guided Robert on his flight home; he flew a hundred times faster than a swallow, speeding on and on till he reached the blacksmith's forge at the four crossroads. He stayed out of sight and waited till midnight for the blacksmith to come out and to take off his human skin.

When the unsuspecting blacksmith shed his skin and jumped into the river in the form of an otter, Robert flew, a hundred times faster than a swallow, to the hollow in the willow tree. He took the human skin and hung it on the third hook of his belt, then he flew over the river:

'Hullo, Blacksmith!'

The blacksmith in the form of an otter stuck his head out of the water:

'What do you want, giant bird?'

Robert cried out:

'Listen, Blacksmith, I bring you news of your daughter, the Queen of all Snakes!'

The otter's head popped up once again from under the water:

'Speak, giant bird!'

Robert exclaimed:

'I am not a giant bird, Blacksmith. I am your apprentice, Robert. For seven years I have had to endure great hardship in the Tower on the shore of the big sea; for seven years I have had to bear your torture, but now I have escaped! Your daughter, the Queen of all Snakes, hangs on the hooks of my belt, her head on one, her body on the other.'

The blacksmith cried out as a mountain eagle does when he is hit by an arrow. But Robert took no notice and continued:

'That is not all, Blacksmith! For seven years you have tortured me in the Tower with hunger and thirst and imprisonment, but now I am here and I have your human skin hooked on the third hook of my belt! You are doomed to remain an otter for ever!'

The blacksmith cried out once more, then plunged into the waves and was never seen again.

Robert flew to his mother's house a hundred times faster than a swallow.

'Rat-tat, rat-tat,' he knocked at the door.

'Who is it?' asked the widow as she went to open the door of her cottage.

'It is I, mother,' Robert cried out.

'My dearest son, you have returned at last,' his mother marvelled, crying with happiness when she saw Robert in the doorway. 'I have been waiting for you for so long.'

'Forgive me, dear mother, but I could not come before this,' Robert apologised. 'Now that I am here, your poverty and my troubles are over.'

He threw the skin of the blacksmith with the head and body of the Queen of all Snakes onto a roaring fire. Before he had time to retell all his experiences to his mother, they were burnt to cinders.

'Now I must go and claim my bride,' he ended, embracing his mother fondly. He put on the gold wings, lighter than feathers, and flew a hundred times faster than a swallow to the Palace of the King of France.

The coffin of the little princess stood in a chapel under a white gravestone. With one hard pull Robert moved the heavy stone aside, and saw his promised bride. She lay in her coffin dressed in a wedding dress. On her head she wore a garland of lilies and a veil, and at her waist a posy of flowers. Robert whispered:

'Come, my beautiful little Princess, it is time to wake up! You have been sleeping for seven long years.'

The moment the princess heard Robert's voice, she opened her eyes:

'Can this really be you, Robert, can this really be you, handsome apprentice? I have been waiting for you so long!'

'Forgive me, my little Princess, I could not come before. But now that I am here, your waiting and my suffering are at an end,' Robert assured her. 'Rise and come with me!'

The dawn was breaking by the time Robert brought his little princess into the royal apartments.

'It is morning already, beautiful Princess,' said Robert. 'Wait for me in your room while I go to see your father, the King of France.'

'Go, Robert, I shall wait for you, my handsome apprentice!' the happy princess replied, as she went into her own room.

Robert went to see the King and Queen of France:

'Good day, French King, good day, French Queen! Do you remember me?'

'We do not recognise you, my friend, but we welcome you!' the queen said in reply.

'I am the apprentice of the blacksmith,' Robert reminded them. 'I worked for you when your elder daughter was preparing for her wedding to the King of the Sea Islands.'

'Now I recognise you, handsome apprentice. Of course we remember you!' the king said.

Robert continued:

'You had another daughter, the little princess. Whom did she marry?' The King and Queen of France sighed sadly:

'Our youngest daughter married no one, handsome apprentice. She died, and we buried her as she asked, in a wedding dress, on her head a garland of lilies and a veil, and at her waist a posy of flowers.'

'If I returned your daughter to you alive and well, would you give her to me for a wife?' Robert asked.

'With pleasure, handsome apprentice!' the king and queen replied. 'To that we swear.'

'In that case, your Majesties, let the wedding preparations begin, for your daughter, the lovely little princess, is waiting for you in her room!' Robert said happily.

The French King and Queen rushed to their daughter's room and could hardly believe their eyes when they saw her alive and more beautiful than before — dressed in her wedding dress, a garland of lilies and a veil on her head, a posy of flowers at her waist. The wedding could go on.

So it came to pass that Robert married his little French princess and lived with her and his old mother in happy contentment till the end of their days. And till the end of his days Robert never grew tired of relating his adventures with the blacksmith to his twelve sons.

THE TWO GIFTS

Once upon a time there was a good king who enjoyed eating, drinking and amusing himself. He was kind to his subjects and loved them all, except the misers and the liars.

One day when the king sat at his table, dining and playing cards, a poor peasant was shown into the room. He carried an enormous marrow on his head, such as the world had never seen and never will see again.

The good peasant bowed to the king, and said respectfully:

'Good day, Your Majesty, and everybody present!'

'Good day, my friend,' the king replied. 'Where are you going with that marrow?'

'To you, dear King!' the peasant said daringly. 'I want you to have it as a gift, so you can taste marrow soup which is really the most delicious dish there is! But please ask your cook to save the seeds. You can give them to your friends, and I should also like a handful to sow for next year.'

'Thank you, my friend,' the king said to the peasant. 'Now go to the kitchen and have a good meal.'

The peasant thanked his king and went to the kitchen with the marrow. While he was feasting on all the food and drink the cook placed before him, the king talked to his jester:

'Do you know, Jester, I rather like that fellow. I think he brought me that marrow because he has a kind heart. How should I repay him?'

The Jester thought for a while, then replied:

'First test him, Your Majesty, to make sure he has not given you a blade of grass hoping you would offer him four cows in return. If he is not greedy, then reward him with the gift of a fine horse.'

'You are right, Jester,' the king agreed and was lost in thought for quite some time. When the peasant had had as much food and drink as he wanted, the king called him back:

'How would you like me to repay you, my friend?'

'Why should you repay me, Your Majesty?' the peasant wondered. 'I only want a handful of seeds after the cook has dried them.'

'I'll give you something better, my friend,' said the king and had a fine horse brought for the peasant.

The peasant thanked him and set off for his home, most content.

It so happened that this peasant was a subject of a certain count who was a terrible miser. He certainly lived up to his name of Grabber.

When Count Grabber heard what the peasant received in payment from the king, he said to himself:

'Ha-ha, tomorrow I will go to the king, but I will bring him a fine horse as a gift. If he gave a horse in return for a marrow, and I present him with a horse, he is sure to promote me to a prince at least, and to give me a barrel of gold.'

158

The very next morning Count Grabber saddled the finest horse from his stable and galloped away to the castle. When he reached it, the king was once again dining and playing cards with his jester. The count entered the chamber, bowed and spoke thus:

'Good day, Your Majesty and everybody present!'

'Good day, my friend,' the king answered. 'What can I do for you?'

'My name is Count Grabber,' the count introduced himself. 'It has come to my ears that yesterday you, your Majesty, repaid my peasant's marrow with a horse. I have brought you another to take its place. It is already standing in your stable.'

'Thank you, my friend,' said the king. 'Go to the stables and I will follow you in a minute.'

When Count Grabber left, the king turned to his Jester:

'Listen, Jester, I rather like that Count Grabber. I really think he gave me the horse because he has a kind heart. How should I repay him?'

The jester thought deeply, then said:

'First test him, Your Majesty, to make sure he has not given you a blade of grass, hoping you would offer him four cows in return. And if he is not greedy reward him with a gift of seven estates and the rank of a Prince.'

'You are right, Jester,' the king agreed, as they walked to the stables. There he asked the count:

'I have never seen such a fine horse, my friend. What would you like in repayment?'

'What would I like, Your Majesty!' exclaimed Count Grabber. 'I would like you to promote me to the rank of a Prince and to give me a barrel of gold.'

'I will give you something better,' the king said, and sent for his cook. When she entered, the king asked:

'Have you dried the seeds from the peasant's marrow?'

'Yes, I have, Your Majesty,' the cook answered.

'Excellent! Pour them into two bags; one will be for the good peasant, the other for Count Grabber who lives up to his name!'

That is how the generous peasant was given a horse for his marrow, and the miserly count the seeds from a marrow for his horse.

BEAUTIFUL MONA AND THE KING
OF THE MORGANS

Once upon a time there was a fisherman and a fisherwoman who had a daughter, an only child of such charm and loveliness that everyone who saw her stopped to admire her.

'You have such a beautiful daughter,' the neighbours would say to the fisherwoman. 'If we did not know she is your very own we would think she was a daughter of some Morgan.'

'God forbid,' the fisherwoman exclaimed when she heard such things. 'Our Mona is an ordinary human being like you and me, she takes after her grandmother in her beauty.'

The fisherwoman did not want to hear another word about the Morgans, and no wonder! They were a mysterious people who lived on the bottom of the sea. They built fine towns with streets, houses and churches and they were famous for their beauty, their long golden hair and huge bright eyes as blue as the sea. At least that is how they were described by fishermen who caught a glimpse of them as they dried their treasures from the ocean, pearls, precious stones and valuable silks, on the beach in the sunshine.

The Morgans were kind to people. They helped many a fisherman to find a good catch and gave many a young maiden a handful of pearls and precious stones for a wedding present. But sometimes a young Morgan lad would take a fancy to such a girl, and then, alas, her parents would never see her again, for she would be carried off to the city at the bottom of the sea.

This is why the fisherwoman did not wish to have anything to do with the Morgans. She watched over her daughter like a hawk, and when she grew up she tried to find her some upright, fine son of a fisherman for a husband. But lovely Mona would not think of marrying. The constant praise had gone to her head, so perhaps she was waiting for someone better than a simple fisherman.

One day she was busy with her friends, collecting sea shells and crabs which had been left by the incoming tide. While they worked, the maidens chatted happily about many things, till their conversation turned to young men. Each of them in turn boasted about her own boy-friend, how kind he was, how handsome, how skilfully he fished. Only lovely Mona remained silent. In the end one of her friends asked:

'What about you, Mona, whom have you chosen?'

Beautiful Mona replied proudly:

'I shall never marry a fisherman! I shall wait till some prince comes for me, or a rich Morgan from the sea.'

The girls laughed, but their laughter did not last for long. For suddenly a huge wave rose from the sea and flooded the beach, and before the maidens realised what was happening, lovely Mona was gone! In vain they called her, in vain they searched for her, in vain they ran for help to their village. Even the fishermen with their boats could find no trace of the beautiful maiden.

How could they have found her when the King of all Morgans himself had pulled her down into the sea! He had been sunning himself secretly behind a rock and had overheard what the maidens were saying. He liked Mona from his very first glance, and after listening to what she had to say he did not hesitate. He commanded the wave to rise and then he carried Mona to his palace at the bottom of the sea. Even the King of France himself did not own such a magnificent palace as did the King of all Morgans. You could see it from a distance, for it glittered with silver, gold and precious stones. A beautiful garden full of strange and beautiful flowers, fruits and trees surrounded the palace and a still, peaceful light shone above, as if the sunlight had penetrated the deep waters. But you could not see the sun, for the palace stood in the centre of a city on the sea-bed.

The King of all Morgans liked the beautiful Mona right from the start, but his son and heir, the Prince of all Morgans, liked her even more. From the moment the lovely maiden entered the palace on the bottom of the sea, he walked around as if in a dream, never taking his eyes off her. Mona also liked the handsome prince, and no wonder, for she could have hardly imagined a better husband -- not even in her dreams!

When the prince realised that the maiden from the earth was fond of him, he went to see his father the king and said:

'Dear father, my King, you wanted me to get married and now I am quite willing to do so. Give me lovely Mona for my bride.'

The King of all Morgans certainly had not expected this. He himself wanted to marry the beautiful maiden and had chosen another bride for his son; the pretty daughter of some powerful Morgan. When he heard his son's request, his eyebrows drew angrily together as he answered:

'The Prince of all Morgans and the future King cannot marry a woman from the earth! I have already chosen your bride and have given my promise. The king's promise can only be broken by death! Go and prepare yourself. Your wedding will take place in three days time.'

The poor prince could do nothing against the will of his father the king. With sorrow in his heart he prepared for his wedding to the pretty Morgan maiden whom his father had chosen for him. A day before the wedding he went to say goodbye to Mona. He found her shut in a tiny room behind the kitchen, sitting by the table, crying bitterly.

'What is the matter?' begged the prince, full of concern.

Sweet Mona replied:

'The king called me to him and commanded me to make a dress for your bride, but he gave me nothing to work with. If I do not finish the dress by morning, death awaits me.'

'Do not cry, dear one, there is a speck of good in every evil,' the prince consoled her. 'Bring me a needle, a thread and a piece of rag.'

Mona brought the needle, the thread and the piece of rag. The prince put them all on the table and said:

'Needle and thread, work fast, make the bride's dress by dawn!'

Then he kissed his beloved Mona and went away.

Early next morning the King of all Morgans went into Mona's room.

'The bride is waiting for her dress. Is it ready?'

'Yes, King of all Morgans,' Mona replied, pointing to the table, where a beautiful white dress was spread, and a veil with gold embroidery.

The King of all Morgans took the dress, examined it from top to bottom, then drew his brows together angrily.

'I can see someone has helped you! But we shall see who will win!'

Then he took the dress to the bride.

Before noon the bride put on her wedding dress and all the guests got into their golden coaches, preparing to leave for the church. At the last minute the prince jumped out of his coach and ran back to the palace.

'I have forgotten the ring for my bride,' he cried out, so they had to wait for him.

But the prince had not forgotten the ring! He ran to say goodbye to his dearest Mona. He found her locked in the kitchen, sitting by the fire, weeping bitterly.

'What has happened?' the prince asked, full of concern.

The lovely maiden replied:

'The king called me to him and ordered me to prepare a wedding feast for your bride, but he did not even give me a pinch of salt to cook with! If I do not have the food ready by noon, death awaits me.'

'Do not cry, dear Mona, there is a speck of good in every evil,' the prince consoled her. 'Just bring me a pan, a little water and piece of wood.'

Lovely Mona gave him the pan, water and wood. The kind prince took them, threw the wood onto the fire, hooked the pan of water over it and said:

'Pan and water, do you work, so the feast is ready by noon.'

Then he kissed his beloved Mona and left.

When the wedding guests returned from church to the palace, the king went to the kitchen to see Mona:

'The bride and bridegroom are waiting. Is the feast ready?'

'It is ready, King of all Morgans,' Mona replied, pointing to all the

163

saucepans, baking tins and trays in which everything was cooking and sizzling merrily.

The King of all Morgans, lifted first one, then another and yet another saucepan lid, then drew his eyebrows crossly together:

'I can tell someone has come to help you. But we shall see who will win!'

He ordered the food to be brought to the table.

The feast lasted till very late that night. When the clock hands were pointing to midnight and it was time for the bride and groom to retire to their room, the prince rose from the table, excusing himself:

'I must just go to make sure that there is plenty of light in our bedroom!'

'Go on then,' said the king with annoyance, because he was beginning to suspect what was happening.

And, of course, the prince did not go to check the lights, but to say good night to his beloved Mona. However she was not in her bedroom, but was standing by the door of his room with a burning candle in her hand, weeping bitterly.

'What is the matter?' the prince asked with concern.

Mona replied:

'The king called me to him and ordered me to stand all night by your door to light up the room for your bride. But he only gave me this tiny candle! It will go out in a minute and that will be the end of me, because if it does not stay alight till morning, death awaits me.'

'Do not cry, my dearest,' the prince soothed her. 'There is some good in every evil. We shall be going to bed very shortly. When we walk past you, ask the bride to hold the candle for you, while you put a match to our fire. Do not worry about anything else.'

He kissed the lovely maiden and went away.

A minute or two later the guests rose from the table and saw the bride and bridegroom to their bedroom. Mona stood inside the door with the dying candle in her hand. She opened the door to let them in, but as soon as it closed behind them, she asked the bride:

'Please, dear Madam, hold this candle for me for just a minute, while I put a match to the fire in your grate.'

The bride took the candle from her, and Mona ran to the grate to light the fire.

At that moment the King of all Morgans himself spoke from behind the door:

'Can you hear me, Mona? Is your candle still burning?'

Instead of Mona — the bride answered:

'Only just! It will die out at any minute!'

'Then let it die now, and you too!' the king exclaimed behind the door. The last flicker of the candle suddenly flamed upwards — and the bride who held it in her hand melted away, too, as if she was made of wax.

The next morning the prince came before the King of all Morgans and said:

'You told me, father, that your promise can only be broken by death. This has now happened to the bride you chose for me. Now you must allow me to take beautiful Mona as my wife!'

The King of all Morgans drew his brows angrily together:

'What are you saying, son? Surely you have not killed your wife?'

The prince explained:

'I did not kill her, my father the King! She was killed by the candle, which she was holding while Mona was lighting our fire!'

The King of all Morgans realised then that his son was more powerful than he himself and that he would not give his beautiful Mona up.

'Have it your own way then,' his father consented. 'Do what you wish, but do not complain when your Mona forsakes you!'

'That will not happen, my father the King,' the prince assured him and rushed away to make preparations for his second wedding.

This ceremony certainly was a far happier occasion for Mona. This time she was not ordered to sew the bride's dress, nor to prepare the wedding feast. This time she herself put on the wedding dress and she herself sat next to the bridegroom at the festive dinner. The bridegroom looked after her during the wedding and after the wedding. He spoiled his lovely Mona with constant presents; he brought her jewels, expensive silks and brocades. The beautiful maiden was indeed treated like a queen.

The first year passed very happily, so did the second and the third, but then Mona began to grow homesick. She sat by the window gazing into the distance and grew more sad every day. She kept thinking of her father and mother, remembering their cottage by the edge of the sea.

The prince guessed what was making his wife so unhappy. He knew she longed to visit her home, but the thought frightened him. He was afraid that what his father had said might come true. But with each day his lovely Mona became more thoughtful, more sad, more tearful, till the poor prince could bear it no longer. One day he said:

'Give me a smile and I will take you wherever your heart desires.'

Beautiful Mona looked at her prince, gave him a brave half-smile, and, mysteriously, in front of her very eyes a beautiful, crystal bridge rose before her, leading from the depths of the ocean to the beach itself.

'Come,' said the prince and holding his beloved Mona by the hand, he led her over the bridge. In just a short while they reached the beach near the cottage of Mona's parents. As soon as they stepped ashore, the crystal bridge disappeared into the waves. The kind prince implored:

'Go along, dearest Mona, but I cannot come with you. Please return before sundown. I shall be here, waiting for you. Let no one kiss you, or, alas, what my father said will come true and I shall die in the sea from a broken heart!'

Mona promised to take care and to return. She kissed the prince and ran to her parent's cottage.

When she walked through the door, they did not recognise this beautiful, richly dressed lady. Mona all at once felt very sorry about everything. With tears in her eyes she stroked the bench, the table, the door and said:

'Here on this bench I used to sit, from this table I used to eat, a broom used to stand behind this door . . .' Then at last her parents recognised their visitor.

'It is Mona, our own Mona!' they cried, throwing their arms around her neck, weeping with joy and kissing her fondly.

'Tell us where you have been all this time!'

But Mona could not tell them. She forgot everything with the very first kiss of her parents; she did not remember the Kingdom of the Morgans beneath the sea, nor their king, nor her own beloved prince, who waited for her in vain. When her parents asked where she had been, who had given her such beautiful clothes and jewels, she just kept shaking her head in bewilderment:

'I cannot remember, I have forgotten everything. I feel as if there is thick mist in my head!'

So lovely Mona remained at home. She helped her mother around the house, with spinning and sewing, but most of all she liked to sit by the window and gaze into the sea, as if she was expecting someone. Days flew by, weeks flew by, nearly a whole year went by and lovely Mona grew more thoughtful day by day.

'What is the matter with you?' her mother asked.

'I do not know, dear mother,' Mona replied. 'But this mood will pass, you will see.'

'You should get married,' the mother advised her daughter. 'You have more suitors than fingers — all you have to do is to choose.'

But Mona would not hear of marriage.

'I am content to be with you,' she would say as she went on sewing and spinning by the window overlooking the sea.

One day she remained by the window late into the night. Her father and mother had gone to bed and were fast asleep and Mona's eyes too began to close, when suddenly, as from a distance, she heard strange cries, as if someone stood weeping on the shore of the sea.

'Probably they are the cries of shipwrecked souls, who have perished in the sea,' Mona thought. She made the sign of the cross and went to bed.

The second night she heard the strange cries again, but this time they were much louder and not so far away. It seemed as if someone stood weeping by the path to the cottage. Mona listened till nearly midnight, then she made the sign of the cross and went to bed.

On the third night she heard the sound of weeping once more, but now it was so strong and so near, that it sounded as if someone was under her very window. Lovely Mona listened till midnight, when, quite unexpectedly, she heard someone calling to her softly:

'Can you hear me, Mona? Can you hear me, Mona? Why did you not keep your promise? Why did you not return before sundown? Why did you let your mother and father kiss you? Why did you forget your husband? Why did you make me wait so long, so very long? Have pity on me, dearest Mona, and return!'

All at once Mona remembered everything — the Morgan Kingdom at the bottom of the sea, the old king and her dear prince, who was waiting for her under the window. She stood up, quietly slipped through the door and ran into his open arms. From that moment she was never again seen by ordinary people.

THE MISERLY FARMER
AND THE ARTFUL FARMHAND

Once upon a time there was a farmer who was so mean that no farm-hand ever stayed with him for long, and no wonder! The farmer not only paid the meanest wages, but he also never fed his farmhands properly. One day, however, he met his match. He took on a new farmhand, who sized his master up in a moment and decided to try and make him into a better man.

Just then the fields needed ploughing. The farmer and his farmhand prepared for their work; each had a pair of bulls and a plough, but there was not even a piece of bread or a drop of wine for their lunch. The farmhand noticed this but said nothing. When it was time for lunch, his master said:

'Dear me, I have forgotten to bring anything for us to eat. I know, farmhand, shall we just pretend we are eating?'

'We shall not get much food that way, master,' muttered the farmhand. 'But as you wish.'

For a while they pretended to eat, then continued ploughing. The farmer suddenly noticed that his worker kept ploughing the same furrow over and over again.

'Hey, farmhand, what are you up to?' said the farmer.

'What do you think, master! If it was all right for us just to pretend to eat, surely it is all right for us just to pretend to plough!'

And he ploughed the same furrow till evening.

That night the farmer said to his wife:

'Our farmhand is more artful than I realised. Tomorrow I shall send him to hoe my vineyard. Give him a piece of bread and a drop of wine for his lunch, but nothing special and not much, so that we don't spoil him.'

The next day the farmer sent the farmhand hoeing in the vineyard.

'Here is the hoe and here is the bag with your lunch,' he said.

The farmhand took the hoe, slung the bag over his shoulder and left for the vineyard. On his way he had a peep at what the farmer's wife had given him for his lunch. All he found was a piece of black bread and a drop of bitter wine.

By then he had reached the vineyard. He bowed smartly and said in greeting:

'Good morning, vineyard!'

The vineyard inquired:

'What is in your sack?'

The farmhand answered:

'Crust of bread, hard and black.'

The vineyard asked:

'What is in that flask of thine?'

The farmhand replied:

'A drop of tepid, bitter wine.'

So the vineyard pronounced:

'Then curl up under the bush and take a nap!'

The farmhand did not wait to be told twice. He made himself comfortable in the shade and slept through the whole day, without doing a single stroke of work.

When in the evening he returned to the farm, his master asked:

'Tell me, how much hoeing did you get done today?'

'I have hoed more than half of the vineyard,' the farmhand answered and went on eating his supper.

'That is a lot,' the farmer marvelled. Early the next morning he went to see if his worker had been telling the truth. He found to his surprise that the vineyard had not been touched.

'What on earth did my farmhand get up to all day long?' the farmer wondered, and hid in the bushes so he could see for himself.

The farmhand arrived a minute later, with the hoe in his hand and the sack of food over his shoulder. He said in greeting:

'Good morning, vineyard!'

The vineyard inquired:

'What is in your sack?'

And the farmhand replied:

'Crust of bread, stale and black.'

The vineyard asked:

'What is in that flask of thine?'

The farmhand answered:

'A drop of tepid, bitter wine.'

After that the vineyard pronounced:

'Curl up under the bush and take a nap!'

The farmhand did not wait to be told twice. He curled up under the bush and slept through the second day.

That evening the farmer said to his wife:

'I can't get my own way with this worker. Tomorrow give him a flask of good wine and a piece of white bread, as if it was meant for me.'

His wife did as she was asked and early the next morning her husband ran ahead of the farmhand to the vineyard and hid in the bushes.

Soon afterwards the farmhand appeared, a hoe in his hand, a sack over his shoulders, and said in greeting:

'Good morning, vineyard!'

The vineyard asked:

'What is in that flask of thine!'

The farmhand replied:
'A good measure of fine sweet wine!'
The vineyard asked:
'And in your sack — what's there to eat?'
The farmhand replied:
'A hunk of fresh bread, from white wheat!'
The vineyard commanded:
'Then do not dilly-dally, set to work in a hurry!'
The farmhand did not wait to be told twice. He worked with relish and by the evening he had finished all the hoeing in the vineyard.

When that night his master asked how far he had got with his work, he answered:
'It is quite finished.'
And it was true. The farmer saw it the next morning with his own eyes. And he was never so mean with his farmhands again.

THE ADVENTURES OF JACK BRAGGER

Once upon a time there was a farmer who had an only son called Jack. Jack was as tall and straight as a young tree, as strong as a bull and as generous as could be. He had, however, one big fault: he loved to sit with his friends for hours on end in some tavern, and even more he loved to talk. Once he began, no one could stop him. He chattered on and on, and after a while he forgot the difference between truth and imagination. His friends would listen and would wink at each other:

'Our Jack is bragging again!'

So it wasn't very surprising that he was soon nicknamed Jack Bragger.

Jack Bragger boasted about many things, but most of all about the good fortune which was just waiting for him with the army in the town:

'You'll see that in just one month they will make me a corporal.'

'And then?' his friends would ask.

'Then I would be made a colonel,' Jack Bragger would reply.

'And after that?' his friends would laughingly continue.

'After that I shall be a general!' Jack Bragger would brag.

'Whatever next?' His friends would press on, bursting with laughter.

'In the end I shall marry a princess and be a king,' Jack Bragger would announce quite seriously, while everyone's sides would be aching from so much laughing. 'You just wait till I get to town!'

'When will that be?' his friends would shout, all together.

'Very shortly,' Jack Bragger would tell them. 'As soon as my father gives me a hundred gold sovereigns for the journey.'

At last his good father had had enough of his son's boasting. One day he put a hundred sovereigns on the table in front of his son and said:

'Here are the hundred sovereigns you wanted; now go! A little experience of the world will do you no harm. Maybe you will even learn some sense and stop boasting so much. But I tell you this: I don't want to set eyes on you until you are at least a corporal!'

So Jack Bragger went to town. He found the army barracks, went to see the colonel and asked to be taken on as one of his soldiers.

'If you accept me, I will take the whole regiment out for a treat!'

You can imagine that the colonel gladly accepted such a generous

soldier! Jack Bragger did not disappoint his colonel or his new army friends. He played host to them in the tavern until he had spent all but one of his hundred gold sovereigns.

'I shall keep the last one for a rainy day,' he thought as he sang merrily on his way back to the barracks. He was stopped at the entrance by an old beggar dressed in rags:

'Have pity on me, soldier, and be kind to an old man!'

Jack had a heart of gold. Without hesitation he put his hand in his pocket, took out his very last sovereign and gave it to the beggar:

'Here you are, old man, may you enjoy it in good health!'

'Thank you, soldier,' the old man called after him. 'Maybe one day I will be able to repay you!'

But Jack Bragger did not hear him; he walked on gaily through the gates of the barracks, and his good humour did not fail him even when the guards took him straight into the guard-house because he had arrived after lights-out.

Jack spent a whole month in the guard-house, but he still did not learn his lesson. The moment they let him out, he could not think of anything better to do than to write to his father to tell him he had been promoted to the rank of a corporal and to ask him for two hundred sovereigns, so that he could celebrate with his friends.

His father was most surprised that his son had been promoted so soon, but he sent the money and Jack Bragger used it all up in exactly the same way as the first time. He treated his friends to food and drink until he had only one sovereign left.

'I shall keep this last one for a rainy day,' Jack decided as he sang a merry song on his way back to the barracks.

An old beggar stopped him in front of the entrance, as before:

'Have pity on an old man, soldier!'

Without hesitation kind Jack put his hand in his pocket, took out his very last sovereign, and gave it to the beggar:

'Here you are, old man, may you spend it in good health!'

'Thank you, soldier,' the old man shouted after him. 'Perhaps I can repay you one day!'

By then Jack was passing gaily through the gates of the barracks and for the second time he ended in the guard-house for coming in after lights-out.

This time Jack spent two months there and had plenty of time to think, but once again he had not learnt his lesson. The moment he was let out he wrote to his father telling him that he was a colonel already and that he needed three hundred sovereigns to celebrate with his friends.

His father was most surprised at his son's swift progress in the army, but eventually he sent him the gold sovereigns. So Jack played host to his friends for the third time, until he had only one sovereign left for a rainy day. He returned to the barracks singing merrily. The old beggar was already waiting for him:

'Have pity, soldier, be kind to an old man!'

Without hesitation kind Jack took the last sovereign from his pocket and gave it to the beggar.

'Here you are, old man, may you enjoy it in good health!'

'Thank you, soldier,' the old man cried after him. 'Perhaps I will repay you for everything sooner than you think!'

By then Jack was passing through the gates of the barracks, and the guards arrested him for third time for coming in after lights-out. He was in the guard-house for three months this time, and during this time he realised that he had gone about things in quite the wrong way. But what could he do now?

While Jack was kept in the guard-house, his father became more and more worried. His son had used to write every month or two, and now for three months there was not a single line from him. In the end the farmer put on his best shoes, took out his best coat, put his best hat on his head and with a walking stick in hand he set out to town.

When he reached the entrance of the barracks he asked the guards if he could see Colonel Jack.

'Colonel Jack?' asked the surprised guards. 'We know no colonel of that name. We do have an ordinary soldier called Jack Bragger, but he is in the guard-house, because he spent his nights drinking away the money his father sent him, and always came in late. We will take you to him.'

'So this is what you have been up to!' stormed the furious father, when he was taken to Jack and saw with his own eyes that his son was still an ordinary soldier. 'Very well then, but remember this: from now on I don't want to know you. I never want to see you again! Do not dare to come near me, unless you really are a General!'

His father returned to his village and Jack Bragger stayed in the guard-house. He would have been shut in there for a long time, if the only daughter of the king, a princess as lovely as the sun, had not been kidnapped. She went out into the forest in her coach with an escort, and did not return. Just one servant ran back to the king's palace and told the sad tale of how the coach had been held up by a band of robbers, how they killed all the escort, how they dragged the princess off somewhere into the mountains, and how he alone had escaped.

Sadness spread through the whole kingdom; in every town and village the town-crier read out the king's proclamation to the sound of drums. The king promised that whoever found and rescued the princess would be given her hand in marriage and half his kingdom.

You can imagine that many men, rich and poor, wanted to win a princess as a prize — and half a kingdom into the bargain! They all tried their hardest to find her, but without success.

'I should like to have a try,' Jack Bragger decided when he heard about all this, and asked to be taken to his colonel:

'Colonel, sir, I should like to try and find the missing princess, if you will just let me out of the guard-house! If I find her and become a king, I shall promote you to a general; if I do not find her, I shall return and you can lock me up again — so really you cannot lose either way!'

'Very well then, Jack Bragger, since you are so bold and cheeky. Go and luck be with you!' said the colonel laughingly. He gave Jack his back pay and allowed him out to search for the princess.

Jack left the barracks very pleased with himself, but he had no idea which way to go and where to start looking for the princess. As he stood wondering in front of the gates, an old man in a worn-out coat came up to him, saying:

'Where are you off to, Jack? Are you going to search for the kidnapped princess too?'

'Yes, old man, I am, but I do not know where to start looking,' Jack Bragger admitted frankly.

'I will tell you something,' the old man said. 'As you have been so good to me, and have given me your very last sovereign on three occasions, I will now give you some excellent advice. Follow this path as far as you can, till you reach a deep forest, where you will find a high rock. When you come to it, knock three times and wait. An old woman will come out — she is the cook of the robbers, who live inside that rock. Tell her you are looking for work and she will employ you. But it won't be an easy task and if you were left to manage by yourself you would fare very badly. But I will help you. Here are three gifts: a whistle, a cloak and a stick. The whistle has such magic power that if you play on it everybody has to dance and cannot stop until you stop whistling. When you place this cloak round your shoulders it will take you wherever you wish to go. One wave with this stick will make you as small as an ant, or as big as a giant — whichever you wish. You will need all these things you will see! Now off you go and luck go with you.'

Jack thanked the old man, put the gifts into his haversack and, singing gaily, marched along the path leading to the forest. In the middle of this forest he caught sight of the rock, surrounded by deep undergrowth. A faint trail led to it over boulders, bracken and streams. Jack followed the trail and when he reached the rock he knocked on it bravely three times with a stone. The rock parted, as if by command, and an old woman popped her head through the gap.

'What do you want, soldier?'

'I am looking for work, old woman,' Jack Bragger replied. 'Do you need a servant?'

'Yes, we do,' the old woman croaked. 'But I doubt if you would take this kind of job. It would only last three days, but if you did not fulfil your duties, you would lose your head!'

'What will I get if I carry out all you ask?' Jack asked.

'Whatever you care to choose from the castle,' the old woman croaked. 'But as yet no one has managed to get that far!'

'I'll manage,' Jack remarked confidently, and stepped through the opening. The rock quickly closed behind him and Jack saw a passage and some stairs before him, with a light shining at the far end. When they climbed the stairs, they came out into a large, beautiful garden, full of bright light, as if another sun glowed underground. In the centre of the garden stood a castle.

'This castle belongs to our master, Captain of the robbers,' said the old woman, as she led Jack into the kitchen. She fed him well, then took him to spend the night in one of the hundred rooms of the castle.

'Your first task awaits you here,' she croaked. 'During the night devils rage inside this room; they make a terrible noise, screaming and

180

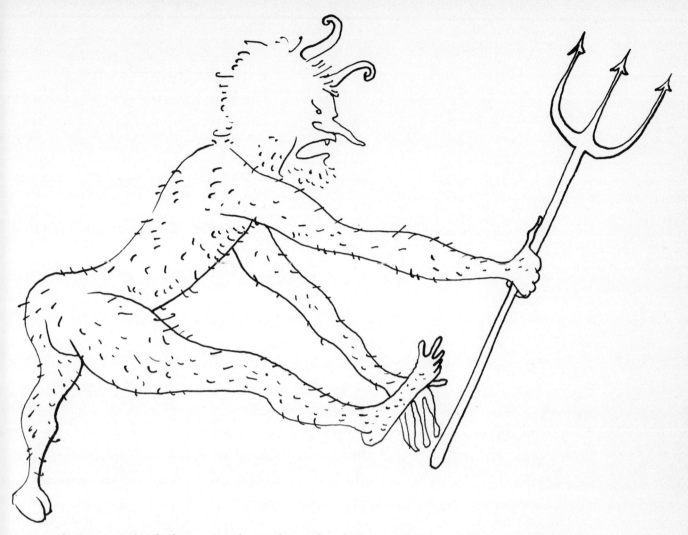

screeching, and if they catch sight of a human being, they tear him to pieces. Stay with them and try to reason with them.'

'With pleasure,' Jack Bragger answered. 'But bring me a jug of wine, so I can gather some strength and then I will show you that I can get the better of them!'

The old woman brought Jack the jug of wine, then locked him inside the room. Jack sat by the fire, with the wine and a glass by his side, drinking merrily. Before long it was midnight, and a gang of devils flew into his room through the chimney.

'How dare you be here, you human worm!' they cried the moment they saw him. 'Take to your heels quickly, or you'll be in for it!'

They began to prod Jack Bragger with red-hot forks.

'Just you take care that you're not in for it, too,' Jack said with annoyance, and taking the old man's whistle from his bag he began to play. The devils just had to dance! At first they were not really worried, and just kept on threatening Jack with how they would punish him when he stopped his whistling. But when Jack did not stop but played on and on, faster and faster, the devils began to pant, then to cry and in the end to plead. But Jack continued without mercy:

'I will go on playing and you will go on dancing until you promise never to come here again!'

What could the poor devils do? They did not want to wear out their hooves and their legs to their very knees, so they had to give in and promise. Only then did Jack put aside his whistle, and the devils, with much noise and commotion, disappeared through the chimney to their blazing hell.

In the morning when the old woman unlocked the room, she could hardly believe her eyes. Jack was tucked comfortably in his bed as if nothing had happened, and was shouting that he was hungry!

'Well done! So your first task is safely behind you,' said the astonished old woman and gave him an enormous breakfast. 'But you are not finished yet. Do you see the high, thin spire over there? Some crows have built their nest right on its very point, and they crow all day long. I want their nest here on this table by this evening, otherwise you'll be in trouble! But I can tell you now that you will not find a ladder or ropes anywhere in this castle.'

'I won't even need them,' Jack Bragger said confidently, and went away to have a nap in the garden under a tree. He dozed all morning and all afternoon. Only when dusk began to fall did he choose a convenient moment to take the old man's cloak out of the haversack and put it round his shoulders. He made a wish to be at the very top of the spire — and there he was! With no bother at all he removed the crows' nest and returned to the garden the same way as he came.

In the evening, when Jack came into the kitchen with the nest in his hands, the old woman could hardly believe her eyes:

'Well done! So your second task is safely behind you,' she marvelled and gave him an excellent dinner. 'But you have not finished yet! Can you see the barred windows up there? Behind those bars lives the princess who has been brought here by our captain. She is imprisoned in her room by seven locks. Tomorrow you must bring me the ring from her finger. But I tell you this: only I have the keys to those locks, and you will not open them with any other keys.'

'I will not even try to,' said Jack Bragger and went to bed happily in his own room.

The next day after breakfast he stretched out in the shade in the garden and lazed away the whole day. When dusk started to close in, he chose a suitable moment to take the old man's stick from his haversack. He waved it once, and immediately shrank to the size of an ant! With no bother at all he crawled under the door which remained locked with the seven locks. In the princess's room, with the second wave of his stick he changed back to his normal size.

When Jack Bragger appeared so suddenly before the lovely princess, she screamed with fright. But Jack quietened her very quickly:

'Do not be afraid, Princess, it is I, soldier Jack Bragger. I have come to rescue you and I shall do so very soon. Tomorrow you will be free, but until then I must have your ring.'

He told the princess what her father had promised anyone who would save her, and what he himself had already done in his search for her.

The princess liked the handsome soldier right from the start, and, blushing deeply, she said to him:

'Thank you, Jack. And if you do rescue me, I shall be very happy to fulfil my father's promise.'

She took off her ring, and gave it to Jack, who put it in his pocket, said good-bye and returned in the same manner as he came.

When in the evening he entered the kitchen with the princess's ring on his finger, the old woman could hardly believe her eyes.

'Well done! I can see you're quite a fellow! You have fulfilled your third task and now it is my turn to repay you. Choose whatever you want from this castle, and it is yours!'

Jack Bragger did not hesitate:

'I want the lovely princess,' he stated firmly, and would not change his mind even when the old woman offered him piles of gold, silver and precious stones instead.

'Very well,' she consented in the end. 'Take her away then. Be careful though, for you are only safe as far as the edge of the rock. As soon as you walk into the forest, our master, Captain of the robbers, will come after you with all his gang and you'll be in for it! Believe me, you won't escape them.'

'I will escape,' said Jack Bragger and he was right! For the rock had hardly closed behind him and his princess when he threw the old man's cloak round his shoulders, took the princess in his arms and in a wink of an eye was standing before the king himself.

'Here is the princess, Your Majesty. I promised my colonel I would rescue her and I have done so.'

The king, with tears in his eyes, embraced his daughter and welcomed Jack as a son-in-law. So that his daughter would not have to marry an ordinary soldier, he promoted Jack straight away to the rank of general and then ordered the wedding preparations to be started.

And so Jack Bragger did become a general after all.

'Perhaps now I dare to let my father see me,' he thought and decided he would go to invite him to his wedding.

The very next day he set out with the whole company to his village. It was not far, only half a day's journey on horseback, but Jack stopped so many times in so many taverns and brought rounds of drinks for so many people that by nightfall he still had not reached his home. He and his company had to spend the night in an inn deep in the forest.

It so happened that this was no ordinary inn for proper travellers, but a tavern for the robbers who had kidnapped the princess. Around midnight, when everyone was fast asleep, the band of robbers pounced upon the unsuspecting soldiers. Before the sleepers were properly awake, they were robbed by the thieves of all they possessed and then chased into the forest clad only in their nightshirts! Even General Jack did not escape this fate. When he saw the commotion and realised that his men were greatly outnumbered, he jumped out of the window, ran through the bushes and made for his home. Before morning he arrived and knocked on the door. An elderly maid opened it. When she saw Jack clad only in a nightshirt, she had an awful fright, thinking he was a ghost. But when Jack spoke she recognised him and let him in.

'If my master sees you, you'll be in trouble! He does not want to lay his eyes on you unless you are at least a general!'

'But I am a general, and I shall marry our princess in less than a week,' Jack assured her, but it was no good the old maid knew of him of old and did not believe a word he said.

'Your father won't believe you either,' she added.

'He certainly won't, if I come to him in a nightshirt! But when my princess arrives in her gold carriage, then he will believe me,' Jack said, taking the princess's ring off his finger. 'This is her ring; take it to her and tell her I have been robbed by those thieves and am waiting for her at my father's house!'

The old maid finally agreed. She found some old trousers for Jack, hid him in the loft and then left for the palace, with the ring wrapped safely in her handkerchief.

You can imagine she was very nervous when she arrived. What if Jack had found the ring somewhere and was just bragging as usual? But the maid need not have worried. As soon as she produced the ring, she was led to the princess herself. The lovely princess nearly burst into tears when she heard what had happened to her Jack.

'I will certainly punish those robbers,' she said and ordered horses to be saddled and a company of Dragoons to be called. An hour later the princess galloped with the company of Dragoons through the gates of the king's palace. Behind them sped the carriage carrying the elderly maid.

Towards the evening they reached the robber's tavern. The princess took Jack's stick out of her saddle-bag, and with a single wave she and her company had shrunk to the size of ants. They slipped into the tavern, completely unseen, and waited.

At midnight the robbers burst into the inn, and were soon lounging round the tables eating and drinking. When their enjoyment was at its height, the princess waved her stick for the second time, and immediately the band of robbers was completely surrounded by a company of Dragoons with unsheathed swords ready to strike! This time it was the robbers who ran away clad in their nightshirts — that is the ones who were not captured or killed by the Dragoons. And since that day the kingdom has remained free from robbers.

The next morning the princess and her company reached Jack's father's house. The farmer rushed out of the building to see what was going on:

'Whom are you looking for, lovely princess?'

'I am seeking my bridegroom, General Jack, and his father,' the princess replied.

'General Jack does not live here,' the worried farmer assured her. 'Only my son, Jack Bragger, used to live here, but he has been forbidden to return, for he did not even manage to be a corporal!'

'Yes he did, father,' said a voice behind the farmer and Jack Bragger appeared in the doorway, clad in his nightshirt and torn trousers. 'I may look like a scarecrow, but I am a General and tomorrow I shall become the son-in-law of the king himself!'

The good farmer could hardly believe his eyes or his ears, but when he saw the princess kiss Jack, clad in a nightshirt and torn trousers, on both cheeks, he realised that his son must have found his fortune in the world.

So it came to pass that Jack did marry a princess and that he did become a king, just as he used to tell his friends. He lived with his wife and with many children in health and happiness till the very end of their lives, and people said that he ruled just as well as all the kings before him.

THE ANIMAL EVEN THE DEVIL COULD
NOT RECOGNISE

Once upon a time a peasant and a devil jointly bought a small-holding so they could farm together. The devil, who was very artful, suggested:

'Man, you can sow and plough, I will look after the weather and we can reap the harvest together.'

'Very well then,' the peasant agreed, 'but how shall we divide the harvest between us?'

'Each of us will get one half,' the devil said.

'Which half do you want?' the peasant asked. 'The bottom half,' the devil stated, because he was thinking of potatoes. But the peasant was more artful than the devil and he sowed corn. He toiled in the field from dawn till dusk and the devil too worked hard, taking care of rain

187

and sunshine, so that the ears of the corn grew to such a size it was a joy to see them.

When the time came to gather the crops, the devil returned hurriedly to take a look at his half. He was certainly not very happy with his share — all he got were roots and stubble!

'You've got the better of me this time, man! You wait, next time I will take the top half!'

'As you wish!' the peasant agreed and next time planted potatoes. It was a pleasure to see such a splendid crop come out of the earth, but once again the devil was far from satisfied, for all he got were stalks and leaves.

'You've got the better of me again, man! You wait, next time I will have the tops and the bottom!'

'As you wish,' the peasant agreed, and sowed maize. The crop was even richer than it had been the first two years, but when the time came to bring in the harvest, the devil was once again most dissatisfied with his share. All he received were useless roots and tops, but the big fat cobs of corn, which grew in the middle, went to the peasant.

'You've got the better of me the third time, man! But he who laughs in the end, laughs the loudest of all! I refuse to farm with you any more. Let the one who can throw a stone higher than the other keep the small-holding. We shall decide tomorrow morning.'

'As you wish,' the peasant agreed and went into the field to catch a lark.

The next morning the devil picked up a stone in the yard and threw it so very high that it flew out of sight into the clouds. A good hour passed before it fell to the ground!

'Man, now it is your turn!'

The peasant pretended to pick up a stone and to swing his arm, but in reality he threw the lark into the air, which he was hiding in his fist. The lark surged upwards into the sky and of course it flew higher than the stone and never fell down again!

'Man, you have won,' the devil admitted. 'But I can't and I won't give up my half of the farm so easily. Let us match our wits again for the last time. Tomorrow morning each of us must bring an animal. If you cannot recognise my animal, the farm will be mine, if I do not recognise your animal, the farm will be yours for ever.'

'As you wish,' the peasant agreed, but this time he was at a loss to know what to do. Where on earth could he find an animal the devil would not recognise?

'Leave it to me,' his wife assured him when he told her his troubles. 'Wake me up nice and early tomorrow — and you will see!'

When early the next morning the peasant woke his wife, she spread honey all over herself, then rolled over and over in feathers from a torn featherbed. As a finishing touch she gripped the tail of a dead cow between her teeth. It was a wonder the peasant himself was not scared of such an unusual animal.

'Now come on, let us hide under the bridge over which the devil will have to pass,' she said.

They heard the devil as soon as they crouched under the bridge. He was walking across, egging on his animal:

'Gee up, Spanish billy-goat, gee up!'

The peasant then left his hiding-place and came towards the devil, leading his feather-covered wife behind him.

'Tell me, man, what animal have I here?' the devil asked.

The peasant pretended to examine the billy-goat from all sides, then he pronounced:

'What else could it be than a Spanish billy-goat!'

'Man, your guess is correct,' the devil had to admit.

'Now, what animal have I here?' the peasant asked.

The devil walked round the man's animal scrutinising it keenly, but he had no idea what it could be:

'It has feathers, but it is not a goose, it has a tail, but it is not a cow; what on earth can it be?'

In the end he just had to give up:

'Man I simply don't know! The farm is yours! Never again will I enter a partnership with a human being!'

Fuming with rage he dived through the earth right down to hell.

HOW JOHNNY PANCAKE DID NOT
MARRY A PRINCESS

Once upon a time there was a young lad whose name was Johnny. But everyone called him Pancake, because he loved pancakes more than anything. He was a thoroughly good-natured fellow, but though his heart was full of kindness, his head was rather lacking in brains and common sense. Everyone pulled his leg, and he fell for it every time for he believed anything he was told. To tell you the truth there were plenty of people who not only teased him, but cheated him too, especially when he was sent by his parents on some errand.

While Johnny had a mother and a father, things were not too bad, but when his parents died, matters went from bad to worse. Though his parents had left a nice house and a smallholding to Johnny, people from near and far soon managed to beg, borrow or steal everything he owned.

'Whatever shall I do, Mary?' Johnny Pancake complained to his one and only faithful friend, his sweetheart Mary, a dairy maid from another farm.

'You must go out into the world and learn some common sense,' his sweetheart Mary advised him sincerely.

'I would perish in the wide world from hunger, long before I learned that,' Johnny Pancake replied, frowning.

'Have no fear of that,' his sweetheart Mary assured him. 'This napkin will save you from hunger. It is made from my fairy godmother's petticoat. She wants you to have it and says it is sure to help you to find good fortune in the world. When you feel hungry you are to unfold it and say: "Napkin, give me this and that," and whatever you asked for will be there before you. But please do not part with the napkin. Now I must say goodbye; return to me soon!'

Johnny Pancake bade his dearest Mary farewell, put the napkin into his pocket and bravely stepped out into the wide world. He walked all day long, following his nose. He picked an apple or a pear off a tree here and there and had a drink from a well or a mountain spring here and there but he gave no thought to the napkin his sweetheart had given him. By the evening, however, when the sun started to go down behind the mountains, he was overcome by an enormous hunger.

'What I would give for a couple of hot pancakes like my sweetheart Mary makes,' he sighed and then remembered the napkin.

'There is no harm in trying it out,' Johnny thought, and he spread the napkin over the grass by the path, saying:

'Napkin, give me a plate of warm pancakes!'

Lo and behold, a full plate of pancakes appeared on the napkin as quick as lightning; they were filled with thick jam and topped with cream. Johnny Pancake ate them with relish, then ordered another plateful, and yet another. When he was just about to tuck into his third portion, he saw a soldier coming towards him. He was striding along, a beret upon his head, a haversack on his back and a stick in his hand.

'Enjoy your food, friend,' the soldier called out in passing.

'Thank you,' Johnny replied, and as he had a heart of gold he invited the soldier: 'If you are hungry, come and have some!'

'With pleasure,' the soldier accepted most gladly and without further ado grabbed the plate and polished off every single pancake! Good-natured Johnny had to ask the napkin for yet another portion of the delicious pancakes. This time they were piping hot and served with sugar and lemon.

'Just look at that!' the soldier marvelled. 'I could certainly put that to good use. Would you not like to exchange it for my magic stick?'

'Certainly not!' Johnny Pancake answered firmly. 'What use could your walking stick be?'

'What use!' the soldier cried. 'Why, five hundred cavalrymen are hidden inside this stick. All you have to do is to command: "Cavalrymen, out you come!" and five hundred armed riders will be at your service and will carry out your orders.'

But Johnny was not really interested:

'What would I do with armed cavalrymen,' he muttered. 'Besides, my Mary told me not to give the napkin to anyone.'

But the soldier was already pushing the napkin into his haversack.

'Whether you like it or not, I am having that napkin,' he stated. 'Here, take my stick and be thankful I did not set my cavalrymen on you.'

The soldier marched away, beret upon his head, haversack on his back and inside the haversack — Johnny's napkin. Johnny Pancake, stick in hand, walked sadly in the opposite direction. When he reached the edge of the wood the stick seemed so heavy he decided to throw it away into a ditch. Then he thought better of it:

'There is no harm in trying it out,' he thought, and so commanded:

'Cavalrymen, out you come!'

Believe it or not, five hundred armed cavalrymen scrambled out of the walking stick, and stood to attention whilst their captain gave Johnny a smart salute, saying:

'What is your order, Commander?'

'My order?' Johnny Pancake stammered anxiously, for he could not think of a single order to give them. Then he remembered the soldier:

'Over there beyond the wood a soldier is marching. Catch up with him and bring me my napkin from his haversack!'

'Charge!' the captain cried out, and the riders galloped swiftly away. A moment or two later they returned with the napkin.

'Here is your napkin,' the captain said, gave the napkin to Johnny and then disappeared with his riders into the stick.

Johnny Pancake heaved a sigh of relief to have his napkin back safely, and to know his sweetheart Mary would have no cause to be angry. He travelled with a light heart, napkin in his pocket, stick in hand, looking for his good fortune. A day or two later he came to a mill. The miller sat on the front doorstep playing a tune on a whistle, and the miller's wife and children danced to the music. When Johnny Pancake was within earshot, he just had to dance himself.

'Enough, enough, stop!' The miller's wife and children were pleading. 'Give us something to eat instead of playing.'

But the miller would not put his whistle down until his wife and children stopped complaining that they were hungry.

Johnny Pancake felt very sorry for the woman and the children. He took the napkin out of his pocket, spread it out right there in the yard and ordered a good supper for them all.

The miller marvelled:

'Just look at that, what a fantastic napkin, I certainly could put it to good use. Would you not like to exchange it for my magic whistle?'

'I certainly would not,' Johnny Pancake assured him. 'What would I do with your whistle?'

'What would you do with it!' cried the miller indignantly. 'Why, when you play a tune on it, everybody has to dance, even the unconscious ones, even the dead!'

But Johnny would not hear of an exchange.

'What would I gain by waking up the dead just to dance?' he muttered. 'Anyway, my Mary implored me not to part with the napkin.'

The miller was, however, already putting the napkin into his own pocket.

'Whether you like it or not, I am keeping this napkin,' laughed the miller. 'Here, take my whistle and be thankful I did not dance you to death.'

Then the miller hurried with his wife and their children inside the mill and locked the door. Johnny Pancake walked sadly along the path away from the mill, whistle in his pocket, stick in his hand. When he reached the edge of the forest, he took hold of the whistle and, burning with anger, decided to throw it into the ditch. But he thought better of it.

'I may as well try it out first. In the meantime my stick will help me.'

He commanded:

'Cavalrymen, out you come!'

Once again five hundred armed cavalrymen scrambled out of the stick, and their captain, giving Johnny a smart salute, said:

'What is your order, Commander?'

'My order?' Johnny Pancake repeated. 'Over there behind the wood stands a mill and in it lives a miller. Go after him and bring me my napkin from his pocket!'

'Charge!' the captain cried out and the riders galloped swiftly away. A moment or two later they were back with the napkin.

Johnny heaved a sigh of relief that his treasured napkin was once again in his possession and that his sweetheart Mary would have no reason to scold him. He continued in his search for good fortune with a light heart, napkin and whistle in his pocket, stick in his hand. Three or four days later he came to a village where wedding celebrations were in progress. The guests were just about to tuck into their feast.

'I could try out the miller's whistle here,' Johnny Pancake thought. The moment he began to play, everyone started to dance, even those who did not want to, because they were tempted by the delicious roast chickens and sucking-pigs which were on the table.

Not only did the guests dance, the dogs under the table danced too, and the geese in the forecourt, and eventually even the roast chickens and sucking pigs! When Johnny stopped whistling, the roast poultry scattered all over the farmyard.

'Look what you've done,' the bride wailed. 'What are we going to eat now?'

'Have no fear,' Johnny Pancake comforted her. 'I will produce a truly wonderful feast.'

The napkin excelled itself. No one from far and wide had ever seen such a feast. The mayor himself was most impressed:

'Just look at that fine napkin, I could certainly do with it. What about exchanging it for a magic cap?'

'Certainly not,' Johnny Pancake replied immediately. 'What could your cap be good for?'

'Good for?' the mayor repeated indignantly. 'If you put it on your head back to front, you can wish for any house or even for a magnificent palace, and it will be built in a trice. If, on the other hand, you put on the cap the right way round, you will become the most handsome youth in the whole world.'

194

Once again Johnny was not really interested in all these promises.

'It is not for me to build magnificent palaces or to be the most handsome youth in the world,' he explained. 'In any case, my Mary told me not to part with this napkin!'

Unfortunately the mayor was already stuffing the napkin inside his shirt.

'I don't care whether you like it or not, but I am having this napkin,' he pronounced sternly. 'Here is my cap. Take it and be grateful I am not having you arrested by my constables.'

The mayor pointed to his constables with sharp swords gleaming at their hips. Johnny Pancake preferred to leave and so, whistle and cap in his pocket, stick in his hand, he sadly followed the path from the village. When he came to the edge of the wood, he grabbed the cap angrily and was just about to throw it into the bushes, when he thought better of it:

'I may as well test it first; in the meantime my stick will help me.'

Then he commanded:

'Cavalrymen, out you come!'

The five hundred armed cavalrymen scrambled out of the stick, their captain giving Johnny a smart salute:

'What is your order, Commander?'

'My order?' Johnny Pancake did not hesitate: 'Behind the wood lies a village and in this village there is a mayor. Go after him and take my napkin away from him!'

'Charge!' the captain cried out, and the riders swiftly galloped away. A moment or two later they returned with the napkin.

'Here is your napkin, Commander,' the captain announced, and giving the napkin to Johnny disappeared with his cavalrymen into the stick.

Johnny heaved a sigh of relief that he had the treasured gift once again in his possession and that his dearest Mary would have no cause to scold him. He continued in his search for good fortune with a light heart — napkin, whistle, and cap safely in his pocket, stick in his hand. Five or six days later he came to the Royal City of Paris and came to a halt in front of the palace of the King of France.

'I could try out the mayor's cap right here,' Johnny Pancake mumbled to himself and waited for dusk to fall. When the last light in the windows of the king's palace flickered out, Johnny placed the mayor's cap on his head back to front and said:

'Build me a castle right opposite the royal palace, one hundred times more magnificent!'

Believe it or not, no sooner was it said that it was done! Right in the main square, opposite the royal palace, stood a castle one hundred times more magnificent. It shone and glittered in the moonlight with dazzling splendour. Johnny walked in through the entrance, dined in the grand dining-hall, went to bed in the luxurious bedroom and slept soundly till dawn.

The next morning Johnny's castle was all aglow in the sunlight. The brilliant radiance awoke the King of France himself. He jumped out of bed, hurried to the window and saw a castle one hundred times more magnificent than his own, made of silver, gold and precious stones. A strange, handsome prince stood on a balcony, dressed in magnificent robes. This was Johnny Pancake, who had put the mayor's magic cap on his head the right way round!

The French king had to pinch himself to see if he was dreaming.

'What audacity, what a nerve to build a castle a hundred times more magnificent than mine, right opposite my palace! Who is this daring fellow? Go to him and bring him here immediately!'

The courtiers obediently rushed to Johnny Pancake:

'Distinguished Prince, the King of France begs you to visit him!'

Johnny Pancake did not feel like visiting the king.

'Tell His Majesty that I want nothing from him, so I do not see the point of visiting him. But if he wants something from me, he may come and call here.'

The courtiers obediently hurried back to deliver Johnny's message.

'Is he coming?' asked the king.

'No, your Majesty,' the courtiers replied. 'He wants nothing from you — that is why he will not come. If you want something from him, you can go and call on him.'

'I shall do just that right now!' the French king decided.

He took all his courtiers and his only daughter with him to Johnny's castle.

Johnny Pancake received them politely and asked them all to sit down at a table prepared for a banquet. This time the napkin surpassed itself; even the French king had not eaten such exciting dishes ever before. When Johnny put on the mayor's cap the right way round, everyone

gasped with amazement. No one had ever seen such a handsome prince, no one had even heard of such a handsome prince.

As a banquet is not a banquet without music and dancing, Johnny took the miller's whistle out of his pocket and played. At once everyone, even the old French king, began to dance. After a while the old and the fat could hardly keep going, so they pleaded:

'Stop, stop, please stop!'

But the young people loved the dancing and the music, and they pleaded:

'Go on, go on, go on!'

Johnny Pancake played on, and on and on, till the perspiration ran down the faces of everyone on the floor. Only then did he stop playing. The young princess ran to her father, the king, and said in front of everyone there:

'Father, I want this prince and no other for my husband!'

'Wait a minute, daughter,' the king pleaded, panting heavily. 'Just let me get my breath back so I can think about it!'

'There is nothing to think about,' the princess insisted. 'I want him for a husband, and that is that!'

So the French king turned to Johnny and announced:

'Dear Prince, I see you are not only handsome and wealthy, but also most powerful, so I shall be happy to give you my daughter in marriage.'

But Johnny had no intention of marrying the princess:

'Thank you, Your Majesty, but I have promised myself to another, and my bride is waiting for me at home.'

'Who is this bride of yours, who makes you refuse the daughter of the French king?' demanded the king, frowning.

'My sweetheart Mary,' Johnny Pancake answered simply, 'she is the most beautiful maiden in the world.'

'This I want to see for myself,' the French king muttered, frowning furiously. 'If she is as lovely as you say, I shall give you a wedding myself. But if you are lying — then heaven help you!'

Johnny was not at all worried.

'Thank you, Your Majesty, but I will arrange my own wedding. But I will let you see how beautiful my Mary really is! Cavalrymen, out you come!'

The five hundred armed cavalrymen immediately scrambled out of the stick, with their captain saluting Johnny:

'What is your order, Commander?'

'My order?' Johnny Pancake repeated. 'In my home village in Brittany, my dearest Mary works on a farm. Go and fetch her back here, but hurry! Take the napkin with you, then she will believe you really are my messengers!'

'Charge!' the captain cried out and the riders swiftly galloped away.

When the cavalrymen had left, the French king and his courtiers relaxed again, for quite frankly, the sight of all those riders had made them feel rather nervous!

The riders soon reached the farm where Johnny's sweetheart Mary was working. She was just taking the pig-wash to the pigs as they rode in, so you can imagine how she must have been dressed. But the captain did not care at all. He gave her a smart salute and said:

'Good day, sweetheart Mary! Our commander Prince Johnny Pancake has sent us to you; we are to take you to him without delay!'

'What are you saying, Captain sir. Surely you must be teasing me,' sweetheart Mary answered laughingly. 'You must give me some proof, if you want me to believe you.'

'Here is the napkin you gave our commander to take on his travels,' the captain said, giving Mary the napkin made from the fairy godmother's petticoat.

Sweetheart Mary realised the cavalrymen really had come from her Johnny. She wanted to run off and change her clothes, but the captain said:

'I am to take you just as you are, for Prince Johnny Pancake is in a hurry.'

With that he lifted sweetheart Mary and sat her in front of him on his horse.

Just a while after the riders had left the castle, the stamping of hooves could be heard by the king and his courtiers; five hundred armed caval-rymen galloped with sweetheart Mary through the castle gates. Johnny Pancake clasped both her hands in his own, kissed her on both cheeks and proudly introduced her to the French king. The king was most surprised, for though Johnny's darling Mary was as pretty as a flower, she was dressed just like a maid who looks after the pigs.

'We shall soon alter that!' Johnny Pancake said happily. 'Return tomorrow for our wedding and you will see!'

The next day the king with all his court came to Johnny's wedding, and when they saw his bride they stood staring in amazement and wonder. Could this breathtakingly beautiful princess at his side really be sweetheart Mary?

It really was Mary. Johnny had clothed her in a robe made of gold, silver and silk, and in her exquisite dress she was a hundred times lovelier than the French king's daughter. The king himself and all his courtiers had to admit it.

So there was a wedding such as the City of Paris had never witnessed before, and at this splendid wedding Johnny Pancake married his sweetheart Mary. When the ceremony was over he sent his five hundred armed cavalrymen to give the magic cap, the whistle and the stick back to their rightful owners. Johnny Pancake and his sweetheart Mary returned to their own village, where they lived in health and in happiness to the very end of their lives.

BALDERDASH AND FIDDLE-FADDLE

Once there was a villager who had a pair of shoes made by the local shoemaker, and then did not feel like paying for them. The shoemaker reminded him of his debt over and over again, but it was of no use. When he met the villager for the fourth time, he'd had enough, so he said:

'Listen to me, friend! It seems to me you haven't got the money you owe me, but never mind! I know a way you can pay me for those shoes without it costing you a single penny!'

'How could I do that?'

'Very simply! All you have to do is to promise me that from now until we meet again you will answer everybody and everything by saying: balderdash and fiddle-faddle! You must not utter any other words, mind you, and you must keep it up till we meet again. Is it a bargain?'

'Balderdash and fiddle-faddle!' the villager shouted merrily and hurried home. Because it was late, his wife was waiting for him in the doorway:

'Where have you been all this time, you vagabond?'

The villager answered:

'Balderdash!'

'What did you say?'

'Fiddle-faddle!'

'Are you crazy?'

'Balderdash!'

'My goodness, my husband has gone mad!'

'Fiddle-faddle!'

'It must be true,' cried the wife and ran to her neighbour: 'Help me, neighbour! My husband has gone crazy! He keeps gabbling the same thing over and over again — balderdash and fiddle-faddle, as if he was out of his mind! Come and see for yourself!'

The good neighbour hurried to have a look at the villager:

'Well friend, what is up with you?'

'Balderdash!'

'What are you talking about?'

'Fiddle-faddle!'

'Bless my soul, he has really lost his mind!'

'Balderdash!'

'The best thing I can is to fetch the mayor.'

'Fiddle-faddle!'

The good woman ran to see the mayor.

'Mr Mayor, my neighbour has gone mad! He answers everything with 'balderdash' or 'fiddle-faddle', as if he was out of his mind! Come and have a look at him.'

So the mayor went to have a look at the villager too.

'Well my friend, what is the matter?'

'Balderdash!'

'Come on, my friend, you must talk to the mayor like this!'

'Fiddle-faddle!'

'Have some sense, friend!'

'Balderdash!'

'Think of what you're saying, friend!'

'Fiddle-faddle!'

'Upon my soul, he really has gone mad,' even the mayor admitted.

It only took one or two days for the tale to spread through the village that the poor villager had gone mad. On the third day the shoemaker met the mayor.

'Good day, Mr Mayor, have you any news?' the shoemaker inquired politely.

'I have no news, shoemaker,' the mayor replied, 'except that one villager has lost his mind.'

'You don't say, Mr Mayor! I don't believe it!'

'Believe it or not, shoemaker, it is the truth! I am quite convinced the man is mad!'

'I tell you, Mr Mayor, that he is not mad!'

'But I tell you he is!'

'He is not!'

'He is!'

'Let us have a bet on that, Mr Mayor!'

'I'll have a bet on that, shoemaker!'

'Very well then, let us bet with fifty gold sovereigns, Mr Mayor!'

'It's a deal, shoemaker!'

Mr Mayor and the shoemaker sealed their wager with a hearty handshake.

Just then, as if someone had called him, the villager in question appeared on the street. The shoemaker called to him:

'Hey, my friend, come over here!'

'With the greatest of pleasure,' the villager answered. 'You cannot know how relieved I am to see you! On account of your shoes the whole village now thinks that I am completely mad. I certainly paid a high price for those shoes!'

Mr Mayor stood glued to the spot like a statue, for he could hardly believe his ears. The villager was chatting away like any other sensible person.

But the shoemaker laughed and laughed.

'Mr Mayor paid an even higher price for your shoes. He now owes me fifty gold sovereigns, instead of you!'

So the shoemaker was paid after all for the shoes he made; but the villager since then has always paid promptly for his shoes, and Mr Mayor has never made bets again.

THE SIX LAZY BROTHERS
AND PRINCESS GOLDENLOCKS

Once upon a time there lived a nobleman who had six sons. They were handsome lads as strong and straight as the beech trees in the grove, but, alas, so very lazy, that the servants even had to feed them! The effort of lifting a spoon or glass to their lips was too great.

At first their wealthy father good-naturedly put up with their idle ways, but he often reminded them that he would not live for ever and that they must learn to fend for themselves. Then came the time when hunger spread through the country and even the father of the six lazy brothers was struck by hardship. He called his sons to him and said:

'My sons, you have been idle for long enough; the time has come for you to mend your ways. Here are one hundred gold sovereigns for each one of you; it is all I have left and all I can give you. Go out into the world and learn to work. I do not want you to return until you have all mastered some kind of trade.'

He accompanied them to the door.

The lads could see they would have to obey. They thanked their father for the sovereigns, kissed his hand and set forth into the world. At first they travelled together, but on the third day the eldest stopped by a cross-roads and said:

'Brothers, we shall not get anywhere like this. We must part and go our separate ways. In a year and a day we shall meet again at this very spot to tell each other how we have fared.'

'You are right,' the others agreed, embraced affectionately, then scattered each in a different direction.

Whilst five of the brothers were still wandering here and there, the eldest came to a town. The main square was crowded with people.

'What is happening here?' the eldest brother asked the citizen next to him.

'Can't you see for yourself?' the citizen replied, pointing to the top of a tall tree. A strong man was swinging from branch to branch, climbing so easily and so nimbly, it was a joy to watch.

'He can climb walls, spires and roof-tops just as cleverly,' the citizen added.

The eyes of the eldest brother shone bright with admiration.

'If only I could climb like him,' he sighed, and when the climber ended his demonstration and slid down to the ground, the youth went over to him and asked:

'Please sir, would you teach me your trade?'

'Why not,' the climber answered. 'If you pay me well, I will teach you all I know!'

'Certainly! I will give you all I have,' the eldest brother assured him.

'How much is that?'

'One hundred sovereigns.'

'A hundred sovereigns is not much, but it will do,' the climber said and took the eldest as his apprentice. He led him from town to town, teaching him his trade, till the lad could climb as nimbly as himself.

Whilst the eldest was learning to climb, the second brother reached a town where a huge crowd had gathered in the main square.

'What is happening here?' the second brother asked the citizen nearest to him.

'Can't you see for yourself?' the citizen replied, pointing to the able fellow in the centre of the crowd. He was sitting on a stool, busily welding and repairing all sorts of broken and damaged things people brought to him. Whether they were made from wood or iron, from glass or gold, he could mend them. Whatever he touched looked as good as new again, even if a moment before it had been completely useless.

The eyes of the second brother shone with admiration.

'If only I could weld and mend as he can!' he sighed, and when the welder had mended all the articles which were before him the brother went over to him and said boldly:

'Please sir, would you teach me your trade?'

'Why not,' the welder replied. 'If you pay me well, I will teach you all I know!'

'Certainly!' the second brother assured him. 'I will give you all I have, one hundred sovereigns!'

'A hundred sovereigns is not much, but it will do,' the welder agreed and took the second brother as his apprentice. They travelled from town to town, and the lad worked hard and learned well till he was as skilled as his master.

Whilst the second brother was busily learning to weld and to mend, the third brother came to a forest where he met an archer — but what an archer! He was such a marksman that he could shoot down anything he fancied from any distance, even a little fly a whole mile away! The third brother could not take his eyes away from such a crack shot.

'If only I could shoot as well as he can,' he sighed, and when the archer had used up all his arrows, he went over to him and said boldly:

'Please sir, would you teach me your profession?'

'Why not,' the archer replied. 'If you pay me well, I shall teach you all I know.'

'Certainly I will pay,' the third brother assured him and gave the marksman the hundred sovereigns.

The archer took on the youth as his pupil; he travelled with him from one forest to another, and taught him to shoot till even the lad could hit a fly a mile off.

Whilst the third brother was busy learning to shoot, the fourth brother roamed the world until one day he met a fiddler, but what a fiddler! When he played on his fiddle, everyone just had to dance. Even the unconscious and the dead would wake up and would hop about gaily when they heard his tune.

When the fiddler stopped playing, the youth went over to him and asked boldly:

'Please sir, would you teach me your profession?'

'Why not,' the fiddler replied, 'that is if you can pay me.'

The fourth brother gave the fiddler his hundred sovereigns and the musician taught him to play until he too was capable of waking the dead with his tunes.

Whilst the fourth brother was learning to play the fiddle, the fifth brother came across a very clever man who was a shipbuilder — but what a shipbuilder! Not only could his vessels sail on water, they could also be driven on dry land. The young watched the craftsman at work with great admiration and eventually asked him:

'Please sir, would you teach me your craft?'

'Why not,' answered the shipbuilder, 'that is if you pay me well.'

So the fifth brother gave his hundred sovereigns to the shipbuilder, who taught him how to make ships which not only sail on the sea, but also travel on land.

This is how five of the brothers mastered their chosen trades. I expect you are wondering what became of the sixth one? He did not waste his time either. While his brothers were busy learning to climb, weld, shoot, play the fiddle and build ships, he reached a certain town, where in the main square he saw a huge crowd of people. An old man sat in the centre with a sack over his head, and he answered any questions the people cared to ask him. He was a seer and a prophet; he could find anything that had been lost, he could guess everything about the past and could foretell the future. The lad's eyes shone in admiration and eventually he went over to him and asked:

'Please sir, would you teach me your profession?'

'Why not,' said the seer, 'If you can pay me well.'

So for the payment of a hundred sovereigns the youngest of the six brothers became the pupil of the seer and he studied and worked until he was as skilled as his master.

A year passed, and the brothers bade their teachers farewell and set off on their return journey home. Exactly a year and a day since they had parted, they met again as arranged at the crossroads.

'What did you learn, brothers?' the eldest one greeted them. 'I myself am now a climber by profession and I have no equal in the whole wide world.'

'I am a welder by trade, who can weld and mend anything under the sun,' said the second brother.

'I am an archer, who can hit a fly a mile away,' said the third.

'I am a fiddler, who can even make the dead rise and dance,' said the fourth.

'I am a shipbuilder, and my vessels sail not only on high seas, but also on dry land,' said the fifth.

'You will all prove very useful,' said the sixth and the youngest, 'for I am a seer and a prophet and I need your help.'

'How can we help you, brother?' the others asked.

'Wait and I will tell you,' and the seer went on to explain: 'I learnt from the books of my master that in the middle of the ocean there is a golden castle which hangs from four golden chains over a certain island. An evil dragon is keeping Princess Goldenlocks a prisoner in this castle. A big, golden bell hangs at the end of a golden chain which is attached to the castle and which reaches the ground. If anyone touches the chains or the castle, the bell starts to ring, and continues until it wakes the dragon. When that happens, the dragon flies out of the castle, circles round it and burns any living thing with his fiery breath. But never mind that now. First we must get to the island in the middle of the ocean.'

'Leave that to me,' said the shipbuilder and in just a day he built the most beautiful ship for his brothers, a ship which could race the wind on sea and on land. The brothers gaily stepped on deck and in a while sighted a green island in the middle of the blue sea. A castle made of gold was hanging from gold chains above the island. A gold bell hung from the castle on a gold chain which reached the ground.

'Now one of us must find a way into the castle to rescue Princess Goldenlocks.'

'Leave that to me,' said the climber. He waited till it was dark, and then very stealthily crept to the bell and carefully wound a coil of rope round its clapper, so it could not raise the alarm. After that he did not hesitate, but swung himself up on to the golden chain and climbed up into the castle. He jumped inside through the window of one of the many rooms, and a moment later entered the Princess Goldenlock's bedroom. She looked so beautiful asleep on her bed of lace and silks, that the climber just stood and stared, forgetting why he had come. Then he came to his senses and, gathering the princess into his arms, he climbed down the chain with her, but so carefully and so skilfully that the princess did not even wake. When the brothers saw her, they too stood like statues, staring with wonder at her loveliness. They would most probably still be standing there today if the youngest one had not urged them on:

'Hurry, brothers, we must be away! In a moment the dawn will break, the dragon will wake and we shall be in real trouble!'

The shipbuilder turned the helm and the ship sailed away faster than the wind. A little later on the bright sun rose over the horizon. Suddenly and unexpectedly it seemed as if an enormous cloud veiled the sun, for the brightness was gone. But it was no cloud!

'The dragon is after us!' the seer exclaimed. 'Now one of us must shoot him down with an arrow which has to pierce a small white circle on his chest. It is the only spot where it is possible to penetrate his thick skin.'

'Leave this to me,' the archer exclaimed. He took out his crossbow, aimed and waited till the dragon flew right over the ship, and then fired. The arrow struck the white circle on the dragon's chest, and went into his heart. But, alas, the body of the dead monster crashed from a great height on to the ship's deck. A high wave swept the princess overboard, as the ship shuddered and broke in two.

'Leave this to me,' the welder shouted and set to work. Before the other brothers had recovered from shock and before the seer, who had jumped in after the princess, and found her in the depths of the sea, the ship was repaired and could continue on her journey. But things did not go so well for Princess Goldenlocks. The youngest brother had saved her from the green depths of the sea, but the poor princess had stopped breathing.

'Leave this to me,' said the fiddler, remembering his fiddle, and he began to play. With the first tune Princess Goldenlocks opened her eyes, with the second tune she sat up and with the third she rose and was as spiritely as ever before. She danced gaily with the brothers until the fiddler put his fiddle away.

So their adventure had a happy ending.

One fine evening the ship came to a stop in front of a house where the elderly father of the six brothers lived. At first the old man did not believe that the six lively young men really were his six lazy sons. He was even more surprised when Princess Goldenlocks stepped off the ship.

'This is the princess we rescued,' the eldest son explained. 'We all like her very much and want to marry her, but we do not know which one of us deserves her most. Please Father, you decide!'

Then they told him what they had done on her behalf:

'I built a ship which took us right to the Golden castle,' said the ship-builder

'I climbed up the golden chain into the castle, and carried the princess down again!' said the climber.

'I slew the dragon who was pursuing us,' said the archer.

'I saved the ship by welding and mending it after the dragon had broken it in half,' said the welder.

'I brought the princess back to life after she fell in the sea and stopped breathing,' said the fiddler.

'I was the one who told you about the princess in the first place, and then rescued her from the depths of the ocean,' said the seer and prophet.

The poor father could not make up his mind which of his sons most deserved the princess. They were all equally worthy, for the princess could not have been saved without any one of them. In the end he turned to her and asked:

'The wisest thing is to ask you to decide. Princess Goldenlocks, which of my sons do you like the most?'

'It is a difficult choice to make,' the princess answered blushingly. 'But as I must choose, I should like to marry the youngest one. To make it up to the others I invite them all to the palace of my father, the King of France. You see, I have five other lovely sisters a little older than myself, and I am sure my father would gladly give them in marriage to such fine brave young men as your sons.'

This proved to be true! When they all reached the royal palace and brought the rescued Princess Goldenlocks before the French king, he was so overjoyed and so grateful that he gladly agreed to give his other five daughters to the remaining brothers. Three days later there was a wedding, a most splendid wedding for, after all, it is not every day that six lazy brothers marry six lovely princesses!

HOW OLD TOM TRIED TO BARTER

Once upon a time there was an old man called Tom, who lived with his old wife Martha in a tiny cottage. They had a little garden, owned a small part of a field, and a cow in their stable — and that was all. No wonder they hardly had enough to live on.

'Why don't you try your hand at bartering, Tom?' Martha suggested one day to her husband. 'Just look at our neighbour, how lucky he has been, and how much money he has made! Go on, have a go!'

'I would rather not,' Tom replied. 'I may strike a bad bargain and then you would be cross with me.'

'Of course I would not be cross,' Martha assured him. 'I know it isn't always possible to make a profit. Tomorrow is market day in town. Take our cow and see what you can exchange her for.'

So it came to pass that the very next day old Tom and his cow set off to the market. On their way they met a man with a goat.

'Where are you going, Tom?' asked the man with the goat.

'To the market, to barter our cow!' Tom answered.

'Would you like to exchange it for this fine goat?' the man with the goat suggested.

'Why not?' Tom thought, and swapped his cow for the goat.

He continued on his way towards the town, leading the goat on a piece of string. After a while he met a man with a goose in a basket.

'Where are you going, Tom?' asked the man with the goose in his basket.

'To the market, to barter this goat!' Tom replied.

'Would you like to exchange it for this fat goose?' suggested the man with the goose in his basket.

'Why not?' Tom thought, and swapped the goat for the goose.

With the goose in the basket he continued on his way towards the town. After a while he met a man with a cockerel under his arm.

'Where are you going, Tom?' asked the man with the cockerel under his arm.

'To the market, to barter this goose,' Tom replied.

'Would you like to exchange it for this young bird?' the man with the cockerel under his arm suggested.

'Why not?' thought Tom, and swapped the goose for the cockerel.

With the cockerel under his arm he continued on his way towards the town. After a while he met an old woman. She was sweeping horse droppings into a sack.

'Where are you going, Tom?' asked the old woman with the sackful of horse droppings.

'To the market, to barter this cockerel,' Tom replied.

'Would you like to exchange it for a sackful of fresh horse manure for your garden?' asked the old woman with the sack of horse droppings.

'Why not?' thought Tom, and swapped the cockerel for the sackful of horse manure.

With the sack of horse droppings over his shoulder, he finally reached town. In the market he met his neighbour. 'What are you doing here, Tom?' asked the neighbour. 'Don't tell me you have come to barter!'

'Certainly I have, neighbour,' Tom replied. 'I have already bartered our cow for a goat!'

'Oh Tom, you are a fool! A cow for a goat.' The neighbour roared with laughter. 'Just you wait and see how your Martha will scold you!'

'No she won't, neighbour!' Tom defended himself. 'Especially when I tell her I bartered the goat for a goose.'

'Oh, Tom, you are a fool! A goat for a goose!' The neighbour roared with laughter. 'Just you wait and see how your Martha will scold you!'

'No she won't neighbour!' Tom defended himself. 'Especially when I tell her I bartered the goose for a cockerel.'

'Oh Tom, you are a fool! A goose for a cockerel!' The neighbour roared with laughter. 'Just you wait and see how your Martha will scold you!'

'No she won't neighbour!' Tom defended himself. 'Especially when I tell her I bartered the cockerel for a sackful of horse manure for her garden.'

'Oh Tom, you really are a fool! A cockerel for a sackful of horse droppings!' The neighbour roared with laughter. 'Just you wait and see how your Martha will scold you!'

'No she won't neighbour!' Tom defended himself. 'I will wager two hundred gold sovereigns on that!'

'Done!' cried the neighbour. 'But if she scolds you with just one little word, you will lose your two hundred gold sovereigns. If she does not scold you, I will give the two hundred sovereigns to you.'

They sealed their bargain with a hearty handshake and went to the cottage to see old Martha.

'Well Tom, did you have a go at bartering?' old Martha asked, waiting at the door.

'I certainly did, Martha,' Tom replied. 'First of all I bartered our cow for a goat.'

'That is better,' Martha was pleased. 'We never had enough hay to feed a cow.'

'That is not all,' Tom continued. 'Then I bartered our goat for a goose.'

'That is better!' Martha was pleased. 'We need feathers for our featherbed.'

'That is not all,' Tom continued. 'Then I bartered our goose for a cockerel.'

'That is better!' Martha was pleased. 'Now we shall have someone to wake us in the morning.'

'But that is not all,' Tom continued. 'Then I bartered our cockerel for a sackful of horse droppings.'

'That is even better!' Martha said happily. 'We need manure for our garden. It will help the roses to grow!'

'So you see, neighbour, my Martha did not scold me,' Tom said, smiling broadly.

'You are right, Tom, she did not tell you off,' the neighbour sourly admitted, and counted the two hundred gold sovereigns out on their table. Old Tom and old Martha bought a fine cow, a goose, a goat and a cockerel with the money. And to crown it all they soon had a garden full of beautiful roses.

HOW THE LITTLE BOY
AND THE LITTLE GIRL
WENT FOR A WALK IN THE MUD
OR THE LONGEST STORY
IN THE WORLD

Once upon a time there was a little boy and a little girl, and one day they decided to go for a walk. As it had just been pouring with rain, there was mud everywhere. And as there was mud everywhere, the path where the little boy and the little girl were walking was muddy too. And because the path was so very muddy, the little girl's feet suddenly slid from under her and — oops! — she fell smack into the mud on her little bottom.

The little boy then felt sorry for the little girl, so he caught hold of her with both his hands and began to pull her to her feet. As he was pulling her, his feet suddenly slid from under him and — oops! — he fell smack into the mud on his little bottom.

Then the little girl felt sorry for the little boy, so she caught hold of him with both her hands and began to pull him to his feet. As she was pulling him, her feet suddenly slid from under her and — oops! — she fell smack into the mud on her little bottom.

And so it went on:

oops! — he sat smack in the mud,

oops! — she sat smack in the mud,

oops! — his bottom in,

oops! — her bottom in,

oops! — he fell,

oops! — she fell,

oops! — his turn,

oops! — her turn,

and oops! . . .

and oops! — . . .

And if they are still alive, they must still be in that mud, going
oops! —
and oops! —
and oops! —
and oops! . . .

Significance of Defects in Welded Structures

SIGNIFICANCE OF DEFECTS IN WELDED STRUCTURES

Proceedings of the Japan-U.S. Seminar, 1973, Tokyo

Edited by
TAKESHI KANAZAWA **ALBERT S. KOBAYASHI**

UNIVERSITY OF TOKYO PRESS

© UNIVERSITY OF TOKYO PRESS, 1974
UTP 3050–68076–5149
Printed in Japan

ISBN   0–86008–114–1

Contents

Program of Technical Session ix
List of Participants... xi
Opening Address
    T. KANAZAWA xiii
Closing Address
    A. S. KOBAYASHI xv

SESSION I

—Present Status of Non-Destructive Inspection Techniques—

Detectable Weld Defects by Current NDT Code
    S. MIYOSHI 3
Status of Non-Destructive Inspection Techniques with Special References to
  Welding Defects
    P. F. PACKMAN... 9
Acoustic Emission Research in Japan for Flaw Detection in Weld
    M. ONOE 22
Recent Developments in Acoustic Emission as Applied to Welding Defects
    K. ONO 48
Non-Destructive Testing for Welded Joints of Huge Hull Construction
    S. KAKU 59
Cracking at the Toe of Welded Joint and Acoustic Emission
    N. OGURA 62
Discussions in Session I... 65

SESSION II

—Fracture Mechanics Approach to the Initiation of Cracks from Welding Defects and Their Growth—

An Application of Fracture Mechanics to Hydrogen Induced Cracking
    K. SATOH AND M. TOYODA 71
Effect of Hydrogen on Fracture Toughness of Steels
    M. FUKAGAWA, M. OHYAMA, H. OKABAYASHI AND M. HIGUCHI............ 82
On the Role of Defects in Crack Initiation in Welded in Structures
    A. J. McEVILY, JR... 96
Micro-Cracking in Consumable-Nozzle Electro-Slag Weld Metal
    T. KUNIHIRO AND H. NAKAJIMA 105
COD Test for Girth Weldment of Linepipe
    K. MATSUSITA, N. NISHIYAMA AND J. TSUBOI 110

Influence of Fatigue Damage of Notch Tip on Brittle Fracture
  N. TANIGUCHI, I. SOYA AND K. MINAMI 114
Discussions in Session II 118

SESSION   III

—Fundamental Researches on Significance of Defects—
(Static and Dynamic)

A Simple Procedure for Estimating Stress Intensity Factor in Region of High
  Stress Gradient
  A. S. KOBAYASHI 127
Brittle Fracture Initiation Characteristics of Twin Notches
  K. IKEDA, K. NAGAI, H. MAENAKA AND K. KAJIMOTO................... 144
COD Approach to Brittle Fracture Initiation in Welded Structures
  S. MACHIDA 156
Some Results of Dynamic COD-Test
  K. NISHIOKA AND H. IWANAGA...................................... 173
Crack Opening Displacement Testing by Use of Acoustic Emission
  M. ARII, H. KASHIWAYA AND T. YANUKI 177
Discussions in Session III.. 182

SESSION   IV

—Fundamental Researches on Significance of Defects—
(Fatigue)

An Analysis of Crack Propagation in Welded Structures
  H. MIYAMOTO, T. MIYOSHI AND S. FUKUDA 189
The Fracture Mechanics Approach to Fatigue
  A. J. McEVILY, JR. 203
Fracture Analysis of Flaws in Welded Bridge Structures
  J. W. FISHER AND G. R. IRWIN 213
Fatigue Strength of Defective Butt Welded Joints
  K. IIDA 224
Fatigue Strength of Fillet Welded Joints of Oblique Crossing Members
  H. INOUE 235
Some Recent Japanese Results in the Fracture Mechanics Approaches to Fatigue
  Crack Problems Related to Welded Structures
  H. KITAGAWA 248
Elastic-Plastic Fracture Mechanics Approach to Fatigue Limit of Welded
  Structures
  A. NISHIOKA AND S. USAMI 260
Deflection-Controlled Fatigue Strength of Fillet Welded Joints with Doubling
  Plates
  K. KISHIMOTO 267
Discussions in Session IV.. 273

SESSION V

—Applications of Fracture Mechanics to Welded Structures—

A Brittle Fracture Criterion Based on the Plastic Zone Size
F. KOSHIGA 283
Effects of Plastic Constraint on the Fracture Mode and COD
A. OTSUKA AND T. MIYATA 292
Present Status on the Evaluation of Fracture Criteria for Structural Steels
T. KANAZAWA AND H. KIHARA 308
Fracture-Control Guidelines for Welded Steel Ship Hulls
S. T. ROLFE 318
Combined Effects of Weld-Induced Residual Stresses and Flaws on the Fracture
Strength of Ti-5Al-2.5Sn
L. R. HALL 340
On the Brittle Fracture Initiation Characteristics of 9% Ni Steel for Spherical
LNG Tank
H. YAJIMA 355
Effects of Notch Size, Angular Distortion and Residual Stress on Brittle Fracture
Initiation of High Strength Steel Welded Joints
K. TERAI AND S. SUSEI 362
Discussions in Session V 367

SESSION VI

—Recommended Future Works—

A Systems Analysis of Significance of Weld Defects
K. MASUBUCHI AND N. YURIOKA 373
Surface Flaw in 9%-Ni Steel Plate under Repeated Load
T. KANAZAWA 392
Determination of Fracture Toughness of Heavy Thick High Strength Steels for
Long Span Bridges
K. IKEDA 395
Toughness Near the Fine Grained Fusion Line of High Strength Steel Developed
for High Heat Input Welding
N. TANIGUCHI, K. YAMATO, A. NAKASHIMA, K. MINAMI AND S. KANAZAWA 397
Applied Fracture Mechanics for Designing Aluminum Alloy 5083-0 Large
Spherical Tank for LNG Carrier
K. TERAI AND S. SUSEI 403
Discussions in Session VI 407

AUTHOR INDEX 415

....

....

....

Program of Technical Session

1. Place
   The Diamond Hall in the building of the Diamond Co. Ltd., Kasumigaseki, Chiyoda-ku, Tokyo

2. Themes of Sessions and Session Officers

   Session I "Present Status of Non-Destructive Inspection Techniques"
   Chairman: Prof. K. Iida
   Co-Chairman: Prof. J. W. Fisher

   Session II "Fracture Mechanics Approach to the Initiation of Cracks from
               Welding Defects and Their Growth"
   Chairman: Prof. A. S. Kobayashi
   Co-Chairman: Prof. A. Otsuka

   Session III "Fundamental Researches on Significance of Defects —Static and
               Dynamic—"
   Chairman: Prof. T. Kanazawa
   Co-Chairman: Dr. L. R. Hall

   Session IV "Fundamental Researches on Significance of Defects —Fatigue—"
   Chairman: Prof. S. T. Rolfe
   Co-Chairman: Prof. K. Satoh

   Session V "Applications of Fracture Mechanics to Welded Structures"
   Chairman: Prof. H. Miyamoto
   Co-Chairman: Prof. P. F. Packman

   Section VI "Recommended Future Works"
   Chairman: Prof. A. J. McEvily
   Co-Chairman: Prof. M. Onoe

3. Program

Monday, Oct. 15, 1973	17:00–19:00	Registration and Opening Reception
Tuesday, Oct. 16	8:55– 9:00	Opening Address
	9:00–12:00	Technical Session I
	14:00–17:00	Technical Session II
Wednesday, Oct. 17	9:00–11:50	Technical Session III
	11:50–18:30	Technical Visit to Products Research and Development Laboratory, Nippon Steel Corporation

Thursday, Oct. 18	9:00–12:00	Technical Session IV
	14:00–17:30	Technical Session V
Friday, Oct. 19	9:00–12:00	Technical Visit to Technical Research Institute, Ishikawajima-Harima Heavy Ind. Ltd.
	14:00–16:55	Technical Session VI
	16:55–17:00	Closing Address
	18:00–20:00	Farewell Party

List of Participants

FISHER, J. W.
Professor
Department of Civil Engineering,
Lehigh University, Bethlehem, Pennsylvania, U.S.A.

FUKAGAWA, M.
Chief Research Engineer
Research Institute, Ishikawajima-Harima Heavy Industries Co., Ltd., Tokyo,
Japan

HALL, L. R.
Senior Scientist
The Boeing Aerospace Company,
Washington, U.S.A.

IIDA, K.
Professor
Department of Naval Architecture,
University of Tokyo, Tokyo, Japan

IKEDA, K.
Manager
Structural Engineering Laboratory,
Kobe Steel, Ltd., Amagasaki, Japan

INOUE, H.
Chief Researcher
Ship Structure Division, Ship Research
Institute, Tokyo, Japan

IWANAGA, H.
Chief Research Engineer
Central Research Laboratory, Sumitomo
Metal Industries, Ltd., Amagasaki,
Japan

KAKU, S.
Principal Surveyor
Hull Department, Nippon Kaiji Kyokai, Tokyo, Japan

KANAZAWA, T.
Professor
Department of Naval Architecture,
University of Tokyo, Tokyo, Japan

KISHIMOTO, K.
Chief Researcher
Chiba Laboratory, Mitsui Shipbuilding
& Engineering Co., Ltd., Chiba, Japan

KITAGAWA, H.
Professor
Institute of Industrial Science, University of Tokyo, Tokyo, Japan

KOBAYASHI, A. S.
Professor
Department of Mechanical Engineering,
University of Washington, Seattle,
Washington, U.S.A.

KOSHIGA, F.
Manager
Technical Research Center, Nippon
Kokan K.K., Kawasaki, Japan

KUNIHIRO, T.
Manager
Technical Research Laboratory, Hitachi Shipbuilding & Engineering Co.,
Ltd., Osaka, Japan

MACHIDA, S.
Associate Professor
Department of Naval Architecture,
University of Tokyo, Tokyo, Japan

MASUBUCHI, K.
Professor
Department of Ocean Engineering,
Massachusetts Institute of Technology,
Cambridge, Massachusetts, U.S.A.

McEVILY, A. J.
Professor and Chairman
Department of Metallurgy, University
of Connecticut, Storrs, Connecticut,
U.S.A.

MIYAMOTO, H.
Professor
Department of Precision Machinery

Engineering, University of Tokyo, Tokyo, Japan

MIYATA, T.
Associate Professor
Department of Metallurgical Engineering, Nagoya University, Nagoya, Japan

MIYOSHI, S.
Chief Engineer
Atomic Energy Engineering Department, Fuji Electric Co., Ltd., Tokyo, Japan

MIYOSHI, T.
Associate Professor
Department of Precision Machinery Engineering, University of Tokyo, Tokyo, Japan

NISHIOKA, A.
Senior Researcher
Hitachi Research Laboratory, Hitachi Ltd., Hitachi, Japan

OGURA, N.
Professor
Institute of Material Science & Technology, Yokohama National University, Yokohama, Japan

ONO, K.
Associate Professor
Materials Department, University of California at Los Angeles, Los Angeles, California, U.S.A.

ONOE, M.
Professor
Institute of Industrial Science, University of Tokyo, Tokyo, Japan

OTSUKA, A.
Professor
Department of Metallurgical Engineering, Nagoya University, Nagoya, Japan

PACKMAN, P. F.
Professor
Department of Engineering Materials, Vanderbilt University, Nashville, Tennessee, U.S.A.

ROLFE, S. T.
Professor
Department of Civil Engineering, University of Kansas, Lawrence, Kansas, U.S.A.

SATOH, K.
Professor
Faculty of Engineering, Osaka University, Osaka, Japan

SUSEI, S.
Manager
Steel Structure Manufacturing Division, Kakogawa Works, Kawasaki Heavy Industries, Ltd., Kakogawa, Japan

TANIGUCHI, M.
Research Engineer
Products Research & Development Laboratory, Nippon Steel Corporation, Sagamihara, Japan

TERAI, K.
Manager
Welding Research Department, Kawasaki Heavy Industries, Ltd., Kobe, Japan

TOYODA, M.
Research Associate
Welding Research Institute, Osaka University, Osaka, Japan

TSUBOI, J.
Manager
Research Laboratories, Kawasaki Steel Co. Ltd., Chiba, Japan

YAJIMA, H.
Senior Research Engineer
Nagasaki Technical Institute, Mitsubishi Heavy Industries, Ltd., Nagasaki, Japan

YANUKI, T.
Engineering Staff
Heavy Apparatus Engineering Laboratory, Tokyo Shibaura Electric Co., Ltd., Kawasaki, Japan

Opening address

T. KANAZAWA

It is my great pleasure to present the opening address for this Japan-U.S. Seminar entitled "Significance of Defects in Welded Structures". First of all, I wish to extend my sincere welcome to the distinguished scientists and engineers who have assembled here to participate this seminar.

The purpose of organizing this seminar is to exchange most recent developments by Japanese and U.S. scientists and engineers and to identify current research problems as well as future research topics associated with the techniques for assessing the significance of defects in welded structures.

For the past decade Japanese progress in fracture research and associated technology has been made mainly on low and medium strength steel structures such as marine structures and storage tanks. The progress in the United States, on the other hand, has been concentrated on high strength welded alminium, titanium and steel components in aerospace structures.

Large quantities of scientific and technical information on fracture and fracture related research works thus exist in the two countries, but these results are used to study only structure of exceptional importance or cases of special difficulty. The enventual goal of such fracture research is to facilitate the economic design and construction of fracture-proof structures, and thus one of the most important tasks is to demonstrate that the results of fracture research can be applied to the design and fabrication of structures. Unfortunately, few attempts have been made to codify the information in a way it can be readily used.

Thus the establishment of a rational acceptance standard of defects in welded structures is one of the most important and urgent problems in welded structure technology. Such standards can be derived through the collaboration of researchers in fracture mechanics, welding mechanics and non-destructive testing techniques. At present, no active international organization which promotes this subject exists except for the Sub-commission in the International Institute of Welding which is dominated by the European scientific community.

With the above factors in mind, planning of this seminar was initiated by Prof. Kobayashi and myself for the purpose of bringing the Japanese and United States expertise in this area together to learn, through presentations and active discussions, of the other's research accomplishments. The primary objective at this seminar will be to review the current status and available technical information related to weld defects. By avoiding duplicate research effort through this exhange of information, both sides can then channel their limited resorces in research to unresolved problems of immediate urgency for coming two or three years.

I believe that for both sides, this multidisciplinary seminar will serve as a valuable background toward establishing appropriate technology for assessing the significance of defects in welded structures. This seminar can only attain its goal through active participation of all attendants who, I am confident, will promote mutual understandings and contribute to the development of fracture research and related technology on both sides.

Finally, on behalf of all the participants, I wish to express our sincere gratitutes to the Japan Society for Promotion of Science and the U.S. National Science Foundation who have lent their support to this seminar. Prof. Kobayashi and I wish to express our thanks to all the participants and their related institutions and organizations for their valuable support offered to this seminar.

As the Japanese main organizer, I feel highly honored to open the Japan-U.S. Seminar on Significance of Defects in Welded Structures. Thank you.

Closing address

Λ. S. Κοβαυλεiii

During the past four days we have discussed a wide range of topics ranging from nondestructive testing techniques for weld defect detection, to crack initiation, crack growth from weld defects, and finally a system analysis to evaluate the significance of weld defects. From the point of fracture research, we have discussed hydrogen cracking, effects of residual stress, fatigue, and fracture of ductile and brittle materials. We have also discussed such practical topics as the adequacy of present codes for brittle fracture prevention, fracture test procedures of welding joints, and fracture control guidelines for welded steel hulls.

A pattern which emerged from this seminar is the clear distinction between the two approaches to ductile fracture used by the US and Japanese engineers. While much of the US efforts in ductile fracture research emphasize an extension of linear fracture mechanics and the J-integral concept, the Japanese efforts are concentrated in the COD approach to ductile fracture. The experimental data on the COD criterion accumulated by the Japanese are certainly impressive and deserve serious study by the US investigators.

Another clear distinction is the Japanese use of full scale tests for establishing crack growth and fracture data. This is in contrast to the US approach of using small scale tests, such as DWT and instrumented Charpy tests, to predict the responses of large specimens. The latter is governed by sheer economic facts in the USA. The possibility of a US-Japan cooperative research program, in which information obtained by these two approaches would be compared, could be valuable in establishing a fracture testing procedure of thick ductile plates.

Although we now recognize these distinct differences between the US and Japanese approaches in failure analysis of structures with weld defects, we probably will each continue along our predestined approaches for the immediate future. It would therefore be interesting to reconvene this same group of engineers and scientists to compare our progress along these two diverse procedures in the future. Perhaps such a seminar could be held in Seattle three years hence.

In closing, on behalf of the US participants, I would like to express our sincere gratitude to Profs. Kanazawa, Iida, Machida and the organizing committee who so graciously hosted this seminar in Tokyo. From the immense task of preparing the preprints to the detailed and precise arrangements of running the seminar, Professor Kanazawa and his colleagues set a superb example difficult to match. And finally but not least, the social events of this seminar will be fondly cherished, particularly by the US participants. I would now like to ask the US participants to join me in a standing applause as a token gesture of our gratitude to our Japanese hosts.

SESSION I

PRESENT STATUS OF NON-DESTRUCTIVE INSPECTION TECHNIQUES

Detectable Weld Defects by Current NDT Code

S. MIYOSHI

Atomic Energy Engineering Department, Fuji Electric Co., Ltd.

1. Introduction

Integrity of a weld is assessed on the basis of informations obtained by non-destructive examination (NDE). The reliability of such assessment is thus greatly influenced by the accuracy of the NDE information provided. Ideally, NDE should meet the following two criteria that:

1) All defects contained in the weld can be detected.

2) Geometries, orientations and positions of the defects can be measured exactly.

Obviously, it is next to impossible to satisfy perfectly these two requirements. In order to approach this idealized condition as much as possible non-destructive examinations are carried out by skilled personnel under correct examination conditions. For this reason, all non-destructive examinations are performed in accordance with codes and standards which specify the qualifications of non-destructive examination personnel and examination procedures.

One of such codes is ASME Boiler and Pressure Vessel Code Sec. III, which specifies various non-destructive examination methods and is most widely used through out the world in nuclear industries. Since nuclear industry derives support from various other industries, the influences of the ASME Boiler and Pressure Vessel Code Sec. III is very wide spread in Japan. Some of the results of our studies in non-destructive examination techniques differ with those of the ASME code. In this paper, we will present some comments on the examination techniques and acceptance standards of weld defects of ASME Boiler and Pressure Vessel Code Sec. III.

2. Examination Technique

Examination techniques considered in this paper are selected on the basis of the highest sensitivity and not necessary from the point of view of economical and operational efficiency. The first example deals with radiography where the contrast of a defect

3

appearing in a radiograph is given as

$$\Delta D = 0.43 \; \gamma \; \mu \; \Delta T/(1+n)$$

where ΔD;   contract

             μ;   absorption coefficient

             γ;   gamma number of film

           ΔT;   defect thickness

             n;   scatter ratio

A higher contrast of ΔD from this equation implies a better detectability of a defect for a constant defect thickness of ΔT. Thus a higher film gamma and a larger absorption coefficient result in easier discrimination of a defect. Generally, fine grain and high contrast films with highest contrast are used for radiographing important weldments. Therefore film contrast due to a defect is mainly caused by the absorption coefficient μ, which is a function of radiation energy. For larger absorption coefficient, the radiation source energy which passes through the weldment must be in as low energy range as possible. The maximum voltage of the radiation source or selection of nuclear radiation source are shown in Figs. IX-3337-1 for steel IX-3337-2 for alloys of copper and/or high nickel and IX-3337-3 for aluminum in ASME Boiler and Pressure Vessel Code Sec. III App. IX. For other materials, this source energies are specified as follows.

"The kilovoltage shall be such that the thickness of material being radiographed shall be no less than two times the second half-value thickness"

According to this ASME specification, maximum voltages of 1 MeV and 5.5 MeV should be used for 1"- and 2"-thick steel plates, respectively. These applicable energies appears excessively high when compared with the radiation source energies normally used in Japan. When such high energy sources are used, the defects cannot be readily detected. Perhaps, this may constitute insignificant matter since radiograph quality is always checked by an image of a properly located penetrameter. It is however well known that penetrameter sensitivity does not always coincide with defect sensitivity. There are many examples in which defects cannot be found in radiographs with good penetrameter sensitivity. Therefore the leveled radiation energy is very important and fundamental concern in radiography when used as a non-destructive examination method for internal defects. The same of problem exists in magnetic particle examination of surface defect.

The most important parameter in magnetic particle examination is the magnetizing current for generating the necessary magnetic flux. The leakage flux generated in the defect area in turn retains the magnetic particle on the surface defect. ASME Boiler and Pressure Vessel Code Sec. III App. IX IX-3531 specifies the following.

"This method of examination consists of magnetizing the area to be inspected to near saturation and then applying the examination medium to the surface".

The code, however, does not indicate the grade of "near saturation" but only specifies the magnetizing current. For instance, a minimum of 100 amperes per inch of prod spacing is specified as magnetizing current in prod method.

Although the magnetic field strength generated by magnetizing current is same for various materials, the induced magnetic fluxes are generally not the same. Defect detectability depends mainly upon the magnetic flux density and the optimum flux density

'B' can be derived from the magnetization curve for each steel. The optimum flux density in Japan is defined as 80% of the saturated flux density. Another reference,[1] however, suggests that this value of B is slightly higher than that for a maximum μ for an ideal state of magnetization created for inspection purpose. Similarly, IIW document[2] mention that optimum sensitivity can be obtained at maximum permeability of the material. This document especially advices that such maximum value is not obtained when using the maximum intensity of magnetizing field. Materials are also classified into three classes of magnetic characteristics in France,[3] and particular magnetizing field strength is recommended for each group. ASME Boiler and Pressure Vessel Code Sec.

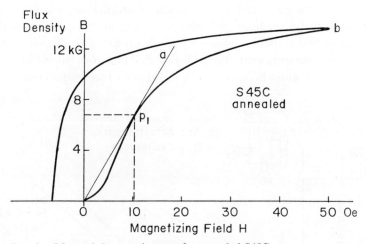

FIG. 1. Magnetic hysteresis curve for annealed S45C.

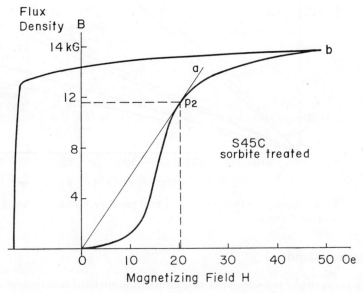

FIG. 2. Magnetic hysteresis curve for heat treated S45C.

III, as mentioned above, disregards the magnetic characteristics of material and thus requires future clasifications. For references, the Japanese procedure for selective optimum intensity of magnetizing field is shown in Figs. 1 and 2.[4] Figure 1 shows the magnetic characteristics of a common carbon steels S45C (annealed) and Fig. 2 shows the magnetic characteristics of the same steel after sorbite heat treatment. The differences in magnetic characteristics are clearly shown. The optimum intensity of magnetizing field 'H' are values corresponding to points P_1 in Fig. 1 and P_2 in Fig. 2; line oa in these figure is a tangent from the origin to the curve ob.

Another problem arises in specifying the optimum magnetizing condition is specified together with the magnetizing current, *i.e.* different magnetizing conditions could exist for different magnetizing device for same indicated magnetizing current. Figure 3 shows relations between meter readings and the actual current.[5] As seen from this figure indicated current of 900 ampere is necessary to obtain meter reading same magnetization for 200 ampere magnetizing current by Device E. Thus both the calibration device and calibration procedure must be specified to avoid such inconsistancies.

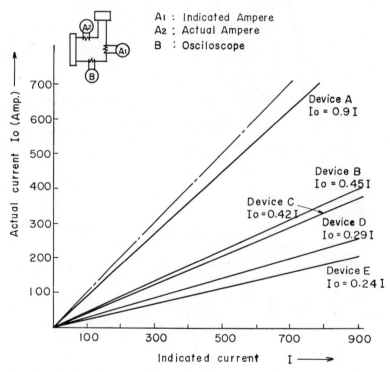

FIG. 3.   Relation between indicated readings from instrument meter and the actual measured current.

3. Acceptance standard

Effectiveness of the non-destructive examination method was then evaluated for the following two cases.

(1)   Production inspection where non-destructive examinations are performed to maintain the weld quality above a predetermined level.

(2)   In-service inspection where examinations are carried out to detect and evaluate the consequence of defects which may occur in service.

ASME Boiler and Pressure Vessel Code Sec. III specifies rules for constructing of nuclear power plant components. The examination procedure and acceptance standard in this code can thus be used in the above case (1). Acceptance standard in the ASME code can be used as a quality control level for weld but level of quality control must be settled first. Since the weld procedure test is performed by welders qualified by welder qualification test and with practical weld procedure be reasonably weld quality can be reasonably measured by the weld procedure test.

Judging from our experiences, the weld quality of weld procedure test plate is generally very good with very small defects if any. The acceptance standard specified in ASME Boiler and Pressure Vessel Code Sec. III NB-5300 in comparison allows larger defects. For instance, a maximum length of acceptable slag inclusion detected by radiography is;

(1)   1/4 inch for thickness up to 3/4 inch inclusive

(2)   (1/3)t for thickness from 3/4 inch to 2.1/4 inch inclusive

(3)   3/4 inch for thickness over 2.1/4 inch.

Detection of such large defect obviously implies a change in weld procedure. These changes may also be due to some differences in environmental condition between weld procedure test weld and practical weld. These acceptable defect sizes are too large and are easily detectable except for cracks by ordinary NDE method. Firstly, it is very difficult to detect cracks by radiography and thus ultrasonic examination method must be used simultaneously to increase the detectability of crack. Yet the combined use of these two methods cannot detect hair crack such as microfissure in most cases. The existence of microfissure, on the other hand, can sometimes be presumed from the existence of fine slag inclusion in the radiography since microfissure are often the generated by the same conditions with cause fine slag. This fact shows that slag inclusion, though very fine, is a very important defect in evaluating weld quality. If only large slag inclusions were considered since fine slag inclusion has no direct connection with failures in weld, there are a risk overlooking some low quality level weld which often accompanies fine slags.

4. Conclusion

Defect existing in weld cannot be predicted nor detected one hundred percent by non-destructive examination techniques. We must, however, do our best to find as many defects as possible and thus use the most sensitive non-destructive examination procedure available to us. Acceptance standard should thus be selected so that weld quality can be evaluated at each fabrication stage.

REFERENCES

1.   Bezer, H. J., " Magnetic Particle Inspection Techniques and their Applications in the U. K.," Brit. J. of NDT. Jan., 2/12 (1971).

2.   " Detection of Sub-surface Defects in Welds using Magnetic Particle Method," *Int. Inst. Weld.*, Document IIW V–424–69/OE.

3.   Perrin, R., "Application des methodes magnetoscopique au controle des pieces coulees a modeles perdus," *Proc. for 3rd World Conference on Investment Casting.* Apr. (1972).

4.   Murakami, Y., " Formation of Defect Indication by Dry Magnetic Powder," *The Japanese Society for Non-Destructive Inspection, No. 3 Research Committee*, Doc. NDI 3403 (1971).

5.   Miyoshi, S., " Detectability of Defects by Prod Magnetization," *The Japanese Society for Non-Destructive Inspection, No. 3 Research Committee*, Doc. NDI 3235 (1968).

Status of Non-Destructive Inspection Techniques with Special References to Welding Defects

P. F. PACKMAN

Department of Material Sciences and Engineering, Vanderbilt University

1. Introduction

The conventional design process for welded structures assumes that the strength values given by tensile tests of typical welds are representative of the properties of the material he will use in his completed structure. He further assumes that the assembled component will be inspected and that the presence of defects that cause significant deviations from the design strength values will be detected and eliminated prior to actual use of the component. The requirements for inspection are different in each case depending upon the particular type of material, thickness, configuration, and intended use.

The designer recognizes that the presence of defects can significantly reduce the strength of his component and uses the inspection as an acceptance criterion following code limits to determine the validity of his weld. The significance of defects in welds and base material on the service life of welded components are largely misunderstood or misinterpreted by practicing engineers as shown by many inspection codes establishing acceptability limits.[1] Great significance is placed on the elimination of some types of defects while others, perhaps more critical, are ignored.

The range of weld defects that can be produced is large and almost every type of defect has been shown to be hazardous under one set of conditions or another. Weld defects can be divided into roughly two classes: (1) defects that are metallurgical, or geometrical in nature that have geometric configuration that result in relatively mild stress concentration effects upon loading, and (2) defects that are crack-like in nature that result in high concentrations of stress upon loading. Typical defects in the first class are: localized arc strikes, local heat affected zones, burn through, surface creasing, crater pits, misalignment of the joint, incomplete fusion, lack of penetration, overlap, porosity, sink or concavity, slag inclusions, undercut weld reinforcement. Typical defects of the second class are: hot cracking, cold cracking microfissures, base metal cracking, lack of penetration, hairline cracks, cracking under fusion crater pits, or arc strikes.

It should be recognized that upon the application of a few stress cycles, the originally

9

mild stress concentration may initiate fatigue cracks that then propagate into the weld or base material. However, this would normally occur after an inspection had been completed and may only be detectable during a second inspection or in the field.

2. Minimum Flaw Detection Capabilities

The use of fracture mechanics-NDT design criterion for critical components has altered the requirements for NDT, both in the preproduction and production inspection process. The fracture mechanics concepts predict when a part containing a flaw will fail or predict the rate of growth of an existing flaw. This then requires the quantification of the NDT process to determine the largest flaw that can exist in a welded component and *yet be overlooked*. The fact that the part is to be designed with the basic premise that flaws do exist and will not grow to critical size within the lifetime of the structure requires detailed information on the size of flaws that can be reliably detected and which cannot be detected. The inverse square root relationship of residual static strength and flaw size can be used to determine what is the criticality of the flaw in the part underload. Assuming a semicircular flaw of length $2c$ and depth a, Table 1 lists the critical size of the flaw that must be detected in order to ensure that failure will not occur below the uniaxial yield strength σ_{TY}. Tensile yield strengths and plane strain K_{IC} values are given as those typical of the material and obtained from numerous sources. Critical flaw sizes range from 0.030" for Titanium alloy 6Al-6V-2Sn at 180 ksi yield to .99" for 2024-T3511 Aluminum extrusion. Parts containing flaws larger than this value, loaded so as to produce plane strain conditions, will fail at gross stresses lower than the tensile yield strength.

It is important to note that these values of initial flaw size are based on the monotonic residual static strength. If the part had to withstand some particular fatigue history, then initial crack sizes considerably smaller than the size given in Table 1 would have to be detected. This would ensure that the cyclic subcritical crack growth would not cause failure during the operating lifetime. Typical aircraft design would require crack growth allowables of 5:1 with the residual strength at 3 cyclic lifetimes equal to 0.8 σ_{TY}.[2]

When knowledge of the initial flaw size, shape, and orientation as determined by the NDT process is available, the techniques of fracture mechanics can be used to estimate the remaining life of the component. Because the assumptions of fracture mechanics use a crack-like defect geometry, emphasis is placed on the ability of the NDT process to detect, measure, and locate these cracklike defects. Hence the major emphasis of this paper will be on detection and measurement of crack-like weld defects.

Two additional factors should be mentioned. First, because the design process involves the determination or the minimization of the probability of failure, the value of the minimum flaw size that can be detected must be given as a probability of detection at a known confidence value, and not just some number. Second, the chosen value of initial (or minimum) flaw size detectable by the NDT process is a design value identical in nature to tensile yield or tensile ultimate.

Accurate knowledge of the sensitivity and reliability capabilities of the major NDT inspection methods is meager. Despite the many studies that have been conducted, the majority of NDT work has concentrated on developing and improving equipment and

TABLE 1. Surface flaw size $2c$ to cause failure at uniaxial yield strength.

Alloy	σ_{TY}	K_{IC}	Surface flaw size 2c (in.)
Aluminum			
2014-T651 (plate)	57	22	.173
2024-T3511 (extrusion)	50	46	.99
2024-T851 (plate)	58	23	.18
2219-T851 (plate)	42	33	.72
2219-T87	48	27	.36
7075-T651 (plate)	77	27	.14
7075-T6511 (extrusion)	72	28	.18
7075-T652 (plate)	78	28	.15
7075-T73511 (extrusion)	58	33	.38
7075-T7352 (forging)	55	31	.37
7178-T651 (plate)	84	23	.09
7178-T6511	82	25	.11
4330V Mod	190	55	.10
4340	230	54	.06
D6AC	250	50	.04
D6AC (salt quench)	205	52	.07
D6AC (oil quench)	205	85	.20
H-11	200	53	.08
H-11	220	24	.014
Marage 250	220	80–100	.15–.29
Marage 300	260	68	.08
9Ni 4Co 20C	180	110–170	.44–1.0
9Ni 4Co 30C	210	115	.35
9Ni 4Co 45C	230	90–110	.18–.22
Titanium			
6Al-4V $(\alpha+\beta)$	150	40–45	.08–.11
6Al-4V (β)	150	60–65	.19–.22
6Al-4V (annealed)	137	50–60	.16–.22
6Al-4V (STA)	158	41	.07
6Al-6V-2Sn $(\beta$ forged)	170	34–40	.05–.07
6Al-6V-2Sn $(\alpha+\beta)$	180	30–35	.03–.04
6Al-6V-2Sn (β)	180	40–45	.05–.07
6Al-6V-2Sn (annealed)	150	35–50	.06–.13
6Al-6V-2Sn (STA)	163	34	.05
7Al-4Mo (β)	160	40–45	.07–.09
8Al-1Mo-1V $(\alpha+\beta)$	126	50–55	.18–.22
8Al-1Mo-1V (β)	122	85	.57
13V-11Cr-3A1 (STA)	168	25	.026
Hylite 60	127	55	.219
Hylite 65	134	93	.56

Note: Properties may be considered typical of alloy in treatment specified. Data taken from AFML TR's and other published information. Not to be considered as statistically valid.

standardizing inspection techniques. Little statistically valid data is available in terms of current needs.

Table 2 lists a summary of selected detection capabilities of some commercial NDT

TABLE 2. Selected detection sensitivities of NDT processes. (sensitivity greater than 90% no confidence limits.)

Ref.	Number	Technique	Material	Size (in.)	Comments
(A)	(1)	Visual	7075-T6511	0.03	Fatigue crack Magnification
	(2)	Ultrasonics	„	0.25	Fatigue 50 MHZ .250″ shear transducer
	(3)	Penetrant	„	0.25	Fatigue No pre etch ZL-2 penetrant ZE-3 emulsifier ZP-4 developer
	(4)	X-ray	„	0.50	Fatigue 110 KVC 5 mil. amps 36″ distance 2 minute exp. D-4 film
	(5)	Visual	4330V	0.03	Fatigue crack Magnification
	(6)	Ultrasonics	„	0.20	Fatigue crack 5.0 MH 0.250″D Shear transducer
	(7)	Penetrant	„	0.35	See #3
	(8)	Mag particle	„	0.30	Fatigue crack Mag 20A 20,000 amp turns
(B)	(9)	Surface wave Ultrasonics	2219-T87	0.20	Fatigue crack Preproof
	(10)	Penetrant	„	0.20	Fatigue crack URE SC O P-133 Dry developer 2L2A penetrant 2E4A emulsifier 2P4A developer
	(11)	Eddy current	„	0.20	Fatigue crack
	(12)	Shear wave Ultrasonics	„	0.25	2.25–15 MHZ Various configurations
	(13)	X-ray	2219-T87 +Welded	0.30	Fatigue crack
(C)	(14)	Delta Scan	D6AC	0.150	Induced flaws
	(15)	Mag rubber	D6AC	0.035	Induced flaws
(D)	(16)	Delta wheel	2014A1	>0.010	Porosity
		60° angle Ultrasonics	2014	>0.010	Porosity
		X-ray	2014 2219	>0.010	Porosity
		Penetrant	7075-T6	0.075	Fatigue P51=2.5 penetrant
		Mag particle	D6AC	0.100	Fatigue Floor mag particle

processes. These are estimates of the size of the smallest flaw that can be detected by a given process at least 90% of the time. It should be recognized that the size of the smallest flaw that can be detected by an NDT technique is not the flaw size that can be reliably used in the design.

The sensitivity of the NDT process is defined as: The ratio of the number of flaws that can be detected by an NDT process divided by the total number of flaws that actually exist in the part, n_{NDT}/N_{TOT}. If only five flaws are detected out of ten samples containing a flaw, the sensitivity is no greater than 50%.

In order to use these flaw sizes in a design, the probability of detection of the flaw at a given confidence level must be determined.

The probability of detection of a given NDT technique can be calculated using a chi square χ^2 distribution approximation of the binomial distribution. This provides the upper confidence limits of the mean number of flaws that can be overlooked by an NDT process out of a given number of trials with a given confidence limit. Hence

$$nq = \frac{1}{2}\chi_c^2 \text{ with } f = 2(x_0+1)$$

where χ_c^2 is the confidence limit fractile of the χ^2 distribution, f is degrees of freedom, x_0 is number of flaws missed, n total number examined, q upper confidence limit for the probability of failure detection. For illustrative purposes, this is shown in Figure 1 at a 95% confidence limit as a function of the number of test inspection trials. In order to establish that a flaw can be detected at a 90% probability of detection at a 95% confidence level, the NDT process must be able to detect at least 29 flaws out of a given group of 30 specimens, all of which contain flaws within the given flaw size range. Thus, although Table 1 may indicate that an NDT process may find 100% of the flaws at 0.050″, the probability of detection is no less than 90% at a 95% confidence factor. By conducting a series of statistically designed experiments, one can obtain a series of curves as shown in Fig. 2. Here the flaw size that is to be used in the design is 0.10″.

During the past two years, a number of such programs have been initiated to determine flaw detection capabilities and typical data are shown in Table 3. These give the minimum flaw size of surface fatigue cracks that can be detected at the given confidence/sensitivity level.

It should be noted here that the sensitivities refer primarily to a fatigue-type crack

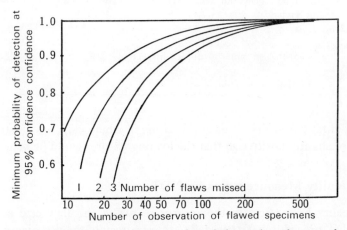

FIG. 1.   Plot of the minimum number of observations that must be made to ensure minimum probability of detection at 95% confidence.

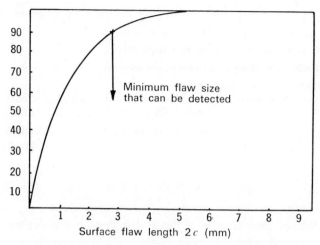

FIG. 2.   Plot of probability of detection at a given confidence level vs. surface flaw length 2c.

TABLE 3.   Flaw sizes detectable at known confidence limits. (in.)

Flaw size range	P. detect.	Confidence levels
.030–0.75 (2c)	75%	95%
.076–.100 (2c)	90%	95%
.101–.150 (2c)	90%	95%
Mag Particle-HP-9 steel. MTL-I-6868 with 0.1 to 0.15 ml per 100 ml SO2		
.030–.075 (2c)	90%	95%
.076–.100 (2c)	90%	95%
P5F-2.5 penetrant system Ti6Al-4V 0.5 mil etch		
.030–.075 (2c)	90%	95%
Instaviz P5F 1.0 penetrant-alum. 0.5 mil etch		
.076–.100 (2c)	90%	95%
P5F-1 penetrant-alum. RHR 65 or better 0.5 mil etch		
.030–.075 (2c)	90%	95%
.076–.100 (2c)	90%	95%
5MhZ 45° and 70° duplex inspection		
.030–.050 (2c)	90%	95%
Mag rubber double inspection		

that was grown at fatigue stress ratios approaching 0, where $\sigma_{MIN}/\sigma_{MAX} \doteq 0$. The value of σ_{MIN} was kept slightly positive so that the loading fixtures could be kept simple.

3.   Flaw Criticality Measurements by NDT

Flaw criticality here refers to the measurements of the flaw size and shape as given by the NDT procedure. We can define the accuracy of the flaw size measurement as[3]:

$$A_{NDT} = 1 - \left| \frac{2c_{NDI} - 2c_{ACT}}{2c_{ACT}} \right|$$

Where $2c_{NDT}$ is the NDT estimate of the flaw size and $2c_{ACT}$ is the actual size of the flaw as measured on the fracture surface. Typical accuracy indexes for several NDT procedures are shown in Figure 2, 3. These measurements were conducted on 7075-T6511 Aluminum and 4330 V Modified Steel.[3] For the penetrant and magnetic particle

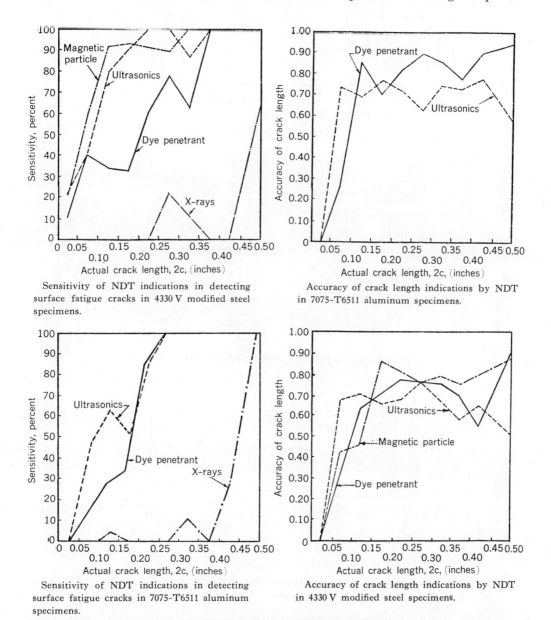

Sensitivity of NDT indications in detecting surface fatigue cracks in 4330 V modified steel specimens.

Accuracy of crack length indications by NDT in 7075-T6511 aluminum specimens.

Sensitivity of NDT indications in detecting surface fatigue cracks in 7075-T6511 aluminum specimens.

Accuracy of crack length indications by NDT in 4330 V modified steel specimens.

Fig. 3. Accuracy and sinsitivity of several NDT techniques for finding and measuring surface flaws in 4330V mod. steel and 7075-T6511 aluminum.

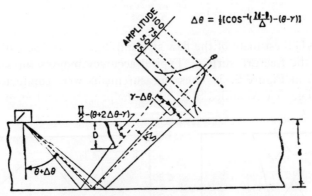

Reflection from the bottom of a crack at an
angle $[(\theta - \gamma) + 2\Delta\theta]$.

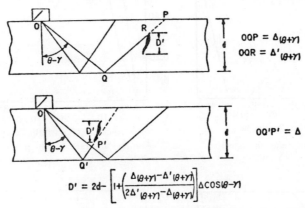

Schematic diagram for estimating defects which
do not come to the surface.

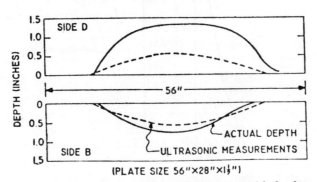

Crack-depth results for first tee-welded plate
specimen.

FIG. 4.   Shematic sketch showing ultrasonic indicium for measuring crack size in welds.

inspection, the surface length of the cracks were measured directly. When the ultrasonics was used to measure crack length, the transducer locations at the half peak height reflections were noted.

Giacomo, Crisci and Goldspiel[4] describe an ultrasonic method for measuring crack depth in structural weldments of high strength steels and titianium. To perform a crack size measurement, the transducer is moved slowly until the reflection signal reaches a lower threshold edge, passes through a maximum when impinging fully on the flaw, and diminishes after passing beyond the crack plane. The crack transducer reflection geometry is used to estimate the size of the flaw. Typical test results are shown in Fig. 4. In almost all cases the ultrasonic estimates of crack size are underestimates of actual crack sizes. These underestimates are attributed to (1) tightness of the crack, (2) crack branching, (3) multiple reflections from the rough surfaces of the crack, and (4) diffraction effects.

Corbly and Packman examined the influence of tightness of the crack on the estimates of crack size.[5] Their results show that increasing the applied stress levels increase the amplitude of the reflected signals from tight cracks. Additional data of Sessler and Weiss[6] show that this increasing amplitude with increasing stress reaches a saturation point, beyond which further increases in stress do not significantly increase

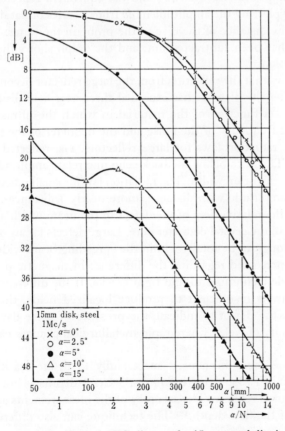

FIG. 5.   Typical AVG diagram for 15 mm steel disc in water.

the signal amplitude. This implied that tight fatigue or microfissures might easily be overlooked by the NDT due to insufficient signal reflection from the crack faces.

Considerable Soviet work has been reported on measurement of defects in welds by ultrasonics; Gurvich[7] uses a scattering indicatrix as a measure of the size and configuration of imbedded defects. The scattering indicatrix of the defect is defined as the normalized function describing the field of an ultrasonic wave reflected toward the probe. A recent review of Soviet ultrasonic methods for defect detection and measurement of defects in welded joints is given in Reference.[8]

Recent ultrasonic work has indicated that the nature of the mismatch making up the defect-base material interface has a significant influence on the amplitude of the reflected signals in ultrasonics. If the acoustic mismatch between the defect and base material is less than 30%, insufficient signal is reflected at the interface to produce a reliable indication.

When the defect is located within a welded structure and is relatively large in comparison to the ultrasonic transducer area, measurements of flaw sizes can be made using the AVG diagram shown in Figure 5. This was introduced in 1959,[9] but is only recently being utilized to any great extent. Essentially the diagram relates the distance from the probe to the flaw (A) the amplification in db (V) and the equivalent reflector diameter (G). The graph is drawn by plotting the amplitude in db from a series of flat disc-shaped reflectors as a function of the distance of the disc to the probe in the water. The ultrasonic attenuation in water has been subtracted out, and the graph shows the reflection conditions with no attenuation.

The backwall echo shows that the reflection from the large reflector becomes linearly decreasing with distance after the distance has exceeded three near field distances. The near field of a transducer is a function of the material in which the ultrasonic signal passes, the major ultrasonic frequency of the pulse and the diameter of the transducer. This confirms the acoustic radiation laws for large reflectors, vis, reflected amplitude proportional to 1/distance. The lines below the back echo line relate amplitude from reflectors that are smaller than the beam width. The radiation law for small reflectors shows a much larger decrease in amplitude with distance, more nearly 1/distance². The term "small reflectors" refers to the relative area of the defect to the beam width at the point of defect reflection, and not to the crystal diameter here. Large defects far away behave as small reflectors when far enough to be totally within the spreading beam width.

Arguments have been presented regarding the difference in magnetic permeability when using magnetic particle techniques to find tight cracks. If the difference between the base metal and the flaw is insufficient to produce localized fields, the magnetic particles will not adhere to the defect to indicate the presence of these flaws. This is particularly true in the vicinity of welds where rapid metallurgical changes can produce many erroneous results.[10]

Eddy current techniques have been used successfully to define crack geometry primarily in 7075 Aluminum in T73 and T651 tempers.[11] Crack depths as low as 10 mils could be detected and measured reliably. The accuracy of the measurements appeared to be relatively independent of the flaw depth.[12] The technique can also differentiate between surface imperfections and cracks.

By far the most commonly used technique for detecting defects in welded structures is that of penetrating radiation.[13] This includes X-rays, gamma rays, and neutron radiography. X-ray techniques vary from simple transmission or attenuation by passage of radiation through materials with different scattering and absorption levels to autoradiographic techniques[14] and back-scattering techniques. Recent radiographic techniques include: (1) radioactive gas penetrant techniques where the beta radiation from absorbed radioactive gasses are concentrated and detected in the vicinity of cracks and pores—radio penetrants; and (2) Positron annihilation where gamma photons resulting from positron annihilation are emitted more readily at loci of microstrain.

The common sensitivities of radiation techniques for welded structures are well documented and reported in many standards manuals. Most evident are the ability to distinguish metallurgical flaws and defects whose dimensions are large with respect to the wall thickness. X-ray sensitivity is usually given in terms of percent of wall thickness, and standard sensitivities of X-ray are on the order of 2% of wall thickness. Hence, defects whose gross dimension is on the order of 2% of the thickness of the wall thickness are theoretically detectable, but practice is limited to 5%. Gamma radiography is usually less sensitive than X-rays, but because of higher penetrating power, is used more extensively for thick sections. The sensitivity of X-ray techniques is limited by several factors: (1) the X-ray source spot size, (2) voltage, (3) exposure time, (4) recording technique, (5) the thickness of the material, and (6) the volumetric nature of the defect. If the defect is crack-like in nature, the crack must be oriented parallel to the beam for best detection. Cracks oriented at angles other than normal to the beam do not register as dark lines on the film and are not readily detectable.

Radiographic transmission techniques are used directly for measurement of the crack length, and triangulation techniques are used for other geometric size estimations. Considerable success has been obtained for large cracks.

Penetrant techniques are commonly used for detection of surface-connected discontinuities. For many components the penetrant inspection is used as a final check on the finished part. The effectiveness of penetrant systems are dependent upon the ability of the penetrant to enter the discontinuities and re-emerge for visual inspection with the proper post-application treatment. In general, the penetrant system technique consists of: (1) cleaning the surface (possible 0.005″ etch), (2) drying of surface, (3) application of penetrant, (4) removal of penetrant, (5) application of post-application technique (emulsifier, developer, etc.), (6) examination of surface, and (7) recording, if necessary.

Even with a simple sequence such as this, the inspection variables can greatly influence the ability of the penetrant to detect the flaws. Typical factors known to reduce the sensitivity of the flaw detection include: (1) the degree of surface preparation, condition of the surface cleanliness, roughness, wetness, (2) the length of time of the penetrant on the surface, wetting ability of penetrant, (3) the use of post-penetrant materials, development time, emulsifier time, (4) the type of developer, dry, wet, nonaqueous, (5) the viewing conditions, and (6) the techniques used to clean the surface after the penetrant has been applied.

At the present time no systematic study has been reported on the factors affecting sensitivity of penetrant systems to find small cracks.[15] Tables 2 and 3 show that penetrant systems, when used effectively, can detect and measure extremely small cracks provided the proper procedures have been followed.

The major difficulty that arises when trying to increase the sensitivity of penetrant techniques is that high sensitivity penetrants may detect small, tight cracks but wash out larger, deeper cracks, and hence, not indicate the presence of these larger cracks. Because of the surface nature of penetrant techniques, the accuracy of the technique in measuring crack lengths is extremely high when used without developer systems.[14] With developer systems the penetrant in the flaw must react with the developer to produce a visible indication. The resulting accuracy of the flaw size indicated decreases considerably.

4. Concluding Remarks

This brief review of the state-of-the-art in NDT with reference to defect detection cannot even begin to do justice to all of the techniques for defect detections and size discrimination available in the literature. It appears that the use of fracture mechanics as a design analysis technique has drastically altered the nature of the NDT research and development process. Most NDT research work is conducted in a manner so that the investigator knows that there is a defect in his specimen and proceeds to develop NDT techniques to characterize that defect.

As a design process, the expectation value for finding defects is low, and hence the NDT process must be optimized to produce the maximum of signal-noise ratio so that the inspector has a definite indication of a flaw. This improves the reliability of flaw detection capabilities for small flaw sizes. Once the flaw has been noted, additional techniques can be used to determine the criticality including the size, shape, and other metallurgical features. The quantitative aspects of NDT are in the rudimentary stages, and clearly considerable development is possible.

ACKNOWLEDGMENTS

The author wishes to express his appreciation to the Air Force Office of Scientific Research (Contract No. F44620–73–C–0073) for their support in portions of this program.

REFERENCES

1. Thielsch, H., " *Defects and Failures in Pressure Vessels and Piping*," Reinhold Pub. N. Y. (1965).
2. Wood, H., " The Role of Applied Fracture Mechanics in the Air Force Structural Integrity Program," AFFDL-TM-60-5 June (1970).
3. Packman, P. F., Pearson, H. S. and Young, G., " NDT Definition of Fatigue Cracks," Journal of Materials, p. 666 (1972).
4. Giacomo, G. D., Crisci, J. R. and Goldspiel, S., "An Ultrasonic Method for Measuring Crack Depth in Structural Weldments," Materials Evaluation, Sept. p. 189 (1971).
5. Corbly, D. M., Packman, P. F. and Pearson, H. S., " The Accuracy and Precision of Ultrasonic Shear Wave Flaw Measurements as a Function of Stress on the Flaw," Materials Evaluation, Vol. 28, p. 103, (1970).
6. Sessler, J. G. and Weiss, V., " Improvement in Crack Detection by Ultrasonic Pulse Echo

with Low Frequency Excitation," ARPA Final Report 8D10, Oct. (1970).

7. Gurrich, A. K. and Shchukin, V. A., " Comparative Evaluation of Methods of Measuring the Apparent Length of Defect," Defectoskopiya, Nov.–Dec. No. 6, p. 685 (1970).

8. *Proceedings Fourth Scientific-Technical Conference on the Ultrasonic Detectoscopy of Welded Joints*, Defectoskopiya Nov.–Dec. No. 6 (1970).

9. Krautkramer, J. and Krautkramer, H., *Ultrasonic Testing of Materials*, Springer-Verlag, New York Inc. (1969).

10. Yee, B. G. W., *Proceedings of NSF/AFML NDT Workshop on Materials Characterization* AFML-TR 73–69, Nov. (1972).

11. Parks, J. W. and Padilla, V. E., " Definition of Fatigue Crack Geometry by Eddy Current Techniques," McDonnell Aircraft Co., presented at *ASNT 7th Symposium on NDT*, San Antonio, Texas (1969).

12. McMasters, R. C. Ed. *Non-Destructive Testing Handbook*, Soc. for NDT, Ronald Press (1963).

13. Masi, O. and Erna, A., " Radiographic Examination of Welds.   A Complete Assessment of Defects in Terms of Tensile and Fatigue Strength," Metallurgica Ital. Vol. 45, p. 273 (1953).

14. Vary, A., " *Non-Destructive Evaluation Technique Guide*," NASA SP 3079.

15. Rodgers, E. H. and Merhib, P., "A Report Guide to Liquid Penetrant Literature," AMRA MS, 64–12, Aug. (1964).

16. Lord, R. J., " Evaluation of the Reliability and Sensitivity of NDT Methods for Titanium Alloys," MDAC A 1920, Oct. (1972).

Acoustic Emission Research in Japan for Flaw Detection in Weld

M. Onoe

Institute of Industrial Science, University of Tokyo

1. Introduction

Acoustic emission (AE) is a transient elastic wave generated by the rapid release of energy within a material. Such a release of energy occurs during, among other things, plastic deformation, crack initiation and propagation. Hence a highly stressed region near a defect or a crack is a good source of AE. Elastic waves thus generated can be detected by an ultrasonic sensor attached on a surface of the specimen. The time rate and the total count of emission are most frequently used measures of AE activities. Amplitude and frequency spectrum are sometimes used as supplementary information. By using several sensors, it is possible to measure differences between arrival time of wave from a single emission and hence to locate the source by triangulation. This technique is very useful for not only locating a defect or a crack but also for rejecting external mechanical noise.

Although early observations of AE in daily life have been numerous, a modern study of AE was only initiated in the early 1950s by Kaiser in Germany. Since that time, much of the AE research has been conducted in U.S.A. At the International Institute of Welding which was held in Kyoto, Japan, in the summer of 1969, several papers on AE were presented and generated considerable interest among the many of us. In response to this interest, the High Pressure Institute of Japan, in co-operation with the Japanese Society for Nondestructive Testing, formed Japanese Committee on Acoustic Emission (JCAE) in December, 1969, for which I have served as the chairman.

JCAE is composed of approximately 40 members, most of whom come from steel makers, plant fabricators and universities. Meetings are held bimonthly. With 21 meetings held so far 88 papers had been presented, of which 8 were survey or review lectures, 40 were literature and conference reports and another 40 were original contributions.

In the summer of 1971, a study mission of 10 members visited about 10 US laboratories which are conducting AE research. In July, 1972, a US-Japan symposium on AE was held in Tokyo where 10 US and 11 Japanese papers were presented. The number of

Japanese participants was 130, which reflected the increasing interest in AE. This summer, July, 1973, 10 members again visited US laboratories and also presented 3 papers at AEWG meeting held in Richland, Washington. Another symposium on AE is being scheduled in Tokyo in September, 1974. JCAE edited two special issues on AE for journals of High Pressure Institute and Society for Nondestructive Testing. JCAE also organized tutorial sessions on AE for various professional societies, such as the National Symposium on Atomic Energy this spring and the National Convention of Electrical Engineers this fall. This paper will review some research works presented at recent JCAE meetings. Particular attention will be paid to the detection of delayed cracking in high tensile strength steel weldments.

2. Basic Studies

Earthquake is often mentioned as an example of large scale AE. Japan being a country of earthquake, it stands to reason that our AE research started from earthquake. Professor Mogi of the Earthquake Research Institute, University of Tokyo conducted,

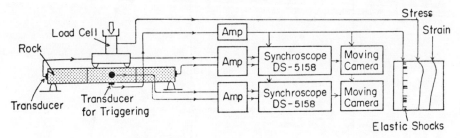

FIG. 1.   Successive development of the source region of elastic shocks in the stages C_1–C_3 and an observed main crack pattern.

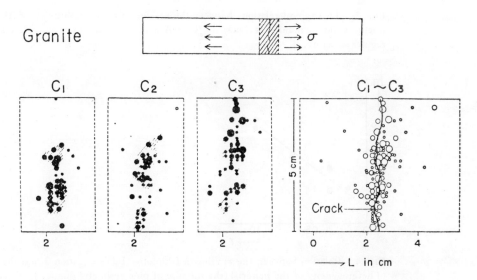

FIG. 2.   Experimental setup for measuring AE caused by microfracturing.

in the early 1960s extensive study of AE in rocks.[1] Figure 1 shows his experimental set up where two to four sensors are used for locating AE sources. Differences in arrival time are directly measured from photographic records of two dual beam oscilloscopes taken by single frame movie cameras. Typical results for source location in granite under constant tensile load are shown in Fig. 2. C1, C2, and C3 show successive development of sources during three time intervals prior to the final failure. Composite figure showing all source locations at the right closely correlates with the macroscopic crack line.

Mogi also pointed out that a log-log plot of the amplitude distribution of AE signal is a useful measure of material property. If the material has a completely irregular structure, the plot will be a straight line as shown in Fig. 3 (A). If any regularity exists, for example a regular network of cracks, the plot will show a bend as shown in Fig. 3 (B). The slope of the plot increases with the degree of non-uniformity of the structure. This is

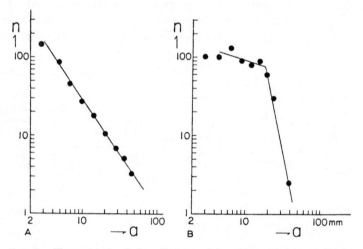

FIG. 3.   Two typical relations between the maximum trace amplitude a of AE during fractures and the number of shocks n.   Case A with irregular structures.   Case B with a regular structure.

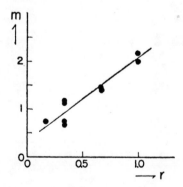

FIG. 4.   Relation between the m value in Ishimoto—Iida's equation 3 and the degree of heterogeneity of the material (the mixture of pine resin and pumice particles). $r=$ volumetric mixing ratio of pine resin medium and pumice particles.

due to the crack propagation rate per event which is proportional to the AE energy and predominantly limited by the presence of discontinuous point. The relation between the slope, m, and the degree of heterogeneity, r, in a resin filled with pumice particle is shown in Fig. 4. The abscissa, r, in this figure is the volumetric mixing ratio of particle and resin.

A major earthquake is usually preceded by many small foreshocks and also ac-

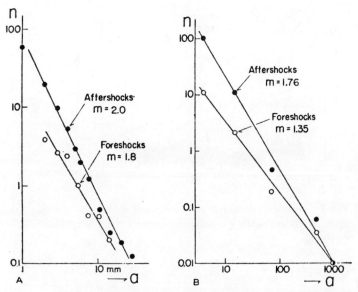

FIG. 5.   Relations between the trace amplitude a of shocks and their number n, in (A) laboratory and (B) field. Closed circle=foreshocks; open circle=aftershocks. B (after Suehiro et al., 1964) has been slightly changed from the original one.

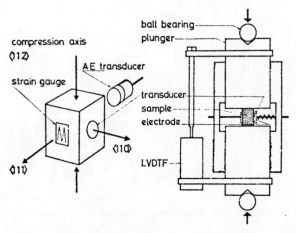

FIG. 6.   Schematic illustration of the arrangement of specimen and transducer for simultaneous attenuation, acoustic emission-deformation measurements and schematic diagram of the specimens used showing sample orientation.

companied by aftershocks. The slopes of the maximum trace amplitude versus shock number plots for aftershocks are larger than those for foreshocks since aftershocks occur at regions already fractured. Typical plots are shown in Fig. 5. for both (a) natural earthquake and (b) simulated laboratory earthquake.

Further detailed study on the source mechanism of AE can be investigated by using a

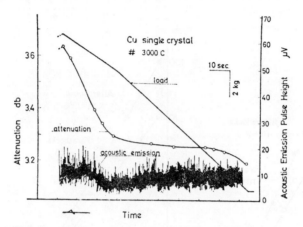

FIG. 7.   Acoustic emission chracteristics and attenuation change vs. time at 2nd loading cycle for copper single crystal. Strain rate: 2×10^{-5} sec^{-1} (continuous type of acoustic emission).

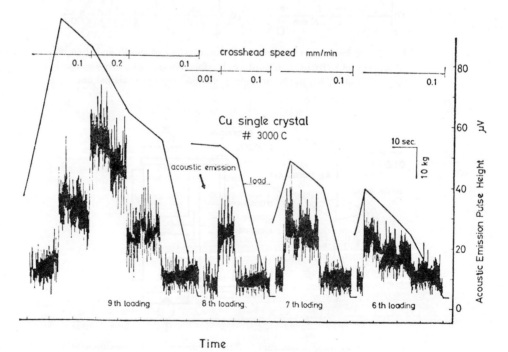

FIG. 8.   Acoustic emission characteristics represented by pulse height for copper single crystal. Strain rate: 2×10^{-5}, 2×10^{-4} and 4×10^{-4} sec^{-1}.

single crystal, which has much simpler structure than rocks. Imanaka, et al. of Kawasaki Steel Corp. established a correlation between AE and dislocations.[2] AE and ultsasonic attenuation at 27 MHz were simultaneously measured during compression test of a single crystal of copper in the set up shown in Fig. 6. A typical record obtained at second loading is shown in Fig. 7. It can be seen that both ultrasonic attenuation and AE increased at the yield point of the load curve. Frequency dependence of ultrasonic attenuation, measured independently in the range from 9 to 225 MHz, agreed well with the Granato-Lucke theory even in the presence of large bias stress. Hence the process of plastic deformation shown in Fig. 7 may be interpreted as follows. As the external stress increases, dislocations are freed from foreign atoms and the segment length of mobile dislocations increases. When this length reaches a critical length of the order of one micron, mobile dislocations multiply abruptly and the crystal yields macroscopically. The increase in ultrasonic attenuation reflects this increase in dislocation density. Hence the origin of AE in this case is the multiplication of mobile dislocations. Figure 8 shows another record of successive loadings with increased strain rate and clearly shows that AE initiates at every macroscopic yield points.

The use of AE during material testing has become a standard practice as shown by the next few examples by Nakasa of the Central Research of Electric Power Industry.[3]

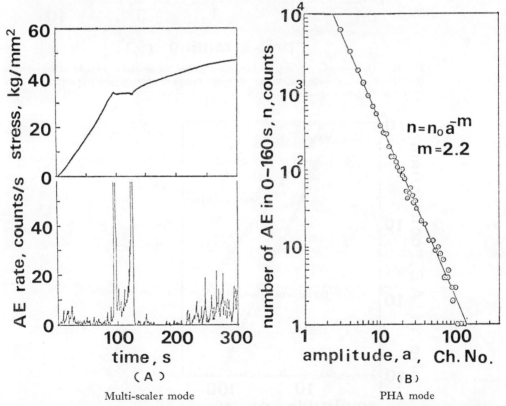

$$n = n_0 a^{-m}$$
$$m = 2.2$$

(A)   (B)

Multi-scaler mode   PHA mode

FIG. 9. AE characteristics of an as-received specimen of low-carbon steel (gauge length: 100 mm, strain speed; 2 mm/min, cross section; 100 mm²).

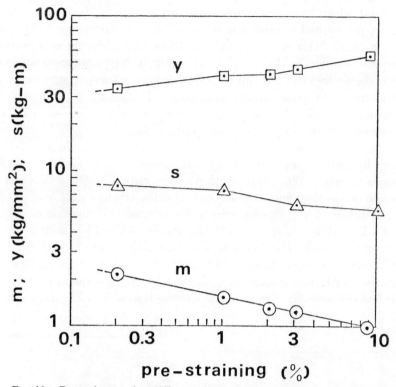

FIG. 10.   Dependency of *m* (AE non-dimensional parameter), *y* (yield stress) and *s* (Charpy-impact absorption energy at room temperature) on the percentage of pre-straining for low-carbon steel.

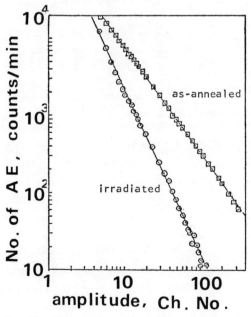

FIG. 11.   PHA mode analysis of the copper specimens.

Figure 9 shows the load curve, AE rate, and a log-log plot of AE amplitude distribution (PHA mode) in a tensile test of low carbon steel. The slope of the log-log plot decreases when prestraining is applied to a specimen before the heat treatment of 250°C for 1 hour. Figure 10 shows the change of slope together with yield stress and Charpy-impact absorption energy at room temperature as functions of the degree of prestraining. This change may be explained by the decrease of plastic deformation and the increase of macro cracks. Figure 11 shows the effect of neutron irradiation on log-log plots of AE amplitude distribution of copper where irradiation causes embrittlement which in turn increases the slope.

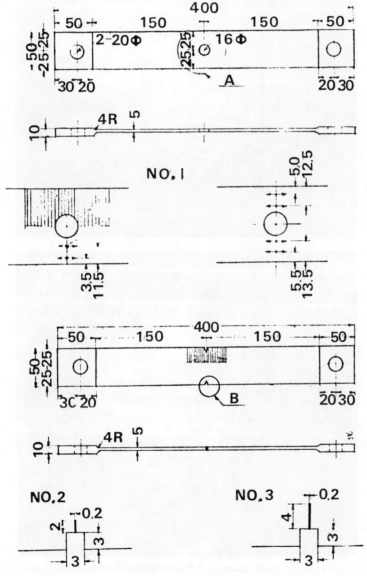

FIG. 12.   Tensile specimens used in AE-Moiré fringe analysis.

AE is generated in the area under plastic deformation. A direct correlation between total emission counts and volume of deformed area was established by Terada, et al. of the Mitsui Shipbuilding Co.[4] Three tensile specimens, one with a central hole and the other two with notches of different depthes, shown in Fig. 12 were used. The material

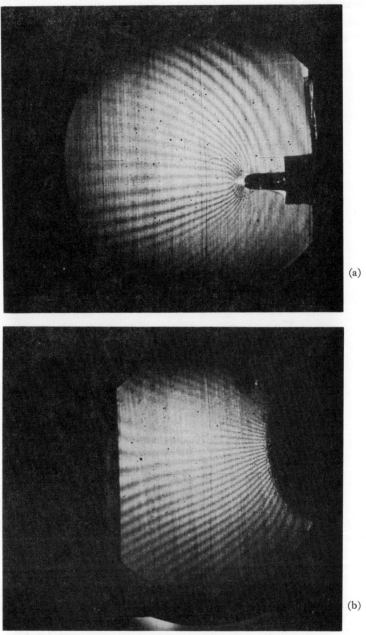

(a)

(b)

FIG. 13.   Moiré fringe patterns in the vicinities of strain concentrations of specimens (a) No. 3 and (b) No. 1.

used was SS41 steel annealed at 600°C. Surface deformation was measured by Moiré fringe technique using a fine grid of 200 lines per centimeter. Figure 13 (a) and (b) show fringes in front of the notch and the hole, respectively. Spatial differentiations of these fringes yield the distributions of strains. Figure 14 shows the successive expansion of the deformed area due to increase in load. Lines in the upper figures represent a 0.1 percent strain, which corresponds to the uniaxial yield strain of the material and lines in the lower figures represent a 1.38 percent strain, which corresponds to initial strain hardening. Figure 15 shows that total emission counts are indeed proportional to the volume of deformed area.

One of the problem in AE research is the need to establish a controlled source of AE for calibrating the instrumentation system. Perhaps one of the simplest source of AE is a bearing ball dropped from a known height. Kanno, et al. of the Ship Research Institute conducted a detailed study of such calibration system.[5,6] Starting from Bowden's theory on the rebound height of a dropped ball, they found that first the dominant frequency of AE is inversely proportional to the diameter of a ball and is independent of the drop height, and second AE signal amplitude is proportional to two third power of the drop height. These facts agreed with experiments as shown in Fig. 16 and 17, respectively. Having calibrated their sensors in this manner, they showed that the energy of AE is

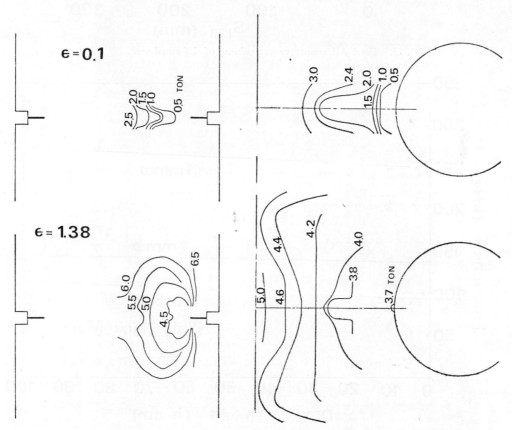

FIG. 14. Maximum strain distributions in specimens No. 1 and 3.

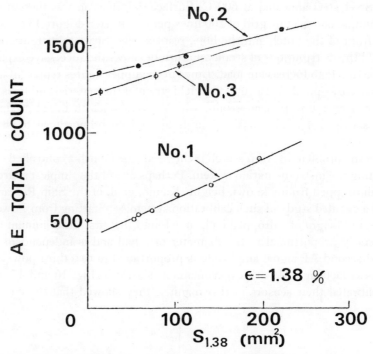

FIG. 15. Total AE counts versus volume of deformed area.

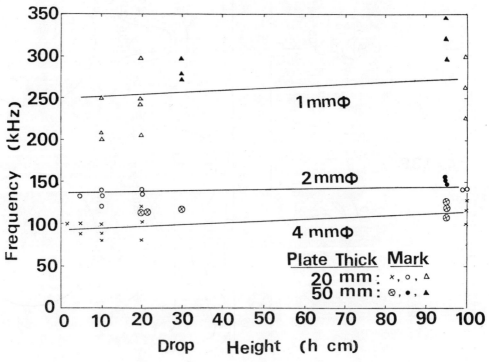

FIG. 16. Frequencies of AE signal for drop test of bearing balls of various diameter.

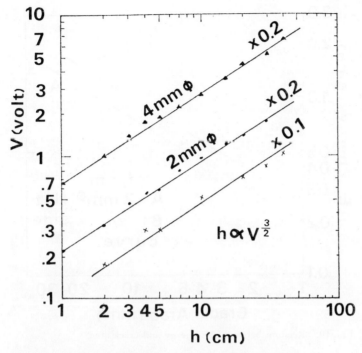

FIG. 17.   AE signal amplitude versus drop height of ball.

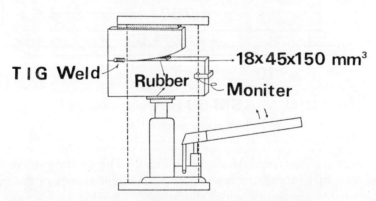

FIG. 18.   Loading setup for cracking TIG welded specimens.

proportional to the area of crack extention within in a weld. The set up for loading TIG welded steel pieces is shown in Fig. 18 with results shown in Fig. 19.

AE is ideally suited for detecting crack initiation and propagation during high speed fatigue testing.[7] A bar specimen shown in Fig. 20 was electromagnetically vibrated in the fundamental free-free flexural mode, where feedback from a pickup coil substains the vibration. The frequency of vibration was a few hundred Herz and fatigue failure was caused within a few hours. This high speed vibration, however, made it difficult to detect crack initiation and monitor its propagation. Hence AE sensors were bonded to nodal

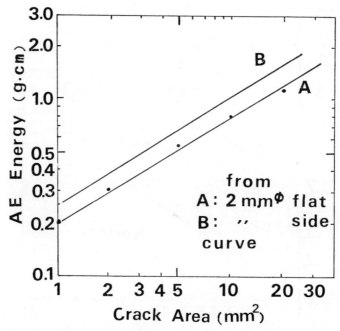

FIG. 19.   Relation between AE energy and crack area.

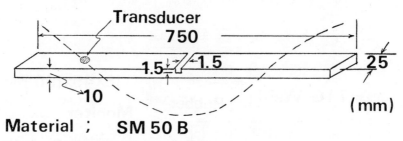

FIG. 20.   Free-free vibration of a notched bar.

area of the bar providing typical AE shown in Fig. 21. During the test, crack initiated at point 1 and thereafter propagated intermittently. A slight change of the vibrating frequency was noted, at the point 3, which was heretofore used as a sign of crack initiation. Hence the AE method enable one to detect cracks in their early stages without stopping the test. The output waveforms of a sensor before and after the crack initiation are shown in Fig. 22 (a) and (b), respectively. Pips in Fig. 22 (a) are switching noise of the driving circuit and can be neglected. AE signals are noted in Fig. 22 (b). Figure 23 shows the waveform just prior to final failure. The period of AE burst is half of the vibration period, which means that AE is generated during both tension and compression cycle.

High temperature fatigue tests of SUS 304 TP stainless steel T-piping to be used in a fast breeder reactor were monitored by Nakasa using AE techniques.[3] Fig. 24 shows the experimental set up. Because of the high temperature up to 550°C, sensors with metal waveguide were used. Figure 25 shows total AE count as a function of fatigue cycles

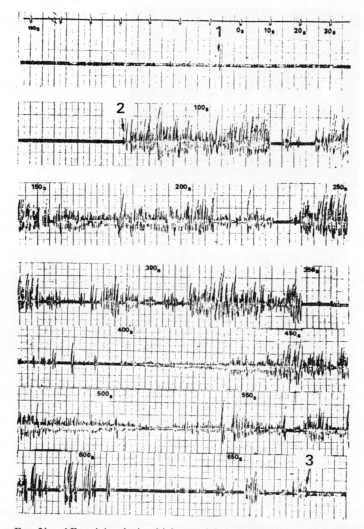

FIG. 21.   AE activity during high speed fatigue test.

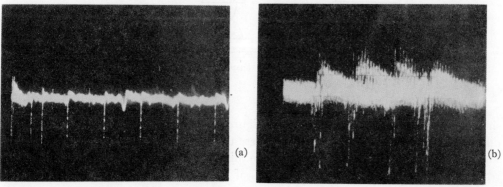

FIG. 22.   Output waveforms (a) before crack initiation and (b) after initiation.

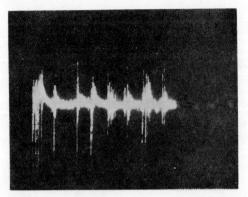

FIG. 23.   AE signals just prior to final failure.

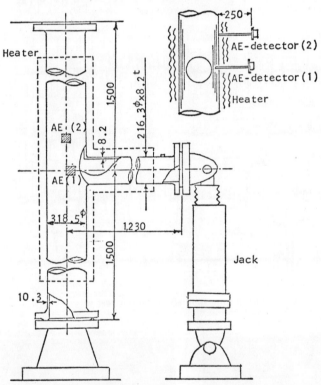

FIG. 24.   Setup of piping for high temperature fatigue test and location of AE detectors.

showing increasing as cracks propagated. Figure 26 compares log-log plots of amplitude distribution at various stages of testing where the slope decreases after crack initiation. Figure 27 shows the effect of temperature. In this particular example, higher temperature resulted in greater numbers and amplitudes of AE signals.

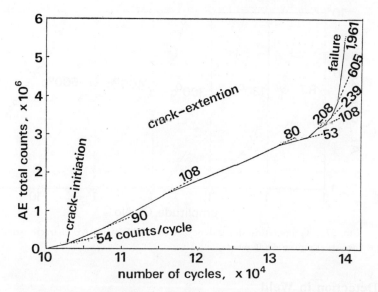

FIG. 25.   Typical test result of high-temperature (550°C) fatigue test of T-piping component.

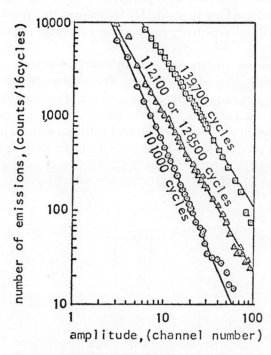

FIG. 26.   Variation of the PHA-mode AE characteristics during high-temperature (550°C) fatigue test of a T-piping component.

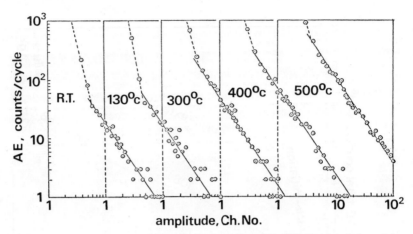

FIG. 27.   Temperature dependency of the PHA-mode AE characteristics of the stainless steel piping component.

3.   Flaw Detection in Weld

Although considerable interests exist in applying AE techniques to real time monitoring of welding operation, little success has been reported so far. This is due to both the electrical noise from large welding current and mechanical noises of flux cracking and sputtering which tend to obscure the real AE signal. Hence our works have been concentrated in detecting delayed cracking in weld. AE techniques are especially suitable for this purpose, because of its high sensitivity and large area coverage without the use of mechanical scanning.

Figure 28 shows the specimen used by Arii, et al. of Toshiba Electric Co. in studying AE characteristics of simplified electroslag welding.[8] The weld metal solidifies in the center hole and is subject to a large constraint. Three sensores of resonant frequency 50, 500 and 1,000 kHz cooled by water are attached to the end of three horizontal arm. High carbon steel S35C and low carbon steel SS41 were tested with and without preheating at 450°C. Sliced crossection of the specimens revealed cracks in all S35C specimens but none in SS41 specimens. Figures 29 and 30 show total AE counts as functions of the elasped time after welding at 50 kHz, and 1MHz, respectively. Slag cracking occurred

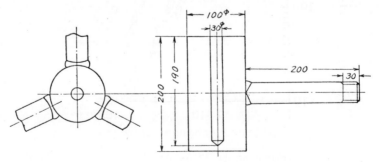

FIG. 28.   Experimental setup for AE monitoring of electroslag welding.

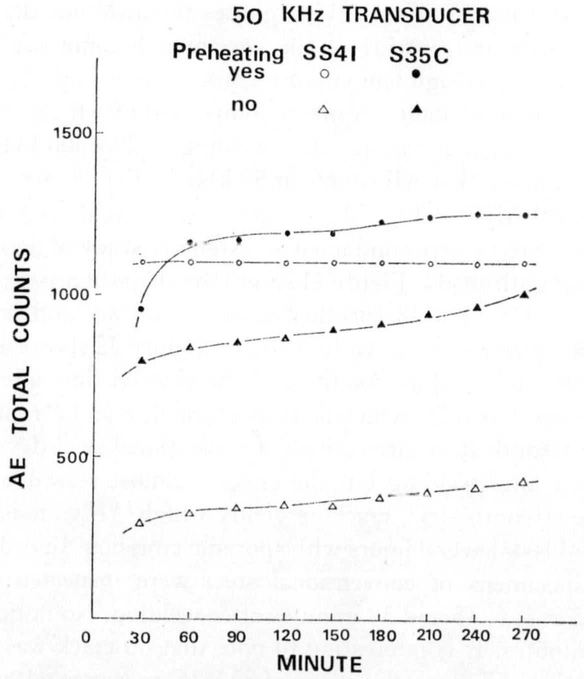

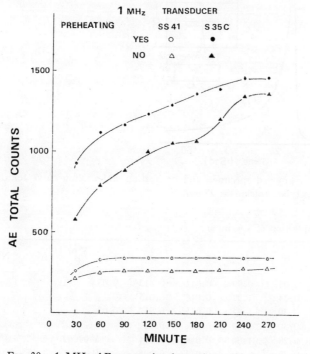

FIG. 29.   50 kHz AE counts in electroslag welded specimens.

FIG. 30.   1 MHz AE counts in electroslag welded specimens.

mostly in the first 30 minutes and lasted up to 150 minutes at which time the temperature difference between the inside and outside of the specimen became negligible. Weld cracking seemed to have started as high temperature cracking and propagated thereafter. Separate measurements of the dominant frequency component of AE signal show that a shift from 90–180 kHz in S35C at 5 minutes after welding to 288–500 kHz at 2 hours. Hence it is reasonable to assume that AE counts at 50 kHz in Fig. 29 are mostly due to slag cracking and counts at 1 MHz in Fig. 30 are mostly due to weld cracking.

Isono et al. of Nippon Steel Corp. conducted an extensive study of delayed cracking in welds of high tensil strenghth steel.[9] Figure 31 shows the shape of a y-groove cracking test specimen specified in JIS Z 3158 together with its heating and cooling curve. Chemical composition of specimen is shown in Table 1. Figure 32 shows a summary of total AE counts for various material as functions of the elapsed time after welding. S represents a conventional steel, SM 50, which is easily cracked, F and P represent 60 and 80 kg/mm² high tensile strength steel, respectively. Conventional steel developed intensive cracking immediately after welding but the craking almost ceased within several minutes. In high tensile strength steel, cracking yields a high AE emission rate 30–60 minutes after welding and lasts several hours with sporadic emission. In order to confirm this observation, few specimens of conventional steel were inspected by magnetic particle NDT technique at 1, 6, 15 and 30 minutes after welding. No noticeable change were observed after 6 minutes. It is interesting to note that no crack was found in the magnetic particle inspection of five cross-sections of SM41C specimen, although positive

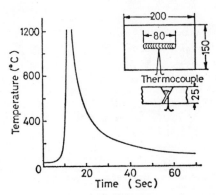

FIG. 31. y-grooved specimen and its heating and cooling curve for under standard conditions (plate thickness: 25 mm).

TABLE 1. Chemical composition of specimen.

	Material	C	Si	Mn	P	S	Cu	V or B	Mo	Nb	Welding rod
1	SM–41C	0.144	0.013	0.99	0.011	0.013	0.05				LH50
2	SM–50B	0.195	0.34	1.37	0.016	0.015					LH55
3	SM–50C	0.177	0.30	1.44	0.015	0.017	0.05				LH55
4	Si–Mn	0.05	0.30	1.00	0.01	0.02					LH50
5	WT 60	0.15	0.28	1.30	0.016	0.004		V 0.062			L62
6	WT 80P	0.13	0.32	1.39	0.015	0.006		B 0.0012	0.55	0.015	LH80

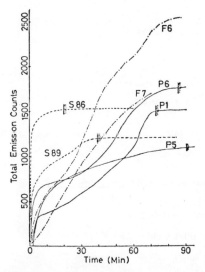

FIG. 32. Change in AE counts after weld.

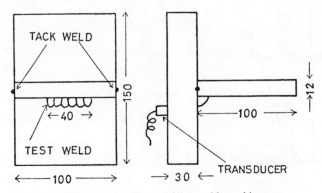

FIG. 33. Non-restraint T-type fillet weld cracking test.

AE activity was recorded. The specimen was polished again and re-examined by micro-scope where tiny cracks less than 0.1 mm were found. This example shows the high sensi-tivity of crack detection by AE technique. X-ray radiographs were also taken at 1, 10 and 60 minutes but little difference was observed in 10 and 60 minutes records.

Preheating up to 150°C tends to delay crack initiation. Cracking ceases within 1 hour in conventional steel, but lasts nearly 20 hours in high tensile strength steel. Preheating of SM50B at 75–150°C does not eliminate cracking, but decreases the cracking rate. Magnetic particle inspection shows cracks only at the ends of welding zone. Preheating of SM41C at 100°C eliminates the craking.

Fuji, et al. of Nippon Kokan Co. studied the effect of preheating on heel cracking and transverse cracking in high tensile strength steel.[10] Figure 33 shows a specimen of 50 kg/mm² high tensile strength steel for non-restraint T-type fillet weld cracking test which simulates heel cracking. Figure 34 shows AE rate and total counts as functions of elapsed time after welding. Post-test inspection showed that the cracking area was 60

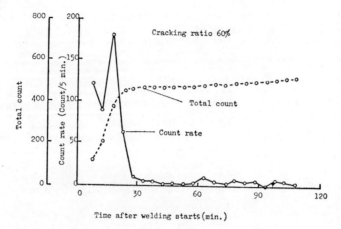

FIG. 34. AE counts in T-type fillet weld.

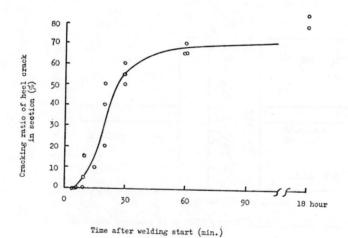

FIG. 35. Crack extension of heel crack.

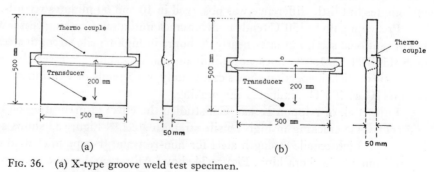

FIG. 36. (a) X-type groove weld test specimen.
(b) V-type groove weld test specimen with backing strip.

per cent of the total area. AE rate peaked at 20 minutes in this case, but delay in peaking was noticed in thinner horizontal plates. The extent of cracked area was checked separately by removing the horizontal plate from the 18 specimens at various time. The result is shown in Fig. 35. Crack extension started at around 10 minutes and saturated at around 60 minutes and is in agreement with the AE data. This AE detection technique has been useful to find the optimum conditions for surface treatment and preheating to prevent heel cracking. A similar study of transverse cracking in 80 kg/mm² high tensile steel was also conducted using X- and V-type groove submerged arc weld test specimens shown in Fig. 36. A typical result for X-type groove is shown in Fig. 37. Delayed cracking started about 1 hour after welding and reached a peak at 3 hours and ceased at 7

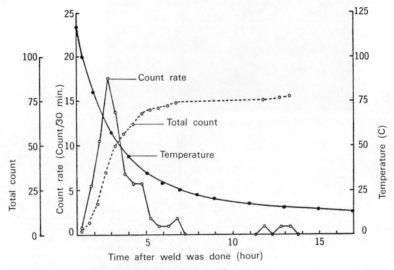

FIG. 37.   AE counts in X-type groove weld.

FIG. 38.   Multi-channel AE system developed by the University of Tokyo.

FIG. 39.   Model of nuclear reactor vessel.

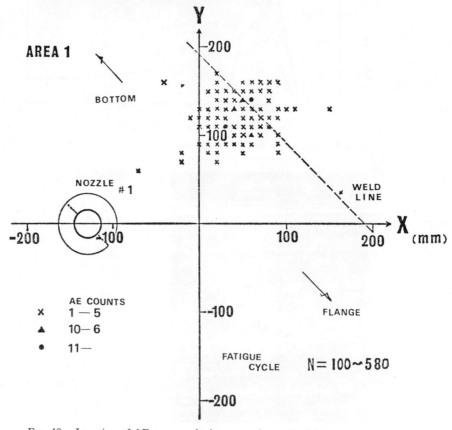

FIG. 40.   Location of AE sources during an early stage of fatigue test.

hours. Around 11–14 hours after welding sporadic emission occurred again. This observation was supported by separate magnetic particle and X-ray tests. With such tests, it was found that the use of alkaline flux, which caused some diffusion of hydrogen, prevented transverse cracking.

Welding is extensively used constructing large pressure vessels. Hence the integrity

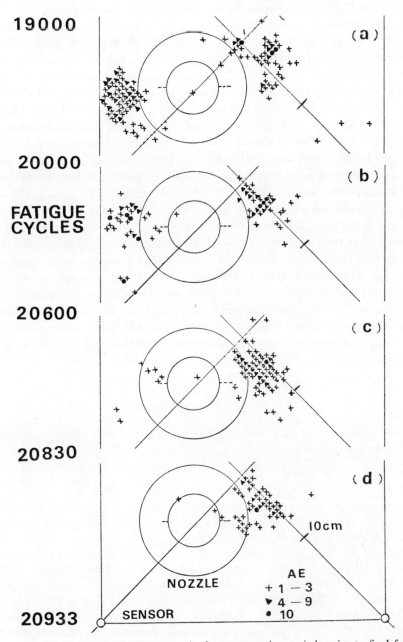

FIG. 41. Location of AE sources in four consecutive periods prior to final failure.

of vessels can only be assured by detecting defects in weld. AE technique is useful in locating defects and in estimating their seriousness. For large vessel, many sensors are required to monitor entire volume of the vessel. Data acquisition of each sensor, AE source location by triangulation, rejection of noises and evaluation of AE activity of each source require substantial data processing and hence a computer for nearly real-time operation. A computerized multi-channel system was developed by Watanabe, et al. of Nippon Steel Corp. and successfully used in hydraulic test of vessels.[11]

Figure 38 shows another multi-channel system developed by the University of Tokyo.[12] This system was used in a fatigue test of models of nuclear reactor vessel conducted by jointly Japan Atomic Energy Research Laboratory and Central Research Institute of Electric Power Industry. Figure 39 shows a vessel model under test. It consists of a cylindrical portion and half sphere. The dimensions of the cylinder are given by: length of 2 m, inner diameter of 695 mm, and wall thickness of 23 mm. The dimensions of the half sphere are as follows: radius of 353 mm and wall thickness of 13 mm. As shown in the figure, four different types of nozzles are installed in the center and are located 90 degrees apart from each other. To initiate fatigue cracks at the inner surface where a nozzle meets the cylinder, two notches were cut in the direction of the cylindrical axis. In total, eight notches were cut. Sinusoidal pressure of zero to 120 kg/cm² were applied at 5 cycles/minute. At an early stage of the test, a considerable AE activity occurred at one of the weld lines as shown in Fig. 40, but soon ceased thereafter. Ultrasonic inspection after the test indeed revealed the presence of minor flaw in the weld. Figure 41 shows four consecutive plots of the location of AE sources at the final stage of the test. In Fig. 41 (a) both notches of 104 mm nozzle exhibited equally strong AE activity. Subsequently the activity of the left crack ceased, whereas the activity of the right crack increased steadily until the crack penetrated the wall at 20933 cycles. These examples show the usefulness of a multi-channel system in fatigue testing of welded vessels. Application of a similar system to in-service inspection and monitoring is also being considered.

ACKNOWLEDGMENTS

The author wishes to thank the JCAE members who kindly supplied materials discussed in this review.

REFERENCES

1. Mogi, K., " Source location of elastic shocks in the fracturing process in rocks (1)," Bull. Earthquake Res. Inst. **46**, 1103/1125 (1968).
2. Imanaka, T., Sano, K. and Shimizu M., " Dislocation attenuation and acoustic emission during deformation in copper single crystal," J. Crystal Lattice Defects, **4**, 57/64 (1973).
3. Nakasa, H., "Application of acoustic emission techniques to material diagnostics," Symp. Nuclear Power Plant Control and Instrumentation, Prague, Jan. 1973.
4. Terada, O. and Tanaka, N., " Relationship between zone of plastic deformation determined by Moiré fringe technique and acoustic emission," JCAE Document 14–52, Jan. 1972.

5. Kanno, A., "Application of standard AE source to calibration of AE from cracks," US-Japan Symp. on AE, Tokyo, July, 1972.
6. Sakaki, M., " Note on frequencies of AE source of dropped steel ball," JCAE Document 20–85, Apr., 1973.
7. Onoe, M. and Yamada, H., " Observation of AE during resonance type fatigue testing," JCAE Document 4–12, Apr., 1970.
8. Arii, M., Kashiwaya, H. and Uchida, K., "AE characteristics of weld cracking in electro-slag welded rod," US-Japan Symp. on AE, Tokyo, July, 1972.
9. Isono, F., Udagawa, T. and Taniguchi, N., "A study of cracking phenomena by AE technique," J. Non-destructive Inspection, **21**, 226/233, Apr., 1972.
10. Fuji, T. and Mori, T., " Study of delayed cracking by AE and its application," US-Japan Symp. on AE, Tokyo, July, 1972.
11. Watanabe, T., Hashirizaki, N. and Arita, H., " Inspection of pressure vessel by multi-channel AE location system, J. Non-destructive Inspection, **22**, 106/107, Feb., 1973.
12. Onoe, M., Yamaguchi, K., Ichikawa, H., Shimada, T. and Noguchi, A., " Multi-channel AE location system," ibid. **21**, 552/553, Sept., 1972 and **22**, 104/105, Feb., 1973.

Recent Developments in Acoustic Emission as Applied to Welding Defects

K. Ono

Materials Department, University of California

1. Introduction

Extensive research and development efforts during the last decade have added acoustic emission (AE) testing to the rank of practical methods of non-destructive evaluation.[1-4] Since the early days of AE testing, the detection of flaws in welded structures was one of the most important goals of AE testing.[5,6] At present, intensive development works are underway in several countries in order to monitor large welded structures for the detection of incipient failure.

Unfortunately, the scientific basis of AE testing is still very poor. This is understandable considering the complicated nature of problems that involve metallurgical aspects: microstructures, dislocations, and fracture toughness; mechanical aspects: the vibration and wave propagation in materials and structures; electromechanical aspects: piezoelectric transducers and coupling; electronic aspects: low level signal processing, arrival time analysis and data storage and presentation. This paper will focus the attention to signal characterization, mechanisms of AE during fracture processes, and flaw location schemes. The first will examine the potential analysis methods that may establish the origin of AE signal, while the second will form the basis for AE testing of welding defects. The third topic is the best example of practicality of this technique and examines a representative testing system and its characteristics.

2. Characterization of AE Signal

The parameters commonly used for the analysis of AE phenomena have been total counts, count rates and RMS voltages, and provided remarkably useful indications of underlying materials processes. However, more information can be deduced from AE signals, and the advanced schemes of signal processing will be essential in order to establish the nature of sources. For this goal, the frequency spectrum and amplitude distribution of AE signals have been studied during the last few years.

The frequency spectrum analysis can most effectively characterize the nature of AE signals, but special techniques are necessary as AE signals are by nature random. One is to use a conventional sweep-type spectrum analyzer in conjunction with a wide-band analogue recorder, such as a video tape recorder and a transient recorder.[7] The same AE signal must be played back repeatedly to obtain its frequency spectrum. Another is to obtain the autocorrelation function of AE signals, which provides the power density spectrum via subsequent Fourier transformation. The autocorrelation function is typically determined by using a hard-wire apparatus, while its Fourier transform can be deduced using a computer or a dedicated Fourier analyzer.[8]

Frequency spectra of AE signals from tensile deformation of 2024 Al alloys, plain carbon and low alloy steels, and Ti and Mg alloys have been determined. Generally, the spectra are close to that of random noice, although certain distinctive features of the spectra have also been noticed. Figure 1 shows the variation of selected frequency components as a function of plastic strain for 2024-T3 Al alloy. The magnitude of relative power density function varied with observed RMS voltage, indicating a maximum at 3% strain. However, the ratios of various frequency components remained nearly identical throughout the test, suggesting the similarity of the frequency spectra at different stages of deformation. On the other hand, Figs. 2A and 2B show similar plots for Beta-III Ti

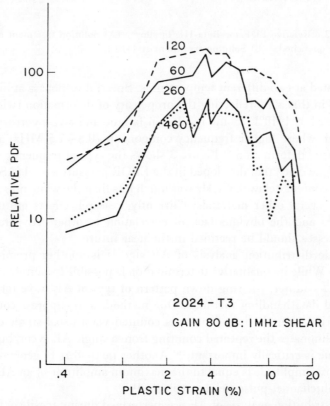

FIG. 1.   Relative power density function (PDF) of AE signals from 2024-T3 Al alloy as a function of plastic strain. Frequencies in kHz are indicated.

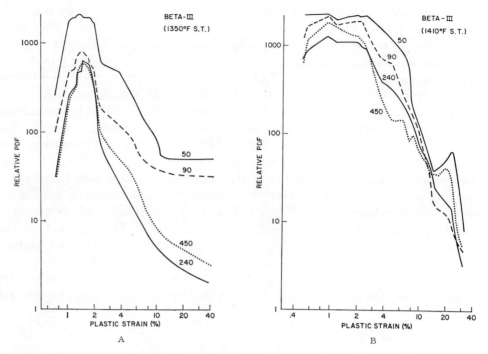

FIG. 2.   Relative PDF for Beta-III Ti alloy.   (A) Solution treatment at 1350°F and water quenched.   (B) Solution treatment at 1410°F.

alloy, solution treated at two different temperatures. Spectral responses at higher strains differ significantly in this alloy reflecting the propensity of deformation twinning in the alloy solution treated at 1410°F. Some results on fatigue and stress corrosion cracking were also reported, where higher frequency components (0.8~1.5 MHz) appear to be higher than in tensile deformation.[9] Figure 3 shows the typical frequency spectrum of the AE from a fatigue crack that developed in the EBOR pressure vessel (ASTM A387B steel). The energy content below 0.5 MHz was much less than the white noise (the dotted line) observed in several other materials. Currently, research efforts are underway at several laboratories and the obvious lack of correlation to other AE parameters and metallurgical processes should be rectified in the near future.

The amplitude distribution analysis of AE signals is another promising tool to characterize them. While its qualitative determination is possible by simply changing the threshold level of a counter, the ring-down pattern of typical AE wave forms requires more sophisticated data handling methods. One method is to suppress counting for a predetermined period after the initial pulse is counted via a usual single channel discriminator. This eliminates the repeated counting from a single AE event, but the choice of suppression time is critically important.[10] Another method is to generate a short (a few μs) pulse, whose amplitude is equal to the maximum amplitude of an AE signal, and to feed it to a multichannel-pulse-height analyzer.[11]

Amplitude distribution analysis of AE was performed during tensile deformation of several materials and fracture testing of *D6ac* steels of varying fracture toughness

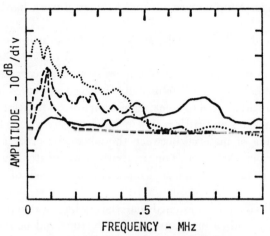

FREQUENCY - MHz

——— Acoustic Emission from fatigue crack
······ San Onofre nuclear reactor noise simulator
- - - - Fatigue pump pressure release noise
-·-·-·- Fatigue pump valve closing-intermittent

FIG. 3.   Frequency spectra of predominant noises encountered during EBOR fatigue test No. 2 (Ref. 9).

values.[10-13] In a latter study,[10] the amplitude distribution of total AE events indicated certain trend with the fracture toughness of a sample; when K_{IC} was high, the amplitude distribution showed a maximum, whereas numerous small amplitude signals tended to predominate in low K_{IC} materials. Nakamura et al.[10] attempted to correlate with the crack growth behavior of the steel samples, but the amplitude distribution from a single sample also varied widely as a function of the stress intensity-factor at the tip of a crack. In separate studies, Pollock and Radon[13] also performed the amplitude distribution analysis on AE during fracture of an Al alloy and a steel. While some differences in the release mode of stored elastic energy may exist, it is hardly possible to draw definite conclusions.

From these preliminary works, it appears that AE signals indeed contain potentially valuable information. More extensive efforts, both qualitatively and quantitatively, will be necessary to utilize these techniques for the identification of AE signal sources.

3.   Acoustic Emission During Fracture Processes

When an unnotched specimen is deformed under a uniaxial tensilon, the acoustic emission activities are greatly reduced in work-hardening stages as compared to numerous emissions observed during the initial yielding of the specimen. Generally, the AE activities are also very low in ductile fracture processes, in which fracture is plastically induced and the propagation of a crack is stable. The crack forms by the coalescence of voids generated in the vicinity of carbides and other nonmetallic inclusions via plastic deformation. The void coalescence comprises the fibrous zone of the cup and cone fracture. Since the crack propagates slowly, few AE are expected.

The shear fracture processes are simply more advanced stages of work-hardening, again producing insignificant AE.

Even in macroscopically ductile materials, such as ferritic-pearlitic steels, micro-cracks form by shear in the pearlite colonies. Cracking of hard second-phase particles often precedes final fracture in many materials. While no systematic correlation of such crack initiation to AE activities has been established, observed increases in AE count rates just prior to fracture were attributed to cracking of cementite in mild steel.[11] Microscopic cleavage cracks nucleates in semibrittle solids in which a cleavage crack propagates discontinuously via the tearing of material between the advancing crack and a micro-crack. The density of the microcracks depends on the ninth power of stress and Tetelman suggested a similar dependence for AE count rates on stress on the basis of cracking: AE event correspondence.[3]

Let us examine the AE behavior of notched materials, which was reported first on 4340 steel and has since been studied on many types of ferrous and nonferrous alloys (for review see Ref. 1–4). In medium-to-high strength materials of limited ductility, AE counts increase with applied stress and the maximum AE count rate is found immediately preceeding the final fracture. At a given stress, more AE counts are generated in a specimen with a longer crack, or with multiple cracks. These experimental results are best correlated with stress intensity factor K (or K_I for the plane strain condition), as shown in Fig. 4. Often the relationship between total (cumulative) AE counts, N, and K can be described by

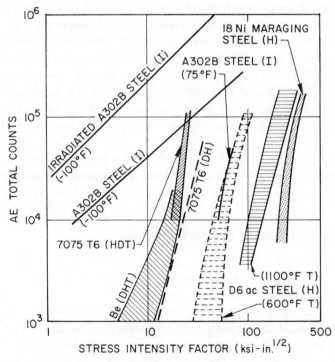

FIG. 4.   AE total counts vs. stress intensity factor for various materials. For the sources of data, see Ref. 4.

$$N = AK^m \tag{1}$$

where A and m are constants. Observed values of m in various materials indicate a large variation among them. Further, m is not necessarily a constant for a given specimen. With increasing K, it increases in Be and D6ac steels, whereas it decreases in a maraging steel and a mild steel. The observed m values depend also on the amplitude of AE signals.

Dunegan et al.[14] offered an explanation for the above power law relation between N and K with $m=4$. Their model essentially assumes that AE counts are proportional to the plastic zone volume at the crack tip. As is well known, AE count rate reaches a maximum at or near the yield stress during tensile deformation of an unnotched sample. Thus, the AE counts of a notched specimen are given as a function of the volume of material that yields plastically. Simply using the proportionality, N is then related to the square of the plastic zone size r_p. The elastic crack approximation provides $r_p = K^2/2\pi\sigma_y^2$, and one obtains $N \propto K^4$. Although some observations of m are close to the above prediction of the plastic zone volume model, experimental results hardly support this model.

As applied stress becomes higher, low-strength materials reach general yield and a crack begins to propagate at the tip of a notch. This fracture is stable and the crack growth is due to the coalescence of plastically induced voids. The ductile fracture produced weak AE activities in mild steels and HY-80 steel. The amplitude and count rate of AE were small. The count rate was maximum immediately after the general yield and was very small during the growth of a ductile crack. In the ductile materials, most of the testing was not under the plane-strain condition. The use of crack opening displacement (COD) or the plastic zone size is more meaningful. Recently, Palmer and Heald[15] demonstrated the AE count from a mild steel to be proportional to r_p as calculated by

$$N \propto r_p = l\,[\sec{(\pi\sigma/2\sigma_1)} - 1] \tag{2}$$

where σ_1 is a characteristic parameter of the material. Figure 5 shows the proportionality between N and COD for a mild steel.[16] Here, the plastic deformation appears to be the source of AE. This was supported by the suppression of AE in a WOL testing of a 10% cold worked mild steel, which manifested the well-known Kaiser effect. At present, however, the meaning of the proportionality between N and r_p or COD is not clear. One possible source of this observation can arise from the cracking of brittle second phase particles during plastic deformation. Since the normal rupture of the particles in the area ahead of the crack leads to the release of elastic energy, the number of AE events should be proportional to the plastic zone area. Spheroidized mild steel samples produced only one-fifth of AE counts found in pearlitic steel samples of the same composition. The total AE counts in vacuum remelted 4335 steels were also reported to be much smaller than those in air melted materials.[17]

Consider next the AE behavior of high toughness, high strength materials, in which low-energy tear fracture is observed. When the thickness of a sample exceeds the value that satisfies the plane strain condition at the tip of a crack, slow growth of a microscopic crack is observed with increasing applied stress. In this region ($K \leq K_{IC}$), stable processes of void coalescence and crack tip sharpening take place, which begin as applied stress produces the critical tensile displacement at the crack tip. Although unstable fracture may occur at $K_I = K_{IC}$, macroscopic slow crack extension is generally found in many struc-

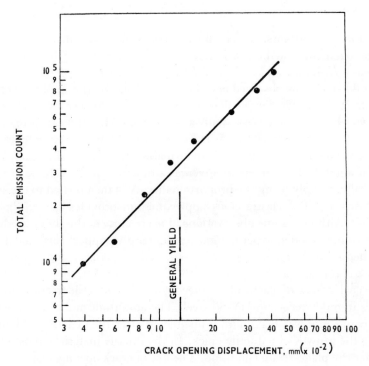

FIG. 5.   AE total counts vs. COD for reactor pressure vessel steel (0.15 C, 0.90 Mn) (Ref. 16).

tures in the range of $K_C>K>K_{IC}$. The void coalescence process can be the main source of AE. Although a similar process also occurs in low strength materials, the released elastic energy increases with the square of the microscopic rupture strength and numerous AE events becomes observable. The number of AE counts is proportional to that of void coalescence. Since the presence of the voids is limited to the area of the large plastic strain, AE counts again depends linearly to the size of r_p. While an accurate estimate of the r_p vs. K relationship for work-hardening materials is not available, qualitative relationships are shown in Fig. 6.[18] When plastic relaxation of the crack tip is considered, the r_p-K relation and consequently N-K relation are expected to be that of finite root radius ($\rho>0$). This agree with the observed N-K relations in $D6ac$ and 18 Ni maraging steels and with the absence of AE below a critical value of K_I. When the number of dimples on the fracture surfaces are compared to that of AE counts, 10^3 to 10^4 dimples correspond to an AE count, indicating numerous low energy events are escaping the detection.

Another important mode of fracture is the discontinuous propagation of cleavage cracks in low ductility materials. Details have to be omitted, but the AE counts are expected to depend on the first to second power of K.[4] This microcleavage crack model is in agreement with AE results of A302B steel at low temperatures and those of low ductility $D6ac$ steels.

In summary, AE during fracture cannot be explained solely by the plastic zone volume model, originally proposed by Dunegan et al. Three possible alternatives are

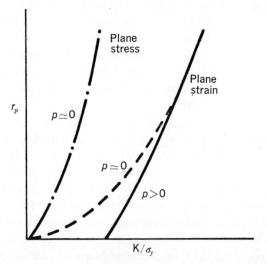

FIG. 6.   Variation of r_p with K/σ_y for notches of varying root radii.

proposed here, although further experimental support for the second-phase cracking, tear fracture and microcleavage crack models need to be developed.

4.   Defects in Welded Structures

The primary industrial applications of AE testing are to detect and locate existing flaws in pressure vessels and to provide early warning of impending failure. The first task relies on triangulation techniques, while the second is based on an empirical correlation between AE and stress intensity factor. These were originally developed for aerospace applications,[5] but are vigorously pursued in nuclear and petrochemical industries.[1,2,19,20] AE testing of a welded pressure vessel is most effective in assuring its integrity during the initial hydrotest, in which the presence of various flaws, gross and local yielding and leakage can be detected. Because of operating environmental noise, continuous AE monitoring is much more difficult, but provides the knowledge on propagating cracks and fatigue crack growth.

The regions of a pressure vessel that emit AE signals and may consequently contain dangerous flaws, can be identified by "*zoning*" techniques. Multiple transducers are used and their outputs are compared for the AE counts, signal intensity, directionality, etc. The area associated with the most active transducer corresponds to a weakened area. This technique cannot, however, match the accuracy provided by triangulation methods, which are based on the differences of arrival times of an AE signal. In one method, time interval data between many pairs of transducers are stored. The time intervals that have been registered many times are then utilized together with those from adjacent transducer pairs to compute unique solution for an AE source.[21] It is also possible to determine the source location for an individual set of time interval measurements. The averaging is performed on the source location data in order to suppress noise. The source location is most often identified by table look-up. This method is real time, and allows continuous display of the source location results. Although differing in details, the majority of source location systems developed so far appears to be of this type (e.g., AET Corp., BNWL, D/E, SWRI). A typical system consists of 10 to 64 channels of transducersignal conditioner combination, a minicomputer for source location processing and for data storage, and display and other data output instrumentation. At present, it can process 20 to 300 source locations per sec. with the number of resolution elements in the system of 500 to 1000.

The flaw detection/location capabilities of triangulation systems have been demonstrated in many tests of pressure vessels as well as in the recent EEI sponsored EBOR testing. Generally, growing cracks that approach criticality and adversely affect the integrity of welded structures can be detected without difficulty. The accuracy of flaw location is typically the wall thickness of the tested vessel. The type, size, and severity of a flaw that can be detected, however, depend on many factors and must be handled case by case. Since AE testing by itself cannot characterize detected flaws, it is essential to correlate the observed AE behavior to other destructive and non-destructive methods of flaw characterization. This step has often been inadequate. Many of identified AE sources were weld seam porosity and slag inclusion, less than a few millimeter diameter, weld and cladding cracks, as small as 0.5 mm long, and noise at support or extension brackets.[21-23]

Some AE sources are impossible to identify by conventional NDT methods. Figure 7 shows the AE count and crack growth as a function of fatigue cycles.[24] The fatigue crack was grown in the 150 mm thick cylindrical section of the EBOR vessel by hydraulic pressurization of a D-shaped saw-cut, 0.6 mm wide, 33 mm deep at the center and 95 mm long. The AE counts were nearly identical to the number of fatigue cycles, whereas no crack growth was detected until 7400 fatigue cycles. Thus, AE can identify growing cracks even when their growth rate is small (much less than 5×10^{-4} mm/cycle). Sub-surface cracks 0.5 to 6 mm long, in cladded steel plates (A508 type) during stress

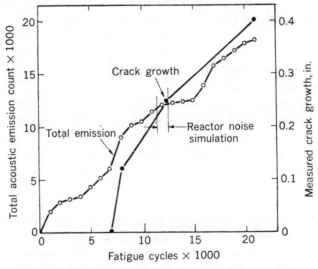

FIG. 7.   Correlation of acoustic emission and crack growth for a fatigue crack (ODF1) in the 6 in. cylindrical section of the EBOR pressure vessel (Ref. 24).

relief anneal were detected by AE. In the majority of the tests, metallographic technique was the only means of revealing the presence of such cracks.[23] Clearly, AE is superior to other known NDT methods in order to monitor growing flaws in welded structures.

Further developments are required in the area of defect characterization and noise discrimination. Changes in the nature of AE signals have been observed and can be applied to identify the AE source involved. Morais and Green[19] found burst type of AE signals at the beginning and just prior to the failure of a steel pressure vessel and continuous type at other times during a rising pressure test. Jolly[24] reported small amplitude (30—60 μV at the transducer), short burst (—50 μsec) signals during a fatigue crack initiation, while large amplitude (1.5 mV at the transducer), longer burst (1—5 msec) signals were found during rapid crack growth in the EBOR vessel test. Systematic studies of AE characteristics in conjunction with metallurgical and fractographic analysis are highly desirable. In the case of noise discrimination, the speed of flaw location processing needs to be increased for better spatial signal averaging results. Since time-intervals for 3 m transducer spacings can be as large as 1 msec, the source location averaging scheme has an inherent upper limit of processing speed (about 10^3/sec). In order to improve the processing speed, extensive instrumentation such as the coincidence detection location system will become necessary. At present, however, this approach appears to be very expensive except for small scale applications. Noise discrimination from AE signal characteristics may also be feasible, but has not been developed.

ACKNOWLEDGMENTS

Work discussed in this paper was supported in part by the Office of Naval Research Acoustic Program.

REFERENCES

1. "Acoustic Emission," *Proceedings of symposium at Bal Harbour, Florida, December 1971, ASTM Special Technical Publication 505*, Philadelphia, Pennsylvania (1972).
2. Liptai, R. G., Harris, D. O., Engle, R. B. and Tatro, C. A., "Acoustic Emission Techniques in Materials Research," Int. J. NDT **3**, p. 215 (1971).
3. Tetelman, A. S., "Acoustic Emission and Fracture Mechanics Testing of Metals and Composites," *Proceedings of U.S.—Japan Joint Symposium on Acoustic Emission*, Tokyo, Japan, July, p. 1 (1972).
4. Ono, K., "Acoustic Emission from Ferrous Materials," Tetsu-to-Hagane **59**, p. 1338 (1973).
5. Green, A. T., "Detection of Incipient Failures in Pressure Vessels by Stress-Wave Emission," Nuclear Safety, **10**, 1, p. 4 (1969).
6. Notvest, K., "Effect of Thermal Cycles in Welding D6ac Steel," Weld. J., **45**, 4, 173s (1966).
7. Graham, L. J. and Alers, G. A., "Frequency Spectra of Acoustic Emissions Generated by Deforming Metals and Ceramics," *1972 Ultrasonics Symposium Proceedings*, 72CH0708 -8 SU, IEEE, New York, p. 18 (1972).
8. Ono, K., Stern, R. and Long, M., "Application of Correlation Analysis to Acoustic Emission," Ref. (1), p. 152.

9. Buck, J. S. and Graham, L. J., "Acoustic Emission Testing Experience at the EBOR Facility," *EEI Project RP79 Addendum Report*, May, p. 17 (1973).

10. Nakamura, Y., Veach, C. L. and McCauley, B. O., "Amplitude Distribution of Acoustic Emission Signals," Ref. (1), p. 164.

11. Nakasa, H., "Application of Acoustic Emission Techniques to Material Diagnostics," *IAEA Symposium on Nuclear Power Plant Control and Inst.*, Prague, Czech., Jan. (1973) (in press).

12. Jax, P. and Eisenblatter, J., "Acoustic Emission Measurements During Plastic Deformation of Metals," Battelle Information **15**, p. 2 (1972).

13. Radon, J. C. and Pollock, A. A., "Acoustic Emissions and Energy Transfer during Crack Propagation," Engr. Fracture Mech. **4**, 2, p. 295 (1972).

14. Dunegan, H. L., Harris, D. O. and Tatro, C. A., " Fracture Analysis by Use of Acoustic Emission," Engr. Fract. Mech. **1**, 1, p. 105 (1968).

15. Palmer, I. G. and Heald, P. T., " The Application of Acoustic Emission Measurements to Fracture Mechanics," Materials Sci. and Engr. **11**, p. 181 (1973).

16. Palmer, I. G., Brindley, B. J. and Harrison, R. P., " The Relationship between Acoustic Emission and Crack Opening Displacement Measurements," Materials Sci. and Engr. (in press).

17. Corle, R. R. and Schliessmann, J. A., "Flaw Detection and Characterization Using Acoustic Emission," Mat. Eval. **31**, p. 115 (1973).

18. Tetelman, A. S. and McEvily, A. J., *Fracture of Structural Materials*, John Wiley, New York, p. 304 (1967).

19. Morais, C. and Green, A., "The Use of Acoustic Emission for Quality Assurance of Pressure Containment Structures," *Proceedings Second International Conference on Structure and Mechanics and Reactor Technology*, Berlin, Sept. (1973) (in press).

20a. "In-Service Inspection Program for Nuclear Reactor Vessels," *EEI Project RP79 Final Technical Report*, May (1973).

  b. *ibid, Technical Report*, Aug. (1972).

21. Jolly, W. D. and Parry, D. L., "Field Evaluation of the Acoustic Emission System," Ref. 20b, p. 97.

22. Hutton, P. H. and Parry, D. L., "Assessment of Structural Integrity by Acoustic Emission," Mat. Res. Std. **11**, p. 25 (1971).

23. Eisenblatter, J., "Acoustic Emission Analysis," Ingenieur Digest **11**, p. 62 (1972).

24. Jolly, W. D., "Field Evaluation of the Acoustic Emission System," Ref. 20a, p. 57.

Non-Destructive Testing for Welded Joints of Huge Hull Construction

S. Kaku

Nippon Kaiji Kyokai

Sampling Test for Large Ships

As a result of recent trend to enlarge a ship size, most of the large tankers ranged in dead weight tonnage from 250,000 to 350,000 with two huge tankers of 470,000 tons in dead weight being constructed in this country. Safety of such huge oil tankers at sea is becoming a serious problem in the world, since damage and the pollution problems associated with such tankers at sea involves a tremendous cost.

On the other hand, the total length of butt weld joint in a ship is estimated to be approximately one hundred thousand meters in length, and therefore more than half a million of radiograph must be prepared if a 100 percent radiography is required for all of the butt welded joints. Thus a tremendous cost is also involved in inspecting these huge ships.

At present, classification societies usually require radiographic sampling tests for butt joints of only primary important structural members of the ship, and the number of these samples is estimated to be from two hundreds to five hundreds. This figure, however, when compared with the above mentioned figure for a 100 percent inspection of the butt weld joint of a hull construction, seems inadequately small.

Hull Damage related to Weld Defects

A quarter of century has passed since the construction of the first all-welded ships, and hull damage related to welding has been remarkably reduced in recent years by improvements in design, workmanship and material.

Investigation of approximately 1200 ships by the Japan Shipbuilding Research Association showed that cracks in butt welded joint of hull structure initiated from continuous two dimensional defects due mainly to poor penetration of welds. Where poor pentration existed in butt welded joint in considerable length, cracks initiated from the top and bottom tips of poor penetration and then extended towards the direction of

59

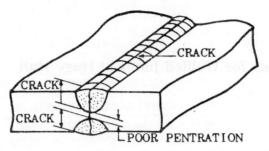

FIG. 1.   Crack intiated from poor penetration.

thickness. Thus a long crack through the welded joint is suddenly generated when the crack reaches both surfaces of the weld as shown in Fig. 1. Such a long crack might result in serious damage to the hull construction.

It has further been shown that any fracture related only to such three dimensional defects as blow holes or slag inclusions has scarcely been found in butt joints of existing hull structures. Furthermore, fractures of butt joints in hull construction related mainly to continuous defects, are also hardly found in those shell and strength deck at half ship length amidship which are considered important primary joints of hull construction and normaly required radiographic inspection by the classification societies. Almost all fractures of butt joints were observed at joints of internal members or outer parts from a half ship length amidship. It is possible that such harmful continuous defects may be included in some weld joints for which special quality control, such as that for important primary joint, is not usually specified.

It must, however, be emphasized that in welded hull structure, serious brittle fractures occur at primary important members, e.g. shell or strength deck plating, even the crack may have initiated from the welded joint of a secondary member, propagated from the secondary member to primary member through a weld connection, therefore, such continuous two dimensional defects should be carefully eliminated from welded joints of structural members, being primary important or not.

Quality Control of Welding for Continuous Defects

Although it is impossible to completely detect two dimensional continuous defects after welding by normal inspection system adopted in shipyards, it is not impossible to avoid such defects in the welded joint of hull structure by normal quality control system during welding.

All butt joints of hull structure are to be welded by qualified welding operators using suitable welding consumables under the welding conditions approved by classification societies. Before welding, all grooves, including the reserve side after gouging, should be carefully checked by a competent person, e.g., foreman in the shipyard, and the names of the welding operators and inspector, should be ascribed close to the relevant joint. Sampling tests of the joint should subsequently be carried out by a simple procedure, using a handy non-destructive testing instrument, e.g., a very small ultra-sonic testing machine, which is designed to detect only to two dimensional continuous defects.

The testing instrument, which is now under development, is not an expensive instrument and will not require a specially qualified personnel but it will be operated by a shop foreman. Writing names next to the welded joint is useful, if it becomes necessary to trace the workmanship as well as to delineate their responsibility.

It is thus, expected that no harmful continuous two dimensional defect exists in butt joints of hull structure. Further radiographic sampling tests, however, may be required to reconfirm the results obtained by the handy non-destructive instrument. The number of such radiographic samples may be kept to a minimum, e.g., to two or three hundreds.

The quality control and inspection system above-mentioned will be adopted in some shipyards in this country, with the cooperation of testing instrument manufacturers.

Cracking at the Toe of Welded Joint and Acoustic Emission

N. Ogura

Institute of Materials Science and Engineering, Yokohama National University

Three recent catastrophic failures during hydraulic testing in Japan, two spherical pressure vessels (1968) and one forged head of a multiple layered vessel (1970), have stimulated study of the condition under which brittle fracture can be initiated.

A major point of interest in these three failures was that failure occurred at the toe and ran along the heat affected zone of a welded joint. Failure was induced by delayed hydrogen cracking at the toe with the crack growing to a critical size before triggering the brittle fracture. The role of dissolved hydrogen in promoting toe crack of a welded joint is thus the object of this investigation.

Two types of specimens were used, rectangular three point bend specimens and compact tension specimens. Both of types have groove for welding as shown in Fig. 1. The steel tested is a high tensile strength quenched and tempered steel with a specified minimum tensile strength of 80 kg/mm². Specimens were welded in a chamber with atmospheric conditions of 30°C temperature and 80% humidity. The electrodes were baked and kept in the same chamber for four hours to induce moisture into the electrode coating.

Figure 2 shows the test system for detecting of acoustic emission in the three point bend test. Acoustic emission instrumentation used was Series 3000 of Dunegan Research Corporation, U.S.A. Amplification of 90–95db and band pass filtering between 100–300 KHz and 1–2 MHz were used. Optical observation of the crack growth were also made during the course of the test at a magnification of 40×.

In the bend tests, bending stress of 80% to 90% of the yield stress was applied. Under these experimental conditions, a slow crack growth was observed until it reaches a critical size at which rapid crack growth occurred.

The acoustic emission signals from the bend specimens have three stages as shown schematically in Fig. 3. In the early stage, no visual crack was observed when acoustic emission signals were recorded. It is not known whether these signals accompany creeping or microcracking or not.

The advanced stage corresponds to slow crack growth. The rate of acoustic emission

62

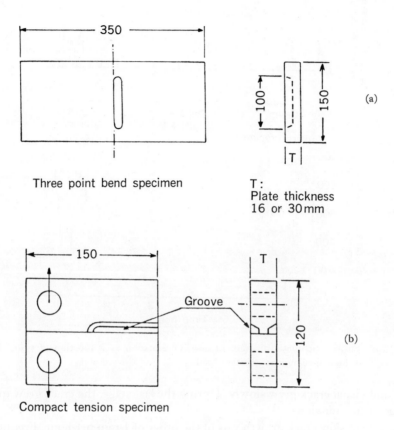

Three point bend specimen

T:
Plate thickness
16 or 30 mm

(a)

Groove

Compact tension specimen

(b)

FIG. 1. Test specimens.

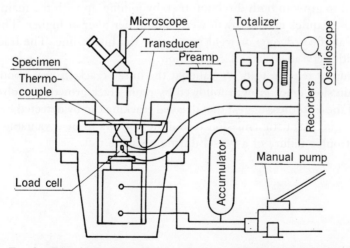

FIG. 2. Experimental system for measuring acoustic emission in welded specimen subjected to three point bend.

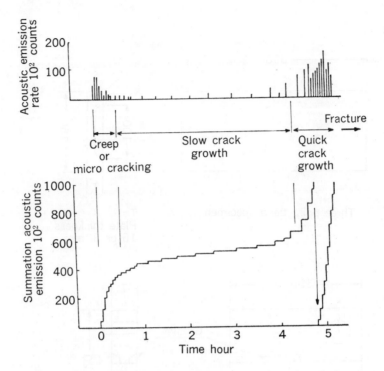

FIG. 3.   Schmatic diagram of acoustic emission as a function of time. Bend test of welded specimen at constant load.

was low and visual crack grew slowly. During the last stage, the crack grew quickly with violent acoustic emissions.

The rate of slow crack growth was of the order of 1 mm per hour. Frequently a new crack was observed to start at approximatly 1 mm in front of the main crack. The new crack continued to grow in both direction thereby joining up with the main crack.

The speeds of quick crack growth were 30 mm per hour or higher. The crack went through the heat affected zone or weld metal near the fusion line. The fracture surface was fibrous with very small lateral contraction.

In the compact tension tests, K value at the initial crack tip was about 250 to 300 kg/mm$^{1.5}$. Again slow crack growth followed by rapid crack growth was observed.

Results of these studies suggest that delayed cracking can be detected by the acoustic emission technique. Acoustic emission technique appears to be a valuable new tool for avoiding catastrophic failure of a vessel during pressure test.

Discussions in Session I

Question directed to Prof. Packman by Prof. McEvily

Question directed to Prof. Packman by Prof. McEvily

I have two short questions of clarification for Prof. Packman. First, are all of the dimensions in your tables in inches? And second, is the surface crack length sufficient to characterize the severity of a defect? Should not something more than the linear aspect be considered in assessing the severity and specification of defects?

Reply to Prof. McEvily by Prof. Packman

The dimensions of all crack length are in inches, yes.

The main question asked is important one, and very difficult to answer simply. In reality, one is not interested in the size of the defect, we are more interested in its criticality in terms of the stress intensity factors associated with the defect. The type of flaw and the loading determines which of the linear dimensions of crack are most important. Consider the part through crack. If one talks about surface flaws, we are not particularly interested in finding a flaw with a given surface length or of a particular depth, but are interested in the ability of the technique to find all flaws of equal criticality, independant of the actual size. If the nondestructive testing technique is limited becasue of the flaw depth, for example, eddy current or surface wave ultrasonic one must design the NDT so that flaws of identical criticality (to the worst case) can be found. Consider

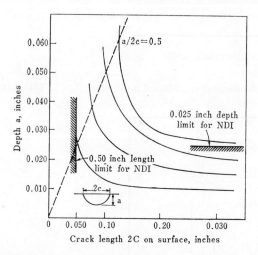

Fig. 1. Flaws of equal criticality that must be detected by NDI for reliable fracture control.

65

66

Fig. 1. These are calculated using the $a/2c$ vs. Q equations for the part through flaws. On the other hand if you were limited by surface length, i.e. penetrant techniques, you must design based on the worst case limited by the $2c$ value. The design analysis is based on the worst case, i.e. the most critical flaw which is for $a/2c=0.5$.

The present NDT techniques do not permit you to discriminate between a depth limited or surface length limited process, and you must consider only the worst case that might be encountered, and yet be missed. That is why a technique such as acoustic emission has such a great potential for analysis. The acoustic emission is not limited to length or depth, but defines the criticality of the flaw by the signal.

Question directed to Prof. Packman by Prof. Kitagawa

I am much interested in your "loading and un-loading" method. To make your method available, the crack tip is probably required to be plastically deformed in large amount.

How can we make out when we apply your method to practical case, or to actual structures?

Can we be permitted to apply a load to such a extent?

Reply to Prof. Kitagawa by Prof. Packman

The effect of stress greatly influences the magnitude of the reflected ultrasonic signal from a fatigue crack. Figure 1 show some work of Coroly & Packman. As the

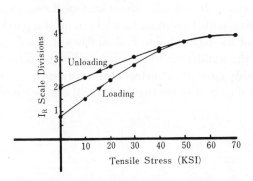

FIG. 1.   Influence of tensile load on reflected pulse height I_R (7075-TG511 AL).

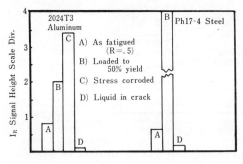

FIG. 2.   Typical values of I_R max after crack has been subjected to treatment indicated.

stress on material containing the crack increases, the signal height increases. It rapidly saturates but upon unloading, does not return to the initial value. Increased signals on unloading are obtained. Thus it is possible that partial proof loading, causing plastic deformation around the crack tip and the resulting increases in crack displacements produce greater signals. Similar results have been found for proof tested pressure vessels examined by X-rays and by shear wave ultrasonics.

Figure 2 shows that the reflected signal intensity from fatigue cracks can be increased significantly by the use of a slight etch prior to inspection. The bar graphs show the relative increases in signal under four conditions for Aluminum, and three for steel. The highest signal is obtained for a crack that has been slightly etched.

It is important that the specimen be cleaned after the etch, since the presence of a small amount of moisture in the crack will result in a severely decreased signal. In this case the presence of the liquid in the crack permits transmission of the ultrasonic signal thru the crack and little signal is reflected back to the transducer. If we equate the magnitude of the reflected signal with a measure of the ability to detect cracks, (in terms of a signal to noise ratio) the crack filled with liquid will be more difficult to detect.

In actual practice it is often possible to apply a load. One example is the pressure vessel that is proof tested. If the NDT used to examine the part for flaws is conducted during the proof test it is possible to find smaller flaws. Another example is the lower wing surfaces of airplaines. The wing is normally in compresion when on the ground and inspected. Improved penetrant inspection is obtained by loading the wing in tension.

Question directed to Prof. Packman by Dr. Miyoshi
How to be sure that etching solution is removed?

Reply to Dr. Miyoshi by Prof. Packman
The question asked was how can you be sure that the etching solution is removed. In practice I don't know. In the laboratory I break the specimen open and do fractography on the surface by replic or scanning microscopy.

Almost all penetrant inspections require etching prior to application of the penetrant. Standard aircraft practice requires a half mil etch before penetrant use. Otherwise you cannot insure detection. The fact that the signal goes up in ultrasonics appears due to the local etching on the surface opening the crack near the surface. You produce most of your reflections from the open part of the cracks since the other portions are still closed tightly.

Question directed to Dr. Miyoshi or Prof. Packman by Prof. Fisher
Most of the discussion by Dr. Miyoshi and Prof. Packman is directed to discontinuities on very smooth surfaces. There are large numbers of civil engineering structures which have the weld reinforcement left in place. In this situation the discontinuity is located at a geometrical stress concentration. Because of the weld profile and geometric change it is difficult to define or detect small cracks. How reliable are non-destructive inspection methods of such discontinuities?

Reply to Prof. Fisher by Prof. Packman

It is much more difficult to find defects in the vicinity of stress concentrations and on rough surfaces than it is on flat sheets. All of the work I have discussed is work conducted by the Air force and on Air force type structures. Aircraft systems do not allow unfinished welds or backups that cannot be fully inspected. Hence all of the surface finishes were representative of those found on aircraft; finished butt welds, relatively clean surfaces, etc.

When you have rough surfaces, geometric changes, reentry etc, the detetectability of the flaw goes down rapidly. I would imagine that increases of detectable flaw sizes to 0.5 inches would not be unreasonable. I don't know how to take into account geometry changes. Every weld inspection becomes an individual problem.

The most difficult problem is to determine what to use for a standard. It has been pointed out that x-ray requirements for flaw detection in welds are in many cases unrealistic. They penalize the welds for defects that may be more critical than those imposed on the parent metal. They may not even consider the truly critical defects in the welds because the x-ray technique cannot detect these tight small defects. All of these studies were conducted using fatigue type cracks. The rason we used fatigue cracks was so that we could control the flaw sizes and depths.

When we came to weld defects we also used a fatigue crack. The crack was placed on the back surface of the plate, and the back was then covered with another plate so that the fatigue crack could not be seen. The inspection had to be conducted from one side only. Because of the nature of the test we could not produce any other type of defect that would be where we said it was going to be, and of a controlled size. One would hope that lack of penetration or microcracking in a weld would be similar in nature to the fatigue crack, i.e. a closed smooth surface.

Question directed to Prof. Packman by Prof. McEvily

Geometrical factors appear to limit the ability of ultrasonic techniques to detect cracks in the toe region of fillet welds. How effective are dye penetrants in detecting such cracks in these regions?

Reply to Prof. McEvily by Prof. Packman

As long as the geometric changes are not too severe, there should be relatively little changes in detection capabilities. If there are no residual stresses acting to close the surface of the crack, there should be little changes in detection capabilities. In titanium, where the structure changes considerably in the weld, the penetrant wetting ability changes. The penetrant techniques with titanium are not as good as other techniques.

Ultrasonic sensitivities change drastically in geometric changes due to the complexity of the ultrasonic path. Magnetic particle defect detection should also become less sensitive for obvious geometric effects.

SESSION II

FRACTURE MECHANICS APPROACH
TO THE INITIATION OF CRACKS
FROM WELDING DEFECTS AND
THEIR GROWTH

An Application of Fracture Mechanics to Hydrogen Induced Cracking

K. SATOH AND M. TOYODA

Faculty of Engineering, Osaka University

Fracture mechanics is used for studying the problem of weld cracking induced by hydrogen under restraint stresses. By considering changes in fracture toughness parameter due to diffusion of hydrogen towards the crack tip, initiation and growth of the delayed cracking are analyzed following the method used in analyzing brittle fracture initiation. Theoretical relation between applied stress and incubation time for crack initiation are also obtained. Stair-like growth of crack is also obtained as functions of applied stresses and specimen rigidity.

1. Introduction

Considerable works on the problem of cold cracking in heat affected zone of steel welds have been conducted to date, where crack formation is believed to be caused by the diffusion of hydrogen in weld metal and its vicinity under restraint stresses. This feature can be shown by the restraint weld cracking tests such as TRC-RRC tests.[1,2] An example of the RRC-test results made on a HT80 steel weld is shown in Fig. 1, in which fracture occurred within a certain incubation time after weld metal had been cooled to room temperature under a constant restraint stress which is governed by restraining gauge length, below yield stress of the material. Root crack is initiated at a certain warm temperature, about 100°C in this test, and grows with a very slow rate as shown in Fig. 2. These results show that the fundamental feature of cold cracking is same as delayed failure under a constant load of notched steel specimens with hydrogen.[3]

In the present paper, fracture mechanics is applied to the problem of initiation and growth of the cold cracking. When the crack grows at a certain slow speed, the stress required for crack growth will be nearly equal to, or a little smaller than, the stress required for crack initiation, and therefore the growth and arrest of the crack could be analyzed by the same method as the analysis of brittle fracture initiation.

In this analysis, influence of the changes in applied load or restraint stress accompanied by crack growth will be considered since crack growth itself is coupled to the

71

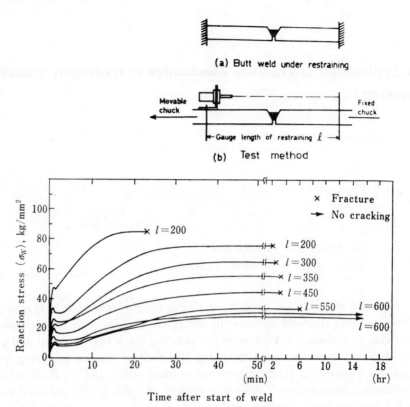

FIG. 1.   Effect of restraint stress on root cracking of HT80 steel weld. (Plate thickness 20 mm, Heat input 13,000 J/cm.)[2]

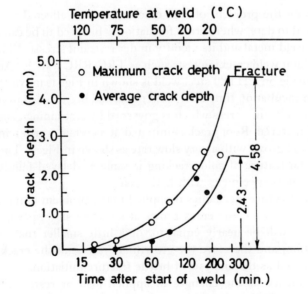

FIG. 2.   Growth of root crack in HT80 steel weld under restraint.

rigidity or restraint intensity of the test specimens and structural elements. In delayed cracking induced by hydrogen, fracture toughness near the tip of the growing crack is changed with hydrogen diffusion around the crack tip. This change in fracture toughness will also be considered in the calculation under simple assumptions.

2. Fracture Mechanics Approach

Analysis by fracture mechanics will be made for a model which consists of a plate (I) with a crack of length $2c$ and a spring (II) as shown in Fig. 3. Both ends of the model are gripped to rigid walls under a certain applied gross stress, σ. Element (I) represents the weld metal and its vicinity in which weld crack is expected to initiate and element (II) represents the rigidity of structural elements around the weld.

If it can be assumed that stress, σ_F, for crack initiation and that stress, σ_M, for crack growth are dependent on the fracture toughness parameter around the crack tip, the σ_F-, σ_M-values can then estimated by either the K_c-, Φ_c- or ρ_c^+-criteria. In the present paper, analysis will be made by the ρ_c^+-criterion[4] which states crack initiation and growth occur when the tensile yield zone size, ρ^+, formed ahead of the crack attains a critical value governed by the material around the crack tip. Relation between the applied gross stress, σ, and the ρ^+-value can be more easily obtained for a plate with finite width W as given by the following equation.

$$\frac{\sigma}{\sigma_Y} = \frac{2}{\pi}\cos^{-1}\left(\frac{\sin(\pi c/W)}{\sin\{\pi(c+\rho^+)/W\}}\right) \tag{1}$$

where σ_r is yield stress of the material.

In the model as shown in Fig. 3, the applied force $P(=\sigma W)$ will change as the crack

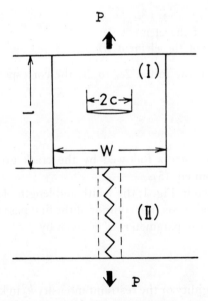

FIG. 3.   Model of a welded tension plate with a crack.

grows at a certain slow rate. The change in force can be obtained by compliance procedure.

The compliances of element (I) without a crack and the element (II) are denoted as $\lambda_1(=1/k_1)$ and $\lambda_2(=1/k_2)$, respectively. For a constant applied displacement loading condition,

$$P\left(1+\frac{\Delta\lambda_1}{\lambda_1+\lambda_2}\right) = \text{constant} \tag{2}$$

where $\Delta\lambda_1$ is the difference in compliance between element (I) without a crack and with a crack of length $2c$. The change in compliance, $\Delta\lambda_1$, is given by the following approximate expression for plane stress condition:

$$\Delta\lambda_1 = \frac{2}{E}\int_0^c \left(\frac{K}{P}\right)^2 dc \tag{3. a}$$

or

$$\Delta\lambda_1 = \frac{1}{E}H\left(\frac{2c}{W}\right) \tag{3. b}$$

where

$$H(\xi) = \pi\int_0^\xi \xi\, sec\left(\frac{\pi\xi}{2}\right)d\xi \tag{3. c}$$

Substituing eq. (3.b) in eq. (2), the change in applied force is related to crack growth by

$$P\left[1+\alpha\beta H\left(\frac{2c}{W}\right)\right] = \text{constant} \tag{4}$$

where

$$\alpha = \frac{W}{l}, \quad \beta = \frac{\lambda_1}{\lambda_1+\lambda_2}$$

W :   Width of the element (I)
l :   Length of the element (I)

When the crack length is increased from the initial $2c_0$ to $2c$, the corresponding gross stress is thus given by

$$\sigma = \frac{1+\alpha\beta H(2c_0/W)}{1+\alpha\beta H(2c/W)}\sigma_0 \tag{5}$$

Figure 4 shows the change of the gross stress followed by the crack growth, when $2c_0/W=0.1$, for various values of $\alpha\beta$ from eq. (5).

In the RRC-weld cracking test shown in Fig. 1, the width and length of element (I) can be considered nearly equal since the cross-section contour of the first pass weld can be approximated as a square, and therefore the parameter $\alpha\beta$ is given by

$$\alpha\beta \fallingdotseq \frac{k_2}{E+k_2} \tag{6}$$

In addition to this approximation, the rigidity or the restraint intensity k_2 in kg/mm·mm is of several ten times the thickness of the welded plates in mm, or usualy less than

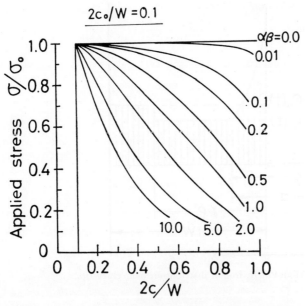

FIG. 4.   Decrease in applied stress, σ, due to crack growth.

2,000 kg/mm·mm in structural elements.[5] As a result the $\alpha\beta$-value is usualy less than 0.08 for steel welds. Figure 4 shows rather small drop in applied stress until the crack length approaches the throat depth.

3.   Hydrogen Concentration at Crack Tip

In the model shown in Fig. 3, fracture toughness near the tip of a growing crack will change with hydrogen diffusion around the crack tip. Consider now the model shown in Fig. 5, in which an uniform initial distribution of hydrogen of constant density C_0 in the shaded portion of $W \times l$ is assumed and hydrogen diffusion occurs under a constant tensile stress, σ_0. Although this model essentially represents a two-dimensional problem in diffusion, this analysis is simplified to a combination of one-dimensional problems as follows:

(1) The average density of hydrogen along the net section ($y=0$) is determined from the solution of a one-dimensional diffusion problem in the y-direction.

(2) Along the net section, hydrogen diffuses one-dimensionally towards the crack tip

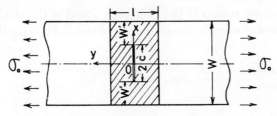

FIG. 5.   Model of a welded tension plate with a crack.

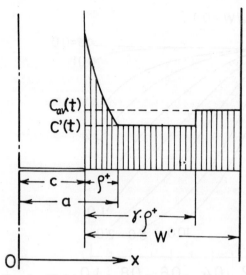

FIG. 6.   Model of hydrogen distribution near crack tip.

under the assumptions that (i) the density of hydrogen is proportional to the amount of plastic strains near the crack tip, and as a result, (ii) redistribution of hydrogen occurs within the zone of $\gamma \times$ (size of tensile yield zone) as illustrated in Fig. 6.

The solution of problem (1) or the average density C_{av} at the net section is given as a function of time t as

$$C_{av}(t) = C_0 \Phi\left(\frac{1}{4\sqrt{t/T_2}}\right) \tag{7}$$

$$\Phi(u) = \frac{2}{\sqrt{\pi}} \int_0^u \exp(-u^2)du$$

$$T_2 = l_2/D, \quad D: \text{ Diffusion coefficient}$$

The solution of problem (2) or the redistribution of hydrogen $C(r, t)$ along the net section is given in Fig. 6 by the following expression

$$C(r, t) = \begin{cases} A(t)f(r) + C'(t): & 0 \le r \le \rho^+ \\ C'(t) & : \rho^+ < r \le \gamma \cdot \rho^+ \\ C_{av}(t) & : \gamma \cdot \rho^+ < r \le W' \end{cases} \tag{8}$$

where $f(r)$ is a function which depends on the distribution of plastic strain near the crack tip and $A(t)$ and $C'(t)$ are functions of time.

If it is assumed that plastic strains in the yield zone ahead of the crack tip are proportional to the opening displacement in the yield zone of the D.M. type, then the function, $f(r)$, is given by

$$f(r) = (c+x)\cosh^{-1}\left|\frac{a^2+cx}{a(c+x)}\right| + (c-x)\cosh^{-1}\left|\frac{a^2-cx}{a(c-x)}\right| \tag{9. a}$$

where

$$x = c+r, \quad a = c+\rho^+$$

An approximate expression of eq. (9.a) is given by

$$f(r) = \frac{2c\ln(a/c)}{1-(c/a)^2} \left\{ \left(\frac{c}{x}\right)^2 - \left(\frac{c}{a}\right)^2 \right\} \tag{9. b}$$

which is used in this paper to simplify the calculations.

As for the time function, $C'(t)$, analogous expression to eq. (7) is assumed by using a time constant, T_1 different from T_2;

$$C'(t) = C_0 \Phi\left(\frac{1}{4\sqrt{t/T_1}}\right) \tag{10}$$

which the time constant, T_1, should be a function of the applied stress. When the applied stress is zero, T_1 is equal to T_2. When the stress is increased, hydrogen diffusion towards the crack tip is hastened and therefore T_1 will decrease. This phenomenon can be expressed as

$$T_1 = T_2 \exp\left(-m\frac{\sigma_N}{\sigma_Y}\right) \tag{11}$$

where σ_N is the applied net stress, σ_Y is the yield stress and m is a numerical factor.

The time function, $A(t)$, in eq. (8) is determined by the condition that the average density of hydrogen over the net section obtained from eq. (8) should be equal to the density C_{av} given by eq. (7). Using eqs. (8), (9.b), (10) and applying the condition mentioned above, the concentration of hydrogen within the tensile yield zone $0 \leqq r \leqq \rho^+$ is obtained as follows:

When $\quad \gamma \cdot \rho^+ \leqq W'$,

$$C(r,t) = C_0 \left[\gamma \frac{a+c}{c} \cdot \frac{\{(c/x)^2 - (c/a)^2\}}{1-(c/a)^2} \left\{ \Phi\left(\frac{1}{4\sqrt{t/T_2}}\right) - \Phi\left(\frac{1}{4\sqrt{t/T_1}}\right) \right\} + \Phi\left(\frac{1}{4\sqrt{t/T_1}}\right) \right] \tag{12}$$

When $\quad \gamma \cdot \rho^+ > W'$,

$$C(r,t) = C_0 \left[\frac{W'}{\rho^+} \cdot \frac{a+c}{c} \cdot \frac{\{(c/x)^2 - (c/a)^2\}}{1-(c/a)^2} \left\{ \Phi\left(\frac{1}{4\sqrt{t/T_2}}\right) - \Phi\left(\frac{1}{4\sqrt{t/T_1}}\right) \right\} + \Phi\left(\frac{1}{4\sqrt{t/T_1}}\right) \right] \tag{13}$$

From eqs. (12), (13), it is found that the density of hydrogen at the crack tip reaches a maximum value at a certain time and then reduces zero after sufficient time has elapsed.

4. Hydrogen Induced Cracking

One of the feature of hydrogen induced cracking is that the fracture toughness parameter such as the critical size of tensile yield zone, ρ_c^+, changes with the concentration of hydrogen at the crack tip. Information on the quantitative relationship between the fracture toughness parameter and hydrogen density has never been obtained. It is, however, reasonable to assume that the ρ_c^+-value decrease with increase in hydrogen density near the crack tip. ρ_c^+ also will increase up to its final value with decrease in hydrogen density. A consistent expression of this phenomenon will be

$$\rho_c^+ = \rho_{CH}^+ \exp\left\{ -n\frac{C(r,t)-C_0}{C_0} \right\} \tag{14}$$

where $\rho_{CH}{}^+$ is the initial value of $\rho_c{}^+$ which depends on the initial density of hydrogen C_0. n is a numerical factor.

As shown in Fig. 2, weld crack induced by hydrogen grows usualy at a constant slow speed, and therefore the fracture toughness $(\rho_c{}^+)^*$ required for crack growth will not become extremely smaller than the fracture toughness $\rho_c{}^+$ required for crack initiation. If it is assumed that $(\rho_c{}^+)^*=0.5(\rho_c{}^+)$, then $\rho_c{}^+$ of eq. (14) is lower than the fracture toughness curves near the crack tip such as curves ①, ② drawn schematically in Fig. 7. These curves move down-wards at first as time elapses; crack initiation will occur at the point A or when the $\rho_c{}^+$-value at the crack tip reaches the ρ^+-value determined by eq. (1), and the crack will stop at the point B. Thus, the applied stress, σ_F, required for crack initiation, the incubation time under a constant applied stress and the increment of crack length Δc can be calculated by using eqs. (1), (12), (13) and (14) for given values of material constants.

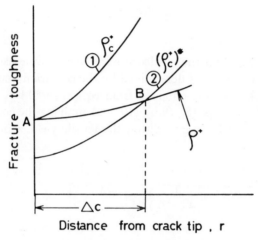

FIG. 7.   Schematic illustration of fracture toughness near the crack tip.

5. Numerical Calculations and Discussions

In order to apply the above analyzes to root cracking of the first pass weld as shown in Fig. 8a, calculations were made for an idealized model shown in Fig. 8b which is the same model as that of Fig. 5. The dimensions used are $W=h+2h_W=34$ mm, $2c=h=24$ mm, $W'=h_W=5$ mm and $l=h_W=5$ mm. The numerical factors and material constants required for the calculation were chosen as $\gamma=4$, $m=n=5$, $\rho_{CH}{}^+=20$ mm and $T_2=4,000$ min*.

Figure 9 shows the hydrogen concentration $C(0, t)$ at the crack tip as a function of time for several applied net stress, σ_N, which were calculated from eqs. (12), (13). As mentioned before, $C(0, t)$ reaches a maximum value at a given time depending upon the

---

* When the hydrogen diffusion coefficient is $D=2\times10^{-6}$ cm²/sec, the time constant T_2 becomes

$$T_2 = \frac{l^2}{D} \approx 10^5 \text{ sec.} \approx 10^3 \text{ min.}$$

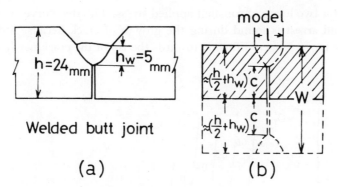

FIG. 8. Joint details and an idealized model.

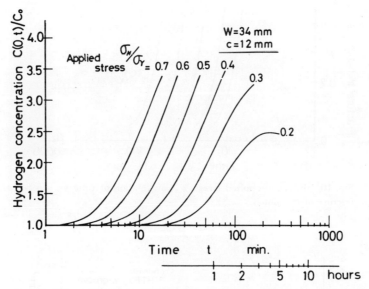

FIG. 9. Time dependence of hydrogen density, $C(0,t)$, of crack tip due to applied stress, σ_N.

applied stresses. The ρ_c^+-value corresponding to the change of $C(0, t)$ can be obtained from eq. (14). The results are shown in Fig. 10, from which the relationship of the net stress, $(\sigma_F)_N$, required for crack initiation vs. incubation time is drawn as a curve with oblique lines in this figure. The incubation time increases with decrease in applied stress and below a critical stress crack does not initiate after sufficient lapse time. This phenomenon is usualy observed in the experiments on hydrogen induced cracking of steels[3, 6] and TRC-RRC weld cracking tests.[1, 2]

Examples of TRC-test results are plotted by open circles in Fig. 11. These experiments were made by Y-groove weld of a HT80 steel of 24 mm thick. The solid line in the figure is the theoretical curve traced from Fig. 10 and is in good agreement with the test results.

Figure 12 shows the growth of crack, which were calculated by the method illustrated in Fig. 7, for two levels of constant applied stress. The step curve or repetition of crack initiation and arrest is found during the growth of crack because a certain time period is required for hydrogen diffusion towards the tip of the crack newly formed.

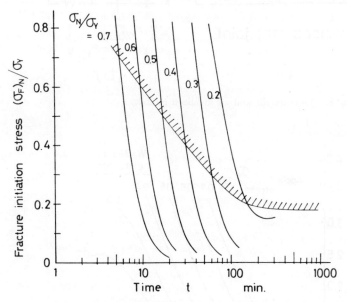

FIG. 10.   Effect of applied stress, σ_N, on relation of time vs. stress, $(\sigma_F)_N$, to initiate fracture at the notch.

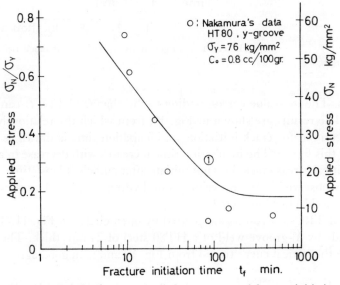

FIG. 11.   Relation between applied stress, σ_N, and fracture initiation time t_f.

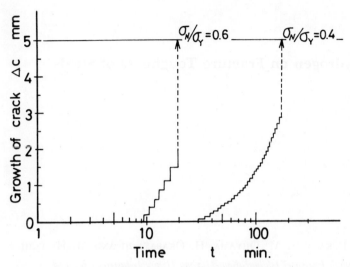

FIG. 12.   Effect of apllied stress σ_N/σ_Y on crack growth rate.

6. Conclusions

Fracture mechanics approach was undertaken as the first step to understand the problem of hydrogen induced cracking often observed in welding of high strength steel. By assuming models of hydrogen diffusion towards the crack tip under a given applied stress, the feature observed in hydrogen induced cracking test such as the relation of applied stress *vs.* incubation time and step growth of crack was obtained by using these model.

REFERENCES

1. Suzuki, H., Inagaki, M., and Nakamura, H., "Effect of Restraining Force on Root Cracking of High-Strength Steel Welds," Trans. Nat. Res. Inst. Metals, **5**, 3 (1963).
2. Satoh, K., and Matsui, S., "Reaction Stress and Weld Cracking under Hindered Contraction," IIW Doc. IX-574-68 (1968).
3. Troiano, A. R., "The Role of Hydrogen and Other Interstitials in the Mechanical Behavior of Metal," Trans. ASM, **52** (1960).
4. Koshiga, F., "A Proposed Mechanism of Brittle Fracture Initiation Influenced by Overstressing Techniques in Terms of Dugdal Model," Jl. Soc. Nav. Archit. Japan, **127** (1970).
5. Satoh, K., Ueda, S. and Kihara, H., "Recent Trend of Researches on Restraint Stresses and Strain for Weld Cracking," IIW Doc. IX-788-72, X-659-72 (1972).
6. Onishi, I. and Kikuta, Y., et al., "Effect of the Diffusivity of Hydrogen in Steel on the Delayed Fracture of Steel," Jl. Jap. Weld. Soc., **38**, 9 (1969).

Effect of Hydrogen on Fracture Toughness of Steels

M. Fukagawa, M. Ohyama, H. Okabayashi and M. Higuchi

Research Institute, Ishikawajima-Harima Heavy Industries Co., Ltd.

1. Introduction

Recent improvements in weldability of high strength steel and the advancement in the welding technique have resulted in considerable expansion in the use of high strength steel in structures, such as spherical gas holders, bridges and ships. Problems due to cold cracking and environmental embrittlement, mainly at the weld heat-affected zone (HAZ), are, however, occasionally encounted, and these cracks on occasion result in the brittle fracture of steel structures.

It is well known that rapid heating and cooling during arc welding of low alloy steels gives rise to extended hardened HAZ, which is mainly composed of martensite and sometimes parts of bainite. The presence of inherent weld defects and hydrogen in this zone may cause delayed cracking when the welded structure is loaded to a comparatively low stress level. Hydrogen embrittlement due to the elctro-chemical diffusion of hydrogen from environment into weldment flaws has also been observed in steel structures in service.

In order to obtain a fundamental understanding of cold cracking and environmental embrittlement, a series of delayed failure tests were performed on some of the commercial carbon and low alloy high strength steels. The results were analyzed using linear fracture mechanics and the effects of metallurgical and mechanical test variables on the susceptibility to delayed cracking were examined.

2. Factors which Affect Delayed Cracking

To assess resistance to fracture initiation, one of the authors[1] performed fracture toughness tests in the temperature range of $-196°$ to $100°C$, using small-size-single-edge-notched specimens and large-size-deep-notched specimens as illustrated in Fig. 1.

Figure 2 shows the test result for carbon steels. This figure shows at low temperatures where brittle fracture occurs, the critical strain energy release rate can be

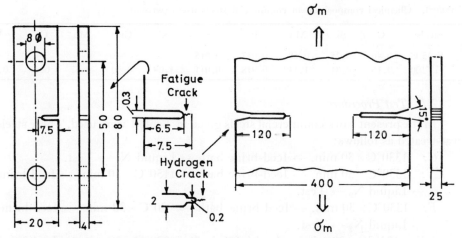

(A) Small-size-single-edge-notched tension test specimen

(B) Large-size-deep-notched specimen

FIG. 1. Fracture toughness specimens.

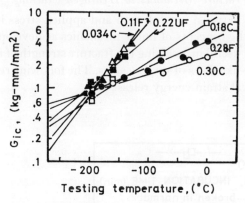

FIG. 2. Relation between testing temperature and G_{ic} of carbon steels after water- and sub zero-quenching.

expressed

$$G_{ic} = G_0 \exp (T/T_0) \tag{1}$$

where, G_0 and T_0 are the material constants, T is the absolute temperature. Inasmuch as hydrogen embrittlement is known to occur down to the ductile-brittle transition temperature range,[2] a quantitative characterization of hydrogen embrittlement should be possible by examining the effect of hydrogen content, test temperature, strain rate, etc. on the material constants, G_0 and T_0 in eq. (1). Thus, the effects of solute hydrogen on the fracture toughnesses of carbon steels and low alloy high strength steels have been evaluated in terms of those factors as follows.

TABLE 1.   Chemical composition of commercial steels used. (wt. %)

Steels	C	Si	Mn	P	S	Ni	Cr	Mo	Cu	V
S 45 C	0.46	0.25	0.58	0.017	0.015	—	—	—	—	—
HT100	0.16	0.31	1.14	0.018	0.011	1.09	0.70	0.37	0.17	0.04

2.1   Test Procedure

In the present work commercial steels given in Table 1 were used. These steels were heat-treated as follows:

C: 1330°C×30 min. → Iced-brine bath → Liquid N_2 → Test.

N: 1330°C×30 min. → Iced-brine bath → 1150°C×30 min. → Iced-brine bath → Liquid N_2 → Test.

F: 1330°C×30 min. → Iced-brine bath → 920°C×30 min. → Iced-brine bath → Liquid N_2 → Test.

UF: 1330°C×30 min. → Iced-brine bath → 920°C×30 min. → Iced-brine bath → 920°C×30 min. → Iced-brine bath → 920°C×30 min. → Iced-brine bath → Liquid N_2 → Test.

2.2   Application of Linear Fracture Mechanics to Hydrogen Cracking

Figure 3 shows the relation between notch length and applied stress in a constant load delayed failure test. Here the concepts of linear mechanics as developed by Griffith[3] and extended by Irwin[4] are useful in assessing the fracture strength of low ductility material that contain initial crack-like flaws of varying sizes. The following relations were thus used in evaluating the critical strain energy release rate.

$$E' G_{ic} \doteq \sigma_{mi}^2 \cdot a \cdot f(a/w) \tag{2}$$

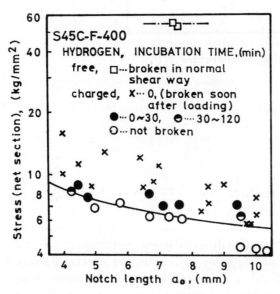

FIG. 3.   Relation between notch length and applied stress to hydrogen-induced crack initiation.

for plane strain, and

$$a = a_0 + E' \cdot G_{ic}/4 \sqrt{2\pi\sigma_{ys}^2}$$
$$E' = E/(1-\nu^2)$$

where, E: Young modulus, G_{ic}: critical strain energy release rate, σ_{mi}: critical value of gross applied tensile stress, a: crack length, $f(a/w)$: a nondimensional parameter governed by the shape of the specimen, σ_{ys}: yield strength, and ν: Poisson ratio.

The $f(a/w)$ value for a single-edge-notched specimen is given by the Gross-Srawley-Brown's equation[5] as

$$f(a/w) = 1/(1-\nu^2) \cdot (w/a \cdot \{7.59(w/a) - 32(a/w)^2 + 117(a/w)^3\} \tag{3}$$

and that for large-size-deep-notched specimen is given by

$$f(a/w) = w/a \cdot (\tan \pi a/w + 0.1 \sin 2\pi a/w) \tag{4}$$

Figure 4 shows the relation between notch length and G_{ic}, as calculated by eq. (2) using the data in Fig. 3.

For hydrogen charged specimens, a nearly constant G_{ic} value was obtained for varied notch lengths, thus indicating that linear fracture mechanics can be applied satisfactorily to hydrogen-induced cracking.

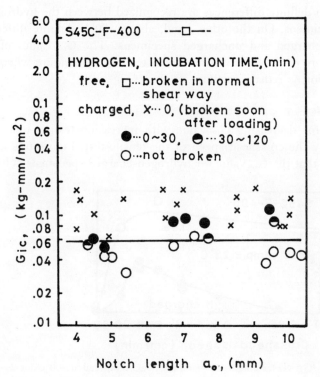

FIG. 4. G_{ic} versus notch length.

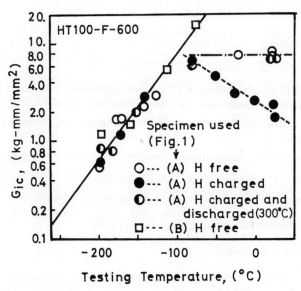

FIG. 5.   Effect of solute hydrogen on G_{ic} of HT100 steel tempered at 600°C for 2 hr.

2.3   Temperature

The effect of temperature on the hydrogen-induced cracking is shown in Fig. 5. Below—80°C it is evident that the G_{ic} values decrease linearly with decreasing testing temperature, and no definite differences are recognized between the hydrogen-charged and uncharged specimens. On the other hand, above—80°C definite differences exist between hydrogen-charged and uncharged specimens. The G_{ic} values of hydrogen-charged specimens are decreased with increasing testing temperature whereas those of the uncharged specimens remain constant.

2.4   Strain Rate

The tendency for decreasing G_{ic} value with increasing testing temperature was markedly affected by the crosshead speed of the tensile test. Figure 6 is a typical example which shows that the G_{ic} value for hydrogen-charged specimens is lowered with

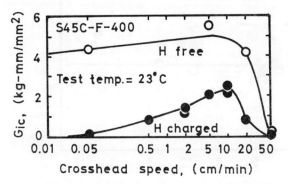

FIG. 6. G_{ic} versus crosshead speed for S45C tempered at 400°C for 2 hr after F heat treatment.

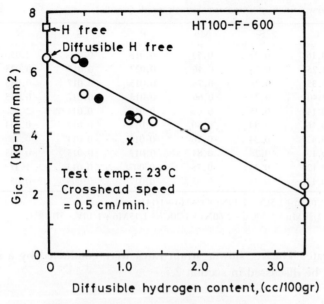

FIG. 7. G_{ic} versus diffusible hydrogen after light charge.

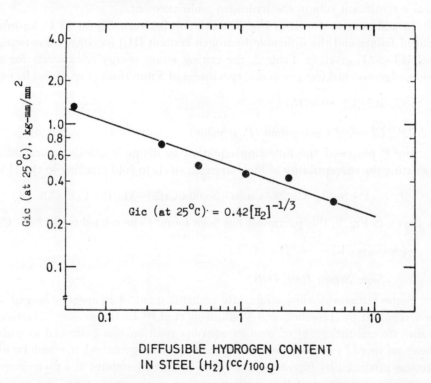

FIG. 8.   Effect of diffusible hydrogen content on G_{ic}.   (HT-80(1), W.Q. with fatigue crack, tested in alcohol, at 25°C.)

TABLE 2.   Chemical composition of commercial steels used. (wt. %)

Steels	C	Si	Mn	P	S	Ni	Cr
S15C	0.16	0.23	0.53	0.018	0.016	0.050	0.18
S25C	0.25	0.23	0.46	0.022	0.017	0.025	0.12
S35C	0.35	0.28	0.78	0.015	0.017	0.085	0.18
S45C	0.40	0.22	0.66	0.013	0.017	0.045	0.092
SNC-21	0.14	0.25	0.63	0.010	0.014	2.26	0.42
SCM-21	0.16	0.33	0.80	0.011	0.013	0.054	1.08
SCM-5	0.47	0.34	0.76	0.019	0.014	0.18	1.04
HT-80(1)	0.13	0.28	0.84	0.013	0.015	0.065	1.08
HT-80(2)	0.12	0.28	0.78	0.007	0.013	1.37	0.53
HT-80(3)	0.13	0.34	0.85	0.017	0.006	0.05	0.78

* $Ceq = C + 1/24Si + 1/6Mn + 1/5Cr + 1/40Ni + 1/4Mo + 1/14V$ (%)

** $P_{CM} = C + 1/30Si + 1/20Mn + 1/20Cu + 1/60Ni + 1/20Cr + 1/15Mo + 1/10V + 5B$ (%)

decreasing strain rate. The yet slower strain rates were conducted by a step loading method which will be discussed in section 2.7.

2.5   Hydrogen

Figure 7 shows the effect of diffusible hydrogen on G_{ic} of HT-100 steel as tempered for 2 hr. at 600°C after heat treatment F. This figure shows that the diffusible hydrogen plays a significant role in the hydrogen embrittlement.

In addition, as shown in Fig. 8, a relation between G_{ic} (at 25°C, kg-mm/mm²) of delayed failure and the diffusible hydrogen content $[H_2]$ (cc/100 g) was found. For the steel HT-80(1) given in Table 2, the critical strain energy release rate for small-size-single-edge-notched (fatigue crack) specimens of 5 mm thick (Fig. 1) can be expressed as

$$G_{ic}(\text{at } 25°C) = 0.48[H_2]^{-1/3} \tag{5}$$

2.6   Chemical Composition (P_{CM} value)

Ito[7,8] proposed the following equation to define a cracking parameter P_{CM} for evaluating the susceptibility of high strength steels to cold cracking in the HAZ.

$$P_{CM} = C + Si/30 + Mn/20 + Cu/20 + Ni/60 + Cr/20 + Mo/15 + V/10 + 5B, (\%) \tag{6}$$

As shown in Fig. 9, this parameter has been found to be related to G_{ic} (at 0°C).

$$log \ G_{ic}(\text{at } 0°C) = -4.9P_{CM} + 0.78 \tag{7}$$

2.7   Slow Strain Rate Tests

Some features of slow strain rate embrittlement of hydrogen-charged steels have been reported by Troiano[9] and Watkinson et al.[10] In the present investigation, slow strain rate embrittlement of steel in aqueous solution was examined at wide range of crosshead speed by continuous loading and step loading method, in which far lower strain rate was produced by increasing the strain in a small amount at a given interval where the average inclination of this curve was taken as the strain rate. The specimen was a notched tensile specimen shown in Fig. 10, machined from HT-80 steel (1350°C×

Cu	Mo	V	Ti	B	C_{eq}*	P_{CM}**
0.12	0.046	<0.01	<0.01	0.001	0.307	0.218
0.022	0.031	0.001	<0.003	—	0.369	0.290
0.13	0.040	<0.001	<0.003	—	0.540	0.418
0.13	0.033	<0.001	<0.003	—	0.547	0.454
0.031	0.036	<0.001	<0.003	—	0.405	0.243
0.047	0.21	<0.001	<0.003	—	0.577	0.282
0.10	0.21	<0.001	0.007	—	0.876	0.593
0.19	0.37	<0.01	<0.01	—	0.593	0.271
0.18	0.35	<0.01	0.023	—	0.492	0.250
0.28	0.43	<0.01	0.28	0.001	0.553	0.271

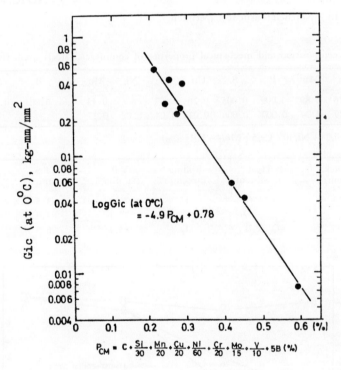

FIG. 9. G_{ic} versus P_{CM} value of quenched steels.

30 min. W.Q. → 150°C×1 hr. A.C. H_V=406) of Table 3. The tests were conducted in a bath containing an aqueous solution of 0.1% H_2SO_4+10 ppm S (as $Na_2S \cdot 9H_2O$) at pH 2. It was found that with decrease in crosshead speed the notch tensile strength values are lowered as shown in Fig. 11 and approach 45 kg/mm² of the lower critical stress (equivalent to K_{ISCC}=54 kg/mm² $\cdot \sqrt{mm}$) which was determined by ordinary constant load testing shown in Fig. 12. This stress intensity factor was calculated using the following equation.[11]

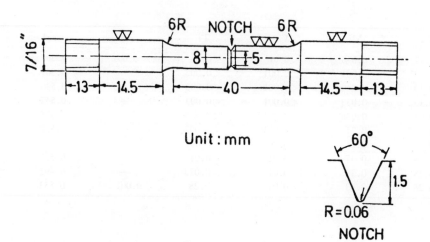

Unit : mm

FIG. 10.   Notched tensile test specimen.

TABLE 3.   Chemical composition and mechanical properties of commercial steels used. (wt. %)

Steels	C	Si	Mn	P	S	Cu	Cr	Ni	Mo	V	B	N	Ceq*
HT-80	0.13	0.26	0.89	0.009	0.005	0.26	0.77	—	0.43	—	0.001	0.008	0.55
SCM-3	0.34	0.29	0.74	0.007	0.006	0.04	1.04	0.08	0.17	—	—	—	0.73

* $Ceq = C + Mn/6 + Si/24 + Ni/40 + Cr/5 + Mo/4 + V/14$ (%)

Steels	Thick. (mm)	Heat treatment	Rolling direction	Y.P. (kg/mm²)	U.T.S. (kg/mm²)	EL. (%)
HT-80	23	Q. & T.	L	76.7	83.5	23
			C	77.1	84.0	23
SCM-3	35	Q. & T.	L	85.1	96.8	21.4

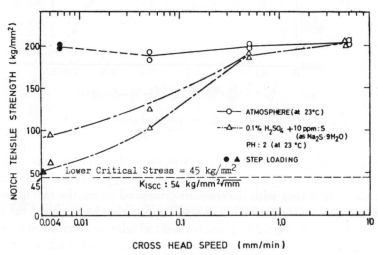

FIG. 11.   Effect of strain rate on notch tensile strength of HT-80 steel.

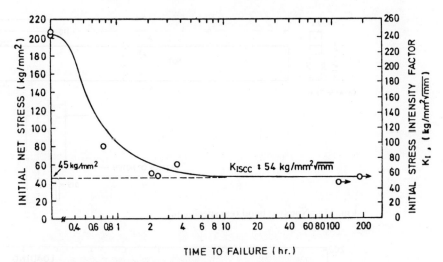

FIG. 12.   Delayed failure characteristics curve for HT-80 steel.
Testing condition of Figs. 11 and 12.
> Material: HT-80, (1350°C × 30 min. W.Q.→150°C × 1 hr. A.C. Hv: 406)
> Solution: 0.1% H_2SO_4 + 10 ppm: S (as $Na_2S \cdot 9H_2O$), pH: 2, tested at 23°C.

$$K_I = \sigma_{net} \cdot (\pi D)^{1/2} \cdot f(d/D)$$

where; D: an outside diameter,
  d: a notched-section diameter,
  σ_{net}:   a net-section stress.

$$f(d/D) = [(d/D)^2 \cdot (1/\pi \cdot \tan \pi/2) \cdot (1 - d/D)^{1/2} \cdot h(1 - d/D)]$$

2.8   Crack Growth Rate

It has been shown by many investigators that the crack growth rate, dc/dt is dependent on the K_I for low alloy, high strength steels.[12–15] In addition, it was recognized in the present work that temperature could also be a contributing factor when K_I values are small. The K_I values were calculated using the following equation for notched bend specimen.[16]

$$K_I = \frac{6M}{(h-a)^{3/2}} \cdot g(a/h) \tag{8}$$

where; M: applied bending moment (per unit thickness)
  a: crack length, h: depth of a beam,
  $g(a/h)$:   stress intensity factor coefficients for notched beams.

Notched bend specimens of SCM-3 steel (930°C × 1 hr. W.Q. → 180°C × 1 hr. A.C.; Hv=582, also see Fig. 13, and Table 3) were used in the experiments. Tests were conducted in a bath containing an aqueous solution of 0.1% H_2SO_4 + 10 ppm, S(as $Na_2S \cdot 9H_2O$) at pH 2. The initial K_I value was 60 kg/mm² · $\sqrt{mm}$.

Figure 14 shows the results in terms of increase in deflection versus time at 10°, 30°, 36°, and 45°C. Following observations were made.

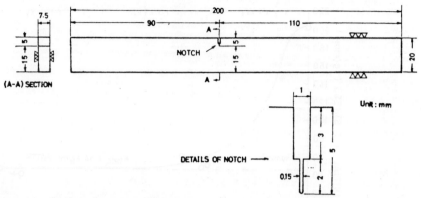

FIG. 13.   Notched bend test specimen.

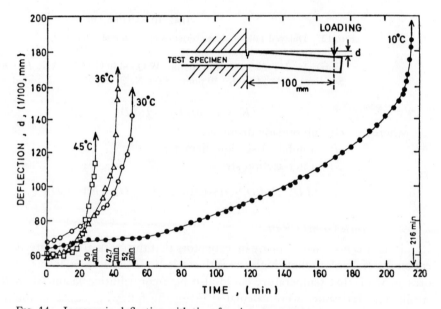

FIG. 14.   Increase in deflection with time for given temperature.

(1)   As shown in Fig. 15, the K_I dependence of slow crack growth rate, dc/dt can be expressed as

$$dc/dt = AK_I + B \qquad\qquad (9)$$

where, A and B are constant.

(2)   Figure 16 shows the relation between dc/dt and the reciprocal of temperature for three K_I values. This result gives an activation energy of 10,700–12,200 cal/g-atom, which is a little higher than that of diffusion of hydrogen.

(3)   A good relation between time to failure and temperature as shown in Fig. 17 was obtained. In the same temperature range of 10°C to 45°C, on the other hand, K_C value was found to show the lowest value at ambient temperature as shown in Fig. 18.

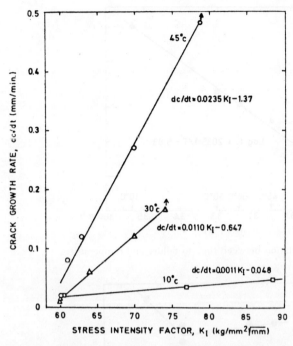

FIG. 15. Crack growth rate for a given temperature as a function of stress intensity factor.

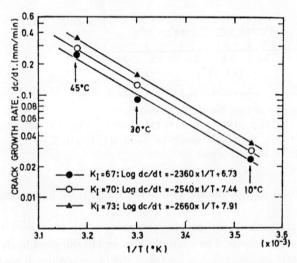

FIG. 16. Relation between crack growth rate and temperature.

3. Conclusion

From the preceding experimental results, the authors conclude that:

(1) Linear fracture mechanics can be applied satisfactorily to hydrogen cracking.

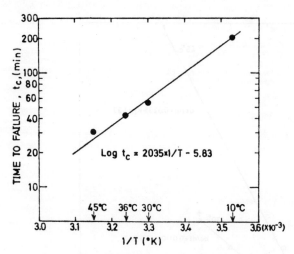

FIG. 17.   Relation between time to failure and temperature.

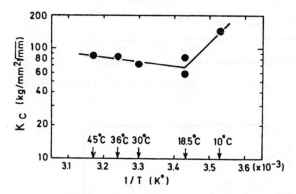

FIG. 18.   Relation between K_C and temperature.

Testing condition of Figs. 14, 15, 16, 17 and 18.
   Material: SCM-3, (930°C × 1 hr. W.Q. → 180°C × 1 hr. A.C. Hv: 582)
   Solution: 0.1% H_2SO_4 + 10 ppm S (as $Na_2S \cdot 9H_2O$), pH: 2
   Initial K_I: 60 kg/mm² · $\sqrt{mm}$

(2)   The critical strain energy release rate is not affected by hydrogen at temperature below —80°C.

(3)   Notch tensile strength values may be surprisingly low at strain rates far lower than those of ordinary test methods. For example, for an HT-80 steel loaded at a mean strain rate lower than 0.005 mm/min. (step loading), the observed notch tensile strength values approached 45 kg/mm² of the lower critical stress determined by conventional testing methods.

(4)   The delayed crack growth characteristics of the quenched SCM-3 steel in aqueous solution may be related to stress intensity factor and test temperature.

REFERENCES

1. Nakamura, H., Naiki, T. and Okabayashi, H., "The Effects of Hydrogen and Carbon on the Fracture Toughness of Low Alloy Steels," Int. Inst. Weld. Doc. No. IX-796-72.
2. Cotterill, P., "The Hydrogen Embrittlement of Metals," Progress in Materials Science, Vol. 9, p. 292 (1961).
3. Griffith, A. A., "The Phenomena of Rupture and Flow in Solids," Philosophical Transactions, Royal Conc. (London), Series A, Vol. 221 p. 163, (1920).
4. Irwin, G. R., "*Fracture*," *Handbuch der Physik*, Band 6, p. 551, Springer (1958).
5. Gross, B. and Srawley, E., "Stress Intensity Factors for Single-Edge-Notch Specimens in Bending of Combined Bending and Tension by Boundary Collocation of a Stress Function," NASA Tech. Note No. D-2603, 1, (1065).
6. Nakamura, H. and Okabayashi, H., "Effect of Hydrogen on Fracture Toughness of Steel," *Proc. 16th Japan National Symposium on Strength, Fracture and Fatigue*, Apr. 3, p. 135 (1971).
7. Ito, Y. and Bessyo, K., "Cracking Parameter of High Strength Steels Related to Heat-Affected Zone Cracking (Report 1)," Journal of the Japan Welding Society, Vol. 37, No. 9 p. 55 (1968).
8. *Ibid.* (Report 2), Vol. 38, No. 10, p. 60 (1969).
9. Troiano, A. R., "The Role of Hydrogen and Other Interstitials in the Mechanical Behavior of Metals," Transactions of the ASM, Vol. 52, p. 55 (1960).
10. Graville, B. A., Baker, R. G. and Watkinson, F., "Effect of Temperature and Strain Rate on Hydrogen Embrittlement of Steel," B.W.R.A. Report, British Welding Journal, June p. 337 (1967).
11. Paris, P. C. and Sih, G. C., "*Stress Analysis of Cracks*," *ASTM. STP. No. 381*, p. 50.
12. Aoki, T., Kanao, M. and Araki, T., "On the Delayed Fracture Crack Propagation Characteristics of Some High Strength Steels," *Proc. 18th Japan National Symposium on Strength, Fracture and Fatigue*, Apr. 4, p. 51 (1973).
13. Nakasa, K., Takei, H. and Asamoto, T., "The Fatigue Crack Propagation Law in Water of Ni-Cr-Mo Martensitic Steel," The Japan Institute of Metals, Vol. 36, p. 1180 (1972).
14. Johnson, H. H. and Willner, A. M., "Moisture and Stable Crack Growth in a High Strength Steel," Applied Materials Research, Jan., p. 34 (1965).
15. Kerns, G. E. and Staehle, R. W., "Slow Crack Growth of a High Strength Steel in Chloride and Hydrogen Halide Gas Environments," Scripta Metallurgica, Vol. 6, No. 12, p. 1189 (1972).
16. Paris, P. C. and Sih, G. C., "*Stress Analysis of Cracks*," *ASTM. STP. No. 381*, p. 42.

On the Role of Defects in Crack Initiation in Welded Structures

A. J. McEvily, Jr.

Metallurgy Department, University of Connecticut

1. Introduction

The subject of defects in welds has been a matter of concern since the advent of the welding process, but our understanding of the nature and significance of these defects has been considerably increased as the result of extensive and continuing investigations. One characteristic of welded joints is that they are never completely defect free; and with increases in resolving power of NDI methods even more defects are likely to be found than ever before. The question then becomes at what size level do such defects affect structural integrity. No doubt some requirements with respect to defect size are overly conservative, and in fact specifications concerning defects in welded regions may be needlessly even stricter than for defects in the parent plate.[1]

The determination of the significance of a particular defect may not be a straightforward matter, and much may hinge on decisions reached. The shutting down of a plant to repair a defect detected in service can be extremely costly, especially if the defect does not really endanger structural reliability. Further, without some rational approach to the assessment of the significance of a defect, the tendency might be to reject or repair all welds in which defects are detected. Further, with the development of the fracture mechanics approach to the analysis of subcritical flaw growth and fracture, we are in a much better position to assess the importance of defects. Nevertheless, the detailed analysis may still be a formidable matter, for we need to know about the loading conditions, the environment, the material and geometry of the part, and the size, location and nature of the defect or defects present in the welded region. In addition, the matter of residual stresses must be given consideration. In many circumstances, as for example when variable amplitude loading of a random nature is involved, previous experience and judgment with particular structural types is extremely useful in setting limits on allowable defect sizes. Experience combined with the fracture mechanics approach, with input from fabricators, inspectors, and consumers as well as technical societies and regulatory agencies should lead to the development of improved codes. It is sometimes argued that

96

present codes are overly conservative and that more emphasis should be placed on the judgment of the inspector. As a general rule this may be a dangerous procedure; I am reminded of the inspector of concrete who claimed to be able to assess the strength of concrete by its smell. Put to the test he failed completely. However, even when following specifications it is sometimes possible for different inspectors to reach different conclusions because of the variation in methods used to detect flaws. In radiographic inspections, for example, the film type and the number of samples being inspected can influence the ability to detect flaws.[1] A serious economic situation can develop if competitors use different procedures for flaw detection. Hopefully, the biasing of inspection procedures to meet set standards is not a widespread practice.

The designer also has a responsibility with respect to blueprint callouts. In the design of certain complex structures it has been observed that all welds were specified as Class II, simply as a convenience for the designer. Some of these welds were virtually unstressed, yet defects had to be removed needlessly to conform with the Class II requirement.[1] Further, there is the danger that the repair welding will decrease rather than increase the quality of the weld.[3]

The above considerations present an overview of concerns with respect to the significance of defects. Clearly the subject is not a closed one. In the subsequent sections, we will review more specifically but briefly the nature and significance of weld defects.

2.   Nature of Deffects

In a broad definition of the nature of a defect, the following categories can be introduced:[4-11]

A.   Geometrical
1.   Undercut and cavity
2.   Overlap
3.   Poor fit-up, mismatch
4.   Excessive reinforcement (height and angle of crown with surface)
5.   Stress concentrations in general
6.   Nature of weld dressing

B.   Weld Character
1.   Lack of penetration
2.   Lack of fusion
3.   Slag inclusions
4.   Oxide films
5.   Delaminations
6.   Tungsten inclusions in GTA welds
7.   Gas porosity
8.   Microsegregation during cellular or dendritic growth
9.   Shape of weld puddle
10.   Arc strikes
11.   Entrapped weld spatter

C.   Metallurgical
   1.   Stress relief cracking
   2.   HAZ hydrogen embrittlement (cold cracking)
   3.   Weld metal solidification cracking
   4.   HAZ liquidation cracking (low melting point segregates)
   5.   Delamination of plate

D.   Residual Stresses
   1.   Constraint
   2.   Repair welding

The influence of geometrical and weld character factors has been extensively treated in the references cited, and we will not review them at this time. However, it is worth noting that geometrical factors may often be the overriding consideration, relegating other defect types to a minor role. For example, during fatigue of fillet weld, cracking at the top of the weld is usually observed. Only after peening, or TIG rewelding, or spot heating can the crack initiation site be made to shift to another location such as the root of the weld. So long as items in categories B and C are not extreme, this geometrical aspect will be dominant.

Metallurgical.   In the listing of defects given above, many of the defects may not be in the form of actual flaws, but are factors which reduce fracture toughness. For example, in a comparison of TIG and SA weldments of 18Ni (250) maraging steel it was found that the SA weld metal was of lower toughness. The lower toughness was attributed to the precipitation of fine dendritic or plate-shaped particles of titanium carbonitride (TiC, N) on boundaries in the austenite, at temperatures near 1500°F. These particles provide a weak path for crack propagation, and result in low-energy intergranular rupture in heat affected regions of the SA weld metal. The embrittlement was much more pronounced in the SA welds because of the higher temperatures, large heating times, and slower cooling rates involved in the SA process.[11] These conditions also favor dendritic growth over cellular growth during solidification of the weld metal,[9] which would also promote microsegregation.

In considering such metallurgical aspects of defects and welding, the following diagram, Fig. 1, is useful in visualizing the effect of a change in metallurgical character on the fracture behavior of ferrous materials. The figure is a three-dimensional plot in which the axes are stress, the reciprocal of the square root of the grain size, and temperature. Region ABC is a surface which is the locus of fracture which occurs when the applied stress reaches the yield stress. For temperature grain size combinations to the right of line BC failure occurs above yield and may be either cleavage or shear initiated. The important fact is that an increase in grain size as in the heat affected zone not only lowers the yield strength but also increases the potential for brittle fracture as can be seen. The presence of a flaw or notch will raise the local yield stress because of plastic constraint with the result that the brittle transition temperature is increased. An increase in the impurity level of a weld will cause a drop in the fracture stress and a resultant increase in transition temperature. Strain aging, irradiation, and increase in strain rate all will raise

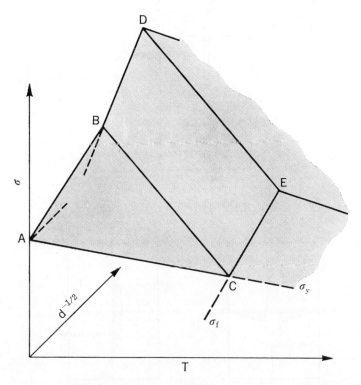

FIG. 1.   Three dimensional stress (σ), temperature (T), and reciprocal of the square root of grain size ($d^{-1/2}$) plot. Cleavage initiated fractures to right of DE. ABC is a surface upon which brittle fracture occures when the applied stress reaches the yield stress.

the yield stress curve again leading to a resultant increase in the tendency for brittle fracture.

Hot cracking due to microsegregation, cold cracking (hydrogen), incomplete fusion, porosity, shrinkage cavities, and arc strikes can each lower σ_f and therefore be deleterious to weld reliability. The role of retained or reverted austenite is not unequivocal. In maraging steels reverted austenite is thought to be deleterious to fracture toughness,[13] but in other steels thin films of austenite have been found to be beneficial.[14,15] If transformation of reverted austenite in the HAZ to another site takes place, internal stresses can develop which could promote hydrogen cracking. Transformation to upper bainite or ferritic structures can also lead to reduction in toughness.

Residual Stresses.   Figure 2 indicates the nature of the residual stress patterns in a butt weld.[10] Of principal concern are the tensile stresses which when added to the applied stresses reduce the apparent fracture toughness and also promote hydrogen embrittlement and stress corrosion cracking processes. Uncertainty with respect to the magnitude of these stresses can have a strong influence on the validity of conclusions reached in a fracture mechanics analysis. The process of fatigue crack growth may relax the tensile residual stresses, whereas the beneficial compressive stresses may be retained

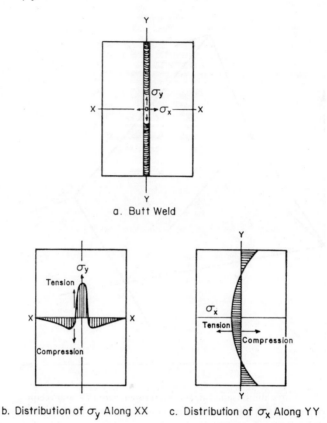

a. Butt Weld

b. Distribution of σ_y Along XX   c. Distribution of σ_x Along YY

FIG. 2.   Typical distributions of residual stress in butt welds.[10]

to some extent. Recent studies have shown that in high toughness steels even tensile mean stresses have little effect in the rate of crack growth.[16] In terms of stress intensities, the effects of mean stress can be schematically shown as in Fig. 3.* Beneficial effects are present when the minimum stress is compressive, since the effects of crack closure are felt. In low toughness alloys the maximum stress intensity in the cycle can trigger static modes of failure and tensile residual stresses may prove to be more important.

3. Significance of Deffects

The following examples of the use of fracture mechanics to assess the significance of defects are based upon a recent article by Gray, Heaton and Oates of the CEGB, NDT Applications Centre.[18]

A. *Distributor Drum Nozzle Cracking.*   The material was a Mn-Cr-Mo-V steel

---

* This diagram should be regarded as a first approximation. Further experimental work is needed to establish detailed dependence of crack growth behavior on mean stress. The sensitivity of the threshold level to mean stress is not reflected in the diagram, for example.

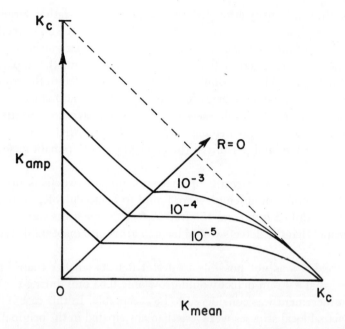

FIG. 3. K_{amp} as a function of mean stress for several growth rates (Schematic). Rates are given in terms of the increment of growth per cycle, $\Delta a/\Delta N$. $R=K_{min}/K_{max}$. Crack closure is assumed at zero load; if it occurs at a positive load, the break in the curves will shift to the right.

welded with low alloy weld metal. The anticipated loading consisted of 15 proof tests at $1.25 \times$ design pressure, 300 cold starts of 0–18.8 MNm^{-2} and 10^4 hot starts of 14.1 MNm^{-2}. Finite element analysis was used to determine stress intensity factors, and the rate of fatigue crack growth at 350°C was estimated to be given by

$$\frac{\Delta a}{\Delta N} = 5.7 \times 10^{-11}(\Delta K)^{2.6} \text{m/cycle,}$$

where a is the crack length, N the number of cycles, and ΔK is the range of the stress intensity factor. The most severe embedded crack had a K/P of 0.36 m$^{-3/2}$. It was predicted that this crack would grow less than 0.1 mm during the service life. The possibility of brittle fracture was evaluated based upon a peak K level of 83 MNm$^{-3/2}$, which value included a contribution due to a possible tensile residual stress which was estimated to be 1/2 of the yield stress. Below 60°C the K_{IC} value of the weld metal was 65 MNm$^{-3/2}$, whereas at higher temperatures the toughness was in excess of 100 MNm$^{-3/2}$.

To guard against fracture, proof testing below 60°C was prohibited, and the plant was kept in operation with the worst of the defects repaired as a precaution during planned maintenance periods. Since unplanned shutdowns involve cost penalties of $50,000–$75,000 per day, substantial savings were realized through this analysis.

B. *Main Steam Drum Feed Nozzle Cracking.*   Initial ultrasonic inspection revealed only intermittent response interpreted as being due to slag lines. However,

12 months later ultrasonic inspection led to the discovery of rather large defects. A fracture mechanics analysis was performed similar in nature to the one described above, but with the inclusion of thermal stresses as well. A maximum fatigue growth rate of but 0.025 mm per year was predicted, a finding not in accord with the apparently much larger increase as determined by ultrasonics. The investigation led to the conclusion that the cracks had been present since fabrication, and that the initial failure to detect them was due to a very low response to ultrasonic compression waves as a result of the geometrical form of the cracks in this instance. The findings allowed more detailed NDT specifications to be written, and permitted the cracked parts to remain in service.

C. *Nozzle Welds.* As a result of analysis, embedded defects up to 5 mm in width and of any circumferential length were found to be acceptable, even if the center line of the defect was only 5 mm from the free surface. Some areas were uninspectable, but analysis indicated that the defects would have to grow into inspectable regions before becoming critical.

In another weld it was not possible to detect defects smaller than 3 mm in size. Analysis indicated that a 3 mm defect would grow only 0.63 mm during the service lifetime and such an increment was considered to be acceptable. In this case it is of interest to note that the actual local stresses were less than anticipated in the original analysis.

D. *Other Examples.* The coarse grained regions of austenitic weldments were difficult to inspect ultrasonically due to high attenuation from grain scatter. Effective examination required a substantial relaxation of the existing defect acceptance standard on the basis of fracture mechanics. The weld geometry was redesigned to allow inspection using compression waves only since the attenuation of shear waves was substantially higher. In this application, defects 15 mm $\times$ 15 mm were found to be acceptable because of the low stresses involved.

Acoustic fatigue as the result of very large numbers of random, low amplitude stress cycles was of concern in the gas circuits of magnox reactors. A repair weld had been made, and the potential for the growth of flaws above a threshold stress-intensity level for crack growth ΔK_{TH} was analyzed. In this case a completely circumferential surface crack several times larger than the limiting NDT size was estimated to grow less than 10^{-2} mm in 10^{12} cycles.

Gray, Heaton and Oates also describe the application of fracture mechanics in the creep range. For 2–1/4 Cr-1Mo at 565°C the rate of growth of macroscopic creep cracks can be given by:[19]

$$\frac{da}{dt} = DK^m,$$

where a is the crack length, t is time, K is the stress-intensity factor, and D and m are constants, with m equal to 5.2 in this case. Somewhat arbitrarily, a defect is considered to be acceptable if the predicted growth rate in 10^4 hours is less than 1 mm. Typical sizes of defects satisfying this condition are 5–10 mm in size depending upon free surface proximity. Repeated inspection is necessary since grain boundary cavitation is invisible ultrasonically and cracks may suddenly appear.

4. Concluding Remarks

This brief review on the role of defects in welds has not done justice to the vast literature on the specifics of the formation and the significance of welds. However, it seems clear that in many cases the nature of potential problems associated with defects have been identified and that rational approaches to safe and economic design are being taken. Finite element analysis, fracture mechanics, and NDI, each of which are developing rapidly, are key ingredients in increasing the realiability of welded structures.

ACKNOWLEDGMENTS

The author expresses his thanks to Battelle, Columbus Laboratories and to the Air Force Office of Scientific Research for their support.

REFERENCES

1. Thielsch, H., "The Sense and Nonsense of Weld Defects," *Weld Imperfections*, ed. by A. R. Pfluger and R. E. Lewis, Addison Wesley, Reading, Mass., p. 129 (1968).
2. Thielsch, H. and Parcel, "Discussion," *ibid.*, p. 610.
3. Bernstein, H., "Experience with Weld Flaws in The Polaris Program," *ibid.*, p. 591.
4. Munse, W. H., *"Fatigue of Welded Structures,"* Welding Research Council, N.Y. (1964).
5. Hall, W. S., Kihara, H., Soete, W., and Wells, A. A., *"Brittle Fracture of Welded Plate,"* Prentice-Hall, Englewood Cliffs, N. J. (1967).
6. Lancaster, J. F., *"The Metallurgy of Welding, Brazing, and Soldering,"* American Elsevier, N.Y. (1965).
7. Lancaster, J. F., *Proc. of Second Conf. on Significance of Defects in Welds*, Welding Institute, Cambridge (1969).
8. Lancaster, J. F., *Proc. of Conf. on Fatigue of Welded Structures*, Welding Institute, Cambridge (1971).
9. Savage, W. F., "What is a Weld?," Ref. 1, p. 13.
10. Tetelman, A. S., "Fundamental Aspects of Fracture, With Reference to the Cracking of Steel Weldments," Ref. 1, p. 249.
11. Masubuchi, K., "Effect of Residual Stresses on Fracture Behavior of Weldments," Ref. 1, p. 567.
12. Pellissier, G. E., "Microstructure in Relation to Fracture Toughness of 18 Ni (250) Maraging Steel Weldments," Ref. 1, p. 427.
13. Steffens, H. D. and Siefert, K., "Microstructure and Fracture Toughness of 18 Ni Maraging Steel Weldments," *Proc. of the Third International Conf. on Fracture*, Munich, Paper III-512 (1973).
14. Averbach, B. L., "Fracture Toughness in High Carbon Steel," *ibid.*, Paper VIII-422.
15. Zackay, V. F., Parker, E. R. and Wood, W. E., "Influence of Some Microstructural Features on The Fracture Toughness of High Strength Steels," *Proc. Third International Conf. on The Strength of Metals and Alloys*, Vol. 1, Paper 35 (1973).
16. Ritchie, R. O. and Knott, J. F., "Brittle Cracking Processes during Fatigue Crack Propagation," *Third Int. Conf. on Fracture, Munich*, Paper V-434A (1973).
17. James, L. A., "Fatigue Crack Growth in Type 304 Stainless Steel Weldments At Elevated Temperatures," ASTM J. of Testing and Evaluation, 1, p. 52 (1973).

18. Gray, I., Heaton, M. and Oates, G., "The Use of Fracture Mechanics to Assess The Significance of Defects in Generating Plant," *Proc. of Conf. on Mechanics and Mechanisms of Crack Growth*, Cambridge (1973).
19. Siverns, M. and Price, A. T., "Crack Growth Under Creep Conditions," Nature, **228**, p. 760 (1970).

Micro-Cracking in Consumable-Nozzle Electro-Slag Weld Metal

T. KUNIHIRO AND H. NAKAJIMA

Technical Research Laboratory, Hitachi Shipbuilding and Engineering Co., Ltd.

1. Introduction

Consumable-nozzle electro-slag welding is widely used as a convenient and efficient method for vertical welding on fablicating steel structures. Micro-cracks, however, are found to occur in the weld metal under certain conditions. The sum of the cracked area is so small in comparison with the total sectional area of the weld metal such that the static strength of the joints will hardly be influenced by the cracks. The fatigue strength, however, may decrease by the cracks. A study was thus carried out to find out the cause of micro-cracks and their influence on fatigue strength.

2. Microscopic Observation

A typical view of micro-cracks found on cross sections of the weld is schematically

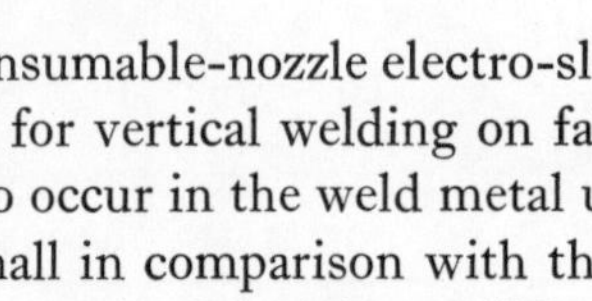

Fig. 1 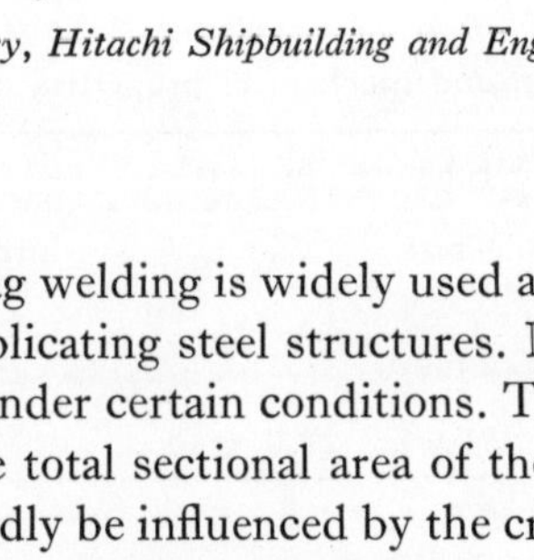   Photo. 1 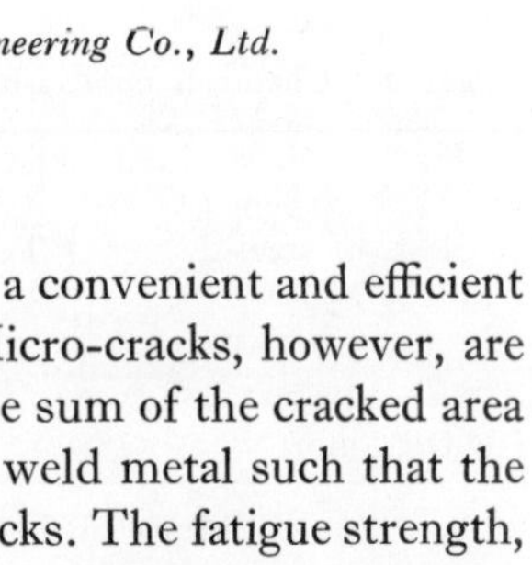   Photo. 2

FIG. 1. Schematic drawing of micro-cracks in cross section of weldment. (No. E), (Total length 11.9 mm).
PHOTO. 1. Microphotograph of micro-crack.
PHOTO. 2. Fractograph of cracked surface.

shown in Fig. 1. Most of the cracks were about 2–3 mm in size, and were distributed in random direction over the entire weld joint.

Photo. 1 shows a typical microphotograph of micro-cracks which extended through the network of ferritic grains precipitated at the boundaries of the original austenitic grains. Hardness was about Hv 115 in the precipitated ferritic phase, and about Hv 200 in the bainitic structure of the matrix.

Photo. 2 shows a typical fractograph of cracked surface where the river patterns suggest the brittle mode of a crack.

3.   Cause of Micro-Cracking

The cause of the micro-cracking was experimentally studied. The chemical composition and the mechanical properties of the plate used are listed in Table 1. Test plates were fixed to restraint blocks as shown in Fig. 2. Backing plates were attached to the both sides

TABLE 1.   Chemical composition and mechanical properties of the plate used.

Class. of steel plate	Mechanical properties					Chemical composition (%)					
	Tensile test			Bend test $(1.5 \times t)$	Impact test $({}_vE_{-7°C}$ kg-m)	C	Si	Mn	P	S	Ceq.
	Y.S. (kg/mm²)	T.S. (kg/mm²)	EL. (%)								
K5D 32 mm N	38.0	54.0	27.0	Good	17.1	.18	.32	1.34	.014	.16	.42

$Ceq.$ (%)$=$C$+$Mn/6$+$Si/24

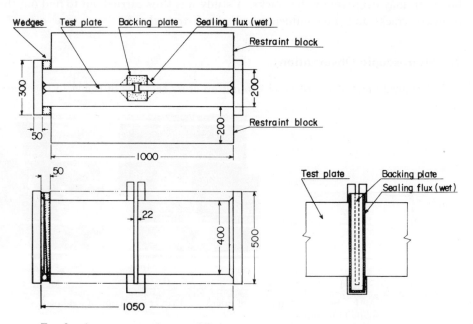

FIG. 2.   Arrangement of test welding.

FIG. 3.   Backing plate and sealing with flux.

TABLE 2. Welding conditions and observed micro-cracks.

Test No.	Backing plate	Heat input Kjoule/cm	Depth of slag pool (mm)	Average length of micro-crack* (mm)	Remarks
A	Graphite	460	18	0	
B		540	49	0	Backing plates were left attached to welds for more than 48 hours and then inspected.
C		570	35	2.9	
D	Copper plate with water cooling	550	27	3.8	
E		580	21	15.0	
F		590	20	0	Condition I.**
G		579	19	0	Condition II.**

* Average length of micro-crack indicates the total of micro-cracks per cross section of 20 inspected sections.

** Condition I: Immediately after air cooled at 100°C, welds were heat treated to 600°C × 2 hr. furnace cooling.

　　Condition II: Immediately after air cooled to 100°C, welds were heat treated to 300°C × 3 hr. air cooling.

of the test joint. Wet sealing flux was plastered around the backing plates as shown in Fig. 3 to protect leakage of molten metal. Two backing plates were used for studying the effect of cooling rate of weld metal on micro-cracking. Copper backing plates with a water-cooling system ($25 \text{ mm}^t \times 70 \text{ mm}^w \times 500 \text{ mm}^l$, the water flow of 20 l/min) were used in one test and solidified graphite backing plates ($45 \text{ mm}^t \times 90 \text{ mm}^w \times 550 \text{ mm}^l$) were used in the other. Backing plates were removed 48 hours after welding and then 20 cross sections were cut out from each weldment and examined for micro-cracks. The welding conditions and the results are summarized in Table 2.

Test results of No. B, C, D and E with copper backing showed that micro-cracks increased with decrease of the depth of slag pool. This tendency can be due to the following reasons: for shallower slag pool, more diffusible hydrogen will penetrate into the

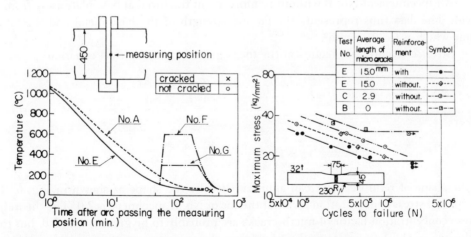

FIG. 4. Cooling curves and thermal cycles of weld metal.

FIG. 5. S-N curves.

molten pool and more inclusions will remain in the weld metal.

Test results of No. A and E showed that the graphite backing plate was more effective for preventing micro-cracking than the copper backing plate. The lower heat conductivity of graphite backing plate increased the temperature of molten pool and decreased the cooling rate of the weld metal. These effects promote refined molten metal and remove diffusible hydrogen in the weld metal.

Figure 4 shows the thermal cycles of No. A, E, F and G. The results of test No. E, F and G suggest that the micro-cracks are hydrogen induced cracks which occur at a temperature below 100°C.

Micro-cracks were produced in soft ferritic grains where internal tensile strain and diffusible hydrogen were concentrated by residual stress. River patterns similar to those in Photo. 1 is observed in a fractured surface of round bar specimen which were taken from a sound CES weld metal and fractured by static tensile load under hydrogen-charged condition.

4. Fatigue Strength

Fatigue tests were carried out to investigate the influence of the micro-cracks on the fatigue strength of weld joints. Specimens were welded under the conditions of No. B, C and E in Table 2. The reinforcement of the weld were removed except with some specimens of type No. E weld. Fatigue tests were conducted by a 100 ton tensile fatigue machine with constant pulsating loads. Test results are shown in Fig. 5.

Fatigue fracture of No. E specimens with weld reinforcement originated at the toe of weld and no fatigue crack initiated from the micro-cracks. Therefore the data indicate that the fatigue strength of CES weld joints with reinforcement is independent of micro-cracks with a fatigue limit of 18 kg/mm[1].

In all specimens of No. C and E without reinforcement, fatigue fracture initiated from micro-cracks near the surface. In these specimens fatigue strength depended on the quantity of micro-cracks.

All specimens of No. B without reinforcement fractured at base plate away from the weld. The data thus represents the fatigue strength of the base metal and the fatigue limit which was 30 kg/mm^2.

Stress concentration factors at the toe is given by an empirical equation[1],

$$\alpha = 1 + (\alpha_0 - 1)\left[1 - \left(1 - \frac{\theta^\circ}{90^\circ}\right)^{\left(1 + \frac{2.4\sqrt{r}}{t}\right)}\right]$$

where,

$$\alpha_0 = 1 + \left[\frac{(b/a) - 1}{2.8(b/a) - 2} \cdot \frac{a}{r}\right]^{0.65}$$

if the shape of reinforcement can approximated by the shape as shown in Fig. 6. The calculated stress concentration factor at the toe of No. E specimens is 2.0. The theoretical stress concentration factor of micro-cracks are probably to be greater than 2.0, but their influence to the fatigue strength is less than the stress concentration at the weld toe. Relation between stress concentration factor and fatigue notch factor in base plate of

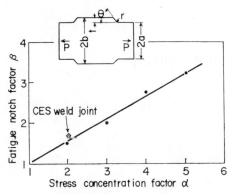

FIG. 6. Relation between α and β of HT50 steel.

50 kg/mm² class steel is shown in Fig. 6.[2] In this figure, the results of No. E specimens show a good agreement with the corelation line.

5. Conclusion

Micro-cracks produced in CES weld metal welded under special conditions are hydrogen induced crack: which can be prevented by increasing the depth of slag pool and decreasing the cooling rate of the weld metal, or by de-hydrogen treatment.

When reinforcement is left on, the fatigue strength of CES weld joint depends on the stress concentration at the toe of weld even in the presence micro-cracks in the weld metal. Micro-cracks, however, reduce the fatigue strength of flushed joints.

REFERENCES

1. Heywood, R. B., " *Designing by photo-elasticity*," Chapman and Hall, 152 (1952).
2. Takahashi, K., et al., " Fatigue strength of base metal and weld joints of high tensile strength steel," Trans. of JSME, **38**, 310, 1154/1167 (1972).

COD Test for Girth Weldment of Linepipe

K. Matsushita, N. Nishiyama and J. Tsuboi

Welding Section, Research Laboratories, Kawasaki Steel Corporation

1. Background

The recent incidence of unstable shear fracture in a high pressure gas pipe-line of large diameter revealed that little is known about the mechanism of pipe-line fracture because of experimental difficulties in duplicating such fracture under laboratory conditions. Metallurgically, fracture was assumed to be based mainly on the mechanical fibering effect due to non-metallic inclusions in steel. These defects are shown by the split in the fracture surface of Charpy or DWT specimens taken from controlled-rolled steel plates. Linepipes pressurized with natural gas to 80 percent of the specified minimum yield strength are usually fabricated from controlled-rolled niobium bearing steels. Often linepipe, and even high-test linepipes, are girth welded with a cellulose type electrode being anxious about hydrogen induced craking.

Unstable brittle or ductile fracture in girth weldment of a linepipe fabricated from niobium bearing steel was studied by measuring the crack opening displacement in a three point bend test specimen and by discussing the results in terms of fracture toughness.

Weldments were made with E7010 and E8018 electrodes for studying the effect of hydrogen on fracture of linepipes.

2. Test Method

2.1 Materials

Two pipes, 48-inch outer diameter, 0.8-inch wall thickness *API* 5*LX*-70 pipes, with the chemistry shown in Table 1, were girth-welded in accordance with the Gas Council Supplementary Specification, *GC/PS/LX*1. Chemistries of all deposited metals made from E7010 and E8018 electrodes are shown in Table 2.

TABLE 1. Chemistry of pipe welded. (wt. %)

C	Si	Mn	P	S	V	Nb	Al	Ni	C.E.*
.11	.21	1.40	.006	.004	.043	.036	.040	.34	.37

$$* \quad C.E. = \%C + \frac{\%Mn}{6} + \frac{\%Cr + \%Mo + \%V}{5} + \frac{\%Ni + \%Cu}{15}$$

TABLE 2. Chemistries of all deposited metals.

Electrode	Dia. (in.)	Components (wt. %)						H cc/100 g	Moisture in coating (wt%)
		C	Si	Mn	P	S	Ni		
E7010	3/16	.07	.07	.30	.010	.017	—	23	15.2
E8018	3/16	.05	.44	.86	.014	.010	2.58	2.5	0.06

2.2 Specimens

The specimens, shown in Fig. 1, for COD measurement were taken from the weldment parallel to the pipe axis. The notch was sawn either at the center or at the fusion line of the weld metal. Test coupons for measuring the temperature dependent yield strength were also removed from the pipe.

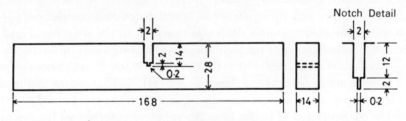

FIG. 1. Geometry of COD specimen (unit in *mm*).

2.3 Measurement of COD

Crack opening displacement at the notch root at the initiation of brittle fracture was measured by a clip gauge. Bending load applied through a center punch of 0.5 inches radius to a 4.5 inches span between 0.5-inch radius support rollers.

Critical COD was calculated from the observed clip gauge COD by using a rotational factor, r, which is based on the geometry of a bent specimen. The rotational factor, r, which was determined by a special experiment using the same grade steel since this value depended on the strength of the specimen.

3. Test Results and Discussion

3.1 Tensile Properties

Reduction in area for the base plate in the direction of wall thickness was different from that in the direction of the plate width. At temperatures above $-20°C$, the pipe material was completely ductile in the direction of wall thickness, and the split was not observed. Nevertheless, the ratio of reduction in area for both directions was most pronounced. Splits were observed only at temperatures ranging between $-62°$ and $-140°C$, where this ratio was almost constant.

Weld metal made from $E8018$ electrodes fractured in a brittle manner at a temperature of $-196°C$. The reduction in area of the weld metal, however, was similar to that of the base plate for the entire range of temperatures. On the other hand, reduction in area for the weld metal made from $E7010$ electrodes increased at temperatures from $20°$ to $-100°C$, and decreased continuously with temperatures below $-100°C$. Fish eye patterns were observed on the fracture surface on the specimen tested at temperatures of $20°$ and $-20°C$. These facts for the weld metal made from $E7010$ electrodes are due to the influence of hydrogen which is twenty times more than the hydrogen in the weld metal made from $E8018$ electrodes.

3.2   Crack Opening Displacement

Several discontinuous drops in load were observed over a range of temperature from $-40°$ to $-160°C$ in the specimen fabricated from the base plate. These drops coincided with splits in the fracture surface of the broken COD specimen.

Specimens tested at temperatures below $-140°C$ fractured without ductile openings at notch roots on the fracture surfaces. Nevertheless, specimens tested at $-140°$ and $-160°C$ could be considered to have fractured in a brittle manner after general local yielding as evidenced by the existence of lateral notch root contraction.

None of the discontinuous drop was observed in the weld metal and the bond of weldment. Brittle fracture of the weld metal was accompanied by ductile opening on the fracture surface at temperature of $-60°C$, and at $-100°C$ in the bond of weldment.

Temperature dependence of the critical COD, δ_{COD}, is shown in Fig. 2. The COD specimens for the bond were of the same quantity of the weld metal and the base plate due to the configuration of fusion line. No split was observed on the fracture surface of the bond specimens even in the base plate. This means that toughness in the direction of wall thickness of the controlled-rolled plate may have been improved significantly through a very short time heating during welding.

Since there are two phases which provide different toughnesses at notch root, results for the bond COD show that when $E7010$ electrodes are used the HAZ toughness is so embrittled by the hydrogen diffused from the weld metal that the bond COD is always same as that of the weld metal. On the other hand, when $E8018$ electrodes are used, the bond COD agrees well with the weld metal COD when the base plate is fractured by either perfectly ductile or perfectly brittle mode. If either the base plate is ductile and the weld metal is brittle or vice versa, the bond specimen brittle fractured following a ductile opening of the notch.

The observed values for COD were compared with the calculated values by Dugdale-Barenblatt's theory and the finite element method by Kanazawa et al.[1] The observed values for $\sigma_N/\sigma_Y \leq 1$ were in good agreement with the calculated values by D.B. theory, and for $1 < \sigma_N/\sigma_Y \leq 2$ by the finite element method. In addition, the observed values for δ_{COD} based on the split, which occured before ductile opening, are in good agreement with the theoretical values of the brittle opening. Relation between crack length of the

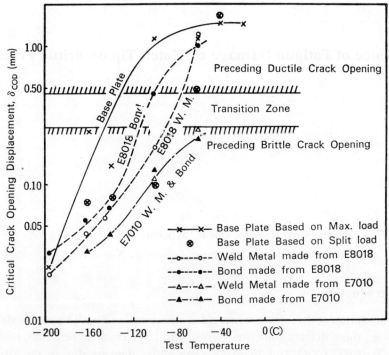

FIG. 2.   Temperature dependence of critical crack opening displacement.

girth weldment and brittle fracture initiation temperature was deduced from the critical COD, δ_{COD}, obtained above.

Resistance to brittle fracture was found to be the largest in girth weldment using $E8018$ and the smallest in the bond of a seam weldment with bulging.

Since the above discussion is based on the condition of no residual stress, the many possible negative factors in girth weldment contribute in increasing the temperature for initiating brittle fracture. Such negative factors include residual stress, angular distortion, poor fitting and offset in pipe ends, and hydrogen induced embrittlement, etc.

In order to avoid these negative factors, girth weld of hightest linepipe should be made with $E8018$ electrode which gives a more reliable weld metal.

REFERENCES

1. Kanazawa, T. and Machida, S., "COD Chart on Bending Test," Doc. TM Committee, Japan Wed. Eng. Soc., Doc. No. TM-114 (1972).

Influence of Fatigue Damage of Notch Tip on Brittle Fracture

N. Taniguchi, I. Soya and K. Minami

Products Research and Development Laboratory, Nippon Steel Corporation

1. Introduction

Various latent defects exist in welded structures and with repetitive stresses or stress corrosion, these defects sometimes grow into large cracks, eventually leading to a fatal brittle fracture. Crack tips in many cases suffer damage due to repetitive stress and generally materials with such fatigue damage have lower resistance against fracture or corrosion.

Brittle fracture characterization tests for ensuring the safety of welded structures normally use large scale specimens without fatigue damage. The results thus obtained may be better than that encountered under actual service conditions. Therefore, the influence of fatigue damage on fracture should be investigated and we are currently working on this subject. Some of our results show a relation between the rate of fatigue crack propagation and plate thickness, differences in fatigue crack propagation at different locations in the weldment, relation between the amount of fatigue damage and fracture strength, and so on. Some of these test results are discussed in this report.

2. Experimental Procedure and Results

(1) *Influence of Fatigue Damage on Brittle Fracture of Butt Welded Fusion Line*

Materials used are HT 60 and HT 80 kg/mm^2 class steel of $t=25$ mm and specimen shape as shown in Fig. 1. Test results of K_c vs. testing temperature is shown in Fig. 2. Starter cracks were fatigued at two load levels. Specimens with machined notch were also tested for comparison. From the above results, fatigue damage due to a higher number of fatigue cycling with low stress had a worse influence on brittle fracture than fatigue damage due to lower cycling number and high fatigue stress. The following are possible reasons for this conclusion; (1) microstructural material deterioration, (2) compressive residual stress at the crack tip, (3) notch tip acuity, and (4) geometrical con-

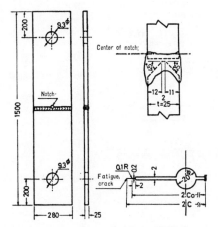

FIG. 1.   Dimensions and notch details of butt welded specimen.

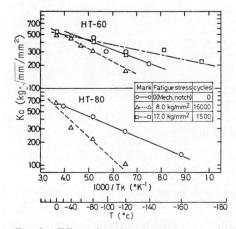

FIG. 2.   Effect of testing temperature on fracture toughness, K_c of HT–60 and HT–80 butt welded joint (corrected for estimated residual stress).

figuration of the notch to plate thickness.

Kanazawa et al.[1] have conducted similar study with hull structural steel plates and concluded that fracture stress of a specimen with lower fatigue cycled crack is appreciably higher than the fracture stress of a machined notch specimen.

For higher fatigue cycled cracks, however, the fracture stress is almost the same or sometimes lower than that of a machined notch. Their rational reason for this result is that the influence of geometrical shape (notch tip inclination to the plate) and the compressive residual stress at the tip is more pronounced than the material deterioration due to fatigue.

The result of this test is mainly due to the compressive residual stress at the fatigue crack tip. Particular emphasis should be made that brittle fracture with a crack of higher number of fatigue cycles and lower fatigue stress can cause lower or unfavorable results in comparison with machined notches.

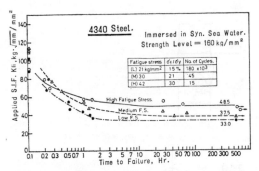

FIG. 3.   Delayed failure curves of 4340 steel, 160 kg/mm² level with different fatigue crack conditions in Syn. Sea Water.

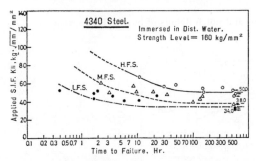

FIG. 4.   Delayed failure curves of 4340 steel, 160 kg/mm² level with different fatigue crack conditions in distilled water.

(2)   *Influence of Fatigue Damage on Delayed Failure*

The influence of fatigue damage on delayed failure in a low alloy martensitic steel (4340) was studied. Fatigue notches were made at the center of a 20 mm square × 200 mm long bar and the specimens were loaded in a cantilever type constant loading machines. Some results are shown in Figs. 3 and 4. with fatigue conditions listed in Fig. 3. The lowest K values which can cause delayed failure, called K_{ISCC}, are the lowest for the highest number of fatigue cycles and the lowest fatigue stress. K_{ISCC} is also the highest for the lowest number of fatigue cycles and the highest fatigue stress. In such delayed failure, the stress corrosion characteristic of the fatigue damage, other than those discussed earlier in the static tensile test of (1), should be taken in consideration. The X-ray microbeam technique of 100 micron square was employed to investigate one such characteristics, namely the magnitude of residual stresses at the notch tip. Little difference in residual stress was observed with different fatigue stresses. Further investigation on other factors which influence delayed fracture should be conducted to.

3.   Discussions

An analysis of the compressive residual stress at the fatigue crack tip for the butt welded joint using Dugdale-Muskhelishvili model was attempted. Figure 5 shows the

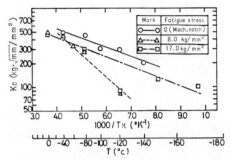

F<small>IG</small>. 5.   Effect of testing temperature on fracture toughness, K_c of HT–60 butt welded joint (corrected for estimated residual stress).

result of a relation between the testing temperature and K_c value which was obtained by subtracting K value due to the residual stress of fatigue loading from the K_c value shown in Fig. 2. The general trend of the result agrees well with the result obtained by Kanazawa et al.,[1] but there is a quantitative difference. In particular, the amount of decreased stress with higher number of fatigue cycles and lower fatigue stress is rather high in this test. One reason could be that the overall fatigue stress level is rather high in Kanazawa et al. test when compared with this test.

Further quantitative analysis of the residual stress and microstructural analysis of material deterioration should reveal new facts and hopefully help understand the phenomena.

4.   Summary

(1)   Brittle fracture stress of specimens with a fatigue crack of higher number of fatigue cycles and lower stress is appreciably lower than the fracture stress of the base metal with no fatigue crack (machined notch). For lower number of fatigue cycles and higher stress the fracture stress is in some cases higher than that of the base metal. This tendency can be enhanced at a lower temperature range.

(2)   The above trend can also be recognized in the delayed failure. Fatigue crack tip with higher fatigue stress is less sensitive to delayed failure. On the other hand, a crack with higher number of cycles and lower fatigue stress is more sensitive to delayed failure.

(3)   Compressive residual stress at the fatigue crack tip is considered as the prime factor which influences fracture. Other factors, however, such as material deterioration at the tip and notch acuity should be investigated further in order to assess quantitatively the degree of influence.

R<small>EFERENCES</small>

1.   Kanazawa, T., et al., " Effect of Low Cycle Fatigue on the Brittle Fracture Initiation Characteristics of Ship Steels," 1st and 2nd report, J. of the Soc. of Naval Architects of Japan, No. 121, June (1967) and No. 126, Dec. (1969).

Discussions in Session II

Question directed to Dr. Toyoda by Prof. Ono

In the Satoh-Toyoda's calculation, it is assumed that the concentration of hydrogen is directly proportional to the plastic strain. Is there any experimental evidence for this assumption?

Question directed to Dr. Toyoda by Prof. Packman

I would like to ask a question of the same paper, if I may. In Fig. 6 you show that beyond the plastic zone the hydrogen is depleted below that of the base material. Would you expect the same distribution of hydrogen to occur if the hydrogen was due to the stress corrosion cracking and not to hydrogen induced cracking, where in the stress corrosion cracking you had hydrogen introduced at the crack tip?

Reply to Prof. Ono by Dr. Toyoda

Thanks for discussing our paper. Behavior of diffusible hydrogen in the strained region around the crack tip has not been known in detail. However, it is well known that diffusible hydrogen is attracted to the stress concentration field of the array in order to decrease its lattice misfit energy. It is also found that hydrogen is trapped at a dislocation array, and the density of dislocation should be proportional to the magnitude of plastic strains. I believe, therefore, the assumption about the density of hydrogen is reasonable.

Question directed to Prof. McEvily by Prof. Iida

1. In Fig. 3 of your text straight lines of a slope of 45° are observed in the range from zero to minus one of the stress ratio. Would you please explain the reason why K_{amp} for a stress ratio of minus one should be twice as that for zero stress ratio? Are there much test results which support construction of such straight lines with a slope of 45°?

2. Some empirical expressions have been proposed with consideration for effects of R ratio on the rate of crack growth. For example, eqs. (10) to (14) are mentioned in the contribution by Prof. Kitagawa. Would the author please explain the interrelation between such equations and K_{amp} versus K_{mean} curves in Fig. 3 in the author's paper?

Reply to Prof. Iida by Prof. McEvily

The 45° line in Fig. 3 is drawn on the basis of the consideration that the compressive portion of a loading cycle is ineffective in promoting crack advance. Closure of the crack during compression allows stress to be transmitted across the crack itself. Only the tension portion of the cycle is considered to be important in growing the crack. The same tensile stress range at $R=-1$ will lead to the same crack growth rate at $R=0$. However, the stress amplitude at $R=-1$ will be twice that at $R=0$. Support for this interpretation comes from work by Illg and myself published in NASA TN D-52. Also, Pook (1972, ASTM STP 513, 106) has recently shown that the tensile stress range at the threshold level is about the same for $R=-1$ as for $R=0$. However, we have also observed that as the amplitude increases there will be some difference between $R=-1$ and $R=0$ behavior, with cracks growing more rapidly under $R=-1$ conditions for the same tensile stress excursion. This difference at higher growth rates would reduce the ratio of stress amplitudes below 2. It was thought that increased plastic deformation at higher amplitudes was responsible for this effect. As a final comment, I would suggest that further experimental work is needed to establish the reliability of the trends indicated in Fig. 3.

Professor Iida has inquired about the agreement or disagreement between the predictions of Fig. 3 in my paper and equations $(10) \sim (13)$ presented in the contribution by Prof. Kitagawa. If the K_{min} value in eq. (10) is zero or greater, this equation might lead to the same prediction but the value of the exponent, A, of K_{max} would have to be set at zero. I expect that the proposers do not mean for A to be zero, and if so the predictions would differ. The next equation (11) appears to be a $\left(\dfrac{K}{\sigma} \right)^2$ modified by a plastic zone size correction. Incidentally, we find that such a correction in our analyses is rarely significant for crack growth below 10^{-4} inches per cycle. Equation (11) does not say much about mean stress specifically, and so in this case over much of the mean stress range of Fig. 3 the two approaches would be similar. Equation (12) is similar to the Forman equation in which mean stress effects can be present over the entire range. In materials of high toughness this approach would be similar to Fig. 3, since in high toughness materials mean stress effects are less important than in low toughness materials. Equation (13) involves a correction factor for mean stress. It appears that mean stress effects above $R=0$ may be present only if static modes of separation are induced as in low toughness materials. Fig. 3 has been drawn for the case of a high toughness material in which case mean stresses should be relatively unimportant until the fracture toughness level is approached.

Comment directed to Prof. Fisher by Prof. Kobayashi

I believe Prof. McEvily has presented an idealized problem in which residual stress is assumed to be nonexistent. The residual stress mentioned by Prof. Fisher can be superposed onto the problems considered by Prof. McEvily to construct the real problem which Prof. Fisher is referring to. Professor McEvily's assessment of the role of defects is thus correct within his postulates but certainly the effects of residual stress mentioned by Prof. Fisher must be considered to complete the assessment of a real situation.

Comment directed to anyone or to Prof. Fisher by Prof. Kobayashi

My comment is addressed to the computation of residual stresses. The state of residual stress in a welded structure is the result of a complex process involving thermal, plastic, and creep strains in a structure with variable material properties due to extreme temperature gradients. I doubt that the state of art in theoretical analysis is advanced enough to analyze such complex process. If such is the case, how much value can we place on analytical results which require large efforts but may provide unrealistic results?

Question directed to Prof. Fisher by Prof. McEvily

In your studies which are presented in your paper did you measure crack growth rates or simply total life? With respect to total life it seems to me that a residual tensile stress could be important insofar as it affects crack initiation, but once a crack and associated plastic zone have formed the residual tensile stresses, as I have indicated earlier, would be less important, particularly if the applied stress ratio is greater than zero.

Comment directed to Prof. McEvily by Prof. Fisher

In welded steel structures, discontinuities are most often located in regions of residual tensile stress. Hence, crack growth is almost always a result of the full load cycle even for the case of stress reversal. The residual stress elevates the minimum stress so that the discontinuity is always subjected to a tensile stress range during the full load cycle. As a result, welded details show essentially no influence of mean stress. The total stress range is observed to fully describe the fatigue strength at all levels of stress range.

When crack growth studies are applied to welded structures, consideration should be given to the residual stresses due to welding. Crack growth rates at high mean stress levels are necessary. Other conditions do not appear to be applicable.

The exception to this condition is discontinuities near the center of groove welds in thicker plate sections. The center of the plate thickness at the weld is often in compression with multi-pass welds. Hence, discontinuities may reside in a region of compressive residual stress. Under this condition the full stress range is not effective and the beneficial effect of a compressive minimum stress suggested by Prof. McEvily may result.

This condition may even be eliminated if a second weld is placed which crosses the first weld. Such a condition occurs in a welded built-up girder. Groove welded flanges are connected to the web by web-to-flange fillet welds which produce a region of residual tensile stress at the web-flange junction.

Discontinuities that reside in weldments or at weld toes appear to have small sharp intrusions of slag or other non-metallic inclusions. Most studies on welded joints indicate that the initial discontinuities at weld toes are sharp enough to be considered equivalent to a microcrack. As a result the crack initiation phase appears negligible and crack propagation accounts for the fatigue life.

Reply to Prof. Fisher by Prof. McEvily

Based upon the results that I have seen in the literature as well as upon our own tests and analysis, it seems to me that for stress ratios of zero or higher that tensile mean stresses, either residual or applied, have little effect on the rate of crack growth provided that the K_{max} of the cycle is well below K_c. However, if an applied mean stress or a residual stress causes the minimum stress in the cycle to be compressive, the crack closure can occur and the effective stress range is reduced. In an $R=-1$ test, a tensile residual stress would be damaging, and the allowable amplitude for a given rate of crack growth would have to be reduced to correspond to the effective R value as indicated in Fig. 3, at least up until the point at which the effective R reached a value of zero. I concur with Prof. Fisher's concern about the influence of residual stress, and believe that further work in elucidating the role of residual stress would be useful.

Crack growth from defects appears to be the approach taken in predicting lifetimes of welded structures. Maddox's work, for example, is a demonstration of the usefulness of this approach in welded structures. In some cases there may be some question as to the severity of a particular type of defect. If it is crack-like, the propagation may start immediately, but if it is not so severe, then an incubation period may be necessary. Lifetime predictions based on crack growth alone should err if at all on the conservative side, a situation usually desired by the designer.

Comment directed to Prof. McEvily by Prof. Rolfe

For structures subjected to fatigue loading (or stress-corrosion cracking), any initial cracks can grow throughout the life of the structure. Fracture mechanics provides a means to analyze the subcritical crack growth behavior of structures using the same general equations and flaw geometries used to analyze conditions at fracture. Thus, an overall approach to preventing fracture or fatigue failures in large welded structures assumes that a small flaw of certain geometry exists after fabrication and that this flaw can either cause brittle fracture or grow by fatigue to the critical size. To insure that the structure does not fail by fracture, the calculated critical crack size, a_{cr}, at design load must be sufficiently large, and the number of cycles of loading required to grow a small crack to a critical crack must be greater than the design life of the structure.

Thus, although S-N curves have been widely used to analyze the fatigue behavior of steels and weldments, closer inspection of the overall fatigue process in complex welded structures indicates that a more rational analysis of fatigue behavior is possible by using concepts of fracture mechanics. Specifically, small (possibly large) fabrication flaws are

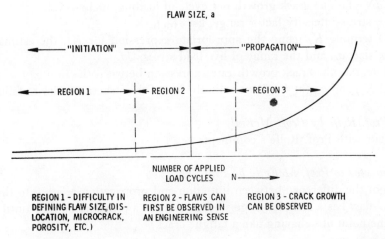

FIG. 1.   Schematic showing relation between "Initiation" life and "Propagation" life.

invariably present in welded structures, even though the structure has been inspected. Accordingly, a realistic approach to designing to prevent fatigue failure would be to assume the presence of an initial flaws and analyze the fatigue crack growth behavior of the structural member. The size of initial flaw is obviously highly dependent upon the quality of fabrication and inspection.

A schematic diagram showing the general relation between fatigue crack initiation and propagation is shown in Fig. 1. The question of when does a crack "initiate" to become a "propagating" crack is somewhat philosophical and depends on the level of observation of a crack, *i.e.*, crystal imperfection, dislocation, microcrack, lack of penetration, etc. An engineering approach to fatigue would be to assume an initial flaw size on the basis of the quality to grow to a size critical for brittle fracture. It is of interest to note that the fracture mechanics approach has been found by Fisher to be compatible with existing S-N fatigue data of welded members.

The procedure to analyze the crack-growth behavior in steels and weld metals using fracture mechanics concepts is as follows;

1) On the basis of quality of inspection estimate the maximum initial flaw size, a_0, present in the structure and the associated K_I relation for the member being analyzed.

2) Knowing K_c or K_{IC} and the nominal maximum design stress, calculate the critical flaw size, a_{cr}, that would cause failure by brittle fracture.

3) Obtain an expression relating the fatigue crack growth rate of the steel or weld metal being analyzed. The following conservative estimates of the fatigue-crack growth per cycle of loading, da/dN, have been determined by Barsom for martensitic steels (for example, A514/517) as wells as ferrite-pearlite steels (for example, A36) in a room temperature air environment.
Martensitic Steels
$da/dN = 0.66 \times 10^{-8}(\varDelta K_I)^{2.25}$
Ferrite-Pearlite Steels
$da/dN = 3.6 \times 10^{-10}(\varDelta K_I)^3$
where
da/dN = fatigue crack growth per cycle of loading, inches/cycle
K_I = stress-intensity factor range, ksi $\sqrt{\text{inch}}$

4) Determine K_I using the appropriate expression for K_I, the estimated initial flaw size, a_0, and the range of live load stress, $\varDelta\sigma$.

5) Integrate the crack growth rate expression between the limits of a_0 (at the initial K_I) and a_{cr} (at K_{IC}) to obtain the life of the structure prior to failure.

Reply to Prof. Rolfe by Prof. McEvily
  I concur with Prof. Rolfe's comments.

Question directed to Prof. McEvily by Prof. Ono
  It is not the difference between initiation and propagation relating to the fact that the original flaw has a rounded edge so that it is not a propagating flaw until it is sharpened to the point of behaving like a fatigue crack?

Reply to Prof. Ono by Prof. McEvily

I agree with Prof. Ono's comments. If the initial flaw is not crack-like, an incubation time may be required before the development of an observable crack takes place. Multiple defects or initial cracks may also affect the rate of growth of cracks if there are interaction effects.

Question directed to Dr. Taniguchi by Prof. Ono

There seems to be an effect of notch root radius depending on the stress level during your fatigue testing program. Is this effect also present in other materials, such as mild steel? Secondly, is the use of the large-sized specimens necessary in observing the effect? Was the scale of specimen size dictated from other considerations?

Reply to Prof. One by Dr. Taniguchi

Thank you very much for your comment, Prof. Ono. The material employed here are three kinds; HT60, HT80, and 160 kg/mm² class martensitic materials, and mild steel is not included, nor has it been done. Through microscopic examination of the specimens among these materials no definite difference at the crack tip in terms of notch acuity was observed.

Regardless of the specimen size one should bear in mind that there is a difference in results with a different stress level of fatigue cracking. Furthermore, the results sometimes might be different from the one which is obtained using a machined notch.

Comment directed to Dr. Taniguchi by Prof. Packman

With respect to the paper by Dr. Taniguchi, similar results have been found by NASA and the Air Force on the effects of fatigue stress levels on the K_{IC} values. Over a period of years the fracture toughness values for 7075-T65 aluminum alloy has dropped from about 32 ksi(in)$^{1/2}$ to a present value of 29 ksi(in)$^{1/2}$. This is due to the changes in the ASTM E-24 requirements for fatigue precracking. I am not sure of the exact values, but ASTM requirements specify the relative maximum stress values for fatigue the last several thousand cycles. This is to sharpen the fatigue crack so that the K_{IC} values will be as low as possible.

Question directed to Prof. Satoh or Dr. Fukagawa by Dr. Hall

I would like to make one comment and ask one question. In the way of comment, I would like to support Dr. McEvily's remark that there are stress ratios effects in fatigue crack growth in high strength steel alloys as well as in high strength aluminum and titanium alloys. There is some concern in my mind at this time that inability to properly account for stress ratio effects at low ΔK levels in airframe alloys may lend to cracking problems in airframe structure.

I would like to direct a question to either Prof. Satoh or Dr. Fukagawa. In your work concerning the effect of hydrogen on cracking in steel, does the hydrogen lower the intrinsic fracture resistance of the material, or does it just appear so because large amounts of slow crack growth that precede fracture are not accounted for in calculation of parameters at critical conditions such as COD on stress intensity factor.

Reply to Dr. Hall by Dr. Fukagawa

We consider that hydrogen does not lower the fracture toughness of whole materials but does lower the fracture toughness only arround the crack tips which are stressed by loading.

Our G_{ic} means the critical strain energy release rate at an initiation of slow crack growth from the crack tip under hydrogen influences. But, in our tests, once slow crack growth starts, the crack usually extends to a final crack. Therefore, it is unlikely that the K value, with the slow crack growth, had become to be equal to the hydrogen-free-K_{IC} value when the final fracture occurred.

Comment directed to Japanese papers in Session 2 by Prof. Satoh

I would like to add a short comment to two Japanese papers, the one given by Dr. Fukagawa and the other by myself. Among these papers, my paper is theoretical, but it includes several assumptions for concentration of hydrogen around the crack tip and numerical values of the material constants, because necessary data were not available at the time this paper was written. Another paper by Dr. Fukagawa is experimental and valuable information about fracture toughness parameter of steels including hydrogen may be led from these experimental results. So, in my opinion, quantitative calculation could be made in the near future by using the data obtained from these test results. About the diffusion of hydrogen around the crack tip, two-dimensional calculation can be made by using computor analysis. Also, FEM analysis can be useful to obtain local stress-strain around the weld defects. These problems are one of the main subjects in the Working Group of IIW Com. X on Welding Stresses, Strains and Other Effects due to Welding, of which the chairman is Professor Masubuchi. I expect that valuable information will be collected by the Working Group soon.

SESSION III

FUNDAMENTAL RESEARCHES ON SIGNIFICANCE OF DEFECTS
—STATIC AND DYNAMIC—

A Simple Procedure for Estimating Stress Intensity Factor in Region of High Stress Gradient

A. S. Kobayashi

Department of Mechanical Engineering, University of Washington

1. Introduction

Often an engineer must estimate the stress intensity factor for a crack in a complex structure for postmortem analysis of a structural failure or for a safe-life design of a structure. Stress intensity factors for such complex problems are normally estimated from available solutions for idealized problems through a succession of judicious engineering reductions of the complex problem to the simple problem in hand. If such reduction cannot be accomplished with confidence, then numerical techniques, such as the finite element analysis, can be used to estimate the stress intensity factor of the crack.

Many cracks are generated in regions of high stress concentrations by fatigue loading and are three-dimensional problems, which cannot be handled effectively by the present generation of finite element codes. Thus there exists an immediate need for estimating stress intensity factors of such crack problems. The purpose of this paper is to present three simple procedures for estimating stress intensity factors of straight cracks and semi-elliptical cracks in regions of high stress concentration.

2. Procedure

Consider a crack in a region of high stress concentration such as a crack emanating from a circular hole in a plate subjected to uniaxial tension as shown in Fig. 1. This problem has been solved by Bowie[1] and can thus be used for assessing the accuracy and limitation of the simplified procedure. The procedure is based on the superposition method which is used to estimate the stress intensity factor by eliminating the residual surface tractions on the crack surfaces which are located in the uncracked region in the vicinity of the hole. These conditions can be approximated by adding a mirror image of the actual crack, as shown in Fig. 1, and then determining the stress intensity by[2]

$$K_I = \frac{1}{\sqrt{\pi a}} \left[\int_{-a}^{o} \sigma_{yy}^{-}(x, o) \sqrt{\frac{a+x}{a-x}} dx + \int_{o}^{a} \bar{\sigma}_{yy}(x, o) \sqrt{\frac{a+x}{a-x}} dx \right] \tag{1a}$$

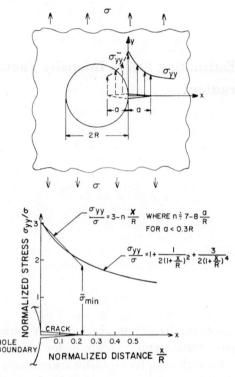

Fig. 1.   Crack emanating from a hole in a plate subjected to uniaxial tension.

where

$$\sigma_{yy}{}^-(x, o) = \sigma \left[1 + \frac{R^2}{2(R+x)^2} + \frac{3R^4}{2(R+x)^4} \right] \tag{1b}$$

$$\sigma_{yy}(x, o) = \sigma \left[1 + \frac{R^2}{2(R-x)^2} + \frac{3R^4}{2(R-x)^4} \right] \tag{1c}$$

The resultant stress intensity factor when $a < R$ is

$$K_I = \sigma \sqrt{\pi a} \left\{ 1 + \frac{1}{2\pi} \left[\frac{aR(-20R^4+9a^2R^2-4a^4)}{(R^2-a^2)^3} + \frac{R^3(8R^4+5a^2R^2+2a^4)}{\sqrt{R^2-a^2}\,(R^2-a^2)^3} \left(\frac{\pi}{2} - \sin^{-1}\frac{a}{R} \right) \right] \right\} \tag{2}$$

A further simplification can be made approximating the distribution of σ_{yy} by a straight distribution of $\sigma_{yy}/\sigma = 3 - nx/R$ as shown in Fig. 1 where n is the slope of line which minimizes stress deviations from the actual stress distribution within the crack length considered. The problem can be further idealized by superposition of two problems, one with the crack uniformly pressurized by $\sigma(6 - \tilde{\sigma}_{min})$ and the other with a linearly varying pressure of $\sigma(3 - \tilde{\sigma}_m) (1 + x/a)$ prescribed onto the crack surface as shown in Fig. 2. This resultant stress intensity factor at the crack tip obtained by this idealization is

$$K_I = \frac{\sigma}{2} (3 + \tilde{\sigma}_{min}) \sqrt{\pi a} \tag{3}$$

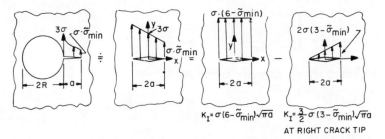

FIG. 2. Idealization of a crack emanating from a hole in a plate subjected to uniaxial tension for $a < 0.3\,R$.

The results of the above two approximations are compared with Bowie's results in the following Table 1.

Of the two procedures proposed here, eq. 2 provides a better estimate for a larger range of a/R ratios while eq. 3 yields tolerable results for a/R ratio of, at the most, 0.3. The cause of the error in the second procedure is mainly due to deviations between the true stress distribution and its linear approximation shown in Fig. 1. The procedure using a linear approximation of the prescribed pressure distribution is, however, a more convenient method to use in estimating the stress intensity factor for a semi-elliptical crack for which available solutions are severely limited.

TABLE 1. Normalized stress intensity factor for a crack emanating from a hole in a plate subjected to uniform tension.

$\dfrac{a}{R}$	$K_{\mathrm{I}}/\sigma\sqrt{\pi a}$					
	0	0.1	0.2	0.3	0.4	0.5
Bowie's Result [1]	3.39	2.73	2.30	2.04	1.86	1.73
Equation 2	3.00	2.63	2.36	2.16	1.98	1.88
Equation 3	3.00	2.69	2.46	2.31	—	—

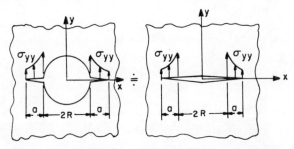

FIG. 3. Idealization of a double crack emanating from a hole in a plate.

The same procedure can also be used to estimate the stress intensity factor of a double crack emanating from both sides of the hole as shown schematically in Fig. 3. The stress intensity factor can be estimated by the following equation

$$K_{\mathrm{I}} = \frac{1}{\sqrt{\pi(a+R)}}\left[\int_{-a-R}^{-R}\sigma_{yy}(x,o)\sqrt{\frac{a+R+x}{a+R-x}}\,dx + \int_{R}^{a+R}\sigma_{yy}(x,o)\sqrt{\frac{a+R+x}{a+R-x}}\,dx\right] \quad (4a)$$

where

$$\sigma_{yy}(x, o) = \sigma\left[1 + \frac{R^2}{2x^2} + \frac{3R^4}{2x^4}\right] \tag{4b}$$

The resultant stress intensity factor is

$$K_I = \sigma\sqrt{\pi a}\sqrt{1 + \frac{R}{a}}\left[1 - \frac{2}{\pi}\left\{\sin^{-1}\frac{R}{R+a} - \frac{R}{R+a}\left[1 + \frac{R^2}{(R+a)^2}\right]\cdot\sqrt{1 - \frac{R^2}{(R+a)^2}}\right\}\right] \tag{5}$$

The results of eqs. 2 and 5 are plotted together with Bowie's results in Fig. 4. Within the range of crack length considered, the maximum errors due to these approximations are 10 percent for the very short crack and also for longer single cracks. Since the stress intensity factors are expected to approach those of an edge crack when $a/R \to 0$, the former error in the proposed approximate procedure can be easily compensated by correcting the stress intensity factor by the edge crack correction factor of 1.12.

Correction for the latter error in longer single cracks is more difficult since the stress intensity factor for the idealized crack in Fig. 1 approaches $K_I = \sigma\sqrt{\pi a}$ as $a/R \to \infty$ while for the corresponding Bowie crack $K_I = \sigma\sqrt{\pi a/2}$. Obviously a better estimate of the stress intensity factors of these two problems and more complex problems can be easily obtained by conventional computer codes of finite element analysis. A recently developed solution procedure by Grandt[3] can also be used effectively and with better accuracy to estimate stress intensity factors in two-dimentional problems. The approximate procedure il-

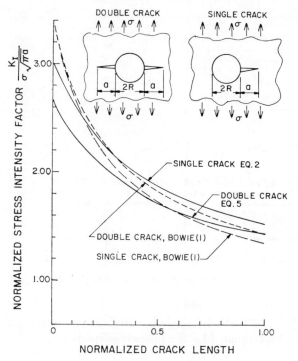

Fig. 4.   Stress intensity factor for cracks emanating from a circular hole in a plate subjected to uniaxial tension.

lustrated by Figs. 1, 2, and 3, however, serves to demonstrate the logic which will be used to estimate factors in semi-elliptical cracks.

Returning to three-dimensional analysis, the only available solution involving linearly varying pressure on a semi-elliptical crack is the stress intensity factor for a semi-circular crack in a beam subjected to bending by Smith[4]. The equivalent idealization of this problem, following the procedure shown in Fig. 2, is to represent the stress intensity factor of this beam bending problem by two solutions of a circular crack, one with a prescribed linearly varying pressure and one with a prescribed uniform pressure. The former solution is obtainable from Kassir and Sih[5] and the latter is a well known solution. The stress intensity factor for this idealized problem is

$$K_I = \sigma\left(1 + \frac{2}{3}\frac{a}{h}\cos\beta\right)\sqrt{\frac{a}{\pi}} \qquad (6)$$

where σ, a, h and β are defined in Fig. 5.

Stress intensity factor computed by eq. 6 is plotted against the results obtained by Smith et al.[4]. In general, good agreement is noticed between the two solutions except in the vicinity of $\beta = 90°$ or when the semi-circular crack intersects the free surface of the beam. This discrepancy is due to the residual normal surface tractions of the free surface which is not eliminated in the solution procedure shown in Fig. 2. This error becomes progressively larger with decreasing a/h ratio as expected. Similar error can be noted in Table 1 when eqs. 2 and 3 underestimate the normalized stress intensity factor by 12

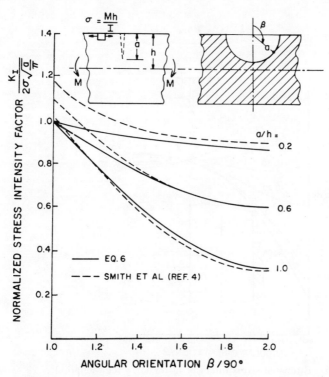

FIG. 5. Stress intensity factor for semi-circular crack in a beam subjected to bending.

percent when $a/R=0$. Table 1 also shows that this error is almost reduced to 4 percent at $a/R=0.2$. One can thus conjecture from Table 1 and Figs. 1 and 4 that while the free surface effect is not negligible in a region close to the circular hole boundary, the idealized procedure described here can be used to estimate the stress intensity factor for a semi-circular crack within ±5 percent accuracy due to other compensating errors involved. It should also be noted that the crack singularity in the near vicinity of the surface traction free surface probably vanishes[6] and thus the calculated stress intensity factor in this proximity region will have no physical significance.

In the following, the above three procedures will be used to estimate stress intensity factors in some problems of practical interest.

3.   Semi-Elliptical Crack Emanating from a Circular Hole in a Plate subjected to Uniaxial Tension

The three-dimensional equivalent of Bowie's crack problem is a semi-elliptical crack emanating from the hole boundary. The stress intensity factor for $a/R<0.3$ and derived on the basis of the simplification shown in Fig. 2 results in

$$K_I = \sigma\left[6-\tilde{\sigma}_{min}-(3-\tilde{\sigma}_{mim})\left\{1-\frac{k^2E(k)\cos\beta}{(1+k^2)E(k)-k'^2K(k)}\right\}\right]$$
$$\times\frac{\sqrt{\pi a}}{E(k)}\left\{\cos^2\beta+\left(\frac{a}{c}\sin\beta\right)^2\right\}^{1/4} \tag{7a}$$

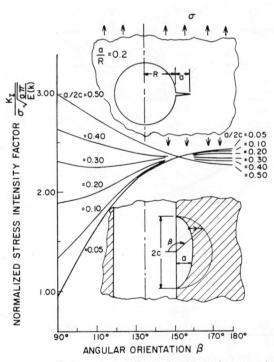

FIG. 6.   Estimated stress intensity factor for a semi-elliptical crack emanating from a circular hole in a plate subjected to uniaxial tension, $a/R=0.2$.

where

$$\tilde{\sigma}_{min} = 3 - n\frac{a}{R} \tag{7b}$$

and

$$n = 7 - 8\frac{a}{R} \tag{7c}$$

Although it is immediately obvious that larger crack depth results in larger stress intensity factors, the variation in K_I along the crack periphery cannot be easily guessed. Figure 6 shows an example of such variations in stress intensity factors along the crack periphery. The differences in the variations in stress intensity factors with crack aspect ratios show that while fracture would tend to originate at the point of maximum depth for an oblong crack, the origin of fracture for a semi-circular crack would be close to the hole boundary. In terms of fatigue crack propagation, both cracks, i.e., $a/2c<0.2$ and the semi-circular crack would tend to grow to a crack with an aspect ratio of approximately $a/2c=0.3$.

4. Cracks emanating from a Circular Hole fitted with a Frictionless Interference Plug

Stress distribution in the near vicinity of the hole is normally fitted with an interference plug in an elastic-plastic state. A crack penetrating the elastic-plastic boundary can cause a complex redistribution of stresses but equilibrium condition suggests that the redistributed stress would probably cause a small change in the available strain energy released and hence the stress intensity factor of a crack, particularly if the crack tip is outside of the plastic yield region. The stress intensity factor determined by the elastic distribution of stresses should thus provide a good estimation of the actual stress intensity factor of such cracks.

The stress intensity for a crack emanating from the hole can be estimated by following procedure similar to that illustrated by Fig. 1 and eq. 1a, by simply using the appropriate stress distributions of σ_{yy} and $\sigma_{yy}{}^-$ which yields for $a<R$

$$K_I = \frac{\delta ER}{2(R^2-a^2)}\left[-\frac{a}{R}+\frac{R}{\sqrt{R^2-a^2}}\left(\frac{\pi}{2}-\sin^{-1}\frac{a}{R}\right)\right]\sqrt{\frac{a}{\pi}} \tag{8}$$

where δ, R, a, and E are defined in Fig. 7.

For a double crack, the procedure illustrated in Fig. 3 and eq. 4 is used to obtain the following stress intensity factor of

$$K_I = \frac{\delta E}{2(R+a)}\sqrt{\frac{2R+a}{R+a}}\sqrt{\frac{a}{\pi}} \tag{9}$$

The results of eqs. 8 and 9 are plotted in Fig. 7. The dotted curve for the double crack shows the expected convergence of the stress intensity factors of the single and double cracks for very short crack lengths. The noted discrepancy is due to the error in modeling the actual problem by the procedure shown in Fig. 3. Contrary to the prob-

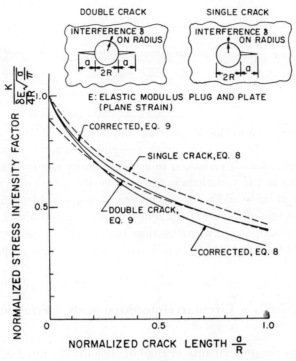

FIG. 7. Estimated stress intensity factor for cracks emanating from a circular hole fitted with a frictionless interference plug, plane strain.

lem of an unfilled hole shown in Fig. 4, stress intensity factors for cracks emanating from interference hole are not expected to converge to 1.12 $\delta E/4R \sqrt{\pi a}$ as $a \to 0$ since the state of stress at the plug-hole interface is such that $\sigma_{xx} (0,0) = -\sigma_{yy} (0,0)$ which is identical to that of the problem of a crack in a plate loaded in tension and not to the boundary condition of a single edge crack.

The stress intensity factor for a semi-elliptical crack emanating from the interference fitted hole can be estimated for $a < 0.3R$ as

$$K_I = \frac{\delta E}{4R} \left[2 - \tilde{\sigma}_{min} - (1 - \tilde{\sigma}_{min}) \left\{ 1 - \frac{k^2 E(k) \cos \beta}{(1 + k^2) E(k) - k'^2 K(k)} \right\}^2 \right]$$
$$\times \sqrt{\frac{\pi a}{E(k)}} \left\{ \cos^2 \beta + \left(\frac{a}{c} \sin \beta \right)^2 \right\}^{1/4} \tag{10a}$$

where

$$\tilde{\sigma}_{min} = 1 - n \frac{a}{R} \tag{10b}$$

and

$$n = 2 - \frac{5}{3} \frac{a}{Rn} \tag{10c}$$

The results for $a/R = 0.3$ are shown in Fig. 8 and exhibit the trend similar to that of Fig. 4 for an unfilled hole.

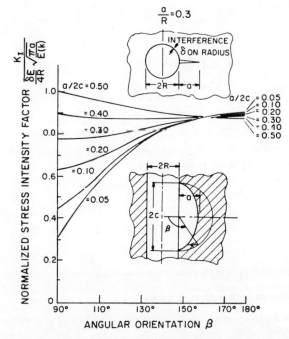

FIG. 8. Estimated stress intensity factor for a semi-elliptical crack emanating from a circular hole fitted with a frictionless interference plug, $a/R=0.3$.

5.   Crack emanating from a Circular Hole loaded with a Concentrated Load

Stress distribution in a plate with a circular hole loaded with a concentrated load is given in Reference 7. Unfortunately the integration process in eq. 1a, although not impossible, was formidable for this particular problem and therefore was not carried out. For double cracks emanating from both sides of the hole, the procedure outlined by Fig. 3 and eq. 4 yields

$$K = \frac{P}{\pi^{3/2}\sqrt{R+a}}\left[\sqrt{1-\{R/(R+a)\}^2}\left\{1-\frac{1}{1+\{R/(R+a)\}^2}\right\}\right.$$
$$\left.+\frac{1+2(R/R+a)^2}{[1+\{R/(R+a)\}^2]^{3/2}}\left\{\frac{\pi}{2}-\sin^{-1}\left(\frac{R}{R+a}\right)^2\right\}\right] \tag{11}$$

Results of eq. 11 are shown in Fig. 9.

For a semi-elliptical crack emanating from a circular hole loaded with a concentrated load, the stress intensity factor becomes

$$K_I = \frac{P}{\pi R}\left[2-\tilde{\sigma}_{min}-(1-\tilde{\sigma}_{min})\left\{1-\frac{k^2 E(k)}{(1+k^2)E(k)-k'^2 K(k)}\cos\beta\right\}\right]$$
$$\times\frac{\sqrt{\pi a}}{E(k)}\left\{\cos^2\beta+\left(\frac{a}{c}\sin\beta\right)^2\right\}^{1/4} \tag{12a}$$

where

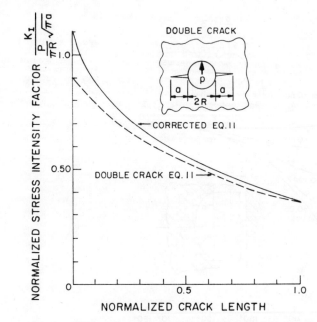

FIG. 9.   Estimated stress intensity factor for cracks emanating from a circular hole loaded with a concentrated load.

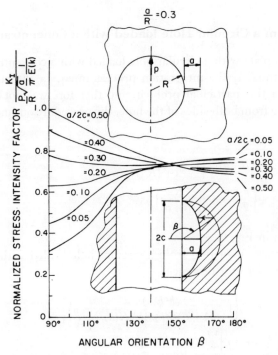

FIG. 10.   Estimated stress intensity factor for a semi-elliptical crack emanating from a circular hole loaded with a concentrated load.

$$\tilde{\sigma}_{min} = 1 - n\frac{a}{R} \tag{12b}$$

and

$$n = 2 - 1.5\frac{a}{R} \tag{12c}$$

The results of equations for $a/R = 0.3$ are plotted in Fig. 10 which shows the characteristic variation in stress intensity factor. A comparison of eqs. 10c and 12c shows that the results of Fig. 10 can also be used to estimate the stress intensity factor for a semi-elliptical crack emanating from an interference fitted hole and vice versa.

6. Crack on the Surface of a Pressurized Cylinder

For surface cracks in pressurized cylinders, the effect of the other wall surface on the stress intensity factor cannot be ignored. The procedure shown in Figs. 1 and 2 must thus be modified to account for the effect of the other surface. For two-dimensional problems the simple integration process of eq. 1a must be replaced by complex numerical procedures such as those discussed in References 8, 9 and 10 or the method of two-dimensional finite element analysis must be used (see, for example, References 11, 12 and 13).

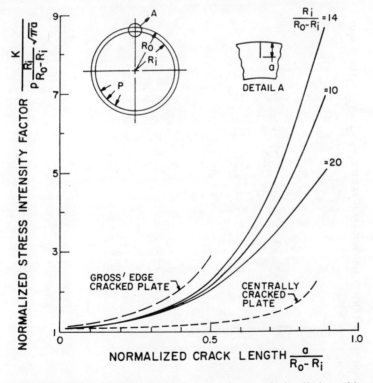

FIG. 11. Stress intensity factor for a surface cracked cylinder subjected to internal pressure.

Figure 11 shows the stress intensity factor for a long surface flaw on the external surface of a pressurized cylinder,[14] which was obtained by finite element analysis. An interesting feature of the variation in stress intensity factor is that it does not approach the single-edge crack solution of Gross[8] monotomically but decreases for cylinder thickness to radius ratio less than 10 percent. More details on this oscillation of stress intensity factor with the thickness to radius ratio can be found in Reference 15.

For a semi-circular flaw on the surface of a pressurized cylinder, available solutions

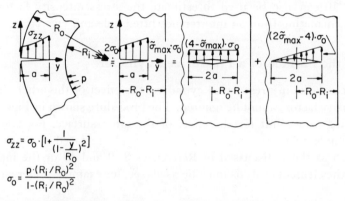

$$\sigma_{zz} = \sigma_0 \cdot [1 + \frac{1}{(1 - \frac{y}{R_0})^2}]$$

$$\sigma_0 = \frac{p \cdot (R_i/R_0)^2}{1 - (R_i/R_0)^2}$$

FIG. 12.   Idealization of a crack on the external surface of pressurized cylinder.

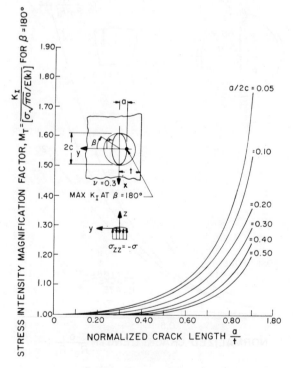

FIG. 13.   Maximum stress intensity magnification factor for an elliptical crack in a semi-infinite solid and subjected to uniform pressure.

involving elliptical cracks in semi-infinite solids and pressurized with uniform and linearly varying pressures can be used.[16,17,18] The procedure is illustrated schematically in Fig. 12 and the two numerical solutions for an elliptical crack subjected to uniform and linearly varying pressures are shown in Figs. 13 and 14, respectively. The maximum stress intensity factor at the deepest penetration of a semi-elliptical crack in a pressurized cylinder can be given in terms of two magnification factors M_T and M_L, in Figs. 13 and 14, for $a/R_O < 0.4$ as

$$K_I = \frac{P(R_i/R_o)^2}{1-(R_i/R_o)^2}\left[M_F M_T(4-\tilde{\sigma}_{max})+M_L(\tilde{\sigma}_{max}-2)\right.$$
$$\left.\times\left\{1+\frac{k^2E(k)}{(1+k)^2K(k)-k'^2K(k)}\right\}\right]\frac{\sqrt{\pi a}}{E(k)} \tag{13a}$$

where

$$\tilde{\sigma}_{max} = 2+n\frac{a}{R_o}$$

$$n = 2+3\frac{a}{R_o}\quad\text{for}\quad\frac{a}{R_o}<\frac{1}{3} \tag{13b}$$

$$M_F = 1.0+0.12\left(1-\frac{a}{2c}\right)^2 \tag{13c}$$

Note that the front surface magnification factor,[16,18] M_F, was incorporated in the above equation to account for the curving front surface which was considered important for a

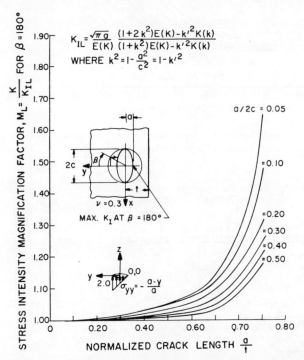

FIG. 14. Maximum stress intensity magnification factor for an elliptical crack in a semi-infinite solid and subjected to linearly varying pressure.

surface crack on the external surface of a cylinder. The maximum stress intensity factor, represented by eq. 13, is shown in Fig. 15.

A similar procedure can be used to estimate the stress intensity factor for a surface flaw on the internal surface of a pressurized cylinder. This problem has also been considered by Underwood[19] and by Emery[20] who only solved for a limited number of two-dimensional cases. The procedure, illustrated schematically in Fig. 16, yields stress intensity factor at the deepest penetration as

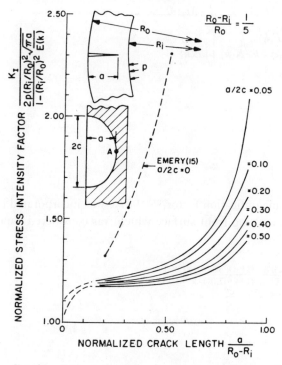

Fig. 15. Estimated maximum stress intensity factor (at point A) for a semi-elliptical crack on the external surface of a pressurized cylinder.

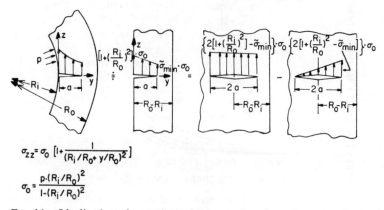

$$\sigma_{zz} = \sigma_0 \left[1 + \frac{1}{(R_i/R_0 + y/R_0)^2}\right]$$

$$\sigma_0 = \frac{p \cdot (R_i/R_0)^2}{1 - (R_i/R_0)^2}$$

Fig. 16. Idealization of a crack on the internal surface of a pressurized cylinder.

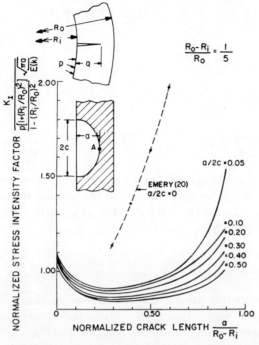

FIG. 17. Estimated maximum stress intensity factor (at point A) for a semi-elliptical crack (unpressurized) on the internal surface of a pressurized cylinder.

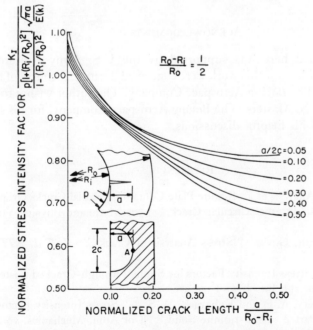

FIG. 18. Estimated maximum stress intensity factor (at point A) for a semi-elliptical crack (unpressurized) on the internal surface of a pressurized cylinder.

$$K_I = \frac{P}{1-(R_i/R_o)^2}\left\{M_T[2+2(R_i/R_o)^2-\tilde{\sigma}_{min}]-M_L[1+(R_i/R_o)^2-\tilde{\sigma}_{min}]\right.$$
$$\left.\times\left[1+\frac{k^2E(k)}{(1+k^2)E(k)-k'^2K(k)}\right]\right\}\frac{\sqrt{\pi a}}{E(k)} \tag{14a}$$

where

$$\tilde{\sigma}_{min} = \left(\frac{R_i}{R_o}\right)^2+1-n\frac{a}{R_i} \tag{14b}$$

$$n = 2-1.5\frac{a}{R_i} \qquad \text{for} \quad \frac{a}{R_i}<\frac{1}{3} \tag{14c}$$

The results of eq. 14 are plotted in Fig. 17 which shows increasing stress intensity factor with deeper crack penetration and is in agreement with the general trend of Emery's results.[20] Figure 18 shows the results for $(R_o-R_i)/R_o=1/2$ which is in qualitative agreement with the results by Underwood.[19]

7. Conclusion

Simple procedures for estimating stress intensity factors of through-cracks and semi-elliptical cracks in regions of high stress gradient have been presented. Stress intensity factors for cracks emanating from an unfilled hole, an interference fitted hole, a hole with a concentrated load, and on the external and internal surfaces of a pressurized cylinder, were determined by these procedures. These procedures should be of practical interest for engineers involved in day-to-day problems in fracture mechanics.

ACKNOWLEDGMENTS

The work reported here was supported by the U.S. Army Research Office—Durham. Some of the ideas for this work were conceived during the course of the author's consulting work with The Boeing Aerospace Company. The author wishes to express his appreciation to Mr. J. N. Masters, The Boeing Aerospace Company, for his support and to Dr. R. C. Shah for his helpful discussions.

REFERENCES

1. Bowie, O. L., " Analysis of an Infinite Plate Containing Radial Cracks Originating from the Boundary of an Internal Circular Crack," J. of Math. and Physics, Vol. 35, 60/71 (1956).
2. Paris, P. C. and Sih, G. C., " Stress Analysis of Cracks," *ASTM, STP 381*, 30/81 (1965).
3. Grandt, A. F., " Stress Intensity Factors for Some Through-Cracked Fastener Holes," to be published in the Int. J. of Fracture.
4. Smith, F. W., Emery, A. F. and Kobayashi, A. S., " Stress Intensity Factors for Semi-Circular Cracks, Part 2—Semi-Infinite Solid," J. of Appl. Mechanics, vol. 34, Trans. ASME, vol. 89 953 / 959, Dec. (1967).
5. Kassir, M. K. and Sih, G. C., " Three-Dimensional Stress Distribution Around an

Elliptical Crack under Arbitrary Loadings," J. of Appl. Mechanics, Trans. *ASME*, Vol. 88, Sept. 601/611 (1966),.

6. Hartranft, R. J. and Sih, G. C.   "Alternating Method Applied to Edge and Surface Crack Problems," *Mechanics of Fracture I, Methods of Analysis and Solution of Crack Problems* (edited by G. C. Sih), Noordhoff Int., 179/238, (1973).

7. Green, A. E. and Zerna, W.,   *Theoretical Elasticity*, Oxford Press, 281/288, (1954).

8. Gross, B., Srawley, J. E. and Brown, W. F., "Stress Intensity Factor for a Single-Edge-Notch Tension Specimen by Boundary Collocation," NASA TM D-2395, Aug. (1964).

9. Bowie, O. L.,   " Solutions of Plane Crack Problems by Mapping Technique ", *Mechanics of Fracture I, Methods of Analysis and Solutions of Crack Problems* (edited by G. C. Sih), Noordhoff Int., 179/238 (1973).

10. Isida, M.,   "Method of A Laurent Series Expansion for Internal Crack Problems," *ibid.*, 56/103.

11. Miyamoto, H., Shiratori, M. and Miyoshi, T.,   "Application of the Finite Element Method to Fracture Mechanics," J. of Faculty of Engineering, University of Tokyo (B), Vol. 31, No. 1, 119/270 (1971).

12. Hilton, P. D. and Sih, G. C., "Applications of the Finite Element Method to the Calculations of Stress Intensity Factors," *Mechanics of Fracture I, Methods of Analysis and Solutions of Crack Problems*, Noordhoff Int., 426/483, (1972).

13. Wilson, W. K.,   " Finite Element Methods for Elastic Bodies Containing Cracks," *ibid.*, 484/515.

14. Kobayashi, A. S., Maiden, D. E. and Simon, B. J., "Application of Finite Element Analysis Method to Two-Dimensional Problems in Fracture Mechanics," ASME Paper No. 69-WA/PVP-12, 1/7, (1969).

15. Emery, A. F., Walker, Jr., G. E. and Williams, J. A.,   "A Green's Function for the Stress Intensity Factors for Edge Cracks and Its Application to Thermal Stresses," J. of Basic Engineering Trans. of ASME, Vol. 91, Series D, No. 4, 618/624, Dec. (1969).

16. Shah, R. C. and Kobayashi, A. S.,   " Stress Intensity Factors for an Elliptical Crack Approaching the Surface of a Semi-Infinite Solid," Int. J. of Fracture, 133/146, June (1973).

17. Shah, R. C. and Kobayashi, A. S.,   " Stress Intensity Factors for an Elliptical Crack Approaching the Surface of a Plate in Bending," *ASTM STP 513*, Sept. 3/21, (1972).

18. Shah, R. C. and Kobayashi A. S.   " On the Surface Flaw Problem," *The Surface Crack: Physical Problems and Computational Solutions*, ASME, 79/124, Dec. (1972).

19. Underwood, J. H.,   " Stress Intensity Factors for Internally Pressurized Thick-Wall Cylinders," *ASTM STP 513*, 59/70, Sept. (1972).

20. Emery, A. F.,   Private communication on unpublished results not incorporated in Reference 14, July (1973).

Brittle Fracture Initiation Characteristics of Twin Notches

K. Ikeda

Structural Engineering Laboratory, Kobe Steel, Ltd.

K. Nagai

Department of Naval Architecture, Hiroshima University

H. Maenaka

Ship Structure Division, Ship Research Institute

K. Kajimoto

Hiroshima Technical Institute, Mitsubishi Heavy Industries, Ltd.

1. Introduction

A notch is needed for brittle fracture initiation and generally several such cracks or defects are located in a welded joint of a structure. When these notches are located close to each other, the brittle fracture initiation characteristics will be different from that of single notch due to the interaction effect of these cracks. Brittle fracture initiation characteristics of twin notches depends on the relative location of notches. In this paper, the interaction effect of notches located in a straight line, parallel and staggered and perpendicular to the loading direction were studied experimentally.[1,2] The interaction effect of these notches on brittle fracture initiation characteristics was evaluated by using the stress intensity factors and the crack opening displacements of these notches. Crack opening displacement at room temperature was measured by means of Moiré method and compared with theoretical crack opening displacement of twin notches previously obtained.

Fracture stress was also investigated by testing wide plate notched test specimens at low temperatures and the crack opening displacements were measured by electrostatic capacitance type COD gages.

2. Theoretical Studies on Twin Notches

2.1 Stress Intensity Factor

The stress intensity factor of a single notch of length $2c$ in a plate subjected to tensile stress, σ, at infinity in the direction perpendicular to the notch is expressed by

$$K = \sigma \sqrt{\pi c} \tag{1}$$

Brittle fracture initiates when the stress intensity factor K is equal to the critical stress intensity factor K_c, which is a function of material quality, temperature and strain

144

TABLE 1. Theoretical solutions of twin notches.

Crack model	$f(\lambda) \cdot g(\lambda)$	Example of $f(\lambda), g(\lambda)$ vs. λ
Equal Length Co-llinear Cracks $\lambda = 2c/h$	From Erdogan [2), 6)] $f_A(\lambda) = \dfrac{(1+\lambda)^2 \cdot \frac{E(k)}{K(k)} - (1-\lambda)^2}{2\lambda \sqrt{1-\lambda}}$ $f_B(\lambda) = \dfrac{(1+\lambda)^{3/2} \left\{ 1 - \frac{E(k)}{K(k)} \right\}}{2\lambda}$ $k = 2\sqrt{\lambda} / (1+\lambda)$ $K(k), E(k)$: Complete elliptic integral of first and second kind associated with k	
$\lambda = 2c/h$ $\sin 2\phi = s/a$ $\sin 2\psi = t/a$ $\dfrac{\sigma}{\sigma_y} = 1 - \dfrac{4(\psi - \phi)}{\pi}$	From Smith [8)] When plasticity has not spread between the two cracks $\Phi_A = \dfrac{8\sigma_y c}{\pi E} \cdot \dfrac{\pi^2 \sigma^2}{8\sigma_y^2} \left(1 + \dfrac{\lambda^2}{2} \right)$ $g_A(\lambda) = 1 + \dfrac{\lambda}{2}$ When plasticity spread between the two cracks $\Phi_A = \dfrac{8\sigma_y c}{\pi E} \left[\log_e \{ \cot(\psi - \phi) \cot 2\phi - 1 \} \right.$ $\left. - \dfrac{h}{2c} \log_e \{ \tan(\psi - \phi) \cot 2\phi + 1 \} \right]$	
Unequal Length Collinear Cracks $\lambda_1 = 2c_1/h$ $\lambda_2 = 2c_2/h$	From Sih [3)] $f_A(\lambda) = \sqrt{\dfrac{(2-\lambda_1+\lambda_2)(2+\lambda_1+\lambda_2)}{(2-\lambda_1-\lambda_2)(2+\lambda_1-\lambda_2)}} \cdot \dfrac{E(k)}{K(k)}$ $k^2 = \dfrac{8\lambda_2}{(2-\lambda_1+\lambda_2)(2+\lambda_1+\lambda_2)}$	
Equal Length Parallel Cracks $\lambda = v/2c$	From Yokobori [4)] $f_A(\lambda) = \dfrac{K_A}{\sigma\sqrt{\pi c}}$	
Equal Length Parallel Staggered Cracks $\lambda = 2c/d$	From Yokobori [5)] $f_A(\lambda) = \dfrac{K_A}{\sigma\sqrt{\pi c}}$	

rate. On the other hand, stress intensity factor of twin notches is influenced by the relative locations of notches and is expressed by

$$K = f(\lambda) \cdot \sigma \sqrt{\pi c} \tag{2}$$

where $f(\lambda)$=interaction effect factor

λ=ratio of notch length to distance between notches

$f(\lambda)$ depends on the relative locations in a straight line, parallel, or staggered. Theoretical solutions for these cases were obtained by Erdogan,[3] Sih,[4] Yokobori et al.[5,6] and Ishida,[7] and are summarized in Table 1.

2.2   Crack Opening Displacement

The crack opening displacement of a single notch of length $2c$ in a plate subjected to tensile stress σ at infinity in the direction perpendicular to the notch was obtained by Bilby, Cottrell and Swinden[8] by using the distributed dislocations model, and is expressed by

$$\Phi = \frac{8\sigma_Y c}{\pi E} \log_e [\sec (\pi\sigma/2\sigma_Y)] \tag{3}$$

When the plastic zone size around the crack tip is small in comparison with the crack length, the following relationship between the crack opening displacement Φ and the stress intensity factor K exists:

$$\Phi \simeq K^2/E\sigma_Y \tag{4}$$

When two notches are closely located, the crack opening displacement as well as the stress intensity factor can be expressed by the following equation:

$$\Phi = g(\lambda)\frac{8\sigma_Y c}{\pi E} \log_e [\sec (\pi\sigma/2\sigma_Y)] \tag{5}$$

where $g(\lambda)$=interaction effect factor

Theoretical solution of $g(\lambda)$ for equal length collinear cracks in a plate subjected to shear stress at infinity was obtained by Smith.[9] By applying this solution to the tension problem in plane stress condition, the theoretical solution presented in Table 1 can be obtained. Here $g(\lambda)$ is a function of λ before general yielding in the notch section. After general yielding, $g(\lambda)$ is not only a function of λ but also of the applied stress.

3.   Test Results and Evaluation

3.1 Interaction Effect of Notches Analyzed by Moiré Method

The authors succeeded in measuring precisely the crack opening displacement by means of Moiré method.[2] The interaction effects of twin notches evaluated by such crack opening displacements in wide plate test specimens tested at room temperature are discussed in the following.

The steel tested is a 10 mm thick (Steel A) 60 kg/mm² high-strength steel quenched and tempered with chemical compositions and mechanical properties shown in Table 2.

TABLE 2. Chemical compositions and mechanical properties.

| Steel | Plate Thick. (mm) | Chemical compositions (%) | | | | | | | | | Mechanical properties | | |
		C	Si	Mn	P	S	Ni	Cr	Mo	V	Y.P. (kg/mm²)	T.S. (kg/mm²)	El. (%)
A	10	0.14	0.44	1.22	0.014	0.014		0.18		0.03	58	68	32
B	20	0.14	0.46	1.21	0.022	0.007		0.17		0.03	58	68	39
C	20	0.13	0.36	1.19	0.016	0.015	0.52	0.05	0.099	0.041	58	66	39

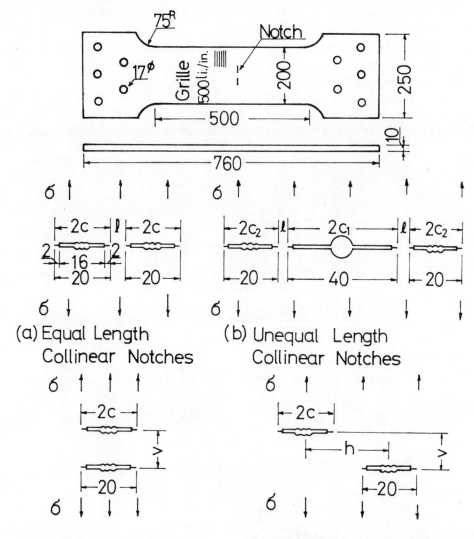

FIG. 1. Small size test specimens of twin notches.

The specimens were 200 mm wide with four types of central twin notches shown in Fig. 1. The equal-length, collinear notches specimen had two 20 mm notches located in a straight line and with variable with distances of l. The unequal length collinear notches specimen had a 40 mm central notch and two 20 mm external notches at a variable distance of l as shown in Fig. 1. The equal length parallel notches specimen had two 20 mm notches at a variable distance of v in the direction perpendicular to the applied tensile load. The equal-length, parallel but staggered notches specimen, two 20 mm notches separated 10 mm apart in the tensile direction and at a variable center distance of h.

The crack opening displacements at the inner and outer notch tips for equal length, collinear notches are shown in Fig. 2. It is noted in Fig. 2 that the crack opening displacement at the inner notch tip, A, is greater than that at the outer tip, B, and increases with stress. The difference between two curves increases greatly as the distance between two notches decreases. In addition, the crack opening displacement at the same stress level increases with decreasing distance, l, between two notches.

It is found at each notch tips of unequal length, collinear notches that the measured crack opening displacement at the tip of the long central notch is the greatest and those of inner and outer tips of the short external notch are smaller and the smallest, respec-

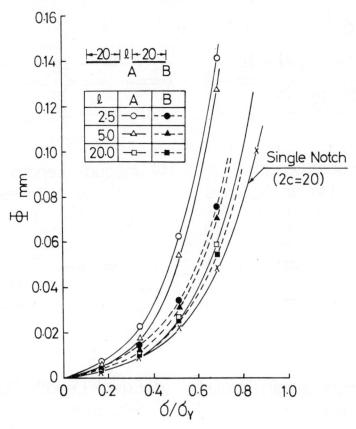

FIG. 2.   Relation between COD and stress ratio for equal length collinear notches.

tively. In addition, the crack opening displacement increases with decreasing distance between the two notches similar to the case of equal length, collinear notches.

The interaction effect of equal length, parallel notches is in contrast to that of collinear notches, and the crack opening displacement at the same stress level decreases as two notches approach each other as shown in Fig. 3. The cricial crack opening displacement, which is expressed by a dotted line in the figure, shows that the fracture stress of an equal length, collinear notch specimen is lower than that of a single notch specimen. In contrast, the fracture stress of an equal length, parallel notch specimen is higher than that of a single notch specimen, and stays on the safe side from the viewpoint of fracture. In addition, the interaction effect factor for crack opening displacement, $g(\lambda)$, can be obtained from this figure. The factor varies with stress as mentioned in the preceding chapter. For equal length, parallel staggered notches, the behavior of crack opening displacements at the each notch tip is complicated. When two notches do not overlap, the behavior of crack opening displacement is similar to that of an equal length, collinear notch specimen, i.e. the crack opening displacement at the inner notch tip is greater than that at the outer notch tip. When two notches overlap, however, the crack opening displacement at the outer tip is greater and this difference becomes greater with increased overlapping. This behavior is due to the fact that each inner notch tip is located behind

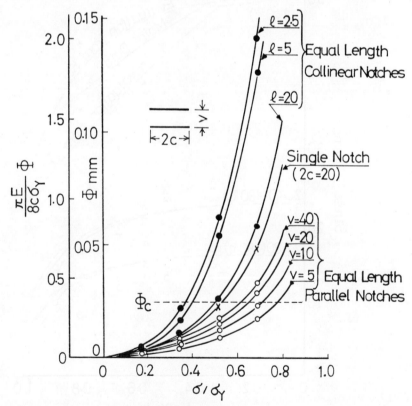

FIG. 3. Relation between COD and stress ratio for equal length, collinear notches and equal length, parallel notches, respectively.

another notch and thus hardly any load is transmitted around the inner notch tip. This tendency becomes greater as the vertical distance between the two notches decreases.

3.2   Brittle Fracture Initiation Characteristics

Brittle fracture initiation test of wide plate test specimen was conducted at low temperatures and the crack opening displacement near the notch tip was measured by means of the electrostatic capacitance type COD gages.[10]

Steels tested are two 20 mm thick 60 kg/mm² high strength steels quenched and tempered (Steels B and C) with chemical compositions and mechanical properties shown in Table 2. Steel B was used for equal length, collinear notch specimen and Steel C was used for unequal length, collinear notch, parallel notch and parallel staggered notch specimens.

The size of test specimens were twice the size of specimens used for Moiré measurement. Equal length, collinear notch specimens with notches of 40 and 80 mm long with

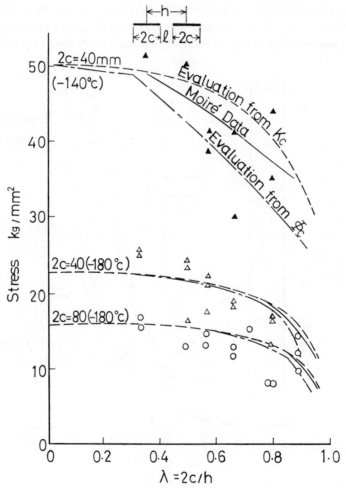

FIG. 4.   Relation between fracture stress and $\lambda = 2c/h$ for equal length, collinear notches.

variable notch distance were tested at -180 and $-140°C$. Figure 4 shows relation between the fracture stress and $\lambda = 2c/h$. Fracture stress decreases with decreased distance between two notches. The two notches do not interact with each other when the distance between inner tips of twin notches is equal to or greater than the notch length ($l \geq 2c$). Curves in Fig. 4 represent the theoretically determined fracture stress from respective theoretical equations based on K_c or Φ_c fracture criteria for a single notch specimen tested at specified temperatures. Also shown are experimentally determined fracture stress estimated from the relation between the stress and the crack opening displacement measured by the Moiré method. Experimental data are in good agreement with these curves. Estimated fracture stress based on crack opening displacement is on the safe side. Since the section between inner notch tips is in general yielding condition at $-140°C$ even for large distance between notches, the fracture stress estimated on the basis of stress intensity factor is irrational.

For unequal length, collinear notches, the fracture stress decreased with decreased distance between the two notches. When the distance is greater than the length of a short notch, the fracture stress is equal to that of a single notch and the interaction effect can be neglected.

Figure 5 shows the relation between fracture stress and length of external notch, $2c_2$, for constant distance between the notches. In this figure, $*$ denotes the estimated

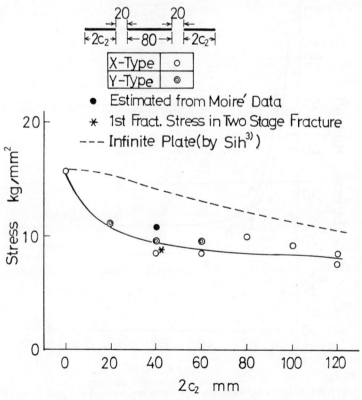

FIG. 5.   Relation between fracture stress and length of external notch.

fracture stress from measured crack opening displacement by means of Moiré method. $2c_2=0$ represents a single notch of 80 mm long. Although the measured critical crack opening displacement near the tip of a central notch is generally greater than that of external notch, the fracture initiates at nearly constant critical crack opening displacement.

For equal length, parallel notches, the relation between the fracture stress and the vertical distance between notches is shown in Fig. 6. ▲ denotes the estimated fracture stress from measured crack opening displacement by means of Moiré method. Since the fracture stress for parallel notch specimen with long vertical distance is equal to that of single notch specimen, the fracture stress for $v=\infty$ is the same as that of single notch.

The fracture stress of a parallel notch specimen increases with decreased vertical distance, v, and the fracture stress is equal to that of a single notch specimen when the vertical distance is greater than half notch length. In addition, when the vertical distance is relatively small, the fracture stress is not influenced by the notch length.

The maximum critical crack opening displacement, Φ_c, measured near the notch tip is shown in Fig. 7. When the vertical distance, v, decreases, the fracture stress increases

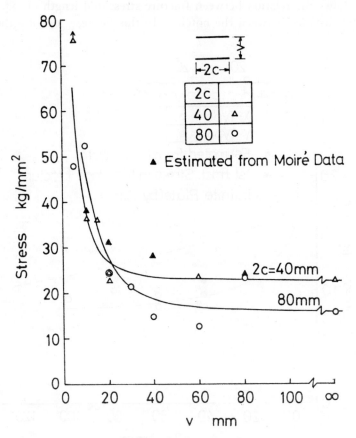

FIG. 6.   Relation between fracture stress and vertical distance for equal length, parallel notches.

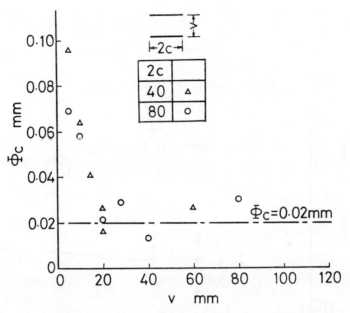

FIG. 7.   Relation between critical COD and vertical distance for equal length, parallel notches.

and consequently Φ_c also increases. Therefore, the phenomenon contradicts the assumption that fracture initiates at a constant critical crack opening displacement, Φ_c, of 0.02 mm for the steel tested.

Next, interaction effect for equal length, parallel staggered notches, which is a combination of equal length collinear with parallel notches, will be discussed. Figure 8 shows the relation between fracture stress and center distance, h, between two notches, where $2c=40$ mm and $v=20, 40$ mm. In this figure ▲ and △ denote the fracture stress at A and B estimated from measured critical crack opening displacement by means of Moiré method for $2c=40$ mm and $v=20$ mm, which are theoretically determined by the solution by Yokobori et al.[6] It is noted that the fracture stress which was estimated from measured critical crack opening displacement by means of Moiré method, at room temperature for B is lower than that for A when two notches overlap ($h<40$ mm). On the other hand, an opposite trend is found when the two notches do not overlap ($h>40$ mm). In other words, fracture initiates at B for the former and at A for the latter cases. The abovementioned tendency and experimental data for $2c=40$ and 80 mm are in good agreement with the theoretical curves by Yokobori et al.

From the critical crack opening displacement, Φ_c, measured near the tip of A and B for overlapped notches ($h/2c<1$), it is found that the critical crack opening displacement, Φ_c, of the outer notch tip is greater than that of a inner notch tip. On the other hand, Φ_c of the inner tip tend to be greater than that of the outer tip when two notches overlap. The critical crack opening displacement, Φ_c, at fracture, however, is nearly equal to 0.02 mm except for $h/2c=0.5$.

Finally, it should be noted that when twin notches are located in a welded joint,

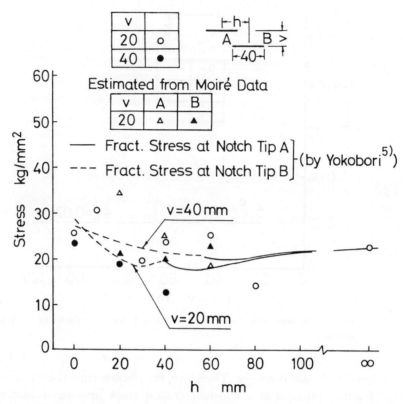

FIG. 8.   Relation between fracture stress and center distance for equal length, parallel staggered notches.

one must consider not only the interaction effect but also the effect of welding residual stress and steel quality at the notch tip in evaluating the brittle fracture initiation characteristics.

4.   Conclusions

Brittle fracture initiation characteristics of twin notches were evaluated from measured crack opening displacements at the notch tip by means of Moiré method at room temperature and by the notched wide plate tests conducted at low temperatures.

The conclusions are as follows:

(1)   Brittle fracture initiation characteristics of twin notches can be evaluated from critical stress intensity factor, K_c, or critical crack opening displacement, Φ_c, at the notch tip of single notch specimen.

(2)   Fracture stress of twin notches specimen can be estimated from measured critical crack opening displacement by means of Moiré method at room temperature.

(3)   When the crack opening displacement criterion is used, the interaction effect factor of twin notches is a function of stress.

(4)   Fracture stress of collinear notches decreases as the two notches approach each

other. On the other hand, fracture stress of equal length parallel notches increases as the two notches approach each other.

For equal length, parallel staggered notches, brittle fracture initiation characteristics represent a combined characteristics of equal, collinear notches with parallel notches. Consequently, variation in fracture stress is a complicated function of the relative locations of notches.

(5)   When notch distances between twin notches are greater than the following these specimens can be considered to be a single notch specimen with a notch $2c$ long:

a) Distance, l, between inner tips of equal length, collinear notches is greater than $2c$.

b) For unequal length collinear notches, l is greater than $2c_2$, where $2c_2$ is the length of short notch.

c) For equal length, parallel notches, the vertical distance, v, is greater than c.

d) For equal length, parallel staggered notches, the vertical distance, v, is greater than c or the horizontal distance, h, between the centers of two notches is greater than $4c$.

(6)   For collinear notches, brittle fracture initiates when the crack opening displacement is equal to a critical value, Φ_c, which can be obtained from single notch specimen. On the other hand, for equal length parallel notches, Φ_c increases with fracture stress for small vertical distance. This fact contradicts the assumption that fracture initiates at a constant Φ_c.

References

1.   Ikeda, K., Maenaka, H. and Kitamura, S.,   " Brittle Fracture Initiation Characteristics of Twin Notches (1st Report)," Journal of Soc. Naval Arch. Japan, Vol. 129, 257 (1971).

2.   Nagai, K., Ikeda, K., Iwata, M., Maenaka, H., Kajimoto, K., Kitamura, S. and Minami, I.,   " Brittle Fracture Initiation Characteristics of Twin Notches (2nd Report)," J. Soc. Naval Arch. Japan, No. 132, 405 (1972).

3.   Erdogan, F.,   " On the Stress Distribution in Plate with Collinear Cuts under Arbitrary Loads," Proc. 4th U.S. Nat. Cong. Appl. Mech., 547 (1962).

4.   Sih, G. C.,   " Boundary Problems for Longitudinal Shear Cracks ", Development in Theoretical and Applied Mechanics, Vol. 2, 117 (1964).

5.   Ichikawa, M., Ohashi, M. and Yokobori, T.,   " Interaction between Parallel Cracks in an Elastic Solid and its Effect on Fracture," Rep. Res. Inst. Strength and Fracture of Materials, Vol. 1, No. 1, 1 (1965).

6.   Yokobori, T., Uozumi, M. and Ichikawa, M.,   " Intesaction between Overlapping Parallel Elastic Cracks," Rep. Res. Inst. Str. and Fract. of Mat., Vol. 6, No. 2, 39 (1971).

7.   Ishida, M.,   "Analysis of Stress Intensity Factors for Plates Containing Randomly Distributed Cracks, " Trans. Jap. Soc. Mech. Eng., Vol. 35, No. 277, 1815 (1969).

8.   Bilby, B. A., Cottrell, A. H., Smith E. and Swinden, H. K.,   " Plastic Yield from Sharp Notches," Proc. Roy. Soc. A 279, 1 (1964).

9.   Smith, E.,   " The Spread of Plasticity Between Two Cracks," Inst. J. Eng. Sci., Vol. 2, 379 (1964).

10.   Ikeda, K., Kitamura, S. and Maenaka, H.,   " New Method of COD Measurement— Brittle Fracture Initiation Characteristics of Deep Notch Test by means of Electrostatic Capacitance Method," J. Soc. Naval Arch. Japan, No. 129, 277 (1971).

COD Approach to Brittle Fracture Initiation in Welded Structures

S. Machida

Department of Naval Architecture, University of Tokyo

1. Introduction

Advancement in technology is demanding a more fundamental and qualitative design procedure in the presence of crack-like defects. Deformation and fracture mechanism in a stressed crack tip region is extremely complex, and have been the subject of intense research efforts from structural engineers to solid state physicists. A fracture design criterion characterized by a single parameter is preferable since any engineering fracture criterion must be able to predict the fracture load through measurements and computations as simple as possible.

Several parameters have been proposed for macroscopic fracture criteria based on continuum mechanics. The parameter K (stress intensity factor) associated with linear fracture mechanics has been very successfully applied to quantative assessment of unstable fracture behavior under small scale yielding condition. For most in-service brittle failures of ordinary welded steel structures, however, defects that lead to catastrophic failures are located at or near a weld joint and/or structural discontinuity where high stress and strain concentrations exist. This implies that the majority of brittle fracture initiation in ordinary welded steel structures would occur under large scale yielding, i.e. a crack is surrounded by extensive plastic yielding prior to unstable fracture initiation. We have thus been very interested in concepts or fracture models which takes into account plasticity around the crack tip. To our present knowledge, the crack opening displacement (COD), Φ, the plastic zone size, $\rho+$, and the path independent contour integral, J, appear to be the three major and different parameters which account for fracture initiation under large scale yeilding condition.

In this report, some of fundamental aspects of the COD concept, its validity and limitation, are briefly reviewed.

2. COD as an Engineering Fracture Parameter Especially under Large Scale Yeilding Condition

Figure 1 shows an example of the notch depth (defect size) dependence of a critical COD (Φ_c).[1] Sharp notches which vary in depth from 3 to 36 mm were machined in each of the 12 mm thick and 90 mm wide specimens. Testing temperature was chosen to ensure that all specimens fractured in a brittle manner after general yeilding. These Φ_c values are mostly independent of notch depth within a certain scatter band.

Relations between Φ_c values of small scale yielding region and those of the general yielding region have been investigated by using large notched tensile specimens with higher transition temperature (fracture stress *vs.* temperature relation) than smaller specimen.[2,3,4] Φ_c values obtained from small specimen compared well with those obtained from large specimens, although the former fractured generally after general

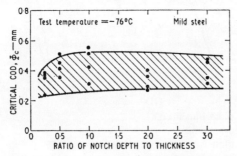

FIG. 1.   Relation between Φ_c and notch depth.

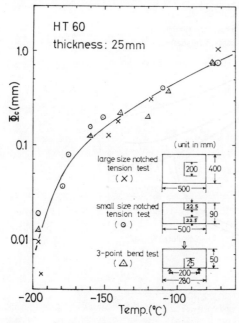

FIG. 2. Φ_c obtained by specimens of various configurations.

yield while the latter fractured at low stress level. Figure 2 shows an example of Φ_c vs. temperature relation for a given material obtained from various testings. The fracture tests included notched slow bend test as well as notched tensile test of various sizes.

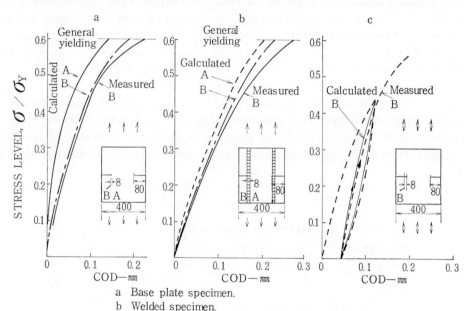

a Base plate specimen.
b Welded specimen.
c Base plate specimen under repeated stress.

FIG. 3. Comparison of measured crack opening displacement versus calculated COD using Dugdale model.

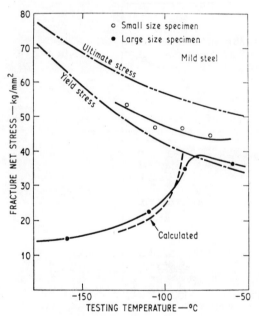

FIG. 4. Fracture stress curves of large and small specimens.

All Φ_c values fall in a single scatter band irrespective of specimen size, loading system, fracture before and after general yielding of the specimens. We can thus conclude that Φ_c is a promising engineering fracture toughness parameter of practical use since the fracture toughness value, Φ_c, can be measured by small specimen which otherwise would fracture under large scale or general yielding condition in the realistic temperature region.

It has been shown that the crack opening behavior calculated on the basis of the Dugdale model, despite its simplicity, compares well with the measured COD (Fig. 3)[14], and that the Dugdale model can be utilized in predicting the fracture strength.[3-5,12-15] Figure 4 shows such typical example. The large and small specimens were of 500 mm width with 125mm side notches and of 90mm width with 20mm side notches, respectively. The thickness of both specimens was 23 mm. The fracture stress for large specimen in low-stress fracture region was calculated from the Φ_c value measured in small specimen using the Dugdale model and is shown by the broken line.

There are many other examples showing the validity of the COD concept which explaines different fracture stress behavior due to the difference in size of specimen and notch.

3.   Applicability of COD Concepet to Fracture Initiation at a Defect in an Initial Stress Field

The above discussion relates to fracture of notched specimen free from initial stresses. Initial stresses can exist, for instance, in a preloaded cracked plate or around a crack in a welding residual stress field, etc. Some macroscopic fracture parameters used in predicting the brittle fracture strength of a defective component at low temperature under the effect of initial stress existing around a defect (crack) are discussed in the following.

Some difficulties can arise in applying a rigorous formalism of the COD concept. For illustrative purpose, consider a cracked plate subjected to tensile preloading. Due to the irreversibile plastic deformation around the crack tip, the crack would have a certain amount of residual COD even if the plate is completely off-loaded, while residual stress near the crack tip would be in a compressive state. It is obvious that this COD has lost its physical meaning as an engineering parameter for characterizing the fracture potential.

In order to circumvent this paradox, Koshiga[6] proposed to take the tensile plastic zone size, ρ^+, as a possible criterion for brittle fracture initiation and explained successfully the strengthening effect due to over-stressing on the basis that fracture occurs when the plastic zone size caused by tensile stress reaches a critical value. Koshiga used the plastic zone size computed from the Dugdale model instead of the actual plastic zone size, which is difficult to measure. It is also to be noted that ρ^+ should be defined as the tensile plastic zone developed at the temperature of fracture initiation.

The above difficulty in applying the COD concept can be avoided if we consider an "active COD" which may be defined as the COD caused by the crack tip plastic deformation developed at the temperature of crack initiation. Such COD corresponds qualitatively to the ρ^+ defined above and thus there is no essential difference between the ρ^+ and the active COD concepts. Even if we use the Dugdale model, however, prediction of fracture stress based on these two concepts may give different results because general unique relationship does not exist between these two parameters computed through the use of the Dugdale crack model under different mechanical and geometrical conditions.[7]

It is to be noted here that the K concept cannot be applied to the fracture behavior of preloaded cracked specimen because the residual stress caused by preloading is inherently associated with the crack tip plastic deformation which cannot be incorporated in the computation of K value. Kanazawa et al.[8] compared three engineering criteria, K, ρ^+ and Φ, and discussed analytically as well as experimentally the applicability of these parameters to the fracture behavior of cracked plates subjected to various initial stresses caused by welding residual stress, preloading, welding residual stress coupled with preloading, etc. Fracture under such complicated conditions can be simulated experimentally in a simple way by subjecting the notched specimens to different stress-temperature history prior to fracture. An example of such experimental results is shown in Fig. 5. Lines with arrows denote the stress-temperature history up to fracture. The thick line shows the fracture stress curve for the virgin state (fracture without any initial stress).

According to the K_c criterion, the specimen is expected to fracture at a point where each stress-temperature history curve crosses the thick line (the fracture curve of virgin state). The experimental results clearly contradict this prediction. The failure of the K_c criterion to explain the fracture stress, especially for cases (2) & (4), may be due to the fact that cleavage of BCC metal is necessarily preceded by plastic deformation. Thus the K_c criterion cannot be used in explaining fracture of complicated cases.

The Φ_c or ρ_c^+ criterion, however, can at least semi-quantitatively explain the experimental results shown in Fig. 5. The fracture stress predicted by the Φ_c criterion shows some differences from that by the ρ_c^+ criterion. Measured fracture stress is compared with calculated stress in Fig. 6. Difference between experimental and theoretical values are tolerable considering the simplicity of the fracture model adopted here. These small differences might be explained by taking into account the effect of cumbersome factors, i.e. triaxiality, work hardening, and blunting of the notch tip, etc.

In conclusion, both the Φ_c and the ρ_c^+ criteria can be used to predict the fracture

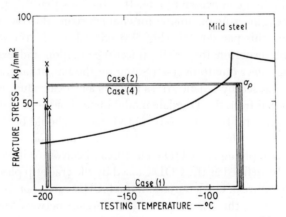

FIG. 5.   Fracture after different stress-temperature histories.

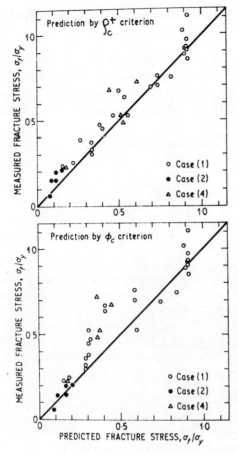

FIG. 6. Comparison between measured fracture stress and calculated stress.

TABLE 1. Salient features of three criteria.

Item	Criterion		
	K_c	ρ_c^+	ϕ_c
The range of application	Only applicable to small scale yielding	Not applicable after general yielding	All ranges
Measurement	Quite simple	Difficult and cumbersome	Simple
Calculation of σ_f with residual stress or preloading	Inadequate		Adequate
Calculation procedure	Complex	Quite easy	Rather easy
Calculating principle	Ambiguous	Clear	Somewhat ambiguous

strength of a structural component which include such complex factors as preloading and/or residual stress. The salient features of the three criteria considered may be summarized as shown in Table 1.

4. COD Concept as Applied to Brittle Fracture of Large Size Welded Specimens

Research works have been carried out to explain the fracture behavior of welded component, especially under the effect of welding residual stress, on the basis of the COD concept. Wide notched tension plate test (Deep Notch Test) with longigudinal welds as shown in Fig. 7 was carried out.[9, 11] The machanical notches were machined after

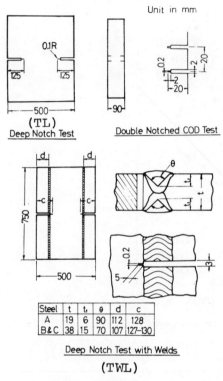

FIG. 7.   Specimens used to investigate the effect of welding residual stress.

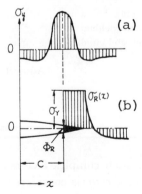

FIG. 8.   A crack in welding residual stress field.

welding with the notch tip located in the region of tensile welding residual stress but hopefully within a region of minimum changes in the material property due to welding. Tests were carried out on several ordinary low and medium strength structural steels. Other specimens shown in Fig. 7 were used for reference tests.

The welding residual stress (as shown in Fig. 8(a)) is assumed to be redistributed due to the machining of the crack and as a result the residual stress on the crack line as shown schematically in Fig. 8(b) was obtained. This residual stress distribution ahead of the crack is calculated using the Dugdale model under arbitrarily distributed stress. Denoting this residual stress by $\sigma_R(x)$, as shown in Fig. 8(b), the crack opening displacement, $\Phi(c)$, at the crack tip in a finite plate subjected to uniform tensile stress σ is given by

$$\Phi(c) = \frac{4}{\pi E}\left[\sigma \int_0^a F(c, a, x)dx + \int_c^a \{\sigma_R(x) - \sigma_{YT}\} \cdot F(c, a, x)dx\right] \tag{1}$$

for

$$\sigma + \sigma_R(x) \leq \sigma_{YT}$$

where

$$F(c, a, x) = \cosh^{-1}\left|\frac{\cos^2 \bar{a} \cdot (\cos^2 \bar{c} + \cos^2 \bar{x}) - 2\cos^2 \bar{x} \cdot \cos^2 \bar{c}}{\cos^2 \bar{a} \cdot (\sin^2 \bar{c} - \sin^2 \bar{x})}\right|, \quad \bar{a} = \frac{\pi a}{2b}, \quad \bar{c} = \frac{\pi c}{2b}, \quad \bar{x} = \frac{\pi x}{2b}$$

σ=applied stress, σ_{YT}=yield stress of the material at the loading temperature, $E=$ Young's modulus and $2b$=plate width.

When $\sigma + \sigma_R(X) > \sigma_{YT}$, the stress that exceeds σ_{YT} must be redistributed to the region where $\sigma + \sigma_R(X)$ is less than σ_{YT} so that the stress distribution obtained thereby would never exceed σ_{YT}. The virtual elastic crack length $2a$ is determined by

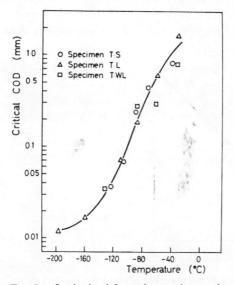

FIG. 9. Φ_c obtained from the specimens show in Fig. 7.

$$\sigma_{YT} \sin^{-1}\left\{\frac{\sin \bar{c}}{\sin \bar{a}}\right\} + \int_c^a \sigma_R(x)\frac{\cos^2 \bar{x}}{(\sin^2 \bar{a}-\sin^2\bar{c})^{1/2}}dx = \frac{\pi}{2}(\sigma_{YT}-\sigma) \qquad (2)$$

where $a=c+\rho$; ρ=plastic zone size.

As illustrated in Fig. 8(b), an initial COD, Φ_R, is produced by the presence of residual stress. In the application of COD criterion, we assume that "the COD produced at the final loading temperature contributes to fracture initiation" as explained in Section 3. If this assumption for COD criterion is accepted, then the measured critical COD would be constant at a certain temperature regardless of the presence of residual stress. By way of an example, this fact was experimentally justified as shown in Fig. 9.

The fracture stress in the presence of residual stress can be estimated from the measured Φ_c at the notch tip of the specimens free from residual stress (TS, TL and possibly small size bend specimen). Relation between the fracture stress obtained in the Deep Notch Test with welds and the one predicted using active Φ computed from eqs. (1) & (2) and Φ_c measured from the specimen without welds is shown in Fig. 10.

Similar experimental works were carried out by Akita et al.[14] and the results were successfully explained on the basis of COD concept. An example is shown in Fig. 11 for the case of wide notched plate test with welding residual stress coupled with the effect of various levels of preloading at room temperature.

Experimental work was carried out on the brittle fracture initiation characteristics of severely constrained structural member with a notch coupled with stress concentration, mechanical constraint due to discontinuous stiffeners and welding residual stress.[9,11] The model specimens tested (Constraint Tensile Test (CTT)), as shown in Fig. 12, may be considered to be under the most possible severe condition simulated in laboratory test for brittle fracture initiation. Deformation at the notch tip in the plate thickness direction is highly constrained and considerable stress concentration is produced due to the discontinuity of the stiffener. Furthermore, welding residual stress may reach a value nearly equal to the yield stress at the neighborhood of the discontinuous part. The machined notches in main plate are also subjected to the thermal cycles due to welding. Typical test results in terms of fracture stress vs. temperature is shown in Fig. 13

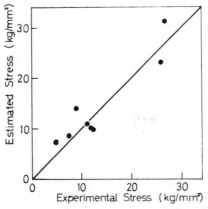

FIG. 10.   Relation between predicted and experimental fracture stress for Deep Notch Test with Welds (TWL).

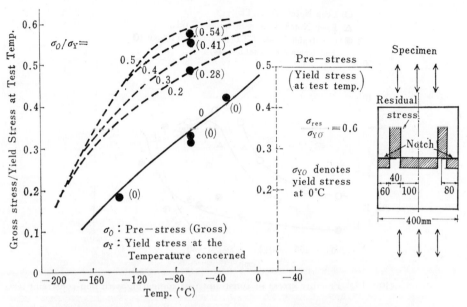

Fig. 11.   Effect of welding residual stress coupled with preloading on fracture stress.

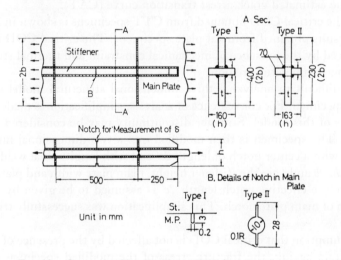

Fig. 12.   Constraint Tensile Test (CTT Specimen).

and are compared with the results of non-constraint test (TL and TWL types as shown in Fig. 7).

In the Constraint Tensile Test, low stress brittle fracture was observed in the temperature range where the fracture beyond the level of general yielding stress was exhibited in the flat plate tests. Rather abrupt increase of the stress at fracture in the Constraint Test was observed. Remarkable elevation of the transition temperature can be obtained in static loading laboratory test superposing various mechanical factors which

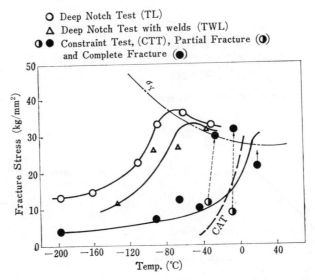

O   Deep Notch Test (TL)
△   Deep Notch Test with welds (TWL)
◐ ● Constraint Test, (CTT), Partial Fracture (◐)
       and Complete Fracture (●)

FIG. 13.   Fracture stress of constraint test comparing with non-constraint tests.

facilitate brittle fracture. In the above example, the fracture initiation transition curve is shifted close to the estimated crack arrest transition curve (CAT).

Example of the critical COD obtained from CTT specimens is shown in Fig. 14 and compared with results obtained from flat plate specimens. The critical COD is shown to be highly influenced by the presence of mechanical constraint and thermal strain ageing, especially in higher temperature region.

It is rather difficult to analyze a three dimensional structural model such as the Constraint Test specimen. For convenience of analysis, simplification is made to estimate the characteristics of this model. Stiffener discontinuity may be considered to have the effect of a notch. The specimen is then modified into a two dimensional finite plate of width $(h+2b-t)$ with a center notch of length $2c'$ and with longitudinal welds, as shown in Fig. 15, where h, $2b$ and t are the stiffener height, main plate width and plate thickness, respectively. Here the effective notch length $2c'$ is assumed to be given by $2c'=h+2c$, where $2c$ is length of main plate notch. This simplification was successfully tried by Yada et al.[15]

With the assumption that critical COD is not affected by the presence of mechanical constraint and strain ageing, the fracture stress of the modified specimen can be calculated using Φ_c measured experimentally in the Deep Notch Test in the same manner mentioned previously. The residual stress distribution in the specimen without the discontinuity and notch was approximated by step-like distribution. An example of the calculated results is shown by solid curve in Fig. 16. Fracture stress of the modified specimen without residual stress is also shown by broken curve in the same figure.

It is found experimentally, that the results of the Constraint Test cannot be explained by the results of the deep notched flat plate specimen with residual stress unless the decrease of critical COD is taken into account. It should be concluded that the direct application of values obtained from laboratory tests with simple flat plate is dangerous

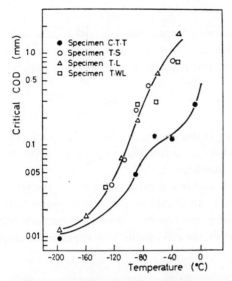

FIG. 14. Φ_c of constraint test comparing with non-costraint tests.

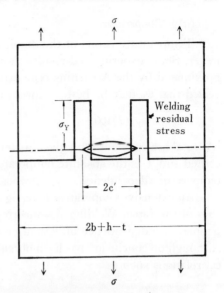

FIG. 15. Two-dimensional model for CTT Specimen.

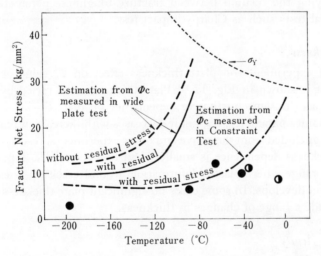

FIG. 16. Estimation of fracture stress of CTT specimen based on COD concept.

from the view point of brittle fracture initiation under highly constrained condition.

5. Factors Affecting the Critical COD

As a macroscopic engineering fracture toughness parameter, the Φ_c value is inherently dependent on several factors. The effect of those factors must be appropriately accounted for in the application of the COD concept.

(a) Temperature

Temperature is one of the dominant factors affecting the material toughness parameter. Some experimental results showed that the temperature dependence can be approximated by the Arrhenius type expression, but further accumulation of data has revealed that Φ_c may be better expressed by

$$\Phi_c = \alpha' \sigma_{YT} (T/100)^5 \qquad (3)$$

where α' is a constant for a given material, σ_{YT} is the yield stress at the temperature concerned and T is the absolute temperature. This expression was implied in the empirical temperature dependence of $\rho_c{}^+$ proposed by Koshiga et al.[16]

An extensive cooperative investigation is now being carried out under the sponsorship of the Japan Welding Engineering Society to obtain empirical expressions for the temperature dependence of Φ_c and/or $\rho_c{}^+$ using test results of various structural steels. Although no conclusion has been obtained as yet, we can establish an appropriate empirical relations such as

$$\Phi_c = \beta T^n \qquad (4)$$

by plotting Φ_c vs. T on a log-log scale within a certain limit of data scatting.

Attempts to formulate an empirical relation for temperature dependence is important for simplifying the relation between fracture toughness parameter and more convenient industrial tests such as Charpy impact test.

(b) Plate Thickness

An example of experiments on plate thickness effect on Φ_c value obtained from small size bend test is shown in Fig. 17.[11] Plate thickness was varied by machining. The critical COD has the same qualitative dependence on plate thickness as does the linear fracture mechanics parameter, K_c, i.e. it decreases with increase in plate thickness. It can generally be concluded from the above and other experimental results that in terms of Φ_c, the plate thickness dependence is smaller than that seen in K_c especially in the higher temperature range where plastic deformation around crack tip is extensive and plane stress condition develops. In some cases no significant plate thickness dependence was observed for wide a range of changes in thickness.

(c) Notch Tip Acuity

Figure 18 shows an example of experimental results using small tensile specimen with various notch tip radius including a fatigue notch.[11] These results show that larger notch tip radius results in larger Φ_c, and the effect of notch acuity on Φ_c is very slight if it is smaller than 0.1 mm. This suggests that fatigue cracking is not necessarily for preparing fracture test specimens. Some other data, however does not support this conclusion. As shown in Fig. 19 by the COD bend test, Φ_c obtained from fatigued notched specimens is considerably smaller than that obtained from specimens with machined notch with tip radius of 0.1 mm. This tendency seems to be observed in high strength steels with high yield ratio.

Available data shows that the notch tip acuity dependence of is different from one steel to another. This problem is important in establishing an industrial and standard procedure to evaluate Φ_c using small specimen. This point is now being investigated in the cooperative research work mentioned above.

(d) Plastic Constraint

In order to clarify the effect of plastic constraint on Φ_c value, several experimental investigations using various specimens which cause plastic constraint around crack tip have been carried out. The results of CTT specimens given in Fig. 14 implies a remark-

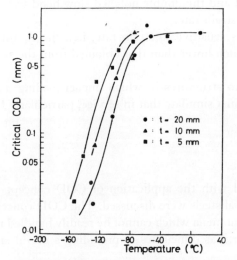

FIG. 17.   Plate thickness dependence of critical COD.

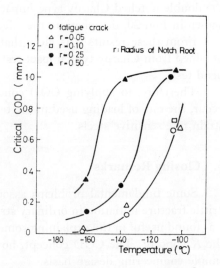

FIG. 18.   Effect of notch acuity on Φ_c.

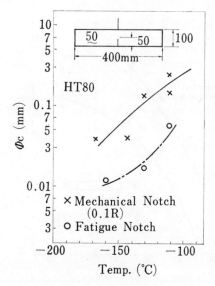

FIG. 19.   Effect of notch acuity on Φ_c.

able effect of plastic constraint on Φ_c. It is to be noted that increase in the intensity of plastic constraint results in decrease in the critical COD value. The applied stress required to produce a given COD, however, becomes larger as the degree of plastic constraint becomes larger. A detailed discussion associated with this problem is given in the present Seminar Report by Otsuka and Miyata.

(e)   Strain Rate

Ordinary structural steels are sensitive to strain rate as most commonly observed by an elevation of trasition temperature with increase of strain rate. Φ_c values obtained from the double notched Charpy type impact test and the double notched slow bend test, as shown in Fig. 20, demonstrate the effect of strain rate.

From these results it is clear that Φ_c is sensitive to strain rate, i.e., the Φ_c value obtained from Charpy type impact test is much lower than that obtained from the slow bend test.

Therefore, in applying COD concept to structures in which impact loading may occur, the rate of loading used in the tests must simulate that in service, particularly for strain rate sensitive steels.

6.   Closing Remarks

Some fundamental problems associated with the application of COD concept to brittle fracture initiation in ordinary structural steels were discussed. The COD concept was found useful in the explaining some phenomena which cannot be readily handled by the K concept. The COD concept, however, has difficulties in providing a useful and simple engineering design basis.

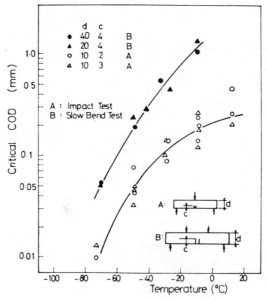

FIG. 20.   Effect of impact loading on critical COD.

It is expected in near future, however, that a more powerful and practical parameter will emerge through further fundamental and critical investigations of the currently proposed parameters possibly through appropriate modification and incorporation of all such parameters.

Despite the many problem left unsolved, this author believes that we should begin an attempt to draft a standard procedure for a critical engineering assessment on the significance of defects in welded steel structures by codifing vast available informations and experiences even if at the risk of oversimplifying the complex situations existing in the actual structures.

For a critical assessment, three major informations are needed, i.e. applied stress and/or strain including primary, secondary and peak stresses and/or strains, fracture toughness of the material concerned in terms of appropriate fracture parameter and geometry of defect. We must establish a standard procedure for estimating fracture toughness parameter of a given material through simple industrial test. We may be able to define an effective flaw size parameter, especially for internal or surface flaw having irregular shape, through certain simplifications and provide a design basis for a relation between applied stress and/or strain and the effective flaw size parameter. If necessary, fatigue crack propagation and environmental effect should be incorporated. No doubt the task is not easy and the first step would include many unsatisfactory formulations, which must be improved by future research and experiences in its application. A major step in this direction has now been taken by British research group.[17] Although the British proposal includes many controversial aspects, it provides us with many important suggestions for the future. A series of fundamental research works associated with above mentioned problems are now being carried out by several research committees in the Japan Welding Engineering Society.

References

1. Kanazawa, T., Machida, S., Momota, S. and Hagiwara, Y., "A Study on the COD Concept for Brittle Fracture Initiation," *Proc. Second Int. Conf. on Fracture*, Brighton, 1 (1969).

2. Kanazawa, T., Mimura, H., Machida, S., Miyata, T. and Hagiwara, Y., " Critical Considerations on the Criteria for Brittle Fracture Initiation," J. Soc. Naval Arch. Japan Vol. 129 June, (1971).

3. Kanazawa, T., Machida, S., Itoga, K. and Tsuchiya, H., "A Study on the Brittle Fracture Initiation with COD Hypothesis," J. Soc. Naval Arch. Japan, Vol. 131, June (1972).

4. Kanazawa, T., Machida, S., Hagiwara, Y. and Kobayashi, J., "A Study on Evaluation of Fracture Toughness of Structural Steels using COD Bend Test," Int. Inst. Weld., Doc. X-702-73 (1973).

5. Sakai, K. and Iino, N., " Study on Crack Opening Displacement and Brittle Fracture Initiation," J. Soc. Naval Arch. Japan, Vol. 127, June (1970).

6. Koshiga, F.,   "A Proposed Simple Theory of Overstressing Technique to Secure Pressure Vessels Against Brittle Fracture," *Proc. Conf. Prac. App. of Frac. Mech. to Pressure-Vessel Tech.*, Inst. Mech. Engineers, London, May (1971).

7. Nishitani, H. and Murakami, Y.,   " Interaction of Elastic-Plastic Cracks Subjected to a

Tensile Stress in an Infinite or a Semi-Infinite Plate," *Proc. Int. Conf. Mech. Behaviors Metals*, Kyoto, Apr. (1971).

8. Kanazawa, T., Mimura, H., Machida, S., Miyata, T. and Hagiwara, Y.,   " Some Critical Consideration on the Criteria for the Onset of Brittle Crack Propagation," *Proc. Conf. Prac. App. of Frac. Mech. to Pressure-Vessel Tech.*, Inst. Mech. Engineers, London, May (1971).

9. Kanazawa, T., Machida, S. and Miyata, T.,   " Brittle Fracture Initiation of Welded Steel Structures," *Proc. 1st. Int. Symp. Japan Weld. Soc.*, Tokyo, Nov. (1971).

10. Kanazawa, T., Machida, S. and Miyata, T.,   "A Study on the Brittle Fracture Initiation in the Constrained Structural Member," J. Soc. Naval Arch. Japan Vol. 129, June (1971).

11. Kanazawa, T., Machida, S., Miyata, T. and Hagiwara, Y.,   "A Consideration on the Variables Included in the Critical COD value in Brittle Fracture Problem of Steel," *Proc. Int. Conf. Mech. Behaviors of Metals*, Kyoto, Apr., (1971).

12. Akita, Y., Sakai, K. and Iino, N.,   " Effect of Slit Size on Brittle Fracture Initiation," J. Soc. Naval Arch. Japan Vol. 128, Dec. (1970).

13. Fujita, Y., Yada, T., Sakai, K. and Iino, N.,   "A Study on Crack Opening Displacement and Brittle Fracture Initiation," Int. Inst. Weld., Doc. X-628-71, (1971).

14. Akita, Y., Yada, T., Sakai, K. and Iino, N.,   " COD Approach for Evaluation of Brittle Fracture Initiation in Residual Stress Field," *Proc. 1st, Int. Symp. Japan Weld. Soc.*, Tokyo, Nov. (1971).

15. Yada, T. and Sakai, K.,   "A Study on Brittle Fracture Initiation from Structural Discontinuities in Arbitrarily Distributed Stress Field," J. Soc. Naval Arch. Japan, Vol. 123, June (1968).

16. Koshiga, F., Tanaka, J. and Kurita, Y.,   " Effects of Stress-Relieving Heat Treatment on the Brittle Fracture Initiation in Welded Structures," Int. Inst. Weld., Doc. X-635-71, (1971).

17. Harrison, J. D., Burdekin, F. M. and Young, J. G.,   "A Report Acceptance Standard for Welded Defects based upon Suitability for Service," *Proc. 2nd Conf. on Significance of Defects*, London, May (1968).

Some Results of Dynamic COD-Test

K. Nishioka and H. Iwanaga

Central Research Laboratories, Sumitomo Metal Industries, Ltd.

1. Introduction

COD-tests have been widely used in recent years to estimate the brittle fracture initiation properties of materials. Most of these COD-tests are usually performed under static loading. For many practical cases, however, brittle fracture initiation is caused by dynamic loading, especially in a structure with a possible fatigue crack.

In this paper, the differences between static and dynamic COD for several steels are discussed.

2. Materials

Materials tested and their mechanical properties are shown in Tables 1 and 2, respectively. Among these materials, only HT70 is quenched and tempered but the others are tested in the as-rolled state.

TABLE 1. Chemical compositions. (%)

	Thick. (mm)	C	Si	Mn	P	S	Cu	Cr	Ni	Mo	V	Nb
HT50	22	0.20	0.33	1.30	0.018	0.015	0.04	0.03	—	—	—	—
X-60	14	0.17	0.46	1.46	0.025	0.016	0.03	—	—	—	0.08	—
X-70	14	0.14	0.41	1.30	0.015	0.005	0.04	0.09	—	—	0.09	0.029
HT70	25	0.12	0.30	0.79	0.014	0.013	0.02	0.43	1.26	0.47	0·03	—

TABLE 2. Mechanical properties.

	σ_y(kg/mm²)	σ_B(kg/mm²)	El. (%)	$_vE_0$(kg-m)	$_vT_S$(°C)	$_vT_E$(°C)
HT50	43.9	66.0	31.0	3.8	46	30
X-60	42.5	64.0	30.0	2.7	2	−11
X-70	54.6	63.3	37.7	22.0	−126	−100
HT70	71.0	77.4	26.7	15.9	−82	−81

3. Testing Procedure

Dynamic COD-test was conducted with the Charpy impact testing machine. Figure 1 shows the test specimen, which is the same as the standard Charpy test specimen except for the notch configuration. Both static and dynamic COD were measured by a specially prepared displacement gage shown in Fig. 2. The gage is a potentiometer, in which 0.10 mm diameter manganin wire is wound around a curved rod. The curvature was determined after a rotational factor, r of 0.40. Displacement according to the deformation was recorded by oscilloscope.

Dynamic load was measured with semiconductor strain gages attached to the hammer of the Charpy machine and calibrated by actual loading. Gage displacement and dynamic load were recorded simultaneously on dual beam oscilloscope.

Sample measurements of gage displacement (upper line) and dynamic load (lower line) are shown in Photo. 1. In the oscillogram, the gage displacement corresponding to the maximum load is considered as the critical load at which brittle fracture initiates. COD is then obtained by multipling 0.314 (rotational factor, $r=0.40$) to the critical gage displacement.

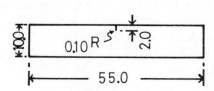

Fig. 1.   Test specimen.

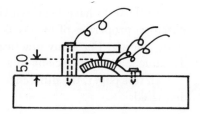

Fig. 2.   Displacement gage.

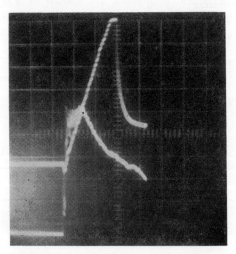

Photo. 1.   An example of oscillogram.
(0.5 m sec/Div, 1.0 mm/Div, 500 kg/Div)

4.   Test Results and Discussions

Test results are shown in Figs. 3 and 4. As can be seen in these figures, the dynamic COD is considerably smaller than the static one at lower temperatures. For instance, in the brittle fracture range, the differences in temperatures which give the same COD values in static and dynamic tests are about 80–100°C. Moreover, in different materials, significant differences in static COD values are noticed but the differences in dynamic COD values are very small.

Impact speed of the Charpy hammer is about 5.6 m/sec, representing a dynamic load which is often imposed on actual welded structures. It thus seems reasonable to recomend the dynamic COD be adopted for the design of welded structures subjected to impact loading.

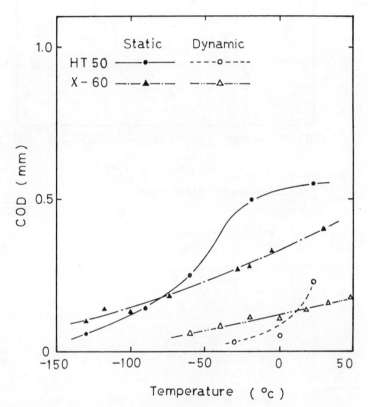

FIG. 3.   Static and dynamic COD-test results.

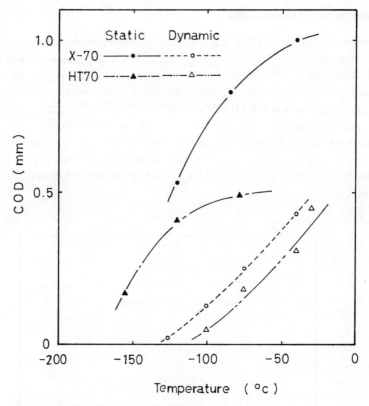

FIG. 4.   Static and dynamic COD-test results.

Crack Opening Displacement Testing by Use of Acoustic Emission

M. Arii, H. Kashiwaya and T. Yanuki

Heavy Apparatus Engineering Laboratory, Tokyo Shibaura Electric Co., Ltd.

1. Introduction

Methods for plane strain fracture toughness (K_{IC}) testing of high strength steels had been established by the A.S.T.M. (E399–70T)[1] and BISRA Fracture Toughness Committee (DD3: 1971).[2] On the other hand, the Crack Opening Displacement (COD) testing is currently being used in U.S.A, Britain and Japan for estimating the fracture toughness of the high-toughness low strength steels. Brittle material fractures at a critical value of stress intensity factor or crack opening displacement without any prior crack growth. In the more ductile materials, however, unstable fracture initiation may be preceded by a period of slow crack growth from the notch tip.

Such slow crack growth may be an essential prelude to unstable fast fracture and thus COD at the start of slow crack growth can also be regarded as a critical value of the fracture characteristics. It is thus desirable to detect the onset of slow crack growth, here COD test may also be used to assess the resistance to fracture initiation of materials. Unfortunately, such information cannot be obtained from the conventional load-displacement diagram in a COD test since the COD is usually taken as that corresponding to the maximum load in the load-displacement diagram. Where the slow crack growth precedes unstable fracture initiation, the critical COD is found by detecting the initiation of slow crack growth which usually occurs prior to the maximum load. This instant of slow crack growth initiation has been detected by using the electrical potential method.[3] We havetried to apply the acoustic emission techniques[4] to the COD test for obtaining the onset of slow crack growth. Our findings are presented in the following.

2. Experiment

Three steels with different strength, namely mild steel (A), quenched and tempered steel (B) and precipitation-hardened steel (C) were used. Chemical compositions and mechanical properties of these steels are shown in Tables 1 and 2, respectively. Single-

TABLE 1.   Chemical compositions of steels used. (%)

Steel	t	C	Si	Mn	P	S	Cu	Ni	Cr	Mo	Nb
A	32	0.16	0.22	0.58	0.016	0.022					
B	35	0.15	0.40	1.16	0.016	0.08		0.26	0.18	0.10	
C	45	0.12	0.34	1.22	0.013	0.006	0.03	0.81	0.023	0.62	0.026

t=thickness, mm

TABLE 2.   Mechanical properties of steels used.

Steel	Yield Strength kg/mm²	Tensile Strength kg/mm²	Elongation %	Reduction of Area %
A	25.7	45.6	40.7	66.2
B	53.7	65.7	27.8	69.2
C	81.1	83.9	24.5	67.6

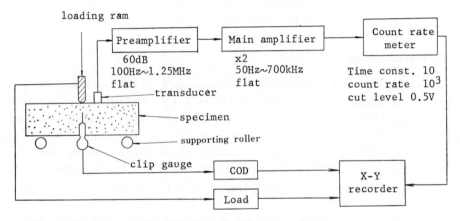

FIG. 1.   Block diagram for COD and A.E. testing system.

edge-notched specimens were tested in three point bending at room temperature. Specimen dimensions (A.S.T.M notation) are B (thickness)=25 mm, W (depth)= 50 mm, a (crack length)=25 mm for the machined notch, and a=24.4~27.8 mm for a notch fatigue pre-cracked in accordance with A.S.T.M E399–70T. During the test COD was recorded by using a clip gauge attached between notch surfaces at distance z= −1.5 mm away from the specimen surface. In addition, sensing transducer with a fundamental frequency of 220 kHz was attached to the specimen surface as shown in Fig. 1. Prior to the COD test, a pre-overloading procedure was devised to eliminate extraneous noise and acoustic emission from the highly stressed portions of the specimen around the supporting rollers and loading ram. The maximum overload was taken to be larger than the anticipated fracture load.

3.   Results and Discussion

The COD, V, measured at the surface was converted to the notch tip COD, δ, by using the following equation[3];

$$\delta = \frac{V}{[3(a+z)/(W-a)]+1}$$

We assumed the following three parameters in defining the fracture characteristics of a COD test conducted by using acoustic emission. First, the COD, δ_Q, corresponding to a load P_Q (A.S.T.M E399–70T notation[1]) in the load-displacement diagram was taken. Second, the COD, δ_C, corresponding to the usual maximum load in the load-displacement diagram was taken. And finally, the COD, δ_{AE}, was taken for a load at which the largest burst of emission occurred prior to the maximum load in the emission count versus time diagram (chart speed 30 mm/min.). The three COD parameters defined above are plotted in Fig. 2 as functions of yield strengths of the tested materials.

The fracture surfaces of the specimen were later examined by a scanning electron microscope, which confirmed that ductile tearing preceded brittle fracture as shown in Fig. 3. This fractograph shows that the slow crack growth was occurring. The acoustic

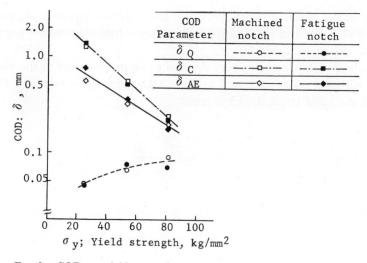

FIG. 2.   COD vs. yield strength.

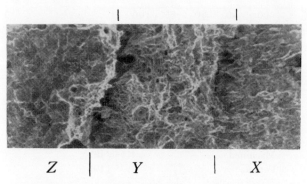

FIG. 3.   Scanning electron fractograph ($\times 100$).
X: fatigue area, Y: ductile tearing, Z: brittle fracture

emission records show that slow crack growth may have started when the largest burst of emission occurred, that is, when the notch tip COD, δ, reached the COD, δ_{AE}, defined above. Figure 2 shows that the difference between the notch tip COD at the initiation of slow crack growth and the subsequently reached maximum load increased as the yield strength decreased. This fact was confirmed by observing the slow crack length. The slow crack length, a_s, at the maximum load was plotted in Fig. 4, which shows that a_s increased as the yield strength decreased (except for the fatigue-cracked specimen of material C). It is thus essential to detect the onset of the slow crack growth in estimating the fracture resistance of materials by means of COD test, in especially low-strength steels.

During the COD test with the monitored acoustic emission, the relation between the total acoustic emission counts, N, and the crack opening displacement, δ, which represents the deformation behavior of a notched specimen was studied and the following relation obtained

$$N = C\delta^n, \quad n = 2$$

following the model describe in reference.[4] C and n in this equation are material constants. Values of coefficient, C, and exponent, n, were obtained from log-log plots of test result and are shown in Table 3.

These values of exponent, n, were deemed to be proportional to the yield strength of materials within a range of 1 to 4 in our COD tests, while values of C varied exponentialy as the yield strength of materials.

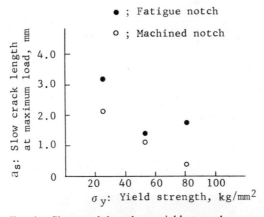

FIG. 4.   Slow crack length vs. yield strength.

TABLE 3.   Values C and n for $N = C\delta^n$ (experimentally determined).

Steel	Notch condition	C	n
A	Machined	7.43×10^4	0.98
B	Fatigue	2.14×10^4	1.20
	Machined	1.54×10^5	1.80
	Fatigue	1.75×10^5	2.01
C	Machined	6.63×10^7	4.08
	Fatigue	3.32×10^7	3.04

4. Conclusion

Our experiments showed that acoustic emission techniques can be used to detect the onset of slow crack growth and to obtain a relation between crack opening displacement and acoustic emission characteristics in the COD test.

REFERENCES

1. *1972 Annual Book of ASTM Standards, Part 31, E-399, " Standard Method of Test for Plane-Strain Fracture Toughness of Metallic Materials,"* American Society for Testing and Materials.
2. *Methods for plane strain fracture toughness (K_{IC}) Testing, DD3* British Standards Institution (1971).
3. *Methods for crack opening displacement (COD) testing, DD19,* British Standards Institution (1972).
4. Dunegan, H. L., Harris, D. O. and Tatro, C. A., " Fracture analysis by use of acoustic emission," Engineering Fracture Mechanics, Vol. 1 (1968).

Discussions in Session III

Comment directed to Prof. Kobayashi by Prof. Fisher

This is a comment related to the stress intensity factors for part-through cracks at welded toes.

It has been experimentally observed that the cracks that grow at the toe of a weld propagate as semi-elliptical cracks through the thickness of the plate during most of a specimens fatigue life.

The solution for the stress-intensity factor for a part-through crack cannot be directly applied because the discontinuity is embedded in a stress field that is affected by the stress concentration of the geometrical change. A comparable stress concentration effect exists at a hole in a plate which has cracks originating from the hole.

In the absence of a crack, the weld geometry acts a stress raiser. The stress concentration effect decays rapidly with increasing distance away from the weld toe.

The stress intensity factor at the weld toe was estimated[1,2] using a finite element analysis to determine the compliance of the joint for various crack lengths. The set of compliances and crack lengths were fitted by least squares to a polynomial of the form

$$EBC = A_0 + \sum_{n=2}^{m} A_{n-1}\left(\frac{a}{t}\right)^n \tag{1}$$

where $C = \Delta/P$ = compliance
B = width
E = Young's Modulus
a = crack length
t = plate thickness

For a plane stress analysis the strain energy release rate was related to the change in compliance

$$G = \frac{P^2}{8EB^2t} \frac{d(EBC)}{d(a/t)} \tag{2}$$

and K was defined by

---

1) Frank, K. H., "The Fatigue Strength of Fillet Welded Connections," PhD Dissertation, Lehigh University, Bethlehem, Pa. 1971.

2) Fisher, J. W., Albrecht, P. A., Yen, B. T., Klingerman, D. J. and McNamee, B. M., "Fatigue Strength of Steel Beams with Transverse Stiffeners and Attachments," NCHRP Report 147 Highway Research Board, 1974.

$$K = (EG)^{1/2} \tag{3}$$

The resulting polynomials that defined K were equated to the function

$$K = \frac{1+0.12(1-a/b)}{\Phi_0} \sigma K_T\left(\frac{a}{t}\right) \sqrt{\pi a} \sqrt{\sec\left(\frac{\pi a}{2t}\right)} \tag{4}$$

This permitted the variation $K_T(a/t)$ to be evaluated as a function of crack length and geometry to be determined for values of a/t equal to 0.02 through 0.70. A best fit of the results yielded

$$K_T\left(\frac{a}{t}\right) = K_T\left\{1 - 3.215\frac{a}{t} + 7.897\left(\frac{a}{t}\right)^2 - 9.288\left(\frac{a}{t}\right)^3 + 4.086\left(\frac{a}{t}\right)^4\right\} \tag{5}$$

where K_T=stress concentration factor. Hence, the stress intensity factor for part-through cracks at fillet weld toes can be estimated by

$$K = \frac{1+0.12(1-a/b)}{\Phi_0} K_T\left(\frac{a}{t}\right) \sigma \sqrt{\pi a} \sqrt{\sec\left(\frac{\pi a}{2t}\right)} \tag{6}$$

Reply to Prof. Fisher by Prof. Kobayashi

Professor Fisher's stress intensity amplification at the deepest penetration of a surface flaw in a toe weld follows the same trend as our results presented today. In fact the $K_T(a/t) \cdot \sigma$ in Prof. Fisher's eq. 4 corresponds to the stress elevated by the concentration factor at the hole in our formulation. The resulting eq. 6 will agree relatively well in magnitude with our results provided that the part-through crack does not extend too close to the other free surfaces in the fillet weld toe. The procedure which was presented today enables one to estimate the stress intensity magnification factor along the periphery of the semi-elliptical flaw where the maximum stress intensity factor may exist close to the hole surface instead of at its deepest penetration for $a/2c > 0.4$.

Question directed to Dr. Iwanaga by Prof. Kobayashi

The rotational factor, $r=.40$ in your report, is presumably determined by static means. Has any attempt been made to estimate the dynamic r for this specimen which is loaded within approximately 0.2 milliseconds? Our experimental results on dynamic COD in a fracturing centrally notched aluminum tension specimen, presented at the 1967 JSME Semi-International Symposium here in Tokyo, show substantial differences between dynamic and static COD's. I thus feel that a dynamic r should be measured and used for proper data evaluation of your experiments.

Reply to Prof. Kobayashi by Dr. Iwanaga

For the slow bend COD-test, we came to the conclusion that the rotational factor, r was about 0.40 by Moirè method. So, for convenience we chose the rotational factor, r of 0.40 both for the static and the dynamic COD-test. We have no solution for the rotational factor of the dynamic COD-test.

Exact rotational factor will be required to be solved for the COD-test by bending load.

Question directed to Prof. Machida by Prof. McEvily

I would like to direct a number of questions for clarification to Prof. Machida.

Is it your finding that the critical COD value is independent of residual stress? What is the magnitude of Φ_R relative to the critical value? How does the introduction of a notch affect the residual stress field in the vicinity of the notch tip? Do you think that spontaneous fracture might occur if a specimen containing a flaw in a residual tensile stress field were subjected to a much lower temperature?

Reply to Prof. McEvily by Prof. Machida

When we discuss about brittle fracture initiation in terms of some macroscopic fracture criteria, any fracture condition is expressed by

(A macroscopic mechanical parameter representing fracture potential)=(Corresponding fracture toughness value of a given material).

In terms of COD concept, the above equation is given by

$$\Phi = \Phi_c . \tag{A}$$

Φ is determined from mechanical and geometrical conditions associated with a given defective structural component. On the other hand, Φ_c is generally a function of temperature, strain rate, constraint, etc. for a given material. Conceptually, residual stress is one of mechanical factors to be involved not in Φ_c value but in Φ value, i.e., residual stress is considered to be independent of the critical COD value. Some secondary effects of residual stress on Φ_c might be expected since residual stress may sometimes cause plastic prestraining resulting in material deterioration and/or may change the degree of constraint which influences Φ_c value. But these secondary effects are considered to be small as compared with its primary effect on Φ value. It is to be noted, however, the effect of residual stress on Φ value affects fracture load. The data of TL and TWL specimens shown in Figs. 9 and 13 supports the above considerations.

When we introduce a notch in tensile residual stress field, a certain amount of Φ_R is produced by the residual stress. If Φ_R exceeds Φ_c at that temperature, fracture would initiate just by the introduction of the notch. If not, a simple formalism suggests that fracture would occur by lowering the temperature to such a level where Φ_c is equal to Φ_R. Our experimental results were aginst this prediction as clearly demonstrated by an example of Case (2) shown in Fig. 5. This suggests that we must discriminate Φ value produced at the temperature where fracture occurs from that produced at a different higher temperature. From this and other experimental works we concluded that fracture initiation requires a certain amount of "Φ value caused by plastic deformations by loading at fracturing temperature (active COD)" irrespective of the magnitude of Φ_R relative to the critical value. Thus a spontaneous fracture would not occur if a specimen containing a flaw in a residual tensile stress field were subjected to a much lower temperature so long as we can avoid any additional plastic deformation by thermal stress which may caused by non-uniform cooling.

It has been revealed from the analysis of several experimental works that the contribution of Φ_R in left-hand term of eq. (A), if any, is small comparing with that of COD produced at fracturing temperature. For the practical simplicity we assumed that Φ_R is "non-active" quantity, and this assumption gave satisfactory fracture load prediction as shown in Fig. 6. Needless to say, the above assumption does not mean that residual stress has no effect on fracture behavior. As schematically shown in Fig. 8, the introduction of a notch in a residual stress field shown in (a) results in a redistributed stress field ahead of the notch as shown in (b). Because of this stress fiield, COD value caused by a given external load is larger than that caused by the same external load for a notch free from residual stress, and this accounts for the decrease of fracture load due to the presence of tensile residual stress as shown in Figs. 11, 13 and 16.

Comment by Prof. Rolfe

In the selection of a test specimen to be used for establishing a toughness criterion for a particular service application, several factors should be noted as follows;

1) As is well known, material toughness is affected by temperature, loading rate, constraint, and notch acuity as shown in Fig. 1.

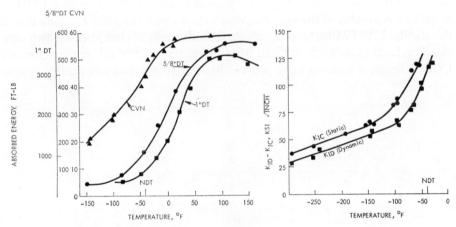

FIG. 1.   Relation between NDT, CVN, DT, K_{IC}, and K_{ID} for A517 steel showing effect of temperature, loading rate, and notch acuity.

2) Most test specimens (K_c, K_{ID}, COD, CVN, DT, etc.) show similar results for the same steel. That is, very tough steels will have low transition temperatures, regardless of the specimen used to measure the transition behavior.

3) The important point is that the *service conditions* should be approximated as closely as possible. That is, to approximate the service performance at a particular temperature, obviously, the test should be conducted at or near that temperature. In addition, the test specimen should be tested at the same loading rate as the structure. Specifically, if the structure can be loaded dynamically, then an impact test specimen, such as the CVN, K_{ID}, or *dynamic* COD loaded at approximately the same strain rate, should be used. If the structure is subjected to static service loading, then a slow test such as K_{IC} or COD should be used to establish performance criteria.

4) If the possibility of sharp cracks in the structure exists, then a sharp-notched specimen (such as the DT or COD) should be used rather than a machined notch

such as the CVN, unless appropriate allowance can be made for loading rate effects.

Thus, a critical decision in developing toughness criteria for service applications is that of determining which of the many toughness test specimens *most closely* models the particular service application. Generally, no single test specimen will do this for *all* structural applications.

Comment by Prof. Ono

I would like to comment on the contention that the COD criterion is a superior concept to the K concept. Robinson and Tetelman[3] have shown that the critical value of COD is directly related to the K_{IC} value of such materials as Ti-6Al-4V, 2024Al 4340 steel and most significantly a mild steel, A533B. They used precracked Charpy specimens and determined the critical COD value in the middle section of the specimen, where the plain strain condition was maintained despite its limited thickness. When the critical COD is less than 0.2 mm, they established that the measured COD is proportional to a K_{IC} value of the material, which agrees with the valid K_{IC} data determined by the standard ASTM method. From these findings, it is clear that the two concepts are closely related to each other. From what I have read and heard on the arguments for the COD concept, it remains to be proven that it is better than comparable approaches.

---

3) Robinson, J. N. and Tetelman, A. S., "The Critical Crack-Tip Opening Displacement and Microscopic and Macroscopic Fracture Criteria for Metals," UCLA-ENG-7360, Aug. 1973.

SESSION IV

FUNDAMENTAL RESEARCHES ON SIGNIFICANCE OF DEFECTS
—FATIGUE—

An Analysis of Crack Propagation in Welded Structures

H. MIYAMOTO, T. MIYOSHI AND S. FUKUDA

Department of Precision Machinery Engineering, University of Tokyo

1. Introduction

In order to analyze crack propagation process in an elastic-plastic material, an elastic-plastic analysis of the crack propagating process into the plastic zone ahead of the crack tip must be conducted. In this paper, the changes in stress and strain distributions, plastic zone and crack opening displacements with crack extension are discussed. Such analysis requires a fracture criterion to establish crack criticality and hence propagation of the crack. The criterion of the critical plastic work was adopted for such purpose in this paper.

Analysis was carried out numerically by the finite element method using the incremental theory of plasticity. In the following, the basic procedure used and results thus obtained are presented for a center cracked tension plate subjected to monotonic and cyclic loadings and without the presence of welding residual stresses. In Section 3, this technique is then used to analyze crack propagation from a defect in welded structure, that is, a center cracked tension plate with an assumed distribution of welding residual stresses.

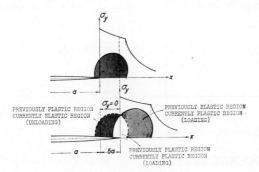

FIG. 1.   Incremental growth of a crack.

2. Elastic-plastic Analysis of Crack-Propagation

In this section, the crack propagation under the elastic-plastic state for both monotonic and cyclic loadings is analyzed by the finite element method using incremental plasticity with the incremental crack growth, δa, being converted into a traction free state when the fracture criterion is satisfied at the crack tip as shown in Fig. 1. In the

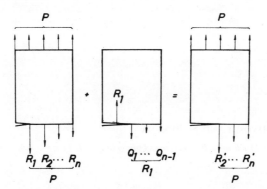

FIG. 2.   Fracture process represented in the finite element analysis.

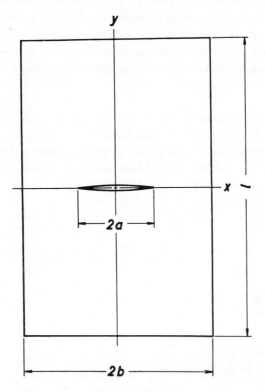

$2b = 20, \ l = 30, \ THICKNESS = 1$

FIG. 3.   Geometry of the specimen, initial crack length, $2a_0 = 8$ mm.

actual finite element analysis, the traction free condition is replaced by a nodal force free condition as shown in Fig. 2 where the nodal force must be eliminated incrementally following the deformation history of the material near the crack tip. Among the many engineering fracture criteria proposed[1,2] the authors chose to use the criterion of critical plastic work[2], in this analysis for both monotonic and cyclic loadings.

Figure 3 shows the geometry of the center cracked specimen composed of 7075-T6 aluminum alloy with the following mechanical properties;

Young's modulus $E=7200$ kg/mm²
Poisson's ratio $\nu=0.33$
Uniaxial yield stress $\sigma_Y=50$ kg/mm²
Strain hardening rate $H'=d\bar{\sigma}/d\bar{\varepsilon}^p=70$ kg/mm²
Critical plastic work per unit area $U_c^{p\ 2)}$

$U_c^p \begin{cases} =0.9 \text{ kg-mm/mm}^2 \text{ for monotonic loading} \\ =90 \text{ kg-mm/mm}^2 \text{ for cyclic loading} \end{cases}$

Fracture criterion based on critical plastic work is given by the following equation;

$$2U_c^p \cdot \delta a \cdot t = U^p \tag{1}$$

in which δa is the length of incremental crack growth, t is the thickness and U^p is the plastic work in the plastic zone near the crack tip for the monotonic loading. For cyclic loading, U^p represents the cumulative work of the total cycle.

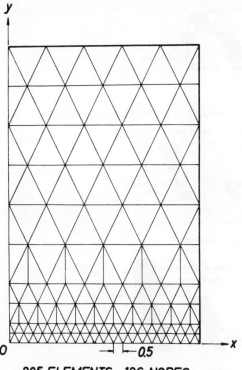

205 ELEMENTS, 126 NODES

FIG. 4.   Nodal breakdown of one quarter of the specimen.

2.1   Monotonic Loading

Analysis was carried out on one quadrant of the specimen only due to the symmetry of the geometry. Nodal breakdown is shown in Fig. 4 and the number of elements and nodes are 205 and 126, respectively. The length of the incremental crack growth, δa, was assumed to be one mesh size, that is, 0.5 mm.

Figure 5 shows the change of the plastic zone ahead of the crack with crack growth where STAGE means the fracture stage and σ represents the applied global stress. In this figure, UNLOADED ZONE, PLASTIC ZONE and NEW PLASTIC ZONE represent previously plastic but currently elastic zone, previously plastic and currently plastic zone and previously elastic but currently plastic zone, respectively.

Figure 6 shows the redistribution of stress, σ_y, on $y=0$ due to the crack growth

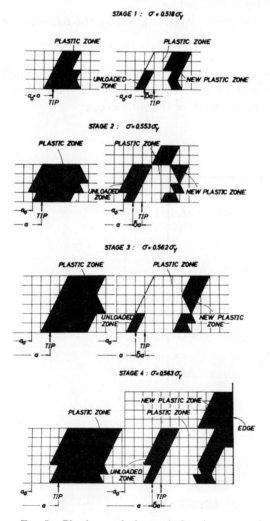

FIG. 5.   Plastic zone before and after the propagation.

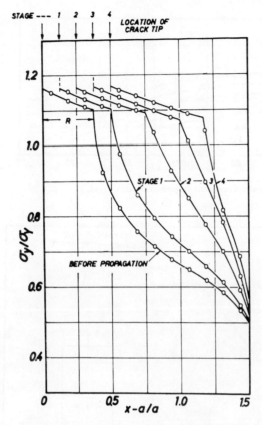

FIG. 6.   Redistribution of stress, σ_y, on $y=0$.

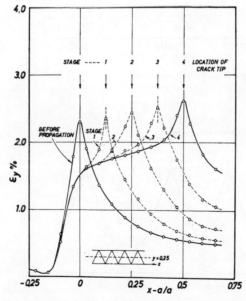

FIG. 7.   Redistribution of strain, ε_y, on $y=0.25$ mm.

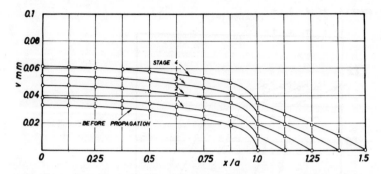

FIG. 8.   Crack opening displacement before and after crack propagation.

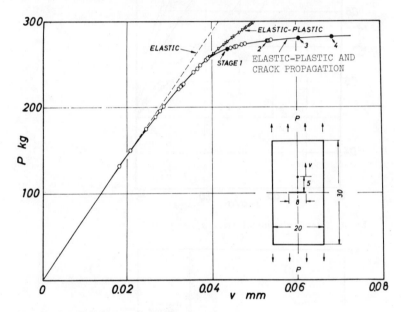

FIG. 9.   Load-displacement curve of specimen.

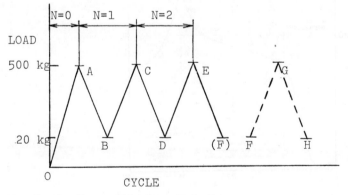

FIG. 10.   Loading condition for cyclic loading.

and the knee points corresponding to the elastic-plastic boundaries on $y=0$. Redistribution of strain, ε_y, on $y=0.25$ mm with crack growth is shown in Fig. 7. From this figure, the process of forming residual strain, ε_y, with crack growth can be understood.

Figure 8 represents changes in crack opening shape due to crack growth. The crack opening shape with crack growth represents the characteristic pivot type. The crack opening displacement with crack growth is smaller than that, at the same distance from the crack tip, without crack growth.

Figure 9 represents the load-displacement curve where the gage points for displacement measurements are on the longitudinal center line at a distance of 5 mm from the crack line. This figure shows that STAGE 1 and 2 are in a condition of stable crack growth while the STAGE 3 and 4 are nearly in a condition of unstable crack growth.

2.2 Cyclic Loading

The analysis was also carried out for one quadrant of the specimen under cyclic loading with the number of elements and nodes being 186 and 115, respectively. The length of incremental crack growth, δa, was again assumed to be one mesh size which was 0.25 mm and the crack was assumed to propagate when the cumulated plastic work in the plastic zone near the crack tip reached its critical value, U_c^p. Loading condition was tension-tension loading with a maximum load of 500 kg and a minimum load of 20 kg.

Table 1 shows the plastic work done in the plastic zone near the crack tip for each cycle where the notations used in this table are presented in Fig. 10. Plastic work based on Dugdale-Barenblatt model of plastic yielding[3] yielded for the first cycle of $N=0$, 0.58 kg-mm which is in good agreement with the value of 0.44 kg-mm obtained by finite element method. Plastic work based on Rice's estimation[2] was 0.69 kg-mm for the cycles of $N=1, 2$ and is one order higher than the value of 0.03 kg-mm obtained by finite element analysis. For cyclic loading, the numerical result obtained by finite element method shows that plastic work per cycle saturates within the first few cycles and thus we can assume the value of 0.03 kg-mm as the saturated plastic work per cycle, ΔU_s^p. The crack thus propagates after a cyclic loading of $N=2U_c^p \cdot \delta a \cdot t / \Delta U_s^p$ which corresponds to point F in Fig. 10.

TABLE 1. Plastic work per cycle in the plastic zone near the crack tip.

Cycle	Path	Plastic work	
N=0	$O \longrightarrow A$	0.44 kg-mm	0.44 kg-mm
N=1	$A \longrightarrow B$	0.018	0.030
	$B \longrightarrow C$	0.012	
N=2	$C \longrightarrow D$	0.017	0.027
	$D \longrightarrow E$	0.010	
	$E \longrightarrow F$	0.016	
	$F \longrightarrow G$	0.14	
	$G \longrightarrow H$	0.005	

Dugdale-Barenblatt Model ($0 \longrightarrow A$) 0.58 kg-mm
Rice Model   0.69 kg-mm

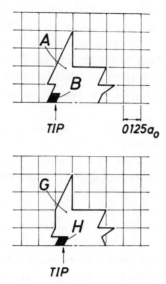

FIG. 11.   Plastic zone before and after crack propagation.

Figure 11 shows the shape of plastic zones for load points A, B, G and H (see Fig. 10). The fatigue plastic zone length ω^* for point B is one-sixth of the length, ω, for point A and this agrees fairly well with the estimation made by using Dugdale-Barenblatt model, that is, $\omega^*=\omega/4$. The fatigue plastic zone size (for point B) before crack growth is same as that (for point H) after crack growth.

Figure 12 shows the crack opening displacements for load points A, B, G and H. Crack opening displacement, v_U, at the first node from the crack tip for point B is one-half of that, v_L, for point A. These results also coincide with the estimation made by D-B model, that is, $v_U=v_L/2$. The important fact is that the crack surfaces close at a load of 94 kg during the cycle of $G \to H$ in spite of the tension-tension loading condition and this does not take place in the loading cycles before crack propagation, for example, during the cycle of $A \to B$. This phenomena is probably due to the smaller crack opening caused by the residual strain generated during crack growth.

3.   Analysis of Crack Propagation from Defects in Welded Structures

In Section 3, the technique of elastic-plastic finite element analysis of crack propagation discussed in Section 2 is extended to the crack propagation in a sheet specimen with welding residual stresses. In the following analysis, the material considered and its mechanical properties are same as those in Section 2 with an additional simplifying assumption that the mechanical properties do not change by heat. The geometry of the specimen, with width, length and thickness of 80 mm, 96 mm and 1 mm, respectively and bead width of 8 mm, is shown in Fig. 13. The initial crack length is 11 mm long. The assumed distribution of the welding residual stress is given in the figure. Nodal breakdown is shown in Fig. 14.

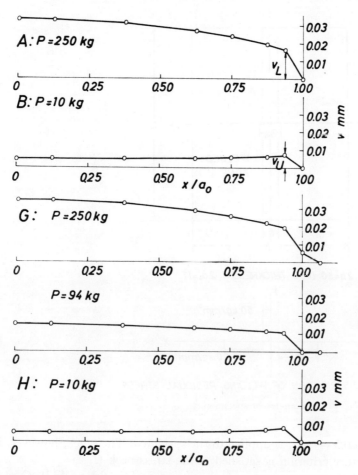

FIG. 12. Crack opening displacement before and after crack propagation. Magnitude of load is one-half the total load due to symmetry of the specimen.

3.1 Monotonic Loading

Figure 15 shows the change of plastic zones with crack growth. At $\sigma=0.544\sigma_Y$, the crack extends one mesh size and at $\sigma=0.560\sigma_Y$, the crack extends one more mesh size.

Figure 16 shows the redistribution of stress, σ_y, with crack growth. Figure 17 shows the redistribution of strain, ε_y, with crack growth. Increase of ε_y, especially at the crack tip is observed.

Figure 18 shows the change of crack opening displacement with crack growth. Due to the welding residual stress, the crack opening shape is quite different from that in Fig. 8 and in this case, the pivot type crack opening is not observed.

3.2 Cyclic Loading

In this analysis, the same loading condition of Fig. 10 with range of stress ratio,

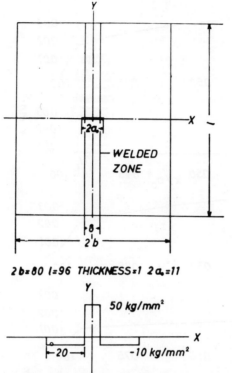

2b=80 l=96 THICKNESS=1 2a₀=11

DISTRIBUTION OF WELDING RESIDUAL STRESS

FIG. 13.   Geometry of specimen.

that is σ/σ_Y is 0.5 ↔ 0.02, is applied to the specimen. The crack, however, is extended when the fracture criterion is satisfied at the stress peak C.

Figure 19 shows the change of plastic zones. The signs, A, B, C and D, in the figure correspond to the same signs in Fig. 10. The maximum plastic zone is small due to the compressive residual stress. The ratio of fatigue plastic zone, ω^*, to the maximum plastic zone, ω, is $\omega^*=2\omega/3$ where ω^* does not change with crack propagation as in Section 2.

Figure 20 shows the redistribution of stress, σ_y, and residual stress with crack growth. Figure 21 shows the redistribution of strain, ε_y, with crack growth. The drop in strain ε_y, of the element A due to crack extension is not large in this case.

Figure 22 shows the change of the crack opening displacements with crack growth. The upper and lower crack surfaces contact in the unloading process so that the analysis had to account for the change in the boundary condition due to the crack closure.[4]

4. Summary

Analysis of the crack propagation in an elastic-plastic material was carried out by the finite element method for both monotonic and cyclic loadings. The conclusions are summarized as follows;

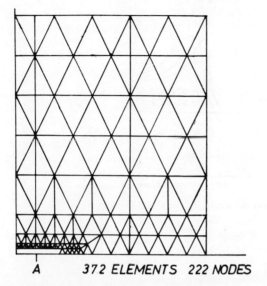

A   372 ELEMENTS   222 NODES

|—4mm—| DETAIL OF A

FIG. 14.   Nodal breakdown of one quadrant of specimen.

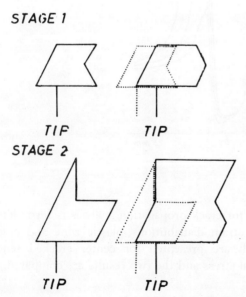

FIG. 15.   Plastic zone before and after crack propagation.

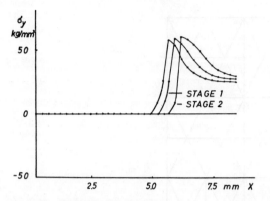

FIG. 16.   Redistribution of stress, σ_y, on $y=0.125$ mm.

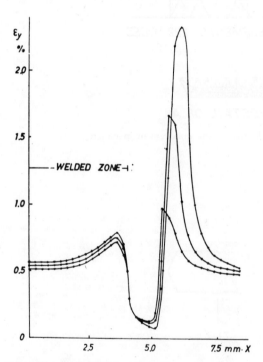

FIG. 17.   Redistribution of strain, ε_y, on $y=0$.

(1)   A numerical procedure for crack propagation analysis is formulated.

(2)   Changes in stress and strain distributions, plastic zone and crack opening displacements with crack growth are presented for center cracked tension plates without and with welding residual stress and the two results are compared.

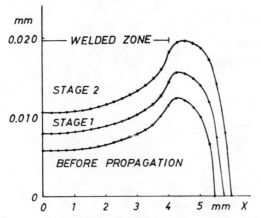

FIG. 18.   Crack opening displacement before and after crack propagation.

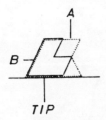

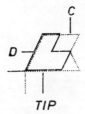

FIG. 19.   Plastic zone before and after crack propagation.

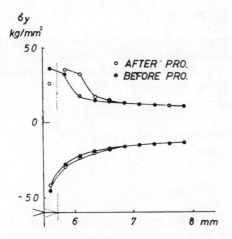

FIG. 20.   Redistribution of stress, σ_y, on $y=0$.

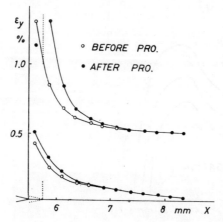

FIG. 21. Redistribution of strain, ε_y, on $y=0$.

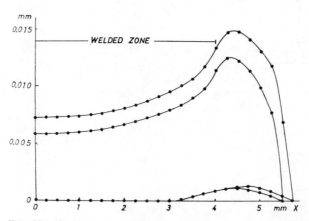

FIG. 22. Crack opening displacement before and after crack propagation.

REFERENCES

1. McClintock, F. A., "*Plasticity Aspects of Fracture*," *Fracture* edited by H. Liebowitz, Vol. 3, Chapter 2, Academic Press, New York, 47/225 (1971).

2. Rice, J. R., "*Mechanics of Crack Tip Deformation and Extension by Fatigue*," "*Fatigue Crack Propagation*," ASTM STP No. 415, 247/311, 1976.

3. Dugdale, D. S., "Yielding of Steel Sheets Containing Slits," Int. J. Mech, Phys. Solids, Vol. 8, No. 100, 100/104 (1960).

4. Shiratori, M., "Study on the Propagation of a Fatigue Crack," Doctral Thesis, University of Tokyo (1971) (in Japanese).

The Fracture Mechanics Approach to Fatigue

A. J. McEvily, Jr.

Metallurgy Department, University of Connecticut

1. Introduction

The analysis of fatigue crack growth rates in terms of stress-intensity factors has gained widespread acceptance in recent years. It has been found that the rate of crack growth in the elastic-plastic range is a single valued function of the stress intensity K, with K given by

$$K = \sigma \sqrt{\alpha \pi a} \tag{1}$$

where σ is the applied stress, α is a factor related to the specific geometry, and a is the crack length. The rate of fatigue crack growth per cycle, $\Delta \varepsilon / \Delta N$ is often expressed in terms of the Paris-Erdogan power law[1];

$$\frac{\Delta a}{\Delta N} = C(\Delta K)^m \tag{2}$$

where C and m are material constants, and ΔK is the range of the stress intensity factor. The appeal of the fracture mechanics approach is that it provides a systematic framework for analysis and permits predictions involving geometries other than those already tested to be made. However, for certain complex geometries of interest K values may not yet be established. Also when multiple flaws on cracks are involved, the analysis may not be straightforward. Nevertheless, it is a very useful approach to the study of the effects of weld variables on the resistance to crack growth. In addition, integration of the growth law permits an estimate to be made of the lifetime for growth of a crack from an initial to a final size, and this capability is useful in assessing the significance of flaws in relation to structural reliability.

With respect to crack growth in welds, heat affected zones and parent plate, the experimental evidence to date does not indicate that any significant differences exist in crack growth mechanisms or rates. For example, Maddox[2] has found that fatigue crack growth in steel plate for the flat mode of growth (plane strain) can be expressed as;

$$\frac{\Delta a}{\Delta N} = 4.32 \times 10^{-9} (\Delta K)^{3.07} \tag{3a}$$

with 95% confidence limits given by;

$$\text{lower limit,} \quad \frac{\Delta a}{\Delta N} = 2.36 \times 10^{-9} (\Delta K)^{3.07} \tag{3b}$$

$$\text{upper limit,} \quad \frac{\Delta a}{\Delta N} = 6.0 \times 10^{-9} (\Delta K)^{3.07} \tag{3c}$$

In eq. (3) Δa is in mm and ΔK is in MNm$^{-3/2}$.

This study involved the testing of six weld metals, a simulated HAZ in mild steel, a simulated HAZ in BS 968 steel, and plain BS 968 steel. Eq. (3) covers the range of growth rates from 5×10^{-6} mm/cycle up to 2×10^{-4} mm/cycle, with ΔK varying from 9.5 to 35 MNm$^{-3/2}$. At any particular K value the scatter in rate of growth from the lower to the upper limit is only a factor of 3.4. This is a relatively small scatter band as compared to the scatter usually found in total life determinations of unnotched fatigue specimens. Maddox also determined the S-N behavior by integration of eq. (3a)and found reasonable agreement between calculated and experimental lifetimes. He concluded that for the specimens he tested crack propagation occupied a significant portion of the total lifetime. For other cases in which the number of cycles spent in the initiation of cracks may be more significant, an estimate of lifetime based on crack propagation alone will be conservative. However such an estimate may approximate the lower life end of the fatigue scatter band, and in such a case may be useful for design purposes.

Only one factor associated with welding has thus far been found which affects in a significant way the rate of crack growth. This factor is the residual stress state which arises as the result of constraints developed on cooling. Insofar as fatigue crack growth is concerned, these stresses appear to be beneficial, and have led to marked reduction in growth rates particularly at the lowest growth rates. As discussed in the companion paper to the present one[3], it appears that the potentially detrimental tensile stresses are relaxed whereas the beneficial compressive stresses are not. The net effect is that residual stresses can retard but not accelerate the rate of crack growth.

It is important to point out that the situation with respect to *crack initiation* may not be so favorable. For example, Gurney[4] cites a case for mild steel where the fatigue strength at 2×10^6 cycles was reduced from ± 122MNm^{-2} to ± 76 MNm^{-2}. The adverse influence of a tensile residual stress will be most pronounced when the peak stresses are low (fully reversed loading, long lifetimes) so that relaxation of residual stresses is not promoted. Under pulsating tension loading, the peak stresses are higher than for fully reversed loading, and residual stresses at lifetimes of 2×10^6 cycles have little effect. On the other hand, in the case of hydrogen embrittlement and stress corrosion, residual stresses may be not only significant but the dominant case of cracking and failure.

To be able to predict the magnitude of residual stress is evidently not a simple matter. For example, Parry, Nordberg, and Hertzberg[5] found that residual stresses can vary from welded plate to welded plate, although all processing had been carried out under nominally the same procedures. They studied crack growth in butt welded plates of

T-1 steel, welded with AX-90 and AX-110 electrodes. Beneficial residual stresses were found in two plates, but were absent in two others. Stress-relief heat treatment eliminated the beneficial effects. Fatigue striation spacing correlated with the general trends of the macroscopic rate data, but in general, the rates as determined by these spacings were lower than the macroscopic rates. Such an observation suggests that other modes of separation were involved, such as ductile tearing, or perhaps cleavage or intergranular separation. In their studies the value of m, eq. (1) was found to be equal to 2.4 for growth rates between 10^{-3} and 10^{-4} mm per cycle.

A more recent investigation by Lawrence and Munse[6], has involved the study of fatigue crack growth in butt welds which lacked complete penetration in the mid-thickness of the plate in the direction of the plate width. This type of weld introduced a compressive stress across the unwelded faces which was sufficient to close tightly the unwelded depth of the joint. The specimens were tested under pulsating tension loading and the average crack length as it extended through the weld to the surface was determined by radiographic means. The specimens were fabricated from ASTM A36 steel plate (ultimate tensile strength of 488 MNm^{-2}). The welding electrode was a 1.6 mm diameter base wire, equivalent to E70 grade electrodes with a minimum ultimate tensile strength of 482.6 MNm^{-2}. They found the rate of crack growth to be less than expected on the basis of plate properties alone. The lower rates which again were most pronounced at low growth rates were due to the presence of the compressive residual stress field. In the range from 10^{-5} mm per cycle to 10^{-3} mm per cycle the crack growth rate was given by;

$$\frac{\Delta a}{\Delta N} = 3.9 \times 10^{-13}(\Delta K)^{5.8} \tag{4}$$

mm per cycle, with ΔK expressed in MNm$^{-3/2}$.

For comparison, the following equations due to Barsom[7] are listed:

A36:

$$\frac{\Delta a}{\Delta N} = 1.45 \times 10^{-9}(\Delta K)^{3.3} \tag{5}$$

Ferrite-pearlite steel average:

$$\frac{\Delta a}{\Delta N} = 5.2 \times 10^{-9}(\Delta K)^{3.0} \tag{6}$$

Martensitic steel average:

$$\frac{\Delta a}{\Delta N} = 9.6 \times 10^{-8}(\Delta K)^{2.25} \tag{7}$$

Here the rate is in mm per cycle, and ΔK is in MNm$^{-3/2}$. For the A36 and the ferrite-pearlite steels the equations are similar to Maddox's. In contrast to Maddox's findings, for the types of specimens used by Lawrence and Munse almost one-half of the lifetime was spent in crack initiation, a stage which probably involved relaxation of some of the compressive stresses as well as the transformation of the initial defect into a fatigue crack.

In the crack growth studies described thus far, cracks were grown parallel to the welding direction, and it is of interest that Parry et al.[5] found no difference in growth rate either with or against the direction of welding. Two other studies have involved the approach of a fatigue crack at angles other than parallel to the weld direction. James[8] has noted the slowing down of a crack as it approached the residual compressive stress field of a weld. Dowse and Richards[9] found in stress relieved weldments that as a fatigue crack approached a heat affected zone which was harder than the parent plate the rate of growth was reduced by a factor of two, an effect associated with a reduction of plastic zone size in the harder material. Further, cracks never followed the weld-parent metal HAZ interface but always deviated to the softer material.

The above provides a broad review of the current states of fatigue crack propagation as affected by weld variables. There does not appear to be any marked difference in character of crack growth in weld metal or parent plate. In the succeeding sections some recent views on fatigue crack growth will be presented which may provide a more complete framework than hereto described for the analysis of fatigue crack growth in general.

2. Fatigue Crack Propagation (Stage II)

In the following sections an analysis of fatigue crack propagation based upon fracture mechanics considerations is given. This treatment of the subject was presented in August, 1973, at the Third International Conference on The Strength of Metals and Alloys in Cambridge.

Elastic-Plastic Fatigue Growth

A schematic variation of the fatigue crack growth rate as a function of the stress intensity factor is shown in Fig. 1. For ΔK values near K_{TH} or K_c, alloys are structure-sensitive. They are much less structure sensitive for ΔK values intermediate between these extremes. The sensitivity near K_c is related to those factors which affect the fracture toughness and bring about micro-void coalescence or other modes of static fracture. Reasons for the structure sensitivity near K_{TH} are less clear. There appears to be a definite mean stress effect in that the ΔK_{TH} value decreases with increasing mean stress level.[10] It is thought that the size of the reversed plastic zone relative to microstructural characteristics such as grain size may affect the level of K_{TH}[10,11]. An aggressive environment can also markedly reduce the threshold level relative to its value in vacuum[12]. An increase in the angle of shear bands to the crack tip with decrease in stress intensity has also been advanced as a factor affecting the threshold level[13]. A dependence of K_{TH} in the elastic modulus and yield strength has been proposed[14], and the threshold level has also been related to the process of crack closure[15]. In this paper we assume the existence of a threshold level without attempting to provide any further explanation for its existence.

With respect to quantitative determination of curves of the type shown in Fig. 1, one approach is to relate the advance per cycle in the striation mode to the crack-tip opening displacement, and to include the threshold effect. This leads to[16]

$$\frac{\Delta a}{\Delta N} = \frac{4A}{\pi \sigma_Y E}(\Delta K^2 - \Delta K_{TH}^2) \tag{8}$$

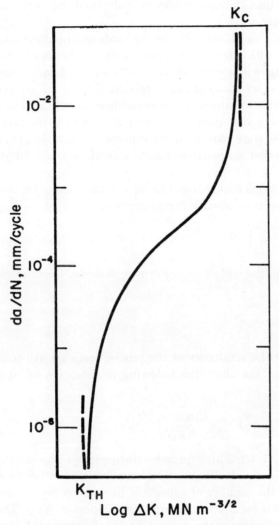

FIG. 1.   Schematic variation of fatigue crack growth rate, da/dN, with alternating stress intensity, ΔK.

Such an expression is useful only in the lower portion of Fig. 1, since static modes of separation are not considered. It has been found that for tests in inert atmospheres for which this type of model is only valid, that A can be expressed as $A = 2\sigma_Y/E$, a finding thought to be related to the rate of strain hardening, so that

$$\frac{\Delta a}{\Delta N} = \frac{8}{\pi E^2}(\Delta K^2 - \Delta K_{TH}{}^2) \tag{9}$$

This equation emphasizes the lack of structure-sensitivity for ΔK values away from the threshold level. Where aggressive environments are present, the rate of growth increases and this fact is reflected by an increase in the constant A. Eq. (9) provides a baseline for growth rates below about 1 μm per cycle under $R = 0$ conditions. If growth rates are significantly higher than th material may be embrittled and/or the environment may be particularly aggressive.

Recent studies by Ritchie and Knott[17,18], by Richards and Lindley[19], and by Pearson[22] have been concerned with effects of R ratio on the rate of crack growth. They find that as the R ratio increases at a given ΔK there is little effect on the rate of growth for tough materials. However, for alloys of low toughness there is a K_{MAX} effect due to the occurrence of static modes of failure in low-toughness materials. The absence of mean stress effects in high toughness materials may be analogous to the case of notched fatigue where the local stress state may be quite different from the applied. Further, Weertman[20] has concluded that mean stress effects should be small for stress intensities below K_c.

To account for K_{MAX} effects Richards and Lindley[19] have found the following empirical expression to be in agreement with experiments on steels;

$$\frac{\Delta a}{\Delta N} = A \left\{ \frac{\Delta K^4}{\sigma_{UTS}^2 (K_c^2 - K_{MAX}^2)} \right\}^n \tag{10}$$

which is somewhat similar to the widely used Forman, Kearny, Engle empirical equation[20];

$$\frac{\Delta a}{\Delta N} = \frac{C(\Delta K)^m}{(1-R)K_c - \Delta K} \tag{11}$$

In view of the fact that the sensitivity of the rate of crack growth to mean stress depends on the toughness of the alloy, the following modification to eq. (9) is suggested, namely that

$$\frac{\Delta a}{\Delta N} = \frac{4A}{\pi \sigma_Y E} (\Delta K^2 - \Delta K_{TH}^2) \left(1 + \frac{\Delta K}{K_c - K_{MAX}} \right) \tag{12}$$

where K_{MAX} is given by $\Delta K/(1-R)$. This expression distinguishes between the two components of crack advance; one the ductile striation component, the other the static mode component. It is noted that the number of adjustable parameters goes to zero for tests in nonaggressive environments for ΔK values large with respect to K_{TH}. The following empirical equation is used to estimate the dependence of the threshold level on the R value;

$$\Delta K_{TH} = \frac{1.2(\Delta K_{TH_0})}{1 + 0.2\left(\dfrac{1+R}{1-R}\right)} \tag{13}$$

where ΔK_{TH0} is the ΔK_{TH} value for $R=0$.

A comparison of calculations based upon eq. (12) with experimental results for aluminum alloys and steels of both high and low toughness is given in Figs. 2 to 4, and the agreement is seen to be reasonable. It is also noted that the L64 alloy, strengthened by GPI zones[22] has a high threshold level but over a certain ΔK range exhibits a higher crack growth rate than does the low toughness RR58 alloy which contains the precipitate $S(AL_2CuMg)$[22]. One can speculate that an instability of the GP structure may be responsible for the unusually high crack growth rates exhibited.

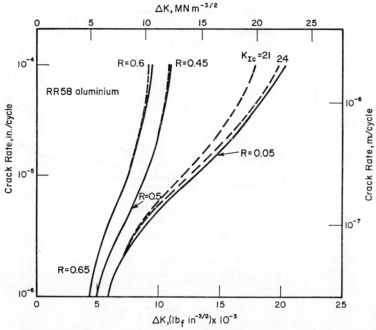

a) A low toughness aluminum alloy, RR58. ΔK_{TH_0} taken as 5 ksi $\sqrt{\text{in.}}$, σ_Y as 60 ksi, E as 10.7×10^6 psi, and the constant A as 0.02, K_c as 21 ksi $\sqrt{\text{in.}}$ except as noted.

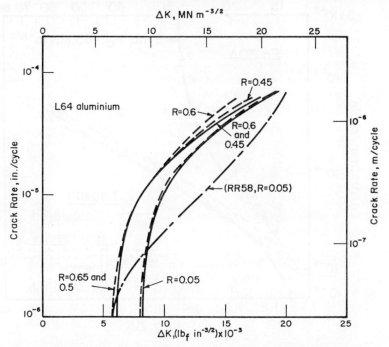

b) A high toughness aluminum alloy, L 64. ΔK_{TH_0} taken as 7 ksi $\sqrt{\text{in.}}$, σ_Y as 52.5 ksi, E as 10.6×10^6 psi, $A=0.08$, $K_c=60$ ksi $\sqrt{\text{in.}}$ RR 58 test results shown for comparison.

FIG. 2. Comparison of experimental[22] and calculated (dashed curves) growth rates for two aluminum alloys.

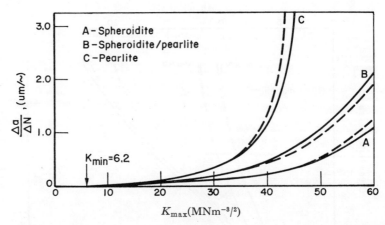

FIG. 3. Comparison of experimental[19] and calculated (dashed curves) growth rates for a 1% carbon steel heat treated to give three different microstructures. K_c values: A–200 MNm$^{-1/2}$; B–90 MNm$^{-3/2}$; C–50 MNm$^{-3/2}$. Constant A taken to be 0.015, $\Delta K_{TH} =$ 11 MNm$^{-3/2}$. $E = 20.7 \times 10^4$ MNm^{-2}; $\sigma_Y = 415$, 455 and 380 MNm^{-2} for A, B, and C, respectively.

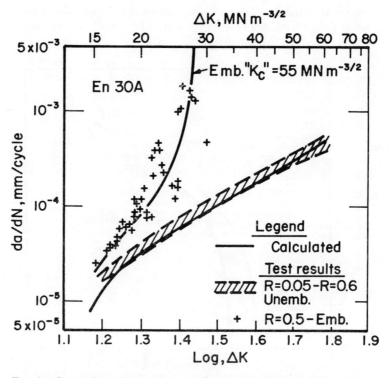

FIG. 4. Comparison of experimental[17,18] and calculated growth rates for En 30a steel in unembrittled and embrittled conditions. σ_Y unembrittled 743 MNm^{-2}, embrittled 735 MNm^{-2}, Constant $A = 0.015$, $\Delta K_{TH} = 11$ MNm$^{-3/2}$, K_c embrittled$= 55$ MNm$^{-3/2}$, K_c unembrittled large with respect to $K_{\max}$.

It should also be mentioned that Pearson[22] has fitted his data of Fig. 2 with an empirical equation of form

$$\frac{\Delta a}{\Delta N} = \frac{CK_c(\Delta K)^3}{[(1-R)K_c - \Delta K]^{1/2}} \tag{14}$$

which resembles eqs. (10) and (11), but has only one adjustable parameter. In reviewing the data for Figs. 2–4 it was of interest to find that K_{MAX} values 50% higher than K_{IC} were reached in the case of the embrittled En30a alloy, whereas for the aluminum alloys Pearson found a much closer correspondence between static and crack growth levels of K_{IC}, although some small variations occurred as indicated in Fig. 2a. Pearson's results are also of interest in that 12 mm thick plate was used to insure that plane strain conditions prevailed throughout the tests.

3. Concluding Remarks

In this paper fatigue crack growth under constant amplitude of cyclic loading has been considered. The important problem of variable amplitude loading has not been discussed since the history efforts involved do not lend themselves to straightforward analysis. More needs to be learned about the mechanisms of crack growth under such conditions. Nevertheless, as pointed out in Reference 3, sufficient information is now available to make design decisions in many cases.

ACKNOWLEDGMENTS

The author expresses his thanks to Battelle, Columbus Laboratories and to the Air Force Office of Scientific Research for their support.

REFERENCES

1. Paris, P. C. and Erdogan, F., "A Critical Analysis of Crack Propagation Laws," J. of Basic Engineering, ASME Transactions, 85, Series D, 528 (1963).
2. Maddox, S. J., Ph. D. Thesis, The Imperial College of Science and Technology, London (1971).
3. McEvily, A. J., "On the Role of Defects in Crack Initiation in Welded Structures," U.S.-Japan Seminar on Significance of Defects in Welded Structures (1973).
4. Gurney, T. R., *Fatigue of Welded Structures*, Cambridge University Press, 153 (1968).
5. Parry, M., Nordberg, H. and Hertzberg, R. W., "Fatigue Crack Propagation in $A514$ Base Plate and Welded Joints," Welding J., Res. Suppl., 485-s (1972).
6. Lawrence, F. V. and Munse, W. H., "Fatigue Crack Propagation in Butt Welds Containing Joint Penetration Defects," Welding J., Res. Suppl., 221-s (1973).
7. Barsom, J. M., "Fatigue Crack Propagation in Steels of Various Yield Strengths," *Proc. First International Congress on Pressure Vessels and Piping*, San Francisco (1971).
8. James, L. A., "Fatigue-Crack Growth In Type 304 Stainless Steel Weldments At Elevated Temperatures," ASTM J. of Testing and Evaluation, **1**, 52 (1973).
9. Dowse, K. R. and Richards, C. E., "Fatigue Crack Propagation Through Weld Heat Affected Zones," Met. Trans., **2**, 599 (1971).

10. Birbeck, G.,Incle, A. E. and Waldron, G. W. S., "Aspects of Stage II Fatigue Crack Propagation in Low-Carbon Steel," *J. Mat. Sci.*, **6**, 319 (1971).

11. Robinson, J. L., Irving, P. E. and Beevers, C. J., "An Analytic Approach to Low Stress Fatigue Crack Growth in Titanium," *Proc. Third Int. Conf. on Fracture*, Munich, Paper V-343 (1973).

12. Irving, P. E. and Beevers, C. J., "The Effect of Air and Vacuum Environments on Fatigue Crack Growth Rates in Ti-6Al-4V," U. of Birmingham Res. Rpt., May (1973).

13. Lindley, T. C. and Richards, C. E., "The Influence of Crack Closure and Plastic Zone Geometry on Fatigue Crack Propagation," *Proc. Third Int. Conf. on Fracture*, Munich, Paper V-431A, (1973).

14. Kitagawa, H., Nishitani, H. and Matsumoto, T., "Fracture Mechanics Approach to Threshold Condition for Fatigue Crack Growth," *ibid.*, Paper V-444A, (1973).

15. Paris, P. C., Bucci, R. J., Wessel, E. T., Clark, W. G. and Mager, T. R., "An Extensive Study of Low Fatigue Crack Growth Rates in A533 and A508 Steels," *ASTM STP 513*, 141 (1972).

16. Donahue, R. J., Clark, H. M., Atanmo, P., Kumble, R. and McEvily, A. J., "Crack Opening Displacement and the Role of Fatigue Crack Growth," Int. J. of Fracture Mech., **8**, 209 (1972).

17. Knott, J. F. and Ritchie, R. O., "Effect of Fracture Mechanisms on Fatigue Crack Propagation," *Proc. Conf. on Mechanics and Mechanisms of Crack Growth*, Cambridge (1973).

18. Ritchie, R. O. and Knott, J. F., "Brittle Cracking Processes during Fatigue Crack Propagation," *Proc. Third Int. Conf. on Fracture*, Munich, Paper V-434A, (1973).

19. Richards, C. E. and Lindley, T. C., "The Influence of Stress Intensity and Microstructure on Fatigue Crack Propagation in Ferritic Materials," Eng. Fracture Mech., **4**, 951, (1972).

20. Weertman, J., "Theory of Rate of Growth of Fatigue Cracks Under Combined Static Stresses," Int. J. of Fracture Mech., **5**, 13, (1969).

21. Forman, R. G., Kearny, V. E. and Engle, R. M., "Numerical Analysis of Crack Propagation in Cyclic-Loaded Structures," Trans. ASME, D89, 459 (1967).

22. Pearson, S., "The Effect of Mean Stress on Fatigue Crack Propagation in Half-Inch (12.7 mm) Thick Specimens of Aluminum Alloys of High and Low Fracture Toughness," Eng. Fracture Mech., **4**, 9, (1972).

Fracture Analysis of Flaws in Welded Bridge Structures

J. W. Fisher

Fritz Engineering Laboratory, Lehigh University

G. R. Irwin

Adjunct Professor of Mechanics, Lehigh University

1. Introduction

In the present design (1973) of steel bridges for fatigue, provisions have been specified in many instances on the basis of limited test data. Previous work had not adequately investigated the behavior of beams in terms of stress, detail and type of steel. The effects of variable such as stress, stress ratio, cover-plate geometry, details and type of steel were not clearly defined.[2,3,4] Equally important to the fatigue life of highway bridges is the significance of such factors as the loading history to which the structures are subjected, the type of materials used, the design details, and the quality of fabrication.

Recognition of these facts lead to the bridge studies on the AASHO Road Test[1] and the development of a comprehensive study of rolled and welded built-up beams with a variety of welded details.[5,6] This program was sponsored by the American Association of State Highway Officials in cooperation with the Bureau of Public Roads, U.S. Department of Transportation under the National Cooperative Highway Research Program, which is administered by the Highway Research Board of the National Academy of Science.

The major objective of this study was to develop suitable mathematical design relationships for between 50,000 and 10,000,000 cycles of loading. Altogether, more than 500 beams with one or more details were studied. The principal design variables for this study were grouped into three categories; (i) type of weld detail, (ii) stress condition, and (iii) type of steel.

Three grades of steel were examined—ASTM A36, A441 and A514—for the details discussed in this paper.

Nine different types of beam details were examined, including cover-plated beams, plain-welded beams with and without attachments, welded beams with groove-welded flange splices and plain-rolled beams[5,6]. Only two details are discussed in this report. One detail is a rolled or welded steel I beam with cover plates which provided a severe

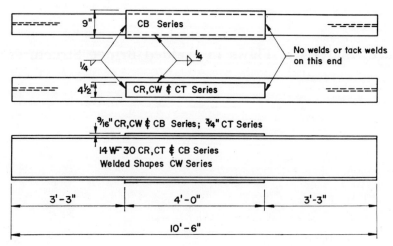

FIG. 1.   Details of the cover-plated beams.

notch producing detail with crack growth from the weld toe and a lower-bound to fatigue
behavior. The second detail discussed is the plain welded beam without attachment
which provided a minimum notch producing detail with crack growth from an internal flaw and an upper bound for the behavior of welded beams.

Details are given in the Final Reports of the study on the effect of weldments on
the fatigue strength of steel beams.[5,6]

Figure 1 shows schematically the basic details considered in the cover-plated beam
study. Cover plates were attached to both rolled and welded beams. The steel beams in
the CR–CW series had 11.4 cm (4–1/2 in.) wide cover plates which had 1.5 times the
flange thickness. Other cover-plated beams were examined with thicker, wider, or
multiple cover plates, but all these were fabricated from A36 steel.

The plain-welded beams were identical in cross section to the cover-plated beams
and were fabricated using the same technique except no cover plates were attached.

All longitudinal fillet welds were made by the automatic submerged arc process.
Tack welds and the transverse end welds on the cover plates were manual welds. All
beams in this study were 320 cm (10 ft. 6 in.) long and were tested on a 305 cm (10 ft.)
span. The ends of the cover-plate details were positioned in the shear spans 30.5 cm
(12 in) from each load point. The plain-welded beams were loaded so that a 106.7 cm
42 in) constant moment region resulted in the center.

Minimum stress and stress range were selected as the controlled stress variables.
This permitted variation in one variable while the other was maintained at a constant
level. Had stress rate (ratio of minimum to maximum stress) been selected as the independent variable, both minimum stress and maximum stress would have to be changed
simultaneously to maintain the ratio at a constant level.

The controlled stress levels were the nominal flexural stresses in the base metal
of the tension flange at the end of the cover plate, and at points of maximum moment
for the plain-welded beams.

2. Initial Flaw Conditions

Experimental fatigue studies have nearly all confirmed that fatigue crack growth commenced at some initial "flaw or defect". In unwelded steel this may be at small mechanical notches, discontinuities in mill scale, surface imperfections and laminations or from gas cut edges. In welded structures small, sharp defects exist at the weld periphery or in the weldment of both fillet and groove welds, and crack growth has invariably started at the weld periphery or at an internal flaw depending on the direction of applied stress.

Signes et al.[7] have shown that fatigue cracks initiated in many details at the toes of fillet welds from small, sharp intrusions of slag that emanated from the welding flux or plate. These findings were further confirmed by Watkinson et al.[8] who showed that these defects exist in most conventional welding processes.

All experimental evidence has confirmed that crack growth does normally initiate at the toe of a weldment starting from the initial micro-flaw when the applied stress is perpendicular to it. Figure 2 shows the cracks which formed in the beam flange at the toes of both longitudinal and transverse fillet welds that connected the cover plate to the beam flange.

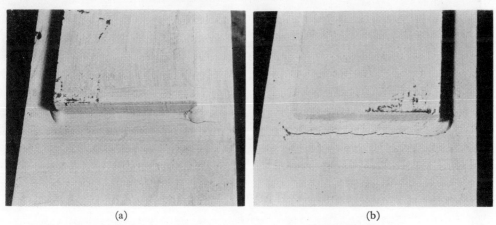

(a)   (b)

FIG. 2a.   Crack in beam flange at end of longitudinal fillet weld.
FIG. 2b.   Crack in beam flange at toe of transverse end weld.

The fracture surfaces are shown in Fig. 3 for several stages of crack growth. Prior to penetrating the flange thickness, the crack grew as a semi-elliptical surface crack.

In some types of joints, however, fatigue cracks may initiate at points other than the weld toe. For example, in joints involving transverse load-carrying fillet welds, cracking can initiate at the weld root with propagation through the weld. Provided that the welds are sufficiently large and their geometry satisfactory, joints will also experience crack growth and failure from the toe. Generally joints failing from internal defects have a relatively high fatigue strength. This was the case for the plain-welded beams. Cracks causing failure initiated at a flaw in the longitudinal fillet welds joining the web to the flanges. Typical initial flaws are porosity (gas pockets) as illustrated in Fig. 4.

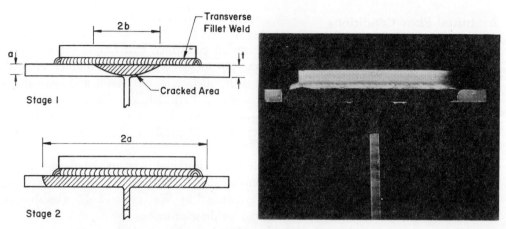

FIG. 3. Fracture surface and schematic of crack growth at end of cover plate with transverse end weld.

(a)   (b)

FIG. 4a. Fatigue crack growing from porosity in the web-to-flange fillet weld.
FIG. 4b. Fatigue crack which has nearly penetrated the beam flange surface.

Other sources of crack growth are at start-stop positions or weld repairs where incomplete fusion or trapped slag exists[2,3,5]. Cracks starting at porosity were initially completely inside the weld and were not visible from the surface until substantial crack growth had occurred.

3. Fatigue Strength of Cover-Plated Beams

The results of tests on cover-plated beams provided data for a severe notch producing detail so that a lower bound to fatigue strength could be examined. When a transverse end weld existed, the crack initiated at the toe of the transverse weld as was illustrated in Fig. 2. During the first stage of growth, the crack grew through the flange in an elliptical shape as illustrated in Fig. 3. Visual observation of these semi-elliptical cracks indicated that the crack maintained its geometric shape at all crack sizes. After

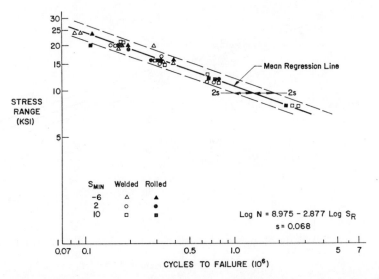

FIG. 5. Effect of stress range and minimum stress on the fatigue strength of cover-plated beams.

penetrating the flange thickness, it grew toward the flange tips and into the web. Cracks initiated at the toe of the longitudinal fillet welds connecting the cover plate to the beam when no transverse end weld was present. These cracks also grew through the flange in an elliptical shape and were similar to the first stage of growth exhibited by cracks at the end with a transverse end weld.

The effects of the controlled variables of minimum stress, stress range and type of steel were analyzed using statistical methods. The dominant variable was stress range for all cover-plate geometries, end details and steels tested.

Figure 5 summarizes the test data for A36 steel beams with an end weld. Cycle life is plotted against stress range for different levels of minimum stress. Also shown are the mean regression line and the limits of dispersion as given by two standard errors of estimate. It is apparent that the variation due to minimum stress is insignificant and that stress range accounted for the variation in cycle life. The mathematical relationship between the applied stress range and cycles to failure for each series and geometry was determined using regression analysis. The analysis showed that the logarithmic transformation of stress range and cycle life provided the best fit to the data.

The effect of type of steel was also evaluated since the experiment design provided equal factorials and sample sizes of A36, A441 and A514 steel beams with cover plates. The test data for all three types of steel cover-plated beams are compared in Fig. 6. The A514 steel beams yielded only a slightly longer life. The variation in life due to type of steel is too small for consideration in the design of structures.

The results of this study have been compared with the earlier work of Wilson[9], Lea and Whitman[10], and Munse and Stallmeyer[11], for both end details. The limits of dispersion provided by two standard errors of estimate included almost all the data.

This study has confirmed that no great differences exist in the fatigue strength of square-ended cover plates; that cover plates affect rolled and welded beams similarly;

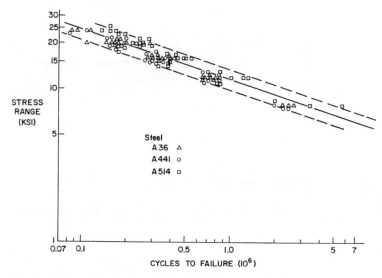

FIG. 6.   Effect of grade of steel on the fatigue strength of cover-plated beams.

that welded cover-plated beams yield about the same fatigue strength for A36, A441 and A514 steels, and that only stress range is the critical stress variable.

4.   Fatigue Strength of Welded Beams Without Attachments

The results of the tests on plain-welded beams provided a minimum notch producing detail and an upper bound to the fatigue strength of welded beams. Nearly all cracks initiated at a flaw in the fillet weld at the flange-to-web connection as illustrated in Fig. 4. The fillet weld flaw was usually a gas pocket or worm hole in the fillet weld caused by gas trapped in the weldment. Cracks were initially inside the weld as shown in Fig. 7, but eventually grew out to the fillet weld surface. They maintained a circular

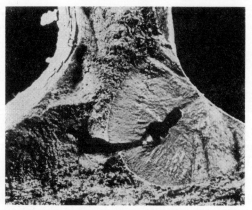

FIG. 7.   Small penny-shaped fatigue cracks which have originated at internal discontinuities the web-to-flange fillet welds.

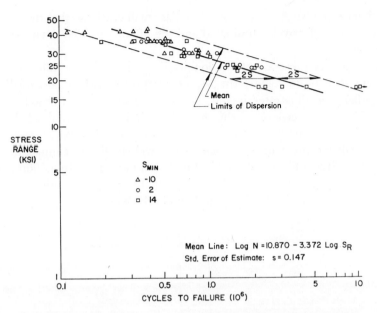

Fig. 8.   Effect of stress range and minimum stress on the fatigue strength of welded gird-ers.

shape as shown in Figs. 4 and 7 until they penetrated the outside flange surface. It is also apparent that the other free surfaces on the weld face and the web did not affect the crack shape. It maintained its circular shape even though free surfaces were inter-sected. After penetrating the outside fibers of the flange, the crack grew on two fronts toward the flange tips as well as up the web.

The effect of the design factors, minimum stress and stress range are illustrated in Fig. 8.   Stress range is observed to account for the variation in cycle life. Multiple regression analysis also indicated that the logarithmic transformation of both stress range and cycle life provided the best fit to the data.

Residual stresses were measured in several of the welded shapes, and all indicated the presence of large tensile residual stresses in the vicinity of the flange-to-web fillet welds. As the strength of the steel increased, there was greater probability of the com-pression flange being subjected to the full tensile stress range in the vicinity of the weld since the residual stresses were about equal to the yield stress. The presence of residual tensile stresses also accounts for the behavior of the welded beams without attachments and cover-plated beams and the fact that their fatigue behavior can be expressed in terms of stress range.

As was the case with cover-plated beams, the experiment design provided equal sample sizes of plain-welded A36, A441 and A514 steel beams. There was no statistically significant difference due to type of steel. All the variation was due to stress range.

5.   Stress Analysis of Crack Propagation

In welded joints the small sharp initial defects at the weld toe and the internal flaws in the weldment (porosity) can be considered as small cracks so that the need for a crack initiation period is effectively eliminated and the life of a welded detail is taken up with crack propagation[7,8].

For example, at the ends of the longitudinal or transverse fillet weld connecting a cover plate to a beam flange, the toe cracks propagated in a semielliptical shape through the flange as illustrated in Fig. 3. The internal flaws in the web-flange connection of a welded beam have taken the shape of a circle and maintained that shape until the bottom surface of the flange was completely penetrated as shown in Fig. 4. A schematic of the advancement of the crack in the web to flange connection after it had penetrated the extreme fibre is shown in Fig. 9 and indicates a transition from a penny-shaped crack with a continuous crack front in the flange-web junction to a three-ended crack with two crack tips in the flange and one in the web.

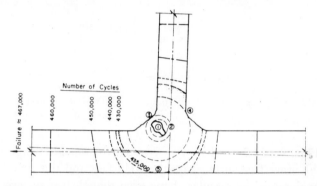

FIG. 9.   Schematic of the growth of a fatigue crack from an internal discontinuity in the web-flange connection.

Hence, two basic stages of growth were observed for cracks originating from pores in the longitudinal fillet weld of welded beams. The first stage is growth in the flange-to-web junction from the initial crack-size up to the point where the crack reached the extreme fiber of the flange. After penetration of the extreme flange-fiber, the crack changed its shape rapidly to become a three-ended crack.

Investigations at Fritz Laboratory, Lehigh University, using a wide range of welded details typical for steel bridge structure, have shown that the observed fatigue crack growth rates correspond approximately to the widely used equation

$$\frac{d\alpha}{dN} = C(\Delta K)^n \tag{1}$$

where α is a measure of the crack size, (crack radius for embedded crack, crack depth for a part-through crack or half-length for a through-the-thickness crack), N is the number of fatigue cycles, ΔK is the variation of the stress intensity factor, K, per cycle, and C and n are constants. In these experiments the nominal stress range per cycle, $\Delta\sigma$, was held constant. Thus ΔK changed slowly with increase of the crack size. Using ΔK in units of ksi $\sqrt{}$ in and α in units of inches, eq. (1) in the form

$$\frac{d\alpha}{dN} = 2 \times 10^{-10}(\Delta K)^3 \tag{2}$$

seemed applicable to a large number of observations conducted using A36, A441, and A514 steels[6,12].

The equation for ΔK can be expressed as

$$\Delta K = q(\Delta\sigma)\sqrt{\alpha}\, f \tag{3}$$

where q is $1.1\sqrt{\Pi}$ for a surface crack with a small depth to surface length ratio, or $2/\sqrt{\Pi}$ for a surface crack of half-circular shape. The factor, f, is an adjustment for the geometrical stress concentration. For example, in the case of a small crack at the toe of a cover plate filled weld, f might have values in the range of 2.5 to 4.5. One would expect the size of the geometrical stress concentration causing stress elevation to decrease with increase of α.

Assuming the proportionality of ΔK to $\sqrt{\alpha}$ remains fixed, eq. (2) can be integrated. The number of cycles, N, for growth of the crack from size α_0 to α is then given by

$$N = \frac{10^{10}}{[qf(\Delta\sigma)]^3\sqrt{\alpha_0}}\left\{1-\left(\frac{\alpha_0}{\alpha}\right)^{1/2}\right\} \tag{4}$$

Consider next the relationship of α_0 to the nominal stress range, $\Delta\sigma$, for fixed values of N and (α_0/α). Evidently $qf(\Delta\sigma)$ is inversely proportional to $(\alpha_0)^{1/6}$. Furthermore it can be noted that, in the case of fatigue life testing for large values of N, the ratio, (α_0/α), is usually small enough so that $(\alpha_0/\alpha)^{1/2}$ can be neglected in comparison to unity. With these considerations in mind several conclusions can be drawn as follows.

(a) A plot of log N versus log $(\Delta\sigma)$ from fatigue life testing should have a slope of about minus three. Such lines have in fact provided satisfactory representations of fatigue tests of I-beams both with and without fillet welded cover plates.

(b) Much of the data scatter shown in the above tests can be attributed to variations in the factors q (for crack shape) and f (for stress concentration), or the initial crack size α_0.

(c) One can observe that, within the range or variability of qf, initial crack depths differing by a factor of $(1.5\times2)^6$ or 730 might have equivalent severity.

With regard to conclusion (c) above, it can be recognized that the factor, f, will tend to decrease as the crack depth grows to a size which is a significant fraction of the size of the geometrical discontinuity responsible for the stress elevation. Thus a small defect in a region such that a large value of f is applicable may undergo only a limited fatigue growth before the effective f value is reduced to 2 or less.

Numerical examples coupled with comparison to direct observations are helpful at this point. Carefully welded beams with no attachments tested at Fritz Laboratory tend, on average, to have a fatigue life of 10^6 cycles at $\Delta\sigma=30$ ksi. Assuming f to be unity, the lower and upper bounds of q give values of α_0 of 0.068 inches and 0.0025 inches respectively. Inspections of the origin regions of fatigue cracks suggest the initial defect sizes were in the range of 0.03 to 0.08 inches.

Beams with welded cover plates tend on average to have a fatigue life of 10^5 cycles at $\Delta\sigma=25$ ksi. Assuming f is unity in this case gives values of α_0 of 21 inches and 0.76 inch respectively for the lower and upper bounds of q. However, inspections of the origin regions of the fatigue cracks suggest the initial defect sizes were in the range of 1 to 20 times 10^{-3} inches. Thus the initial size of α_0 appeared to be smaller than 21 inches by a factor about equal to 730. These examples confirm the sensitivity of the detail to the initial geometrical stress concentration condition and the overriding influence of the initial flaw size α_0.

From the above discussion it is clear that control of fatigue life quality based upon efforts to detect or estimate initial starting crack sizes may be impractical in large welded steel structures. Clearly any initial cracks large enough to be consistently found, depending on location and stress range, may cause undesirably large reductions of fatigue life. Otherwise satisfactory control of fatigue life quality is most likely to be acheived by uniform high quality welding and the avoidance of stress elevating features.

The relationship of fatigue crack growth rate to ΔK has shown negligible sensitivity to strength level of the steel. Correspondingly shorter fatigue lives are observed if a heat treated high strength steel, such as A514, is used in a design which allows larger values of $\Delta\sigma$ in service. This inherent disadvantage can be countered by judgment in the use of the steel. Experience has shown that the presence of substantial fracture toughness capabilities of A514 (and similar steels) should not be assumed without verification. Attention to this aspect is desirable both with regard to cracking during fabrication as well as the residual fracture hazard of the completed structure. Relative to design, use of a steel of the A514 type may be desirable in a component which supports a large fraction of the dead weight load of a bridge structure. If the ratio of live load to dead weight load is quite small, as is often true for situations of this kind, the expected fatigue life of the component may be satisfactory simply because the applicable values of $\Delta\sigma$ and ΔK remain relatively small.

As a numerical illustration of the above comment, consider a situation in which the tensile stress acting across an overlooked surface crack is 50 ksi and assume the dead weight load is responsible for 95 percent of this stress. Estimates using eq. (2) show that a half-circular surface crack with a depth of one inch would increase in size by less than 5 percent in 10^7 cycles with $\Delta\sigma$ equal to the entire live load. The corresponding increase in the value of K at the leading edge of the crack would be 2.3 percent or less. The crack size for this illustration is, of course, an arbitrary choice. With the reasonable assumption that the fracture toughness quality of the steel would be substantially larger than the expected K values for the largest overlooked cracks, the percent increase of K noted in the above illustration would not be dangerous to the structure.

REFERENCES

1. Fisher, J. W. and Viest, I. M., "Fatigue Life of Bridge Beams Subjected to Controlled Truck Traffic," Preliminary Publications, 7th Congress, IABSE, 497/510 (1964).
2. Gurney, T. R., "*Fatigue of Welded Structures*," Cambridge University Press (1968).
3. Munse, W. H. and Grover, L. M., "*Fatigue of Welded Steel Structures*," Welding Research Council, New York (1964).
4. ASCE Task Committee on Flexural Members, "Commentary on Welded Cover-Plated Beams," Journal of the Structural Division, ASCE, Vol. 93, No. ST4, Aug. (1967).
5. Fisher, J. W., Frank, K. H., Hirt, M. A. and McNamee, B. M., "Effect of Weldments

on the Fatigue Strength of Steel Beams," *Final Report, NCHRP Report 102*, Highway Research Board (1970).

6. Fisher, J. W., Albrecht, P. A., Yen, B. T. and Klingerman, D. J., "Fatigue Strength of Welded Steel Beams," *Final Report Phase II NCHRP* 12-7, *NCHRP Report 147*, Highway Research Board (1974).

7. Signes, E. G., Baker, R. G., Harrison, J. D. and Burdekin, F. M., "Factors Affecting the Fatigue Strength of Welded High Strength Steels," British Welding Journal, Vol. 14, Mar. (1967).

8. Watkinson, F., Bodger, P. H. and Harrison, J. D., "The Fatigue Strength of Steel Joints and Methods for its Improvement," *Proceedings, Fatigue of Welded Structures Conference*, The Welding Institute, England, Paper No. 7, July (1970).

9. Wilson, W. M., "Flexural Fatigue Strength of Steel Beams," Bulletin No. 377, University of Illinois, Urbana, Illinois (1943).

10. Lea, F. C. and Whitman, J. G., "The Failure of Girders Under Repeated Stresses," Welding Journal, Vol. 18, Jan. (1939).

11. Munse, W. H. and Stallmeyer, J. E., "Fatigue in Welded Beams and Girders," Bulletin No. 315, Highway Research Board (1962).

12. Hirt, M. A. and Fisher, J. W., "Fatigue Crack Growth in Welded Beams," Engineering Fracture Mechanics, Vol. 5, No. 2, June (1973).

Fatigue Strength of Defective Butt Welded Joints

K. IIDA

Department of Naval Architecture, University of Tokyo

NOMENCLATURE

S_R: Range (=double amplitude) of net section stress (calculated on net section area obtained by subtracting the sum of areas of weld defects from the total cross sectional area at the fractured section). (kg/mm²)

N_f: Number of cycles to failure.

α_s: Degree of weld defect severity defined on a fracture surface by direct observation. Percentage of the sum total of weld defect areas to the gross area of the fracture surface. (%)

α_x: Degree of weld defect severity defined on a given area of radiograph. (%)

α_c: Value of α_s indicating the parameter of a median line on which any data lies (see Fig. 9).

σ_u: Ultimate tensile strength. (kg/mm²)

1. Introduction

Effects of weld defects on fatigue strength of butt welded joint have been one of the important problems in the field of fatigue design and quality control of welded structures. In recent years tens of papers have reported on the effects of external geometry, porosities, slag inclusions, incomplete penetration and crack. Harrison[1,2] summarized these papers by plotting available results taken from a number of literature references. Figure 1 shows an example in which straight lines dividing a S–N diagram into five arbitrary area labelled V, W, X, Y and Z are drawn with a slope of 1/4 with the assumption that a fatigue crack will propagate following the 4th power law. Based on such figures, the WEE/37 Committee of the British Standards Institution proposed the limits given in Table 1 for inclusions and porosities in weldments.

Analyses by Harrison, however, were based on some questionable facts which require further discussion. These facts are: (1) Some results quoted in the analysis

224

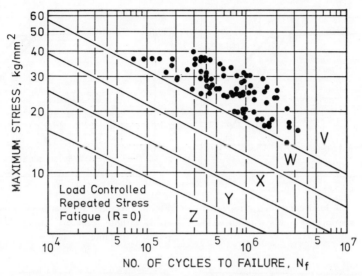

FIG. 1.   Fatigue test results for minimum porosity levels up to 3% [after Harrison].

TABLE 1.   Limits for inclusions and porosity [after Harrison].

Fabrication quality	Inclusion length (max.) as-welded (mm)	Inclusion length (max.) stress relieved (mm)	Porosity-Percentage of projected area on radiograph (%)
V	0	0	0
W	1.5	6	3
X	10	No maximum	5
Y	No maximum	No maximum	5
Z	No maximum	No maximum	5

were obtained from test specimens of uncertain weld defect severity, namely volume percentage for one case and area percentage for the other case, (2) the slope of a S–N diagram is not always equal to $-1/4$ and (3) the analysis does not cover intermediate fatigue life range.

In the present paper, test results obtained previously by the author and his co-workers[3,4,5] are briefly summarized, and a new classification of butt welded joints containing porosities and slag inclusions is proposed.

2.   Fatigue Strength of Defective Butt Joint and Proposed Design Curves

Fatigue strength, in the failure life range of 0.5 to 5×10^6 cycles, of a butt welded, transverse joint containing various weld defects was investigated by Ishii and Iida.[3] Defects studied were porosity, slag inclusions, incomplete penetration, longitudinal crack and undercut. These weld defects were deliberately introduced by various methods, and the weld defect severity α_s was defined for a full cross sectional area of the test section, 50 mm in width multiplied by plate thickness ranging from approximately 10 mm to nearly 50 mm. Specimens, with base metal satisfying the specifications of ASTM standard A533 Class 1, were subjected to repeated or fluctuating axial load

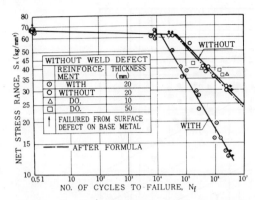

FIG. 2. Results of load-controlled, repeated stress fatigue tests on butt welds without weld defect.

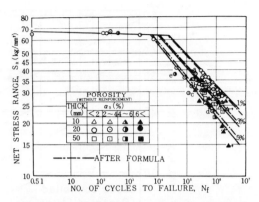

FIG. 3. Results of load-controlled, repeated stress fatigue tests on butt welds containing porosity (parameter: α_s).

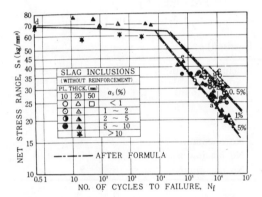

FIG. 4. Results of load-controlled, repeated stress fatigue tests on butt welds containing slag inclusions (parameter: α_s).

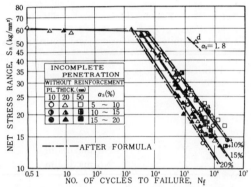

FIG. 5. Results of load-controlled, repeated stress fatigue tests on butt welds containing incomplete penetration (parameter: α_s).

in a load controlled fatigue test with a minimum stress within 3 kg/mm². Cycling rate was generally kept between 1 to 10 cpm when the failure life was expected to be less than 10^4 cycles, and 220 to 500 cpm for other tests.

Fatigue tests of butt welded joint without internal defects were carried out as a standard of comparison. The results are shown in Fig. 2, in which it is clearly observed that the fatigue strength of the butt joint with reinforcement is considerably lower than that of the flushed joint. The strength ratio of the former to the latter is approximately 0.58 at 2×10^5 cycles of N_f, and 0.45 at 2×10^6 cycles.

Figures 3 to 8 show test results of defective butt joints where reinforcements were machined flush with the specimen surface. Static tensile strength of the defective butt joint was an average of 66.8 kg/mm². By disregarding the effect of specimen thickness, the most probable median lines are drawn with α_s as a parameter. Exponent k and constant C in the exponential relation of S_R versus N_f were plotted against α_s, and faired values of k and C were determined as a function of α_s from the faired curves. The

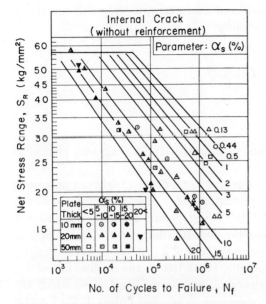

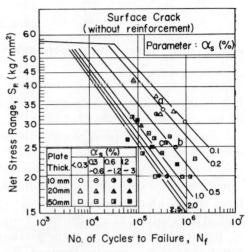

FIG. 6. Results of load-controlled, repeated stress fatigue tests on butt welds containing internal crack.

FIG. 7. Results of load-controlled, repeated stress fatigue tests on butt welds containing surface crack.

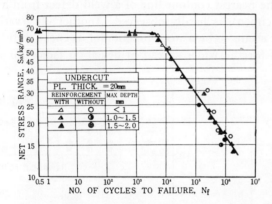

FIG. 8. Results of load-controlled, repeated stress fatigue tests on butt welds containing undercut (parameter: maximum depth of undercut).

intermediate fatigue strength of butt welds containing weld defects was expressed in terms of α_s as follows:

For reinforcement-less welds containing undercut

$$S_R = 454(N_f)^{-0.239} \tag{1}$$

For reinforcement-less welds containing longitudinal crack

$$S_R = 340(N_f)^{-\exp(0.01448a_s - 1.697)} \tag{2}$$

For sound welds without reinforcement ($\alpha_s=0$) and reinforcement-less welds containing porosity, slag inclusions or incomplete penetration

$$S_R = 390(N_f)^{-\exp(0.03284\alpha_s - 1.749)} \quad \text{when } 0 \leq \alpha_s \leq 5 \tag{3}$$

$$S_R = 390(N_f)^{-\exp(0.01480\alpha_s - 1.659)} \quad \text{when } 5 \leq \alpha_s \leq 20 \tag{4}$$

and for sound welds with reinforcement

$$S_R = 965(N_f)^{-0.278} \tag{5}$$

Dot-dash lines in the above-mentioned figures represent S–N diagrams calculated by the empirical formulas (1) to (5).

From a practical point of view, the application of eqs. (1) to (5) should be limited since these equations represent only a 50% probability of failure. The range of deviations in results was examined by Ishii and Iida[4] for proposing a fatigue design curve which lies on the safe side. Figure 9 illustrates the deviation factor for α_s value of 2%. Open circles, which represent results of specimens with 2% α_s, lie on the respective median lines with α_s as a parameter. For example, Point 1 is on the median line of 1% α_s. By the definition that α_c is the parametric value, α_s, of a median line on which any data lies on, α_c/α_s is easily obtained. The values of α_c/α_s for Points 1, 2, 3 and 4 in Fig. 9 are 0.5, 1, 2.5 and 5, respectively for a given value of 2% α_s. As an example, relations between α_s and α_c/α_s for specimens containing porosities or slag inclusions are plotted in Fig. 10. The parametric significance of defect location factor in thickness direction, h_s/t ($h_s=$depth to the nearest contour line of a weld defect from a plate surface, and $t=$thickness of specimen), is hardly observed. Another observation is that the maximum deviation factor seems to be a steep function of α_c enclosed by the dotted curve in Fig. 10. The reason for the wider spread in deviation factor for a lower α_s

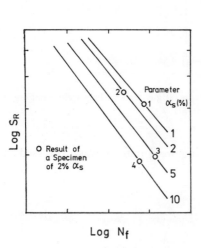

FIG. 9.   Sketch defining deviation factor.

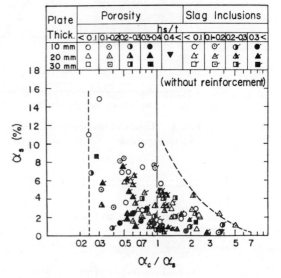

FIG. 10.   Relation between data deviation factor and α_s (porosity and slag inclusions).

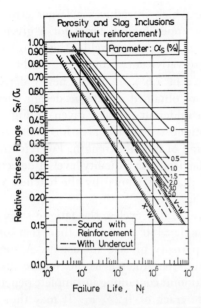

FIG. 11. Proposed S–N curves for sound butt joint with reinforcement, and reinforcement-less butt joint containing porosity, slag inclusions or undercut (R=0).

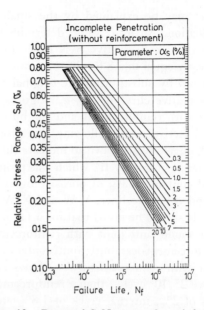

FIG. 12. Proposed S–N curves for reinforcement-less butt joint containing incomplete penetration (R=0).

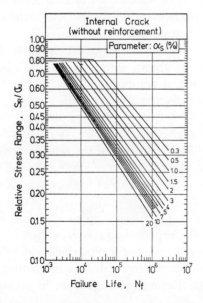

FIG. 13. Proposed S–N curves for reinforcement-less butt joint containing internal crack (R=0).

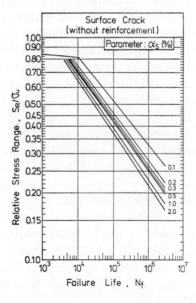

FIG. 14. Proposed S–N curves for reinforcement-less butt joint containing surface crack (R=0).

value may be explained by the smaller α_s value which introduces a larger error in evaluation. An α_c/α_s value determined from this upper bound curve for a given α_s provides a conservative S–N curve for design use. For porous welds, the α_c/α_s value is nearly equal to 3.8 for 2% α_s, from which a conservative curve for 2% α_s can be constructed by substituting the original median curve of 7.6% α_s by the newly derived conservative curve of 2% α_s. Figures 11 to 14 are obtained as fatigue design curves joint with reinforcement and for butt joint with undercut are also given in Fig. 11. for defective welds following this procedure. Fatigue strength curves for sound butt Both curves were drawn to indicate the lower bound of fatigue strength. For reference, the range of quality W, which was proposed by Harrison[1] as a quality level of defective weld containing 3% of porosity by volume percentage, is shown by the hatched area bounded by two lines, V-W and X-W lines in Fig. 11.

It should be noted that for a failure life above 2×10^5 cycles, the fatigue strength of a sound butt joint with reinforcement (toe angle $\simeq 150°$) is lower than that of a reinforcement-less butt joint containing 5% of porosity or slag inclusions. A sound joint with reinforcement also shows lower fatigue strength, when the failure life is above 2×10^5 cycles, than a reinforcement-less butt joint containing incomplete penetration of 2%, internal crack of 1.8% and a surface crack of 0.2% α_s. It may thus be concluded that the reinforcement itself, would act as a dominant factor in reducing the fatigue strength to a certain percentage rather than the internal defects.

3. Proposed Classification of Butt Joints Containing Porosities and Slag Inclusions

The S-N diagrams given in Fig. 11 are used in the calculation of fatigue strength ratio of a defective butt joint with a certain percentage of porosities and slag inclusions. Fatigue strength ratio is defined as the ratio of fatigue strength of a defective joint without reinforcement to that of a reinforcement-less joint without weld defects. In Fig. 15 relations between fatigue strength ratio and α_s are shown with failure life as a parameter. Fatigue strength ratio is naturally a function of failure life and α_s. It may thus be unreasonable to define the quality level of a defective welded joint by only one factor of the defect percentage.

A proposed classification of defective joints is given in Table 2. The quality level is divided into five grades, which correspond to 0.9 to 0.5 times of the fatigue strength of a sound butt joint without reinforcement. Acceptance levels of porosities and slag inclusions are given as a function of upper limit of the number of load cycling as well as a grade of required quality.

It should be emphasized that porosities and slag inclusions up to 5% of α_s have no influence on the fatigue strength, provided the expected life is less than 5×10^3 cycles. Also if the reinforcement is left as it is, requirements for repairing weld defects of a certain level are meaningless when the service stress in a structure is less than the stress range which may cause a possible fatigue fracture in fatigue life in excess of 2×10^5 cycles.

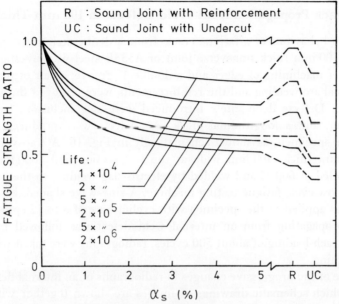

FIG. 15. Fatigue strength ratio versus α_s.

TABLE 2. Upper limit of defect area percentage as a function of expected life and quality level.

Quality	F.S.R.	Upper limit of life					
		1×10^4	2×10^4	5×10^4	2×10^5	5×10^5	2×10^6
A	0.9	1.7	0.5	0.2	0.2	0.1	0.1
B	0.8	5.0	1.6	0.7	0.5	0.4	0.3
C	0.7	—	5.0	1.7	1.3	0.9	0.7
D	0.6	—	—	5.0	3.2	2.3	1.5
E	0.5	—	—	—	5.0	5.0	5.0

F.S.R.: Fatigue strength ratio to sound welds without reinforcements.

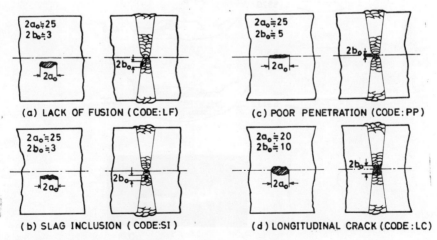

FIG. 16. Schema of location and size of various defects.

4.   Fatigue Crack Propagation from Weld Defects in 100 mm Thick Butt Joint

Propagation behaviour of a fatigue crack from a deliberately introduced internal weld defect in 100 mm thick transverse joint of A533B steel was investigated by Iida and Fujii.[5] After machining of edges and a double-U groove, a pair of plates was butt welded by manual arc welding and the reinforcements were removed flush to the level of plate surface. Defects deliberately introduced were slag inclusion, lack of fusion, poor penetration, and a longitudinal crack. All defects were produced at the mid-thickness of the specimen, as shown schematically in Fig. 16. A transverse butt joint specimen, 100 mm thick, 400 mm wide at the test section and 1000 mm in length, was stress annealed at 600°C and welded by electro-slag welding to the loading plates of a 3,000 tons low cycle fatigue testing machine. A sine-wave shaped, zero-to-tension, axial loading was applied to the specimen with cycling rate of 3 to 12 cpm. An internal fatigue crack propagating from an internal weld defect was followed by a 15 MeV betatron. After each loading of about 500 cycles, radiographs were taken while stopping the testing machine.

An example of the progressive changes in radiographs of an internal defect is shown in Fig. 17, in which schematic drawings of images are shown together with the number of cycles imposed as a parameter. Figure 18 shows an example of a fracture surface. A pattern similar to an annual ring indicates a contour line of a momentarily arrested crack front, which might be formed as a result of a rest period and possible under- and

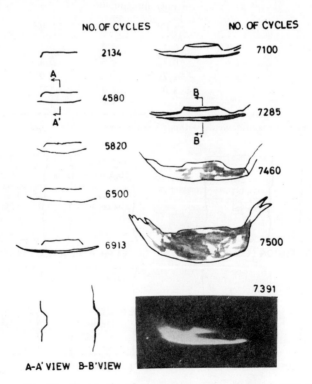

FIG. 17.   Progressive change of images in radiograph (LC-4 specimen).

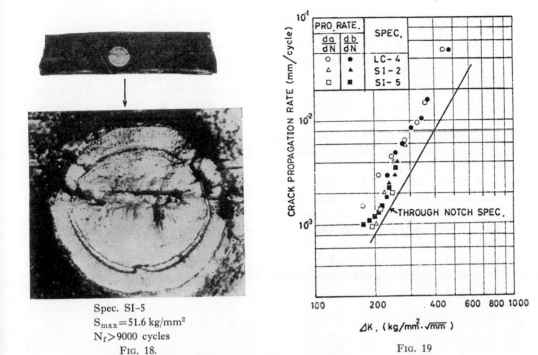

Spec. SI-5
$S_{max} = 51.6$ kg/mm^2
$N_f > 9000$ cycles

FIG. 18.   FIG. 19

FIG. 18.   Example of fracture surface.
FIG. 19.   Crack propagation rates in thickness and crosswise directions (weld metal containing internal weld defects).

over-loadings due to unexpected disturbance in the control system of the testing machine. These patterns were very helpful in evaluating the crack propagation rate in the thickness direction. In Fig. 19, fatigue crack propagation rates in the thickness as well as in the crosswise directions are plotted against ΔK value, that is calculated by equations given by Shah and Kobayashi[6] for an embedded elliptical crack. A fatigue crack which propagated from an internal weld defect showed no remarkable difference in propagation rates in the crosswise and thickness directions, while the propagation rate of a crack from a weld defect was higher than that from a through thickness notch at a given value of stress intensity factor range.

Another observation on the propagation behaviour of a fatigue crack, which started from an internal weld defect in horizontally linear shape, is that generally the length ratio of longitudinal axis to vertical axis is much larger than unity in the beginning stage of propagation, while it becomes approximately unity in its final stage.

5.   Concluding Remarks

Fatigue strength of defective butt joints and propagation behaviour of a fatigue crack, which started from an internal weld defect were described. Acceptance standards based on the expected fatigue life and required quality level for porosities and slag inclusions were proposed.

REFERENCES

1. Harrison, J. D., "The Basis for a Proposed Acceptance Standard for Weld Defects, Part 1; Porosity," Submitted for *Commission XIII of the International Institute of Welding*, Doc. XIII–624–71 (1971).
2. Harrison, J. D., "The Basis for a Proposed Acceptance Standard for Weld Defects, Part 2; Slag Inclusions," Submitted for *Commission XIII of the International Institute of Welding*, Doc. XIII–663–72 (1972).
3. Ishii, Y. and Iida, K., "Low and Intermediate Cycle Fatigue Strength of Butt Welds Containing Weld Defects," J. Society of Nondestructive Testing in Japan, Vol. 18, No. 10 (1969).
4. Ishii, Y. and Iida, K., "An Analysis of Intermediate Cycle Fatigue Strength of Defective Welded Joints," Trans. Japan Welding Society, Vol. 3, No. 2 (1972).
5. Iida, K. and Fujii, E., "Fatigue Crack Propagation from Weld Defect in 100 mm Thick Joint," Submitted for *the Second International Conference on Pressure Vessel and Piping Technology* held in Oct. 1973 in San Antonio, U.S.A.
6. Shah, R. C. and Kobayashi, A. S., "Stress Intensity Factors for an Elliptical Crack Approaching the Surface of a Semi-infinite Solid," Int. J. of Fracture Mechanics, June (1973).

Fatigue Strength of Fillet Welded Joints of Oblique Crossing Members

H. INOUE

Ship Structure Division, Ship Research Institute, Ministry of Transport

1. Introduction

Fillet welded joints of oblique cross members are commonly used in ship structure. A survey by Nippon Kaiji Kyokai[1] reports many cases of fatigue cracks originating at oblique fillet welded joints. Also, fatigue strength of oblique fillet welded joints was studied experimentally by K. Takahashi and his coworkers[2], Y. Takahashi[3-5], and the author and his coworkers[3-5].

This paper discusses the results of a series of fatigue tests in which angle of the cross members and welding procedure were varied.

2. Specimens and Test Methods

The specimen material was a 10 mm thick, rolled mild steel plate for welded structure, SM41, with chemical compositions and mechanical properties as shown in Table 1.

TABLE 1. Chemical compositions and mechanical properties.

Chemical composition					Tensile test			Bend test
C	Si	Mn	P	S	Y.P. (kg/mm²)	U.T.S. (kg/mm²)	Elong. (%)	
0.16	0.02	0.81	0.007	0.019	28	42	31	Good

Two series of specimens were tested; one with straight bevels and some lack of fusion (Type *A*), and the other with bevels prepared in such a way to eliminate the lack of fusion (Type *B*). Configurations and dimensions of the specimens are shown in Fig. 1. For each series, specimens with four different cross angles, 90° (cruciform joint), 75°, 60° and 30°, at the center plate were provided. Longitudinal direction of the speci-

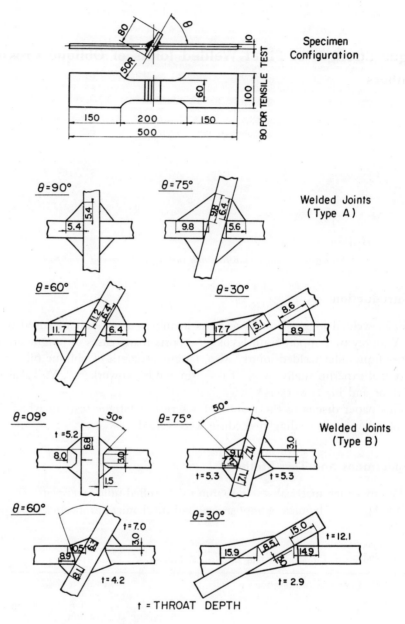

FIG. 1.   Specimen configuration.

men was parallel to the rolling direction of the plate. Welding condition and bevel shapes are tabulated in Tables 2 and 3. Specimens were welded following standard shipyard practice with no heat treatment after welding.

Static tensile tests were carried out in a 50 ton universal testing machine. For each tensile test, stress concentration and rotation of the center plate were measured

TABLE 2.   Bevel shape, welding sequence and condition (Type *A*).

Bevel Shape and Welding Sequence	Pass No.	Diameter of Electrode	Welding Current	Welding Voltage
Butt Joint	1 ~4	mm 4	amp 165	volt 27
$\theta = 30°$	1 ~ 2 3 ~10	26 4	100 165	22 27
$\theta = 60°$	1,2 3,5 4,6 7,9 8,10	4 4 4 4 4	170 165 170 165 165	27 27 27 27 27
$\theta = 75°$	1 ~ 10	4	165	27
$\theta = 90°$	1,2 3,5 4,6	4 3.2 4	165 135 165	27 25 27

by electric resistance strain gages with gage length of 1 mm and dial gages, respectively. Hardness distribution was measured with Vickers hardness tester (weight: 10 kg).

Fatigue tests were carried out under zero-to-tension load at room temperature. A cycling rate of about 2,300 cycles per minute was obtained by a resonance type mechanical driving mechanism for fatigue tests of more than 10^6 cycles. For fatigue tests of less than 10^6 cycles, a servo-hydraulic driving mechanism was used at a cycling rate of about 120 to 180 cycles per minute. No difference in fatigue life in tests conducted by the two driving mechanisms was observed.

TABLE 3.   Bevel shape, welding sequence and condition (Type B).

Bevel Shape and Welding Sequence	Pass No.	Diameter of Electrode	Welding Current	Welding Voltage	Arc Travel Speed
BUTT JOINT 2 GOUGING		mm	amp	volt	cm/min
	1	4.0	210	26	15
	2	"	220	27	"
	3	"	"	"	"
	4	"	210	"	13
	5	"	"	"	15
	6	"	"	"	13
θ = 30°	1,2	3.2	180	25	12
	5,3	"	180	"	15
	6,4	4.0	200	"	16
	7,8	"	"	"	15
	9~22	"	220	27	"
θ = 60°				volt	cm/min
	1,2	3.2	150	24	15
	5,3	"	"	"	"
	6,4	4.0	200	25	16
	7,8	"	180	24	"
	9~14	"	220	27	15
θ = 75°	1,2	3.2	150	24	15
	5,3	"	"	"	"
	6,4	4.0	200	25	16
	7,8	"	190	"	"
	9~14	"	220	27	15
CRUCIFORM JOINT	1,2	3.2	180	25	12
	3,4	4.0	"	27	16
	5~12	"	220	"	"

3.   Test Results

3.1   Static Tensile Tests and Hardness Distribution

Yield points, ultimate tensile strength and fracture stresses obtained from static tensile tests are shown in Fig. 2. The main cracks which led to final failure initiated at roots of welds in specimens with cross angles of 90°, 75° and 60° of Type A, and in the base metal for the other specimens. Specimens of Type A-90° had a lower ultimate tensile strength than the other since these specimens had longer regions of lack of fusion at the weld roots.

An example of the hardness distribution is shown in Fig. 3. The highest Vickers hardness number was about 190 in the obtuse angle side, and about 170 in the acute angle side.

3.2   Fatigue Tests

Fatigue test results are shown as S-N curves in Fig. 4. Initiation points of the main cracks are designated with letters adjacent to the plotted points in Fig. 4, where r stands

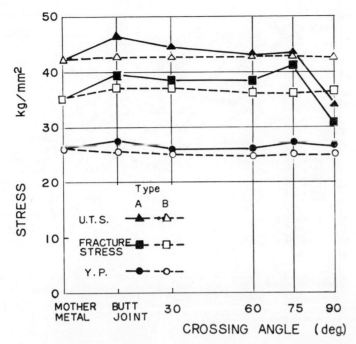

FIG. 2. Tensile test results.

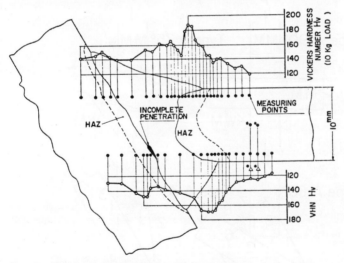

FIG. 3. Hardness distribution.

for root, t for toe, w for surface of weld metal, m for base metal, and subscripts 1 and 2 for obtuse angle side and acute angle side, respectively. Type A-90° specimens fractured by cracks initiated from the roots. Type A-75° specimens fractures by cracks which initiated mostly from r_2. Type A-60° specimens fractured by cracks which initiated from t_1 at low stress level, but by cracks from r_1 or t_2 at relatively high stress level. Type A-30° specimens fractured by cracks which started from t_1. All butt joint speci-

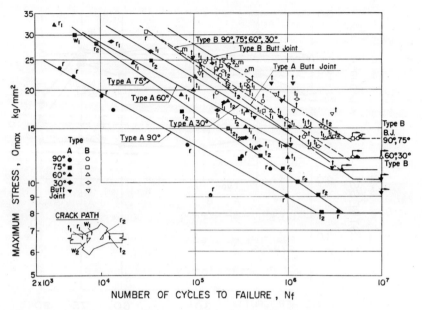

FIG. 4.   S-N curves.

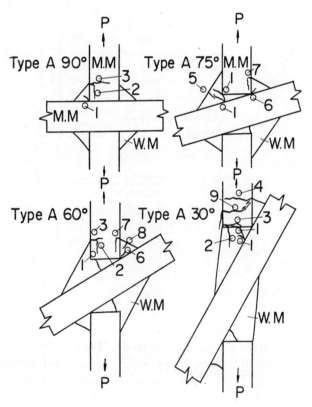

FIG. 5.   Typical crack paths.

mens fractured by cracks from toes. For Type B specimens, t_1 was almost always the initiation point of main cracks. Typical crack paths are shown in Fig. 5. In many cases, cracks were observed to initiate at critical points other than the initiation points of main cracks.

For Type A specimens, fatigue strength increased with decreased cross angle, while little difference in fatigue strength was observed among the Type B specimens with four different cross angle.

4. Discussion

4.1 Finite Element Analysis

It is widely known that the flank angle at toe has significant effect on the fatigue life and that a larger flank angle results in higher fatigue strength[6]. As shown in Fig. 4, however, almost all Type B specimens and Type A-30° specimens fractured by cracks starting form t_1. The toe with larger flank angle had a lower fatigue strength than the toe with smaller flank angle. This phenomenon was also observed by K. Takahashi[2] in Type B specimens, and he experimentally found that stress concentration at toe of obtuse angle side was higher than that at the toe of acute angle side. This means that stress concentration at the toe is determined not only by flank angle and the toe radius, but also by the overall behavior of the welded joint as a structure, such as the unbalanced compliance of fillet welds, the unbalanced partition of load on fillet, and the development of static indeterminate moment.

By means of finite element method, stress concentration factors at critical points and specimen deflections were calculated for cruciform fillet welded joints with equal or unequal leg length and Type A-60° specimen (Fig. 6). The result of this computation is shown in terms of relations between leg length and stress concentration factor as shown in Fig. 7. Soete and his coworker[7] obtained experimentally optimum fillet size for cruciform joints, such as those of Type A-90° specimen, from view point of fatigue strength as follows;

$$f/t = 0.85 \tag{1}$$

where f is the leg length of fillet, and t is the plate thickness. Ouchida and Nishioka[8] made a more comprehensive study of the optimum size of fillet also from the view point of fatigue strength, and obtained the optimum size for specimens with lack of fusion as follows;

$$
\begin{aligned}
f/t &= 1.0, && \text{for } t = 16 \, \text{mm} \\
f/t &= 0.875, && \text{for } t = 32 \, \text{mm}
\end{aligned}
\tag{2}
$$

The mesh used in the present FEM analysis was not fine enough to obtain stress concentration at the root. By assuming that the condition for stress concentration at toe is equivalent to that at root for an optimum size of fillet, $f/t = 1.0$, stress concentration factors at the roots were modified by multiplying the ratio of stress concentration factor at toe to that at root for $f/t = 1.0$, and are plotted with an asterisk in Fig. 7. Figure 7 shows that, for an equal leg length, stress concentration factor at the root is larger than the corresponding factor at the toe for $f < t$. For an unequal leg length,

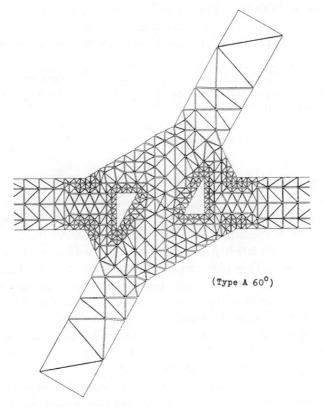

(Type A 60°)

FIG. 6.   Example of mesh division.

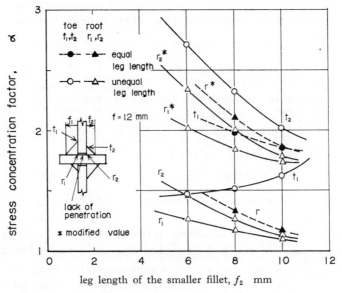

FIG. 7.   Relation between stress concentration factor and leg length (FEM analysis).

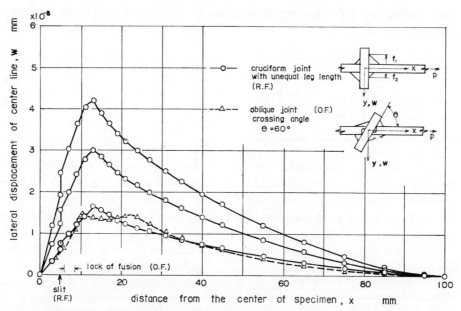

FIG. 8.   Deflections of cruciform joint specimen with unequal leg length and Type A-60° oblique joint specimen.

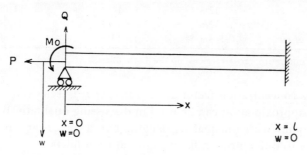

FIG. 9.   Cantilever beam model.

however, the stress concentration factor at the toe of a smaller fillet is higher than the corresponding factor at the root of a small fillet in spite of this modification.

Deflections of cruciform joint specimens with unequal leg length and Type A-60° specimen were obtained by FEM and are shown in Fig. 8. Assuming that half of a specimen can be replaced by a cantilever beam as shown in Fig. 9, relation between deflection, $w(x)$, and static indeterminate moment, M_o, was obtained as follows;

$$\frac{w(x)p}{M_o} = \frac{kl\sinh(kl)-\cosh(kl)+1}{kl\cosh(kl)-\sinh(kl)}\sinh(kx)-\cosh(kx)$$
$$-\frac{(\cosh(kl)-1)kx}{kl\cosh(kl)-\sinh(kl)}+1 \tag{3}$$

where, $k^2 = p/EI$, E is Young's modulus, I is moment of inertia, and p is tensile load.

Substituting the deflection, $w(x)$, obtained by FEM into eq. (3), M_o's were obtained as follows;

	Cruciform joint with unequal leg length			Oblique joint Type A-60°
Leg length, f_1 mm	12	12	12	—
Leg length, f_2 mm	10	8	6	—
Moment, M_o kg-mm	43.07	79.69	118.73	41.37

The bending stress caused by the bending moment, M_o, is about 1% of p/A for $f_1=12$ mm and $f_2=6$ mm, where A is the cross sectional area at the parallel part of the specimen. Therefore, the contribution of the moment to an unbalanced partition of the load can be ignored and both fillet welds may be assumed to sustain almost the same loads.

The followings are ratios of stress concentration factor to that at the corresponding site of the other angle side.

	f_1/f_2	S.C.F. at t_2 / S.C.F. at t_1	S.C.F. at r_2 / S.C.F. at r_1
Cruciform joint	12/10	1.25	1.03
With unequal	12/8	1.53	1.08
Leg length	12/6	1.84	1.14
Oblique joint Type A-60°	5.8/5.8*	1.19	0.90

* Thickness ratio at the minimum cross sections of the both fillets.

The ratio of stress concentration factor at t_2 to that at t_1 is relatively close to the value of f_1/f_2, and this approximation can be used in discussing qualitatively the fatigue strength of cruciform joint with unequal leg length. For Type A-60° specimen, this error will partly be due to differences in flank angles at both fillets.

Iida[9] analysed the effect of flank angle on stress concentration factor in a butt joint by means of the FEM procedure; For a trapezoid reinforcement, of which height was a half of the plate thickness, the stress concentration factor was 2.13 for flank angle of 60° and 1.72 for 30°. Applying those values directly to the oblique fillet joint the S.C.F. ratio at t_2 and t_1 of 1.24 is obtained. This value is close to 1.19 in the preceding table. The effects of flank angle and mean stress at the minimum cross section of fillet must, therefore, be considered in estimating the toe liable to initiate crack the most. On the other hand, the ratio of stress concentration at the root is not as sensitive as that at the toe.

4.2   Fatigue Strength of Oblique Fillet-Welded Joint

Relation between cross angle and fatigue strength is shown in Fig. 10. The ordinate stands for the ratio of the fatigue strength of fillet-welded joing to that of Type B butt joint for the same life. Fatigue strength of Type A specimens decreases with increasing cross angle and relates to the size of the region of lack of fusion. Fatigue

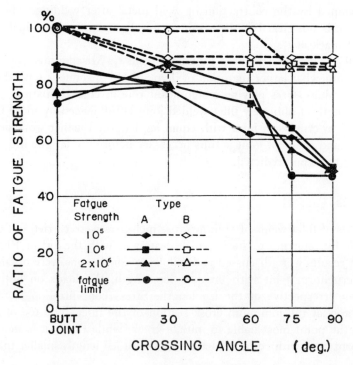

FIG. 10.   Relation between fatigue strength and cross angle of center plate.

strength of Type *B* specimens is about 85 to 90% of that of butt joint, irrespective of cross angle. The qualitative relation, however, is not applicable to the fatigue limit.

Thickness at the minimum cross section of fillet, *b*, and flank angle, α, at toe of Type *A* specimens are listed in the following.

Cross angle	Obtuse angle side		Acute angle side	
	b mm	α°	b mm	α°
75°	5.1	37	4.7	57
60°	5.8	30	5.8	60
30°	8.4	6.5	8.4	71

Type *A*-75° specimens fractured mostly by cracks from r_2 or t_2. In this case, relevant discussion in the preceding section is applicable, since the cross angle is not much different from 90°. As seen in the table, *b* of the acute angle side was somewhat smaller than that of the obtuse angle side, resulting in fracture of the fillet in the acute angle side. Therefore, fatigue strength of this type of specimen can be improved, by increasing the size of the fillet on the acute angle side.

For the Type *A*-60° specimen, FEM analysis predicted that t_2 was more liable to initiate crack than t_1. However, specimens of this type fractured almost always by cracks from the toe of obtuse angle side (t_1). In spite of careful fabrication, some misalignment developed by the contraction of weld metal after welding. The reason for this contradiction is not clear but the resultant misalignment and residual stress aided the initiation of crack at t_1.

Type A-30° specimens fractured by cracks from t_1. Misalignment of this type of specimens was somewhat larger than that of Type A-60° specimens with the misalignment and the residual stress playing a significant role in crack initiation.

Fatigue strength of obliquely fillet-welded joint is influenced by more factors than those considered in cruciform joint with equal leg length. Further work on the effect of misalignment and shape of joint is thus necessary before the fatigue life of obliquely fillet-welded joint can be predicted.

5. Conclusions

Fatigue tests of fillet welds of oblique cross members were carried out under zero-to-tension load. By referring to static tensile tests and with the aid of FEM analysis, the fatigue test results were discussed and following conclusions were obtained:

(1) For cruciform joint with unequal leg length, the loads on both fillets are almost the same irrespective of the leg length. Stress concentration factor at toe is related to the area at the minimum cross section of the fillet. The toe of the smaller fillet is always the point most liable to initiate crack, while the root is more liable for fillet in cruciform joint with equal leg length and with leg length smaller than the plate thickness.

(2) Concentrated stress at the toe of oblique joint is influenced by the flank angle.

(3) Fatigue strength of oblique joint depends on the size of the region of lack of fusion. When it is eliminated, fatigue strength more than 85% of that of butt joint for an oblique joint is attainable.

(4) The effect of static indeterminate moment due to an unbalanced compliance of fillet to fatigue strength can almost be ignored.

(5) Misalignment of specimen and residual stress are thought to influence the fatigue strength of oblique joint. Further research on the effects of misalignment and residual stress and the effect of shape of joint is necessary.

ACKNOWLEDGMENTS

The present study was carried out from 1969 to 1972 as a part of the research program of SR109 Committee of Shipbuilding Research Association of Japan. The author is grateful to the chairman of the committee, Prof. K. Terazawa, and to the members of the committee for their valuable discussions of fatigue test results. Material was provided by Nippon Steel Corporation, and specimens were fabricated by Ishikawajima Harima Heavy Industry Co., Ltd. FEM analysis was made by the FACOM 270-20 of the Ship Research Institute. The author is also grateful to Mr. M. Sakuma and Mr. H. Endo of Ship Structure Division, Ship Research Institute, for their assistance.

References

1. Kaku, S., "Damages in Welded Parts of Ship Hull and their Causes," Report of SR109 Committee (Studies of the Effects of Welded Defects and Misalignment to Strength of Ship Hull), Shipbuilding Research Association of Japan, Doc. No. 111, 1/19 (1970) (in Japanese).
2. Takahashi, K. et al., "Fatigue Strength of Obliquely Crossed Fillet Welded Joints," Int. Inst. Weld. Doc. No. XIII–570–70, (1970).
3. Takahashi, Y. and Inoue, H., "Fatigue Strength of Obliquely Crossed Fillet Welded Joints," Report of SR109 Committee, Shipbuild. Res. Assoc. of Japan, Doc. No. 111, 56/75 (1970) (in Japanese).
4. Takahashi, K. and Inoue, H., "Fatigue Strength of Obliquely Crossed Fillet Welded Joints," Report of SR109 Committee, Shipbuild. Res. Assoc. of Japan, Doc. No. 126, 57/101 (1971) (in Japanese).
5. Takahashi, Y. and Inoue, H., "Fatigue Strength of Obliquely Crossed Fillet Welded Joints," Report of SR109 Committee, Shipbuild. Res. Assoc. of Japan, Doc. No. 144, 47/82 (1972) (in Japanese).
6. Sanders, Jr., Y. W. W., Derecho, A. T. and Munse, W. H., "Effect of External Geometry on Fatigue Behavior of Welded Joints," Welding Journal, Vol. 44, No. 2, 49s/55s (1965).
7. Soete, W. and van Crombrugge, P., "A Study of the Fatigue Strength of Welded Joints," Welding Journal, Vol. 31, No. 2, 100s/103s (1952).
8. Ouchida, H. and Nishioka, A., "A Study of Fatigue Strength of Fillet Welded Joints," Hitachi Review, 3/13, Apr. (1952).
9. Iida, K. and Yamaguchi, I., "Effect of External Geometry of Reinforcement on Fatigue Strength of Welded Joints," Report of SR109 Committee, Shipbuild. Res. Assoc. of Japan, Doc. No. 126, 31/40 (1971).

Some Recent Japanese Results in the Fracture Mechanics Approaches to Fatigue Crack Problems Related to Welded Structures

H. Kitagawa

Institute of Industrial Science, University of Tokyo

1. Looking Back upon Japanese Researches on Fatigue Crack Problems

Fatigue strength of materials with a crack or a flaw had been investigated thoroughly by the late T. Ishibashi[1] and others since the 1950s following the same methods used for studying fatigue of notched specimens.

The prevailing design concept in Japan for a long time was not to allow a crack or a flaw to originate nor grow. The main objective in fatigue research was to establish the conditions for crack nucleation, fracture due to fatigue, fatigue limits, and a non-propagating fatigue crack at a notch root. Thus, fatigue crack growth was investigated only as an academic interest. During this period, the research effort in U.S. centered on fatigue crack growth studies and analysis of residual static strength of cracked structures. The results of this systematic work in Japan were collected and published by Research Committee for Surface Effects on Fatigue of the Japan Society of Mechanical Engineers in 1965[2] and by the No. 129 Committee of the Japan Science Promotion Society in 1970.[3]

Since the concept of finite fatigue life was introduced into design against fatigue, the whole S-N curve as well as the fatigue limit became important in Japan. For this, we cite two sets of data for weld defects.[3,4] The latter set of data was prepared by the 001 Committee of the Japan Society of Non-destructive Inspection and was the bases of design charts proposed by Iida, et al.[5]

Since 1950, analytical method has been used in studying fatigue crack growth in Japan too. At nearly the same time when the most significant law for fatigue crack growth rate was proposed by Paris, et al.,[6,7] and McEvily, et al.,[8,9,10] in U.S., the following law was proposed by Ishibashi[11] in Japan.

$$\frac{da}{dN} = C\left(\frac{\sigma \sqrt{a}}{\sqrt{\xi}}\right)^m \tag{1}$$

It is interesting that these three laws were proposed independently at about the same time and were based essentially on the same concept.

During this one decade, the fracture mechanics approach to fatigue crack growth studies have become increasingly popular in Japan. Some of these results related to defects in welded structures will be presented in the following from the mechanical engineering viewpoint.

2. Some Recent Results of Fatigue Problems Related to Welds by the Fracture Mechanics Approach

2.1 Basic Law of Fatigue Crack Growth

Dependency of fatigue crack growth rate on stress intensity factor (SIF), K, has been examined for various cases. The relation.

$$\frac{da}{dN} = C(\Delta K)^m \tag{2}$$

could be well applied to fatigue data of in-plane-bending of a beam,[12] out-of-plane-bending of a plate[13,14,15] and rotary bending[16] (with not-too-deep circumferential crack) as well as tension plates. This relation was reported to be valid for not only the second stage of crack growth or the first mode of crack tip deformation, but also for the mixed

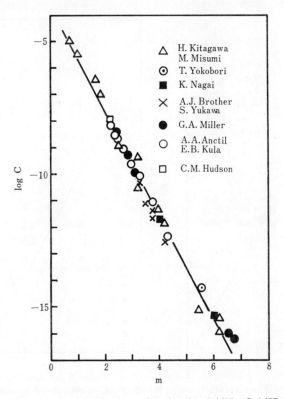

FIG. 1.   Relation between C and m for $da/dN = C \cdot (\Delta K)^m$.

modes of first and second, and first and third by Nakazawa, Kobayashi, etc.[17]

For the nominal stress range of $\sigma_n/\sigma_y < 0.9$, another relation,

$$\frac{da}{dN} = C \cdot r_s \qquad (3)$$

was proposed by Ouchida, Nishioka & Usami[18] where r_s is a cyclic plastic zone size at a crack tip.

As for the constants "C" and "m" of eq. 2, by Kitagawa and Misumi[19] established the following relation,

$$C = A/B^m \qquad (4)$$

B is about 55 for various metals, and A is about 0.5×10^{-4} for steels for ΔK represented in kg$\cdot$mm$^{-3/2}$ and da/dN in mm$\cdot$(cycle)$^{-1}$. This relation is also shown in Fig. 1. Koshiga and Kawahara[20] showed that this relation was also good for a wide range of structural steels and fairly good for all b.c.c. metals. For f.c.c. metals including austenitic steels and non-ferrous metals, the same relation can be applied, but "A" should be larger than 0.5×10^{-4}, where B is 55, as shown in Fig. 2.[20]

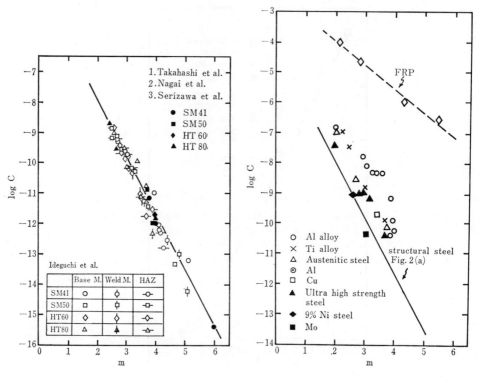

FIG. 2(a).   C-m relation of structural steels.   Fig. 2(b).   C-m relation of various materials.

In the fatigue crack growth law based on the kinetic theory by Yokobori, et al.[21,22] these parameters were formulated,[21,22] for example, as

$$m = \frac{2\beta}{1+\beta} \frac{1}{nkT} \tag{5}$$

where, "β" is a cyclic strain hardening exponent, "k" is the Boltzman constant, "T" is the absolute temperature, "n" is a material constant, $1/n = 2.26\pi\{v/(1-\nu^2)\}^{2/3}\rho$, "$v$" is effective volume created by the separation of a pair of atoms, "ν" is Poisson's ratio, and "ρ" is specific surface energy. By eq. 5, "m" was given as 4.0 for mild steel.

2.2 Fatigue Crack Growth Rate at Low Temperature

Fatigue crack growth rates at $0° \sim -160°C$ in 50 kg/mm² medium tensile strength steel plates were obtained by Hasegawa and Kawada[23] as shown in Fig. 3. It should be noted that growth rates do not change with temperature change in low temperature range.

2.3 Lower Threshold Stress Intensity Factor

"Very-slow crack growth conditions" or "no-growth conditions" had been studied prior to the emergence of fracture mechanics. Recently, a large amount of data on

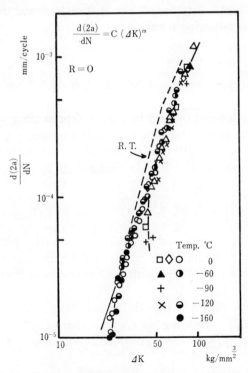

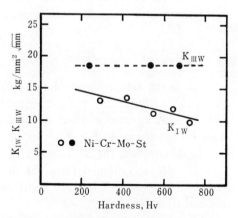

FIG. 3. Fatigue crack growth rate at low temperature ($R=0$).

FIG. 4. Dependency of K_{IW} (ΔK_{TH} of 1st mode) and K_{IIIW} (ΔK_{TH} of 3rd mode) on hardness (Vickers).

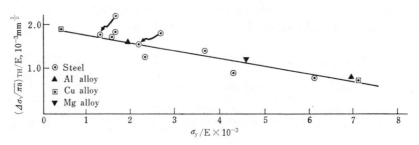

FIG. 5. Dependency of $(\Delta\sigma\sqrt{\pi a})_{TH}$ on E and σ_Y.

threshold stress intensity factors, ΔK_{TH}, were obtained by systematically conducted tests. Using data on fatigue limits of steel specimens, Ouchida and Ando[24,25] obtained ΔK_{TH} for the third mode, K_{IIIW}, and ΔK_{TH} for the first mode, K_{IW}. K_{IIIW} was independent of the hardness, and K_{IW} decreased slightly with increase in hardness, as shown in Fig. 4.

By the out-of-plane-bending fatigue tests on ten different steels, two different Al alloys and Cu alloys, and the others being Mg alloy and Ni alloy, Kitagawa and Matsumoto[26,27] obtained ΔK_{TH}. They decreased ΔK stepwise by a small amount, and finally achieved no-growth for more than 10^7 cycles, over test periods of 2 to 3 months and 2 to 3 specimens being used for each materials. All data for all the materials tested fell nearly on one line in Fig. 5, resulting in the following relation,

$$\Delta K_{TH}(\cong \Delta\sigma\sqrt{\pi a}) = A\cdot E - B\cdot\sigma_Y \tag{6}$$

where E is Young's modulus, δ_Y is yield strength and $A=1.905\times10^{-3}$, $B=1.655\times10^{-1}$ mm$^{-1/2}$ for ΔK_{TH} in kg·mm$^{-3/2}$

The notch root radius (ρ_o) at the branch point $(\alpha=\alpha_o)$ in Fig. 6, representing σ_W (fatigue limit) versus α (stress concentration factor) diagram for notched specimens, is a constant for each material. Kitagawa and Nishitani[26] then related ΔK_{TH} indirectly to σ_{w2}, fatigue limit of cracked specimen, as shown in Fig. 7, and calculated ΔK_{TH} in eq. 7 as

$$\Delta K_{TH} = C'\cdot\sigma_{wo}\cdot\sqrt{\rho_0} \tag{7}$$

σ_{wo} is the fatigue limit of unnotched specimen, and $C'\cong1.2$ for wide steel plate with double edge cracks under tension. The value of ΔK_{TH} calculated for various steels with $38\sim142$ kg/mm^2 in yield strengths, fitted fairly well with the test results of Paris, et al.,[28,29] as shown in Fig. 8.

In determining the ΔK_{TH} value by tests, the followings should be noticed;

(1)　ΔK_{TH}, obtained from the $\log(\Delta K)$ versus $\log(da/dN)$ diagram of constant load and increasing K fatigue tests, can vary with the test conditions and is not a material constant.

(2)　A crack, started from the root of a notch or a slot, will not accelerate smoothly. After a large acceleration and then decceleration, the crack can grow smoothly. Such growth are sometimes observed and affect the data.

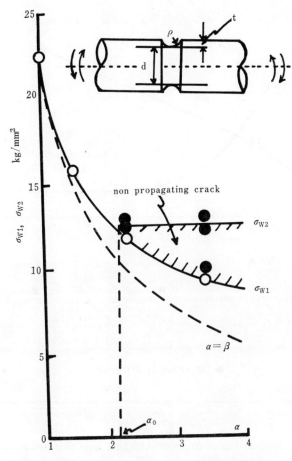

FIG. 6. Relation of σ_{W1} and σ_{W2} to stress concentration factor, α, and branch point ($\alpha = \alpha_0$).

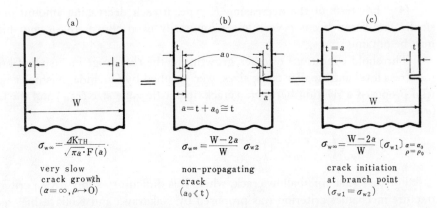

FIG. 7. Proposed model for relating stress intensity factor and the fatigue limit of notched specimen with non-propagating crack.

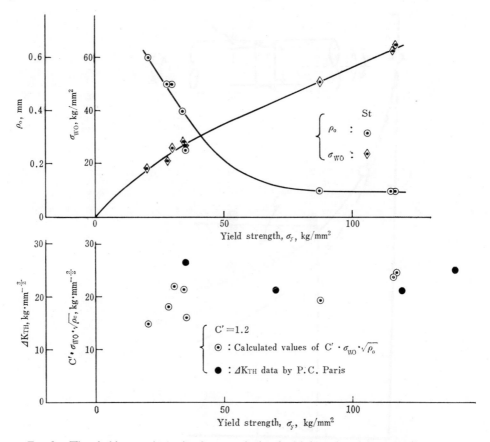

FIG. 8.   Threshold stress intensity factors calculated with branch point root radius ρ_0.

(3)   When starting from a fatigue pre-crack, over-loading larger than the test loads for pre-cracking can affect the initial crack growth rate.

(4)   For tests of the decreasing K type, if each decreasing amount or rate is not small, da/dN can become very low temporarily even above ΔK_{TH}, and higher ΔK_{TH} may be obtained.

Threshold conditions of crack growth, for the test range inclusive of higher nominal stress level and smaller crack sizes, were studied by Ouchida, Nishioka and Usami[30] who proposed a relation between a crack tip plastic zone size (r_{PW}) and the fatigue limit (σ_W) as

$$r_{PW} = \frac{K}{\pi\sigma_w{}^2}\left(\sec\frac{\pi\sigma_w}{2\sigma_Y}-1\right) = \frac{90}{\sigma_Y{}^2} \qquad (8)$$

For very small or shallow crack, where it is difficult to apply ΔK_{TH} criterion, a non-fracture mechanics criterion was proposed by Nakazawa and Kobayashi[31] as

$$(\Delta\sigma)^4{\cdot}a = \text{const} \qquad (9)$$

for fatigue limits of annealed steel obtained by cracked specimens under rotary bending and plate-tension conditions.

2.4 Effects of Mean Stress (σ_m, K_m) and Stress Ratio (R)

Based on the results of well prepared tests mostly on steels, many experimental and semiexperimental formulas have been proposed by:

a) Hasegawa·Kawada[23]

$$\frac{da}{dN} = C'(K_{\max})^A (K_{\max} - D \cdot K_{\min})^B \tag{10}$$

where A, B, D: const., $A + B = m$

b) Ouchida · Nishioka · Usami[18,32]

$$\frac{da}{dN} = C\left(\frac{K}{\sigma}\right)^2 \left\{ \sec\left(\frac{\pi\sigma}{2\sigma_Y}\right) - 1 \right\} \tag{11}$$

where true stress;

$$\sigma = \begin{cases} \sigma_{max} - \sigma_{min} : (\sigma_{min} \geqq 0) \\ \sigma_{max} \quad\quad (\sigma_{min} \leqq 0) \end{cases}$$

c) Isida·Terada, et al.[33]

$$\frac{da}{dN} = \frac{C(K_a)^A (K_{\max})^B}{(1-R)K_c - \Delta K} \tag{12}$$

where $K_a = 1/2\,(\Delta K)$, A, B: const.

d) Nakazawa · Homma[34]

$$\frac{da}{dN} = C\left(1 + \frac{K_m}{K_a}\right)^2 (\Delta K)^m \tag{13}$$

for torsion and diagonal crack

e) Kitagawa · Misumi[35,36]

$$\frac{da}{dN} = C(K_e)^m = C(K_{\max} - K_{\mathrm{com}})^m \tag{14}$$

where K_e is the effective stress intensity factor and K_{com} is the compensatory stress intensity factor

$$K_{com} = \begin{cases} C_1 K_m : & (\sigma_m > 0) \\ C_1 K_{mo} : & (\sigma_m \leqq 0) \end{cases}$$

$$C_1 = \begin{cases} 0.5 : & \text{steel} \\ 0.6 : & \text{Al alloy} \end{cases}$$

K_{mo} is initial value of $K_m\left[= \frac{1}{2}(K_{max} + K_{min}) \right]$ proportional to σ_m.

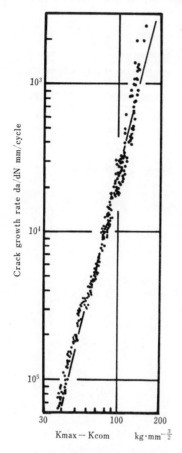

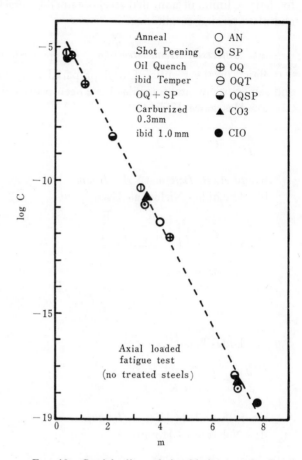

FIG. 9. $da/dN \sim \Delta K_e$ Relation for various R by author's method.

FIG. 10.   Straight line relationship between $log\ C$ and m for $d(2a)/dN = C \cdot (\Delta K)^m$ for the steels treated by various methods.

Formulae listed in a), b), d) and e) are based on the tests in the range from $R \leqq 0$ to $R \geqq 0$. In a) and e), crack closure was taken into consideration and the formulas are similar to that by Elber.[37] Results of e) are shown in Fig. 9 for various values of R.

2.5   Effects of Residual Stress

Kitagawa and Misumi[38-42] measured crack growth rates in steel plates with residual stresses generated by carburization, decarburization, shot-peening and high frequency induction hardening. A relation between the constants "C" and "m", which is same for annealed steel, is shown in Fig. 10. Effects of spot-welding, local heating were studied by Kawada, Kodama and Hasegawa,[43] and tufftride by Terazawa, Yoshioka, et al.[44]

2.6   Crack Growth under Variable Loads

Kitagawa and Fukuda[45] showed that da/dN in a steel plate under random loads is different from the results of Al alloys by Paris and Rice,[46] and that da/dN is larger than the theoretical value obtained by a linear accumulation law, that is, stress intensity factor for the same da/dN obtained by a sine wave loading is lower than this K_{eq}.

$$\frac{da}{dN} = C \int_{K_{TH}/\sqrt{\bar{K}_{TH}^2}}^{\infty} \left(\frac{K}{\sqrt{\bar{K}^2}}\right)^m P\left(\frac{K}{\sqrt{\bar{K}^2}}\right) d\left(\frac{K}{\sqrt{\bar{K}^2}}\right) = C\left(\frac{K_{eq.}}{\sqrt{\bar{K}^2}}\right)^m \tag{15}$$

For cyclic loads with periodically gradually varying amplitudes, Okamura and Naito[47] showed that da/dN can be well calculated by a "full wave method[48]"

3. Concluding Remarks

For more suitable and wider application of fracture mechanics to fatigue crack problems, the accumulation of data is required on the following problems.

(1) Fatigue crack growth under bi-axial or tri-axial loads, or given variable loads.

(2) Effects of plate thickness, high or low temperature, unusual variation of K, the second or the third mode of K, environment and structure of materials on the da/dN and ΔK_{TH} values of wide range of materials.

(3) Growth of a two or three dimensional crack, including a surface crack, and change of direction of crack growth in fatigue.

References

1. Ishibashi, T., *"Fatigue of Metals and Protection of Failure,"* Yokendo Ltd., Tokyo (1954)
2. *"Design Data of Fatigue Strength,"* Vol. II, Sec. 3 "Cracks and Surface Flaws" (arranged by J. Hoshino) Jap. Soc. Mech. Engrs. (1965).
3. Japan Science Promotion Society, Committee 129, *"Strength and Fatigue Data of Metallic Materials,"* Vol. 1, edited by Yokobori, Kawasaki & Kawada, Maruzen Ltd., Tokyo (1960).
4. Ishii, Y. and Iida, K., "Low and intermediate cycle fatigue strength of butt welds containing weld defects," J. Jap. Soc. Non-destructive Inspection, Vol. 18, No. 10, 1 (1969).
5. Ishii, Y. and Iida, K., "An analysis of intermediate cycle fatigue strength of defective welded joints," Trans. Jap. Weld. Soc., Vol. 3, No. 2, 243 (1972).
6. Paris, P. C., "Crack propagation caused by fluctuating loads," ASME-paper, 62-MET-3 (1962).
7. Paris, P. C. and Erdogan, F., "A critical analysis of crack propagation laws," Trans. ASME, D, Vol. 85, No. 4, 528 (1963).
8. McEvily, A. J. and Illg, W., "The rate of fatigue crack propagation in two aluminium alloys," NACA TN 4394 (1958).
9. Hardrath, H. F. and McEvily, A. J., "Engineering aspects of fatigue crack propagation," *Proc. Crack Prop. Symp.*, Cranfield, 231 (1961).
10. McEvily, A. J., A discussion to Paris and Erdogan's paper, "A critical analysis of crack propagation," Trans. ASME, D, Vol. 85, No. 4, 533 (1963).
11. Ishibashi, T., "Recent problems on fatigue crack propagation," Science of Machine (Kikai-no-Kenkyu), Vol. 10, No. 5, 609 (1958).
12. Muro, H., et al. "Observation of fatigue crack growth in high hardness steel," J. Jap. Soc. Str. & Frac. of Mat., Vol. 5, No. 3, 75 (1970).
13. Kitagawa, H. and Matsumoto, T., "A X-ray study on fatigue crack growth," 1st Jap. Nat.

Symp. Frac. Mech., Jap. Soc. Mech. Engrs., preprints No. 710–7, 25, June (1971).

14. Kitagawa, H. and Matsumoto, T., "Generalized law of fatigue crack growth in various metallic materials," to be published.

15. Matsumoto, T., "Studies on dependence of fatigue crack growth and its threshold upon the materials," Doctoral thesis, University of Tokyo (1973).

16. Nakazawa, H., Kobayashi, H. and Yamamoto, H., "Fatigue crack growth rate in notched specimens under rotary bending," Jap. Soc. Mech. Engrs., preprint No. 203, 149 (1969).

17. Nakazawa, H., Kobayashi, H., et al., "Fracture mechanics examination on fatigue crack growth behaviors in large steel plates," Jap. Soc. Mech. Engrs. preprint No. 720–9, 61, Aug. (1972).

18. Ouchida, H., Nishioka, A. and Usami, S. "*Proc. 3rd Intern. Cong. Fracture,*" München Vol. 6, V–442/A (1973).

19. Kitagawa, H. and Misumi, M., "An estimation of effective stress intensity factors by a crack model considering the mean stress," 1st Jap. Nat. Symp. Frac. Mech., Jap. Soc. Mech. Engrs., preprints, No. 710–7, 17, June (1971).

20. Koshiga, F. and Kawahara, M., "A proposed design basis with special reference to fatigue crack propagation," J. Jap. Soc. Naval Archtecture, Vol. 133, 249, June (1973).

21. Yokobori, T. and Ichikawa, M., "Some complementary notes to the kinetic theory of fatigue crack propagation," Rep. Res. Inst. Str. & Frac. of Mat., Tohoku Univ., Vol. 5, No. 2, 43 (1969).

22. Yokobori, T., "A kinetic approach to fatigue crack propagation," *Physics of Strength and Plasticity*, Orowan Anniversary Volume, MIT, 327 (1969).

23. Hasegawa, M. and Kawada, Y., "Fatigue crack growth rate in low temperature range and effects of mean stress," Jap. Soc. Mech. Engrs. 227th Kansai-Lecture-Meeting, preprint No. 714–10, 73, Nov. (1971).

24. Ouchida, H. and Ando, S., "The relation of fatigue strength and hardness in high carbon low alloy steels," *Proc. Symp.*, *Micro-Structure, Strength and fatigue of Medium and High Hardness Steel*, 158, Nov. (1969).

25. Anado, S., "Application of fracture mechanics to brittle fracture and non-fatigue crack propagation of steels," *Proc. 1st Intern. Conf. Mech. Beh. of Mat.*, Kyoto (1971).

26. Kitagawa, H., Nishitani, H. and Matsumoto, T., "Fracture mechanics approach to threshold conditions for fatigue crack growth," *Proc. 3rd Intern. Cong. Fracture*, München Vol. 6, V–444/A (1973).

27. Kitagawa, H. and Matsumoto, T., "Thrshold stress intensity factor for fatigue crack growth in metallic materials," Jap. Soc. Mech. Engrs., 48th Ann. Kansai-Meeting, 76, Mar. (1973).

28. Paris, P. C., "Testing for very slow growth of fatigue cracks," Closed Loop, Vol. 2, No. 5 (1971).

29. Paris, P. C., et al., "Very slow fatigue crack growth rates in a steel alloy," *3rd U.S. Nat. Symp. Fracture Mechanics*, Lehigh (1969), "Very low fatigue crack growth rates in A533 steels," "On the threshold for fatigue crack growth," ibid., 5th, Illinois (1971).

30. Ouchida, H., Nishioka, A. and Usami, S., "Initiation and growth of a fatigue crack (3rd Report; fatigue limit of steels with a crack-line flaw)," Jap. Soc. Mech. Engrs., preprint No. 710–9, 37, Oct. (1971).

31. Nakazawa, H. and Kobayashi, H., "Cyclic stress required for fatigue crack growth in carbon steels," Jap. Soc. Mech. Engrs. preprint No. 203, 141, Apr. (1969).

32. Ouchida, H., Nishioka, A. and Usami, S., "Fatigue crack growth in flat plates. (2nd Report; Effect of mean stress on fatigue crack growth rate)," Jap. Soc. Mech. Engrs. pre-

print, No. 700–2, 159, Apr. (1970).

33. Isida, M. and Terada, H., "Fatigue crack growth in metallic materials for aeroplanes," Jap. Soc. Mech. Engrs., preprint No. 710–9, 49, Oct. (1971).

34. Nakazawa, H. and Homma, H., "Effects of mean stress on fatigue crack growth rate," Jap. Soc. Mech. Engrs., preprint No. 370–1, 37, Apr. (1973).

35. Kitagawa, H. and Misumi, M., "Estimation of effective stress intensity factor considering the mean stress, " *Proc. 1st Intern. Conf. Mech. Beh. of Mat.*, Kyoto, Vol. II, 225 (1971).

36. Kitagawa, H. and Misumi, M., "Effective stress intenstity factor for fatigue crack growth rate including the effect of mean stress," Jap. Soc. Mech. Engrs., 227th Kansai Lecture Meeting, 67 (1971).

37. Elver, W., "The significance of fatigue crack closure," *ASTM STP 486*, 230 (1970).

38. Kitagawa, H. and Misumi, M., "Fatigue crack propagation due to plane bending cyclic stresses," Seisan, Inst. Industrial Science, Univ. Tokyo, Vol. 23, No. 5, 195 (1971).

39. Kitagawa, H. and Misumi, H., "Fatigue crack propagation due to plane bending cyclic stresses in carburized and quenched specimens," ibid., Vol. 23, No. 6, 244 (1971).

40. Kitagawa, H. and Misumi, M., "Fatigue crack propagation due to plane bending cyclic stresses in surface decarburized specimens," ibid., Vol. 23, No. 9, 404 (1971).

41. Kitagawa, H. and Misumi, M., "The behaviors of fatigue cracks in a high frequency induction hardened steel," Jap. Soc. Mech. Engrs. preprint No. 213, 73, Oct. (1969).

42. Kitagawa, H., Misumi, M. and Sato, K., "Effects of surface residual stresses on fatigue crack growth," Jap. Soc. Mech. Engrs., preprint No. 700–12, 277, Oct. (1970).

43. Kawada, Y., Kodama, S. and Hasagawa, "The effect of residual stress on fatigue crack propagation rate," J. Jap. Soc. Str. & Frac. Mat., Vol. 4, No. 1–2, 17 (1969).

44. Terazawa, M., Yoshioka, Y. and Asami, K., "A study on fatigue fracture of tufftride steels (1st Report; Fatigue of notched materials)," Trans. Jap. Soc. Mech. Engrs., Vol. 38, No. 310, 1142 (1971).

45. Kitagawa, H., Fukuda, S. and Nishiyama, A., "Fatigue crack growth in steels under random loading considering the thereshold condition," *Proc. 1st Intern. Conf. Mech. Beh. of Mat.*, Kyoto Vol. II, 508 (1971).

46. Paris, P. C., "The fracture mechanics approach to fatigue," *Fatigue-An Interdisciplinary Approach*, 107 (1965).

47. Naito, Y., "Studies on fatigue crack growth in various structural materials," Doctoral thesis, University of Tokyo (1974).

48. Kawamoto, M., Ishikawa, H. and Onoe, T., "On counting and programing procedures for random load by full wave method," Trans. Jap. Soc. Mech. Engrs., Vol. 37, No. 296, 658 (1971).

Elastic-Plastic Fracture Mechanics Approach to Fatigue Limit of Welded Structures

A. Nishioka and S. Usami

Hitachi Research Laboratory, Hitachi Ltd.

1. Introduction

Welded structures have an inherent strength even in the presence of defects. Thus, an optimum allowable defect size should be determined rationally with due consideration of the balance between safety and economy. This report first relates the fatigue limit of a cracked specimen and a specimen with natural defects, and then presents, as an example, a design diagram for butt welded joints with lack of penetration.

2. Fatigue Limit of Cracked Specimens[1]

Chemical compositions and mechanical properties of mild steel (JIS SM41) tested are shown in Table 1. Figure 1 shows the details of fully annealed specimens with double edge cracks. Figure 2 shows the results of alternating fatigue test. An effective

TABLE 1. Chemical composition and mechanical properties of material. (%, kg/mm²)

C	Si	Mn	P	S	σ_y	σ_B	ϕ	ψ
0.18	0.01	1.04	0.016	0.026	25.6	49.3	43.2	66.4

crack length, a_e, shown in this figure represents the half crack length of an infinite plate with the same stress and strain conditions at the crack tip as that of the specimen under the same net spection stress, σ_n. a_e is given as follows;

$$a_e = \frac{1}{\pi} \left(\frac{K}{\sigma_n} \right)^2 \tag{1}$$

where K is the stress intensity factor.

Figure 3 shows the crack tip state before and after the test. This figure clearly shows that the crack has not propagate at all in the specimen which has not failed, and that the persistent slip band zone was nearly equal to the grain diameter at the fatigue limit.

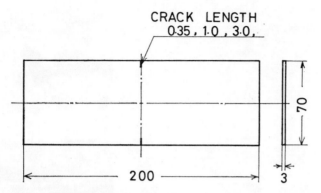

FIG. 1.   Details of test specimens.

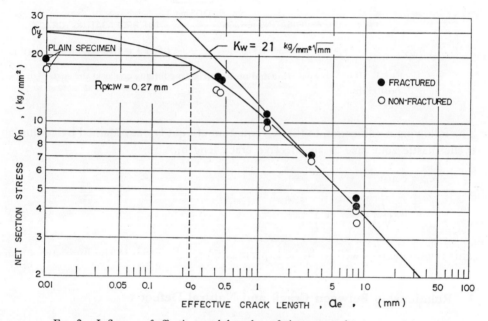

FIG. 2.   Influence of effective crack length on fatigue strength.

Hence, the cyclic plastic zone size, $R_{p(c)}$, at the crack tip must have an inherent constant value of $R_{p(c)w}$. From the results of Fig. 2, this constant value is given by the following;

$$R_{p(c)w} = \text{const.}$$

$$= a_e\left(\sec\frac{\pi\sigma_w}{2\sigma_Y} - 1\right) \tag{2}$$

This equation can also be expressed in terms of the stress intensity factor, K, when the net section stress, σ_n, is lower than 50% of yield strength, σ_Y, as;

$$K_w = \text{const.} \tag{3}$$

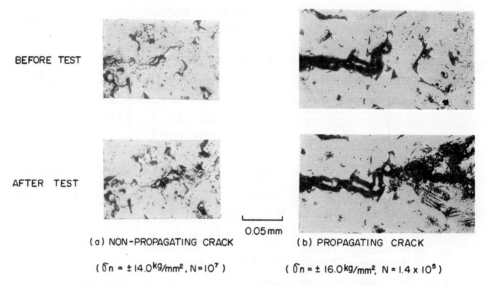

BEFORE TEST

AFTER TEST

0.05 mm

(a) NON-PROPAGATING CRACK

(b) PROPAGATING CRACK

(σ_n = ± 14.0 kg/mm², N = 10⁷)

(σ_n = ± 16.0 kg/mm², N = 1.4 x 10⁵)

FIG. 3.   Tip of propagating and non-propagating fatigue cracks at the surface of specimen a=0.35 mm.

The following modification to the K_w equation of eq. (4) was obtained by adding on the cyclic plastic zone size as an effective crack length.

$$K_w = \text{const.}$$
$$= \sigma_w \sqrt{\frac{\pi a_e}{1 - \frac{\pi^2}{8}\left(\frac{\sigma_w}{\sigma_Y}\right)^2}} \tag{4}$$

This relation agrees well with the experimental results, even in the high stress range.

3. Relationship Between Crack and Natural Defect

Figure 4 shows the fatigue limits for cracked specimens of three steels. The results in Fig. 5 for approximately 40 steels show that SM41 mild steel has the highest K_w value when σ_w/σ_Y is lower than 0.5 and the lowest and medium K_w values were obtained in quenched Cr-Mo steel[2] and eutectic steel[3], respectively.

Figure 4 also shows the test results of natural defects steel. The effective crack length, a_e, of an elliptical plane defect is expressed by

$$a_e = a/Q$$
$$Q = \frac{1}{M}\left[\int_0^{\pi/2}\left(1 - \frac{c^2 - a^2}{c^2}\sin^2\theta\right)^{1/2}d\theta\right]^2 \tag{5}$$

where M is 1 or 1.26 for the internal and the surface cracks, respectively. Specimens with natural defects, such as inclusions (SCM4, SF55), blow holes (SC46 cast steel)[4] lamellar tear defect (SM41) and lack of penetration of fillet welded joint

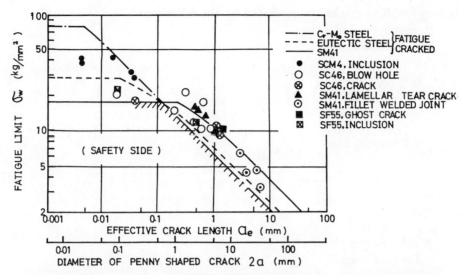

FIG. 4.   Relationship between fatigue cracked specimen and natural defect specimen.

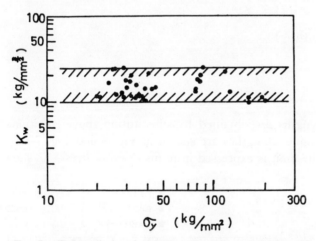

FIG. 5.   Fatigue limits of various steels with crack ($\sigma_w/\sigma_Y \ll 1$).

(SM41)[5]', have strength close to that of fatigue cracked specimens. In as-welld specimens of SM41 steel, the fatigue strength of toe is identical to that of the penny shaped crack of 3 mm in diameter and 7 mm in diameter for pulsating and alternating fatigues, respectively.

4.   Fatigue Strength of Butt Welded Joint

The strength of weld deposited metal of mild steel is very close to that of the base metal (Fig. 2). The geometry of butt welded joint with lack of penetration can be approximated with a center cracked or a side cracked plate specimen. The stress intensity factors for these cracks are expressed by the followings:

A center cracked plate;

for tensile load[6]

$$K = \sigma_n \sqrt{\pi a \sec \frac{\pi a}{T}} \left(1 - \frac{2a}{T}\right) \tag{6}$$

$$\sigma_g = \sigma_n \left(1 - \frac{2a}{T}\right)$$

for bending load[7]

$$K = \frac{\sigma_n}{2} \sqrt{\pi a \left(1 - \frac{2a}{T}\right)} \left[1 + \frac{1}{2}\left(\frac{2a}{T}\right) + \frac{3}{8}\left(\frac{2a}{T}\right)^2 - \frac{11}{16}\left(\frac{2a}{T}\right)^3 + 0.464\left(\frac{2a}{T}\right)^4\right] \tag{7}$$

$$\sigma_g = \frac{\sigma_n T}{2a} \left[1 - \left(\frac{2a}{T}\right)^3\right]$$

A side cracked plate;

for tensile load[7]

$$K = \sigma_n \sqrt{\pi a}\, k_t$$

$$\sigma_g = \sigma_n \left(1 - \frac{a}{T}\right) \tag{8}$$

for bending load[7]

$$K = \sigma_n \sqrt{\pi a}\, k_b$$

$$\sigma_g = \sigma_n \left(1 - \frac{a}{T}\right)^2 \tag{9}$$

The effective crack lengths are obtained by substituting above equations to eq. (1). The corresponding fatigue strengthes are shown in Fig. 6 and Fig. 7 respectively. In these figures the fatigue limit is expressed in terms of gross stress. As shown in Fig. 6

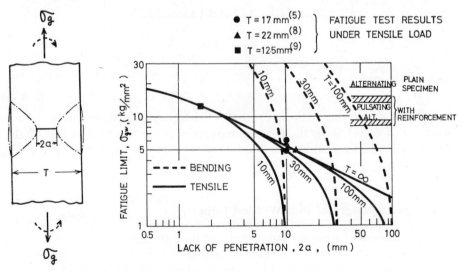

FIG. 6.   Fatigue strength of double grooved butt welded joint with lack of penetration.

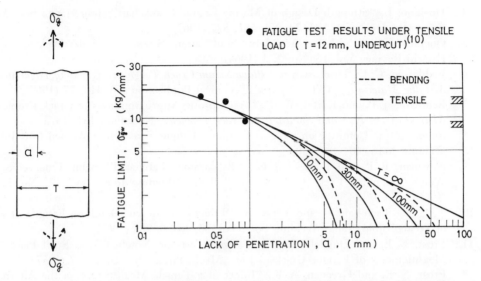

FIG. 7.   Fatigue strength of single grooved butt welded joint with lack of penetration.

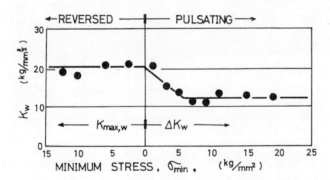

FIG. 8.   Effect of mean stress on fatigue strength of cracked 0.22%C steel.

and 7 the test results of specimens with lack of penetration[5,8,9] and with undercut[10] have strength close to the above theoretical values.

Figure 8 shows the effect of mean stress on fatigue strength of cracked 0.22% carbon steel[11,12].

REFERENCES

1. Ouchida, H., Nishioka, A. and Usami, S., "Elastic-Plastic Approach to Fatigue Crack Propagation and Fatigue Limit of Material with Crack," Preprint of 3rd International Conference on Fracture, München V–442/A (1973).
2. Ando, S., "Brittle Fracture Strength and Non-Crack Propagation," *Proc. International Conference on Mechanical Behavior of Materials*, Kyoto, Vol. 1, 331 (1972).
3. Kobayashi, H. and Nakagawa, H., "Stress Criterion for Fatigue Crack Propagation," ibid., Vol. 2, No. 199 (1972).

4. Hoshino, J., "Strength Design of Marine Engine Crankshaft," Jour. Japan Soc. Mech. Engrs. (in Japanese), Vol. 70, No. 581, 827 (1967).

5. Ouchida, H. and Nishioka, A., "A Study of Fatigue Strength of Fillet Welded Joints," Hitachi Review, Vol. 13, No. 2, 3 (1964).

6. Feddersen, C. E., Discussion to *Plane Strain Crack Toughness Testing of High Strength Metallic Materials*," ASTM Special Technical Puplication No. 410, 77 (1967).

7. Benthem, J. P. and Koiter, W. T., "Asymptotic Approximations to Crack Problems," *Method of Analysis and Solutions to Crack Problems*, Noordhoff 131 (1973).

8. Report of the Comittee on Fatigue Testing, "Fatigue Strength of Welded Butt Joints," Welding Jour., 404–S (1950).

9. Newman, R. P. and Dawes, M. G., "Exploratory Fatigue Tests on Transverse Butt Welds Containing Lack of Penetration," British Welding Jour., Vol. 12, No. 3, 117 (1965).

10. Tada, T., Tachibana, I. and Terao, S., "Effect of Undercut Depth on Fatigue Strength of Welds," Jour. Japan Welding Soc., Vol. 30, No. 6, 387 (1961).

11. Frost, N. E. and Dugdale, D. S., "Fatigue Tests on Notched Mild Steel Plates with Measurements of Fatigue Cracks," Jour. Mech. Phys. Solids, 5, 182 (1957).

12. Frost, N. E. and Greenan, A. F., "Effect of a Tensile Mean Stress on the Alternating Stress Required to Propagate an Edge Crack in Mild Steel," Jour. Mech. Engng. Sci., Vol. 9, No. 3, 234 (1967).

Deflection-Controlled Fatigue Strength of Fillet Welded Joints with Doubling Plates

K. KISHIMOTO

Chiba Laboratory, Mitsui Shipbuilding and Engineering Co., Ltd.

1. Introduction

Fillet welded joint with doubling plate, which is commonly used in ship structures, has a long sharp notch whose length depends on the width of the plate and is

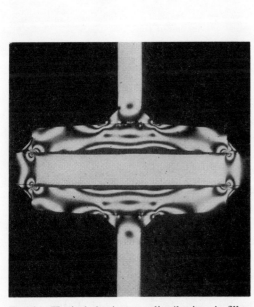

FIG. 1.   Typical elastic stress distributions in fillet joint with doubling plate under tensile load.

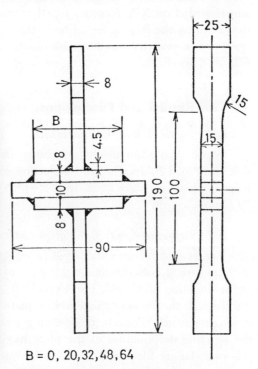

B = 0, 20,32,48,64

FIG. 2.   Dimensions of specimens.

subjected to deflection due to wave force. Fatigue failure of the fillet joint may occur at the notch tip, that is root of weld, or any toe of the fillet weld which are location of stress concentrations as shown in Fig. 1. This paper reports results of fatigue tests of fillet joints under deflection-controlled conditions.

2. Test Procedures

2.1 Specimens

Chemical compositions and mechanical properties of material used for specimens are shown in Table 1. As shown in Fig. 2 dimentions of the specimens varied from 0 to 64 mm in width of the doubling plate with thickness of 8 mm. The leg length of fillet weld was regulated to 4.5 mm by cutting. Hardness of the deposited metal was H_v 150–160 after postweld heat treatment.

TABLE 1. Chemical compositions and mechanical properties.

C	Si	Mn	P	S	YP (kg/mm^2)	UTS (kg/mm^2)
0.18	0.01	0.48	0.012	0.041	27.4	41.5

2.2 Test Method

Cyclic deflections in gauge length of 50 mm was measured by a deflection gauge and recorded on X-Y recorder together with axial load. It was held within a constant range during the fatigue test. Local strain range and strain distributions in the fatigued specimen were determined by the photoelastic coating which was applied to the surface of a specimen.

3. Test Results and Discussions

3.1 Static Tensile Characteristics

Static tensile test results are shown in Fig. 3 and 4. The maximum load P_m and flow limit load P_f decrease and deflection at the maximum load δ_{pm} increases as the slit length, which is nearly equal to the width of the doubling plate B, increases above 20 mm in length.

3.2 Deflection-Controlled Fatigue Strength

Figure 5 shows an example of failed specimen, in which locations of fatigue crack initiation are at both the root and the toe of fillet welds. Final failure occurred generally at the doubling fillet weld. For Type D($B=48$ mm) specimens, however, failure occurred through thickness of the doubling plate at the toe of Tee fillet welds. When a toe crack propagated through the doubling plate, the load range suddenly decreased since the bending deformation of the plate increased under a constant deflection range. In this case, failure life was defined as the number of cycles where a sudden drop in absorbed energy, defined as area surrounded by hysterisis loop, occurred. Fatigue tests could not be carried out due to buckling for Types A and B specimens.

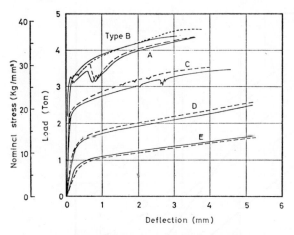

FIG. 3. Static load-deflection curves, $G.L. = 50$ mm.

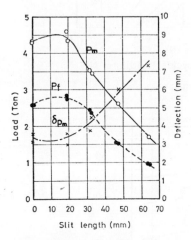

Fig. 4. Results of static tensile tests.

FIG. 5. Example of failed specimen.

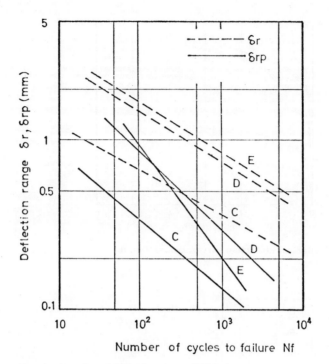

FIG. 6.   Results of deflection-controlled fatigue test.

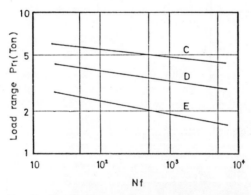

FIG. 7.   Representation of the test results in terms of load range.

Results of deflection-controlled fatigue tests are shown in Fig. 6. Note that Type E($B=64$) mm specimen has the highest strength in terms of total deflection range, δ_r, but in the plastic deformation range, δ_{rp} for Type D specimen is the highest. On the other hand, representation in terms of the initial load range, P_{r1} ($N=1/4$–$3/4$), vs. failure life shows that Type C($B=32$ mm) specimen has obviously the highest strength as expected from the statical features (Fig. 7). Hysterisis energy W_1 for the initial cycle ($N=1/4$–$1^1/_4$) are represented in terms of failure life in Fig. 8.

It is clear from this figure that Type D specimen is superior in energy absorption.

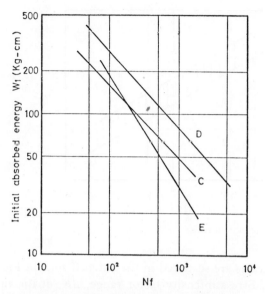

FIG. 8.   Initial absorbed energy vs. failure life.

This means that plastic deformation in Type D specimen is produced relatively uniform. The same tendency is shown for the accumulated hysterisis energy to failure, W_f, which increases with failure life as $W_f \propto N_f^{0.2\sim0.3}$

As generally known, fatigue strength might depend on cycling range of the local plastic strain, ε_{rp}, or on the stress intensity factor range, ΔK, as follows;

$$\varepsilon_{rp} \cdot N^n = \text{Const.} \quad \text{or} \quad N_p = \int_{a_0}^{a_f} \frac{da}{C(\Delta K)^m}$$

An attempt was made to determine the local strain range, ε_r, by the photoelastic coating method. A typical strain distribution at the maximum cycling load is shown in

FIG. 9.   Typical strain distributions under cycling load (Type D).

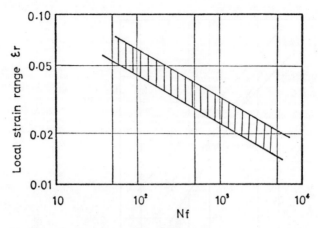

FIG. 10.   Strain range *vs.* failure life.

Fig. 9. The measured local strains are scattered in the hatched zone in Fig. 10 and are not related to the slit length. Stress intensity factor range, ΔK, at the tip of the slit could be predicted from the measured elastic stress distributions, such as that in Fig. 1.

The results represented in terms of ΔK showed that failure life was not too dependent on ΔK as predicted. This may be due mainly to the excessive plastic strain in failed region.

4. Concluding Remarks

Fatigue tests on the fillet welded joints with the doubling plates with thickness of 8 mm and width from 0 to 64 mm were carried out under deflection-controlled conditions. The results showed that optimum dimensions for fatigue strength, in which the plastic deformation is uniformly produced absorbing the deformation energy, do exist and that the failure life depends on the local strain range as predicted. Future study should include study of fatigue strength in the higher cycle region and improvement in the accuracy of the local strain measurements.

Discussions in Session IV

Question and comment directed to Prof. Iida by Prof. Fisher

In groove welded joints the residual stresses through the thickness are such that the midpoint of the weldment is in a region of residual compressive stress. This is particularly true with thicker plates and small plate type specimens. Will this not result in an overestimate of the fatigue strength in butt welded joints with discontinuities in the residual compression zone?

Design curves for defective joints should consider this fact, since a large class of joints may have residual tensile stresses superimposed from other welded sequences or restraint conditions.

It also appears that the slope of the S-N curve should be independent of the function α_s. Since structural grade steels exhibit a common growth rate, changes in the slope are more likely related to difficulties in defining the initial crack size a_0, the residual stress field and an accurate estimate of the state of stress that the discontinuity is subjected to.

Also, could the residual stresses account for some of the differences associated with internal flaws and surface flaws?

Reply to Prof. Fisher by Prof. Iida

In response to the first question raised by Prof. Fisher, the author would like to mention, first of all, that residual stresses in a specimen used in the tests, of which results are described in section II of the author's paper, may be negligibly small from the viewpoint that residual stresses should be taken into account as an influencing factor in decreasing or increasing high cycle fatigue strength, because both width and thickness of the specimen are small. This author, as a general consideration, agrees with Prof. Fisher's suggestion that residual compression stress in the midpoint of the weldment may contribute in increasing the high cycle fatigue strength in butt welded joints containing internal weld defects in a region of compressive residual stress, as compared with the case where they exist in a region of tensile residual stress. This author, however, should like to emphasize that both the increasing effect of residual compressive stress and the decreasing effect of residual tensile stress on the high cycle fatigue strength may be a small extent as compared with the value of residual stress itself. It may be helpful to refer here to an example of the influencing effect of residual stress on the high cycle fatigue strength. The example is given by a work by Prof. Serensen et al.[1], who reported

---

1) Serensen, S. V., Trufiakov, V. I. and Koryagin, J. A., "Residual Stresses and Fatigue Resistance of Welded Joints," International Institute of Welding, Doc. No. XIII-436-66 (1966).

that the endurance limit in repeated axial load fatigue S_o was related with the residual stress σ_{res} with the relation of

$$S_o = 14.7 - 0.36\,\sigma_{res} \quad \text{(kg/mm}^2\text{)}$$

in the range of residual stress -2 to 15 kg/mm², where yield point and ultimate tensile strength of the material were 34.5 kg/mm² and 52.3 kg/mm², respectively.

This author also agrees with Prof. Fisher that design curves for defective butt joints in actual structures should include the effect of residual tensile stresses that are introduced by highly restrained conditions in welding. But a question naturally arises here as to what extent the effect of tensile residual stress should be taken into account as a decreasing factor of the fatigue strength. An exact reply to this question should be based on the value of estimated or measured residual stresses as well as results of investigations on the effect of residual stresses on fatigue strength.

As to the slope of S-N curve, this author can not agree, from an academic viewpoint, with Prof. Fisher's opinion that the slope of the S-N curve should be independent of the function α_s. Test results shown in Figs. 2 to 8 in my paper are ploted against the failure life, which consists of fatigue crack initiation life and propagation life. In general, it is well known that the slope of a S-N curve depends upon such factors as notch sharpness, material, stress ratio and others. The author has the feeling that the function of α_s may be a kind of notch sharpness. However, it may be an easy way to assume the slope of the S-N curve to be the same from the practical viewpoint of constructing design curves for defective butt welded joints.

As for the last comment by Prof. Fisher, this author's feeling is that the residual stresses can not be helpful in evaluating the differences associated with internal flaws and external flaws, by the reason mentioned in the opening sentences. The difference in fatigue strength may be due to the difference in the stress concentration factor.

Comment directed to Mr. Inoue by Prof. Fisher

In welded joints with $\theta=0$ and partial penetration, the stress intensity factor at the weld root can be estimated by[2]

$$K = \frac{\sigma_{pl}}{(1+2h/t)}\,[C_1 + C_2\{a/(t/2+h)\}]\,\sqrt{\pi a}\,\sqrt{\sec\left(\frac{\pi a}{t+2h}\right)}$$

Where

$$C_1 = 0.528 + 3.287\frac{h}{t} - 4.361\left(\frac{h}{t}\right)^2 - 3.696\left(\frac{h}{t}\right)^3 - 1.875\left(\frac{h}{t}\right)^4 + 0.415\left(\frac{h}{t}\right)^5$$

$$C_2 = 0.2184 + 2.717\frac{h}{t} - 10.171\left(\frac{h}{t}\right)^2 + 13.122\left(\frac{h}{t}\right)^3 - 7.755\left(\frac{h}{t}\right)^4 + 1.783\left(\frac{h}{t}\right)^5$$

The joint geometry is shown in Fig. 1.

σ_{pl}=stress in the plate
h=weld height
t=plate thickness
$2a$=degree of partial penetration or crack size

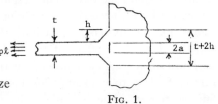

FIG. 1.

---

2) Frank, K. H., "The Fatigue Strength of Fillet Welded Connections," PhD Dissertation, Lehigh University, Bethlehem, Pa., 1971.

Although crack growth at the weld toe is directly related to the stress concentration factor K_T (see discussion of stress-intensity factors for part-through cracks at weld toe session 3), the condition at the weld root appears to be more easily related to the stress intensity factor K for a through thickness crack.

The relative severity of the weld toe can be compared to the weld root by considering the stress intensity factors for these locations.

Reply to Prof. Fisher by Mr. Inoue

Thank you for your suggestive discussion. I think that we still have a difficulty in applying K-value approach to the cracks to initiate at weld toe, as far as the initiation of fatigue crack concerns. Anyway, I am planning to re-examine the data, and I will try to apply K-value approach to the problem.

Comment directed to Prof. Kitagawa by Prof. Fisher

Care needs to be exercised in determining crack growth rates for fatigue life estimates of welded built-up structures. Most structural components will have initial discontinuities and applied stress ranges that result in crack growth rates less than 10^{-6} inches/cycle.

Measurements of crack growth are often made at rates greater than 10^{-6} inches/cycle. The extrapolation of these rates into the lower crack growth rate levels can result in substantial error predictions of fatigue life.

Figure 2 shows crack growth rates in A36 steel above and below 10^{-6} inches/cycle. It is visually apparent that the exponent in the region between 10^{-8} and 10^{-6} inches/cycle differs from the slope between 10^{-6} and 10^{-4}. A transition to a crack growth threshold appears to occur between 10^{-8} and 10^{-9} inches/cycle.

Since most welded structural details exist in structures where crack growth will occur at the lower crack growth rates it appears desirable to focus crack growth studies in that region.

Comment directed to Prof. Iida by Prof. Kabayashi

Dr. Shah and I have recently computed the stress intensity magnification factor for an elliptical crack in a finite thickness plate. This paper will be presented at the coming ASME 1973 Winter Meeting, Detroit. The new magnification factor will shift the data points in Fig. 19 in Prof. Iida's paper and will bring the experimental points closer to the straight line marked "through notch specimen." This correction will be in the opposite direction of that just mentioned by Prof. Fisher.

Reply to Prof. Kobayashi by Prof. Iida

The author gratefully acknowledges Prof. Kobayashi's interesting comment, which may be a great stimulus for further discussion of Fig. 19 in the author's paper.

Question directed to Prof. Miyamoto by Prof. Kobayashi

Was a kinematic strain hardening used in the elastic-plastic finite element analysis? Has the author compared the unloaded states in isotropic and kinematic strain hardening materials?

I also wish to congratulate the authors for their timely analysis of an important problem of crack closure which is currently commanding much attention in the United States. I look forward to seeing further results from these authors.

276

Reply to Prof. Kobayashi by Prof. Miyamoto

We used isotropic hardening. We have not yet compared the unloaded states in isotropic and kinematic strain hardening materials. But the comparison may be not hard, and we would like to try it in near future.

Comment directed to Prof. McEvily by Prof. Fisher

In his concluding remarks Prof. McEvily has noted that variable amplitude loading has not been discussed. Only constant amplitude cyclic loading was considered. Recent studies by Barsom[3] have shown that the crack growth rate in structural steels under

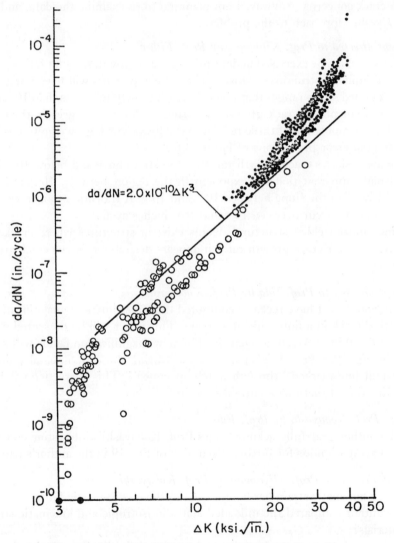

FIG. 2.   Crack growth rates in A36 steel near crack growth threshold.

3)   Barsom, J. M., "Fatigue-Crack Growth Under Variable Amplitude Loading in ASTM A514-B Steel," *ASTM STP 536*, 1973.

variable amplitude loading is the same as constant amplitude cyclic loading when the rootmean square (*RMS*) of ΔK is used. Thus

$$\Delta K = \Delta K_{RMS} \tag{1}$$

provides the same growth rate.

Thus in structural steels, a direct relationship can be obtained. These crack growth studies are also compatible with fatigue tests on structural details where random variable loading was used.[4,5]

Reply to Prof. Fisher by Prof. McEvily

I think Prof. Fisher's comments with respect to Barsoms' findings on the use of a *RMS* value of ΔK to analyze crack growth under variable amplitude loading are of interest. However, there are loading conditions which lead to either significant or complete retardation of crack growth, and it is particularly with respect to this problem area that I think some additional insight which results in quantitative analysis would be useful.

The example which you have cited of crack growth in a nominally compressive region is somewhat difficult to understand. How do the rate of crack growth in this region compare with that of cracks in the nominally tensile region? On another point, with respect to the lifetime plots, the lines are of the order of 10^6 cycles or less. In such a case what were the initial growth rates involved. It seems to be that they should be above 10^{-7} inches per cycle, but perhaps rates as low as 10^{-9} inches per cycle were involved in your analysis. It has been my experience that where the environment is not a factor, the threshold level expresses a strong influence in retarding growth rates between 10^{-8} and 10^{-6} inches per cycle, and I wondered therefore about the effect of the threshold level in your calculations. If for the steel investigated initial crack growth rates of the order of 10^{-9} inches per cycle are involved, then I would think the lifetime might be 10^8 cycles or so. For civil structures such a lifetime might be quite satisfactory.

Reply to Prof. McEvily by Prof. Fisher

In welded structures with their normal fabrication discontinuities most of the life is consumed propagating the crack at growth rates less than 10^{-6} inches/cycle. Figure 9 of my paper shows the stages of crack growth in a plain welded beam. More detailed discussion is given in a paper by Hirt et al.[6]

At a bending stress range of 18 ksi crack growth rates varied from 10^{-8} to 5×10^{-6} as the discontinuity grew from its initial size through the flange thickness as illustrated in Fig. 3. Approximately 5 million cycles of stress range were applied during this change in crack size.

4) Fisher, J. W., Frank, K. A., Hirt, M. A. and McNamee, B. M., "Effect of Weldments on the Fatigue Strength of Steel Beams," NCHRP Report 102, Highway Research Board, 1970.

5) NCHRP Project 12–12, "Fatigue Strength of Steel Beams under Random Loading," Highway Research Board, work now in progress.

6) Hirt, M. A. and Fisher, J. W., "Fatigue Crack Growth in Welded Beams," Engineering Fracture Mechanics, Vol. 5, 415/429 (1973).

278

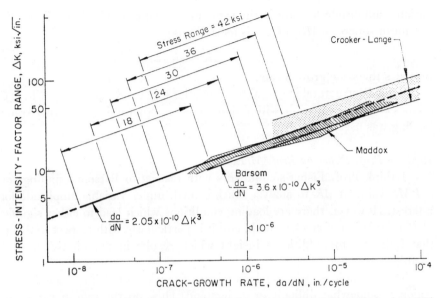

FIG. 3. Ranges for crack growth in welded girder from an initial discontinuity (a_i=0.04 in. radius) to its penetration of flange.

Comment by Prof. Rolfe

Regarding the selection of a particular test specimen to analyze the fracture behavior of a material, you have to model the particular service condition. There are cases where, for example, the very high strength steels, the fracture mechanics approach works best. There are other cases where it does not work, and then some other test specimen such as the COD should be used. But, I think fracture mechanics did tell us one very quantitative thing, which we knew qualitatively, and that is that if you know the stress, and you have a flaw and you know the K_c of the material, you can establish a failure curve. As long as you are at some K_I level where the combination of stress and flaw size is less than K_c, your structure is safe. Now fracture mechanics gave us the initial quantitative understanding to be able to quantitatively relate stress, flaw size, and material toughness. Then as you have very properly pointed out, there are cases where the K_c concept does not work, but we'd like to be able to substitute a COD Value or a J_c value. Thus when we have a situation where we know the stress and flaw size, and they are both large, we can state the need to increase the material toughness, whether it's in terms of K_c, K_{IC}, COD or J. We'd like to be albe to get to a point of being able to handle this analysis analytically for the lower strength materials in the same way that for the very high strength materials we can handle the K concept analytically. But fracture mechanics did one very large thing and that's put it on a basic quantitative level for those materials for which it works. Fortunately, fracture mechanics does not work for very many low-strength structural materials, because if it did, we should not be using them.

Comment by Prof. Packman

I think the point made with regard to threshold fatigue crack growth is very significant. The existence of fatigue crack growth threshold and then questions of how you measure it. One must remember that when one measures growth rates of 10^{-9} inches per cycle, we are integrating the growth over a large number of cycles. Obviously anything that is growing at 10^{-9}, 10^{-10} inches per cycle is not growing continuously, but growing intermittently.

There is a phenomena known as acoustical fatigue in which there is crack growth rates on the order of 10^{-12} inches per cycle because the crack is growing under the influence of acoustical stress pulses which are extremely small. Thus there may be some question as to the existance of a threshold stress intensity range below which a crack "will not grow".

Professor Fisher's comment with regard to Dr. Barsom's work primarily refers to a randomly applied load spectrum, in which there is no prior sequencing of loads. In that type of fatigue crack growth, using the *RMS ΔK* value for growth prediction would be most appropriate, since there is an almost pure random loading sequence. However as Prof. McEvily has pointed out there are situations, particularly aircraft and pressure vessel loading condtions for which the sequence is not truly random. The loading sequence in an aircraft engine or a pressure vessel is very well known, or at least the sequence is less random than loading of a bridge. In these cases, Prof. McEvily's comment that the crack growth predictions under these specific load level interactions are not well acounted for using *RMS ΔK* values, but have to be accounted for using the appropriate retardation analysis.

To discuss Prof. Fisher's comment, there are significant fatigue crack load interaction phenomena even though the peak loads are not more than 10 to 20% above the baseline loads. If the peak overload gets above twice the baseline, you may get complete stoppage of the crack. So you may get significant life prediction changes even though the overloads are relatively small *ΔK* changes.

SESSION V
APPLICATIONS OF FRACTURE MECHANICS TO WELDED STRUCTURES

A Brittle Fracture Criterion Based on the Plastic Zone Size

F. Koshiga

Nippon Kokan Kabushiki Kaisha

1. Introduction

Defects in welded structures are often surrounded by well-developed plastic zones. The COD concept[1] is more suitable for evaluating the significance of such defects than the concept of linear elastic fracture mechanics[2]. When compared with K-value calculation, however, COD determination for in-service conditions requires a much more complicated calculation. Fracture philosophy by means of the plastic zone size is similar to the COD concept, but has the added advantage that the zone size is easily determined by K-value cancellation of the Dugdale crack model.[3] The present paper begins with an introductory note on the plastic zone size concept. Next, several examples involving practical applications of this concept are described. Finally, a simple method of determining the material toughness in terms of the plastic zone size approach, in combination with the critical COD measurement, is proposed.

2. A Note[4] on Plastic Zone Size Concept

The Dugdale crack model is usually applied to the COD calculation. Theoretically speaking, however, no basis exists for its applicability to problems of any quantity other than stresses. On the other hand, plastic zone size, ρ^+, as defined in Fig. 1 is not accompanied with such a logical difficulty, for it is derived from stress calculation only. The symbol σ_Y in this figure means the yield strength of material. While the plastic zone size is symbolized as ρ by Hahn et al.,[5] the superscript $(+)$ is attached in the present paper for a special reason. The surface traction along the zone ρ^+ should be equal to the yield strength at the temperature the material is exposed to.

Consider, for example, the crack tip plastic yield region shown in Fig. 1. If the material is uniformly cooled under constant applied tensile load, the superscript $(+)$ should be removed since the yield strength increases as the temperature decreases while the stress distribution remains constant. Any additional tensile load will provide

283

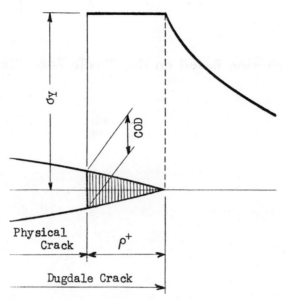

FIG. 1.   Conditioned plastic zone size ρ^+.

a new ρ^+. If the tensile load is lowered or removed, a compressive yield zone (denoted by ρ^-) is formed. The fracture criterion in the present paper states that brittle fracture initiates when ρ^+ attains the upper limit (denoted by ρ_c^+) which can be sustained by the material. The ρ^+ concept is related not only to deformation but also to force, since the extent of the plastic zone as a deformation measure is conditioned by the super-script (+) for the tensile yield stress as a force measure.

3.   Practical Applications of ρ^+ Concept

3.1   Effects of Welding Residual Stress on the Failure Stress of Welded Structures[6]

Using the deeply notched tension specimens shown in Fig. 2 (a), ρ_c^+ can be determined as a function of temperature through the relation;

$$\sin (\pi c/W)/ \sin [\pi(\rho_c^+ + c)/W] = \cos (\pi\sigma/2\sigma_Y). \tag{1}$$

By varying the dimensions of c and W and the steel (yield strength of 30 kg/mm² to 80 kg/mm² at room temperature), the author has found a simple empirical expression, i.e.

$$\rho_c^+ = \alpha(T/100)^5, \tag{2}$$

where T is the absolute temperature and α is a material constant. If the distribution of welding residual stress around a defect in welded structure is known, the ρ^+-value corresponding to any applied load σ can be calculated by using the Dugdale model. Substituting the ρ_c^+ in eq. (2) for this ρ^+-value, the failure load of welded structure can be determined as a function of temperature.

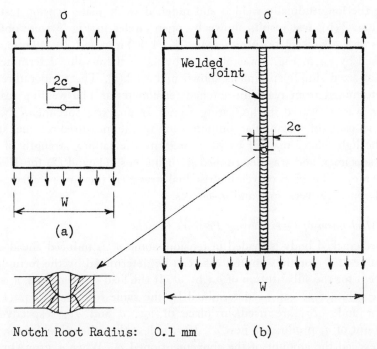

Notch Root Radius: 0.1 mm

FIG. 2. (a)   Deeply notched tension test specimens and (b) Welded-and-notched wide plate tension test specimen.

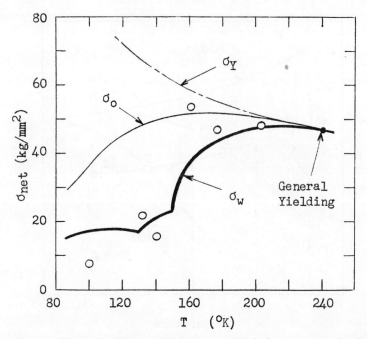

FIG. 3.   Effect of welding residual stress on brittle fracture strength of structure.

Using the longitudinally welded and notched, wide plate, tension test specimens shown in Fig. 2 (b), test results shown by open circles in Fig. 3 were obtained. The dimensions of the wide plate specimen are $W=1,000$ mm and $2c=40$ mm. The heavy curve marked by σ_W in Fig. 3 was obtained by using the α-value determined by small- and medium-sized simple specimens shown in Fig. 2 (a). The temperature-dependent σ_Y was determined from plain un-notched tension tests. The welding residual stress distribution was measured in the testing section of an extra specimen. Two cusps on the σ_W-curve came of rectangular simplification of the measured residual stress distribution. The light curve marked by σ_o represents the failure strength of a residual stress free specimen and was determined by using eqs. (1) and (2) for $W=1,000$ mm and $2c=40$ mm. The effect of welding residual stress, viz the Greene effect is illustrated by the difference between σ_W- and σ_o-curves.

3.2   Mechanism of Overstressing Pressure Vessels[4)]

If a pre-cracked body is loaded in tension, some ρ^+ is induced ahead of the crack tip. The value of ρ^+ for the simplest case can be determined by the formula similar to eq. (1) except for the substitution of ρ_c^+ by ρ^+. If the load σ is removed, a ρ^- is brought about. The value of ρ^- can be determined by the same formula as eq. (1), provided that ρ^-, $-\sigma$ and $-2\sigma_Y$ are used in place of ρ_c^+, σ and σ_Y, respectively. Reload by the amount of σ_1 produces a new ρ^+. If σ_1 is less than the initial load σ, the new ρ^+ can never exceed the amount of the abovementioned ρ^-. When σ_1 grows beyond σ, the ρ^+ increases with a jump from ρ^- to the initial ρ^+.

These preliminaries are concerned with any fixed temperature, but they are very useful to understand the mechanism of overstressing for reducing the risk of brittle

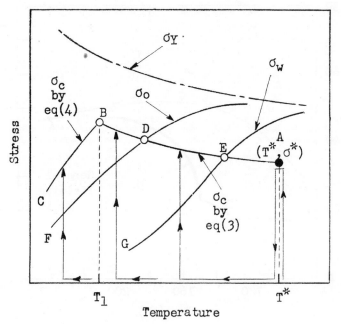

FIG. 4.   Mechanism of overstressing.

fracture at lower temperatures. Figure 4 shows schematically the characteristic curves, where σ_Y, σ_o and σ_W correspond to those values defined in Fig. 3. In this figure, brittle fracture strength of any welded structure is considered regardless of the particular test specimen shown in Fig. 2 (b). Suppose that the structure is initially subjected to a loading, σ^*, followed by an unloading at temperature T^* as shown in Fig. 4. If the structure is subsequently loaded at temperatures lower than T^*, the load to failure coincides with the knuckled curve of ABC. The part AB of the curve is given by

$$\sigma_c = \frac{1}{2}[1+(\sigma_Y/\sigma_Y^*)]\sigma^*, \tag{3}$$

where σ_Y and σ_Y^* are the yield strength at temperatures of failure and preloading, respectively. The remainder of the curve, BC, is represented by

$$\sigma_c = [1+(\sigma_Y^*/\sigma_Y)]\sigma_o. \tag{4}$$

Equation (3) can be easily deduced from failure which should occur when ρ^+ due to reloading attains the size ρ^- given by the initial loading cycle. This result can be easily reasoned by the aforementioned preliminaries. If the toughness, ρ_c^+, is less than the said, ρ^-, eq. (3) is no longer valid and eq. (4) should be used. The effective yield strength used for deducting eq. (4) as well as eq. (3) is of course $\sigma_Y^*+\sigma_Y$. The curve representing eq. (3) intersects the curve of eq. (4) at temperature T_1 as illustrated in Fig. 4. In other words, ρ_c^+ coincides with ρ^- at T_1. It is of practical significance that eq. (3) is independent of the original stress distribution around the defect. In fact, safety of an as-welded structure is remarkably improved by the overstressing (T^*, σ^*)

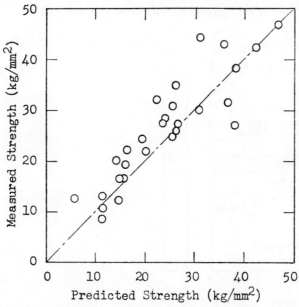

FIG. 5.   Measured strength *vs.* predicted strength for notched tension specimens subjected to various sequences of loading and cooling.

as shown by the region *CBEG*, while for completely stress-relieved structures this gain is limited as shown by the region *CBDF*.

The above discussion is concerned with a particular sequence of on-load → off-load → cooling → re-load to failure, but the ρ^+ concept is also applicable to other sequences, *e.g.* on-load → cooling → off-load → re-load to failure, on-load → cooling → additional load to failure, etc. By means of deeply notched test specimens shown in Fig. 2 (a), failures were predicted for various sequences of loading. These results are shown in Fig. 5.

3.3   Strength- and Toughness-Dependence of Brittle Fracture Path[7]

Needless to say, the path of brittle fracture is predominated by the directions of principal stresses. It is also well known that Charpy-*V* tests often fail in evaluating weld fusion boundary embrittlement because of curved fracture path. The ρ^+ concept is also applicable towards interpreting such undesirable phenomenon. Figure 6 shows the test specimen employed for this study. The notched section is located on the weld fusion boundary. The weld metal (denoted by the material *A*) is a 2-1/4% *Cr*-1% *Mo* steel, and the base metal (the material *B*) is an *Al*-killed mild steel. Welding residual stresses are relieved by heat treatment at 600°C ×5 hrs with subsequent cooling in furnace.

High-strength with low-toughness and low-strength with high-toughness charac-teristics are obtainable in materials *A* and *B*, respectively, after heat treatment. Net average stress to failure of the specimen, shown in Fig. 6, is plotted against temperature in Fig. 7. Closed circles indicate that fracture propagated in the weld metal, open circles represents crack propagation in the base metal, and fracture along a weld fusion bound-ary is shown by a semi-open circle. In other words, the brittle fracture propagates through softer zones at higher temperatures, and along relatively brittle zones at lower temperatures.

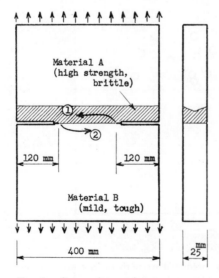

Fig. 6.   Composite specimen.

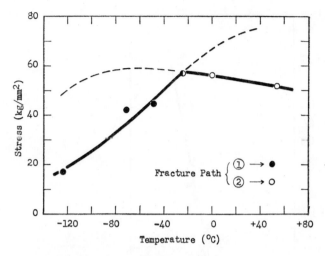

FIG. 7.   Results of composite specimen tests.

These empirical findings can be adequately interpreted by the ρ^+ concept. In fact, eqs. (1) and (2) suggest that fracture stress of material A shows higher value of upper shelf and higher transition temperature when compared with those of material B when each material is tested separately. The curves of fracture stress *vs.* temperature of these two materials, therefore, should intersect each other. This fact implies that the composite specimen as shown in Fig. 6 should bring forth test result which bears a close resemblance to the lower branches of the abovementioned intersecting curves. Experimentally obtained curves in Fig. 7 are suitably extended with broken curves for the sake of better understanding.

4.   Toughness Determination in Terms of ρ^+ Concept[8]

Fracture toughness in terms of COD concept is usually denoted by δ_c, which is a measurable quantity. On the other hand, the value of ρ_c^+ is not easily determined by direct measurement. The following simple formula, however, has fortunately proven adequate for converting the measured δ_c to ρ_c^+, *i.e.*

$$\rho_c^+ = (\pi E/8\sigma_Y)\cdot\delta_c \qquad\qquad (5)$$

where E is the Young's modulus. This relation is identical with the limit form of δ *vs.* ρ^+ for $\sigma/\sigma_Y \to 0$ on the basis of a Dugdale model, and its general applicability, irrespective of σ/σ_Y value, has been verified experimentally.

Figure 8 shows an example of data analysis of a medium strength structural plate steel. Closed circles indicate data obtained from three-point bend COD tests, and open circles are data obtained by deeply notched tension tests of various sized specimens. W and $2c$ as defined in Fig. 2 (a) range from 70 mm to 400 mm and from 50 mm to 160 mm, respectively. Numerals attached to the open circles are identification marks for specimen size. Data obtained at and beyond general yielding of notched tension

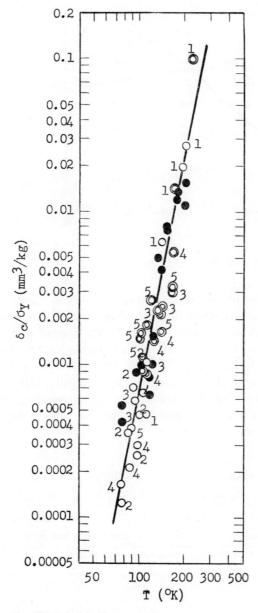

FIG. 8. δ_c/σ_Y vs. T.

specimens are marked by double circles. A straight line is drawn through all data points in Fig. 8. The slope of this straight line is 5 : 1 after eq. (2). Regardless of the loading in tension or in bending, fracture below or beyond general yielding, and specimen size changes, this straight line appears to be the best fitted line for all data plotted. Similar analyses have been carried out on various types of structural steel rendering a strong support to general applicability of eq. (5).

5. Closing Remarks

When compared with the COD approach, the ρ^+ approach provides an easier understanding of fracture behavior and a simpler calculation for the example studies. These merits are proven by several practical applications in the present paper. The fracture toughness parameter, $\rho_c{}^+$, also was shown to be easily obtainable by a simple conversion from the directly measurable critical COD, δ_c. The plastic zone size approach, therefore, is considered most promising in assessing failures due to defects in welded structures.

REFERENCES

1. Wells, A. A., "Application of Fracture Mechanics At and Beyond General Yielding," British Welding Journal *10*, 563 (1963).
2. Irwin, G. R., "Fracture," *Handbuch der Physik*, Springer, *VI* (1958), 551.
3. Dugdale, D. S., "Yielding of Steel Sheets Containing Slits," Jnl. Mech. Phys. Solids *8*, 100 (1960).
4. Koshiga, F., "A Proposed Mechanism of Brittle Fracture Initiation Influenced by Over-stressing Techniques in Terms of Dugdale Model," IIW Doc. X–566–70 (1970); Koshiga, F., "A Proposed Simple Theory of Overstressing Technique to Secure Pressure Vessels against Brittle Failure," Paper C50/71, *Instn. Mech. Engrs.*, London (1971).
5. Hahn, G. T. and Rosenfield, A. R., "Local Yielding and Extension of a Crack under Plane Stress," Acta Met. *13*, 293 (1965).
6. Koshiga, F., Tanaka, J. and Kurita, Y., "Effects of Stress-Relieving Heat Treatment on the Brittle Fracture Initiation in Welded Structures," IIW Doc. X–625–71 (1971).
7. Koshiga, F., Tanaka, J., Watanabe, I. and Akiyama, T., "On the Path of Brittle Fracture (in Japanese) I and II," *Weld. Res. Comm.* Doc. 1–209–72 and 1–211–72, Soc. Nav. Arch. Japan (1972).
8. Koshiga, F., Akiyama, T. and Iwasaki, T., "Consistency of Critical COD and a Proposed Method of $\rho_c{}^+$ Determination," J. Soc. Nav. Arch. Japan *134* (1973), to be published.

Effects of Plastic Constraint on the Fracture Mode and COD

A. OTSUKA AND T. MIYATA

Department of Metallurgical Engineering, Nagoya University

1. Introduction

Recent progress in general yield fracture mechanics has produced a possibility of its practical application in preventing failure of steel structures constructed of ductile material, such as low strength structural steels.[1] Although the validity of COD concept, for brittle fracture following large scale yielding has been already confirmed in many respects[2], there are still some unsolved problems left before this concept can be used in practical applications.

One problem arises from the fact that a critical COD value is not a material constant in the strict sense but rather a variable depending on mechanical factors since the COD criterion is not necessarily a direct representation of a fracture mechanism. Another problem arises from the fact that the analytical expression of COD, as a function of defect size and applied load, has not been obtained in the general yield region in which the COD concept will be the only appropriate fracture criterion.

This paper relates to the former problem where some experimental investigations on the effect of plastic constraint around the crack tip, and the validity and limitation of the COD criterion have been studied with relation to the fracture mechanism.

2. Materials

Chemical composition of the three steels used in this investigation is shown in Table 1, and mechanical properties and results of V-Charpy impact test are shown in

TABLE 1. Chemical compositions of tested materials. (%)

Material	C	Si	Mn	P	S
A (JIS-SS41)	0.118	0.22	0.39	0.011	0.030
B (JIS-SS41)	0.21	0.25	0.47	0.013	0.028
C (JIS-SM50C)	0.16	0.30	1.40	0.013	0.013

TABLE 2. Mechanical properties and V Charpy impact test result of tested materials.

Material	Mechanical properties				V Charpy test vTrs (°C)
	σ_y (kg/mm²)	σ_u (kg/mm²)	Elong. (%)	R.A. (%)	
A	26.7	43.9	23.0	67.0	+12
B	27.0	47.4	32.0	57.2	+29
C	34.7	52.2	32.7	71.9	−38

Table 2. Structural mild steels designated as Materials A and B, and high strength steel of 50 kg/mm² class designated as Material C were used. Materials A and C are hot rolled steel plates of 22 mm and 25 mm in thickness, respectively, and Material B is a hot rolled steel bar of 60 mm in diameter.

3. Test Specimens and Experimental Details

The following four series of experimental investigations were conducted:

a) Effect of plastic constraint on the critical COD value was investigated in center-notched tension plates of various thickness, side-grooved tension plates and circum-

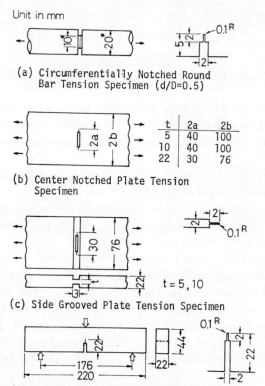

Unit in mm

(a) Circumferentially Notched Round Bar Tension Specimen (d/D=0.5)

t	2a	2b
5	40	100
10	40	100
22	30	76

(b) Center Notched Plate Tension Specimen

(c) Side Grooved Plate Tension Specimen   t = 5, 10

(d) Three Points Slow Bend Specimen

FIG. 1. Test specimens for Material A.

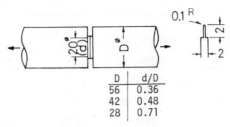

D	d/D
56	0.36
42	0.48
28	0.71

FIG. 2.   Test specimens for Material B.

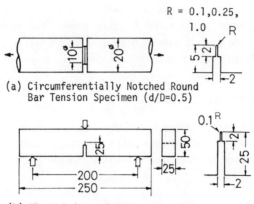

(a) Circumferentially Notched Round
    Bar Tension Specimen (d/D=0.5)

(b) Three Points Slow Bend Specimen

FIG. 3.   Test specimens for Material C.

ferentially-notched round bars. Specimen details are shown in Fig. 1 and Material A was used.

b)   Circumferentially-notched round bars with different ratios of notch depth to specimen diameter were tested for investigating the effect of notch depth on the plastic constraint. Specimen details are shown in Fig. 2 and Material B was used in this series of tests.

c)   As a standard test on the Materials A and C, three-point notched bend tests were made with appropriate specimens shown in Figs. 1 and 3.

d)   Effect of notch acuity was studied by testing circumferentially-notched round bar specimens with different notch root radius. Specimen details are shown in Fig. 3 and Material C was used in this series of tests.

COD values were measured by using a clip gauge in all tests. In circumferentially-notched round bar specimen and notched plate specimen with or without groove, two clip gauges were inserted at a distance of 2 mm from the notch tip. For Materials A and C, the COD values measured by clip gauges were corrected to the COD values at the notch tip by using calculation obtained by finite element method, FEM. Clip-gauge COD agreed well with the calculated COD at the measured point. For Material B, FEM calculation was not performed and thus the test results are shown in terms of clip gauge COD.

In slow bend tests, the notch tip COD for a range of low stress level was calculated from the fracture load using the FEM results by T. Kanazawa et al.[3] For the range

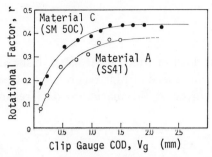

FIG. 4.   Variation of rotational factor r with clip gauge displacement for bend tests.

of high stress level, the notch tip COD was calculated from the clip gauge COD measured at notch end using the rotational factor, r. Measured rotational factor r as a function of clip gauge COD is shown in Fig. 4 and the notch tip COD is given by the following equation,

$$\delta = \frac{V_g}{1+(z+a)/r(d-a)} \tag{1}$$

where δ=notch tip COD, V_g=clip gauge COD, d=specimen depth, a=notch depth and z=knife edge thickness. The notch tip COD values obtained by this method agreed well with those obtained by using the Wells' formula[4] in a wide range of stress levels.

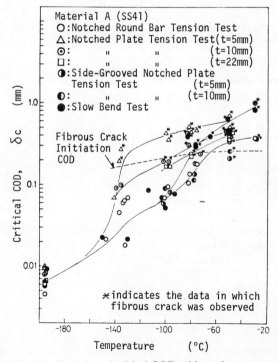

FIG. 5.   Variation of critical COD with testing temperature (Material A).

4.   Results and Discussion

a)   COD at Maximum Load

Critical COD, δ_c, at the maximum load of Material A and C tests are shown in Figs. 5 and 6. Clip gauge COD at maximum load of Material-B test is shown in Fig. 7. Unstable brittle fracture initiation occurred at the maximum load regardless of the

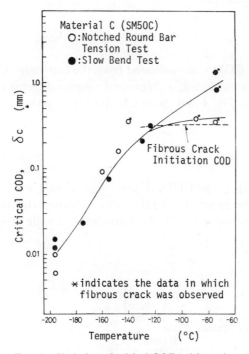

FIG. 6.   Variation of critical COD with testing temperature (Material C).

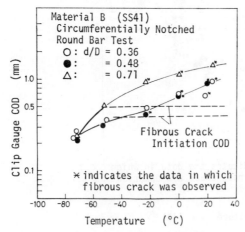

FIG. 7.   Variation of clip gauge displacement with testing temperature (Material B).

material tested, with the exception of the circumferentially-notched round bar tested in the high temperature region.

Broken lines in the figures show the COD values at fibrous crack initiation from the notch root. These fibrous crack initiation, as shown in Fig. 8, occurred before the load reached the maximum point, and therefore COD values which are larger than the COD values at fibrous crack initiation are no longer the critical COD which indicates the fracture toughness of the material. In fact, it is shown by some authors[5,6] that those COD values are affected by specimen size and geometry. The COD values at fibrous crack initiation were obtained by the off-load method described later. It should

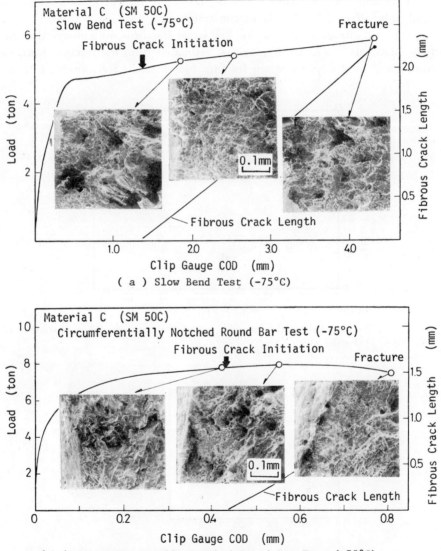

(a) Slow Bend Test (-75°C)

(b) Circumferentially Notched Round Bar Test (-75°C)

FIG. 8.   Load-displacement curve and fibrous crack initiation (Material C).

be noticed that fibrous crack usually initiates at an early stage where the COD still shows about 1/2–1/4 of the COD value at unstable fracture, as shown in Fig. 8. This phenomenon is not confined to the case where the load drops before unstable fracture, as seen in Fig. 8.

From the test results of Material A, critical COD values for fracture, which was initiated by an onset of cleavage crack, were found to be affected considerably by the plastic constraint at the neighbourhood of a notch tip. To show the intensity of plastic constraint accurately, a three-dimensional analysis will be necessary. Figure 9 shows an example of the relation between critical COD, δ_c, and the ratio of general yield stress to uniaxial yield stress, which expresses indirectly the intensity of the plastic constraint. In addition, the temperature region where fibrous crack initiation occurs was found to be affected by the plastic constraint.

At liquid nitrogen temperature, low stress fractures were observed in all specimens of the Materials A and C. K_{IC} values, estimated from the fracture load, satisfied the requirement for the plane strain fracture toughness, $2.5(K_{IC}/\sigma_Y)^2 < t$ or a if such re-

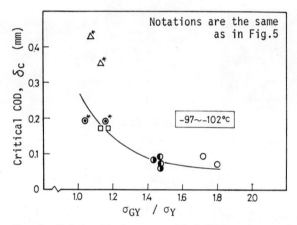

FIG. 9.   Relationship between critical COD and general yield stress of the specimens (Material A).

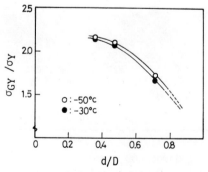

FIG. 10.   Relationship between general yield stress of circumferentially notched round bar specimen and d/D (Material B).

quirement is applicable to low strength steel. In this region it was observed that the various specimens exhibited about the same K_{IC} or COD values.

Results of circumferentially-notched round bar tests for Material B show that critical COD obtained by specimens with the ratios of $d/D=0.357$ and 0.476 was smaller than that obtained by specimens with the ratio of $d/D=0.714$ in a wide range of the temperature. Conclusive discussion, however, cannot be made at the present time because the notch tip COD was not determined. Figure 10 shows the relation between d/D and the ratio of general yield stress of the specimen to uniaxial yield stress. Intensity of the plastic constraint appears to be about the same if $d/D<0.5$.

b) COD and Fibrous Crack Initiation

For fibrous fracture initiation in low strength steel, COD at the instant of fibrous crack initiation, δ_i, takes almost a constant value, regardless of specimen geometry such as specimen width[5,6], specimen thickness[7], and the ratio of notch depth to specimen depth[5], while the COD at maximum load varies with these parameters. Also S. Kanazawa et al.[8] recently reported that δ_i is not affected even by strain rate and test temperatures. If δ_i can be proven to be a general characteristic parameter or if conditions for its existence can be determined, δ_i will be a very good fracture criterion from the points of view of design application and study of fracture mechanism.

In this report, the values of δ_i were obtained at various temperatures on circum-

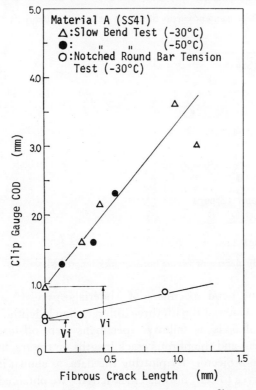

FIG. 11.   Clip gauge displacement versus fibrous crack length (Material A).

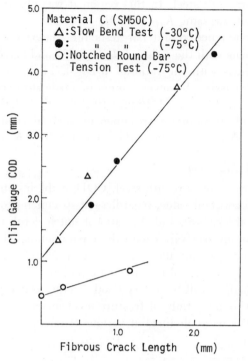

FIG. 12.   Clip gauge displacement versus fibrous crack length (Material C).

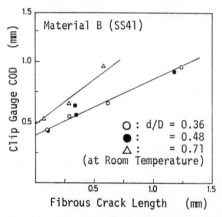

FIG. 13.   Clip gauge displacement versus fibrous crack length (Material B).

ferentially-notched round bar and bend specimens of Materials A and C, and circumferentially-notched round bar of Material B with three different notch depths. The method used to obtain the values of δ_i is as follows: specimens were off-loaded during loading, broken in liquid nitrogen, and the fibrous crack lengths on the fracture surfaces were measured by Nikon Profile projector. By plotting the data, as shown in Figs. 11–13, and by extrapolating the curves to zero fibrous crack length, we obtained the values of COD for zero crack length. This value thus obtained is used as δ_i in this report.

Examples of fractographs by SEM are shown in Fig. 8. Fractographs were also used to identify the fibrous crack. These results are shown in Figs. 14 and 15. Plots of COD at fibrous-cleavage transition are also included in these figures. These values are obtained by plotting these values of δ_c for each fibrous crack length from the data obtained at various test temperature and extrapolating the δ_c vs. fibrous crack length curve obtained from the above plot. The COD value at the intersecting point namely the point of zero fibrous crack length, represents the COD value at fibrous-cleavage transition. This value is δ_i at the lowest temperature where fibrous crack occurs, but it may also be used as a representative value of δ_i for this material since δ_i hardly varies with temperature as mentioned before. This method will be referred to as the " transition point method" since the other method was described as the "off-load method". For plate specimens of different thickness shown in Fig. 14 of Material A, δ_i was obtained by this transition point method only. For all specimens of the other series, the values of δ_i were obtained by the both transition and the off-load methods.

What is most remarkable in these figures is that δ_i of different specimens shows

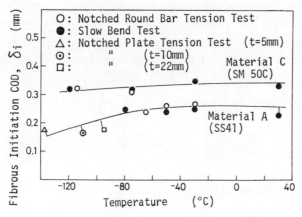

FIG. 14.   Variation of fibrous crack initiation COD with temperature (Materials A & C).

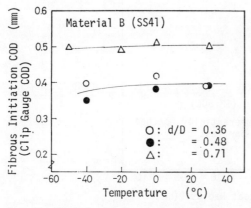

FIG. 15.   Variation of clip gauge displacement at fibrous crack initiation with temperature (Material B).

about the same value and that only a slight increase with increase in test temperature is noted as long as the temperature is in the fibrous crack initiation region.

One test involving the least-depth notch of Material B, however, shows a considerably different trend from the other tests. This may in part be due to the fact that correction for measured COD value to notch tip value was not made for this series of tests. Or it would be more reasonable to assume that notch depth, too, had some influence if it is too shallow.

Figure 16 shows the relation between clip gauge COD, V_g, and notch root radius. It is seen in this figure that the relation is almost linear both crack initiation and final fracture. The data by Smith and Knott[7], however, shows that COD at fibrous crack initiation is proportional to the slot width (COD is zero when slot width is zero). This difference in behavior may be due to the fact that in Fig. 16, V_g (clip gauge COD) is used but in the data by Smith and Knott, δ_i (corrected value to notch tip) was used.

Further investigation will be necessary to clarify the effects of notch acuity on δ_i.

c) Critical COD and Fracture Condition

Fracture mode transition has a significant effect, as Barsom and Rolfe[9] pointed out, on the fracture toughness of medium strength steel and low strength steel. Fracture condition and critical COD at various temperatures will thus be discussed with particular attention to fracture mode.

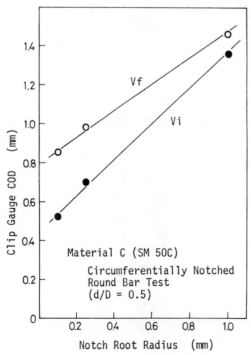

FIG. 16.   Effects of notch root radius on COD at fracture and COD at fibrous crack initiation.

Figure 17 is a schematic illustration of the relation between critical COD and fracture mode. Because a detailed study of fracture behavior at various temperatures is given for smooth round bars by Hahn et al.,[10] the analyses of the present results described in (a) and (b) are made in reference to their results.

Fracture initiation mode is divided by line BD; above this line or at higher temperature than T_i fracture occurs by fibrous type crack, and by cleavage below this line or at lower temperature than T_i. In the temperature region higher than T_i, fibrous crack occurs when COD reaches the value BD and unstable fracture occurs at the curve BC. For low constraint and high temperature, unstable fracture could occur in fibrous type, but usually in notched low strength steel specimens unstable fracture coincides with fibrous-cleavage transition. The former and the latter cases are named regions A and B, respectively by Hahn et al. It has already been shown that the fibrous initiation curve BD shows little dependence on temperature and specimen geometry.

It is well known that fibrous crack occurs by void coalescence, McClintock[11] showed, at least in principle, that void growth is enhanced by both shearing stress and hydrostatic tension. The present experimental results which showed that δ_i has little dependence on specimen geometry in spite of the large variation in plastic constraint, however, seems to imply that hydrostatic tension has little influence on fibrous crack initiation at the notch tip.

In the intermediate temperature region, region II and III, fracture occurs by cleavage crack with considerable amount of COD. These regions, where cleavage occurs after plastic deformation, correspond to Hahn's regions of C and D. These regions are characterized, as already mentioned in (a), by the large dependence of δ_c on specimen geometry (or plastic constraint of the specimen). Hahn et al. also reported that many micro-cracks are observed in regions C and D, and thus the theory by T. Yokobori[12] appears appropriate to explain this case. Yokobori considers the propagation of micro-crack in one grain by traversing the grain boundary as the critical event in fracture in this temperature region. The condition of the fracture is given by

$$A\sigma + B(\tau - \tau_i) = R \qquad\qquad (2)$$

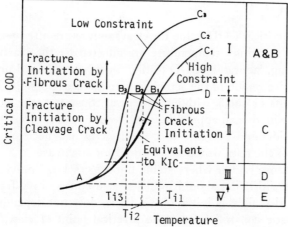

FIG. 17.   Schematic relations between COD and fracture mode transition.

where A, B and R are the constants which depend on the material and geometry of the specimen.

In the lower temperature part of region III, however, the mechanism given by Stroh[13], Cottrell[14], and Smith[15], in which the critical stage is considered to be initial growth of the first micro-crack, seems to be more appropriate. The fracture condition is given as

$$\sigma(\tau - \tau_i) = C \tag{3}$$

where τ_i=frictional stress

C=material constant

In eqs. (2), (3), σ and τ is the local tensile and shearing stresses in the element at the notch root induced by applied load. The most interesting fact in the above discussion is that fracture condition involves both σ and τ, whether the fracture condition is given by eq. (2) or by (3). This means that if the ratio of σ/τ in the element at the notch root varies, the values of τ and σ at fracture must also vary. In other words, the larger the constraint (the larger σ/τ), the smaller the τ at fracture. This explains the present results related to the effects of constraint on δ_c in that the larger the constraint, the smaller δ_c becomes since COD is determined by the amount of plastic deformation at the notch root. If the condition of fracture is further clarified together with the critical parameters, the estimation of δ_c for a given constraint will be possible.

In the region of relatively low temperature and high constraint, Fig. 5 shows that COD at fracture approaches some limiting value which depends on temperature. In the region where the value of COD attains this limiting value, the condition of plane strain is satisfied and thus this limiting value, as shown in Fig. 17, would correspond to K_{IC}. K_{IC} approach would thus be preferable to COD-approach in such a region.

The fracture condition in region IV is considered to be τ=constant because this region corresponds to Hahn's region E where fracture occurs at the instant of initiation of yielding. In this region, the COD at fracture takes an almost constant value regardless of specimen geometry and temperature.

5.   General Discussion

It is shown that the critical COD value for cleavage fracture after general yielding and the cleavage-fibrous transition temperature are affected by the plastic constraint. Therefore, strictly speaking, laboratory COD testing must be conducted under the conditions close to the defective region of the actual constructions as possible. In evaluating defects in plane butt joints or shells without structural constraint, the slow bend test with full plate thickness will give an appropriate COD value. For a severely constrained structural member, considerable decrease in critical COD had been observed[16] and thus careful assessment of the data would be required for such case.

In the high temperature region where stable fibrous crack is observed, the COD value at the fibrous crack initiation should be taken as a conservative fracture toughness. It can be assumed that fibrous initiation COD, δ_i, does not depend on the temperature and on the plastic constraint from the practical point of view, and thus its value can be obtained by simple methods. Off-load method, mentioned previously, at room temperature is one such possible methods. In the slow bend test, relation between clip gauge COD and notch tip COD does not vary with temperature because the rotational factor, r, is nearly a constant value in the transition region and linear correlation between the clip gauge COD and fibrous crack length has been observed as shown in Fig. 18. On the basis of the above facts, δ_i can be obtained also from fracture test in the transition temperature region by the transition point method explained in 4 (b).

Table 3 shows the results of usual tensile tests and Charpy tests along with δ_i and the lowest fibrous initiation temperature, T_i, of circumferentially-notched round bars. δ_i, as well as the reduction of area, is one of the parameters which represent ductility; and the lowest fibrous initiation temperature is, of course, a fibrous-cleavage transition temperature like that of Charpy test. An interesting fact shown in Table 3 is that the order of ductility and transition temperature from conventional tensile test and

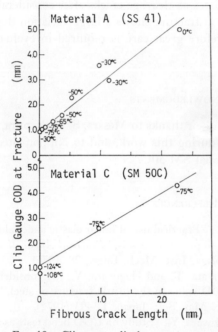

FIG. 18.   Clip gauge displacement versus fibrous crack length at various temperatures (Slow bend test).

TABLE 3.   Characteristics of fibrous crack initiation, reduction of area of the material and V Charpy transition temperature.

Material	δ_i (at T_i, mm)	T_i (°C)	R.A. (%)	vTrs (°C)	vTr5% (°C)
A	0.24	−65	67.0	+12	−38
B	0.17	−40	57.2	+29	−15
C	0.32	−114	71.9	−38	−74

* T_i: Lowest fibrous crack initiation temperature in circumferentially notched round bar test.

Charpy tests agrees well with those from δ_i and T_i, respectively for all materials tested. If more data are accumulated, it will be possible to establish some empirical correlations between these parameters.

6. Conclusions

Condition of fracture initiation from a notch was investigated using low strength steels with particular attention to the fracture after large scale yielding.

Main conclusions are as follows:

a) The present results show that COD at fibrous crack initiation, δ_i, is a very important and effective criterion of ductile fracture initiation, due to its early initiation and little dependence on temperature and specimen geometry. From the practical view point, the value of δ_i can be obtained easily, without any special technique, from the data of conventional fracture tests at various temperature by adding only the measurement of COD.   b) When fracture initiates as cleavage cracks after considerable amount of plastic straining, the value of COD at fracture shows a large variation depending on the degree of plastic constraint. Therefore great care is required in evaluating cracklike defects in such a region.

ACKNOWLEDGMENTS

The authors would like to express their thanks to Messrs. S. Nishimura, M. Ohashi and Y. Kashiwagi for their assistance during this work, and to Nippon Steel Corporation for kindly supplying the test material SM 50C.

REFERENCES

1. Burdekin, F. M. and Dawes, M. G., "Practical use of linear elastic and yielding fracture mechanics with particular reference to pressure vessels," *Practical Application of Fracture Mechanics to Pressure Vessel Technology*, Inst. Mech. Engr., 28 (1971).
2. Kanazawa, T. and Machida, S., Miyata, T. and Hagiwara, Y., "A consideration of the variables included in the critical COD value in the brittle fracture of steel," *Proc. Inter. Conf. Mech. Behavior of Mat.*, Soc. Mat. Sci., Japan, **1**, 493 (1972).
3. Kanazawa, T., Machida, S. and Hagiwara, Y., "Study on COD bend tests as an engineering brittle fracture initiation characteristics test," J. Soc. Nav. Arch. Japan, **132**, 361(1972).
4. " Methods for Crack Opening Displacement (COD) Testing, *DD*19 ", British Standards Institution (1972).
5. Terry, P. and Barnby, J. T., "Determining critical crack opening displacement for the onset of slow tearing in steels," Metal Const. and Brit. W. J., **3**, 343 (1971).
6. Fearnehough, G. D., Lees, G. M., Lowes, J. M. and Weiner, R. T., "The role of stable ductile crack growth in the failure of structures," *Practical Application of Fracture Mechanics to Pressure Vessel Technology*, Inst. Mech. Engr. 119 (1971).
7. Smith, R. F. and Knott, J. F., "Crack opening displacement and fibrous fracture in mild steel," *Practical Application of Fracture Mechanics to Pressure Vessel Technology*, Inst. Mech. Engr., 65 (1971).
8. Kanazawa, S., Minami, K., Miya, K., Sato, M. and Soya, I., "An investigation of static

COD and dynamic COD," J. Soc. Nav. Arch. Japan, **133**, 257 (1973).

9. Barsom, J. M. and Rolfe, S. T., "K_{IC} transition temperature behavior of A517–F steel," Eng. Frac. Mech., **2**, 341 (1971).

10. Hahn, G. T., Averbach, B. L., Owen, W. S. and Cohen, M., "Initiation of cleavage microcracks in polycrystalline iron and steel," *Fracture* ed. by Averbach et al., MIT Press, 91 (1959).

11. McClintock, F. A., "On the mechanism of fracture from inclusions," *Ductility*, ASM, 255 (1968).

12. Yokobori, T., *An Interdisciplinary Approach to Fracture and Strength of Solids*, Wolters-Noordhoff, 164 (1968).

13. Stroh, A. N., "The formation of cracks as a result of plastic flow," Proc. Roy. Soc., Ser. **A 223**, 404 (1954).

14. Cottrell, A. H., "Theory of brittle fracture in steel and similar metals," Trans. AIME, **212**, 192 (1958).

15. Smith, E., "Cleavage fracture in mild steel," Inter. J. Frac. Mech., **4**, 131 (1968).

16. Kanazawa, T., Machida, S. and Miyata, T., "Brittle fracture initiation of welded steel structures," *Proc. 1st Intern. Symp. of Japan Weld. Soc. on Precution of Cracking in Welded Structures Based on Recent Theoretical and Practical Knowledge, Session III*, Japan Weld. Soc. (1971).

Present Status on the Evaluation of Fracture Criteria for Structural Steels

T. Kanazawa

Department of Naval Architecture, University of Tokyo

H. Kihara

Welding Research Institute, Osaka University

1. Introduction

The Japan Welding Engineering Society has established the WES standard, "Evaluation Criterion of Structural Steels for Low Temperature Application", based on the correlations between small-scale tests (V-Charpy test, Pressed Notch Charpy test) and large-scale propagation arrest tests (Double Tension test) as expressed in terms of K_c-value. In this standard, steel plates are classified into two classes of G and A, where G is generally usable for welded structures where hazard of brittle fracture is anticipated and A is used for arresting a propagating crack.

It is well-known that the linear elastic fracture mechanics concept, on which the above mentioned WES standard is based, is valid only when fracture occurs under a small scale yielding condition, that is, the yielding zone size at the tip of a pre-existing crack is small compared with the crack size. In ordinary structural steels, however, in-service failure of steel structures are more often caused by fracture initiation from pre-existing crack under large scale yiedling. Consequently, G class steels in the WES standard should be revised to account for fracture under large scale yielding condition. To our present knowledge, the COD concept or the ρ_c^+ concept* proposed by Koshiga[1] is considered a very promising engineering concept of brittle fracture initiation under large scale yielding.

In order to establish a revised WES standard, the TM Committee of the Japan Welding Engineering Society has conducted a comprehensive cooperative research works since 1971 and the conclusions of this Committee are forthcoming soon. In this paper, the present status of this cooperative research work will be briefly reported with particular emphasis on the correlations between COD bend tests and notched tension tests and related problems.

---

* ρ_c^+ is the critical plastic zone size under tensile yield stress at the tip of pre-existing crack.

2. Experiments

2.1 Materials

Materials tested are 18 charges of mild steel, 50 kg/mm² class, 60 kg/mm² class and 80 kg/mm² class high strength steel plates with thickness varing from 18 mm to 50 mm. The temperature dependent yield stresses and tensile strengthes of each steel were obtained by using round bar tension specimens.

2.2 Tests and Test Procedures

In order to clarify the effects of specimen size and testing method on a critical COD measurement as well as other related problems, various tests, which included 3 point and 4 point bend tests and notched tension tests, were carried out for each steel. Examples of the specimen configurations used in these tests are shown in Fig. 1. COD was measured by a ring-type clip gage where measurements were made at the knife edges attached to the notch end for a bend specimen and at a certain distant from the notch tip (for example 7 mm) for a tension specimen.

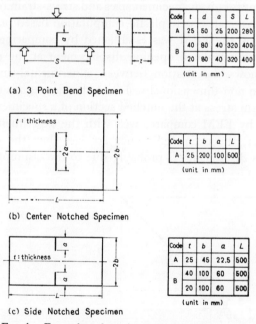

Code	t	d	a	S	L
A	25	50	25	200	280
B	40	80	40	320	400
	20	80	40	320	400

(unit in mm)

(a) 3 Point Bend Specimen

Code	t	b	a	L
A	25	200	100	500

(unit in mm)

(b) Center Notched Specimen

Code	t	b	a	L
A	25	45	22.5	500
B	40	100	60	500
	20	100	60	500

(unit in mm)

(c) Side Notched Specimen

FIG. 1.   Examples of specimen configurations.

3. Determination of Notch Tip COD

COD value is usually measured by a clip gage for convenience of continuous and simple recording. Since the clip gage cannot be mounted at the notch-tip because of its blade thickness, procedure must be established for reducing the clip gage reading, V_g, to the notch tip COD value, Φ, Some of these procedures will be discussed in the following.

3.1   Tension Test

Using the Dugdale-Barenblatt crack model the opening displacement of a crack caused by the applied load can be calculated at an arbitrary point.[2] The opening displacement, V_g, on a crack where the clip gage is attached is calculated and compared with experimental values as shown in Fig. 2. In this figure, E is the Young's modulus, σ_Y the yield stress of the test steel at the test temperature and 2a or a is notch length of center or side notched specimen, respectively. This figure shows that the calculated V_g value compares well with the measured ones and implies that the D-B model simulates well the actual opening displacement of a crack.

Thus the opening displacement, Φ, at the crack tip can be obtained from experimental V_g values using the D-B model for tension tests.

For the bend test, however, a universally accepted procedure for converting V_g to Φ has not successfully been established yet. This will be considered in the following.

3.2   Bend Test

3. 2. 1   Computation by FEM (Finite Element Method)[3]

Crack opening displacement for given specimen sizes and stress-strain relations were calculated using the two-dimensional, elastic plastic computation based on FEM. The validity of such computation by the FEM was established by comparing the experimental clip gage reading to the calculated opening displacement at the point of clip gage attachment. Figure 3 shows the relation between experimental and calculated critical clip gage reading, V_g, in non-dimensional scale. In this figure, d is the specimen depth and σ_N is the nominal skin stress at the notched section of a specimen.

The V_g values estimated by FEM compares well with the experimental values at the lower load level. However, the estimated values are less than the experimental values for $EV_g/d\sigma_Y \gtrsim 3.0$. This discrepancy is probably due to the assumption of linear

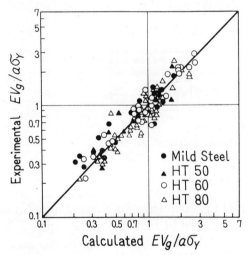

FIG. 2.   Relation between measured clip gage and calculated CODs using the D-B model for tension test.

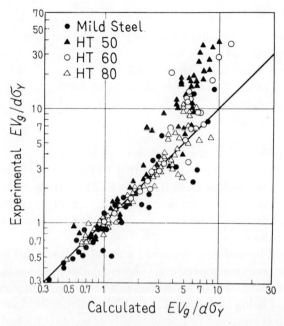

FIG. 3. Relation between measured clip gage and calculated CODs using FEM for bend test.

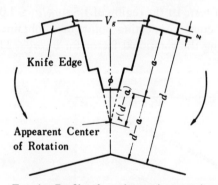

FIG. 4. Profile of notch opening associated with the rotational factor.

strain hardening in the FEM calculation which resulted in the calculated strain being less than the actual one in the highly strained region. It is concluded from this figure that the FEM results are valid for $EV_g/d\sigma_Y \lesssim 3.0$ which corresponds approximately to the condition of $\sigma_N/\sigma_Y \lesssim 1.5$

3. 2. 2   Rotational Factor

Another method for determing COD value at the crack tip of a bend specimen is the concept of rotational factor. In this concept, a notched specimen is assumed to deform about a "pivot", the location of which depends on the applied load. After the rotational factor, r, is experimentally determined, clip gage readings can be reduced to COD values at the notch tip using a simple proportional relation given by (see Fig. 4)

$$\Phi = V_g/\{1+(z+a)/r(d-a)\}$$

This rotational factor was determined theoretically[4] and experimentally[5] and was found to depend on the applied load in the lower load level and tend to approach a constant value at higher applied stress ratio (say $\sigma_N/\sigma_Y \gtrsim 2.0$). r, however, is highly dependent on stress in the region of $\sigma_N/\sigma_Y \lesssim 2.0$. For the sake of simplicity, the value of r is taken to be 1/3, which is approximately the lower bound of the experimentally obtained r values, for $\sigma_N/\sigma_Y \gtrsim 2.0$ in this paper.

3. 2. 3   The Proposed Method

The discussions in the previous sections show that COD at a notch tip can be determined by using elastic plastic crack analysis based on FEM for stress ratio $\sigma_N/\sigma_Y \lesssim 1.5$, and for $\sigma_N/\sigma_Y \gtrsim 2.0$ the method based on the rotational factor ($r=1/3$) is useful. In the region of $1.5 \lesssim \sigma_N/\sigma_Y \lesssim 2.0$, COD could be estimated by taking the intermediate values obtained from these two methods.

A typical result obtained by using the proposed method is shown in Fig. 5 in terms of the critical COD Φ_c vs. testing temperature. The solid line represents the critical COD obtained from the tension test. The dotted and broken lines represents curves obtained from the bend test using the methods of FEM and rotational factor, respectively. Temperatures which correspond to fracture loads of $\sigma_N/\sigma_Y=1.5$ and 2.0 are also indicated. As shown in this figure, Φ_c determined for $\sigma_N/\sigma_Y \lesssim 1.5$ using FEM in the bend test and Φ_c determined for $\sigma_N/\sigma_Y \gtrsim 2.0$ using the rotational factor compares well with the Φ_c curve obtained from the tension test. In the region of $1.5 \lesssim \sigma_N/\sigma_Y \lesssim 2.0$, Φ_c for the bend test may be estimated by a faired curve connecting points of Φ_c obtained by FEM for $\sigma_N/\sigma_Y=1.5$ and Φ_c obtained by using the rotational factor for $\sigma_N/\sigma_Y=2.0$.

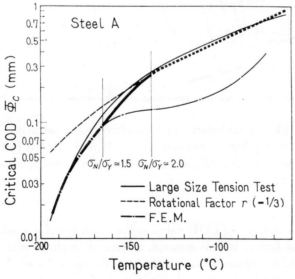

FIG. 5.   A comparison of critical COD determined from bend test using the methods of rotational factor and FEM with that obtained for tension test.

4.   Relation between COD Bend Test and Notched Tension Test

In this section, the validity of COD concept and COD bend test is investigated by studying that the Φ_c value is practically independent of specimen size and type of loading.

Figure 6 shows an example of the relation between fracture stress *vs.* testing temperature for large size deep notch test. The solid curve in this figure shows the predicted fracture stress of large size specimen calculated from the experimental Φ_o values of small size tension test using the D-B model. Similar results are obtained for the other steels tested. In Fig. 7, a correlation between the experimental and predicted fracture stress is shown. This figure shows that good estimation can be made for the fracture stress of large specimen on the basis of COD concept using the experimental value obtained from small specimen.

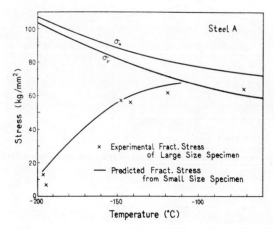

FIG. 6.   Relation between measured and estimated fracture stress.

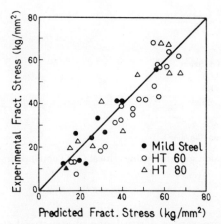

FIG. 7.   Fracture stress for large size tension specimen using critical COD obtained from small size tension specimen.

The effectiveness of COD bend test was also investigated. Figure 8 shows a comparison of experimental data of large and small tension tests with predicted curves from bend test. In Fig. 9, fracture stress of large size notched tension tests are plotted against those estimated from the results of COD bend test for various types of steel. Fracture stresses of tension specimens predicted from COD bend test compared well with the experimental values. These results show that from practical and industrial points of view, COD bend test could be a very useful test for evaluating brittie fracture initiation characteristics of steels, since the specimens can be made smaller and can be fractured at considerably lower load than that of tension test.

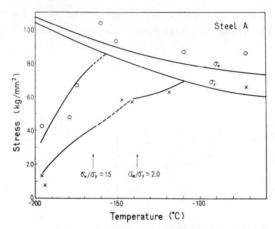

FIG. 8.   Relation between measured and estimated fracture stress for COD bend test.

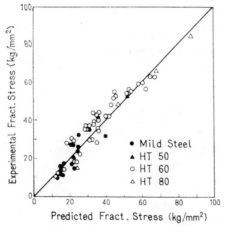

FIG. 9.   Fracture stress for tension specimen using critical COD obtained from bend test.

5. Temperature Dependence of Φ_c

Koshiga[6,7] has shown that the temperature dependence of structural steels can be expressed by

$$\rho_c{}^+ = \alpha(T/100)^5$$

or

$$\Phi_c/\sigma_Y = \alpha'(T/100)^5$$

where T: testing temperature in $^\circ$K, α and α': $\rho_c{}^+$ and Φ_c/σ_Y value at 100° K, respectively.

Data obtained by the TM Committee were checked against these relations and Fig. 10 shows the results of tension tests with various width specimens of 50 kg/mm² class high strength steel. Irrespective of specimen size, Koshiga's expression compares well with experimental results. Similar results are also obtained for other steels. For the bend test, temperature dependence of Φ_c/σ_Y(or $\rho_c{}^+$) is also expressed by the sameformula, and Figures 11 (a) and (b) show examples involving 50 kg/mm² and 80 kg/mm² classhigh strength steels. These illustrations demonstrate that we can always evaluate Φ_c/ σ_Y(or $\rho_c{}^+$) value for various steels, irrespective of testing method and testing temperature.

6. Concluding Remarks

It is shown that COD bend test is one of the most effective and useful test methods for evaluating notch toughness of structural steels.

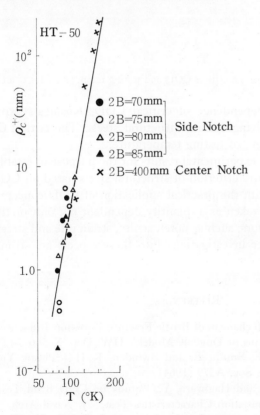

FIG. 10.   Relation between $\rho_c{}^+$ and testing temperature for tension test.

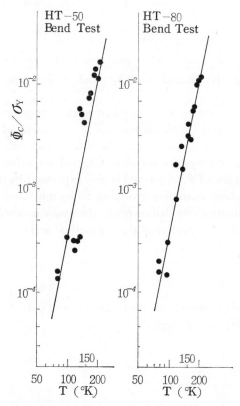

FIG. 11.   Relation between critical COD and testing temperature for bend test.

As for the temperature dependence of critical COD, Koshiga's expression fits well with the test results involving various structural steels. The critical COD values thus can be evaluated irrespective of testing temperature.

We are now evaluating the experimental results for the purpose of establishing final conclusions on the brittle fracture criterion of structural steels based on COD concept.

One problem associated with the practical application of COD concept is the fact that the critical COD must be taken as a quantity dependent not only on the temperature but also on mechanical factors, such as notch acuity, strain rate and stress triaxiality (plastic constraint), etc. Further investigations into these aspects are strongly recommended for futuer works.

References

1. Koshiga, F., "A Proposed Mechanism of Brittle Fracture Initiation Influenced by Over-stressing Techniques in Terms of Dugdale Model," IIW. Doc. X–566–70 (1970).
2. Bilby, B. A., Cottrell, A. H., Smith, E. and Swinden, K. H., "Plastic Yielding from Sharp Notches," Proc. Roy. Soc. A279 (1964).
3. Kanazawa, T., Machida, S. and Hagiwara, Y., "Study on COD Bend Test as an Engineering Brittle Fracture Initiation Characteristics Test," J. Naval Arch. Japan, No. 132 (1972).

4. Alexander, J. M. and Komoly, T. J., "On the Yielding of a Rigid/Plastic Bar with an Izod Notch," J.M.P.S. 10 (1962).

5. Ingham, T., Egan, G. R., Elliott, D. and Harrison, T. C., "The Effect of Geometry on the Interpretation of COD Test Data," *Proc. Conf. Prac. Appl. of Frac. Mech. to Pressure Vessel Tech.* London (1971).

6. Koshiga, F., Tanaka, J. and Kurita, Y., "Effects of Stress-relieving Heat Treatment on the Brittle Fracture Initiation in Welded Structures," J. Naval Arch. Japan No. 129 (1971).

7. Koshiga, F., "A Brittle Fracture Criterion Based on the Plastic Zone Size," *Session V, 283/291 in this Proceedings.*

Fracture-Control Guidelines for Welded Steel Ship Hulls

S. T. ROLFE

Department of Civil Engineering, University of Kansas

1. General Problem of Brittle Fracture in Ships

Although welded ship failures have occurred since the early 1900's, it was not until the large number of World War II ship failures that the problem was fully appreciated.[1] Of the approximately 5,000 merchant ships built during World War II, over 1,000 had developed cracks of considerable size by 1946. Between 1942 and 1952, more than 200 ships had sustained fractures classified as serious, and at least nine T-2 tankers and seven Liberty ships had broken completely in two as a result of brittle fractures. The majority of fractures in the Liberty ships started at square hatch corners or square cutouts at the top of the sheer strake. Design changes involving rounding and strengthening of the hatch corners, removing square cutouts in the sheer strake, and adding riveted crack arresters in various locations led to immediate reductions in the incidence of failures.[2] Most of the fractures in the T-2 tankers originated in defects in bottom shell butt welds. The use of crack arresters and improved workmanship reduced the incidence of failures in these vessels.

Studies indicated that in addition to design faults, steel quality also was a primary factor that contributed to brittle fracture in welded ship hulls.[3] Therefore, in 1947, the American Bureau of Shipping introduced restrictions on the chemical composition of steels and in 1949, Lloyds Register stated that "when the main structure of a ship is intended to be wholly or partially welded, the committee may require parts of primary structural importance to be of steel, the properties and process of manufacture of which have been specially approved for this purpose.[4]"

In spite of design improvements, the increased use of crack arresters, improvements in quality of workmanship, and restrictions on the chemical composition of ship steels during the later 1940's, brittle fractures still occurred in ships in the early 1950's.[5] Between 1951 and 1953, two comparatively new all-welded cargo ships and a transversely framed welded tanker broke in two. In the winter of 1954, a longitudinally framed welded tanker constructed of improved steel quality using up-to-date concepts of good

318

design and welding quality broke in two.[6]

During the 1950's, seven Classification Societies responsible for the classification of ships (American Bureau of Shipping, Bureau Veritas, Germanischer Lloyd, Lloyd's Register of Shipping, Nippon Kaiji Kyokai, Det Norske Veritas, and Registro Italianno Navale) held numerous meetings and in 1959 published the Unified Requirements for Ship Steels.[4] These requirements specified various manufacturing methods, chemical composition, or Charpy V-Notch impact requirements for five grades of steel.

Since the late 1950's (although the actual number has been low) brittle fractures have still occurred in ships as is indicated by Boyd's description of ten such failures between 1960 and 1965 and a number of unpublished reports of brittle fractures in welded ships since 1965.

Therefore, although it has been approximately 30 years since the problem of brittle fracture in welded ship hulls was first recognized as a significant problem for the shipbuilding industry, brittle fractures still occur in ships. While it is true that during this time considerable research has led to various changes in design, fabrication, and materials so that the incidence of brittle fractures in welded ship hulls has been reduced markedly,[8] nonetheless, brittle fractures continue to occur in welded ship hulls fabricated with ordinary-strength steels. With the use of higher-strength steels, there is a definite concern that brittle fractures may occur in these steels also.

Currently there are no specific fracture-control guidelines or overall toughness criteria available for the practicing naval architect to specify in designing welded steel ship hulls of all strength levels. Therefore, the purpose of this report is to provide rational fracture-control guidelines consistent with economic realities which, when implemented, will minimize the probability of brittle fractures in welded ship hulls. Although the fact is rarely stated, the basis of structural design in all large complex structures is an attempt to optimize the desired performance requirements relative to cost considerations (materials, design, fabrication) so that the probability of failure (and its economic consequences) is low.

For reasons developed in the following sections, the guidelines are primarily material oriented. This does not relieve the naval architect of responsibility for good ship design, but recognizes the fundamental importance of using good quality structural steels in large complex welded structures.

2.   General Problem of Brittle Fracture in Welded Structures

An overwhelming amount of research on brittle fracture in welded steel structures has shown that numerous factors (e.g., service temperature, material toughness, design, welding, residual stresses, fatigue, constraint, etc.) can contribute to brittle fractures in large welded structures such as ship hulls.[5-16] However, the recent development of fracture mechanics[16-20] has shown that there are three primary factors that control the brittle fracture. These three primary factors are:

2.1   Material Toughness (K_c, K_{IC}, K_{ID})

Material toughness can be defined as the ability to deform plastically in the presence of a notch and can be described in terms of the static critical stress-intensity factor under conditions of plane stress (K_c) or plane strain (K_{IC}). K_{ID} is a widely accepted measure of the critical material toughness under conditions of maximum constraint (plane strain) and impact-loading. In addition to metallurgical facsors such as composition and heat treatment, the notch toughness of a steel also depends on the application temperature, loading rate, and constraint (state-of-stress) ahead of the notch.

2.2   Flaw Size (a)

Brittle fractures initiate from flaws or discontinuities of various kinds. These discontinuities can vary from extremely small cracks within a weld arc strike, (as was the case in the brittle fracture of a T-2 tanker during Warld War II) to much larger weld or fatigue cracks. Complex welded structures are not fabricated without discontinuities (porosity, lack of fusion, toe cracks, mismatch, etc.), although good fabrication practice and inspection can minimize the original size and number of flaws. Thus, these discontinuities will be present in all welded ship hull structures even after all inspections and weld repairs are finished. Furthermore, even though only "small" flaws may be present initially, fatigue stressing can cause them to enlarge, possibly to a critical size.

2.3   Stress Level (σ)

Tensile stresses, (nominal, residual, or both) are necessary for brittle fractures to occur. The stresses in ship hulls are difficult to analyze because ships are complex structures, because of the complexity of the dynamic loading, and because of the stress concentrations present throughout a ship which increase the local stress levels. The probability of critical regions in a welded ship hull being subjected to dynamic yield stress loading (σ_{yD}) is fairly high, particularly in regions of stress concentrations where residual stresses from welding may be present.

All three of these factors must be present for a brittle fracture to occur in structures. All other factors such as temperature, loading rate, residual stresses, etc. merely affect the above three primary factors.

Engineers have known these facts for many years and have reduced the susceptibility of structures to brittle fractures by applying these concepts to their structures qualitatively. That is, good design (lower stress levels by minimizing discontinuities) and fabrication practices (decreased flaw size because of proper welding control), as well as the use of materials with good notch-toughness levels (e.g., as measured with a Charpy V-notch impact test) will and have minimized the probability of brittle fractures in structures. However, the engineer has not had specified design guidelines to evaluate the relative performance and economic tradeoffs between design, fabrication and materials in a quantitative manner.

The recent development of fracture mechanics as an applied science has shown that all three of the above factors can be interrelated to predict (or to design against) the susceptibility of a welded structure to brittle fracture. Fracture mechanics is a method of characterizing fracture behavior in terms of structural parameters familiar to the engineer, namely, stress and flaw size. Fracture mechanics is based on stress analysis and thus does not depend on the use of empirical correlations to translate laboratory results into practical design information. Fracture mechanics is based on the fact that the stress distribution ahead of a sharp crack can be characterized in terms of a single parameter K_I, the stress-intensity factor, having units of ksi $\cdot \sqrt{\text{inch}}$ (MN/m³/²). Various specimen geometries have been analyzed, and theoretical expressions for K_I in terms of applied stress and flaw size have been developed. Three examples are presented in Fig. 1. In all cases, K_I is a function of the nominal stress and the square root of the flaw size. By knowing the critical value of K_I at failure, K_c, for a given steel of a particular thickness and at a specific temperature and loading rate, the designer can determine flaw sizes that can be tolerated in structural members for a given design stress level. Conversely, he can determine the design stress level that can be safely used for a flaw size that may be present in a structure.

This general relation is presented in Fig. 2 which shows the relationship between material toughness (K_c), nominal stress (σ), and flaw size (a). If a particular combination of stress and flaw size in a structure (K_I) reaches the K_c level, fracture can occur. Thus there are many combinations of stress and flaw size (e.g., σ_f and a_f) that may cause fracture in a structure that is fabricated from a steel having a particular value of K_c at a particular service temperature, loading rate, and plate thickness. Conversely, there are many combinations of stress and flaw size (e.g., σ_o and a_o) that will not cause failure of a particular steel.

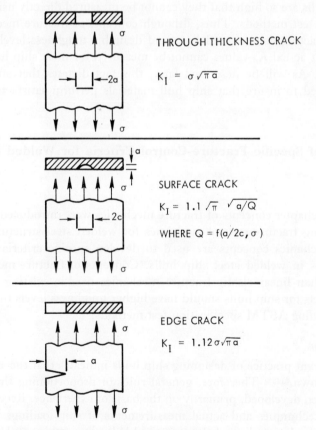

THROUGH THICKNESS CRACK

$$K_I = \sigma \sqrt{\pi a}$$

SURFACE CRACK

$$K_I = 1.1 \sqrt{\pi} \ \sqrt{a/Q}$$

WHERE $Q = f(a/2c, \sigma)$

EDGE CRACK

$$K_I = 1.12 \sigma \sqrt{\pi a}$$

FIG. 1. K_I values for various crack geometries.

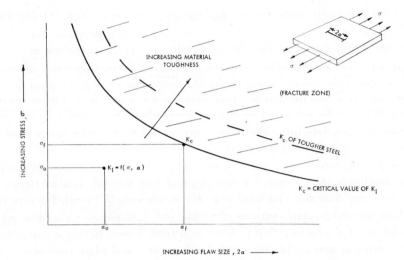

FIG. 2.   Schematic relation between stress, flaw size, and material toughness.

At this point, it should be emphasized that (fortunately) the K_c levels for most steels used in ship hulls are so high that they cannot be measured directly using existing ASTM standardized test methods. Thus, although concepts of fracture mechanics can be used to develop fracture-control guidelines and desirable toughness levels, the state of the art is such that actual K_c values cannot be measured for most ship hull steels at service temperatures. As will be described later, this fact dictates that auxiliary test methods must be used to insure that ship hull materials perform satisfactorily under service conditions.

3.   Development of Specific Fracture-Control Criteria for Welded Steel Ship Hulls

General

In the previous chapter concepts of fracture mechanics were introduced as the best method for developing fracture-control guidelines for welded steel structures. In this chapter, fracture-mechanics concepts are used to develop specific criteria to prevent catastrophic fractures in welded steel ship hulls. Concepts of fracture mechanics are emphasized rather than linear elastic fracture mechanics used in existing ASTM test methods because steels for ship hulls should have higher toughness levels than can currently be measured suing ASTM specification test methods.

Service Conditions

A review of current practice of designing ship hulls indicates that the actual loadings are not well known.[21, 22] Therefore, general rules of proportioning the cross section of ships have been developed, primarily on the basis of experience. Recent developments in analytical techniques and actual measurements of ship loadings have led to improvements in the understanding of the structural behavior of ships.[23] However, the design of ship hulls is primarily an empirical proportioning based on satisfactory past experience rather than a systematic analytical design and therefore calculated design stresses for specific sea states are rarely found.

Strain measurements on actual ships have indicated that the maximum vertical wave-bending-stress excursion (peak-to-trough) ever measured was about 24 ksi (165 MN/m²). Also the maximum bending stress for slender cargo liners is about 10 ksi (69 MN/m²) and for bigger ships such as tankers and bulk carriers, about 14 ksi (97 MN/m²).[22,24] Therefore, 14 ksi (97 MN/m²) appears to be a reasonable maximum nominal stress level in ship hulls. Although this stress is less than one-half the yield stress of most ship hull steels, the local stress level at stress concentrations reaches the yield strength level, particularly when the additional effects of residual stress are considered. Furthermore, because of the particular nature of ship hull loadings and the number of brittle fractures that have occurred in service, it is reasonable (and conservative) to assume that ships can be loaded under impact conditions, i.e., the loads can be applied rapidly enough so that the dynamic yield stress is reached.

The dynamic yield stress under impact loading is approximately 20 ksi (138 MN/

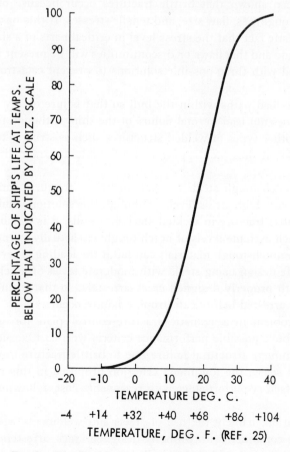

FIG. 3.   Distribution of service temperature for ships (Ref. 25).

m²) higher than the static yield stress as measured in standard tension tests. The actual loading rate for ship hulls is probably between the limits of "static" loading (strain rate approximately 10^{-5} sec⁻¹) and dynamic or impact loading (strain rate approximately 10 sec⁻¹). However, in view of the general service behavior of ships, and the lack of information on specific loading rates, the conservative assumption that ships are loaded dynamically is made.

Studies have shown that ships operate at temperatures less than 32°F (0°C) only about 3% of the time, Fig. 3.[25] Therefore, a design service temperature of 32°F (0°C) for welded steel ship hulls appears realistic. For special applications, such as icebreakers, the design service temperature should be lower.

Therefore, from a fracture-control standpoint, the probability is very high that critical regions in welded ship hulls can be subjected to impact loadings at 32°F (0°C) such that the dynamic yield stress of the material can be reached. Thus, the use of dynamic fracture parameters, K_{ID}/σ_{yD}, rather than static fracture parameters, K_{IC}/σ_{ys}, is justified.

Required Performance Characteristics

Previously, it has been shown that brittle fractures occur because of particular combinations of material toughness, flaw size, and tensile stresses. If this basic principle is combined with the realistic fact that the stress level in critical parts of a ship hull will reach yield stress magnitude and that flaws or discontinuities will be present in the hull, the naval architect is faced with three possible solutions to prevent catastrophic brittle fractures in ships[26]:

1) Develop multiple-load paths within the hull so that failure of any one part of the cross section does not lead to total failure of the ship. Although this solution is satisfactory for other types of welded structures such as stringer-type bridges with concrete decks, it does not appear to be feasible for monolithic welded steel ship hulls.

2) Use extremely notch-tough steels so that no brittle fractures can initiate or propagate, even at very high stress levels. Although this solution would eliminate the problem of brittle fracture in welded steel ship hulls, it is economically unfeasible because such extreme levels of notch toughness actually are not required. Furthermore, even notch-tough materials can fail if the loading is severe enough.

3) Provide a fail-safe design using steels with moderate levels of notch-toughness in combination with properly designed crack-arresters, so that even if a crack initiates, it will be arrested before catastrophic failure occurs.

The fundamental problem in a realistic fracture-control plan for welded ship hulls is to optimize the above possible performance criteria with cost considerations so that the probability of complete structural failure due to brittle fracture in welded ship hulls is very low. In that sense, the toughness criterion proposed in this report is an attempt to optimize satisfactory performance with reasonable cost, following a fail-safe philosophy.

Thus, the third solution, namely the use of steels and weldments with moderate levels of notch toughness combined with properly designed crack arresters, is recommended as a fracture criterion for welded ship hulls.

In line with this general fracture-control plan, the following items are noted.

1) As has been well documented during the past 30 years, the definite possibility of brittle fracture in welded ship hulls exists because welded ship hulls are complex structures that can be subjected to local dynamic loading of yield point magnitude at temperature as low as 32°F (0°C).

2) Because of current limitations in fabrication practice and inspection at shipyards, a large probability exists that large undetected flaws will be present at some time during the life of welded ship hulls. Even with improvements in control of welding quality during fabrication,, some discontinuities will still be present prior to the service life of the structure and fatigue may cause these discontinuities to grow in size during the life of the structure. Thus, it is assumed that flaws are present in all welded ship hulls.

3) The naval architect generally does not have absolute control over the fabrication of a welded ship hull. Thus, he should establish material and design controls during the design process that are adequate to prevent the occurrence of brittle fractures in welded ship hulls. Although the designer tries to avoid details that act as stress raisers, this is an impossible task in large complex welded structures. Hence, the emphasis in this fracture-control plan is on the choice of proper materials (toughness specifications for steels and weldments) and design (proper use of crack arresters), even though quality fabrication and inspection of welds are extremely important.

4) Although specifying solely the metallurgy and manufacturing process, including composition, deoxidization practice, heat treatment, etc., has been used as one method of controlling the level of notch toughness in a steel, the only method of measuring the actual toughness of a steel is a toughness test. A direct measure of toughness is better for the user because he is ultimately concerned with the performance of the steel or weldment, and this performance can best be determined by a notch-toughness test. Also a specification based on a notch-toughness test would appear to be more equitable for steelmakers in that it leaves them some latitude to adopt the process best suited to their particular operation in satisfying the toughness requirement. However, a toughness test does have the disadvantage in that a test value pertains to only one location in a plate whereas proper processing control should pertain to the entire plate. However, because this may not always be true, a toughness test is no less effective as an indication of the service performance of the entire plate.

5) Because of the difficulties in conducting a toughness test on a composite weldment, notch-toughness specimens should be taken from each of the following regions: base metal, weld metal, and heat-affected zone. While there is no "one" heat-affected-zone, an average measure of toughness can be obtained by notching the test specimen so that the tip of the notch is at approximately the center of the heat-affected zone region. Existing ABS Rules[27] specify that five sets of impact specimens be taken during welding Procedure Qualification Testing for weldments used for very low-temperature service. The notches for the specimens are located at the centerline of the weld, on the fusion line, and in the heat-affected-zone, 0.039-in (1 mm), 0.118-in (3 mm), and 0.197-in (5 mm) from the

fusion line. For weld qualification tests it may be desirable to follow this practice.

The specific requirements to implement these fail-safe fracture-control guidelines consist of 1) establishing a satisfactory level of notch toughness in the steels and weldments, and 2) development of properly designed crack arresters. It should be re-emphasized that improper fabrication can still lead to structural failure regardless of the level of notch-toughness. Thus good quality welding and inspection must be followed.

4. Materials Performance Characteristics

General

In general, the primary load-carrying members of steel ship structures are the plate members within the center .4L of the hull that comprise the upper deck, bottom shell, side plating, and longitudinal bulkheads. Because these members are the primary load-carrying members, material toughness requirements should be specified for them. Although stiffeners can also be primary load-carrying members, they are not connected to each other and thus failure of one stiffener should not lead to failure of adjacent stiffeners. Therefore they need not be subject to the proposed criteria.

Stresses in a ship hull vary from extreme levels in the upper deck and bottom shell to essentially zero at the neutral axis as indicated in Fig. 4, which illustrates an idealized stress distribution in the section. As shown schematically in Fig. 2, the critical crack size for a given material is influenced by the nominal tensile stress level. Because stresses in the main-stress regions (Fig. 4) can reach critical levels, the materials performance characteristics of the primary load-carrying plate members in these areas should be specified by a toughness requirement. Stresses in the secondary-stress region are somewhat lower, and for primary load-carrying plate members in this area, a less-stringent toughness requirement is needed.

Development of Toughness Requirement for Main-Stress Regions

Traditionally, the fracture characteristics of low-and intermediate-strength steels have been described in terms of the transition from brittle to ductile behavior as measured by impact tests. This transition in fracture behavior can be related schematically to various fracture states as shown in Fig. 5. Plane-strain behavior refers to fracture under

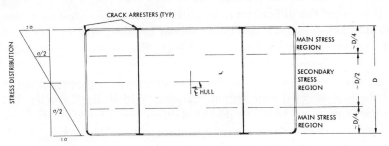

FIG. 4. Schematic cross section showing primary load-carrying members in main- and secondary-stress regions.

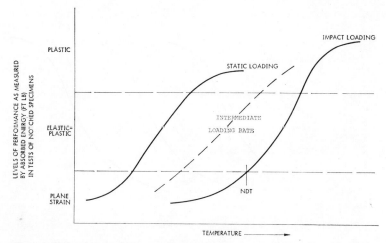

FIG. 5. Schematic showing relation between notch-toughness test results and levels of structural performance for various loading rates.

elastic stresses with little or no shear-lip development and is essentially brittle. Plastic behavior refers to ductile failure under general yielding conditions with very large shear-lip development. The transition between these two extremes is the elastic-plastic region which is also referred to as the mixed-mode region.

For static loading, the transition region occurs at lower temperatures than for impact (or dynamic) loading, depending on the yield strength of the steel. Thus, for structures subjected to static loading, the static transition curve should be used to predict the level of performance at the service temperature. For structures subjected to impact or dynamic loading, the impact transition curve should be used to predict the level of performance at the service temperature.

For structures subjected to some intermediate loading rate, an intermediate loading rate transition curve should be used to predict the level of performance at the service temperature. Because the actual loading rates for ship hulls are not well defined, and to be conservative, the impact loading curve (Fig. 5) is used to predict the service performance of ship hull steels. As noted on Fig. 5, the nil-ductility transition (NDT) temperature generally defines the upper limit of plane-strain behavior under conditions of impact loading.

A fundamental question to be resolved regarding a fracture criterion for welded ship hull steels is; "What level of material performance should be required for satisfactory performance in a ship hull subjected to dynamic loading?" That is, as shown schematically in Fig. 6 for impact loading, one of the following three general levels of material performance must be established at the service temperature for the steels that are primary load-carrying members:

1) Plane-strain behavior—Use steel (1)—Fig. 6
2) Elastic-plastic behavior—Use steel (2)—Fig. 6
3) Fully plastic behavior—Use steel (3)—Fig. 6

Although fully plastic behavior would be a very desirable level of performance for

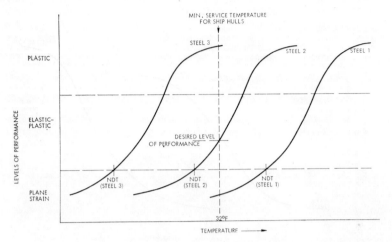

FIG. 6.   Schematic showing relation between level of performance as measured by impact tests and NDT for 3 arbitrary steels.

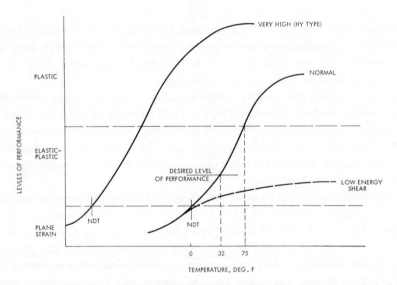

FIG. 7.   Schematic showing relation between normal-high, and low-energy shear levels of performance as measured by impact tests.

ship hull steels, it may not be necessary, or even economically feasible. A reasonable level of elastic-plastic behavior (steel 2—Fig. 6) should be satisfactory to prevent initiation of most brittle fractures. (If fractures do initiate, they should not lead to catastrophic failure of a ship as long as properly designed crack arresters are used.) Specifying that the NDT temperature of all steels and weldments used in primary load-carrying members in the center 0.4L of ships be equal to or less than 0°F (−18°C) (32°F [18°C] below the minimum service temperature) should establish the required performance level, if the materials follow the general behavior of steel 2 in Fig. 6.

Thus, the primary material specification in an overall fracture-control plan for welded steel ship hulls is that all steels and weldments used in primary load-carrying plate members in the main-stress regions of ships have a maximum NDT of 0°F(−18°C) as measured by ASTM Test Method E-208-69.[28]

Although necessary, this primary NDT requirement alone is not sufficient, since an additional toughness requirement is necessary to insure that the resistance to facture of the steels and weldments whose NDT is 0°F (−18°C) (or lower) is actually satisfactory at 32°F (0°C). That is, this additional requirement is necessary to guarantee that materials follow the general performance level shown in Fig. 6, rather than exhibit a low-energy shear behavior. Figure 7 shows the relationship of low-energy performance to normal behavior and very-high level behavior (HY-80 type behavior for military applications).

Low-energy shear behavior usually does not occur in low-strength steels but is sometimes found in high-strength steels. Thus the additional toughness requirement is necessary to eliminate the possibility of low-energy shear failures, primarily for the higher strength steels.

In terms of fracture-mechanics concepts, the critical dynamic toughness, K_{ID}, is approximately equal to 0.6 σ_{YD} at NDT, where σ_{YD} is the dynamic yield strength of the material. Thus for the ship hull materials that satisfy the criterion that NDT be equal to or less than 0°F (−18°C),

$$\frac{K_{ID}}{\sigma_{YD}} \geq 0.6 \text{ at } 0°F(-18°C)$$

At the minimum service temperature of 32°F (0°C) K_{ID}/σ_{YD} is estimated to be about 0.9 because of the rapid increase in K_{ID} with temperature in the transition temperature

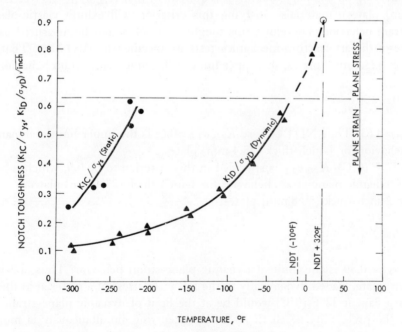

FIG. 8. Crack-toughness performance for ABS-C steel.

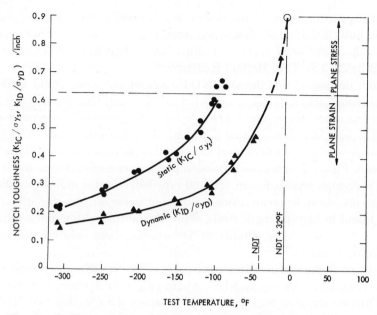

FIG. 9.   Crack-toughness performance for A517-F steel.

region. Although the value of 0.9 cannot be established theoretically, experimental results for various steels,[29] including ABS-C and ASTM A517 steels, Figs. 8 and 9, indicate that this is a realistic value.

It should be emphasized that although concepts of fracture mechanics have been used to develop an auxiliary toughness requirement that $K_{ID}/\sigma_{YD} \sim 0.9$ (for 1-inch-thick [25.4 mm] plates), materials satisfying this criterion will exhibit elastic-plastic, non-plane-strain behavior. Therefore, this toughness level cannot be measured using existing state-of-the-art fracture-mechanics tests as specified by ASTM.[30] That is, for 1-inch-thick [25.4 mm] plates, the upper limit of dynamic plane strain behavior is

$$1.0 = 2.5 \left(\frac{K_{ID}}{\sigma_{YD}} \right)^2$$

$K_{ID}/\sigma_{YD} = 0.63$. Thus NDT (where $K_{ID}/\sigma_{YD} \simeq 0.6$) is the upper limit of dynamic plane-strain behavior for 1-inch-thick (25.4 mm) plates.

At 32°F (0°C), K_{ID}/σ_{YD} is specified in this criterion to be 0.9, which is beyond the limits of dynamic plane-strain behavior for 1-inch-thick (25.4 mm) plates.

For 2-inch-thick (50.8 mm) plates,

$$2.0 = 2.5 \left(\frac{K_{ID}}{\sigma_{YD}} \right)^2$$

or $K_{ID}/\sigma_{YD} = 0.89$ is the limit of dynamic plane-strain behavior. Thus, a 2-inch-thick (50.8 mm) plate, loaded dynamically to the full yield stress of a material in the presence of a sharp flaw at 32°F (0°C) would be at the limit of dynamic plane-strain behavior. Because the probability of all these factors occurring simultaneously is minimal, the requirement that $K_{ID}/\sigma_{YD} \geq 0.9$ appears to be satisfactory for all thicknesses of plate 2 inches (50.8 mm) or less. However, the required toughness levels for plates thicker than 2 inches (50.8 mm) should be increased.

Using concepts of fracture mechanics, as well as engineering experience, the following observations can be made regarding the level of performance at 32°F (0°C) for steels and weldments that satisfy the primary toughness requirement of NDT≤0°F (−18°C) and the auxiliary toughness requirement that $K_{ID}/\sigma_{YD} \geq 0.9$ at 32°F (0°C):

1) The start of the transition from brittle to ductile behavior will begin below the minimum service temperature of 32°F (0°C) Therefore, at the minimum service temperature, the materials will exhibit some level of elastic-plastic non-plane-strain behavior in the presence of a sharp crack under dynamic loading.

2) Although not specified in the proposed toughness requirement, the materials will exhibit some percentage of fibrous fracture appearance at 32°F (0°C). Service experience has shown that fracture appearance is an effective indicator of the resistance to brittle fracture. Thus, this criterion is consistent with service experience of ship hulls.

3) Although precise stress-flaw size calculations cannot be made for material exhibiting elastic-plastic behavior, estimates of critical crack sizes for 40 ksi (276 MN/m²) yield strength steels can be made as follows;

a) For a $K_{ID} \geq 0.9 \ \sigma_{YD}$ and a nominal stress of 14 ksi (97 MN/m²) the critical crack size at 32°F (0°C) is estimated to be 8–10 inches (203–254 mm) as shown in Fig. 10.

b) For one of the largest stress ranges (peak-to-tough) ever recorded in ships, i.e., about 24 ksi (165 MN/m²), the critical crack size is estimated to be 3 inches (76 mm).

c) For the worst possible case of dynamic loading of yield point magnitude, the dynamic critical crack size is estimated to be 1/2 inch (12.7 mm).

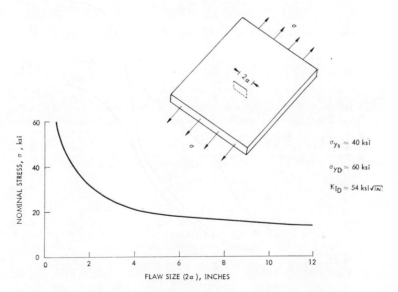

FIG. 10.   Estimate of stress-flaw size relation for *ABS* steel with $K_{ID}/\sigma_{YD} \simeq 0.9$.

Ideally, the auxiliary toughness requirement that $K_{ID}/\sigma_{YD} \geq 0.9$ at 32°F (0°C) sould be established by conducting a K_{ID} test at 32°F (0°C). Unfortunately, no inexpensive standard K_{ID} test specimen exists. Furthermore, research test procedures to obtain K_{ID} values directly are currently too complex for use in specifications. Thus some other test specimen must be used to insure that $K_{ID}/\sigma_{YD} \geq 0.9$ at 32°F (0°C).

The test specimen should be loaded dynamically, easy to use, standardized, and the results should be readily interpretable. In addition, the specimen should have a sharp notch to closely approximate the sharp crack conditions that exist in large complex welded structures such as welded ship hulls. Finally, the test specimen should be as large as practical because of the effect of constraint on the fracture behavior of structural steels.

After careful consideration of which of the various fracture test specimens (e.g., CVN, pre-cracked CVN, Crack-Opening Displacement-COD, DT, and K_{ID}) would be most applicable to the particular requirement for welded ship hulls, the 5/8-inch(15.9mm) thick dynamic tear (DT) test specimen[31] is recommended as the auxiliary test specimen.

For the ship hull steel application, the DT test specimen currently satisfies all of the above requirements better than any other test specimen. The DT test is an impact test (high-loading rate) that has a sharp pressed notch with residual tensile stresses (thus the strain concentration is larger than for machined notches). The beginning of the elastic-plastic transition occurs at NDT as shown in Fig. 11, 12, and 13 for representative ABS-B, ABS-C, and A517 steels, respectively. Thus the DT test specimen results can be easily related to the NDT values for ship steels.

For the plate thicknesses normally used in ship hull construction (less than 2-inches [50.8 mm] thick), thickness has a second-order effect on the toughness behavior in the transition temperature region compared with the first-order effects of loading rate

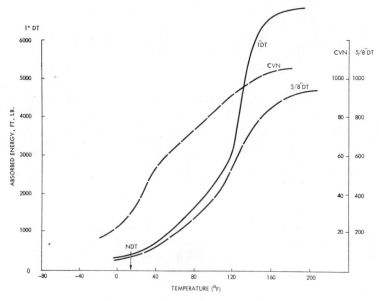

FIG. 11.   Relation between NDT, CVN, and DT test results for ABS-B steel.

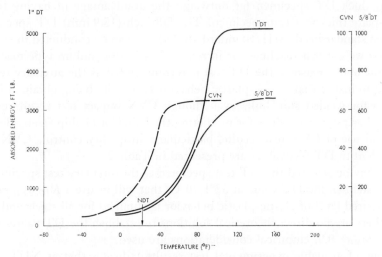

FIG. 12.   Relation between NDT, CVN, and DT test results for ABS-C steel.

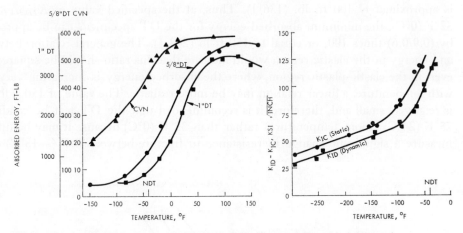

FIG. 13.   Relation between NDT, CVN, DT, K_{IC}, and K_{ID} for A 517 steel.

of notched steel specimens raises the transition temperature as shown in Fig. 8 and 9.[32] Increasing the notch acuity (from that in a machined CVN specimen to that in a pressed-notch DT specimen) also raises the beginning of the transition temperature range as shown in Fig. 11–13 and 26–29. The second order effect of thickness (namely the very small change in transition behavior between 5/8 [15.9 mm] and 1 inch [25.4 mm] thick DT specimens) is shown in Figs. 11, 12, and 13. There are larger changes in transition temperature for much thicker plates (e.g., 3– to 12-inch (76 to 305 mm) thick plates used in thick-walled pressure vessels) but for the ship hull application (plates less than 2-inches [50.8 mm] thick), the effects of specimen thickness are second order and can be ignored.

Therefore, although it would be technically more desirable to use full-thickness DT specimens to specify the behavior of ship steels, only the 5/8-inch (15.9 mm) thick DT specimen is being recommended because the practical aspects of testing the 5/8-inch

(15.9 mm) thick DT specimen far outweigh the disadvantage of having to use a less than full-plate thickness test specimen. The 5/8-inch (15.9 mm) DT specimen has recently been standardized (MIL Standard 1601[31]) and can be conducted in existing NDT type falling weight test machines or in relatively small pendulum type machines.

For the above reasons, the DT test is recommended as the auxiliary test specimen to be used to insure that elastic-plastic behavior is actually being obtained in steels and weldments for welded ship hulls even though CVN impact test results currently are widely used as reference values for predicting the behavior of ship steels. Because of the wide-spread use of CVN test results, particularly in quality control, CVN values that are equivalent to DT test values are presented in Table 2.

After having selected the DT test specimen as the auxiliary test specimen, the next step is to establish the DT value at 32°F (0°C) that will insure a K_{ID}/σ_{YD} ratio of 0.9 so that the desired level of elastic-plastic behavior is obtained for all steels and weldments. Because there are no direct theoretical solutions to establish the DT values corresponding to $K_{ID}/\sigma_{YD}=0.9$, empirical considerations are used.

A review of available experimental test results indicates that at NDT, where $K_{ID}/\sigma_{YD}\simeq0.6$, the amount of absorbed energy for 5/8-inch (15.9 mm) thick DT specimens is approximately 100 ft. lb. (136 J). Thus, at the specified value of $K_{ID}/\sigma_{YD}=0.9$ at 32°F (0°C), the minimum absorbed energy for the DT specimens can be approximated by (0.9/0.6) times 100, or equal to 150 ft lb (203 J). The general relation between K_I and energy in the elastic region would indicate that this ratio should be squared. However, in the elastic-plastic region, where the absorbed energy is increasing very rapidly with temperature, a linear relation may be more realistic. The value of 150 ft lb (203 J) is relatively small and, therefore, it is recommended that the DT test be conducted at 75°F (24°C) (room temperature) rather than 32°F (0°C) because it may be difficult to measure a significant change in resistance to fracture between 0°F (−18°C) (limit of

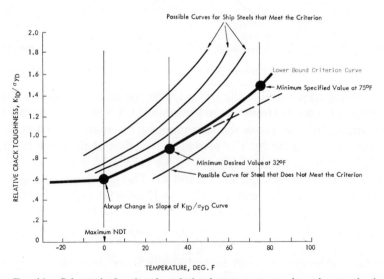

FIG. 14.   Schematic showing the relation between proposed toughness criterion for members in the main-stress region and behavior of actual ship steels.

plane-strain behavior) and 32°F (0°C) (a moderate level of elastic-plastic behavior). Although from a technical viewpoint it would be preferable to conduct the DT test at both 32°F (0°C) and 75°F (24°C), the practical considerations of the specification suggest that the DT test be conducted at +75°F (24°C) (room temperature).

If the test is conducted at 75°F (24°C), the minimum K_{ID}/σ_{YD} ratio should be 1.5 on the basis of a non-linear extrapolation from 0.9 at 32°F (0°C) as shown in Fig. 14. Thus, the minimum DT value should be (1.5/0.9) times 150, or equal to 250 ft lb (339 J). Fig. 14 also shows a schematic representation of the lower-bound specification curve of required values (NDT=0°F (−18°C) and $K_{ID}/\sigma_{YD}>1.5$ at 75°F (24°C) actually 250 ft lbs (339 J) in a DT test) and the minimum desired values of $K_{ID}/\sigma_{YD}=0.9$ at 32°F (0°C) compared with possible curves for ship steels that either do or do not meet the criterion. This figure shows that by meeting both of the toughness requirements at 0°F (−18°C) and 75°F (24°C) the desired behavior at 32°F (0°C) ($K_{ID}/\sigma_{YD}\geq0.9$) should be met.

Assuming that the dynamic yield strength is approximately 20 ksi (138 MN/m²) higher than the static yield strength of a steel, the required DT values at 75°F (24°C) $K_{ID}/\sigma_{YD}\geq1.5$) can be proportioned for strength level as shown in Table 1. This adjustment is necessary to insure that high-strength steels have the same relative toughness levels as lower strength steels.

Thus, the auxiliary material specification in an overall fracture-control plan for welded steel ship hulls is that all steels and weldments used in primary load-carrying plate members in the main-stress regions of ships exhibit the levels of absorbed energy in a 5/8-inch (15.9 mm) dynamic tear (DT) specimen as presented in Table 1.

The values presented in Table 1 should be the minimum values of specimens oriented in the same direction as the primary stress level (notch oriented perpendicular to the direction of primary stress). In most cases, the specimens will be longitudinal to the rolling direction. However, if the transverse stress level becomes significant, then the test specimens should be oriented in the transverse direction. CVN values (using a stan-

TABLE 1. Dynamic tear (DT) requirements at +75°F (24°C) for steels and weldments in main-stress regions for primary load-carrying members* of ship hulls.

Actual static yield strength σ_{Ys}		Assumed dynamic yield strength σ_{YD}		Proportionality factor for strength level	Absorbed energy requirements** for 5/8-inch (15.9 mm) thick specimens	
ksi	MN/m²	ksi	MN/m²		ft-lb	J
40	276	60	414	(60/60)	250	339
50	345	70	483	(70/60)	290	393
60	414	80	552	(80/60)	335	454
70	483	90	621	(90/60)	375	508
80	552	100	689	(100/60)	415	563
90	621	110	758	(110/60)	460	624
100	689	120	827	(120/60)	500	678

* These members must also meet the requirement of NDT≤0°F (−18°C).
** Dynamic elastic-plastic behavior approximating $K_{ID}/\sigma_{YD}\simeq1.5$.

TABLE 2. Equivalent CVN values for $K_{ID}/\sigma_{YD} \geq 0.9$ at 32°F (0°C) for primary-load carring members using CVN-DT correlation.

Static yield strength σ_{Ys}		Dynamic yield strength σ_{YD}		Required DT value		Equivalent CVN value	
ksi	MN/m²	ksi	MN/m²	ft-1b	J	ft-1b	J
40	276	60	414	250	339	20	27
50	345	70	483	290	393	24	33
60	414	80	552	335	454	28	38
70	483	90	621	375	508	32	43
80	552	100	689	415	563	36	49
90	621	110	758	460	624	40	54
100	689	120	827	500	678	44	60

dard notch) that are equivalent to a K_{ID}/σ_{YD} value of 0.9 at 32°F (0°C) are presented in Table 2. It should be emphasized that the values presented in Table 1 or 2 are not fully plastic "shelf-level" values, but rather, are values that should insure the desired level of elastic-plastic behavior.

Development of Toughness Criterion for Secondary-Stress Regions

The toughness criteria developed thus far in this section are applicable to areas of maximum stress levels which include critical members in the main-stress regions of the hull. Primary load-carrying members within the secondary-stress region (central D/2 portion-Fig. 4) will now be considered.

In this vicinity, nominal stresses can usually be expected to be less than one-half the maximum normal hull stress in the deck. Because low stresses (5 to 8 ksi [34 to 55 MN/m²]) have been known to initiate brittle fractures in steels at temperatures less than NDT[5], and flaws are present in ships, it accordingly follows that a moderate notch-toughness criterion is required even in secondary-stress regions of primary load-carrying members.

Because the same size flaws can exist throughout the entire hull section, the toughness criterion for the secondary stress regions should result in the same required stress-intensity factor (K_{ID}) for both primary-and-secondary-stress regions. Thus, for the main-stress region, $K_{ID} \sim \sigma \sqrt{a_{cr}}$ and for the secondary-stress region, $K_{ID} \sim \sigma/2 \sqrt{a_{cr}}$. A comparison of these relations shows that required K_{ID} for the secondary-stress region is one-half that of the main-stress region. Accordingly, the required K_{ID}/σ_{YD} ratio is equal to 0.45 (K_{ID}/σ_{YD} is 0.9 for the main-stress regions). However, a history of welded steel fractures indicates that a design for this particular level of toughness (<NDT) would not be desirable because fractures have initiated from very small flaws when service temperatures are lower than NDT, even when the applied stresses were quite low.[5]

Thus, even though a tolerable flaw size can be numberically computed for a K_{ID}/σ_{YD} ratio of 0.45, it would be very small (~0.1 inch [2.5 mm]), and a minimum service temperature coincident with NDT ($K_{ID}/\sigma_{YD}=0.6$) appears to be the lowest realistic design-toughness level. A graphical representation of this design-toughness level is presented in Fig. 15.

A review of several hull cross sections indicates that primary load-carrying mem-

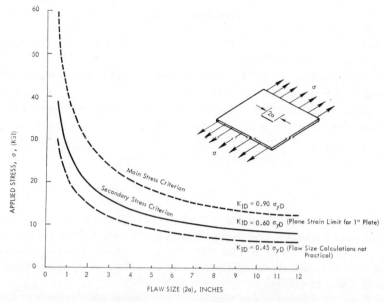

FIG. 15.   Schematic comparison of main-stress and secondary-stress criterion.

bers in the secondary-stress regions usually have nominal-section thicknesses less than or equal to one inch (25.4 mm).[33] This is due to the fact that the steel in these members is seldom a higher grade than ABS Grade B, which is restricted by ABS rules[25] to a one-inch (25.4 mm) thickness for this application. Thus a one-inch (25.4 mm) section thickness would appear to be the maximum thickness used. As mentioned previously, NDT essentially represents the upper limit of plain-strain behavior for this thickness.

Because the material-toughness requirement of $K_{ID}/\sigma_{YD}=0.6$ at the minimum service temperature (32°F [0°C]) is coincident with the NDT temperature, it can be conveniently established by using the NDT test. Such a marginal toughness level does not require an auxiliary test to evaluate transition behavior. However, past experience with the NDT testing procedure indicates that a margin of at least 10°F (6°C) be allowed, particularly for a specification that is based solely on NDT. For all practical purposes, an NDT temperature of 20°F (−7°C) should be sufficient to assure that $K_{ID}/\sigma_{YD}=0.6$ at 32°F (0°C).

Thus, all steels and weldments used in primary load-carrying plate members in the secondary-stress regions must satisfy a less stringent material-toughness requirement of NDT<20°F (−7°C).

As stated previously, the above material specifications for either the main-stress regions or the secondary-stress regions will not guarantee the complete absence of brittle fractures in welded ship hulls. Therefore, a fail-safe philosophy that incorporates properly designed crack arresters fabricated from steels with very high levels of notch toughness must be used in conjunction with the above material requirements.

ACKNOWLEDGMENTS

The work discussed in this report was sponsored by the Ship Structure Committee by means of the Naval Ship Engineering Center Contract N00024-72-Q-7071 (S) and will be published in late 1974 as SSC Report No. 244. The present report is a condensed version of SSC Report No. 244.

The opinions and conclusions presented in this paper are those of the author and not necessarily those of the Ship Structure Committee nor of the Department of the navy.

REFERENCES

1. Bannerman, D. B. and Young, R. T., "Some Improvements Resulting from Studies of Welded Ship Failures," Welding Journal, Vol. 25, No. 3, Mar. (1946).
2. Acker, H. G., "Review of Welded Ship Failures," (Ship Structure Committee Report Serial No. SSC–63), Washington, National Academy of Sciences–National Research Council, Dec., 15 (1953).
3. *Final Report of a Board of Investigation*—"The Design and Methods of Construction of Welded Steel Merchant Vessels," 15 July, 1946, Government Printing Press, Washington, D.C. (1947).
4. Boyd, G. M. and Bushell, T. W., "Hull Structural Steel—The Unification of the Requirements of Seven Classification Societies," Quarterly Transactions, The Royal Institution of Naval Architects (London), Vol. 103, No. 3, Mar. (1961).
5. Parker, E. R., "*Brittle Behavior of Engineering Structures*," New York, John Wiley & Sons, Inc., (1957).
6. Turnbull, J., "Hull Structures," The Institution of Engineers and Shipbuilders of Scotland, Transactions, Vol. 100, pt. 4, Dec., 301/316 (1956-7).
7. Boyd, G. M., "Fracture Design Practices for Ship Structures," *Fracture* edited by H. Libowitz, Vol. 5, "Fracture Design of Structures," Academic Press, New York and London, 383/470 (1969).
8. Heller, S. R., Nielsen, R., Lytle, A. R. and Vasta, J., "Twenty Years of Research Under the Ship Structure Committee," (Ship Structure Committee Report, Serial No. SSC–182), Washington, U.S. Coast Guard Headquarters, Dec. (1967).
9. Welding Research Council, "*Control of Steel Construction to Avoid Brittle Failure*," edited by M. E. Shank, Mass. Inst. of Technology (1957).
10. Hall, W. J., Kihara, H., Soete, W. and Wells, A. A., "*Brittle Fracture of Welded Plate*", Prentice-Hall, Inc., Englewood Cliffs, N.J. (1967).
11. The Royal Institution of Naval Architects, "*Brittle Fracture inSteel Structures*," edited by G. M. Boyd, London, Butterworth & Co., (Publishers) Ltd. (1970).
12. "*Fracture, An Advanced Treatise*," Vols I–VII, edited by H. Libowitz, Academic Press, New York and London.
13. Tipper, C. F., "*The Brittle Fracture Story*," Cambridge University Press (Great Britain), (1962).
14. The Japan Welding Society, "Cracking and Fracture in Welds," *Proceedings of the First International Symposium on the Prevention of Cracking in Welded Structures*, Tokyo, Nov. 8–10 (1971).
15. Pellini, W. S., "Principles of Fracture—Safe Design," (parts I and II), Welding Journal

(Welding Research Supplement), Mar. 91–S/109–S, (1971), and April, 147–S/162–S, (1971).

16. American Society for Testing and Materials, "Fracture Toughness Testing and its Applications," *ASTM, Special Technical Publication* No. 381 (1964).

17. American Society for Testing and Materials, *"Plane Strain Crack Toughness Testing of High Strength Metallic Materials,"* edited by Brown, W. F., and Srawley, J. E., ASTM-STP No. 410 (1966).

18. American Society for Testing and Materials, "Review of Developments in Plane Strain Fracture Toughness Testing," edited by Brown, W. F., *ASTM-STP* No. 436 (1970).

19. American Society for Testing and Materials, "Fracture Toughness," *Proceedings of the 1971 National Symposium on Fracture Mechanics, Part II, ASTM-STP* No. 514 (1971).

20. American Society of Civil Engineers, "Safety and Reliability of Metal Structures," *ASCE Specialty Conference* held in Pittsburgh, Pennsylvania, Nov. 2–3 (1972).

21. Hoffman, D. and Lewis, E. F., "Analysis and Interpretation of Full-Scale Data on Midship Bending Stresses of Dry Cargo Ships," (Ship Structure Committee Report, Serial No. SSC–196), Washington, U.S. Coast Guard Headquarters (1970).

22. Nibbering, J. J. W., "Permissible Stresses and Their Limitations," (Ship Structure Committee Report, Serial No. SSC–206), Washington, U.S. Coast Guard Headquarters, (1970).

23. Nielson, R., Chang, P. Y. and Deschamps, L. C., "Computer Design of Longitudinally Framed Ships," (Ship Structure Committee Report Serial No. SSC–225), Washington, U.S. Coast Guard Headquarters (1972).

24. Steneroth, E. R., "Reflections Upon Permissible Longitudinal Stresses in Ships," Transactions, Royal Institution of Naval Architects (London), Vol. 109, No. 2, Apr. (1967).

25. Hodgson, J. and Boyd, G. M., "Brittle Fracture in Welded Ships—An Empirical Approach from Recent Experience," Quarterly Transactions, The Royal Institution of Naval Architects (London) edited by Capt. A.D. Duckworth, R.N., Vol. 100, No. 3, July (1958).

26. Pellini, W. S., "Design Options for Selection of Fracture Control Procedures in the Modernization of Codes, Rules and Standards," *Proceedings of Joint United States-Japan Symposium on Application of Pressure Component Codes*, Tokyo, Japan, Mar. 13–15 (1973).

27. The American Bureau of Shipping, *"Rules for Building and Classing Steel Vessels,"* 45 Broad Street, New York, N.Y. (1973).

28. 1972 Annual Book of ASTM Standards, Part 31, E-208, *"Standard Method for Conducting Drop-Weight Test to Determine Nil-Ductility Transition Temperature of Ferritic Steels,"* American Society for Testing and Materials 594/613.

29. Shoemaker, A. K. and Rolfe, S. T., "Static and Dynamic Low-Temperature K_{IC} Behavior of Steels," Transactions of the ASME, Journal of Basic Engineering, Sept. (1969).

30. 1972 Annual Book of ASTM Standards, Part 31, E-399, *"Standard Method of Test for Plane-Strain Fracture Toughness of Metallic Materials,"* American Society for Testing and Materials, 955/974.

31. *Method for 5/8-Inch Dynamic Tear Testing of Metallic Materials,"* MIL-STD-1601 (ships), 8, May (1973).

32. Shoemaker, A. K., "Notch-Ductility Transition of Structural Steels of Various Yield Strengths," Transactions of ASME, Journal of Engineering for Industry, Paper No. 71-PVP-19 (1971).

33. *Higher-Strength Steels in Hull Structures*, Technical & Research Bulletin 2–19, Society of Naval Architects and Marine Engineers, 74 Trinity Place, New York, N.Y. (1971).

Combined Effects of Weld-Induced Residual Stresses and Flaws on the Fracture Strength of Ti-5Al-2.5Sn

L. R. HALL

Research and Engineering Division, Boeing Aerospace Company

1. Introduction

Crack growth in residual stress fields is a problem of considerable practical significance. For example, fusion welds are a common source of both crack-like defects and residual stresses. Hence, potential detrimental effects of residual stresses on crack stability must be quantitatively understood so that better estimates of quality requirements and service performance can be made for structures containing residual stresses.

This experimental program was undertaken to study the effect of weld-induced residual stresses on crack stability in 5Al-2.5Sn (ELI) titanium alloy base metal and weld metal. Static fracture tests were conducted on tension loaded specimens containing part-through cracks. The test program, summarized in Table 1, was divided into three series of tests. In Series 1, the surface cracks were located at the centerline of a GTA weld with the crack plane parallel to the weld. In Series II, the surface cracks were located in base metal with the crack plane perpendicular to the rolling direction. In Series III, the cracks were located in a GTA weld with the crack plane perpendicular to the weld centerline. Surface cracks having two distinctly different sizes were used to effect failure stresses at two different levels including one level at or near, and one level well below the tensile yield strength. The smaller cracks had crack depth-to-specimen thickness (a/t) ratios of about 0.3 and the larger cracks had a/t ratios of about 0.5. Tests were conducted under three different residual stress levels including one baseline or reference value, and two other values including one greater than and one less than the baseline value. All tests were conducted at $-320°F$ $(-195°C)$ in liquid nitrogen.

A number of previous investigations[1-5] have dealt with the effects of weld-induced residual stresses on brittle fracture in steel alloy specimens. Tests are usually conducted at low temperatures on specimens consisting of pairs of rectangular steel plates joined by butt welding after placing saw cut notches in the prepared edges. Such tests have shown that: the presence of tensile residual stresses in the vicinity of the notch reduces the applied stress required to initiate crack propagation; propagating cracks can be ar-

340

rested by residual compressive stresses;[4] and both mechanical and thermal stress relieving can increase the fracture strength of notched and welded steel plates.[6,7] Results of
steel plate fracture tests have been quantitatively evaluated by several investigators.[8-10]
This was accomplished through combining the effects of residual and applied stresses
using linear elastic fracture mechanics. Tests conducted on cracked titanium alloy
specimens[11] have demonstrated that fatigue crack growth rates can be diminished by
residual compressive stresses acting near the crack tip.

2.   Materials

Al specimens were cut from 0.375 by 36 by 84 inches (0.95 by 91 by 213 cm) plates
purchased in the mill annealed 1500°F (816°C)/0.5 hour/air cooled condition. Ingot composition is given in Table 2 and base metal mechanical properties are included in Table
3. Mechanical properties for the weld metal were obtained by testing specimens having
all weld metal test sections with a 0.20 by 0.25 inch (5.1 by 6.4 mm) rectangular cross-
section. The longitudinal axes of the test specimens coincided with the weld centerline.
The resultant mechanical properties are included in Table 3.

TABLE 1.   Test program for evaluating residual stress effects in 5Al-2.5 Sn (ELI) titanium.

Test series	Flaw location and orientation	Flaw geometry		Test temp. °F (°C)	Residual stress level		
		Type	Depth Thickness (a/t)		Reference + Tensile	Reference	Reference + Compressive
I	Weld Center flawplane ‖ to longitudinal weld axis	Surface flaw	0.25	−320 (−195)	2	2	2
			0.50		2	2	2
II	Parent metal flawplane ⊥ to rolling direction	Surface flaw	0.25	−320 (−195)	2	2	2
			0.50		2	2	2
III	Weldment flawplane ⊥ to longitudinal weld axis	Surface flaw	0.25	−320 (−195)	2	2	2
			0.50		2	2	2

Note: Numbers indicate duplicate tests.

TABLE 2.   Chemical composition of Ti-5Al-2.5 Sn (ELI) plate.

Material	Chemical composition (% by weight except as noted)								
	Mg	Fe	C	N	O	H	Sn	Al	Ti
Ti-5Al-2.5 Sn (ELI) 0.375—inch-thick plate—heat No. 294327	0.01	0.19	0.02	70 ppm	940 ppm	94 ppm	2.50	5.10	Bal

TABLE 3   Mechanical properties of Ti-5Al-2.5 Sn (ELI) base metal and weld metal.

Material	Condition	Grain direction	Temp. °F/°C	Ultimate tensile strength (ksi/kg/mm²)	0.2% Offset yield strength (ksi/kg/mm²)	Elongation in 2.0 inch gage length (%)
Base metal	Mill annealed (1500F/0.5HR)	Long.	72/22 −320/−195	122/86 187/131	113/79 180/126	15 8
Weld metal	Stress relieved 1200F/1HR	—	72/22 −320/−195	126/89 192/135	117/82 184/129	11 9

3. Procedures

Procedures for welding, precracking, generation of residual stresses, and measurement of residual stresses are briefly described in the following paragraphs.

Welding: All welding was accomplished using the mechanized GTA process with no filler wire additions. All welds were deposited using one pass from each side. Weld parameters were chosen to result in 100 percent penetration for the first pass with no measurable underfill along the edges of the weld bead as determined by visual inspection, and 90 percent penetration for the second pass. Argon gas was used for underbead shielding and helium gas was used for top side shielding. All welds were machined just enough to clean up the weld bead.

Precracking: All surface cracks were prepared by growing fatigue cracks from starter slots. Starter slots were produced using an electrical discharge machine and 0.06 inch (1.5 mm) thick circular electrodes; electrode tips were machined to a radius of about 0.003 inch (0.08 mm) and an included angle of about 20 degrees. Fatigue cracks were initiated from the periphery of the starter slots at room temperature using peak cyclic stresses of 50 ksi (35.2 kg/mm²) and a stress ratio of 0.06. The fatigue cracks extended about 0.02 inch (0.5 mm) from the root of the starter notch. The resultant flaw geometry and nomenclature is illustrated in Fig. 1. All flaws had depth-to-length ($a/2c$) ratios of 0.2.

Generation of Residual Stresses: Specimen configurations and methods of generating residual stresses for test Series I and II are illustrated in Fig. 2. After the specimens were machined and precracked, electron beam (EB) welds were used to generate the residual stresses. Circular welds completely surrounding the surface crack were

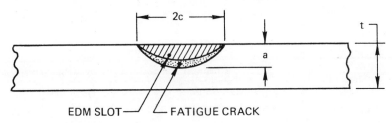

Fig. 1.   Surface flaw geometry.

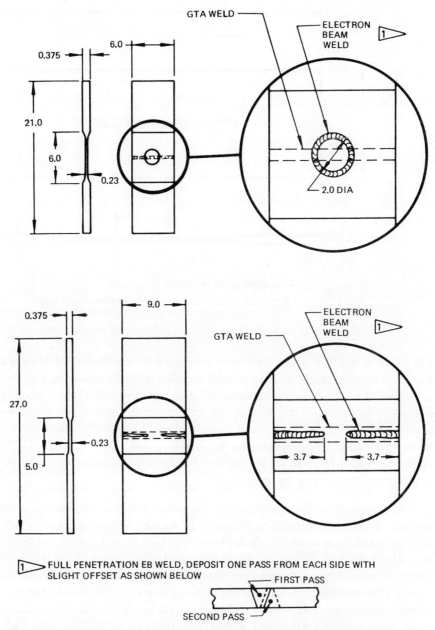

FIG. 2.   EB welding for 5Al-2.5 Sn (ELI) titanium test series I and II (All dimensions in inches).

used to generate tensile residual stresses as illustrated in the upper part of Fig. 2. Linear welds in the plane of the surface crack were used to generate compressive residual stresses as illustrated in the lower half of Fig. 2. After EB welding, the gage area widths of the specimens were reduced from 6 to 4 inches (15.2 to 10.2 cm) for specimens containing circular welds, and from 9 to 6 inches (22.8 to 15.2 cm) for specimens containing linear

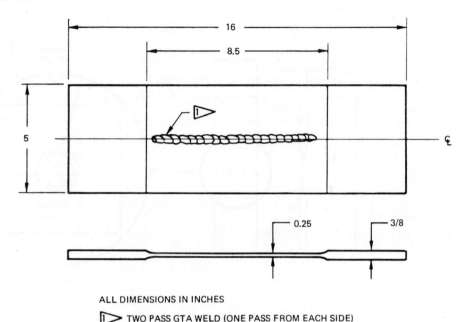

ALL DIMENSIONS IN INCHES

▷ TWO PASS GTA WELD (ONE PASS FROM EACH SIDE)
    DEPOSITED WITHOUT EDGE PREPARATION

FIG. 3.   5Al-2.5Sn (ELI) titanium test specimen for residual stress test series III.

EB welds in the flaw plane. Specimen configuration for Series III tests is illustrated in Fig. 3. The magnitude of longitudinal tensile residual stresses in the weld metal was controlled by subjecting specimens to different thermal cycles. Maximum residual stresses were obtained by leaving specimens in the as-welded condition. A 1000°F (538°C)/4 hour/retort cool thermal cycle was used to partially relieve residual stresses in some specimens. Other specimens were fully stress relieved using a 1300°F (704°C)/1 hour/retort cool thermal cycle. Surface cracks were introduced at the centers of the specimens after thermal treatment.

Measurement of Residual Stresses: Residual stress measurements were made using the hole drilling compliance technique[12] in which measurements are made of strain relaxation resulting from drilling a flat bottomed hole in successive increments at the location where residual stresses are to be measured. The center of the 0.125 inch (0.32 cm) diameter hole coincided with the intersection of center lines drawn longitudinally through two mutually perpendicular strain gages positioned such that their active grid edges were located 5/32±0.010 inch (0.40±.03 cm) from the hole center. Incremental strain gage readings were read during interruptions in drilling after each 0.005 inch (0.013 cm) increment up to a depth of 0.050 inch (0.013 cm), and after each 0.010 inch (0.025 cm) increment thereafter. Holes were drilled from only one side of each panel.

4.   Reults and Discussion

Residual Stress Measurements: The resultant distributions of residual stress in Series I and II specimens are shown in Fig. 4. The transverse residual stresses in the

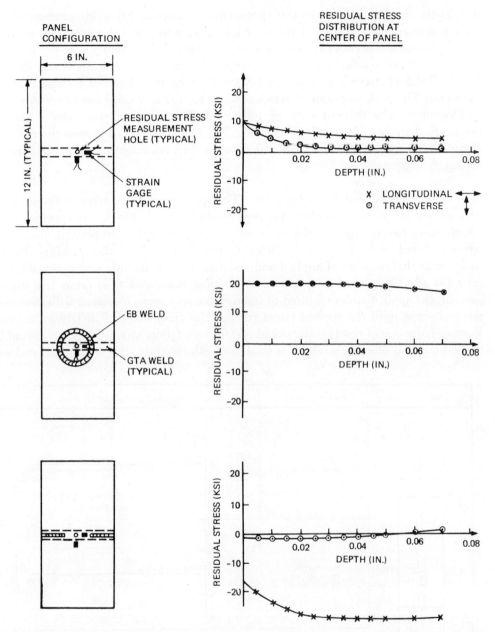

FIG. 4. Residual stress measurements for 5Al-2.5Sn (ELI) titanium alloy test series I
and II.

stress relieved weld were less than 2 ksi (1.4 kg/mm²) except over a 0.02 inch (0.5 mm)
layer next to the panel surface where the stresses increased to about 6.5 ksi (4.6 kg/mm²).
In panels with circular EB welds, transverse and longitudinal tensile stresses of 19 ksi
13.4 kg/mm²) were measured. In panels with the linear EB welds, peak transverse residual
compressive stresses of about 29 ksi (20.4 kg/mm²) were measured. It was concluded

that, at the flaw location in the test specimens, the circular EB welds generated transverse tensile residual stresses of about 17 ksi (12 kg/mm²), and the linear EB welds induced residual compressive stresses of about −30 ksi (21.1 kg/mm²).

Results of residual stress measurements for Series III specimens are shown in Fig. 5. Residual stresses were reasonably constant up to a depth of at least 0.07 inch (0.18 cm). The peak longitudinal residual stress for the as-welded condition was 70 ksi 49.2 kg/mm²). The thermal cycle of 1000°F (538°C) for four hours reduced the peak longitudinal stress to 24 ksi (16.9 kg/mm²). The 1300°F (704°C)/one hour thermal cycle completely stress relieved the weld and reduced the peak longitudinal tensile stress to 0.4 ksi (0.3 kg/mm²).

Static Fracture Test Series I and II: The applied gross area stress at failure for all Series I and II specimens is plotted against residual stress in Fig. 6. For specimens containing flaws having depth-to-thickness ratios (a/t) greater than 50 percent, the applied stress required to fracture the specimen increased with decreasing residual stress in such a way that the sum of applied and residual stress at fracture was reasonably constant for all specimens. For specimens containing flaws with (a/t) ratios less than 50 percent, the applied stress required to fracture the specimens increased with decreasing residual stress until the applied stress reached the yield stress of the flawed material. Further reduction of residual stress had no effect on failure stress. Since the spread between yield and ultimate strength is small for both titanium alloy base metal and weld

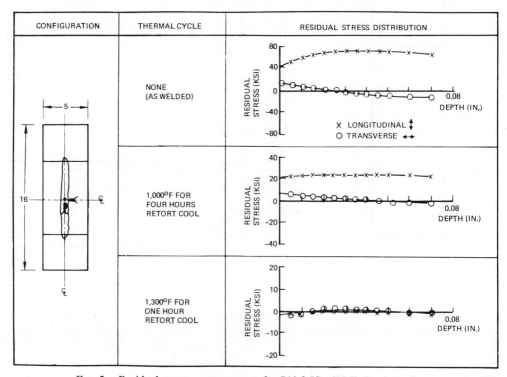

FIG. 5.   Residual stress measurements for 5Al-2.5Sn (ELI) titanium alloy test series III.

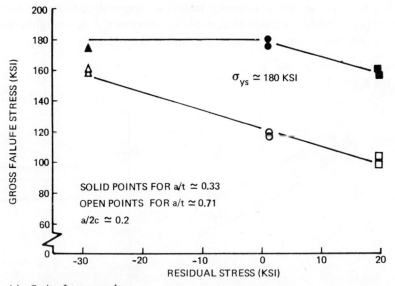

(a)   Series I test results

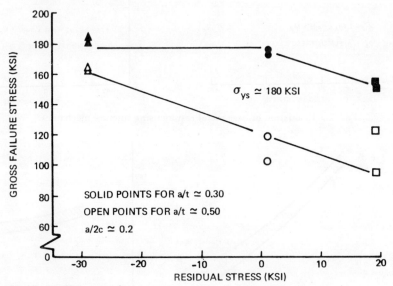

(b)   Series II test results

FIG. 6.   Effect of residual stress on gross failure stress for 5Al-2.5Sn (ELI) titanium test series I and II.

metal, it is not possible to obtain fracture stresses much in excess of yield stress, particularly in the presence of flaws.

Test results were used to evaluate the validity of a failure criterion for surface flaws subjected to combined applied and residual stresses. The criterion was based on the assumption that failure would occur when

$$K_{IR} + K_{IP} = K_{cr} \qquad (1)$$

where K_{IR} and K_{IP} are stress intensity factors corresponding to residual stress (σ_R) and load stress (σ_P), and K_{cr} is the critical stress intensity or fracture toughness of the flawed material. Stress intensities were calculated using the equation

$$K_I = 1.1\sigma\sqrt{\pi a/Q} \cdot M_K$$
$$Q = E(k)^2 - 0.212(\sigma/\sigma_{ys})^2$$

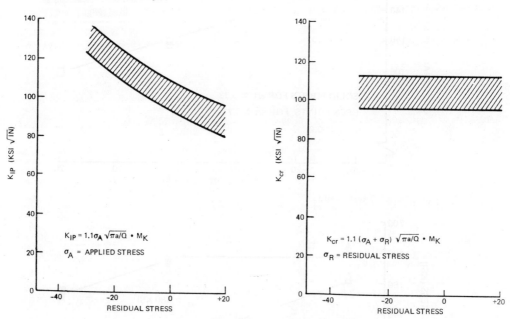

FIG. 7.   Evaluation of base metal results using fracture mechanics.

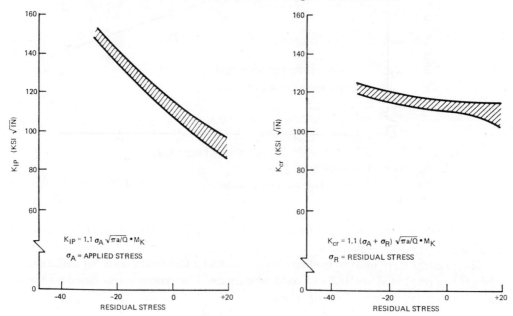

FIG. 8.   Evaluation of weld metal results using fracture mechanics.

where $E(k)$ is the complete elliptical integral of the second kind.

σ is the applied stress

σ_{ys} is the yield strength of the material

M_K is a scalar factor depending on crack depth-to-thickness ratio and crack depth-to-length ratio used to account for effects of the stress free back specimen surface.

Values of M_K were taken from Fig. 57 of Reference 13. The M_K values used were evaluated experimentally using $-320°F$ ($195°C$) tests of Ti-5Al-2.5Sn (ELI) base metal and weld metal surface flawed specimens. Values of K_{IR} and K_{IP} were calculated by respectively substituting $\sigma = \sigma_R$ and $\sigma = \sigma_P$ into eq. 1.

Scatterbands including all values of K_{IR} and K_{IP} for specimens failing at elastic stress levels are included in Figs. 7 and 8. Figure 7 includes results for Series II (base metal) tests and Fig. 8 includes results for Series I (weld metal) tests. For base metal, K_{cr} values ranged from 94 to 113 ksi·$\sqrt{in}$ (333 to 400 kg/mm$^{3/2}$). If residual stresses had not been accounted for in K_{cr} calculations, i.e., if K_{cr} had been set equal to K_{IP}, K_{cr} would have ranged from 81 to 136 ksi·$\sqrt{in}$ (287 to 482 kg/mm$^{3/2}$). For weld metal, K_{cr} values ranged from 103 to 127 ksi·$\sqrt{in}$ (368 to 450 kg/mm$^{3/2}$) whereas K_{IP} values ranged

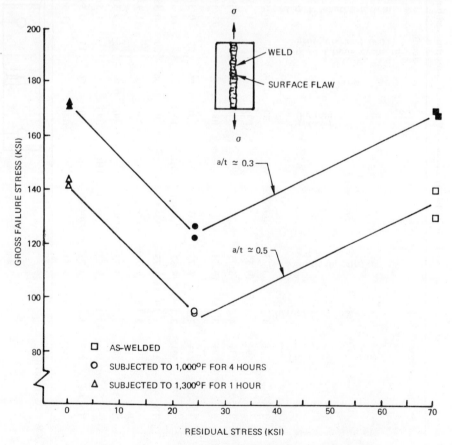

FIG. 9.   Gross failure stresses for 5Al-2.5Sn (ELI) titanium test series III.

TABLE 4.   Fracture test results for 5Al-2.5Sn (ELI) titanium GTA weld centerlines subjected to various thermal cycles.

Type	Identification	Thickness in. (cm)	Width in. (cm)	Length in. (cm)	Thermal processing	$(K_f)_{MAX}$, ksi-in$^{1/2}$ (kg/mm$^{3/2}$)	$(K_f)_{MAX}/(K_f)_{MIN}$	No. of fatigue cycles to grow crack (1,000's)	Crack length, in. (cm)	Environment	Temperature, °F(°C)	Loading rate, (1,000 lb/min.)	Failure load, lb (kg)	P_Q lbs (kg)	K_Q, ksi-in$^{1/2}$ (kg/mm$^{3/2}$)
Single edge notched tension	TX-1	0.234 (0.594)	1.254 (3.185)	3.75 (9.53)	NONE (AW)	30 (106)	0.06	37	0.570 (1.45)	LN$_2$	−320 (−195)	6	8,180 (3,710)	7,700 (3,490)	86.5 (306)
	TX-2	0.234 (0.594)	1.253 (3.183)	3.75 (9.53)		30 (106)	0.06	50	0.585 (1.49)	LN$_2$	−320 (−195)	6	7,180 (3,260)	6,000 (2,720)	71.1 (252)
	TX-3	0.234 (0.594)	1.254 (3.185)	3.75 (9.53)	AW+ 1,000°F−4HR. (538°C)	30 (106)	0.06	27	0.570 (1.45)	LN$_2$	−320 (−195)	6	5,060 (2,290)	4,750 (2,150)	53.6 (190)
	TX-4	0.236 (0.599)	1.256 (3.190)	3.75 (9.53)		30 (106)	0.06	20	0.580 (1.47)	LN$_2$	−320 (−195)	6	5,000 (2,270)	5,000 (2,270)	58.0 (205)
	TX-5	0.233 (0.592)	1.254 (3.185)	3.75 (9.53)	AW+ 1,300°F−1HR. (704°C)	30 (106)	0.06	15	0.595 (1.51)	LN$_2$	−320 (−195)	6	5,980 (2,710)	5,600 (2,540)	69.0 (244)
	TX-6	0.235 (0.597)	1.256 (3.190)	3.75 (9.53)		30 (106)	0.06	15	0.590 (1.50)	LN$_2$	−320 (−195)	6	6,060 (2,750)	5,800 (2,630)	68.9 (244)

AW = As welded.

from 86 to 154 ksi· $\sqrt{\text{in}}$ (305 to 546 kg/mm³/²). Since materials are known to exhibit reasonably constant values of fracture toughness for given conditions, and since eq. 1 did yield reasonably constant values of fracture toughness, it was concluded that eq. 1 is a useful criterion for evaluating potential effects of residual stresses on stability of surface cracks.

Static Fracture Test Series III :   Applied gross area stress at failure for all Series III specimens is plotted against peak residual stress level in Fig. 9. The nature of the variations in failure stress with residual stress led to the conclusion that the thermal cycles used to vary residual stress levels also effected changes in fracture toughness of the titanium welds. To evaluate this conclusion, six single-edge-notched-tension (SENT) specimens were prepared and tested. Two specimens were subjected to a 1300°F (704°C)/ one hour/furnace cool thermal cycle. Two other specimens were subjected to a 1000°F (538°C)/4 hour/furnace cool thermal treatment. The remaining two specimens were left in the as-welded condition. Specimens were precracked at the weld centerline, instrumented with a clip gage, and loaded to failure at −320°F (195°C) in liquid nitrogen. Specimen dimensions, cracking details, and results are summarized in Table 4. The P_Q loads correspond to pints at which a 5 percent secant offset interected the load-deflection test record and K_Q values were calculated using published[14] stress intensity factor calibrations for single-edge-notched tension specimens. The K_Q values show that both thermal cycles decreased the fracture toughness of the weld metal with the 1000°F (538°C)/4 hour cycle being most detrimental.

Results of the SENT tests used to estimate fracture toughness values for the Series III test specimens. It was decided to base estimates of fracture toughness on SENT specimen failure loads rather than P_Q loads since calculations of fracture stresses for SF specimens relate to failure load. For specimens stress relieved at 1300°F (704°C) for one hour, SENT and SF specimens yielded average K_{cr} values of 69 and 89 ksi· $\sqrt{\text{in}}$ (244 and 315 kg/mm³/²), respectively. It was assumed that the ratio between fracture toughness for SF and SENT specimens subjected to as-welded and 1000°F (538°C)/4 hour thermal cycles was the same as that for the 1300°F (704°C)/one hour thermal cycle, i.e., 89/69=1.29. The resulting estimates of fracture toughness for SF specimens subjected to as-welded and 1000°F (538°C)/four hour thermal cycles were 1.29 (88)=114 ksi· $\sqrt{\text{in}}$ (404 kg/mm³/²) and 1.29 (58)=75 ksi· $\sqrt{\text{in}}$ (266 kg/mm³/²).

The estimated fracture toughness values for the Series III SF specimens were used to calculate applied stresses at failure using eq. 1 and the known initial flaw dimensions. Calculations were made that either accounted for residual stresses by taking $K_{cr}=K_{IR}+K_{IP}$, or ignored residual stresses by taking $K_{cr}=K_{IP}$. Both calculated and actual applied failure stresses are plotted as a function of residual stress level in Fig. 10. Results for specimens having flaw depth-to-thickness ratios of approximately 0.3 are included in Figure 10a. Failure stresses predicted without accounting for residual stresses were limited to the yield strength of the weld metal at −320°F, (184 ksi or 130 kg/mm²) since ultimate and yield strength for the weld metal differ only by a small amount. When the residual stress level was 70 ksi (49.2 kg/mm²) the actual failure stress had an intermediate value between the two predicted values. This result is probably due to the fact that the 70 ksi (49.2 kg/mm²) residual stress level was a peak value and some areas near the flaw

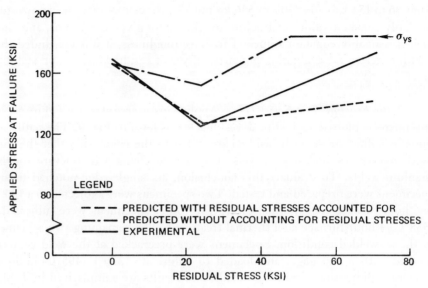

(a) For flaw depth-to-thickness ratio≃0.3

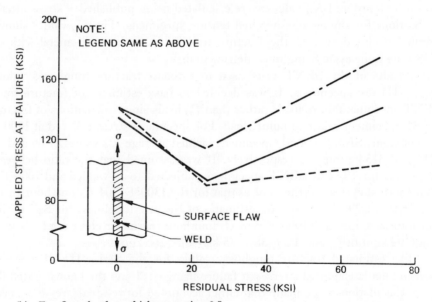

(b) For flaw depth-to-thickness ratio≃0.5

FIG. 10.   Comparison of predicted and actual failure stresses for test series III.

tip were under the influence of residual stresses somewhat less than the peak value. When the residual stress level was 24 ksi (16.9 kg/mm²), the actual failure stresses were in good agreement with the failure stress that was predicted by accounting for residual stress. Results in Fig. 10b for specimens having flaw depth to thickness ratios of about 0.50 are similar to those described above.

On the basis of the results for Test Series III, it appears that eq. 1 can be used to account for the effects of residual stresses on crack stability in metallic alloy weld metal as long as the sum of residual and applied stresses is less than the yield strength of the weld metal. Variations in fracture toughness from specimen to specimen and variations in residual stress level within each specimen made the applicability of eq. 1 to the Series III results difficult to evaluate.

5. Summary and Conclusion

Residual stresses were shown to have a significant effect on fracture stress of surface-flawed specimens fabricated from 5Al-2.5Sn (ELI) titanium alloy. For specimens in which failure stresses were elastic, residual stresses at the flaw location changed the applied fracture stress by an amount equal to the residual stress. Tensile and compressive residual stresses respectively lowered and elevated applied fracture stress relative to residual-stress-free specimens. For specimens in which yield stress levels were reached prior to failure, residual stresses had a smaller effect on applied fracture stress than in specimens in which no yielding occurred. Finally, it was found that the effect of residual stress on applied fracture stress of surface-flawed specimens could be quantitatively evaluated using eq. 1.

The foregoing information leads to the conclusion that residual stresses should be taken into account in estimates of critical flaw sizes for peak proof test stress levels. Tensile residual stresses can reduce critical flaw sizes from those calculated for nominal stress fields and place more stringent requirements on sensitivity of nondestructive inspection techniques required to avoid proof test failures. If the peak nominal proof stress levels are at or near the yield strength of the parent metal, mechanical stress relieving should substantially reduce both the magnitude and effects of tensile residual stresses during subsequent loadings. If peak proof stress levels are significantly below the parent metal yield strength, tensile residual stresses may be unaffected by the proof overload and continue to reduce critical flaw sizes during subsequent operation of the structure.

ACKNOWLEDGMENTS

The author wishes to acknowledge the support of NASA Lewis Research Center through contract NAS3-12016, and Mr. Gordon T. Smith, NASA Program Technical Manager. The author also wishes to acknowledge the invaluable help of R. W. Finger and A. A. Ottlyk who coordinated and conducted the tests performed in this program.

REFERENCES

1. Wells, A. A., "The Brittle Fracture Strength of Welded Steel Plates," Quarterly Transactions Institute of Naval Architects, Vol 48 (1956).
2. Wells, A. A., "Influence of Residual Stresses and Metallurgical Changes on Low Stress Brittle Fracture in Welded Steel Plates," Welding Journal Research Supplement, Apr. (1961).
3. Martin, D. C., Ryan, R. S. and Preppel, P. J., "Evaluation of Weld-Joint Flaws as Initiating Points of Brittle Fracture," Welding Journal Research Supplement, Vol. 37 (1957).

4. Hall, W. J. and Chamberlain, A. D., "Studies of Welding Procedures Part III," Welding Journal Research Supplement (1966).
5. Kennedy, R., British Welding Journal, 4 (1957).
6. Kihara, H. and Masubuchi, K., "Effect of Residual Stresses on Brittle Fracture," Welding Journal Research Supplement (1959).
7. Greene, T. W., Welding Journal Research Supplement (1949).
8. Wells, A. A., "Effects of Residual Stress on Brittle Fracture," *Fracture—"An Advanced Treatise,"* Vol. 5, Chap. 7. Academic Press (1969).
9. Boyd, G. M., "The Conditions for Unstable Rupturing of a Wide Plate," Trans. Inst. Naval Arch., 99, (3), Part II, July (1957).
10. Masubuchi, K., "Effects of Residual Stress on Fracture Behavior of Weldments," *Proceedings of Symposium on Weld Imperfections,* Palo Alto, California, Sept. 19–21(1966).
11. Robelloto, R., Joy A. and Lambase, J., "Investigation of Magnitude and Distribution of Stresses in Welded Structures," AFML Technical Report AFML-TR-67-293, Sept. (1967).
12. Mathew, J., "Determination of Initial Stresses by Measuring the Deformation Around Drilled Holes," Trans., ASME, Vol. 56 (1934).
13. Masters, J. N., Haese, W. P. and Finger, R. W., "Investigation of Deep Flaws in Thin Walled Tanks," NASA CR-72606, Dec. (1968).
14. Gross, B., Srawley, J. E. and Brown, W. F., "Stress Intensity Factors for a Single-Edge-Notch Tension Specimen in Boundary Collocation of a Stress Function," NASA TN D-2603, Jan. (1965).

On the Brittle Fracture Initiation Characteristics of 9 %Ni Steel for Spherical LNG Tank

H. Yajima

Ship Strength Research Laboratory, Nagasaki Technical Institute, Mitsubishi Heavy Industries, Ltd.

1. Introduction

The Moss Rosenberg-type spherical LNG tank is equipped with a safety device called "small-leak protection system" for providing an early warning of accidental leakage of cargo. For this reason, a reduced secondary barrier has been approved by classification societies. This means that any fatigue crack, if it should ever form in the tank wall, would be detected and repaired before it reaches a critical length which induces a fatal unstable brittle fracture. To put it another way, the tank steel is required to offer sufficient ductility so that any fatigue crack, when measured at the time of repair some time after its formation during sea service, will remain well below the critical length.

To determine the interrelation of critical crack length and brittle fracture initiation for the 9%Ni steel plate, we conducted some through-notch tensile tests[1-3] on plain, welded, and line-heated 9%Ni steel plate specimens which were approximately the same in thickness as the actual tank shell plating. We studied also the initiation of brittle fracture from the surface fatigue crack produced at the toe of fillet weld forming the plate-stiffener joint. It was found through these tests that critical crack lengths which could give rise to the brittle fracture were invariably so great for the base metal, heat-affected zone of welded joint (heat input of about 4×10^4 Joule/cm) and line-heated zone that the use of "small-leak protection system" would be fully justifiable.

2. Estimated K_c Values for Base Metal, Heat-Affected Zone of Butt-Welded Joint, and Line-Heated Zone

As the parameter of fracture toughness for brittle fracture initiation, K_c values were determined from the test results and used to calculate the critical crack lengths.

2.1 Base Metal and Heat-Affected Zone of Butt-Welded Joint

Plain and butt-welded test specimens were prepared from seven quenched and

355

Plate No.	Plate Thickness (mm)	Heat Treatment	Chemical Compositions						Tensile Properties			Impact
			C (%)	Si (%)	Mn (%)	P (%)	S (%)	Ni (%)	Y.S. (kg/mm²)	T.S. (kg/mm²)	Elong. (%)	vE-196°C (kg-m)
I	20	QT	0.06	0.20	0.34	0.010	0.005	8.86	T 66.5 / B 68.5	70.4 / 70.9	42.0 / 42.0	21.1 / 18.4
II	20	QT	0.08	0.17	0.48	0.008	0.008	8.65	69.3~70.0	74.2~74.3	38.0~42.0	17.5
III	23	QT	0.06	0.24	0.53	0.007	0.004	9.10	67.9	72.8~73.1	31.4~31.8	16.3
IV	23	QT	0.07	0.27	0.52	0.007	0.005	9.10	72.5~71.2	77.2~76.3	26.0~28.0	9.5
V	23	QT	0.07	0.24	0.53	0.006	0.006	8.88	72.2~73.4	79.0~80.1	26.0~27.0	18.4
VI	24	QT	0.06	0.24	0.47	0.011	0.008	8.87	68.4	72.3	31.0	19.8
VII	25	QT	0.07	0.20	0.60	0.013	0.007	8.95	72.8	78.3	28.5	8.3

Y.S. : 0.2% Proof Stress   T.S. : Tensile Strength

Mark	Plate No.	Plate Thickness (mm)	Type of Notch	Location of Notch	Empirical Formulae
①	I	20	Side Notch	Base Metal	$\ell nkc = -0.047(\frac{10^3}{T_K}) + 7.43$
②	II	20	Side Notch	Base Metal	$\ell nkc = -0.018(\frac{10^3}{T_K}) + 7.03$
③			Side Notch	Bond	$\ell nkc = -0.014(\frac{10^3}{T_K}) + 6.86$
④			Side Notch	Bond	$\ell nkc = -0.018(\frac{10^3}{T_K}) + 6.86$
⑤	III	23	Side Notch	Base Metal	$\ell nkc = -0.014(\frac{10^3}{T_K}) + 7.07$
⑥			Center Notch	Base Metal	$\ell nkc = -0.014(\frac{10^3}{T_K}) + 6.99$
⑦	IV	23	Center Notch	Base Metal	$\ell nkc = -0.026(\frac{10^3}{T_K}) + 7.04$
⑧	V	23	Center Notch	Base Metal	$\ell nkc = -0.028(\frac{10^3}{T_K}) + 7.09$
⑨	VI	24	Side Notch	Base Metal	$\ell nkc = -0.101(\frac{10^3}{T_K}) + 8.09$
⑩			Side Notch	Bond	$\ell nkc = -0.101(\frac{10^3}{T_K}) + 7.80$
⑪	VII	25	Side Notch	Base Metal	$\ell nkc = -0.046(\frac{10^3}{T_K}) + 7.40$

Mark	Welding Condition
③	Flat Position Manual Welding NIC-709N, 4⌀,11Passes,11,800 Joule/cm
④	Vertical Position Manual Welding NIC-709N, 4⌀6Passes, 39,300 Joule/cm
⑩	Flat Position Manual Welding YAWATA WELD-B,18Passes,15,000 Joule/cm

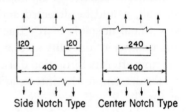

Side Notch Type   Center Notch Type

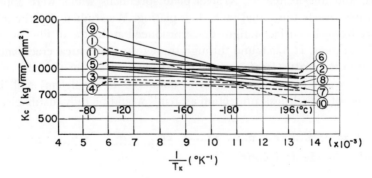

Fig. 1. Brittle fracture initiation characteristics of 9%Ni steel. (Base metal. Heat-affected zone of butt welded joint.)

tempered 9%Ni steel plates produced from different furnace charges and ranging from 20 mm to 25 mm in thickness. Chemical compositions, tensile properties, summarizes of through-notch tests, test results (relation between K_c value and test temperature), etc., are shown in Fig. 1. In the diagram showing the K_c value-test temperature relation, solid lines denote the plain test specimens and dotted lines the welded test specimes.

2. 2   Line-Heated Zone

Line-heated test specimens were prepared from 23 mm thick quenched and tempered 9%Ni steel plate. Each specimen was given one pass of line heating on both face and back and through-notched within the line-heated zone. The line heating was provided up to 800°C max. and water cooling from 550°C downwards. Chemical compositions, tensile properties, shape of test specimen, test results (relation between K_c value and test temperature), etc., are shown in Fig. 2.

2. 3   Consideration

K_c value at -162°C can be calculated using applicable empirical formula shown in Figs. 1 and 2. The critical crack length may then be given by the following equation which

Plate Thickness (mm)	Heat Treatment	Chemical Compositions						Tensile Properties			Impact
		C (%)	Si (%)	Mn (%)	P (%)	S (%)	Ni (%)	Y.S. (kg/mm²)	T.S. (kg/mm²)	Elong (%)	vE-196°c (kg-m)
23	QT	0.08	0.23	0.53	0.008	0.006	8.80	71.0	77.6 ⌠ 77.8	24	18.4

Y.S.: 0.2% Proof Stress
T.S.: Tensile Strength

Mark	Plate Thickness	Type of Notch	Location of Notch	Empirical Formulae
⑫	23	Center Notch	Base Metal	$\ell nkc = -0.072\left(\frac{10^3}{T_k}\right) + 7.60$
⑬	23	Center Notch	Line-Heated Zone 800°C $\xrightarrow{A.C.}$ 550°CW.C.	$\ell nkc = -0.072\left(\frac{10^3}{T_k}\right) + 7.53$

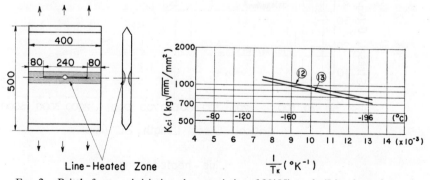

Line-Heated Zone

FIG. 2.   Brittle fracture initiation characteristics of 9%Ni steel. (Line-heated zone.)

expresses the relation between the applied stress and the critical crack length as;

$$K_c = \sigma \sqrt{\pi c} \tag{1}$$

where K_c=fracture toughness for brittle fracture initiation, kg$\cdot \sqrt{mm}$/mm²
  σ=applied stress, kg/mm²
  c=1/2 crack length, mm

Diagrams in Fig. 3 show the relation between the applied stress and the critical crack length for each of plain, butt-welded, and line-heated test specimens.

In regards to the allowable stresses for the spherical tank, the following values can be adopted.

The membrane stress in accordance with ASME Boiler Code, Section VIII, Div. 1

$$\sigma_{all} = \frac{T.S.}{4} \times 0.95 = \frac{70.3}{4} \times 0.95 = 16.7 \ (kg/mm^2)$$

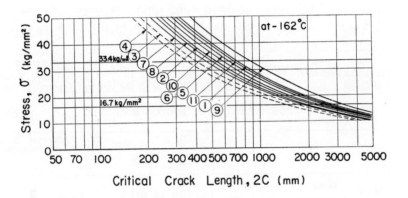

Base metal, Heat-affected zone of butt welded joint

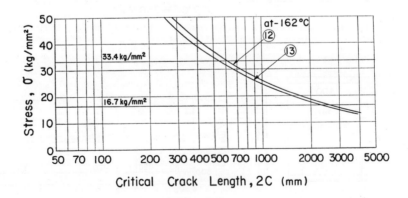

Line - heated zone

FIG. 3.   Applied stress *vs.* critical crack length.

where $T.S.$=tensile strength ($=70.3\,kg/mm^2$)

The surface stress including stress concentration factor, in accordance with ASME Boiler Code, Section VIII, Div. 2

$$\sigma_{all} = 1.5 \times \frac{T.S.}{3} \times 0.95 = 1.5 \times \frac{70.3}{3} \times 0.95 = 33.4\,(kg/mm^2)$$

At the above-mentioned stress levels, Fig. 3 shows the allowable critical crack lengths for brittle fracture initiation are very large.

When determining the allowable critical crack lengths from Fig. 3 for the applied stress levels, the effect of residual stress induced by welding may be viewed as follows.

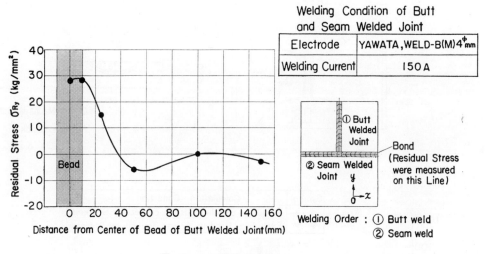

T-cross welded joint

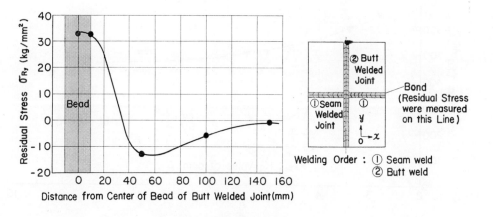

Cross welded joint

FIG. 4.   Distribution of residual stress in " T-cross " and " cross " welded joint.

(1)　Our study shows that the residual stress induced in the "T-cross" or "cross" welded joint made with *YAWATA WELD-B* (M) 70%Ni electrodes is approximately 30～35 kg/mm² at the maximum (see Fig. 4).

Plate Thickness (mm)	Heat Treatment	Chemical Compositions						Tensile Properties			Impact
		C (%)	Si (%)	Mn (%)	P (%)	S (%)	Ni (%)	Y.S. (kg/mm²)	T.S. (kg/mm²)	Elong (%)	vE-196°C kg-m
23	QT	0.07	0.24	0.53	0.006	0.006	8.88	71.8	78.6	26.5	18.2

Y.S. : 0.2% Proof Stress
T.S. : Tensile Strength

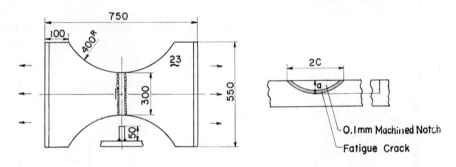

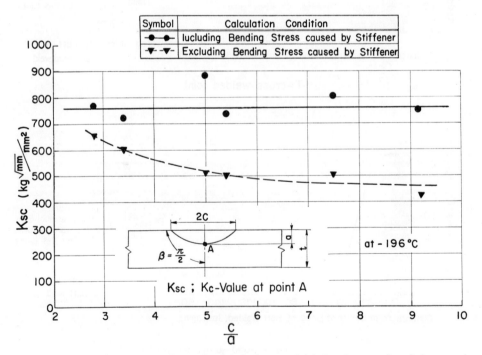

FIG. 5.　Fracture toughness for brittle fracture initiation from surface fatigue crack at toe of stiffener fillet weld.

(2) Such a high tensile residual stress in the "T-cross" or "cross" welded joint is limited to within about 40 mm on each side of the weld bead.

(3) The fatigue crack which may start in the welded joint will not be affected by the residual stress once it propagates in excess of about 80 mm across the weld bead. As can be seen from Fig. 3, the critical crack lengths are all far in excess of 80 mm, so that it will hardly be necessary to consider the effect of the residual stress induced by welding.

3. Estimated K_c Value for Surface Fatigue Crack at Toe of Stiffener Fillet Weld

Test specimens were taken from 23 mm thick 9%Ni steel plate. Across the surface of each test specimen, a stiffener was fillet-welded normal to the direction of test load, and a surface fatigue crack was produced under constant pulsating tensile stress at room temperature. Test specimens were then tensile-tested to fracture at $-196°C$. Chemical compositions, tensile properties, test results, etc., are shown in Fig. 5.

The parameter of fracture toughness for brittle fracture initiation from surface crack, K_{sc}, remained constant regardless of the shape of the surface crack when calculated with the effect of bending stress caused by the stiffener. It should also be mentioned that the calculated K_{sc} values were very great.

4. Conclusion

(1) Critical crack lengths which induce brittle fracture are invariably so great for the base metal, heat-affected zone of butt-welded joint (heat input of about 4×10^4 Joule/cm) and line-heated zone that the use of "small-leak protection system" is fully justified.

(2) The surface fatigue crack produced at the toe of fillet weld forming the plate-stiffener joint also is safe against the brittle fracture because of its great allowable critical crack length.

REFERENCES

1. Ikeda, K., Akita, Y. and Kihara, H., "The Deep-Notch Test and Brittle Fracture Initiation," Welding Journal Vol. 46, No. 3, 133–S, Mar. (1967), and International Institute of Welding Document No. X–404–67, Mar. (1967).

2. Ikeda, K. and Kihara, H., "Brittle Fracture Strength of Welded Joints," Welding Journal Vol. 49, No. 3, 106–S, Mar. (1970), and International Institute of Welding Document No. X–521–69, Mar. (1969).

3. KMN Committee (composed of members from Kawasaki Heavy Industries, Ltd., Mitsui Shipbuilding & Engineering Co., Ltd., Mitsubishi Heavy Industries, Ltd., and Nippon Steel Corporation), "Studies on 9-Percent Nickel Steel for Moss-Type Liquefied Natural Gas Carriers".

Effects of Notch Size, Angular Distortion and Residual Stress on Brittle Fracture Initiation of High Strength Steel Welded Joints

K. Terai and S. Susei

Welding Research Department, Kawasaki Heavy Industries, Ltd.

1. Preface

In many cases, brittle fracture in welded steel structure originates from local defects in the high stress field of a weld joint. Such local defects include weld crack, lack of penetration and other weld defects, fatigue crack, stress corrosion crack, segregation of steel, and flame cutting notch, etc.

Normally cracks generated in the process of material working are relatively small. Toe cracks developed in welded joints and hydrogen embrittled cracks developed in the inside welds of LPG spherical pressure vessels fabricated from high strength steel, on the other hand, are large oblong surface cracks. Such cracks grow to several meters in length by the time the crack penetrates through the plate thickness.

Many of these local defects are not through cracks but are part through cracks. These part through cracks are most likely to have serious effect on the structure.

In addition to local defects, other stress raisers must be considered in actual structures; these stress raisers include local material deterioration due to welding (especially bond embrittlement), welding deformation, tensile residual stress, and others.

This paper reports the size effect of part through notch on wide tension specimens, and the effects of superposed defects, angular distortion of welded joints, and tensile residual stress due to welding on brittle fracture initiation.

2. Test Materials

Steel plates used in this investigation were 25 mm thick quenched and tempered high strength steel plates of 60 kg/mm² and 80 kg/mm² classes. For the 60 kg/mm² class steel A which fully satisfies *WES* 135-1964, HW50 standards. Also steel B (plate thickness 27 mm) with remarkable work hardening characteristic and inferior notch toughness which represent the lower limit of the standards were partially used for tests.

3. Test Specimens

A typical notched, cross welded tension specimen with angular distortion is shown in Fig. 1. Standard specimens used were 400 mm wide ($=2b$) and 500 mm long, and had cross welded joints. The specimen had an angular distortion with the ridge at the butt weld. The specimen was welded at the seam line after butt welding. After welding, the notch was machined and then the specimen was bent to provide the prescribed angular distortion.

The notch was a surface notch of semi-elliptical type with a notch root radius of 0.1 mm. The notch length $2c=160$ mm, and the notch depth i.e. relative notch depth t_1/t varied from 0.1 up to 0.6. Special attention was made to positioning the notch tip at the heat affected zone (bond).

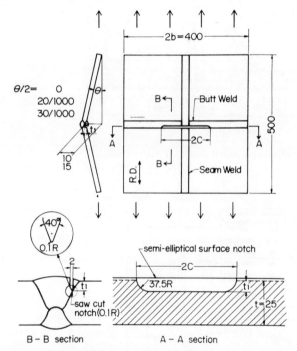

FIG. 1.   Cross welds tension specimen.

4. Results and Discussions

4. 1 Effect of Notch Depth

Relation between fracture stress and temperature for surface notched base plate or wide tension specimen with a butt weld are shown in Fig. 2. Results of wide tension specimens of HT60 show that the fracture stress tends to decrease with an increase in t_1/t within the test temperature range. On the other hand, results of wide tension specimen of HT80 show that when $t_1/t \geqq 0.4$, the fracture stress in terms of net stress is equal to the tensile strength of the base metal at the same temperature. Furthermore, the fracture stress decreases with a drop in temperature.

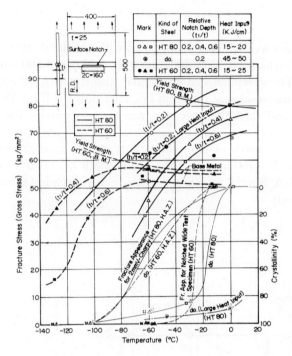

FIG. 2.   Effect of relative notch depth on fracture stress.

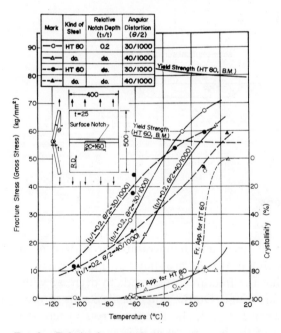

FIG. 3.   Relation between fracture stress and temperature in surface notched tension specimen with angular distortion.

4. 2   Effect of Surface Notch and Angular Distortion

Relations between gross stress and temperature for a wide central surface notched tension specimen with a welded joint and angular distortion are shown in Fig. 3. When the relative notch depth of t_1/t is 0.2 and the initial angular distortion, $\theta/2$, changed from 30/1000 to 40/1000, fracture stress sharply decreased with a drop in temperature, and also with greater amount of distortion. When these test results are compared with cases with only a notch without any angular distortion, the fracture stress at $-60°C$ for example, is reduced to about half of that with angular distortion. The bending stress added to the tensile stress in specimens with angular distortion have undesirable effect on the initiation of brittle fracture, especially, in a low temperature region.

4. 3   Effect of Surface Notch, Angular Distortion and Welding Residual Stress

Relation between fracture stress and temperature in a HT60 wide tension specimen with cross welded joint together with the presence of high tensile residual stress and angular distortion are shown in Fig. 4. Note that the fracture stress-temperature curves for specimens with surface notch, angular distortion and residual stress shifted towards the higher temperature in comparison with the notched specimens and notched and angular distorted specimens.

When the notch depth increased to 20% and 30% of the plate thickness $(t_1/t=0.2$ and 0.3), the fracture stress-temperature curve moved about 10 to 20°C towards higher temperature respectively, while maintaining the same inclination for $t_1/t=0.1$. The

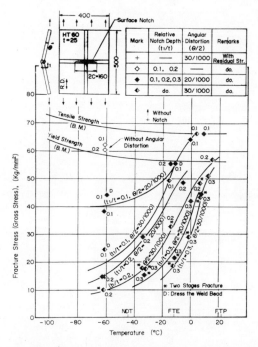

FIG. 4.   Relation between fracture stress and temperature in cross weld tension specimen with surface notch, angular distortion and residual stress (HT60).

upper limit of fracture stress, however, is almost at the yield point of the base metal. For a notch depth of $t_1/t=0.3$ and angular distortion of $\theta/2=30/1000$, which are the most severe conditions imposed in this experiment, the fracture stress was low even at the normal temperature and was about $1/2\ \sigma_y$ near 0°C.

5. Conclusions

The following conclusions were obtained as a result of this experimental study.

(1)   Wide tension specimens with a surface notch in the welded joint fractured at low applied stress levels (below yield stress levels) at service temperature where commercial test data of those steel plates and their welded joints exhibited satisfactory notch toughness.

(2)   Brittle fractures were reproduced in specimens with various stress concentration such as toe notch, angular distortion of the welded joint and welding residual stress.

(3)   From these test results, surface notched specimens with large notch size, angular distortion, welding residual stress have low fracture resistance. It is thus necessary to establish a upper bound on these stress concentration factors commensurate with the service conditions of the structure.

Discussions in Session   V

Question directed to Dr. Koshiga by Dr. Toyoda

I pay my respect to Dr. Koshiga for the discussions held concerning the plastic zone size approach. Would you please give further comments on the following questions?

Needless to say, the COD- and ρ^+-concepts are more appropriate than the concept of linear elastic fracture mechanics for discussing the significance of the defects which are surrounded by a well-developed plastic zone. Especially, using ρ^+-concept, the estimation of the fracture initiation stress can be made easily. But in that case, I have one thing which weighs on my mind. In ρ^+-concept, ρ^+-value is calculated on the basis of the Dugdale model. As you may know, if we calculated the fracture stress using ρ^+-concept (or COD-concept) in the infinite plate (or $2c/W \ll 1$), the calculated curve which shows the relationship between the fracture stress and temperature, draws near to the temperature-depended σ_Y-curve as temperature increases; that is to say, the fracture stress does not become equal to the general yield stress. I think that calculated results do not coincide with reality. As temperature increases sufficiently, it can be said ductile fracture, in which strength is larger than the yeild stress, occurs in the infinite plate including a notch. I think this contradiction is caused by applying the Dugdale model to calculate ρ^+-value in the range of extreme large scale yielding. I may be wrong, but I think that ρ^+-concept (COD-concept) cannot be applied to sufficient large scale yielding range, when the fracture toughness parameter (ρ^+ or δ) is calculated on the basis of the Dugdale model. Would you give your comments on this matter?

To go a step further, it would be very important in discussing the significance of defects in welded structures to clarify the behaviors of notch specimens after general yielding. I think the evaluation of ductility of welded joints including defects after general yielding is a basic problem.

Dr. Koshiga, may I hear your opinion about this problem and would you give us an outline of your forthcoming study on this matter?

Reply to Dr. Toyoda by Dr. Koshiga

The argument pointed out by Dr. Toyoda is indeed of some importance. If the toughness parameter ρ_c^+ can only be determined by the fracture stress of notched tensile test specimen, we must urgently tackle that problem from the viewpoint of testing material. However, I have fortunately found a very simple method of converting the critical COD value into the said ρ_c^+ as I introduced in my paper. As to the service failure of welded structures, on the other hand, we need not consider so much the deformed situation because the brittle fracture to be discussed is in general preceded by minor deformation in a macroscopic sense. By the way, I think better understanding of the effect of constraint on the brittle fracture initiation may be possible if any solution is found to Dr. Toyoda's comment.

Comment directed to Dr. Susei by Prof. Kobayashi

The B/C ratio in your specimen is barely 3 and could introduce bending effect which is not accunted for in an infinite plate solution for the surface flaw. Moreover your flat crack front could have a K_I approximately 15% larger than that of a semi-elliptical crack as shown by recent three-dimensional photoelasticity results by Prof. C. W. Smith, Virginia Polytechnic Institute and State University.

Reply to Prof. Kobayashi by Dr. Susei

I wish to thank so much for Prof. Kobayashi's useful suggestions and discussion.

Question directed to Dr. Hall by Prof. McEvily

To what extent does the introduction of a flaw tend to relax the stress field in vicinity of the flaw?

Reply to Prof. McEvily by Dr. Hall

In our work, Prof. McEvily, the specimens were designed so that the sources of the residual stresses were sufficiently far away from the cracks that the introduction of the crack did not perturb the source of residual stress. The cracks did relieve the residual stresses in the immediate vicinity of each crack by introducing a source of displacement. However, the displacements due to the crack should have been very small at the location of the welds which generated the residual stresses. Hence, the source of residual stresses was not greatly altered by the introduction of the crack.

Comment directed to Prof. Rolfe by Mr. Kaku

We generally agree to the philosoply explained to us this afternoon session by Prof. Rolfe.

I suppose that NDT obtained from the dynamic tear test would be higher than that of the old Pellini Test.

According to our survey of the existing hull structural steels of Grade B, C, D and E steels, excluding Grade A steels, it has been observed that NDT of the old Pellini test for these steels distribute between $-10\,°C$ and $-50\,°C$, as shown in Fig. 1.

On the other hand, based on the requirement proposed by your philosophy, NDT of dynamic tear test for these steels is required to be lower than $-18\,°C$, which would probably correspond to NDT temperature of -25 to $-30\,°C$ of the drop weight test. Consequently, more than half of the existing hull structural steels would be rejected by the requirements, in spite of their satisfactory results in service.

Therefore, we are afraid that your proposal would be an overly stringent requirement for the hull structural steels.

We, of the classification societies, have discussed the up-grading of the existing requirements for hull structural steels, and it was concluded last year that the testing temperature of Grade D steels should be lowered from $0\,°C$ to $-20\,°C$, however, this

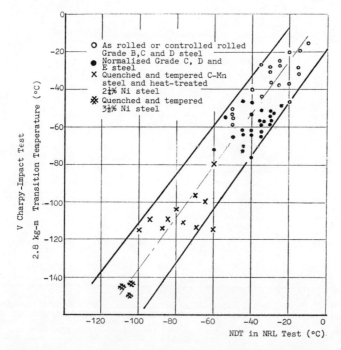

Fig. 1. Relationship between 2.8 kg-m transition temperature and nil ductility temperature of NRL drop weight test.

has been flatly refused by European steel manufacturers, as this results in high cost. Then, we attempted to adopt another notch toughness test, i.e. D.T. test or pressed notch impact test, in lieu of the V Charpy impact test, for the purpose of up-grading of the steels.

Question directed to Prof. Otsuka and Prof. Kanazawa by Prof. Packman

I have a question for Prof. Otsuka and Prof. Kanazawa. In your discussions you mentioned ring type clip gage. Could you explain the difference between that gage and the ASTM double cantilever gage.

Reply to Prof. Packman by Dr. Koshiga on behalf of Prof. Otsuka and Prof. Kanazawa

The ring type clip gage Prof. Packman mentioned was designed by me about five years ago. Nowadays this commonly used in Japan because of a wider range of linearity of output against displacement, up to 3 mm or more, and a special configuration of claws which is suitable for insertion into a narrow slit, 2 or 3 mm in width. The accuracy of measurement by using this ring gage is similar to that obtained from U.S. type double cantilever clip gage.

SESSION VI

RECOMMENDED FUTURE WORKS

A Systems Analysis of Significance of Weld Defects

K. Masubuchi

Department of Ocean Engineering, Massachusetts Institute of Technology

N. Yurioka

Products Research and Development Laboratory, Nippon Steel Corporation, Formerly a Graduate Student at MIT.

1. Introduction

In the past several days, we discussed various aspects of significance of defects in welded structures. Significant advancement has been achieved in techniques of detecting defects in weldments and analytical methods for analyzing significance of weld defects, especially in the application of fracture mechanics. Obviously there are a number of subjects related to non-destructive testing and applications of fracture mechanics which need to be developed further.

When we think about the future, it is often worth-while to think in a broad manner about what we have accomplished, where we stand, and where we should set our goals in the future.

Before presenting technical discussions, we would like to mention a non-technical story. Recently, one of the authors watched a television program shown on the "Today Show" on NBC. The guest speaker was the president of the Rockefeller Foundation, who was formerly the director of the Massachusetts General Hospital. The topic was "hospital killing." The speaker mentioned that "over 50 percent of all surgeries done in the United States today are unnecessary and some patients are even killed due to complications caused by unnecessary surgeries." He went on to say that "even if a patient did die after a surgery which does not seem to have been necessary, it is almost impossible for the family of the dead patient to sue the doctor who performed the surgery unless there was a gross mistake in the surgery itself, something like leaving a surgical instrument in the body."

It is felt that a similar situation exists with weld repairs. We are convinced that over 50 percent of all repair welds done today are unnecessasy. Some repairs are even detrimental to the structure and the current trend, unfortunately, appears to be making more repair welds.

In the past, many weldments were accepted because of the lack of adequate non-destructive testing methods. Due to improvements in NDT techniques, an increasing number of small defects can be detected today. Consequently, the development of NDT techniques often cause more repair work. If this idea were carried to an extreme, we find ourselves in a ridiculous situation; the finer the testing equipment we have for finding smaller defects, the more repair welds we will make. We must also realize that no repair weld is perfect, because it causes repeated heat effects on the material and concentrated residual stresses. Repair of a large, expensive structure often causes a huge economical loss, primarily due to loss in operational time.

Dr. Richard Weck published an article in 1966 entitled "A Rational Approach to Standards for Welded Construction."[1] He pointed out the backwardness of many specifications and codes. He mentioned that "in the light of modern scientific crtieria, some of the basic ideas in standards are naive and primitive in the extreme." The paper presents various examples of how present standards are irrational, especially when they are applied to welded structures. It discusses the significance of weld defects and cites irrational attitudes of classification societies on this subject.

We have very high regard for Dr. Weck's courage in presenting the paper which discusses such a fundamental issue. However, we cannot help but feel that his paper falls short midway toward the goal. His paper cites various examples of how present standards are imperfect or irrational; however, the paper does not propose a better way of dealing with the subject. What we are proposing here is a systems approach.

This paper first reviews the present state of weld quality control and repair. It proposes a systems approach of evaluating reliability of a welded structure.

Then, the paper describes, as an example of a systems analysis, results of a study conducted recently at the Massachusetts Institute of Technology on the reliability of a pressure hull of a deep submersible.

2.   Present State of Weld Quality Control and Repair

There are a number of technical and managerial problems in quality control and inspection of welded structures.

An ideal procedure for weld quality control would be to inspect the joint conditions before welding and control welding conditions during welding so that all welds made are of satisfactory quality. Unfortunately, we do not have reliable techniques to ensure that all welds are made satisfactorily. The entire problem related to non-destructive testing and significance of weld defects could be reduced, or even eliminated, if we could develop a more reliable production control system.

However, since we cannot entirely rely on the present process control, we use non-destructive inspection techniques. Many inspection techniques, such as radiography and ultrasonic techniques, are, unfortunately, after-the-fact inspections. Many NDT techniques detect some material discontinuities such as pores, slag inclusions and cracks. However, they do not give direct evaluation about the degradation in weld performance. In other words, present NDT techniques also are not perfect in assuring that all welds are of satisfactory quality.

In order to fabricate welded structures under these adverse conditions, engineers have developed the concept of "safety factor" and "joint efficiency." Codes and specifications also have been developed by classification societies to assist fabricators of structures and their users. Most of welded structures thus constructed performed satisfactorily. However, some structures experienced failures, some of which were catastrophic. Well-known structural failures include those of welded ships during World War II and the British Commet jetliners in the 1950's.

In order to prevent structural failures, much research has been conducted in many countries during the last two decades. Many research programs have been carried out with various objectives.

1. Studies have been conducted to better understand mechanisms of fracture. The fracture mechanics theories, as they are often called today, represent and important outcome of the studies.

2. Efforts have been made to improve fracture toughness of strural materials. Many ferrous and non-ferrous alloys with high strength and excellent fracture toughness have been developed.

3. Efforts have been made to improve non-destructive testing techniques. With a proper use of present NDT techniques, we can detect very fine defects.

4. Experimental and analytical studies have been made of influence on weld defects on service behavior of structures. Many data have been accumulated.

The extent to which weld defects affects reliability of a structure depends upon various factors including; (a) nature and extent of defects; (b) material properties, and; (c) type of loading.[2] When the material is ductile and the load is static, even a large defect can be tolerated. On the other hand, even a short crack can not be tolerated when the material is brittle and the structure is subjected to repeated loading. During the last several years, significant efforts have been made in analyzing this subject by use of fracture mechanics theories.

Although many studies have been made of these various subjects, little has been done, at least on the basis of published papers, to integrate results of these studies to develop a system which could assist fabricators of structures and their users.

The need for such a system is apparent if one considers procedures for design and fabrication of a welded structure. Although construction of an actual structure involves complex procedures, Figure 1 illustrates a simplified procedure. First, the initial design group determines an initial design which satisfies requirements by the customer. Then the structural design group prepares a detailed structural design which includes material selection. During this period, some iteration processes may take place between the initial design group and the structural design group and even the fabrication group to modify the initial design, and finally the design is completed.

Then, the production starts. The production stage includes a number of operations including machining, cutting, forming, welding, etc. After welding is completed, the welds will be inspected, perhaps by the quality assurance group which is independent of the production group. A representative of the customer may be involved in the inspection. Welds which do not pass the inspection will be sent back to the production group for repair.

After the fabrication is completed, the structure will be subjected to the final testing, such as a pressure testing of a vessel. When the structure passes the final testing, it wil be delivered to the customer.

In the fabrication of large, ctitical structures, be they space rockets, submarines,

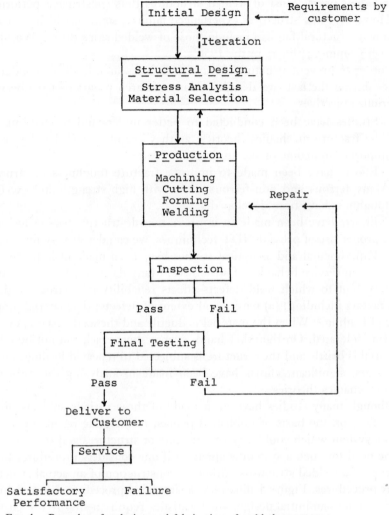

FIG. 1. Procedure for design and fabrication of welded structures.

nuclear pressure vessels, the fabricator cannot afford risking failures during service. In fact, they cannot even afford having major repairs at later stages of construction. Even though the direct cost for the repairs may not be high, the cost by the delay in production can be enormous.

Obviously the fabricator tries hard to avoid major repair jobs. As a safeguard against major repairs, they will try to have a good structural design, a right selection of materials, and good production control so that necessary repairs will be minimized.

Therefore, the real objective of the study of significance of weld defects is not to develop knowledge to be able to tell the fabricator whether or not a structure which they are making will perform satisfactorily during service but rather to provide them with a system which could prevent them from being trapped by a messy situation caused by major repairs and/or failures.

When one tries to develop a system which could assist the fabricator in dealing with this subject, he will soon find that there are a host of complex problems which must be dealt with.

For example, suppose that a defect is found in a weld. It is perhaps possible to apply the fracture mechanics theory and to estimate how many cycles of repeated stress at a certain level would be required before the crack grows to a certain size. However, the fracture mechanics theory alone cannot tell the fabricator whether the weld should be repaired or should be left as it is. What is needed is a different kind of analysis which can assist the fabricator to make such a decision.

To decide to repair a weld, the fabricator must consider various things as follows;

(1)   There is no guarantee that the repair weld would be acceptable—probability of repeated rpair jobs.

(2)   By repair welding, the heat-affected zone properties may be degraded.

(3)   Repair welding may produce highly concentrated residual stresses.

(4)   Time and cost required for the repair, including the cost for delay in construction.

In fact, many failures of actual structures did start from repair welds.

To decide *not* to repair, the fabricator must consider the following;

(5)   Variation of material properties. What happens if properties of the material near the defects are not as good as they should be?

(6)   Unexpected loading. What happens if stresses higher than predicted are applied to the structure? A probabilistic approach is necessary.

(7)   Extent of damage and risk. What is the possible extent of a damage, if a fracture occurs from the defect? How much is the probability of having damages?

In order to make decisions for accepting or rejecting a defect, the above problems must be analyzed.

Since no explicit, analytical system has yet been developed for making decisions for repair welding, decisions have been made on empirical bases. Currently, decisions are usually based upon codes and specifications. Sometimes defects which are apparently harmless are rejected simply because the specification being used does not accept such defects. With the proper use of a systems approach, it is hoped that the number of unnecessary repair welds could be reduced.

A systems approach can also be very useful for design and fabrication of a very critical structure using complex, high-strength alloys. For example, the M.I.T. study presented in this paper deals with deep submersibles fabricated with high-strength steels.

3.   M.I.T. Study on Crack Growth in Heavy Weldments

A study has been conducted at the Massachusetts Institute of Technology to develop a system which could assist a fabricator in making various decisions. Although the system developed so far does not deal with the decision-making for repair welding, it is presented in this paper as an example of a system analysis on welding fabrication.

The system that has been developed covers the following subjects;

1.   Material Selection.   A designer must select a material most suitable for the particular application. It may be wiser to select a material with a slightly lower strength, but higher fracture toughness and better fabricability.

2. *Allowable Flaw Size and Repaire.* The inspection standard for acceptable flaws must be severe enough to obtain adequate reliability of the structure. However, if the standard is too severe, it will cause unnecessary repair jobs, which will result in delay in fabrication and higher costs. One must not forget that the repair weld may not be defect-free and the repair may cause further degradation of the material.

3. *Stress Relieving.* One must decide whether or not the structure be stress-relieved. If it is stress-relieved, how should it be done? As the stress relieving temperature increases, more complete reduction of residual stresses can be achieved. However, a treatment at a certain temperature for a certain period may result in material degradagtion.

Since there has been no published analytical system on this subject, the major emphasis of the M.I.T. study has been to develop an overall system. It is recognized fully that the system that has been developed so far is far from complete. However, we believe that once it is proven that an analytical system could be developed, the system can be improved later by improving each step and/or by adding more steps.

The current study covers the following subjects;

1. Analysis of crack growth in heavy weldments in high-strength steels.
2. Establishment of rational standards for permissible crack size, weld repair, and stress relieving treatment.
3. Optimization of material selection for a pressure hull of a deep submersible.

This paper presents a brief summary of results obtained in the M.I.T. study. Details are given in the M. S. thesis by Yurioka.[3] A paper by Yurioka and Masubuchi[4] also presents some of the results.

3. 1   Analysis of Crack Growth in Heavy Weldments

When a weldment which contains an initial flaw is subjected to cyclic loading, the crack grows after each cycle. This fatigue crack growth may result in brittle fracture when the crack size exeeds the critical size. For some critical structures such as pressure hulls of deep submersibles, the structures are considered to fail, when a crack grows to become a through-the-thickness crack.

Analysis were made of fatigue growth of surface and embedded cracks in weldments of high-strength steels, including HY–80, HY–100, HY–130, HP–9–4 and maraging steels. Fatigue life of structures subjected to hoop stresses was obtained by the iteration method of the crack growth under nonuniform welding residual stresses in weldments.

Unique characteristics of crack growth in a weldment compared to that in an unwelded material are;

(1) A weldment contains residual stresses.
(2) A weldment is heterogeneous metallurgically, being composed of the weld metal, the heat-affected zone, and the unaffected base metal.

Although many studies have been conducted on the use of fracture mechanics theories for analyzing the crack growth under repeated loading, no published papers have considered both residual stresses and the nonuniformness of material properties, including fracture toughness.

Analysis. The analysis employed the fracture mechanics approach. The crack growth rate is known to be a function of the stress intensity factor, K. Kraft[5] proposed the following law of crack growth rate:

$$\frac{da}{dN} = A\left(\frac{K_{max} - K_{min}}{K_{max}}\right)^4 \cdot K^4_{max} \tag{1}$$

When an uniform tensile stress, σ, is applied to a plate with a finite width, W, containing a central through-the-thickness crack, a stress intensity factor of the mode I (tension mode), K_I, is expressed as follows:

$$K_I = \sigma\sqrt{\pi a}\left[\frac{2W}{\pi a}\tan\frac{\pi a}{2W}\right]^{1/2} \tag{2}$$

When stress distribution normal to a crack is not uniform, a stress intensity factor at the right hand of a crack in an infinite plate is obtained as the form of the following equation.[6]

$$K_I = \frac{1}{\sqrt{\pi a}}\int_{-a}^{a}\sigma(x)\left(\frac{a+x}{a-x}\right)^{1/2}dx \tag{3}$$

For a weldment, $\sigma(x)$ should be the sum of the nonuniform weld residual stress, $\sigma_R(x)$, and the applied cyclic stress, σ_H.

Masubuchi[7] has given the following expression for a longitudinal residual stress distribution in butt welds;

$$\sigma_R = \sigma_{RO}\{1-(x/f)^2\}\exp^{(-1/2(x/f)^2)} \tag{4}$$

where σ_{RO} is the maximum tensile longitudinal residual stress caused by welding, and f is half the width of a tensile residual stress region.

For water- and air-tight structures such as, pressure vessels and pressure hulls of submersibles, the structures are considered to fail when the cracks grow to become through-the-thickness cracks. Therefore, a partially through-the-thickness crack growth problem becomes more important for such structures. Irwin[8] has proposed the following expression for a stress intensity factor of an elliptical crack embedded in a plate.

$$K_I = \frac{\beta\sigma\sqrt{\pi a}\,(a^2/b^2\cdot\cos^2\theta+\sin^2\theta)^{1/2}}{\sqrt{\Phi^2-0.212(\sigma/\sigma_Y)}} \tag{5}$$

where

$$\Phi = \int_0^{\pi/2}(a^2/b^2\cdot\cos^2\theta+\sin^2\theta)^{1/2}d\theta$$

a=length of a crack along the minor axis
b=length of a crack along the major axis
β=1.0 for an embedded crack
β=1.1 for a surface crack.

Stress intensity factors for a part-through crack can be obtained from eqs. (3), (4) and (5), when the initial central location of a crack is x_o from the weld center line.

A stress-intensity factor term in the crack growth rate equation is too complicated to be integrated to obtain a fatigue crack growth curve. When a small number of cyclic loads are chosen, the crack growth rate can be rewritten as:

$$\Delta a = f(a, b, x_0, f, \sigma_{RO}, \sigma_H)\Delta n \tag{6}$$

Fatigue life can be predicted by continuing the iteration based on the above formula until the stress intensity factor attains the critical value, K_{IC}, or the depth of a crack becomes as long as the plate thickness.

Example of Analysis. A study was made to analyze effects on fatigue life of various factors, including the level of applied stress, profiles of welding residual stresses, variations of fracture toughness in a weldment. Computer programs have been developed to handle complex calculations required.

As an example of the analysis, Fig. 2 shows the effect of initial location of a crack

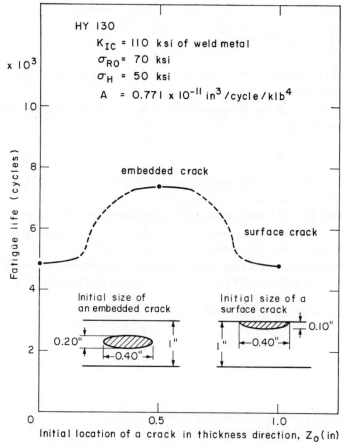

FIG. 2. Effect on fatigue life of various factors including the level of applied stress, profiles of welding residual stresses, etc.

in thickness direction on fatigue life of a pressure vessel in HY–130. The analysis was made under the following conditions;

Plate thickness, $t=1$ inch

Applied hoop stress $\sigma_H=50$ ksi

Maximum residual stress at weld center, $\sigma_{RO}=70$ ksi

Fracture toughness of weld metal, $K_{IC}=110$ ksi-in$^{1/2}$

Coefficient of crack growth rate,* $A=0.771\times10^{-3}$ in^3/cycle/klb^{-4}

The figure shows that a surface crack is more dangerous than an embedded crack.

3.2 Rational Standards for Acceptance Criteria of Heavy Weldments

Uncertainty in Fatigue Life. Fatigue life is influenced by many factors, including testing methods, material properties, residual stresses, surface conditions of structures and environmental conditions. Therefore, fatigue life for a structure must be probabilistically distributed. Yokobori[9] investigated the deviation of fatigue life from the bending test of carbon steels, and he concluded that the fatigue life distribution is close to the normal distribution of logarithm of fatigue life at any acting stress levels. Based upon his observation, the distribution function of fatigue life in a given applied stress level is assumed to be;

$$p(x) = \frac{1}{2\pi\sigma_D} \exp \{-(x-E(x))^2/2\sigma_D{}^2\} \tag{7}$$

where $x=\log N$

$\sigma_D=$ the standard deviation of log N

$E(x)=$ logarithm of the mean fatigue life.

Utility of a Pressure Vessel. The utility can be defined as the value in use of a set of goods in terms of their quantity or of their attributes.[10] It is more logical to make use of a utility function to compare the alternatives with respect to their quantity or attributes. Their general utility function may be of the form;

$$u(x) = u_0(1-e^{-x/\tau}) \tag{8}$$

The constant, γ, is related to how much diminishing marginal utility should be assessed by the analyst. If an infinitely large number is assessed to γ, the utility function becomes linear so that there is no diminishing marginal utility as shown in Fig. 3.

Since the designed stresses for pressure vessels are relatively high and the fatigue of pressure vessels is thus considered to be low cycle-high stress type, the maximum utility for pressure vessels may be given when a number of cycles of loading become 10^5. Defining the maximum utility within the sequence range as a unit for convenience, the utility function for pressure vessels can be expressed by;

$$u(x) = u_0(1-e^{-x/\tau}) \tag{9}$$

where

$u_0 = 1/(1-e^{-1/\tau})$

$x = N\cdot10^{-5}$, N is fatigue life.

---

* $da/dN = A(\varDelta K)^4$

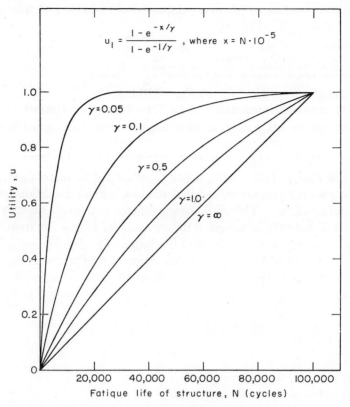

$$u_1 = \frac{1 - e^{-x/\gamma}}{1 - e^{-1/\gamma}}, \text{ where } x = N \cdot 10^{-5}$$

FIG. 3.   Utility of a structure with respect to fatigue life.

As the predicted fatigue life is probabilistically deviated following the log-normal distribution function, the expected utility for pressure vessels should be given as;

$$E[u(N)] = \int_0^\infty u(x') \cdot p(x) dN \qquad (10)$$

where $x = N \cdot 10^{-5}$ and $x = \log N$.

Rational Standards for Permissible Crack Size.   The permissible crack size should be determined in a term of the expected utility as noted above. The expected utility is numerically computed for various initial crack size in HY–130 weldments, and Fig. 4 shows the equi-utility curves for various initial cracks as a result of numerical computation.

Although higher utility is given for a weldment with smaller initial cracks, the effort to make no-defect welds does not seem rational. Considering that it is very difficult technically to obtain welds without any weld flaws, it would be rational to set up the permissible crack size in welds for a certain amount of utility which ought to be the minimum satisfactory value decided from the designing point of view.

In this study, (a, b) represents an initial crack with the half length of a inch along the minor axis and b inch along the major axis. Provided that an initial surface crack of

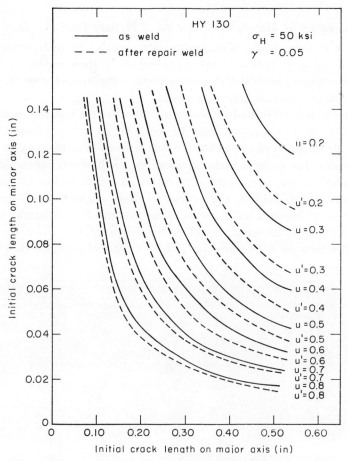

FIG. 4.   Utility of pressure vessel with various initial crack size after welding or repair welding.

size (0.10, 0.10) or (0.02, 0.35) located near the weld center line can be inevitable in the current welding techniques and that the objective utility for vessels is 0.83, which is equivalent to 8,700 of the mean fatigue life, the permissible crack sizes would be inside the 0.83 equi-utility line in Fig. 4.

Acceptable Criteria for Stress Relieving Anneal. The stress relieving temperature for the quenched-and-tempered steels (QT-steels) should be less than the tempered temperature. SR-treatment, therefore, cannot completely eliminate weld residual stresses, and stresses of 25 ksi would remain for HY–130 as the unrecovered stresses. It must be noticed that a temper embrittlement is accompanied by stress relieving anneal of QT steels. Based on the investigation of stress relief embrittlement of HY–100 and HY–130,[11,12] the critical stress intensity factor of HY–130 is estimated to be 70 ksi-in$^{1/2}$ after SR-treatment.

Based upon the above values for residual stresses and fracture toughness, expected utility is obtained for a HY–130 pressure vessel after SR-treatment.

3.3   Optimization of Material Selection for a Pressure Hull of a Deep Submersible

Fatigue of a Pressure Hull.   Compressive stresses due to hydrostatic pressure is subjected to the pressure hulls of deep submersibles in their excursion in deep sea. Such compressive stresses are believed not to enhance fatigue crack growth. Only tensile stresses can contribute to crack extension forces.

If a pressure hull is fabricated by welding and not stress relieved, it contains high tensile residual stresses in the region near the weld. When a deep submersible is at the sea surface, tensile stresses exist at welds. Tensile stresses in welds are compensated by compressive stresses due to hydrostatic pressure as a submersible dives into deep sea and tensile stresses are recovered again in its return excursion to the sea surface. Thus, cyclic loading is caused to welds in a pressure hull after each service performance. Some of the weld flaws in weldments will grow by cyclic loading. Such a fatigue crack growth problem might have an influence on the life of submersibles.

Required Thickness for a Pressure Hull.   Important technological factors of a deep

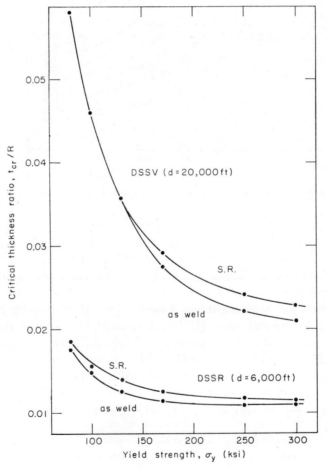

FIG. 5.   Required thickness for pressure hulls of deep submersibles.

submersible are buoyancy and possible operation number (life) of a pressurre hull. These attributes are closely related to the thickness of a pressure hull. The required thickness for pressure hulls of deep submersibles is obtained according to DTMB Report[13] as shown in Fig. 5, based on the following assumptions:

a) The maximum operating depth, d, is assumed as:
$d=6,000$ ft. for the rescue vehicle
$d=20,000$ ft. for the search vehicle

b) The designing thickness, t, is assumed as:
$t=t_{cr}/0.75$

c) Hull materials are:
HY–80 ($\sigma_y=80$ ksi),
HY–100 ($\sigma_y=100$ ksi),
HY–130 ($\sigma_y=130$ ksi),
HP9–4 ($\sigma_y=170$ ksi),
Marage 250 ($\sigma_y=250$ ksi),
Marage 300 ($\sigma_y=300$ ksi).

The buoyancy factor, B, that is, the the ratio of the hull weight to the weight of displaced water is expressed by:

$$B=\text{Hull weight/Displacement}$$
$$= (S \cdot R/V)(t/R)(1+W_p/W_s)(\rho_h/\rho_w) \qquad (11)$$

where $S=$Surface area of the hull structure
$R=$Radius of the hull structure
$V=$Volume of the hull structure
$W_p=$Payload weight of the hull structure
$W_s=$Shell weight
$\rho_h=$Density of material 490 lb/ft³ for steels
$\rho_w=$Density of sea water 64.4 lb/ft³

A less buoyancy factor is desirable for a pressure hull. Where a pressure hull is spherical and the payload weight is neglected, the buoyancy factor is expressed by;

$$B = 22.9(t/R) \qquad (12)$$

Utility Function for a Pressure Hull.   As noted above, the important attributes of a deep submersible are buoyancy as well as the number of excursions without a failure or collapse. Thus, an analysis of the optimization of material selection should be made by means of a two-dimensional utility function.

According to Keeney's multi-attribute utility theory,[14] the utility function for a pressure hull is given as;

$$u(x, y) = (0.10+1.125y)\left(\frac{1-e^{-x/r}}{1-e^{-1/r}}\right) \qquad (13)$$

where

$y = 1.10-B$ (variable of a buoyancy factor)
$x = N\times10^{-5}$ (variable of fatigue life)

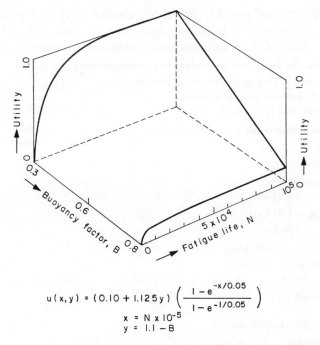

$$u(x,y) = (0.10 + 1.125y)\left(\frac{1-e^{-x/0.05}}{1-e^{-1/0.05}}\right)$$
$$x = N \times 10^{-5}$$
$$y = 1.1 - B$$

FIG. 6.   Two dimensional utility of a pressure hull of a deep submersible.

Two-dimensional utility surface of eq. (13) is graphically shown in Fig. 6. If $p(x)$ is the probabilistic distrbution function of the predicted fatigue life, the expected utility of a pressure hull is given as;

$$E[u(x, y)] = (0.10+1.125y) \int_0^\infty \left(\frac{1-e^{-x/\tau}}{1-e^{-1/\tau}}\right)p(x)dx \qquad (14)$$

Optimization of Material Selection for a Pressure Hull.   Assuming that weldments in all high-strength steels contain initial weld flaws of (0.1, 0.2), expected utility is computed by substituting obtained fatigue life and its distribution into eq. (14). Results are shown in Figs. 7 and 8. Figure 9 shows reliability of predicted fatigue life obtained by deviation of material properties including A, σ_{RO}', and K_{IC}.

When expected utility and the reliability of life are compared, important findings are as follows;

   a)   Stress relieving treatment increases utlity for all steels.

   b)   HY–100 and HY–130 have high utility for a rescue vehicle as a weld condition.

   c)   Predicted fatigue life of pressure hulls in Marage 300 steels is zero at 99.9 percent reliability, in spite of possessing high utility.

   d)   Only stress relieved HP9–4 and aged Marage 250 steels can be applicable to a pressure hull of a search vehicle.

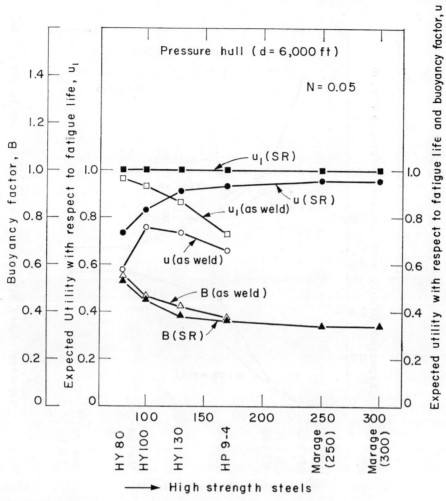

FIG. 7.   Optimization standards of material selection for pressure hull of deep submersible.

4.   Closing Comments

This paper first discussed the need for a systems approach for analyzing signifi-cance of weld defects and then presented a system developed at M.I.T. on welding fabrication. The M.I.T. study analyzed material selection and related subjects for deep submersibles. The authors believe that a similar system can be developed for analyzing acceptance levels of weld defects.

A systems analysis will be very useful in establishing standards for large, new pro-jects for constructing critical structures. For example, a huge project like the Trans-Alaska and Trans-Siberia pipelines involves many technical-managerial decision-making problems;

(1)   Fracture toughness requirement. How much fracture toughness should be required for the base plate, the heat-affected zone, and the weld metal?

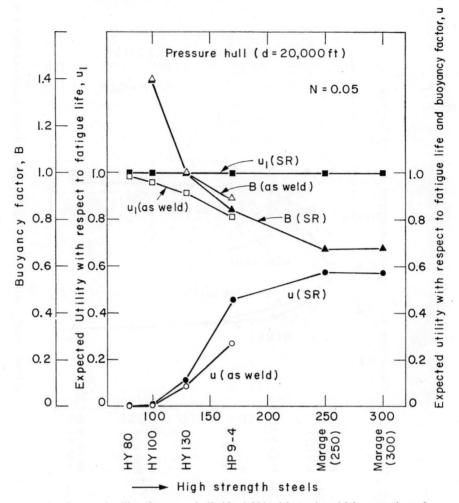

Fig. 8.   Expected utility of pressure hulls ($d=6,000$ m) in various high strength steels.

(2)   Weld quality. How stringent requirements should be imposed upon the weld quality?

(3)   Treatment. Preheating, post-heating, stress relieving, etc.

One may say that the pipeline is so critical that we should use the best material available, apply the most stringent quality control, and use the most careful fabrication procedures. However, one must also recognize that there is an economical limit for this approach. If this approach is pushed too far, the construction cost becomes so high that the project is no longer economically feasible.

A simple subject such as preheating temperature may require a careful analysis. Under normal shop fabrication, an increase in the preheating temperature from 150°F to 250°F may not add to much to the cost. However, the increase in preheating temperature for a pipeline which may extend over several thousand miles in the arctic means a tremendous cost. In such a case, the fabricator must evaluate carefully the benefit which

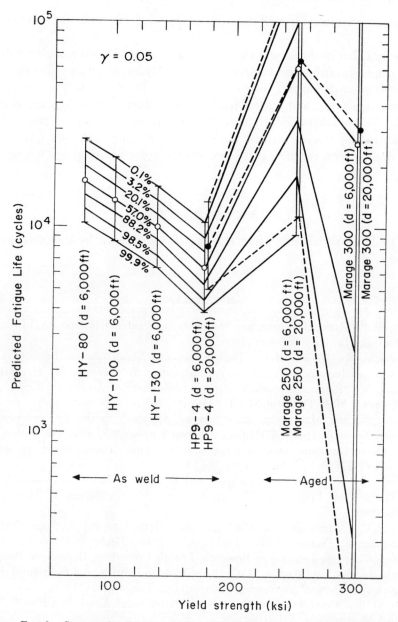

FIG. 9. Structural reliability of pressure hulls in various high strength steels.

may result from the increase of preheating temperature such as lowering the hardness of the heat-affected zone, less cracking tendency, etc., over the cost required.

When we think about the trend in fabrication tehnology, much emphasis during the last two decades was placed on the use of higher and higher strength materials. They were often used for aerospace and military structures, including space rockets, supersonic fighters, and submarines, most of which were funded by the government. In fabricating these structures, high cost can be justified for achieving superior performance.

We believe that in the future, the trend will be somewhat different from that of the past. The emphasis of the world activity will probably be placed on such subjects as the energy crisis and environment. Important projects in the future will be pipelines in the arctic, ocean structures, and nuclear reactors rather than space rockets and deep-diving submarines. In the fabrication of these new structures, construction cost and liability due to failures may become crucial issues. A systems approach may prove to be essential in dealing with complex problems which involve technical and managerial subjects.

ACKNOWLEDGMENTS

The study on which this paper is based was supported by the National Science Foundation.

REFERENCES

1. Weck, R., "A Rational Approach to Standards for Welded Construction," British Welding Journal, Nov., pp. 658–668 (1966).
2. Masubuchi, K., "Weld Defects, Their Effects and Nondestructive Testing," Chapter 6 of a text on *Analysis of Techniques for Fabricating Structures*, under preparation.
3. Yurioka, N., "Rational Approach to the Establishment of Acceptance Levels of Heavy Weldments," M.S. Thesis at M.I.T., May (1972).
4. Yurioka, N. and Masubuchi, K., "Rational Approach to the Establishment of Acceptance Levels of Heavy Weldments," a paper presented before the Second International Ocean Development Conference and Exhibition, Tokyo, Japan, pp. 1059–1084, Oct. 4–9 (1972).
5. Kraft, J. M., "On Prediction of Fatigue Crack Propagation Rate from Fracture Toughness and Plastic Flow Properties," Transactions of American Society of Metals, Vol. 58, p. 691 (1965).
6. Paris, P. C., "Application of Mushelishvilli's Method to the Analysis of Crack Tip Stress Intensity Factors for Plane Problems," *Fracture Mechanics Research for the Boeing Airplane Company*, Institute of Research, Lehigh University, Bethlehem, Pennsylvania.
7. Masubuchi, K. and Martin, D. C., "An Analytical Study of Cracks in Weldments," *Research on Structural Engineering*, University of Tokyo Press (1968).
8. Irwin, G. R., "Crack-extension Force for a Part-through Crack in a Plate," Journal of Applied Mechanics, p. 651 (1962).
9. Yokobori, T., "*Structural Strength*," Giho-do, Tokyo (1955) (in Japanese).
10. de Neufville, R. and Stafford, J. H., "*Systems Analysis for Engineers and Managers*," McGraw-Hill, New York (1971).
11. Rosenstein, A. H. and Asche, W. H., "Stress Relief Embrittlement of High-Strength Quenched-and-Tempered Alloy Steels," *Temper Embrittlement in Steels*, ASTM STP 407, American Society for Testing and Materials, p. 46 (1968).
12. Porter, L. G., Carter, G. C. and Manganello, S. J., "A Study of Temper Embrittlement during Stress Relieving of 5Ni-Cr-Mo-V Steels," *Temper Embrittlement in Steels*, ASTM STP 407, American Society for Testing and Materials, p. 20 (1968).

13. Krenzke, M., "Potential Hull Structures for Rescue and Search Vehicles of the Deep-Submergence Systems Project," DTMB Report 1985, 1965, Structural Mechanics Research and Development Center, Washington, D.C..

14. Keeney, R. L., "Multidimensional Utility Functions: Theory, Assessment, and Application," Technical Report No. 43, Operation Research Center, Massachusetts Institute of Technology, Cambridge, Massachusetts (1969).

Surface Flaw in 9%-Ni Steel Plate under Repeated Load

T. KANAZAWA

Department of Naval Architecture, Univeristy of Tokyo

Because of the scarcity of oil, natural gas has recently attracted our attention as a natural resourse of energy, and liquified natural gas (LNG) carries are now under construction. LNG when transported is held at a low temperature, as low as $-160°C$, and thus special material for low temperature use, such as 9%-Ni steel, must be used in constructing the vessels. 9%-Ni steel has a high fracture toughness at very low temperature, but the possibility exists that a fatigue crack growing from a defect, caused by welding or stress concentration, becomes sufficiently large to be critical.

We thus investigated fatigue crack propagation from various shape notch in 9%-Ni steel plates under pulsating bending and tensile load using a surface notch to simulate a welding defect. The results of fatigue crack propagation rate are analysed by the following expression:

$$\frac{dl}{dN} = C(\Delta K)^n$$

where l: part-through crack size (depth or half length at the plate surface, mm)

   N: number of cycles

   ΔK: range of stress intensity factor (kg$\cdot \sqrt{mm}$/mm^2)

   C, n: material constants

The magnification factor proposed by Kobayashi is used to calculate the stress intensity factor of the part-through cracks which are assumed to be semi-elliptic cracks. We obtained material constants, C and n, which are 1.19×10^{-9} and 2.57, respectively. Using these values, fatigue life is calculated by the following relation:

$$N_f = \int_{l_i}^{l_c} \frac{dl}{C(\Delta K)^n}$$

where l_i: initial defect size

   l_c: critical defect size

Figure 1 shows a comparison between the prediction from the above formula and

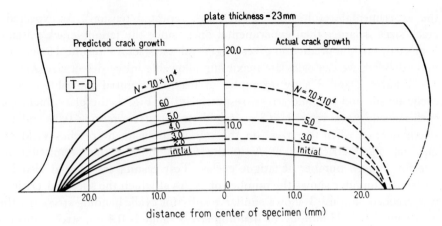

FIG. 1. Comparison of calculated and actual fatigue crack growths.

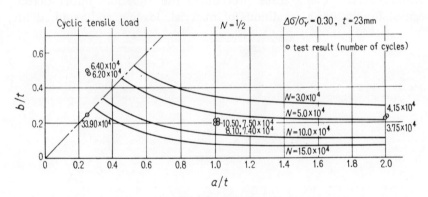

FIG. 2. Calculated maximum initial defect size under cyclic tensile load. (a=half length of defect at plate surface, b=depth of surface defect.)

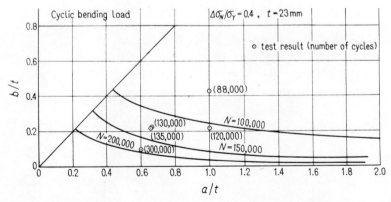

FIG. 3. Calculated maximum initial defect size under cyclic bending load. (a=half length of defect at plate surface, b=depth of surface defect.)

the experimental results ($\Delta\sigma$=20 kg/mm², repeated tension). As expected, calculated crack sizes is larger than experimental ones, since the fatigue crack initiation life was neglected, but the prediction gives in general satisfactory result. Hence if N_f is properly defined, we can calculate maximum allowable initial defect size, l_i.

Figures 2 and 3 show examples of maximum initial allowable defect size under cyclic tensile and bending stress, respectively. In Fig. 2, the plate thickness is 23 mm, cyclic tensile stress range is 0.3 σ_Y (yield stress), stress ratio is 0.09 and crifical crack size is defined when the stress on the minimum ligament reaches yield stress of the material. Parametric lines of N in the figure indicate the permissible initial defect size for a given number of fatigue cycles. Test results are plotted also in the figure where the number shows the number of cycles at which the specified critical crack size was reached. Figure 3 shows similar results for cyclic bending stress. In this case, the plate thickness is 23 mm, cyclic bending stress range is 0.4 σ_Y, stress ratio is 0.09 and a critical crack size is reached when its depth becomes 0.7×plate thickness. These figures show that these calculations satisfactorily predict fatigue crack growth from a surface defect. Using these procedures the allowable initial defect size can be specified for the given conditions of material, loading and required life, etc.

Determination of Fracture Toughness of Heavy Thick High Strength Steels for Long Span Bridges

K. Ikeda

Structural Engineering Laboratory, Kobe Steel, Ltd.

The long span Gerber truss type bridge called Osaka Port Bridge has been under construction in Osaka Port area. The main span length is 510 m, and the main box girders consist of 75 and 50 mm thick HT 80 (or 80 kg/mm² high strength steel) and HT 70 plates. Some presently planned long span bridges between Honshu (Main) and Shikoku Islands will use these high strength steel plates.

Material specifications for these bridges require a fracture toughness based on the brittle fracture initiation characteristics of the bond of a welded joint under given boundary conditions. Such brittle fracture initiation characteristics is influenced by various factors, such as steel quality, plate thickness, temperature, crack size (length and depth), welding heat input, restraint stress, welding residual stress in cross or T-joints, misfabrication such as angular distortion and misalignment of welded joint. Effects of these factors can be evaluated by using large size specimens including the deep notch test specimen with a welded joint. The good correlation between the critical fracture toughness and the V notch Charpy criterion, with due consideration to the yield ratio and effect of plate thickness, is also used for determining the required fracture toughness in Charpy data expressed by the fracture appearance transition temperture, $_vT_{rs}$, or the absorbed energy at 0°C, $_vE_o$.

For Osaka Port Bridge, the specifications for fabrication are: the maximum welding heat input is controlled to 45,000 Joule/cm and the permissible angular distortion and misalignment are 10 mm/1,000 mm and 3 mm respectively. The presumed maximum crack size in a cross joint, where the welding residual stress exists, is assumed to be 85 mm long and 5 mm deep. This is the crack discovered during the inspection of a spherical storage tank. The requested fracture toughness of bond, which is required for preventing brittle fracture at the lowest atmospheric temperature of −10°C under the conditions abovementioned, is expressed by $_vT_{rs}<0$°C in V notch Charpy impact test for the bond.

For the long span bridges between Honshu and Shikoku Islands, the conditions for evaluating fracture toughness of bond for HT 80 and HT 70 of 75 and 50 mm thick plate are as follows:

    Welding heat input: 45,000 Joule/cm

    Angular distortion: 10 mm/1,000 mm

    Misalignment for plate thickness greater than 50 mm: 5 mm

    Restraint stress: 15 kg/mm^2

    Crack length: 80 mm

    Crack depth: 8 mm

    Tensile welding residual stress is superposed.

    The lowest atmospheric temperature or brittle fracture initiation temperature:
      −10 and 0°C

(These values are under discussion)

Toughness Near the Fine Grained Fusion Line of High Strength Steel Developed for High Heat Input Welding

N. Taniguchi, K. Yamato, A. Nakashima, K. Minami and S. Kanazawa

Products Research and Development Laboratory, Nippon Steel Corporation

1. Introduction

Many of the recent welded strutures, such as ships, crude oil storage tanks, etc. are fabricated by high heat input welding methods for the purpose of decreasing the cost of construction. Unfortunately the toughness of a welded fusion line in high tensile strength steels decreases with increasing heat input. This paper describes a new steel developed specifically for improving the deteriorated toughness in the region adjacent to the fusion line. With the dispersion of fine TiN into the plate, austenite grain growth is prevented even if the steel is exposed to high temperature along the fusion line. Improved toughness is then obtained by transforming the structure into fine grained ferrite and pearlite.

The paper also reports test results of fracture behavior of welded junction, especially in the embrittled region. Methods for assessing brittle fracture initiation and propagation characteristics of welded joints are not as yet firmly established and part of this paper adresses itself to this problem.

2. Metallurgy of the Newly Developed Steel

Generally, the decrease in toughness adjacent to the fusion line with high heat input is due to grain growth of austenite and to transformation to large grained upper bainite caused by the low cooling rate and subsequent transformation following the high heat input welding. In order to prevent embrittlement, the region surrounding the fusion line should be transformed to either a lower bainite of good toughness or a ferrite-pearlite structure. To obtain the former lower bainite structure under low cooling rate and high heat input welding conditions, the alloying elements must be enriched which then causes a tendency of cold cracking under regular heat input welding. However, if the austenite grain can somehow be fine grained, the ferrite plus pearlite structure can be easily obtained. In the following, it will be clearly demonstrated that the fine particle of TiN in HT 60 class steel is very effective for this purpose.

a) Austenite grain growth prevention adjacent to the fusion line by the precipitated fine TiN particles.

Figure 1 indicates the effects of various precipitates on the austenite grain growth, which was prepared by a synthetic weld thermal cycle, where the TiN precipitates are effective in making the austenite grains smaller. This fact has been well known, but the most significant point is the difference between Ti–1 and Ti–2 of the same Ti–steel in Fig. 1. Figure 2 shows results of new findings in which austenite grain size varies widely with different amount of TiN particles in dimensions smaller than 0.1 micron.

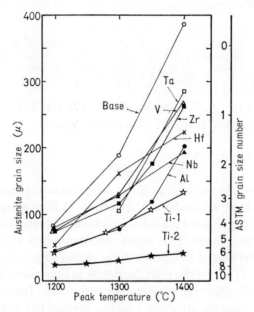

FIG. 1.   Relation between austenite grain size in welding and various precipitates.

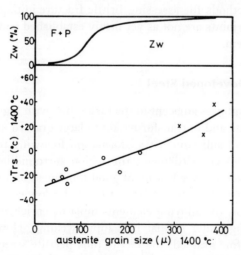

FIG. 2.   Relationship between $_vT_{rs}$ for synthetic weld fusion zone of SAW (100 kJ/cm) and austenite grain size.

b) Improved toughness of the region adjacent to the fusion line of fine grained austenite produced with fine TiN particls.

Figure 3 illustrates the relation between austenite grain size and toughness of the fine grained austenite by TiN steel (symbol ○) and non-Ti steel (symbol ×). Charpy test results of specimens taken from an actual welded joint with high heat input is shown in Fig. 4 where remarkable improvement in the new steel (A) with fine TiN in

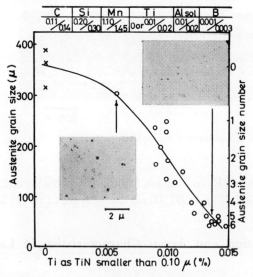

C	Si	Mn	Ti	Al sol	B
0.11/0.14	0.20/0.30	1.10/1.45	0 or 0.01/0.02	0.01/0.02	0.0001/0.0003

FIG. 3. Relationship between austenite grain size at 1400°C in synthetic weld thermal cycle and Ti% as TiN smaller than 0.10 μ in steel plate.

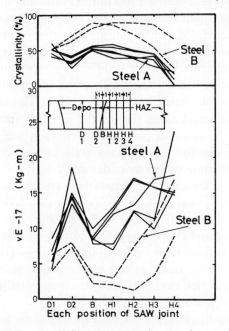

FIG. 4. V Charpy test results at various position of one side SAW-joints.

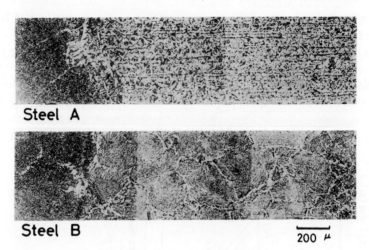

Steel A

Steel B $\overline{200\ \mu}$

PHOTO. 1.   Micrograph of sub-merged arc welded joints.

comparison with conventional steel (B) is noticed. Photo. 1 depicts the microstructure near the fusion line of both steels (A) and (B). Here, the heat input is 131 kJ/cm.

3. Brittle Fracture Propagation and Arrest Characteristics in Large Scale Specimens

Proper assessment of the toughness of a welded joint has not been well established because of the many complexities involved. A new procedure of assessing the propagation and arrest properties of the welded joint has been recently attempted at our laboratory and a report on the test results, hopefully, would indicate direction of future study.

Consider now brittle fracture of an actual welded structure due to appreciable crack extension along a welded joint. Such fracture behavior is difficult to reproduce with the Robertson type test on a laboratory scale because the brittle crack which initiates from the welded joint is usually arrested after deviating into the base metal. The new method is to force the crack to propagate and arrest along the welded joint by machining the side grooves in the specimen. Figure 5 illustrates such test specimen which was tested with a gradient type of temperature distribution. In most tests using this specimen, cracks ran along the fusion line but in some cases cracks deviated.

The new test method was used to compare differences between the newly developed Ti-steel (HT–60S) and the conventional steel (HT–60). Figures 6 and 7 show, in terms of K_c (brittle crack arresting toughness) vs. testing temperature, the results of specimens with submerged arc welding and electro gas arc welding joints. It is obvious from these figures that the arresting toughness of the new steel is considerably better than the steel commercially available. Test result of the base metal is also shown in Fig. 6. Arresting characteristics of the region near the fusion line is appreciably different from that of the base metal and should not be compared.

The current WES (Japan Welding Engineering Society) specifications for assessing plate properties based on the assumption that "brittle crack propagating along the weld-

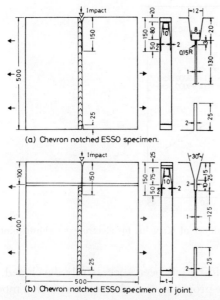

(a) Chevron notched ESSO specimen.

(b) Chevron notched ESSO specimen of T joint.

FIG. 5.   Specimen configuration and notch details.

(a)   Chevron notched ESSO specimen.

(b)   Chevron notched ESSO specimen of T joint.

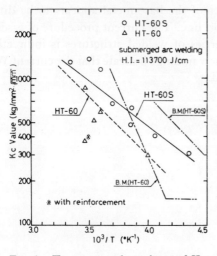

FIG. 6.   Temperature dependence of K_c value for submerged arc welding joints.

ed joint deviates eventually to the base metal" must, therefore, be reviewed in view of the above findings. New data must be accumulated and a proper procedure for assessing new material characteristics should be studied and established.

4.   Summary

(1)   With fine TiN particles, a new steel of good toughness in the region adjacent

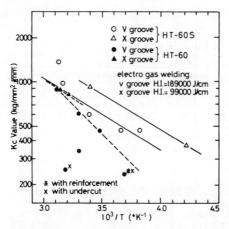

FIG. 7.   Temperature dependence of K_c value for electro gas welding joints.

to a fusion line of high heat input welding has been successfully developed.

(2)   An improved brittle fracture propagation and arrest test with a modified ESSO type specimen in assessing these characteristics in regions adjacent to the weld fusion line is reported. Improvement in the brittle fracture characteristics of the new steel in comparison with the conventional steel has been demonstrated.

(3)   Brittle fracture characteristics of the base metal appears to be different from those in the region adjacent to a fusion line. The current procedure of assessing brittle fracture propagation and arrest properties of welded structures is indirectly based on the test results of the base metal. Our new findings indicate that the current WES specifications should be reviewed and revised.

Applied Fracture Mechanics for Designing Aluminum Alloy 5083-0 Large Spherical Tank for LNG Carrier

K. Terai and S. Susei

Welding Research Department, Kawasaki Heavy Industries, Ltd.

Aluminum alloy 5083-0 is considered one of the most suitable structural material for tanks in LNG carrier. A LNG carrier of 29,000 M³ capacity with aluminum alloy tanks is being built at the Moss Rosenberg yard. 125,000 M³ LNG carrier with five tanks of aluminum alloy will be produced and 125,000 M³ carriers are also to be built under licensed by General Dynamics USA. For spherical tanks in 130,000 M³ LNG carrier heavy aluminum alloy 5083-0 plates of 40–200 mm in thickness are to be used.

For this type of tank, without a secondary barrier, "leak before failure" becomes one of the major design criteria, which requires as a necessary condition an evaluation of the critical crack size. The following requirements must be fulfilled to satisfy the "leak before failure" criterion.

1. The critical crack size can be determined.
2. Fatigue cracks shall penetrate the tank wall before reaching a critical size.
3. Critical crack size for through cracks shall, with ample margin, be large enough to allow safe sailing from the time of detection of leak until discharge and repair is possible.

To meet these requirements, fracture mechanics and accurate detailed stress analysis must be used.

Figure 1 shows results of tensile test using notched specimen of aluminum alloy 5083-0 at cryogenic temperature. For all tests, the fracture stress was above 0.2% proof stress and test specimens was broken after general yielding.

Valid K_{IC}-values for aluminum alloy 5083-0 cannot be defined from data involving large scale yielding and thus it is difficult to calculate the critical crack size. Linear fracture mechanics is not strictly applicable for determination of critical crack size and neither is the COD method (Fig. 2). Kaufman of ALCOA Research Laboratories estimated the critical K_{IC}-value of aluminum alloy 5083-0 from the relation between K_c-values and unit propagation energy in tear test of more brittle aluminum alloy. As shown by Fig. 3, however, the validity of this method has not been proven yet.

If tensile tests of notched wide specimens show that no unstable fracture occur at

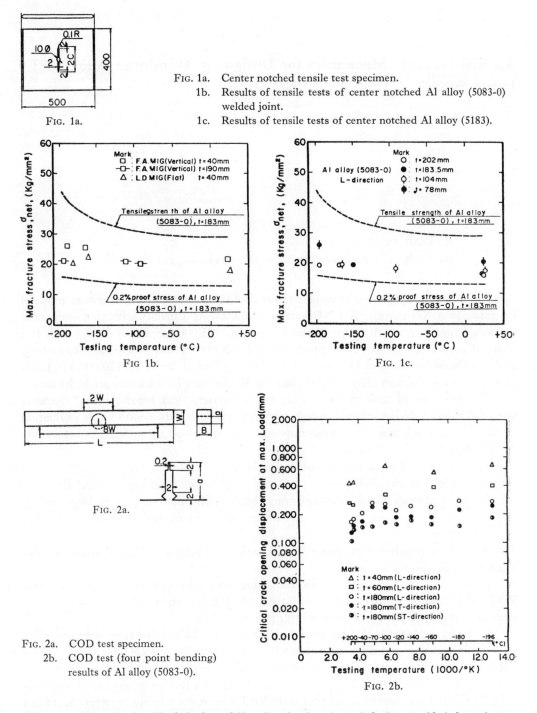

FIG. 1a.   Center notched tensile test specimen.

1b.   Results of tensile tests of center notched Al alloy (5083-0) welded joint.

1c.   Results of tensile tests of center notched Al alloy (5183).

FIG. 1a.

FIG 1b.

FIG. 1c.

FIG. 2a.

FIG. 2a.   COD test specimen.

2b.   COD test (four point bending) results of Al alloy (5083-0).

FIG. 2b.

a low stress level, the "leak before failure" criterion is satisfied even if defects larger than the detectable defect exists. No fracture at a low stress level occured in wide notched tensile specimens of 180 mm in thickness, 400 mm in breadth and 160 mm in noch

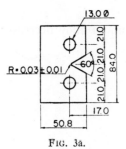

Fig. 3a.

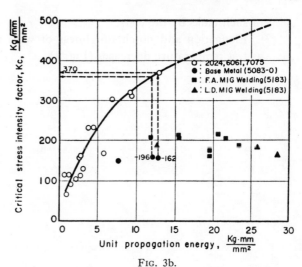

Fig. 3a.   Tear test specimen.

3b.   Critical stress intensity factor, K_c vs. unit propagation energy for 1 inch Al alloy plate.

Fig. 3b.

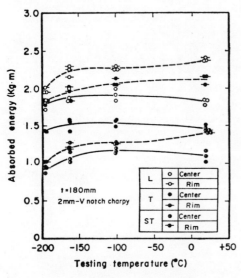

Fig. 4a.   Impact value of Al alloy (5083-0) ($t=$ 180 mm).

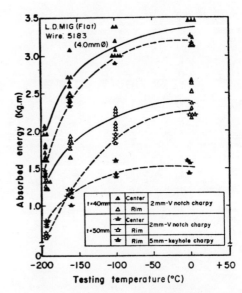

Fig. 4b.   Impact value of Al alloy (5183) welded joint.

length. The fracture surface was fibrous and shear lips was also observed. Fracture speed, however, approached that of unstable fracture and fracture surface plane was normal to tensile direction when the crack ran, thus exhibiting a semibrittle fracture after general yielding of the specimen. These fracture phenomena do not seems to seriously affect the design of aluminum alloy tanks for LNG carrier but some problems remained to be solved in future. These are as follows;

(1) If the LNG tank is large with large tank wall thickness and the detectable defect size becomes larger than one meter, it is then difficult to prove to the safety

of such tanks by the tests.

(2) Elongation and notch toughness of weld metal in aluminum alloy decrease as test temperature decreases (Fig. 4).

Discussions in Session VI

Comment by Dr. Toyoda

I would like to speak concerning the problems in application of fracture mechanics to weld cracking. Weld cracking usually is one of the fatal defects in welded structures and energetic efforts to prevent weld cracking are being made. In order to determine the correct welding conditions for prevention of weld cracking, the behaviors of it must be evaluated quantitatively, for example using the calculated analysis applied by fracture mechanics.

Weld cracking is divided roughly into two parts, hot cracking and cold cracking. In the case of cold cracking, the application of fracture mechanics may be more simple than in the case of hot cracking, because initiation of it is at a certain warm temperature and the behaviors of the stress and strain in the welded joints will be stationary.

It has been pointed out by many researchers that the cold cracking is a kind of "Hydrogen Induced Creacking", and it is a phenomenon called "Delayed Cracking". In the case of hydrogen induced cracking, the first step of the fracture mechanics approach was already given my collaborator, Prof. Satoh, in Session 2. On the other hand, a great deal of researches on the hydrogen embrittlement has been made by many researchers. They have been making every effort to clarify the mechanism using notched steel specimens with hydrogen. However, even in the case of macroscopically homogeneous and simple notched specimen in which hydrogen induced cracking occurs, there are many difficult problems in an application of fracture mechanics.

To take into consideration the change of fracture toughness due to hydrogen diffusion is one of the means of solving problems in using the fracture mechanics approach to hydrogen induced cracking. But it is very difficult to determine the behaviors of change of fracture toughness by means of experiments. Following, I shall show some examples of these difficult problems.

Figure 1 shows the calculated results and the relation between the fracture net stress required for crack initiation and holding time under a constant load of notched steel specimen with hydrogen. But this fracture net stress can hardly be obtained by the experiment, that is, it is only the imaginary fracture strength. Figure 2 shows two results of experiments that the notched steel specimen with hydrogen which were held under a constant load. The solid curve shows the relationship between applied stress and incubation time, and the dotted curve shows the relationship between the imaginary fracture stress under a certain constant load, or σ_o, and holding time. On the other hand, even if after a certain holding time the notched specimen is stretched rapidly by force, the fracture initiation stress is the almost same value of the specimen not including

408

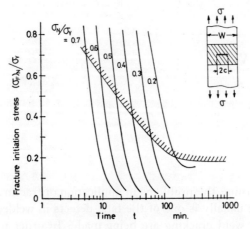

FIG. 1. Effect of applied stress, σ_N, on relation of time vs. stress, $(\sigma_F)_N$, to initiate fracture at the notch.

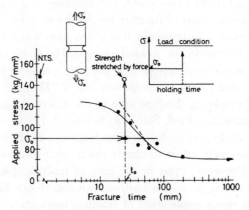

FIG. 2. Relation between applied stress, σ_N, and fracture initiation time.

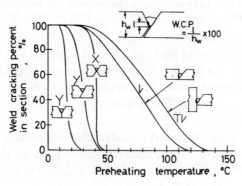

FIG. 3. Effect of groove shape on relation of weld cracking percentage vs. preheating temperature.

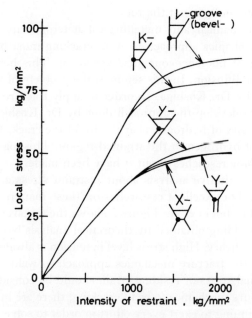

FIG. 4. Effect of groove shape on relation of local stress vs. intensity of restraint.

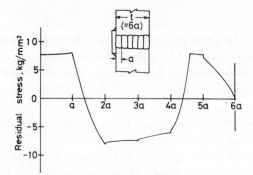

FIG. 5. Residual stress distribution in multi-pass welding.

hydrogen and becomes a larger value than the expected strength given by the analysis. The experimental results depend upon strain rate, so it is difficult to clarify these phenomena by experiments.

Next let us consider the problems of fracture mechanics applied to weld cracking. In welded joints, there are many difficult conditions that are different in homogeneous material and a simple loading condition.

The first of these problems is the effect of the groove shape. Figure 3 shows the relationships between weld crack percentage and preheating temperature for various kinds of groove shapes. Thus the initiation behaviors are influenced by groove shape. Figure 4 shows the results calculated about the local stress by the elastic-plastic analysis using FEM. In weld cracking, the calculated method of the fracture toughness parameter becomes difficult, because the shape of the specimens is complex and the macroscopic stress or strain concentration occuring at the root.

Then, next, there exists mechanical and metallurgical heterogeneity in welded joints. Therefore, the fracture mechanics approach to weld cracking must be different from hydrogen induced cracking of homogeneous steel specimen. This heterogeneity must also have effect on hydrogen diffusion. In this seminar, the problem of the heterogeneous material was considered by Dr. Koshiga. In order to apply fracture mechanics to weld cracking, it is necessary to develop the approach done by Dr. Koshiga.

The third problem is the density of hydrogen near the tip of the crack. It is necessary to make clear the diffusion of hydrogen in the strained region. This may be a very difficult problem, but recently, some reseaches about it have been made.

The forth problem is the quantitative analysis about restraint stress and residual stress caused in the welded joint. The excellent researches on these matters have been made by Prof. Satoh, and Prof. Masubuchi et al.. Figure 5 shows the transverse residual stress distribution in multi-pass welding obtained by theoretical analysis based on one-dimensional thermal elastic-plastic theory. High stress level in tension is always produced slightly below the final layer. In the fracture mechanics approach to weld cracking, it is a problem as to how this residual stress or residual strain should be considered.

Thus in order to apply fracture mechanics to weld cracking, there are many things yet to be made clear. We are continuing to exert every effort in order to solve these matters.

Comment by Prof. Packman

One of the topics discussed during this program has been fatigue crack growth and the prediction of life for a structure subjected to fatigue. In most cases we conduct our tests at constant amplitude fatigue or constant load fatigue. The real world structure rarely sees constant amplitude fatigue.

If the load interaction effects on fatigue crack growth are not considered, very large errors in life prediction can occur. In this discussion I shall confine my remarks to relatively high strength materials. If one just considers constant amplitude fatigue and plots the crack length vs. the number of cycles applied, one obtains the typical parabolic shape that results from the integration of the da/dN curve, and the life can be predicted based on the crack growth to failure.

If however, during the constant amplitude cycles, there is introduced an occassional peak overload, the introduction of the overload reduces the rate of crack growth at the subsequent lower stress level below that rate which would have occured had the overload not been applied. If the fatigue life analysis only considers the incremental crack excursions that occur for each value of load and number of cycles at the load, and does not consider the load interaction retardation, the life prediction will be grossly in error. The life prediction considering no interaction of loads will be much shorter than the actual life.

In the U.S. there are many people working on studies of the load interaction effect. The process was first brought to the forefront with the life prediction for the F-111 aircraft. The crack growth rates calculated for the high strength D6AC steel were not observed in the laboratory spectrum load tests. Subsequently these load-interaction crack growth retardation phenomena were found in many other aircraft materials.

Three major phenomena have been reported;

1.   Delayed retardation, in which the degree of retardation of crack growth is reached some number of cycles after return to the lower stress level.

2.   Monotonic retardation, in which the return to the unaffected crack growth rate is continuous, and maximum retardation is found immediately after returning to the lower load level.

3.   Crack acceleration, in which the crack grows faster that predicted at constant amplitude da/dn vs. ΔK curves upon immediate application of the overload.

Examination of electron fractographs reveals some measure of the influence of the number of applications of the same peak overload on the crack growth rates. Results found for 7075-T6511 show that the amount of retardation is stongly dependant on the number of applications, i.e. 12 applications of a peak load produce less retardation than 50 applications of the same peak load. As the number of peak overloads increases however, the retardation effect rapidly saturated (for N_{peak} over 100)

Hence I had listed about 10 items for needed future works, and I never got beyond fatigue crack-load interaction studies. For example;

1.   A point raised by Professor Fisher regarding the degree of randomness of the load applications. As the degree of randomness increases the RMS ΔK values accurately predict the crack growth and the subsequent life. One program should consider how random does the load sequence have to be before we do not have to consider the load interaction process.

2.   Another problem is the length of time that the structure is kept at the peak load. If the time of hold at the peak is short, the time dependant creep deformation is minimum, and no relaxation can occur and there is a difference between the subsequent crack growth and that observed if held for a long time.

3.   Consider the role of compressive loads. If you apply compressive loads it appears to wipe out the retardation effect.

4.   The influence of the number of applications of the peak load. It is not a simple process, how many applications produce saturation.

5.   The environmental effect during the load applications. If the peak loads are applied when wet, does that influence the subsequent crack growth?

6.   The temperature changes during the fatigue spectrum. Do we simply use the da/dN curve obtained at constant amplitude loading for each temperature?

7.   The effect of yield stress. Lower strength materials do not exhibit as much interaction effects as higher strength materials.

8.   The influence of overloads on threshold stress intensity.

9.   The role of strengthening mechanisms on the retardation.

10.   The role of peak overloads on stress corrosion susceptibility.

Comment directed to Prof. Packman by Prof. Kitagawa

Your results in relation to the effects of variation of K on the fatigue crack growth is much interesting and useful for us all.

We have the several data relating to your results. Mr. Matsumoto in my lab. changed ΔK step-wise from $(\Delta K)_0$ to $\eta(\Delta K)_0$ and measured da/dN (Fig. 6). When we take 100% $\geq \eta \geq 80\%$, da/dN changes at once to the new crack growth rate level governed by $\eta(\Delta K)_0$

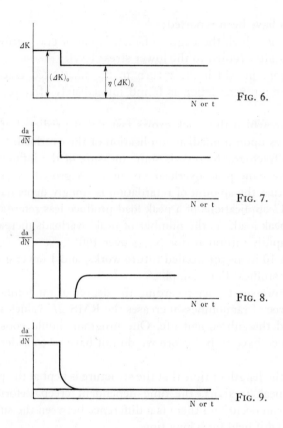

FIG. 6.

FIG. 7.

FIG. 8.

FIG. 9.

(see Fig. 7). If we take $\eta < 80\%$, for instance, $\eta = 50\%$, da/dN descends rapidly to zero and the crack stops growing temporarily, and after some repetitions of loads it starts growing again and grows at the expected value of da/dN, as Fig. 8, and in the case of the materials with much ductility, da/dN approaches gradually to the expected value, as Fig. 9. We made it sure on steels and non-ferrous alloys.

Question directed to Prof. Masubuchi by Prof. Fisher

In your presentation you indicated that more effort should be given to quality control. Will a significant increase in effort for quality control actually eliminate the random occurrence of discontiuities? It would seem that increased effort may decrease the number of flaws but cannot eliminate them. Would it not be better in bridges, buildings and ships to balance design, quality control and material rather than overemphasize quality control?

Reply to Prof. Fsher by Prof. Masubuchi

The question is, how important the quality control is. In some cases, additional quality control may not help you at all, while in other cases, it is important. I think that you are referring to ordinary structures such as bridges and ships.

In the fabrication of ordinary structures made in low-carbon steel, I probably have to agree with you. Additional quality control may not result in significant improvement in structural reliability. Perhaps Mr. S. Kaku of Nippon Kaiji Kyokai may care to make a comment.

However, when you are fabricating a critical structure in a titanium alloy, as an extreme example, you will find that you are in a completely different ball park. In such a case, a good quality control is essential.

Let us think, for a moment, about what current non-destructive testing techniques do. As you know, there are a number of NDT techniques using X-ray, ultrasonic, magnaflux, etc. However, all they do is to look for discontinuities such as porosity slag inclusions, lack of fusion, etc. This is based upon an assumption that a weld which does not contain discontinuities has acceptable metallurgical properties.

Here, I would like to discuss three different cases, an ordinary steel structure, a critical structure in an aluminum alloy, and a critical structure in a titanium alloy. You will find that situations change radically when you move from steel to aluminum and further on to titanium.

When you are fabricating ordinary steel structures using proper welding techniques, you can probably assume that the level of control of metallurgical structures is reasonably good. In such a case, you may want to use NDT methods to insure that welds are being made under satisfactory conditions. Then, your statement is probably correct. In other words, additional quality control may not be an effective way of improving structural reliability.

However, when you are fabricating structures, such as huge fuel and oxidizer tanks of the Saturn V rockets, used for the Apollo program, the situation is different. Unless you use very strict process control, it is extremely difficult to obtain welds without porosity. Aerospace companies experienced this problem during the fabrication of the Saturn V. NASA spent so much money for improving welding process control.[1] In such a case, there is a definite benefit of having a better control.

When you are fabricating critical titanium structures, process control becomes essential. In welding titanium, you may have a weld which has no discontinuity, but the material is embrittled due to contamination by oxygen. An ordinary NDT technique, therefore, cannot guarantee that a weld which passes the inspection will perform satisfactorily during service.

In summary, when you are welding ordinary carbon steel, I probably have to agree with you. In welding aluminum, there is a benefit of having a better process control. In welding titanium, it is absolutely necessary to have a very good process control.

Question directed to Mr. Susei by Prof. McEvily

Your results indicate that welded aluminum exhibits a loss in toughness with decrease in temperature. Do you have an explanation for this behavior?

Reply to Prof. McEvily by Dr. Susei

The Charpy results of welded joint with large heat input is shown in Fig. 4. Namely, aluminum plates of 40–50 mm in thickness welded by one pass welding from both sides.

---

1) Masubuchi, K., "Integration of NASA-Sponsored Studies on Aluminum Welding," NASA Contractor Report CR-2064, National Aeronautics and Space Administration, Washington, D. C., June, 1972.

In this case, the heat input reached about 6–7 kjoule/cm. Therefore, I think that the effect of heat input on Charpy results is very remarkable and the impact value decreases at a low temperature. The main reason that the impact value is low at a low temperature is perhaps due to the influence of segregation such as Al_2Mg_3, Al_2Mn_3, etc.

Author Index

Arii, M. 177

Fisher, J. W. 213
Fukagawa, M. 82
Fukuda, S. 189

Hall, L. R. 340
Higuchi, M. 82

Iida, K. 224
Ikeda, K. 144, 395
Inoue, H. 235
Irwin, G. R. 213
Iwanaga, H. 173

Kajimoto, K. 144
Kaku, S. 59
Kanazawa, S. 397
Kanazawa, T. xiii, 308, 392
Kashiwaya, H. 177
Kihara, H. 308
Kishimoto, K. 267
Kitagawa, H. 248
Kobayashi, A. S. xv, 127
Koshiga, F. 283
Kunihiro, T. 105

Machida, S. 156
Maenaka, H. 144
Masubuchi, K. 373
Matsushita, K. 110
McEvily, A. J. Jr. 96, 203
Minami, K. 114, 397
Miyamoto, H. 189
Miyata, T. 292

Miyoshi, S. 3
Miyoshi, T. 189

Nagai, K. 144
Nakajima, H. 105
Nakashima, A. 397
Nishioka, A. 260
Nishioka, K. 173
Nishiyama, N. 110

Ogura, N. 62
Ohyama, M. 82
Okabayashi, H. 82
Ono, K. 48
Onoe, M. 22
Otsuka, A. 292

Packman, P. F. 9

Rolfe, S. T. 318

Satoh, K. 71
Soya, I. 114
Susei, S. 362, 403

Taniguchi, N. 114, 397
Terai, K. 362, 403
Toyoda, M. 71
Tsuboi, J. 110

Usami, S. 260

Yajima, H. 355
Yamato, K. 397
Yanuki, T. 177
Yurioka, N. 373